'If *Night of the Living Dead* was the first word in the dead rising field, *The Living Dead* is the last word. A monumental achievement'
ADAM NEVILL, author of *The Ritual*

'The ultimate tribute to a remarkable career. For George A. Romero, that's a wrap. For the rest of us, we are once again reminded to "Stay Scared"'
NEW YORK JOURNAL OF BOOKS

'Every zombie movie lives in the shadow of Romero, but he never got the budget to work at the scale he deserved. Fortunately, Daniel Kraus delivers the epic book of the dead that Romero began. That shadow just got a whole lot bigger'
GRADY HENDRIX, author of *My Best Friend's Exorcism*

'A spectacular horror epic laden with Romero's signature shocks and censures of societal ills. A blockbuster portrayal of the zombie apocalypse and a fitting tribute to the genre's imaginative progenitor'
KIRKUS REVIEWS

'There's a weight and a depth to this that shows respect for the material, for Romero and for the genre. The authors know what readers want – and deliver. Pleasingly impressive'
SFFWORLD

THE LIVING DEAD

GEORGE A. ROMERO
DANIEL KRAUS

CORGI BOOKS

TRANSWORLD PUBLISHERS
Penguin Random House, One Embassy Gardens,
8 Viaduct Gardens, London SW11 7BW
www.penguin.co.uk

Transworld is part of the Penguin Random House group of companies
whose addresses can be found at global.penguinrandomhouse.com

Penguin
Random House
UK

First published in the United States by Tor Books

First published in Great Britain in 2020 by Bantam Press
an imprint of Transworld Publishers
Corgi edition published 2021

A CIP catalogue record for this book
is available from the British Library.

ISBN
9780552177603

Typeset in 10/14.5pt Minion Pro by Jouve (UK), Milton Keynes
Printed and bound in Great Britain by Clays Ltd, Elcograf S.p.A.

The authorized representative in the EEA is Penguin Random House Ireland,
Morrison Chambers, 32 Nassau Street, Dublin D02 YH68.

Penguin Random House is committed to a sustainable
future for our business, our readers and our planet. This book
is made from Forest Stewardship Council® certified paper.

For George.
I never got to thank you.

— DK

Now the vulture has eaten the dove, the wolf has eaten the lamb; the lion has devoured the sharp-horned buffalo; man has killed the lion with the arrow, with the sword, with the powder; but the Horla will make man into what we made the horse and the steer: his thing, his servant and his food, by the simple power of his will. Our woe is upon us.

– Guy de Maupassant, *The Horla*

Though the night be dying / May the day endure!

– *The Tales of Hoffmann*

ACT
ONE

The Birth of Death

2 WEEKS

JOHN DOE

Absovle Me Iff Yuo Can

Within the early months of the twenty-first century, before the terrorist attacks of 9/11, hospitals, nursing homes, and police departments in the United States, except for rural outposts too remedial to be computer-equipped, were mandated to join the Vital Statistics Data Collection network. This cyber-system instantly downloaded all inputted information to a division of the Census Bureau known as the American Model of Lineage and Dimensions, or AMLD, often dubbed *A Matter of Life and Death* by those who, back then, could afford black humor. Be it either one – a birth or a death – the event was entered by a doctor, nurse, or registrar, who simply clicked a link that uploaded the statistic to the VSDC.

John Doe's VSDC case number, 129–46–9875, was recognized by the system twice on the night he died: October 23. It was initially and unremarkably input by St Michael the Archangel, a Catholic hospital in San Diego, California. The second entry, the one that made the case notable, came three and a half hours later from the Medical Examiner's Office in San Diego County. It reached VSDC central computers at 10:36 p.m., Pacific standard time, but went unnoticed for another forty-eight hours, until a quiet, offish AMLD statistician named Etta Hoffmann found it while searching for abnormalities in recent files.

Hoffmann printed a hard copy of the record. Even then, she had a sense of foreboding about the systems upon which humans had come to depend.

No matter what program, typeface, or font size was originally used by an entrant, a default conversion was made, for the sake of standardization, by the VSDC system. John Doe's file was spat from an AMLD printer in a font called Simplified Arabic. Years after the launch of VSDC, there had been a Senate spat over whether it was appropriate for a government agency to adopt a typeface designated as 'Arabic'. The Democratic majority defeated the Republicans lobbying for Franklin Gothic. Upon prevailing, the Democrats indulged in satisfied winks and jolly backslaps.

None who survived the weeks after John Doe remembered this petty victory. It was but one of a million tiffs that had been tearing the country into pieces for generations. In the dark days to come, some former Congress members would wonder, if they'd only listened closer, if they might have heard America's tendons pinging apart like snapped piano wire and been able to do something to heal the wounds before the whole body politic had been ripped apart.

Thousands of files sharing similarities with 129–46–9875 were received during the three days following John Doe's death. Etta Hoffmann discovered John Doe's file while trying to determine the starting point of the phenomenon. The VSDC system did not organize entries by date and time; the original designers hadn't believed that function would be needed. Hoffmann and her coworkers had to search manually, and only later, when comparing the findings they'd thrown into a folder labeled *Origin,* did the time stamp on John Doe's dossier indicate it preceded all others. She was not 100 percent confident of it, but at some point even she had to stop searching.

There were other, more pressing matters.

By the end of that third night following John Doe's death, only two men and two women remained at AMLD's Washington office, clicking, scribbling, and filing. The quartet pulled together adjacent desks and worked in ragged, lopsided shifts, none more tirelessly, or with such enviable composure, as Etta Hoffmann.

Hoffmann had always been AMLD's oddball. Every statistician forced to work with her presumed her personal life, like her work life, was full of leaden, blank-stare interactions.

Unlike Hoffmann, the other three lingerers had knowable reasons for staying. John Campbell's recent years had been traumatic – the death of a child, a divorce he hadn't wanted – and he had no one left to run to. Terry McAllister had gotten into government work with dreams of single-handedly saving the day; he wasn't going anywhere. Elizabeth O'Toole had a husband she feared, especially during stressful times, and the hope that this event could be her escape kept her bolted to her seat.

In addition, Terry McAllister and Elizabeth O'Toole were in love. Etta Hoffmann had figured that out some time before the crisis. She did not understand this. Both were married to other people. That was something Hoffmann understood. Marriage revolved around legal documents, co-owning property, and joint tax returns. Love and lust, though, had always been illogical puzzles to Hoffmann. They made the afflicted unpredictable. She was wary of Terry McAllister and Elizabeth O'Toole and gave them additional space.

Etta Hoffmann's reason for staying? The others could only guess. Some at AMLD, miffed by Hoffmann's lack of emotion, believed her stupid. Those aware of the staggering volume of work she did speculated she was autistic. Others thought she was simply a bitch, though even that gendered slur was suspect. Besides her first name and choice of restroom, there was little evidence of how Hoffmann identified. Her features and body shape were inconclusive, and her baggy, unisex wardrobe offered few clues. Watercooler speculation was that Hoffmann was trans, or intersex, or maybe genderqueer.

A temp worker, under the influence of his English major, once referred to Etta Hoffmann as 'the Poet' because she reminded him of Emily Dickinson, pale and serious, gazing into the depths of a computer screen as Dickinson had gazed down from a cloistered berth.

Perhaps Hoffmann, as inscrutable as Dickinson, found in everyday monotony the same sort of vast morsels.

The nickname served to excuse Hoffmann's distant manner and deadpan replies. Such were the prerogatives of the Poet! Who could hope to understand the Poet's mind? It was fun for the whole office. It attributed sweeping, romantic notions to an androgynous, sweatpants-wearing coworker who joylessly keyed data while drinking room-temperature water and eating uninspiring sandwiches assembled in what was undoubtedly the blandest kitchen in D.C.

During the three days after John Doe, the Poet proved herself the best of them all, stone-faced when others broke down, eyes quick and fingers nimble when others' heavy eyelids slid shut and their hands trembled too much to type. Hoffmann, the least inspiring person anyone had ever met, inspired the other three holdouts. They dumped cold water on their heads and slapped their cheeks. Powered by cheap coffee and adrenaline, they recorded what was happening so that future denizens might find evidence of the grand, complicated, flawed-but-sometimes-beautiful world that existed before the fall.

Forty-eight hours later, five days after John Doe's 129–46–9875 report, John Campbell, Terry McAllister, and Elizabeth O'Toole agreed that there was nothing more to be done. Although AMLD's emergency power kept their office fully functional, the VSDC network was in collapse. The reports still dribbling in were little more than unanswerable cries for help. John Campbell shut down his computer, the black monitor reminding him of his lost child and lost wife, went home, and shot himself in the head. Elizabeth O'Toole began obsessively doing push-ups and sit-ups, preparation for an uncertain future. Terry McAllister, his dreams of heroism faded, made a final entry in his work log. It strayed from the usual facts and figures into something, should anyone ever find it, that might have read as gallows humor: 'Happy Halloween.'

It was three days before that spooky holiday, three weeks before Thanksgiving, two months before Christmas. Millions of pieces of candy, instead of being doled out to trick-or-treating children, would become emergency rations for those too afraid to leave their homes. Those who bought Thanksgiving turkeys early would jealously hoard them instead of inviting loved ones over to share. Thousands of plane tickets, purchased to visit families for Christmas, would molder in in-boxes.

Terry McAllister and Elizabeth O'Toole did not shut off their computers as John Campbell had; the overheated hum sounded to them like breathing, albeit the strained gasps of hospice-bed bellows. Before they left for Terry McAllister's apartment in Georgetown, Elizabeth O'Toole asked Etta Hoffmann to come with them. Terry McAllister had told Elizabeth O'Toole not to bother, but Elizabeth O'Toole did not want to leave the other woman alone. Terry McAllister was right. Hoffmann stared at Elizabeth O'Toole as if her coworker were speaking Vietnamese. The Poet showed no more emotion at this final appeal than when being handed a cube of cake at an office birthday party.

While Terry McAllister and Elizabeth O'Toole prepared to leave, they heard the dull *clack, clack, clack* of Hoffmann's robotic typing. Elizabeth O'Toole decided that Hoffmann's lifeless, dogged work ethic reminded her of the lifeless, dogged attackers described in the reports that had flooded into the office. Maybe Hoffmann, already so much like Them – even this early, *Them* and *They* had become the terms of choice – was the perfect one to understand, process, and respond to Their threat.

On the seventh day, inside Terry McAllister's apartment, Elizabeth O'Toole used her phone, which clung to a single bar of signal, to text her cousin, a priest in Indianapolis, to confess her sins. She added that she and a lover, who was not her husband, were going to try to get out of Washington. Because she had little time and battery to spare, the text was rife with misspellings. Elizabeth O'Toole wasn't watching when the phone died, so would never know if her confession had been sent or if it were one more unheard whimper at the end of the world. As she and Terry McAllister stepped from the blood-smeared foyer of the building onto a sidewalk scorched with gunpowder, with no plan other than to follow his hunch to 'head north', Elizabeth O'Toole saw her final message everywhere she looked, the letters like carrion birds daggering the November sky.

I parobalgy wont see yu agaon so Absovle me iff yuo can dfrom where you are if it is legal8 bc I hae tried to make an act of contritiojn but I cant mreember all the owrds and isnt that the scareiest thign of all how lilttel I can remember alreyad like none of itever happened? lieka ll of the life we evre lived wsa all a dream?

A Gray Murk

Luis Acocella was chasing white beans around his *caldo gallego* when the front window of Fabi's Spanish Palace exploded. As San Diego's assistant medical examiner, Luis was versed in all manners of glass contusions. He knew the meaty, grinding pocks left in cheeks by windshield safety glass, the chilling, swanlike beauty of a suicidal wrist slash performed with a chunk of broken mirror. Fabi's front window promised the latter, with its typhoon of translucent lancets catching glints from the cheap chandeliers before arrowing toward him like hornets.

Any other meal, eaten anywhere else, and Luis would have been half-dead to the world, scrolling through Facebook, Instagram, Twitter, YouTube, Snapchat, and Reddit. But *caldo gallego* was too messy, so his phone, for once, was stowed. At first, its absence kindled something like panic; his eyes kept flicking to the phone's rightful place on the tabletop, and his fingers twitched to scroll. In five minutes, however, he'd settled down and found the lack of sensory input intriguing. The piped-in mariachi music had ended and the staff hadn't gotten around to restarting it, and in its wake were the noises of real life: feet scuffling, people sighing, or laughing, or simply breathing.

Luis sat near the kitchen when he ate alone. He liked to scroll, like, comment, and post along to the comforting sizzle of kitchen sounds, and when he made an observation in Spanish, the Spanish-speaking staff became different people. The waitress would relax her neck and hips; the cooks would beam from the kitchen in a way that made Luis think, *Ah, now I'm going to get the goods.* It warmed him as much as any earthen bowl of *caldo gallego.* Language: it connected people. He wondered if his beloved phone might actually be counterproductive.

For all these reasons, Luis was too far from the window to be hurt by the detonating glass. He covered his face anyway and bailed from his chair. His instinct was good: concurrent with the deafening shatter was the chesty bellow of a gunshot.

It was 5:54 in the afternoon, early for Fabi's on a Thursday, and the other customers were protected by the tall-backed booths. No one in the restaurant had been injured; Luis knew that immediately. He'd lived long enough in San Diego – and excavated enough bullets in the course of his work – to know that rarely was one shot not met by several more.

He squatted under his table, eyes fixed to the sugar packets used to steady the table's gimpiest leg, and listened to a spray of gunshots, followed by a man's scream. There was a pause before the bubble-wrap rippling of police returning fire, too many shots for Luis to count. He heard a moist crunch – the chrome pop of one vehicle ramming another – and that was the end of it.

Luis stayed with the sugar packets. For how long, he wasn't sure. Time had a different quality when life was under threat; the seconds ticked by like little knife cuts into his flesh.

At last, he got up and dashed toward Fabi's door, glass scrunching under his heels, and plunged into the looser acoustics of a cool, violet California dusk. He unlocked his car and withdrew his emergency med kit. He'd heard a man scream, and that man might still be alive. Luis jogged along the line of parked cars until he reached Mission Bay Drive and the classic post-shooting tableaux of burned rubber on pavement, clouds of exhaust gone red and blue with swirling police lights, and abrupt gridlock beneath traffic lights blithely unaffected by the violence.

Maybe it was because of his phone-free dinner, but the next thing Luis noticed was the utter lack of reaction from pedestrians. Gunfire had ripped through the area only minutes ago. At least one car had been struck. Yet people had already returned to their gadgets, preferring bullets of information they could control with their flicking thumbs. Some took photos of the glut of police cruisers; a few framed them as selfies. They'd upload these pictures instantly, as Luis had uploaded so many of his own, proof of life in captioned boxes.

Hitting the street, Luis saw the perpetrator's vehicle, an old panel truck with south-of-the-border plates, its front fender interlocked with the side of a station wagon. The truck's passenger door was thrown open, and a man was perched on the edge of the seat. Luis knew a dead man when he saw one. The butt plate of a rusty Uzi was jammed against a chest black with blood, yet the corpse clung to the magazine as if unwilling to relinquish the behaviors that had driven him while alive.

The pedestrians had their gadgets, the shooter his Uzi. Luis wondered why, tonight, both tools looked so much alike.

There was movement in the cab, but the black-and-whites had the truck surrounded, and officers had guns pointed from behind SDPD cruisers. Dismissing the confrontation from his thoughts, Luis swept his gaze from curb to curb, searching for anyone who wasn't staring at a gadget. Ambulance sirens had intensified by the time he spotted what he was looking for. Luis trotted into the shadow of an overpass, where a man lay crumpled amid moist grime and the gleams of discarded snack bags and broken bottles.

The man was sixtysomething, and from his soggy clothing and sour odor, Luis judged him to be homeless, though he felt certain the streets hadn't been this man's home for long. There was a *T* shape to his shoulders and spine the lifelong destitute rarely had. Beneath the beard scruff were lips that, rather than draping over gums, rested upon a full set of teeth. Even his overgrown hair kept to combing contours. Most telling of all was the man's bedraggled clothing: a tailored suit, leather shoes, and a dress shirt, complete with one sur-viving cuff link. This man, Luis thought, had once been wealthy. He'd once had everything America had to offer.

Luis felt none of the serenity of his lab work as he set down his med kit, took the man by the wrists, and began articulating the limbs to get a better sense of the overall situation. He noted four bullet holes, all on the right side of the body. One high on a thigh, one high on the belly, one low on the shoulder, and the fourth low on the neck. He pushed aside the shirt collar and pressed his fingers through slip-pery blood to check for a pulse. By the temperature of the flesh alone, he knew he might be too late. He glanced at his watch. It was 6:07 p.m. Based on body temperature, death had likely occurred in the last couple of minutes. If Luis was filling out the standard paperwork, he would have given the ETD – estimated time of death – as 6:05 p.m.

Fuck – those extra minutes Luis had spent cowering under the table.

A detective was already hovering. He gruffly introduced himself as Detective Walker. He had the straight, sandy hair of fairy-tale princes and seemed as eager to get out of there as the pedestrians and motorists. He barked for a subordinate to string up police tape and then, after getting Luis's name and qualifications, ripped a sheet from a clipboard and tried to hand it to him.

'Pronounce him dead,' Walker said. 'He's part of my crime scene.'

Luis stared at the form while anger foamed in his gut. In a few hours, this dead man would be a one-sentence news item people scrolled past in their news feeds without a prick of emotion.

He displayed his bloody hands. 'I am not ready to pronounce.'

Detective Walker pointed. 'You see that cross street? I got three ambulances trying to shove through that mess. This guy's going to be ice cold by then. You haul him to a hospital, you cause me a whole night of headaches, amigo. Leave him here, where he can do some good, huh?'

'These aren't necessarily kill shots,' Luis said. 'We get this man to a hospital, we might be able to resuscitate—'

'You understand English? I said, we're in a bottleneck. Every car you see is filled with people trying to get home and binge their shows. So help me out here. I would hope you'd give a shit. It's your kind that killed this guy.'

Luis turned, his heel squishing through coagulating blood.

'My kind?'

Detective Walker was as forthright with his prejudices as he was with his work.

'Fucking A, José,' Walker growled. 'Mexicali gangbangers killed this man. Later on, we'll be counting on you to prove it. So wipe that cherry pie off your hands and fill out this fucking form.'

The anger in Luis's belly thickened. 'What do you mean you're counting on me?'

The detective loomed over him. His features were compact, a thumbprint pressed into dough. His starched collar dug deep into his neck flab, threatening bisection. Spit fizzed at the corners of his lips.

'We get these greasy perps on a murder charge, we got an airtight case.'

'Are you saying you *want* this man dead? Because it'll help your case?'

Detective Walker shrugged. 'I didn't say that. I didn't say nothin'. I didn't say nothin' about some worthless homeless fuck nobody's ever going to miss.'

The simple tools in Luis's med kit couldn't save a man riddled with bullets, but Luis had a notion they'd do a fair job mutilating this asshole cop. The kit's tourniquet would look quite smart twisted around the detective's neck. The scissors would be a stylish accent when planted in the detective's jugular. Luis tamped down his rage, old hat in a long career of taking shit. He glanced left and saw the lights of the closest ambulance.

Luis's boss, San Diego medical examiner Jefferson Talbot, was at a convention in Las Vegas. There was no way to pass the buck. Luis was stuck with this case, and that meant he had to do it right or suffer consequences from JT worse than Detective Walker's. Luis stood and waved his med kit at the ambulance down the block, hoping an EMT would see and come running. He turned to Walker, concealing neither disgust nor hope.

'I believe this man can still be saved, if we move our asses,' Luis said. 'I'll do it without you. But it'll be easier if you help. Come on. Grab his legs. Let's get him to that ambulance. You and me. Right now. What do you say?'

Everyone was a gray murk. Luis had learned that maddening lesson on the job. Blowhard assholes saved the day by knowing CPR, loathsome politicians pulled kids out of car wrecks, ex-cons with child-porn raps saved people from burning buildings. Detective Walker was the same as any of them – when you came down to it, the same as Luis Acocella. The cop unleashed a swarm of filthy phrases as he tossed aside his clipboard and grabbed the homeless man's filthy ankles. Together, they rushed the dead-or-dying man down the sidewalk until two EMTs met them, releasing the wheels from their gurney.

Luis didn't hang around after that. Other ambulances were arriving. His work here was done. That didn't mean his work for the night was even close to finished. If the sawbones at St Mike's pronounced the man dead, and they probably would, then Luis would be obligated to perform a forensics exam. But he'd be damned if he was going to let it ruin his weekend trip to see his family in La Paz. He'd do the autopsy tonight, get it over with. He pulled out his phone and texted Rosa the news. There wasn't a damn thing to do but go back to the morgue and await the call. He'd do it with Charlene if she was willing, by himself if necessary. *Just one more body to chop up,* he told himself. One more VSDC record to file. One more John Doe.

This Is the Place

The plaque had hung in his office for so long, Luis should have stopped seeing it. He couldn't count how many times a perfectly forgettable lunch hour, spent trawling through alarmist political posts, had been disrupted by its unblinking presence. It pissed him off. The plaque was shorter than most social media updates, but because Luis couldn't click it into oblivion – it was bolted to the wall above the door – it managed to draw his dry, news-feed-reading eyes back into active service.

HIC LOCUS EST UBI MORS GAUDET SUCCURRERE VITAE

His chief regret of his time as assistant medical examiner was that, roughly six months after taking the job, he'd googled the translation. Now, apparently, he was doomed to obsess over it. It was just the kind of open-ended Ouroboros proclamation he'd hated since medical school, expressly designed to drive readers mad.

THIS IS THE PLACE WHERE DEATH REJOICES TO HELP THOSE WHO LIVE

On the most basic level, he got it. The dead assisted the living by offering their bodies for autopsy. He should have quit there, wrenched the plaque from the wall, and chucked it in the dumpster. But the dead didn't really 'give' their bodies to 'help' us, did they? We *took* them. Luis thought of other Americans who had been taken as 'help': women as wives and property, Africans as slaves, the disabled and deformed as medical playthings.

The idea that death 'rejoiced' felt true. It gave voice to a thought Luis had always kept private. Anytime he opened the chest of a corpse, the vivid colors and textures beneath seemed *excited* to finally show off. The confetti of sinew sprayed by a bone saw; the blinding brightness of blood; the wet wink of the brain; the bloomed chrysanthemums of mammary glands; the balloon-animal arteries of the heart; the high-fashion leather satchel of the stomach; the golden surprise of the pancreas. His rational mind knew these were not celebrations. They were the first blushes of the mushrooming spoil to come.

It was the plaque's final three words that got Luis most turned around. It was peculiar phrasing, wasn't it? Not 'those who are alive' – a low bar that even he, a lethargic lunchtime screen-scroller, surmounted – but 'those who live'. That was an active phrase, refer-ring to those *celebrating* existence. Luis wondered if he, in this too-dark morgue in too-bright San Diego, qualified as one 'who lived'. The plaque suggested an equality between the dead and the living, a relationship that, if properly handled, would result in transcendence.

His desk phone rang, and Luis was glad. Circular thinking was pointless. He closed out his news feeds (if 'news' was what you could call animal GIFs, subtweet backbiting, fine-dining humblebrags, and sponsored shopping), checked the time, and snapped up the receiver at what his gadgets agreed was 8:22 p.m.

The news was what he'd expected; death, once you were familiar with it, held few surprises. St Michael the Archangel had pronounced John Doe dead at 7:18 p.m., with an ETD of 6:10 p.m. The source of this pronouncement, Luis learned after several questions, was an intern. A fucking intern. First, Detective Walker herds John Doe toward the grave like a rude usher, and then St Mike's lets a pimpled idiot, probably eager to beef his résumé, make the final call. If John Doe hadn't been homeless, it wouldn't have gone down like this.

Luis Acocella, at least, would get a second chance to do right by John Doe. The body was on its way to their unhappy reunion. Honestly, Luis was starting to look forward to it. He'd flay John Doe head to foot if it meant finding proof the gunshots had been survivable and that John Doe's death had, at least in part, been Detective Walker's fault. If he could sink Walker, and every SDPD fuck like him, then truly he'd be one 'who lived'.

Luis dialed Charlene Rutkowski, his diener. Being a regular human being with a life, she didn't pick up. He texted instead, giving her the straight dope. He had a gunshot victim to slice, it had to be done tonight, and she had every right to ignore this message. He hesitated before adding a final sentence, because he knew Charlie as well as he knew anybody, and if he made it personal, she'd drop everything and come. Luis hated having this kind of sway over a subordinate. But he also didn't want to cut up this guy alone. It'd been a hell of a day. He'd almost been shot, for Christ's sake.

St mikes had an intern call it. A FUCKING INTERN.

The response was immediate:

Bastards. Be there in 30.

The warm gladness Luis felt was subsumed by hotter flames of shame. Charlie knew Luis's moods better than Luis's own wife, and even though he enjoyed that intimacy, he felt a stab of guilt every single time he fostered it.

On that night of October 23, the night of John Doe, Luis Acocella was forty and had been married for sixteen years to Rosa del Gado Acocella. They had met when she was sixteen, undocumented from El Salvador, and he was a Mexican-born twenty-six-year-old who'd become a US citizen five years earlier. Though it was another four years before they began dating, the age gap haunted him, particularly when he thought of the attraction he'd felt for her when she'd been a teenager and illegal in more ways than one.

Back then, Rosa was scheduled to be deported along with her mother, who had paid everything she had to coyotes in order to smuggle the girl into the States. Luis took pride in riding to the rescue like John Wayne. Scholarships and help from his family had seen him through med school, and though he'd intended to specialize, he had loans to repay. So he opened a humble office near Los Penasquitos, studying at night and working as a GP by day, mostly for Spanish speakers, seeing Rosa whenever he could.

Rosa told her mother that Luis was 'muy hombre', a 'simpático' who had done his best over the years to help the undocumented. Mama del Gado had wanted Luis to tell deportation officials Rosa was sick and couldn't be moved until she was well again. It was a ridiculous plan, though Luis admired the woman's spunk. Instead, Luis used every trick he knew to delay deportation hearings. Over time, he slowly decided the best way to save Rosa was to marry her.

She was beautiful. So there was that. Delicate bones, honey skin, dark eyes. She claimed to love Luis, and he had no reason to doubt her beyond the obvious protections he offered. But those eyes – he never did manage to penetrate them, and, to add to his other shames, he came to prefer not to. She fit into his life every way a wife ought to, brought him the right kind of social capital, all that.

But Rosa couldn't fix his professional quandaries. His early experiences in general surgery failed to switch on any surgical lamps of enlightenment. With every disappointment on the operating table, what he hoped to get out of helping people only became obscurer. It was part of why Luis was looking forward to this weekend's trip to La Paz. With his brother, Manolo, now living in Bangor, Maine, strapped to a paralegal position that ate up his nights and weekends, Luis had been forced to turn to his father, Jeronimo, for advice. Fifty-five at the time of Luis's marriage, he'd looked fifteen years older; sixteen years later, nothing had changed. But somehow, the man's overall ill health had lifted from him old-world prejudices, leaving behind a plain-talking, white-mustached monk who delivered replies like shots of tequila. He didn't give a shit if you drank them or not.

'It's the most helpless job in the world,' Luis had explained, years earlier. 'If someone keels over on the sidewalk and you, Papá, can't save them, it's not your fault. But I've got all the training. All the tools. All the assistance I need. I've spent my whole life preparing. And they still die, right under my hands.'

'They do not go away,' his father said. 'God takes them when it is their time.'

'A boy, five. A girl, three. In the last month, Papá. How could it have been their time?'

'God's plan takes centuries to unfold.'

'We're an ant on a blade of grass, I know, I know.'

'You understand your relationship to God. Let this bring you peace.'

'Maybe I understand it. But I don't like it. If this is the God I know, I prefer not to know him. I should be able to *give* life, Papá. Even if people die, if I do my job well enough, I should be able to bring them back from death.'

No anger remained in Jeronimo Acocella, only resolve. 'That is God's job.'

Conversations like these guided Luis toward his specialty. While still a practicing GP, he took night courses. With a prodigious stamina he didn't know he had, he managed a four-year internship, emerging with a degree in pathology. As time passed, and with Rosa by his side, he found himself increasingly surrounded by Latino supporters whose goal was to see him become San Diego's first Latino medical examiner.

He ran. The competitive streak that made him excel as a med student compelled him to fight for the job with both fists. When he lost, it hurt.

The winner was Jefferson 'JT' Talbot, who, Luis believed, got the knee-jerk support of both the Black and gay communities. Luis had the Latinos, of course, but they weren't enough. Thinking of the race in racial terms – a race about race – made Luis feel shitty, but he couldn't help it. America was crisscrossed with ley lines upon which ethnic groups gathered, locked arms, and stuck together, no matter what.

JT was magnanimous. Luis swallowed his pride and took the offered post as assistant ME. Medical examiner was a *position,* with esteem, authority, and deference. Assistant medical examiner was a *job.* Instead of JT's battery of fine suits, Luis required white smocks, rubber gloves, and plastic visors to keep viscera off his face.

While JT was his boss, Luis found it impossible to think of the man as *superior* in any way. The disgruntlement got under his skin, as surely as if he'd scalpeled himself open and stuffed it in there. Was it any coincidence his relationship with Rosa also deteriorated over the years as if by cancerous infection? Her physical changes felt like a betrayal. Her honey skin grew patchy. She gained weight, a lot of it. Those deep, dark eyes that once seemed to hide secrets now failed to hide her naked desire for care and comfort.

They were the worst years of Luis's life. Was he really an asshole who cared about physical appearance more than anything? He diagnosed himself with clinical depression. Instead of seeking treatment, he drank. That Rosa accepted the change in him without a word only deepened his self-hatred. She'd expected this. All along, from the day they'd exchanged vows, she'd expected him to recede from her, to fade away, like every other husband she'd ever witnessed.

Luis didn't like admitting that his marriage might be one more reason he so readily decided to spend tonight in his chilly chop shop. He retracted his feet from his desk, stood up, and took one more look at the plaque: THIS IS THE PLACE WHERE DEATH REJOICES TO HELP THOSE WHO LIVE. Curiously, for all the times he'd ruminated over the morphemes of the Latin phrase, he'd never focused on the first four words: THIS IS THE PLACE. There was something foreboding about the phrase. As if this unassuming morgue in some bland San Diego neighborhood had been ordained as the site of something miraculous or dreadful.

Outside, a car door slammed shut. Either Charlie arriving from the Gaslamp Quarter or the corpse arriving from St Mike's. The living and the dead – they sounded the same if you didn't listen close enough.

It's the Twixt That Gets You

Luis snapped on blue latex gloves from the cardboard dispenser.

'A fucking intern,' he reminded.

'You,' Charlie said, 'are a complainer.'

'I don't deny it.'

'Deny it? You enjoy it.'

'Yes, I do.' He pointed. 'Scalpels, please, diener.'

The telltale cymbal of sharp objects dropped to a metal tray.

'Complaining raises blood pressure, Acocella. Causes insomnia. In my medical opinion, you need another hobby.'

'I don't agree. If you have a taste for, say, caviar, foie gras, Château Latour, you get enjoyment from it one, two, maybe three times a year. A perfect steak, a Cuban hand-rolled on a woman's bare thigh, sex itself – all too rare. The secret to leading the most satisfying life possible is to find enjoyment in something you can indulge in every day. Now what might that be, diener?'

Charlie's tone was dry. 'Your captivating seminars?'

'Good answer! Here's an even better answer. Each and every day, there are hundreds of moments that drive our moods into the dirt. Thus and so, if we wish to get the most out of life, we must learn to twist those moments to our advantage. To enjoy the act of not enjoying!'

'And what are you not-enjoying right now?'

'An intern. A fucking intern!'

Luis and Charlie were prepping Autopsy Suite 1 for John Doe. It was a square room dominated by six autopsy tables and bordered by counter workstations. Stainless steel, all of it, smeary in the violet fluorescents. Charlie took a sprayer and hosed down the first table, gently, so as not to conjure an aerosol of effluvial droplets. The liquid drained to a catch basin, which was tubed to a biohazard sink. Luis finished calibrating the organ scale and began making room inside a curing cabinet, where bits of clothing from homicide cases were drip-dried for later testing.

Sharpening his anger into darts of humor aimed at Detective Walker and the racist pigs he represented alleviated pressure. Charlie helped the catharsis by snatching those darts midair and hurling them back. They were playing roles for each other and knew it, but Luis wouldn't give it up for the world. As the sign above his office door said, this was life, humming right along in a place where it was supposed to have vacated the premises.

Luis glanced at Charlie affectionately. He'd pegged her wrong when she'd started two years ago. Something of a floozy, he'd thought. Charlene Rutkowski, Bronx-born with big, country-western blond hair and the swagger to go with it, was as out of place in a morgue as a cadaver would be at the Grand Ole Opry. Charlie seemed to enjoy the dichotomy. Outside the autopsy suites, she wore playfully patterned dresses that showed off cleavage and thighs. Scrubs were required in the labs, but Charlie was a magician with the shapeless green bags – they weren't shapeless on her.

Part of their routine was interspersing bawdy interplay (verboten in most workplaces, but rather common in jobs dealing with the dead) with faux-serious boss-to-underling directives, punctuated by Luis calling Charlie by her title of *diener* – an attendant responsible for cleaning and preparing corpses, handling tools, and helping with record keeping. Charlie relished repeating the word back to him in a

French accent: *dee-en-ay*. Despite all their ribbing, Luis knew its limits; he hadn't the heart to tell her the word was actually German and meant *servant*.

'Don't be so hard on interns. We were both interns once,' Charlie said.

'And our internships included lessons on how to bottle up youthful enthusiasm. We've both come a long way since then.'

'Have we? Let's see.' Charlene tapped her chin with a latex-gloved finger. 'I'm less happy, get less respect, and am paid less money. I made more waiting tables. My mom used to tell me if I fucked guys in good positions, I'd wind up in a pretty good position myself. My mom said that! Mrs Mae Rutkowski!'

'Didn't work, huh?'

'Well, look around. I've fucked my way to the bottom.'

'That's an offensive characterization of my lab.'

'Ah yes. Your lab. On a Friday night. I feel like a princess.'

'Roll me a drum of formalin, will you, Your Highness? And you might as well prepare the shears. We've got four bullets to hunt down.'

'See, this is what I'm saying. Hand me this, get me that. Men always have to be on top.'

Even by morgue standards, this was ribald, so Luis kept his reply to a noncommittal 'Mmmmm.' He was gratified by Charlie's pout. She'd gone on record saying anytime she conquered him conversationally, he retreated to a professorial *Mmmmm*. Now he made the sound as often as possible. He chuckled, slipped his phone from his pocket to check the time, as well as the news-feed notifications, and tried to use fingerprint identification to open it. He cursed. Damn latex.

'Acocella. Enough already. Seek help, you addict.'

His battery was low. Luis walked to a counter where he kept a spare charger, plugged in the phone, and switched it to mute.

'Addict,' he repeated. 'That reminds me.' He kneeled, pulled open a junk drawer, and rooted through it. 'All I'm saying is you and I, as lowly interns, wouldn't have had the bowling-ball cojones to make a call like that. This is a man's life we're talking about.' He stirred the contents of the drawer more vigorously. 'Those shots – you'll see. I mean, they're close to lethal. The jugular, the axillary, the femoral, maybe the kidney. But – what's the phrase? "There's many a slip . . ."'

'"Twixt the cup and the lip",' Charlie finished. 'It's the *twixt* that gets you.'

Luis found the dented pack of Marlboros he'd been hunting as he pictured the blood all over John Doe's ragged suit. A lot of blood, but not that much when you considered the man had absorbed four bullets. The pack took on an anvil's weight. Was all of it pointless, a doctor's perpetual raging against death? When he found himself splitting hairs between a *lot* of blood versus a *whole* lot of blood, it sure *felt* pointless.

'As much as I despise your phone, I prefer it to the smoking,' Charlie said. 'JT would fire you if he knew you lit up in here.'

'It's just . . . You should have seen this man's suit, Charlie. Like something from JT's closet. And his hair. He had good hair. And cuff links! He was somebody. Not all that long ago, he was somebody.'

'Oh, and the somebodies deserve better treatment, is that it? Would you be crumpled on the floor like the Pietà if it'd been some needle-marked panhandler in secondhand Padres sweats?'

'That's insulting.'

'You know what an expensive, tailored suit says to me, a humble diener? It says white-collar crime. It says to me, here's a guy who had sacks of money, probably sat on the board of some corporation, and got caught screwing over the workingman. Luis, come on. You tell stories about playing in the dirt in Mexico without a cent to your name. Me and my sisters used to gather used needles in the park and stick our dolls with them. Now *that's* fucked. *That's* unfair. You're feeling sorry for the wrong people.'

'If we're right, and this guy was some bigwig, why doesn't anyone know his name?'

Charlie quit tabbing through blank death certificates. 'St Mike's didn't figure it out?'

'First name John,' Luis confirmed, 'last name Doe.'

Charlie crossed her arms. 'You know who else wears a fancy suit?'

'Who?'

'A dead man. Any dead man. In a casket.'

Luis pulled out a stale cigarette, placed it between his lips – *betwixt,* he corrected – and began rooting for a light. He came up with a dusty box of matches. He tried to strike one. It snapped in two. He tried to strike another. The tip came off. A third left a red residue on the striking surface but never ignited.

'Fuck,' he muttered.

A shadow interrupted the bright overhead lights. Charlie had moved next to him. She'd already taken her gloves off and was holding out her hands in a cupping gesture. This was the other Charlene Rutkowski: absent of ego and quick to apologize when she felt she'd hurt any feelings. Luis relinquished the matchbook. Charlie tore free a match and, with great care, pressed the phosphorus head to the strip. It lit. She shielded the flame and touched it to his cigarette.

He took a needy puff. The nicotine made him dizzy, and for a moment, Charlie turned into two or three dieners. He didn't like that; Charlie, and Charlie alone, deserved his focus. He stood, grunting, and with repentance dipped the cigarette into yesterday's coffee.

'If I hadn't packed such a shitty med kit,' he said quietly.

'Acocella,' Charlie said.

Luis sighed. 'Or if I were still a doctor. A real doctor.'

'*Luis.*'

The tenderness in her voice was a soft stroke against his cheek. He gazed at her through smoke that looked like a ghostly replica of the rib cage they'd soon sever. It wasn't only Charlie's tone that had changed. It was her stance, thrust forward and yearning, every point of sarcasm smoothed. With the chugging from the cooler's air ducts and the buzzing of the refrigerated cabinets, there was never silence in the morgue. But this came close.

Both retreated from the moment, eyes and hands suddenly busy.

'So what's the deal? When's the stiff arrive?' She spoke hurriedly.

Luis looked at a watch that didn't exist – his phone performed that service now.

'Any time now,' he said.

Charlie brusquely swiped the back of her hand under her nose, as if trying to be unappealing. Her eyes had gone pink, giving her usual heavy mascara a hellish glow.

'Gotta pee,' she mumbled.

Luis nodded and watched his diener move across the lab with an adolescent awkwardness. It only made Luis like her more. She had no idea she'd just given him a gift. He was energized to have been the object of her desire. He felt worthy of the office plaque: THOSE WHO LIVE. At the same time, he felt a surge of affection for Rosa. He couldn't wait to crawl into their bed and expound upon every detail of this long day.

Even the intricacies of inner body systems, he marveled, could not match the pinprick sensitivity of emotions, those little slips of twixt that made the living so difficult to predict. He gazed at the cigarette in his coffee, disintegrating just as his life might if he made the wrong choices in this lab. It would be good to get started on John Doe. There was no twixt with the dead. The dead didn't want, didn't lust, didn't hunger, and frankly, Luis couldn't wait to get reacquainted.

Who's Got the
Last Laugh Now?

The delivery bell rang at 9:42, the same digital *ding-dong* as the chimes at Charlie's hairdresser, and Charlie's instinct was the same: to take the opportunity to check herself in the mirror. She'd tidied her mascara as best she could with the washroom's toilet paper, but some must have melted into her pores. She was gray-skinned, dark-socketed. It was a look she saw five days a week, on faces rolled from the cooler and unzipped from bags.

Luis's voice rumbled through the washroom door.

'Charlie? They're here.'

She'd stared herself down in circumstances direr than this. She pinched both cheeks, one of her mother's tricks. Crying eyes looked less pink when the cheeks beneath them were pink as well. As a side benefit, the sting braced her like a pull of whiskey. She swallowed the final, hot, sorry-for-herself tears, chose a smile of the determined variety, and bounded out the door.

'I'm here too,' she announced.

Luis stopped pacing between the third and fourth operating tables. He had a serious, tentative expression that'd be no good at all for a late-night cut-up. She hated that she'd caused it.

'Hey,' he said. 'I can handle this one. Why don't you head home? It was shitty of me to drag you out this late.'

'No. I'm in.'

'I was doing my drama bit before. This is straightforward stuff. I really don't need you.'

'Yes, you do, Acocella.' She picked up a pair of forceps and snapped them at him. 'You just don't know it yet.'

He gave her a doubtful look, maybe wondering which part of him she was picturing caught in the forceps, before trundling to the loading doors. Charlie opened a cabinet and withdrew a death certificate and autopsy report. The form was printed with the outline of a human figure, upon which she would draw circumcision, identifying moles, birthmarks, tattoos, scars, abrasions, and wounds. This sketch work was as vital as the more intrusive tasks. Once, she'd failed to notice a decedent's missing fingertips – lost from frostbite when he'd rescued a friend from an icy lake – a detail so significant to his family they refused to believe Luis and Charlie had cut up the right guy. Complaints like that reached JT and got ugly quick.

Her purposefully raucous dropping of knives, chisel, mallet, bone saw, and bowel scissors into the tray blocked out the distant conversation of the St Mike's paramedics. They blocked out Charlie's emotions too. She brought out her sticker-decorated PM40, the best scalpel in the biz, and set it beside Luis's own. She laid out the remainder of their PPE (personal protective equipment): nylon aprons, plastic sleeve protectors to cover them from wrists to biceps, and plastic visors, which they'd need if things got messy. From all indications, things would.

She was piling her thick blond hair into a hairnet when Luis rolled their lucky gurney into Autopsy Suite 1. By the orca squeak of the front left wheel, she could gauge the decedent's weight – 170, 180 tops. She nabbed Luis's hairnet and slingshotted it at him. He caught it.

'No booties,' he said.

'Tsk, tsk. Protocol.'

'If I have to slip and slide in booties at this hour, I'm going to cry.'

'Wow, special occasion,' Charlie monotoned. 'Had I known, I would've worn heels.'

She put on her booties anyway. It was a pleasure to submerge into work. At this hour, there were no young doctors fulfilling residencies, no touring med students, before whom Luis and Charlene would have to conduct themselves like professionals. Carrying out their tasks in easy, crisp concert had a calming effect on Charlie. Kicking down the gurney wheel stoppers, those four metallic clucks. The *one-two-three-lift* of transferring the body to the autopsy table. The crinkle of unwrapping heavy-duty blue-roll paper towels. Luis had a fussy way of adjusting every elastic strap of his PPE that rivaled a ballplayer's batting-box ritual. And, of course, the long, slow purr of the zipper splitting open the white plastic body bag.

John Doe was naked. His suit, scissored apart at St Mike's, was packed separately. Luis and Charlie husked John Doe of his bag and shifted him to the steel table. Death had been too recent for the body to have started smelling. That was good. What was bad was Charlie could feel the body's warmth through her gloves. She hated cutting into warm corpses. She figured any sane person hated it. Dead flesh ought to be cold and claylike, not indistinguishable from living.

She maneuvered an overhead arm that enabled a Pentax to shoot angles front, right, and left. Luis was close beside her, checking John Doe's hospital bracelets, yet the work, now that it had begun in earnest, allowed her to think of him at more of a distance. She'd never known anyone like him, that was true. But wasn't that her fault? Wasn't that the side effect of the places she'd placed herself and the people who habituated those places?

Charlie couldn't think of a single man other than Luis Acocella who hadn't, at some point, made her uncomfortable. This experience stretched back as far as kindergarten and as recently as today's morning coffee run. She'd been the kind of teen who'd gotten charges from flipping off catcallers and shouting at friends' dads to quit looking at her boobs. They were thrilling days, screaming with girlfriends in cars with the windows down, half-excited, half-terrified, electric with their own vulnerability, feeling every moment as if running fast down a steep hill. Every bit of it, though, had been preemptory resistance against infringing males.

Crushing on her superior made her feel like a stupid kid. At the same time, disregarding society's views on proper behavior brought back the windswept stimulation of her youth, when doing the wrong thing felt like it kept her definitively alive. Few spurned her advances then; few spurned them now, even the married ones. Luis was different. Even thinking of his potential rejection hurt. The body on their slab was an excellent distraction.

John Doe had to be turned onto his belly so the camera could photograph his back. Luis helped, and Charlie watched the delicacy with which he held the man's shoulder and hip. It looked fatherly to Charlie, though she knew that was only aggravating emotions again. Gentleness was just smart doctoring; you never knew what to expect from a decedent's back – gaping stab wounds, maggoty bedsores, she'd seen it all. John Doe's back, though, had a babyish perfection.

The autopsy table was also a scale. Just as she'd estimated, John Doe weighed 176 pounds. Charlie let herself shift into autopilot. Took measurements. Shot X-rays. Drew blemishes on the autopsy report's blank model. It was like the mnemonic jobs of her youth. Bartending, mopping up a country club, operating a blow-mold machine at a factory. She'd felt as dead as John Doe at those jobs. One exhausted night, she remembered, she could have sworn everyone on the factory floor was a corpse, propped up alongside whirring machines, a grotesque *tableau vivant*.

She never got that feeling at the morgue. Procedures were routine but vital; Luis knew the stakes of his job. Stakes were what Charlie had desired when she'd shocked her mother by announcing she, the girl her own mom called 'a Bronx bombshell', was going back to school for medicine. Only upon seeing Mae Rutkowski's look of pity – utter disbelief that Charlie had the brains or dedication – did she know she meant it. Having a job of actual import must underlie her feelings for Luis. The theory made enough sense that she planned to run with it.

Only one part of her job bothered her. She didn't talk about it; to give it air was to risk it blooming into full-scale neurosis. Charlie knew it was part of why she depended on Luis's presence.

Charlene Rutkowski, professional diener, lipsticked-and-tattooed commander of her own destiny, was still afraid to be alone with a dead body.

She did whatever she could to avoid it. Little things other people would never notice. Kept strict business hours so the morgue was always bustling when she was working. Timed her trips into the cooler so someone else was already there. If that was impossible, she drew the door open to its widest extent, so it would take extra seconds to close, during which she chattered to herself like a madwoman about frivolous bullshit – TV shows, pet memories – as she unshelved the corpse and rolled it toward the door with careless speed, the fear in her chest coagulating into a cold certainty that the cooler door wouldn't open.

The fear was rooted in a recurrent nightmare. The type of dream didn't matter. It could be a flying dream, a school anxiety dream, a sex dream. It could take place anywhere. An office building, a supermarket, a public pool. All that was costuming. The nightmare was sharking under the surface. At some point in the proceedings, Charlie would walk through a door and learn the truth: the nightmare had been there all along.

The nightmare was always the same but for two details.

Charlie steps into an autopsy room. It is very dark, save a center table, where a high-intensity surgeon's lamp throws a circus spotlight on a dead man. She comes closer. Each time, it is the same dead man dressed in a snappy tuxedo. His face seems vaguely familiar, but she can't identify it.

It takes a moment for her to realize the room is sealed off. The door through which she entered is gone. No other doors exist, no windows, no escape. The corpse speaks.

'Hello, Charlene.' He has a musical voice.

He sits up.

The dreaming Charlene races around the room, slapping at walls, looking for a hidden seam. She glances over her shoulder and sees the corpse swing his feet, clad in shiny dress shoes, onto the floor. She watches him stand. Sees him walk toward her with unexpected spryness. She backpedals into a corner, and the second her back hits the wall, she thinks how stupid she's been, that if she could control her fear and stay in the middle of the room, she might be able to evade him. In the corner, of course, he gets her every time.

Inches away, the corpse lifts his slender arm, elbow relaxed, palm up.

'Shall we dance?' he asks with a smile.

The smile changes into a snarl. Then back to a smile. It wavers like water.

The most frightening aspect of the dream was not knowing if the dead man was safe. Wasn't that all men, though? Except Luis Acocella? After suffering the nightmare for a year, Charlie visited her mother in Parkchester, near the Whitestone Bridge, and found herself alone in the dining room, gazing at the plastic, three-dimensional depiction of Jesus on the cross that had lorded over the family meals of her youth. Charlie moved her head slightly to the left, then right. The depiction seemed to change. A smiling, benign Jesus appeared from one angle, while from the other, his face was wrenched in agony.

Was it an illusion of light and perspective? Charlie didn't know, but figured the corpse's shifting face in her nightmare began with this likeness of another walking, talking corpse. After two years as a diener, how could she picture the risen Christ in any other way? Youth Bible groups (only memorable to Charlie for the passing around of V. C. Andrews books) taught her Jesus rose on the third day. Her medical training translated *third day* to *seventy-two hours*. Jesus's membranes would have ruptured. The limbs with which he'd performed miracles would be stiff with rigor mortis. When Jesus appeared to Mary Magdalene outside his tomb, so said the gospels, she didn't recognize him. Of course she didn't, thought Charlie. The savior would have been purple-hued, obese with gases, leaking bloody foam from nose and mouth.

Jesus wasn't the only face Charlie recognized during that visit to her mother. Mae Rutkowski, age fifty-four, had settled into the sofa with a glass of green crème de menthe, the only booze she kept in the house. The veins of her skinny wrists pushed through papery skin as she pressed buttons on the TV remote. Channels blabbered for attention. Charlie rubbed the aching temples that came free with every visit and, too tired to think better of it, mentioned the workplace nightmare that was ruining her sleep.

'Why do you stick?' Mae asked. 'Doing what you're doing, I mean. All my life, I didn't like a job I was doing, I quit!'

'Money's good,' Charlene replied robotically. The money, of course, wasn't good, not nearly enough to chip away at med school loans. Charlie knew the real reason she wasn't trading up for a better job, but there was no way she was telling Mae Rutkowski about Luis Acocella and the three strikes against him. He was Charlie's boss. He was married. He was Mexican.

'Remember Carol Springer?' her mother shouted over the TV. 'Lived over on the Grand Concourse? She became a flight attendant. Her mother told me Carol has nightmares every night. Her plane goes down in flames every single night!'

Charlie knew this line of conversation too well. She was

thirty-five. In Mae's view, the years spent becoming a diener would have been better used locking down a husband and having babies. But Charlie's interest in children began to putrefy the day she'd assisted Luis in the autopsy of a pregnant car-crash victim. Opening the woman's uterus had revealed a fetus that, in contrast to the mother's pulverized body, was in immaculate shape, its features as delicately rendered as a china doll. Holding the tiny human in a single palm froze a part of Charlie's mind that had yet to thaw; Luis had to instruct her twice to put the fetus back into the uterus. He would be buried like that, inside his mother. For the rest of the autopsy, Charlie's mind spun in infinite spirals. The fetus, living for a while inside a dead mother; the dead mother being planted into live earth; the Earth existing inside the death of space; space existing within God's supposed life-giving embrace.

Luis registered her discomfort and gently explained how, for some fetuses, a womb could be a tomb.

Charlie never forgot that comparison. A womb, a tomb.

Had Jesus's interment spot been both?

'Oh, now *here*,' Mae Rutkowski cried.

She'd happened upon a black-and-white movie, a skinny man in a black suit with tails, white bow tie, and white boutonniere, tap-dancing across a glossy stage, making marionette jerks in front of black-gowned women all wearing identical masks. Charlie's reaction was one of repulsion – this must be a horror film – but her mother spilled her crème de menthe in excitement.

'This is a good one,' Mae said. '*Shall We Dance.*'

Charlie recognized the man from her nightmare, the corpse who stood, walked, and extended a hand to take hers.

It was Fred Astaire.

Mae bobbed her head, following the dancer's twirling with Ginger Rogers. Charlie felt like Ginger, caught in Fred's bony grip and spun so quickly she was sick to her stomach. The duo turned to the camera, arms interlocked, Ginger having been transformed into the same sort of mindlessly grinning creature as Fred. They offered their free arms to the audience, inviting them to join the dance inside a grayscale world that hadn't rotted in decades and might withstand age forever. In unison, their jaws unhinged and loosed the number's last, uncomfortable lyrics.

But oh-ho-ho, who's got the last laugh now?

'I always loved Fred Astaire,' Mae sighed.

'Not me,' Charlie said, looking away. 'He always looked to me like . . .'

'Like what?' Mae didn't look away from the cursive title that had taken over the screen: THE END.

Charlie noted how her mother's green liquor looked like something that might drain from a liquifying corpse. Regardless, she wished she'd accepted a pour of it when asked.

'I don't know,' she said. 'Like a guy who's been dead for a while.'

Invisible Hands

Charlie made the first incision at 10:17 p.m. Ignoring all bullet wounds for now, she began with a notch behind the left ear before drawing her PM40 toward the breastbone in a *Y* cut. John Doe's flesh split like dough. She copied the cut from the left ear and proceeded down the abdomen, dodging the navel with a juke to the right before stopping at the pubis. There was blood, but barely any. Dead hearts don't pump. She reflected back the skin and tissues of the chest like saloon doors. Revealed were a set of ribs not so different from the sauce-slathered racks Charlie and Luis often shared at Damon's #1 Ribs.

John Doe was old enough that his rib cartilage had begun to morph into bone. Charlie used a serrated knife to saw through the fused cartilage, then took up the stainless steel rib shears. She liked operating these two-handed chrome-glossed scissors; like riding motorcycles and changing her oil, the act felt outsized and brash. She notched the jaws around individual ribs and cut through them. It was the loudest part of any autopsy. Wet cracking noises echoed about the room.

'Maybe we should *all* go topless,' she suggested.

Luis smiled and gestured with his chin.

'Just Mr Doe,' Luis said. 'Look sharp now.'

Charlie lifted the man's breastplate in a single piece and set it in a steel pan on the counter. When she returned, Luis was hovering over the open body, inhaling. If you were good, he always said – inferring he was, in fact, good – you could smell the sweetness of diabetes or the bar-floor stink of alcoholism. This sniff looked indecisive.

'What do you see?' he asked, and his tone brought Charlie joy. His questions had become less pop quizzes, more requests for a know-ledgeable second opinion.

'Bit of green fluid.' Her mother's crème de menthe flashed through her mind. 'Pneumonia, probably.' She raised a reproachful eyebrow at Luis. 'And he was obviously a smoker.'

'Yeah, yeah. Based on the entry wound, your best guess.'

'Right lung.'

'Prove it, querida.'

With a steadiness she was proud of, Charlie cut through the pleu-ral adhesions gumming the lungs to the chest interior, typical of an older man in a stricken condition. She severed the trachea and esophagus. At last, she slid her hand past the warm ball of the heart and made two long incisions on either side of the spine to release the lungs. She scooped out the right lung first. You had to be careful with internal organs. The little suckers liked to weasel away. Especially livers, especially from alcoholics. Fatty growths made them as slip-pery as water balloons.

She carried the right lung to a dish near John Doe's feet, then did the same with the left. However, she could not, as Luis had requested, 'prove it'. The right lung was black with nicotine and showed signs of pleurisy but was free of contusions that would indicate a bullet impact. She glanced at Luis, who winked. He'd known the airbags were a dead end. Charlie didn't accept defeat; she went back for the entrails, almost hungry for them. She parted the bottom of John Doe's Y cut, detached the rectum, and snipped through the web of fat that kept the intestines in place. She reeled the long, ropy organ into a steel mixing bowl.

The intestines were not her quarry. The liver, she'd decided, was where the abdominal bullet was hiding, and with the intestines cleared, no organ was easier to extract. Three vessels and a few ligaments later, the big, blubbery organ was in her hands. She settled the liver in the pan alongside the lungs and massaged it.

'Touchdown,' she said. Picking up her forceps, she began to extract the bullet.

'Vital?' Luis pressed.

'Nyet. I'd say a rib stopped it.'

'Uh-*huh*.' Luis punched a fist into his opposite hand. His gloves, wet with fluid, smacked. 'And that was the likeliest kill shot.'

Charlie got the picture. Did she ever. Luis wanted to prove the four GSWs – gunshot wounds – weren't what, in Luis's phraseology, 'shut this guy down'. Charlie had zero interest in interdepartmental San Diego civics, but couldn't deny the dented bullet she let plunk into a specimen jar.

'I'm coming around to your paranoia, Acocella. Bed rest, a little hospital mush, some light narcotics, this dude walks home.'

'Hot damn. That Walker fuck is history.'

Charlie smiled uneasily. Antiestablishment oaths spoken in a state facility made her wonder if, among all the high-tech equipment, there was hidden a secret microphone. More likely, their words would be picked up by the mic Luis wore. With the touch of a button, it recorded his comments and transcribed them to text. The completed, full report would be uploaded to a prescribed list of city and county agencies; a separate command could email the same text to the VSDC system in D.C. That was the last thing Charlie needed, some upstart at the Census Bureau flagging her morgue for rebellion.

'City living's what killed this guy,' Charlie said. 'Wrong place, wrong time.'

'Mmmmm,' Luis replied, touching a finger to the Record button.

The voice-recognition processor was designed to make the

pathologist's job easier, but the technology was, to say the least, imperfect. Long after the day's dirty work was done and the cadavers rolled back into the cooler, Luis could be found in his office, correcting transcripts he claimed had a 20 percent error rate. He was rigorous with autopsy reports; that's why he let Charlie do the wet work while he made vocal notes into the mic and ink ones into a binder.

'White male,' he said. He took his finger off the button and smirked at Charlie. 'Let's see how they fuck that one up. *Flight meal? Wire mule?*'

'You have an accent, Acocella. Might as well accept it.'

'Lord forbid someone in this country has an accent.'

'Hey, I have one too, so I'm told.'

'I'd love to see how this doohickey would manhandle your lovely brogue.'

'Machines, man.' Charlie shuffled over to John Doe's neck, the second of the four shots. 'That mic? That phone attached to your hand? You realize it's all going to fuck us in the end, right? Have you ever had a single problem understanding me?'

She glanced up from the body and watched his Record-button hand halt. Her body went just as still; she hadn't realized what she'd said. It might be late, this might be a morgue, and their activities might be suffused in malodorous smells, but this pause of theirs was abundant in soft, sandy textures and floral scents, better even than the night's earlier cigarette-lighting intrigue.

'Never,' Luis replied.

Charlie lowered her plastic visor to hide her face.

'Mmmmm,' she said.

He laughed and she was relieved, though her heart was racing.

Within forty minutes of John Doe's arrival in the autopsy room, while Luis Acocella took fastidious notes and spoke into his mic, Charlene Rutkowski, working roughly from the head down, removed a total of three bullets and several more vital organs from the corpse, taking breaks to razor off samples that she submerged in preservatives for later testing. Luis's insistence that John Doe was 'somebody' dug at her, but she had to admit he'd been on to something. Teeth were a corpse's capsule history, and John Doe's molars showed evidence of good dental work. Charlie finished by digging into the body's right thigh, not even close to the femoral, and pulling out a bloody lump of lead.

'There you have it,' Luis celebrated.

'What do you figure?' Charlie asked. 'Heart attack?'

'Dig it out. Let's see.'

Charlie raised her visor and patted at perspiration with blue-roll.

'We hardly need to,' she said. 'Nothing hit this guy's vitals. He's old. Out of shape. Smoker's lungs. Alcoholic's liver. A kid in a Halloween costume could have scared this guy to death. Four bumps from an Uzi? Forget about it. Heart attack. Hundred percent chance.'

Luis surveyed the notes in his binder and clicked the Record button on his earpiece with obvious gusto.

'Cause of death not – repeat, not – ballistic insult. Proceeding with examination of the heart. Checking for occlusion. Cardiomyopathy. And not just on the left. Could be an arrhythmogenic right ventricle. Or could be purely electrical. An inherited condition. Brugada, possibly.'

He sounded genuinely happy. Charlie knew this had nothing to do with her fine performance and everything to do with what she saw as a petty grudge. With reluctance, she picked up her PM40, purple with blood. She didn't want the autopsy to end, she didn't want to have to grab the suction tubes and start cleaning up. Was there any sillier thing? She wanted to be happy alongside Luis, to suggest they celebrate over drinks, maybe even a second cigarette.

She sliced John Doe's pericardial sac, then finned her hand beneath the heart and wrapped her fingers around it. Warm as a desert rock. She used the PM40 to disjoin the vascular attachments, set down her scalpel, and lifted the organ out. She cradled the tired, brown-red muscle in her cupped hands and carried it to the examination basin, only to find she wasn't ready to let it go.

How many times had she held someone's whole heart in her hands? Such a corny sentiment had no place in the mind of the cynical Charlene Rutkowski. While Luis droned into his mic, oblivious to her melancholy, she let the heart's ripe warmth cloud her senses until she saw the heart not only as John Doe's but her own as well. The throb in her chest slowed, beat by shuddering beat, until it was as inert as the hunk of meat she held. Charlie had the strange notion an invisible hand had reached inside her – billions of invisible hands, maybe, inside everyone on the planet – hands belonging to dieners skilled beyond comprehension, sifting, prodding, slicing, and determining if humans were truly alive or if the whole herd of them had been dead on their feet for some time.

Days later, when she had a moment to dwell upon anything beyond survival, Charlie would tell herself if only she could have kept cradling that heart, things might have turned out differently. The invisible hands would have cradled her back, cradled everyone, given humanity a chance to correct course. But she couldn't hold on. The eviscerated corpse next to her moved, entirely on his own, and Charlie dropped the heart. It fell to the floor, landing with a light thump. Instantly, the invisible hand became visible. It was the slender white hand of Fred Astaire, and with dawning horror, Charlie saw she'd taken it and couldn't pull free from its grip.

Fred smiled. He had no teeth, no tongue, nothing but a black hole.

'Shall we dance?' he asked.

The Miscarriage

The neck torqued. Luis's finger, instantly sweaty, slipped from the Record button of his earpiece and landed on a binder full of notes that seemed to lose all factual status.

The corpse's neck was striped with gore from Charlie's incisions. The right-side cord, known to medical texts as the sternocleidomastoid, was taut as a bridge cable. Three separate drops of blood snailed down it toward the slab. The rest of the world, in a tease of things to come, had gone dead – the silence was absolute. Luis's breath and Charlie's breath held tight; it felt like the fate of the world hung on that single flexed neck muscle. Then, a dull gonging: John Doe's skull knocking against the table.

'Jesus,' Luis whispered. His hand moved across his chest in a holy sign he hadn't made in decades. 'Madre de Dios.'

He heard a soft thud on the floor and noticed in his peripheral vision the skid of a dropped human heart, bumped by Charlie's bootie-covered shoe. He tore his eyes from John Doe – it felt like his eyes were being spooned out, what doctors called *enucleation* – and found Charlie holding her empty, blood-slicked, gloved hands before her.

Nothing upset Luis more than the slide-whistle tone of his stalwart diener.

'How long,' she gasped, 'after . . . after a—'

'Muscle contractions. The muscles—'

'—after a body dies—'

'There's cases. I mean, I've *read*—'

The corpse opened his eyes with a sound like the *tsk* of a tongue, a swift damnation of the stupid sputtering of an outdated race. Luis's last, worthless word banged around metal surfaces as the corpse flexed his neck again, harder this time, and turned his head, attention apparently drawn by Luis's voice. And there he was: John Doe, looking at Luis Acocella. Beneath drooping lids, the corpse's eyes were clouded with mucus. Irises once the color of black coffee had turned mocha from some internal milk. Luis swayed his body to the left as he might to test an unleashed dog's intent, and the eyes followed. The movement was uneven, but of course it was – the vitreous humor was skipping across dry sockets.

'Is this . . . ?' Charlie looked at Luis. 'Acocella. Luis. Is this . . . ?'

He did not respond, because whatever Charlie's question was, the answer was simultaneously *absolutely yes* and *no way in hell.* John Doe, however, did respond. The corpse redirected his head in Charlie's direction. More blood, cool and thick, syruped from the hole in his neck. His white eyes landed on hers. There was something soft there, like the cataracts of an old dog; they were also as unreasonable as stone.

Luis's hand again moved by instinct, not to sign the cross but to touch his earpiece. Whatever this was, it must be recorded; Jefferson Talbot might have won the election for ME, but it would be Luis Acocella who handled this right. Doing so might also save his sanity. He depressed the button.

'John Doe is moving.' His voice was distant and pipsqueak. 'That's John Doe forwarded to the San Diego Medical Examiner's Office by St Michael the Archangel on October 23. It's been four . . .' He consulted his binder: comforting checkboxes and fillable blanks. 'Nearly four and a half hours since ETD and' – he looked at his watch – 'three and a half since pronouncement. Vital organs have been extracted.

But he is moving. Repeat: John Doe is moving and in a most deliberate—'

The corpse lifted his right arm toward Charlie.

Luis's first impression of the gesture, one he would carry until the end, was not one of violent threat. John Doe had awakened, and his first instinct was to reach out. Who could say why? For contact, for help, for security. But his right deltoid, having been victim to first a bullet and second Charlie's scalpel, hadn't the integrity to finish the gesture. The arm sagged.

Nothing was wrong with the corpse's hand flexors. His fingers tightened, relaxed, tightened. This motion seemed radically different. This was no open-palmed yearning. These were claws out to snag, an idea worsened by John Doe's splintered, yellow nails. However he had longed for Charlie in his first seconds, now he craved her in a different way. His half-lidded eyes bulged in her direction, and she took a step back, rattling the tray of surgical tools.

Luis heard the *zing* of Charlie swiping her PM40 from the cart. Though he could diagnose her fear from her blanched face and shaking hand, she did not look to be panicking. She held the scalpel at her side. That was good, though he did not like the way she stared at John Doe's clenching fingers. It was the expression of a woman on the edge of a dance floor being offered the hand of a poisonous man.

Keep talking, he told himself. He hit his headset button.

'I've read cases,' he continued, 'of contractions. Twitches. But we're four and a half hours in, here. The arm, the head – they're moving in concert. This is—'

'I *know* what this is,' Charlie snapped. 'It's a man staring at me.'

'That's . . . ridiculous.'

'Put that in your report,' Charlie said.

The corpse tried to sit up. He couldn't, of course; the Y cut had robbed all strength from his abdominals. But there was no mistaking the effort. The flabby obliques quivered beneath a cake of drying blood. The gluteus maximus, flattened to the table, drew taut. John Doe rocked slightly, side to side, testing his equilibrium. He looked like an infant, innocent and ambitious, trying to roll over for the first time.

This realization sliced Luis with a PM40's ease. He thought of Rosa, in bed by now, the cherubic smile of her sleeping face. She'd been pregnant once, an event they'd celebrated with thoughtless enthusiasm until her miscarriage. Rosa had called him at work, saying she didn't feel well. Instead of going home, he'd suggested phoning their ob-gyn. After she hung up with Luis, Rosa miscarried in the upstairs bathroom. She scrubbed the room afterward so he never had to see a spot of blood. Subsequent exams diagnosed Rosa with uterine abnormalities that made bringing a baby to term unlikely, even risky. Luis assured Rosa he didn't mind, but sometimes when he had to navigate the bathroom by moonlight, his sleep-fogged peripheral vision caught the aborted baby coyly hiding in the bathtub, behind the toilet, in the towel closet, somehow living off trash bits, waiting to reintroduce itself to the family.

For a moment, John Doe was that child born anew, this time right in front of Luis, where he could do something about it. If his diener got out of the way, he could slide in beside the corpse, put a gentling hand on the straining body, whisper calming words, apologies, whatever it took.

'Charlie, step back,' Luis said.

Her eyes were locked on the corpse, her hand squeezing the scalpel.

'Rutkowski,' he hissed. 'Step *back*.'

It was the miscarriage all over again: he waited too long to offer help. Rocking, John Doe achieved enough momentum to allow his torso to slip across his own bodily fluids and topple over the lip of the table. It was an ugly, profane fall, stiff limbs flailing, genitals flopping, the curtain of parted chest flesh rippling on the way down.

John Doe landed on his back with a loud slap, spattering tissue across Charlie's legs. She scuttled backward, her free hand pulling the instrument cart with her. John Doe's arms and legs kept moving, the legs of an upturned beetle.

'Not dead,' Charlie said. 'What did I do?'

'He *is* dead,' Luis said.

'I cut out his insides!' she cried. *'What did I do?'*

'You dropped his heart on the fucking floor!' Luis shouted. 'He's dead! He's dead!'

Was he trying to convince himself? Or the people who might listen to this recording? He looked down. The heart, flat as a purse, was two feet away. Impulse gripped him, and he kicked the heart to prove to Charlie she was talking madness. The heart wept red tears on impact and bounced against John Doe's side, a pool-table bank shot. It got the corpse's attention. John Doe found Charlie, now upsettingly far away. Lodged against table legs, the corpse had more leverage and was able to flop himself over. He began to pull himself along on his split belly. *My baby,* Luis thought wildly, *is crawling already.*

John Doe pulled himself forward with first one elbow, then the other, functioning despite the dissected shoulder.

'What does it want?' Charlie begged.

Luis found it an astute question. Because the corpse *did* want; he wanted palpably, achingly. Luis pictured the pedestrians after John Doe's shooting, how little they'd cared about life versus death, how quickly they'd gone back to the Novocain glow of the same gadgets he adored, how little they, or he, wanted anything real at all. The corpse had brought *want* slamming back into the world: *his* want to get closer to them, *their* reawakened want to survive.

John Doe's limbs, slathered with autopsy ooze, fought for traction. He slid closer to Charlie, who did not look capable of further movement.

'Stop,' she ordered.

The corpse did not stop. His jaw opened. Bloody drool sluiced down his chin. He heaved himself forward. His spine sank, and Luis wondered if the emptied torso and extracted ribs might result in total skeletal collapse. Not yet, anyway – John Doe's left hand snagged Charlie's tennis shoe.

Charlie flung the instrument cart. Scalpels, probes, forceps, knives, and scissors all hit the floor with clacks and clangs Luis believed would reverberate forever. He watched John Doe's right hand land atop one of the scalpels. Again, it was as with a baby: put something in baby's hand and baby grabs it. The corpse's fingers closed around the PM40. The blade, kept razor-sharp by Charlie, cut through all four fingers so deeply they folded against the back of the corpse's hand.

Luis winced with a father's urge to console, but John Doe's expression reflected no pain. He didn't seem to mind losing half his fingers. He kept inching toward Charlie. Luis, meanwhile, just stood there, blandly narrating the bald facts of the matter ('He is crawling. I can see the hamstring muscles flexing through the exit wound in his thigh.'), while doing nothing whatsoever to affect them.

Charlie did; she always did. Luis had always felt that she operated in the real world while he bobbed in the ether of ideas. Charlie never ran out of stories of youthful partying, drinking, and getting high, all while navigating creeps and gropers, from crap-job supervisors to med school professors. She'd been mugged three times in the Bronx. She'd defended her drunken old man, Maury Rutkowski, twice in bar brawls. She'd once tackled a burglar robbing a liquor store.

Now Charlene Rutkowski reared back and made one hell of a kick. Her sneaker struck the corpse square in the chin. John Doe's head snapped back. The weight of his skull twisted him sharply right. His pelvic bone pivoted through his own lubricating sludge until he faced Luis. Two teeth fell from between John Doe's lips, borne on a cascade of pink slime. As if nothing had happened, he recommenced crawling, now toward Luis.

The movement broke Luis's paralysis. Unlike Charlie, he had no hero in him, but if he held it together, he could still be of use – his recording of this event, whatever it was, must be delivered before the next impossible event prevented it. He whipped off his earpiece and rushed to the computer. He jumped on the stool so fast he nearly bounced off it. His gloved hand smeared blood, a hallucinogenic red, against the mouse's white plastic. He cursored for the VSDC app, overshot it, tried again, overshot in the other direction.

'Sux!' Charlie cried. 'We'll shoot him with sux.'

'Get it,' he confirmed.

Luis heard bootie-coated shoes rush away, followed by the creak of an opening autoclave. A small *clink* indicated the removal of a hypodermic. A squishing noise drew Luis's attention, and he glanced to the left to see that John Doe had followed him. Behind the corpse trailed a foot-wide smear of blood and fluids. Luis cursed, then single-clicked the VSDC app, then triple-clicked it, neither of which did squat.

'Shit!' he shouted.

A blur: Charlie darting past Luis. He heard her keys jangle as she unlocked the glass door of a pharmacy. With hands this unsteady, it would have taken him ten tries to do the same. He looked back at John Doe. The thing had halved the distance toward him, ten feet away now. The dead man's back was beginning to droop into his vacant body cavity, his spine becoming a reptilian ridge. The milk white of the corpse's eyes glowed as the monitor brightened with the VSDC app.

Luis hissed in victory and stabbed his earpiece with a cable connected to the desktop. He cursored across the interface, clicked open a menu, and slid down to choose an option. Too far, the wrong option.

'Shit shit shit shit!'

He clicked Back and was met by the Circle of Hell, that ubiquitous, pulsing wait symbol. He swung his head back. John Doe was six feet away, having trouble with the corner of a cabinet jabbing into his side. The left flap of his chest had adhered to a dry patch of floor. The flesh stretched as John Doe struggled. Luis watched hairy epidermis rip unevenly, revealing beige fat beneath.

Back to the computer: the Circle of Hell still circled.

A crisp crack, a scream. He looked up to find Charlie in a posture of comic terror, both hands clutching the air beside her ears, the hypodermic shattered at her feet.

'Fuck me!' she wailed.

'Plastic!' he shouted. 'Use a plastic one!'

'Don't yell at me!'

'You dropped the heart! You dropped the syringe! Stop dropping things!'

Charlie ran for another needle. Back to the monitor. The app's home screen again. Luis pulled down the menu with arduous care and clicked to load the VSDC's entry page.

A meaty ribbon of flesh lay by the cabinet corner like a dead snake. John Doe had pulled his love handle straight through it. The dead body was five feet from Luis. John Doe used his good arm to pull himself a few inches closer and reached for Luis despite the distance. When his fingers closed on nothing, he returned to crawling. The thing was stupid, Luis realized. For some reason, the idea stung, as if he'd just indicted himself and everyone he knew.

Now beside Luis, Charlie inserted her fresh needle into a drug bottle and raised the plunger, filling the translucent hypodermic with liquid. Succinylcholine, a neuromuscular paralytic that took mere seconds to kick in, was used by anesthesiologists to relax a patient's muscles to allow insertion of an endotracheal tube. Too much could be fatal. Tonight, Luis had lost all sense of *fatal*. He watched Charlie fill the entire barrel.

Back to the computer once more. The icon of his transcribed voice file was waiting, as innocuous as the hundreds of others he'd sent during his time on the job. He clicked it and hit Send. He waited for the confirmation, prayed for it, but never got to see it.

Cold flesh enveloped his ankle.

John Doe had grabbed Luis with his right hand, the one sliced by the scalpel. When Luis kicked, the front halves of the corpse's fingers, attached by strands of flesh, flopped like loose shoelaces.

This corpse couldn't hurt him, Luis thought, feeling a thin rod of scientific curiosity seep through his panic. Maybe he'd sent the file to the VSDC too soon. Maybe there was more to learn here. Something historic. Isn't that what the sign in his office suggested? THIS IS THE PLACE.

John Doe's head jerked forward. Teeth clacked, chiming like china, along Luis's pant cuff.

Luis retreated a few feet from his stool.

'The fuck was that?!' he yelled.

'He tried to bite you,' Charlie said in astonishment.

'The fuck!'

'Move.' Her voice had gone hard. 'I'm loaded.'

She lifted the syringe, thumb to plunger, and began to crouch. Luis coiled his right arm around her waist to hold her back.

'Charlie,' he said, 'wait.'

John Doe kept coming. His left hand happened upon a leg of the stool. He pulled experimentally. The stool tipped onto a single leg before settling back. The corpse's white eyes studied the curious development. Baby stuff again, toying with objects, observing outcomes. No, Luis couldn't think that way, not if they were going to put this thing down.

'Don't get close,' Luis said. 'You could get infected.'

'You think this is some kind of disease?'

The stool fell, the loudest crash of the night. John Doe didn't flinch, though it hit the tile an inch from his face. He stared at the stool for a few seconds as if evaluating prey. His neck cranked again, and he looked at Luis and Charlie. His mouth opened and closed, opened and closed, strands of mucus stretching from upper to lower jaw. He planted his hands on the floor and moved toward them.

'I'll get him from behind,' Charlie said. 'Intramuscular.'

'Do not do that!'

'Why the hell not?'

Luis drew back a few feet, out of John Doe's range, tugging Charlie with him.

'What if it doesn't work?'

'Acocella! There's enough curare in here to drop a T. rex!'

'Think! He's not breathing. He doesn't have lungs. He doesn't even have a heart! What's sux going to do?'

'What's he on, then? Batteries?'

Luis scolded himself for his sharp tone. *There are answers. Be calm. Be professional.* He scrutinized the thing – no, the *cadaver*. John Doe's eyeballs shifted their weird white gaze between him and Charlie. His lips wrinkled back from his teeth. A muscle along his side spasmed uncontrollably. Batteries: Charlie had to be correct. Some kind of power source had plugged into this thing's cerebellum. Following the trail of the corpse's grotesque slither to the beginning, Luis noticed his smartphone resting on the counter, aglow from missed alerts.

'What about wireless?' he whispered. 'We're all holding little computers, soaking up who knows what. Maybe some kind of bad signal gets sent, hits this John Doe like a tuning fork.'

'This is crazy enough,' Charlie said, 'without you going crazy too.'

She was right, Luis told himself. This wasn't something to be strapped to a table or slid onto a rack for study. It was a miscarriage, if not *the* Miscarriage – a flawed rebirth on a tidal wave of rotten amniotic fluid. Like Rosa in the bathroom, perhaps Luis's job was to take care of this miscarriage so no one else had to see it.

'You won't think less of me,' he asked softly, 'if I kill it?'

Charlie turned to face him. Her smock crinkled against his.

'It's like you said,' she replied simply. 'He's already dead.'

Luis looked toward the northeast corner of the room and felt Charlie following his gaze. Though she'd never asked about it, she had to be aware of the cabinet there, black-and-yellow striped and labeled *SDPD*. Some questions had obvious answers, especially in a country where mass shootings barely crested the news-feed froth. Luis remembered voting against the need for the police magazine, saying he'd rather have a bigger latex-glove budget. Now he needed what was inside. It felt like failure, capitulating to a savage mind-set that had always been his job, as a doctor, to fight against.

He gently took hold of the key ring in Charlie's hand. He pulled, but she pulled back. It had the same effect as some scenes in the romances he occasionally watched with Rosa, when a woman pulled a man's tie to bring him closer.

'Let me do it.' She smiled as best she could and shrugged. 'I'm your diener.' She pronounced it perfectly. Luis realized she'd known all along how to say it and had been doing it wrong for comic effect – or to feed his ego. He hated that he'd ever thought an iota less of her than she deserved.

His effort to smile back was disrupted by the hard, wet smack of John Doe's hand on the tile.

Luis broke toward the corner. His hands, as predicted, were less steady than Charlie's, but on the third try, he slotted the key into the cabinet lock. Unlatching a bolt burred with rust from nonuse, he opened the door. He knew what was inside, expected to see what he saw, but still paused before peeling off his gloves. He didn't dare wear latex when he needed a grip this sure.

He took the preloaded .38 revolver from the shelf.

Irregular thumps – Charlie stumbling – echoed across the room. Luis hurried. The gun was so heavy he imagined the floor cracking under its weight, the building's concrete foundation pebbling, the earth crumbling as humanity fell. He blinked the vision away along with sweat as he turned. Charlie, gaze fixed to the floor, had retreated from the corpse, which, pursuing, had become entangled in computer cords. John Doe bit at the wiring, raking incisors down a printer cable hard enough to peel the plastic coating.

Next to Charlie, Luis took the safety off the revolver and pointed it at John Doe's head. It was the right thing to do, yet he expected Charlie to stay his hand. She did not. Luis focused on the crenellations of the trigger instead of the whisper at the back of his brain that this was the wrong response to the Miscarriage and that, once done, there could be no going back.

He shot, and for the second time that day, John Doe died.

Sixty-Four Floors

The corpse's skull broke into irregular pieces scattered across John Doe's back and legs. Pink-gray matter, once the brain of someone who'd mattered, splattered across tile. The dull light that had animated John Doe's white eyes dimmed. The body sagged to the floor, limp as a steak, except for the head, which was still noosed in computer cables. Bloody drool, the last thing John Doe would ever offer, skimmed down a power cord.

Luis slumped against the counter. Charlie slumped against him.

They panted until their pounding chests synchronized.

'The fuck, right?' Charlie rasped.

'That's right,' Luis said. 'The *fuck*.'

Luis surveyed across the lab. Blood and fluid, red and yellow, smeared everywhere. Autopsy tools displaced, as if by explosion. An overturned stool. A prone body, dead from a bullet he'd fired – he, Luis Acocella, assistant medical examiner of San Diego, had *shot* someone. What would local media make of that? He felt the gun in his hand and hissed like it was hot. He looked about, wishing for a supernatural vortex to whisk it away, and settled for putting the safety back on and placing it carefully into the pocket of his scrubs.

Charlie audibly swallowed. 'Wireless signals. Batteries. Whatever. Something made his brain send signals to his limbs. To his . . . mouth.'

'With rigor mortis setting in? Cut up all to hell?'

Charlie shivered against him. He felt her bring individual muscles into military formation before using the counter to guide her toward the office phone. She barked a laugh. 'Who do I even call?'

'My father told me God takes people when it's their time.'

'Don't start talking God shit.'

'He said God's plan takes centuries to unfold.'

'Acocella, look at me. I can't have you having a spiritual crisis right now.'

Despite feeling any movement would make him vomit, Luis rotated his head. Charlie stood by the phone. Her familiar pugnacious expression saturated Luis with gratitude.

'What have you always told me?' she asked.

Luis shrugged through exhaustion the weight of chain mail. 'Smoking. Quit smoking.'

'You told me this job isn't about the dead. It's about the living. What just happened – I know it's hard to think. I feel that way too. But we need to tell people. We need to tell them right away. I know you were an altar boy, Acocella, but this is science. Not God shit.'

He peered into the table's polished steel. A gorgon doppelgänger stared back. Luis nodded in agreement with Charlie; his twin's gesture was less conclusive.

'Good,' Charlie soothed. 'Now tell me who to call.'

There was no protocol for this, which meant the emergency call list was one name long. Luis inhaled sharply. He had to be the one to make the call, so he'd better do as Charlie said and piece his shit together. The process was like puzzling extracted organs back into their home cadaver.

Fighting dizziness, he went the long way around the corpse, passing the glutinous ring of bio-matter where John Doe first hit the floor, the upset tray of instruments, the muculent trail of the corpse's progress. He avoided bits of skull and brain as he dislodged his phone from its charger.

Messages awaited. A lot of them. He flicked his thumb and a train of notifications scrolled by, all voice mails from Rosa, caboosed by a single text: *CALL ME*. Annoyance flickered. She'd bombed his phone like this before, once when a broken pipe flooded the kitchen, once when a squirrel had gotten inside the house. Whatever her current emergency was, it would have to wait.

He tapped over to his favorites, though conversing with Jefferson 'JT' Talbot could hardly be considered a favorite task. While JT's phone rang, Luis stared at the bottoms of John Doe's feet. It didn't matter who you were, captain of industry or homeless beggar, the soles of your feet returned you to the infant you once were, the baby-fat wrinkles, the knobby little piggies.

You didn't kill something defenseless, he told himself. *This wasn't a miscarriage.*

JT picked up on the fourth ring.

'Acocella,' he said.

JT had a vivacity Luis coveted, along with the ability to adapt to his surroundings, to deploy gayness or blackness or concerned profession-alism as needed. Tonight, Luis encountered a JT he'd never met before, empty and lumpen of tongue. Luis hesitated, wondering if somehow his smartphone, not so smart after all, had dialed incorrectly or if he'd woken JT from sleep. Impossible: it was midnight in Vegas, equivalent to six o'clock anywhere else, especially for a night prowler like JT.

'I know it's late,' Luis said. 'I'm putting you on speaker.'

He set the phone alongside the bowl of intestines.

'Why?' JT's spike in caution was a sign of life. 'Who's there?'

'Just Charlene Rutkowski. My diener.'

'I can't – Acocella, I can't do it. No speaker.'

Luis and Charlie stared at each other. Both knew Jefferson Talbot rarely turned down an audience, and when he did, he let the excluded know damn well why they were being excluded. This was, again, out of character for their boss.

'All right,' Luis lied. 'You're off speaker. What's wrong?'

JT laughed – a goblin's cackle. 'You tell me, Acocella. It's *your* name on *my* phone.'

'You don't sound so good, JT. Is there something we need to know about?'

JT was silent. Luis detected voices in the background, and not the boisterous discord of the casino or private-suite soirée JT would have sought out. These were unpleasant rumbles, terse officials in a closed environment.

'You had a body revive,' JT said, almost sadly. 'Am I close?'

If the lab could get any colder, it did. Luis felt a *Y* cut unzipping his torso; everything inside collapsed outward, leaving him as weightless as an empty body bag. Luis mourned his thoughts of only minutes ago, when he'd believed the horror of what they'd witnessed could be contained, disinfected, burned, whatever it took. But JT already knew about it. Which meant it was bigger. Luis felt his femurs and tibias pop from his decomposing legs. He was going down. They were all going down.

'JT . . . ?' It came out like a plea, lackey to boss man.

'How long since ETD?' The query sounded programmed.

'Four and a half? Five? JT, he got up. He came after us.'

'*Après la mort,*' JT chuckled direly. 'Am I right?'

'You gotta tell us what you know,' Luis said.

The background discussions grew louder. Sharp thumps shot through the audio, the sound of a phone being jostled, perhaps moved to a stealthier position. JT's voice resumed in a louder, more sibilant rasp, likely amplified by a cupped hand.

'I've heard shit,' he hissed. 'There's a couple guys here who work at the – I can't talk about it.'

'Who?' Luis demanded. 'Where are you?'

'A party?' JT said, then laughed again, another crazed sound. 'Talk to me, Acocella. Because those men, they're looking at me. I can't say the words I want to say.'

Luis's fantasy of a desperate JT had come to pass, but he couldn't relish it. He felt he'd do anything to resurrect the haughty, self-centered Jefferson Talbot. He looked to Charlie for help, but she shook her head. She'd removed her hairnet, and her python curls swayed over a heaving chest. Luis cleared his throat.

'We had a . . . John Doe.'

'SDPD?'

'Yeah.'

'I knew that's why you were there so late. You guys cut him?'

'Uh-huh.'

'Head case?' JT asked. 'Tell me about the brain.'

Luis recalled the .38's puff of smoke. He didn't want to admit he'd shot John Doe. Not to JT, and not to himself either.

'There was no reason to examine the brain,' he said carefully.

JT's exhale crackled the phone speaker.

'Same. Damn. Thing.' His voice hardened. 'You send in anything yet?'

Luis looked at Charlie. Her thumbs-up injected him with a few cc's of confidence.

'Yes, sir,' he replied. 'Local and VSDC.'

'Oh, shit, man!' The sanguine voice that held so many state workers in thrall went squeaky. 'Every single VSDC record is going to get combed through. Call them. Do it now. Retract the report. Mark my words, Acocella. Shit is going to rain down, and the storm is headed straight our way.'

Confusion was as thick as viscera; Luis tried to wipe it away.

'What was I supposed to do? JT, what *am* I supposed to do?'

JT's audio was overwhelmed with basso tones. Whoever was in the room with JT had come closer. Luis heard his boss talking to the other person and angled his head to hear better. Charlie came closer, toeing around John Doe's hog-tied head. The deep voice was a subaudible rumble. JT returned, the phone crackling like a cleared throat.

'Acocella. You're still in the autopsy suite?'

'Yes. But—'

'I need you to stay put. Stay with the body. We're going to . . . send help.'

Charlie gestured fiercely for Luis to end the call. He felt trapped, light-headed.

'Who's *we*?' Luis managed.

'Just do it, Luis,' JT whimpered. 'It's all about to . . . there's nothing you or I—'

'Don't call me *Luis*. You've never called me Luis in your life. I'm bowled over you even know my name.'

'Kill the call,' Charlie hissed.

'Please,' JT begged. 'How long have we been friends?'

'Since never!'

JT's voice splintered. *'Listen to me, you wetback little shit! You stay right fucking there where I told you to stay! Don't you move one fucking muscle!'*

'Fuck you, queen!' Luis shouted.

'Disobedient spic motherfucker!' JT fired back.

'House negro company-man fairy!'

'Kill the call!' Charlie yelled.

A strange gurgling bubbled from the phone, like the brook of blood that poured from a fresh cadaver after he incised a major vein. Luis half expected blood to spurt from the phone's speaker. After a moment, he identified the dreadful sound as soft, weeping laughter.

'Yes, Luis, I know your name. Always have. Even when we both ran for office. I always liked you. I don't expect you to believe that. You're good at what you do. All I've got is . . . what? A nice smile?

'I'm sorry, Luis. I'm not in control. Do you understand? I'm not in any kind of . . . control here. And I'm so sorry. For *all* of us, man. For all of us.'

There was no mistaking it: this was goodbye. Charlie waved her arms in semaphore, sliced a finger across her throat, anything to get Luis to hang up. Her pantomime was useless. A good doctor didn't hang up on a man this despondent, even if it was Jefferson Talbot.

'JT. Stay with me.'

The reply was a series of hard thumps – the sound of a phone being dropped. In most cases, said phones were picked up. Who willingly abandoned the device linking them to the wider world? In this instance, however, Luis heard receding footsteps. He never could have foreseen the sudden, acute concern he felt for his boss.

'JT!' His shout vibrated a hanging scale. 'Get out of there! Get out!'

Luis snapped his mouth shut; he sounded hysterical. He and Charlie stared at each other for one minute, maybe two. He expected Charlie to shout that, like JT, they needed to run. He anticipated his reply: that there were protocols, always protocols.

The speaker rustled as someone picked up JT's phone.

The voice was so deep as to be almost bottomless.

'Who's there? Acocella, I think he said?'

Who's there indeed. Luis's head spun with possibilities. All sorts of power brokers frequented Las Vegas; no place was better at keeping secrets. Anyone could be in that room, from any level of government. On their orders, there could be FBI agents racing toward the Balboa Park morgue right now, sirens screaming. Or, if they preferred, in predatory silence.

'Who is *this*?' Luis asked back.

'Lindof.' The man said it with mild surprise, like Luis should have recognized his voice. Luis tried to think. Was there a Lindof in the California governor's office? Was there a Lindof in Homeland Security? He didn't think so, but everything in his head was static.

'Good for you,' Luis said. 'Put JT back on.'

'Sorry, baby. Doesn't look possible.'

'Listen here, Mr Lindof. You fetch Jefferson Talbot and put him back on this phone, *his* phone, or my next call is going to be to the *New York Times.*'

'Oh yeah? What are you going to tell them? How would you pitch it?'

The man's playfulness was maddening. But he had a point. There was nothing Luis could tell a reporter that wouldn't get him shunted to the voice mail oblivion reserved for crackpots.

'Is this your fault?' Luis asked. 'The government?'

Lindof chuckled. 'What makes you think I work for the government?'

'Maybe you don't. But you know whose fault this is, don't you?'

Expensive fabric rustled in a shrug. 'Not really.'

'Then why the fuck are you wasting time talking to *me*? Start figuring this shit out!'

'You sound like you're panicking.'

'Fucking-A right I'm panicking! What do you think the mood is over here right now? We're not sitting around playing UNO!'

'We?' Lindof paused. 'You got someone else there, Acocella?'

Luis glanced at Charlie, ready to lie, but she nodded.

'That's right,' he said. 'We.' Charlie beamed. 'And we can be out of here in thirty seconds. You want to talk about panic? We can spill what happened here to the first guy we pass on the street. You know how fast photos can spread? You know how many we can take before we leave? We're scramming, gringo, unless JT tells me why we shouldn't.'

'Interesting stuff,' Lindof said. 'But I'm afraid Mr Talbot is gone.'

'Get him back.'

'No can do. We're on the top floor of Trump International Hotel in Vegas. And I think your buddy Mr Talbot just took a swan dive off the balcony. Jesus Howard Christ. That's sixty-four floors.'

The silence that descended over Autopsy Suite 1 reminded Luis of the time he and Rosa had vacationed in Colorado and stepped outside one morning to find a world gone mute with five feet of new-fallen snow.

Jefferson Talbot, medical examiner, dead? That figure of such brio and panache, perhaps duplicitous, perhaps promiscuous, but luminous with life, splashed across some gold-painted terrace? Luis's unraveling reached completion. With JT gone, was he in charge? Hadn't that been what he'd always wanted? In the suite's suffocating silence, he rejected not only the promotion but everything toward which his career had headed.

But the silence wasn't silence. Metallic pinging sounds Luis had attributed to air circulation vents began to grow. The sounds were being duplicated, not with the uniformity of rain against window-panes but with the irregularity of palms slapping against a locked door.

Charlie acknowledged the noise seconds later. Both assistant ME and diener gazed with trepidation at John Doe, tensed for some grotesque new evolution, but the sounds came from elsewhere. Together – as if joint movement made it less frightening – they looked toward the source.

Often called a *freezer* or *refrigerator,* the staff here preferred the hipper, jail-cell connotations of *cooler.* Supermarket-style automatic doors provided easy passage for workers pushing gurneys into the temperature-controlled room, where metal shelving held bodies for initial examination, family identification, autopsy, or upcoming legal orders. Two battery-charged hydraulic lifts allowed bagged cadavers to be placed on or removed from the highest shelves. Right now, more than a hundred corpses lay in the cooler, in all states of decay.

From the sound of it, They had begun to awake.

The pinging became thumping, the thumping a banging. The details of the cooler shelves presented themselves to Luis. Metal stoppers prevented trays from shifting. But nothing strapped the bodies to the trays. There was no need to restrain a corpse. A thin gong sounded; Luis and Charlie flinched at the unmistakable sign of a head butting the shelf above it. Another gong, then another, each corpse picking up the cue. At last came a sloppier, awfuller sound: a series of heavy, loud slaps, along with the sharp crackling of body bags.

Corpses were rolling Themselves off shelves and onto the floor.

Luis would have to use the .38 again, on himself this time, to stop the spiraling visions. He imagined dozens of body-bag lumps worming along the cooler floor like eyeless newts. If he and Charlie could stay quiet, he thought, those horrors might wander blind for a long time.

'Hello? Acocella? You still out there?'

Lindof's voice was startling. Luis dropped his phone, like JT. Unlike JT, he caught it.

'My condolences for Mr Talbot,' Lindof said. 'He seemed like a fun little gay guy.'

Luis saw black. He had to hold it together. He thought back, as he often did, to the time an imperious staff physician had discounted Luis, back then an idealistic resident, as lacking 'the stuff'. An insult, but the physician had nevertheless taught Luis a lasting lesson.

Even the loneliest dead body, the doctor expounded, without a single loved one to identify it, affected the living. His example: a shut-in gets shot during a break-in. Think of the first responders who'd have to live with the memories of the mess they found; the surgeons, nurses, orderlies, and interns whose quiet night would be disrupted; the detectives who'd spend weeks chasing the truth; the DA's staff, under pressure to close cases, who'd become personally involved; the insurance agents who'd labor to evade responsibility; the landlord stiffed on the victim's back rent and in sudden possession of hills of detritus. All those people formed a second family of the deceased, and as a family, they had to pull together if they wanted to survive. Luis, Charlie, Lindof, whoever – they had to get along.

Charlie, however, decided to explode.

'Did JT jump, Mr Lindof? Or did someone give him an assist?'

'Charlie!' Luis hissed.

From the cooler, another crackly rasp.

'Oh, a lady,' Lindof said. 'To whom do I owe the pleasure, baby?'

Charlie's mouth opened, teeth flashing.

'No!' Luis cried. 'Don't give him your name!'

Rarely did the *whoosh* of the cooler's automatic doors even register in Luis's brain. Now he looked at the open doors as he'd looked at his open closet while in bed as a kid, Manolo asleep beside him and no help at all. He'd known something unspeakable was waiting inside.

Rippling into view was a white body bag distended into abstract shapes by the hands, feet, and head trapped inside it.

'Now,' Luis croaked. 'Charlie, we're leaving now!'

He snatched his keys from the counter, and on second thought, his phone charger. Without hesitation, Charlie ran to pluck her purse from another counter, avoiding the gore centered on John Doe. Her path brought her close to the cooler, and Luis thought he might shriek in fear. Two more body bags had appeared behind the first, the heads inside straining against zippered plastic like babies against placental sacs. They might be born any second, Their jellied decay spilling from the bags as They crabbed forth, reaching out with unfolded arms.

Luis ran, holding his hand out to Charlie. They'd never held hands before, but her palm sealed to his, sweaty and strong, and it was as if he, like John Doe, was leavened with renewed life. He grew steadier, determined. They would escape these crawling atrocities. They would evade whoever the Vegas contingent had sent to shut them down.

Luis dropped his phone into his scrubs pocket, right alongside the .38, and ripped off his hairnet, apron, and sleeve protectors. Charlie did the same. Declothing was not easy with hands joined, but neither had any intention of breaking the bond.

'Where to?' Charlie asked.

'Rosa – I have to see if Rosa's all right. Okay?'

'I'm with you, all right? Let's get the fuck going!'

When they reached the parking lot, California's nighttime warmth made its usual ambush after the frigid morgue. Luis's sweat sizzled like bacon grease. The air felt thick and smelled of soot. The police and ambulance sirens in the distance might be the normal amount for this time of night, but it might not be.

Only two cars were in the lot. Luis's silver Prius was the more reliable, and Charlie made no objection. When they unlocked their hands to get in, Charlie swiped his keys and it was his turn not to object. Right now, an aggressive driver was who they needed behind the wheel.

Inside the Prius's quiet, Luis realized Lindof's voice was still audible; neither party had ended the call. Lindof was talking quite happily, clearly not caring if anyone was listening. Luis wanted to shut it off, more so with Lindof's every word, but his attention was focused on traffic congestion that shouldn't exist at this hour, and smoke from an uncleared accident, and a distressing quantity of pedestrians darting across the highway. Helping Charlie navigate, he mumbled to himself, 'Not God shit. Not God shit. Not God shit.'

Yet he still heard Lindof, beneath. 'Even if you know who I am, you're wrong. I'm not who I was an hour ago, I can tell you that. I'm better, baby. I'm better, and here's the one thing I know for sure: you're worse. Should you be panicking? The answer is yes. Yes, you really should. You should be pissing your shitty little diapers. Because you know what I think? I think your world is about to fall into the ocean, Acocella, and my world is about to rise up like a fucking mountain. Jesus Horatio Christ, it's going to be glorious.'

Go Redskins

When Etta Hoffmann discovered VSDC case number 129–46–9875 on October 25, she brought it, with characteristic lack of emotion, to the attention of fellow statisticians John Campbell, Terry McAllister, and Elizabeth O'Toole. They huddled in Hoffmann's cubicle – closer than she liked, though she was adept at keeping such discomfort to herself. Not yet confident about AMLD's emergency power, she had printed the report and handed it to Elizabeth O'Toole. Elizabeth O'Toole read the second half aloud, a voice-to-text transcription sent in by a Dr Luis Acocella in San Diego. Terry McAllister, who had given up hiding his feelings and held Elizabeth O'Toole by the waist, knew the glitchy software by heart and translated.

'Write meal . . .'

'White male.'

'Cause of debt . . .'

'Death.'

'Not . . . repeat, not barristic . . .'

'Ballistic.'

'. . . ballistic insult. Preceding . . .'

'Proceeding.'

'. . . with examination of the fart . . .'

'God, that one's my favorite. Heart.'

'Will check for confusion.'

'Too late for that. Occlusion.'

'. . . and car dee oh, my empathy . . .'

'It's poetry. Someone make this Acocella guy poet laureate, stat.'

Hoffmann knew people at AMLD called her 'the Poet'. She was not deaf. This joke, however, was not being made at her expense. Elizabeth O'Toole laughed quietly, perfect round tears enlarging the corners of her eyes. Hoffmann was glad to see this reaction. She understood laughing was a necessary relaxant for most people. It had been forty-eight hours since so much as a smile had been seen in the office, which had begun to trouble even Hoffmann.

By then, there was nothing novel about the content of 129–46–9875. It relayed the same news about *They* and *Them* that had been reported 300,642 times over the past two days. The report's only notable detail (beyond its bonkers translation) was its time stamp. Hoffmann slid it into the *Origin* folder and applied a Post-it to it, bearing a tidy red-ink notation: *Zero-00:00*. The next oldest one, which the VSDC had recorded four hours and twenty-one minutes later, would be labeled *Zero-04:21*. And so on, a new organization for a new age. It brought Hoffmann the sort of relaxation that laughing had brought Elizabeth O'Toole.

Zero-00:00 had a different effect on Hoffmann's coworkers. Instead of seeing a starting point, they saw the beginning of the end.

'I used to celebrate every year around this time, when the holidays kicked off, how I'd made it another year, you know?' John Campbell said with a wistful grimace. 'Then I always said to myself, "Well, fine, but will you be here next year?" That was the whole deal, wasn't it? Worrying about whether you're going to be here tomorrow kept you going.'

Hoffmann knew that John Campbell was not faring well. He'd lost a child to leukemia and a wife to divorce in the span of twenty-one months. It made for a shaky foundation. He was barely eating, existing on coffee. Though he'd lasted to the final four, a feat that impressed Hoffmann, she knew he'd be next to vacate. She was fine with that.

She looked forward to it. John Campbell always stood too close to her.

'Are *any* of us going to be here tomorrow?' Elizabeth O'Toole wiped away her tears. Hoffmann was strangely disappointed not to have seen them fall.

'That's what I'm saying,' John Campbell insisted. 'If there's no tomorrow, we're just left here with our mistakes. Everything we did before the Poet reset our clock to zero-zero-zero-zero-zero. Now we get to stare at those mistakes. With no hope of a new day coming. You see what I'm saying? It's a huge goddamn reckoning for everything we ever did wrong.'

'Sounds like church,' Terry McAllister muttered.

'What do you mean?' John Campbell pressed.

'Isn't that what they tell you in church? You sin, you go to hell, and Satan parades your sins before you like that old TV show.'

This Is Your Life, Hoffmann thought. She liked old TV shows. She watched them, episode after episode, with food and bathroom breaks, until either it was precisely midnight – bedtime – or there were no more episodes in the series, at which point she changed to a different program.

'Except we haven't gone to hell,' John Campbell said. 'We're still here.'

'But so are They,' Terry McAllister replied.

'All that means is They took it away from us! The promise we were told that, when we die, we could go to a better place. They, Them – They're telling us no. This is it. *This is it.*'

'Stop,' Elizabeth O'Toole said. 'You're not making sense.'

'Life was a gift.' John Campbell was gripping the back of Hoffmann's chair. She could feel his hot breath and wished he would go away. 'And as a gift, it belonged to us. We're the only ones who can take it away. It's our choice. Not Theirs.'

John Campbell left two days later. Hoffmann believed he had

gone to kill himself. She felt no sorrow. He would not have survived out there anyway. Shortly thereafter, Elizabeth O'Toole said it was the end of the world, and Terry McAllister responded that, if that were true, why the fuck were they hanging around here when he had good tequila at his place? Despite everything, Elizabeth O'Toole smiled. The two of them could live together, if only for a short while.

Asking Hoffmann if she'd like to come with them, Elizabeth O'Toole added, 'The only obligation we have left is to ourselves.'

Hoffmann appreciated the sentiment. She looked up at Elizabeth O'Toole's red eyes, hollowed sockets, and stringy hair. She would not miss the woman, but she wished her well. Elizabeth O'Toole had always defended Hoffmann when others had mocked her. Hoffmann knew this. She was not deaf.

She glimpsed the outdoors when Terry McAllister and Elizabeth O'Toole left. Dead leaves skittered across the street, adding themselves to berms of litter accumulated over five days without street cleaning. There was a distinct lack of traffic. The most troubling sight was a dead horse curled around a fire hydrant. Hoffmann felt an urge to go see it. She'd never been close to a horse. But it was missing its entire midsection. It was only legs, a head, and a spine.

The Census Bureau, of which AMLD was a part, had maintained offices in Suitland, Maryland, since 2006, and though other satellites moved into those headquarters, AMLD had remained in D.C. This had been a great relief to Hoffmann. Change in routine upset her. Even thinking about the two bus lines she would have to take to Suitland made her feel ill. Others had hoped for relocation, griping about their office building, a small, two-story, functionalist, windowless concrete box decorated with abstract formations of brick and iron. Hoffmann had never given the architectural qualities a thought until she locked the door behind Terry McAllister and Elizabeth O'Toole and bolstered it with a furniture barricade.

The AMLD office was an impregnable bunker.

Hoffmann wandered the building. She'd never done it before. She'd never been curious. In the basement, inside walk-in pantries and coolers, she discovered ponderous stacks of nonperishable food and staggering reserves of bottled water. Although it bothered her to leave her computer post, she devoted an entire afternoon to cataloging the food. By her estimates, she could live off the stockpile for twenty-two years.

Not until she had spent several hours back at her usual post could she classify what she was feeling: the serenity of perfect belonging. She might never again have a face-to-face interaction with another person. This filled her with a lightness she did not think she had ever felt. Amputated from the unpleasant heat, bodily smells, sharp voices, alarming clothing, jarring arrivals, unpredictable physical positionings, and confusing sexual energies of the human race, Etta Hoffmann felt true happiness for the first time.

Days passed. She did her job. She fixed herself three meals a day. Canned soup. Frozen pizza. Peanut butter on bread until the bread went bad. Each midnight, she went to bed on a sofa. Weeks passed.

By a month after the rise of 129–46–9875, roughly nine out of ten VSDC network members had gone off-line. By Hoffmann's calculations, that was 92 percent of hospitals, 95 percent of nursing homes, and 74 percent of police departments. There was less data for her to upload, less to print, less to log, less to file. Never had she known empty queues, but now, even though she was the sole statistician left, half the day could pass without a blip from the outside world. She hit the Refresh icon until her fingertip hurt. She felt adrift for the first time in many years.

The idea came gradually, as ideas always did to Etta Hoffmann. AMLD was unique among government organs, linking the internal data systems of the census, medical, and law enforcement bureaus. AMLD staff might be lowly in terms of Beltway status, but they had nearly unique access to ancillary government interfaces, unprecedented outside of intelligence agencies. These digital inroads were shallow but plentiful. Over the years, Hoffmann had glimpsed them, just as she'd glimpsed hallways she had no interest in exploring.

She remembered a statistician who had been fired eight years earlier for sneaking the phrase *GO REDSKINS* onto the home pages of NASA, the Forest Service, the Patent and Trademark Office, the Food Safety and Inspection Service, and, most lamentably, the Office of Native American Affairs. Hoffmann had not joined in the appalled watercooler gossip that followed the firing. But she was not deaf. *She was not deaf.*

Modifying other government sites was forbidden. But there was no one left to punish her. Accessing outside agencies' control panels should have been impossible, but most AMLD employees had fled the office without shutting down their workstations. Like too many other government agencies, their tech was outdated, so dormant computers did not automatically log off. Hoffmann had been raiding the unprotected drives for weeks.

The mother lode, she suspected, was inside the password manager of a senior statistician named Annie Teller. Hoffmann recalled Annie Teller. She was Black, tall and athletic, had an English accent, wore colorful clothing, and walked with a limp, her dark eyes trained on a distant point. She did not seem to notice anyone she passed. Usually, she did not say hello. Hoffmann hated when people said hello; thus, Annie Teller had been her favorite person to pass in the hall.

Hoffmann set about mining Annie Teller's personal email, open in a separate browser window. Annie Teller tagged nothing, and a search of *password* did not help, so Hoffmann had no choice but to begin reading every email. She had no qualms about this. Once, a woman had left her purse in an AMLD bathroom stall, and Hoffmann, sitting on the toilet, went through every item. She knew such behaviors were considered 'invasions', but she never felt like an invader. She felt like what her job title said she was: a statistician, gathering information, cataloging data, and drawing objective conclusions.

Annie Teller sent and received a lot of personal emails. Did everyone send so many? An ongoing music-recommendation thread between Annie Teller and two friends was over three hundred messages long. Hoffmann, hunting for password clues, took note of the artists Annie Teller referenced most, as well as favorite food items and movies. Annie Teller had a hard-to-tabulate number of nieces and nephews both in the UK and the US; Hoffmann noted each name. Annie Teller had suffered a spinal injury a few years back; Hoffmann wrote down the name of a chiropractor who'd become Annie Teller's friend.

Receipts: there were thousands. Digital music, clothes, shoes, personal care products, and a surprising number of picture frames – Hoffmann imagined Annie Teller's home as filled with framed photos of two countries' worth of friends, siblings, grandparents, all those nieces and nephews. Annie Teller did not appear to have pets, which was unfortunate. Even Hoffmann knew pet names were password gold.

Annie Teller was single. There were pings from online dating sites as well as emails from relationships that had progressed into the physical world. A few were sexually explicit; some employed a playful, coy voice that did not seem like Annie Teller at all; some were angry and in all caps; some were heartbroken and sloppy with spelling errors. None of the men seemed worthy of password status.

One relationship rose above all others. The woman's name was Tawna Maydew. Annie Teller had met Tawna Maydew at Disney World in Florida. Even the mention of the theme park made Hoffmann's stomach roil. All those strange people jammed chest to back inside snaking, inescapable queues – she could think of nothing worse. Annie Teller, though, seemed to have had a wonderful time there with one of her nieces, mostly because of being seated alongside Tawna Maydew on a ride called the Tower of Terror. The ride, Hoffmann gathered from contextual clues, emulated a plummeting elevator, which sounded hellacious but apparently forged camaraderie among riders.

The first emails between Annie Teller and Tawna Maydew were brief and tentative. Annie Teller: *Hope you made it home safe to LA, just wanted to say thanks for being a friend at Disney!* Tawna Maydew: *No problem, limey! Did your lovely niece get that stain out?* Annie Teller: *Hahaha! I think that shirt will have to be burned. Btw, I did what you suggested and signed up for that service. I'm so hard to buy for. Too tall! I'll let you know how it goes!* Tawna Maydew: *Not too tall – perfect. And you have the shoulders of a runway model. (The accent too.) Own it, mama.*

Hoffmann's least favorite old TV shows were romances. Not only did she feel nothing in terms of passion, she felt vaguely threatened by the physicality of larger men descending on smaller women. She wondered if this was why she felt an unusual investment in the burgeoning online affair of Annie Teller and Tawna Maydew. Annie Teller was the tall one, though Tawna Maydew's selfies, of which there were plenty, showed her as fairly tall herself, a pale-skinned, pale-haired Nordic type with strong thighs and biceps. Even when Annie Teller resorted to expletives in frustration with her career or life, there was an honesty to her communication that had been missing from her stilted exchanges with dating-site men.

They loved each other. It took them one year to say it. Tawna Maydew sent photos of things the two of them could do together in LA: green hills, ornate movie theaters, her bed. Eighteen months into their email relationship, Tawna Maydew sent a flurry of photographs from the La Brea Tar Pits. Taken at night, with Los Angeles streetlights rainbowing across bubbling tar, the pictures were unlike anything Hoffmann had seen, phantasmagoric and illusory, yet as real as the desk at which she sat. Tawna Maydew: *Only one block from my home. We can kiss by the gooey ruins of prehistoric Earth!* Annie Teller: *Can we make that our emergency plan? If the world goes gooey, we'll meet on the banks of beautiful La Brea!* Quickly it became their standby joke, deployed each time their plans to reunite fell apart. *Oh well,* one of them would write, *we'll still have La Brea.*

Hoffmann believed it was the only in-joke she'd ever felt on the inside of. Suddenly, Hoffmann wanted nothing more than the two lovelorn women to find each other as planned at La Brea, now that the world had indeed gone gooey. If their story were an old TV show, even one of the romantic ones, Hoffmann knew she would watch as many seasons of it as she could.

The odds of success were infinitesimal. Hoffmann knew this and accepted it. Washington, D.C., and Los Angeles, California, were 2,674 miles apart. With her distinctive limp, Annie Teller had left the AMLD building when most others had, during the afternoon of October 24, by which time flights were being canceled by the hundreds. Interstates were worse; cars would dissolve to rust powder before the roads were clear again. Hoffmann suspected Annie Teller had died in her home, probably violently, probably screaming, while her framed loved ones kept on smiling.

Etta Hoffmann never felt sad, but this brought her close. Her exploration into Annie Teller's daily trivialities was the nearest she had come to understanding a person's raw feelings, naked insecurities, frank aspirations, and knotty contradictions. It was like *This Is Your Life,* but with stakes. Annie Teller had touched something inside Hoffmann neither her parents nor childhood psychiatrists had believed she would be able to reach.

Hoffmann felt a twinge of loss when she figured out Annie Teller's major password. It was LaBr3aTarP1t$. Annie Teller had used the password years ago to open a few one-off merchant accounts. She'd quit using it, perhaps because it was emotionally charged. The La Brea Tar Pits were an unresolved goal for Annie Teller, but for Hoffmann, LaBr3aTarPlt$ resolved everything. It unlocked Annie Teller's password manager, the key to all other keys.

Most federal agency websites remained active, though they had not been updated in weeks. With Annie Teller's password cache, Hoffmann could access home pages of dozens of agencies. She spent days pondering what to post. This was no *GO REDSKINS*. Her first thought was to supply detailed explanations of how to find VSDC portals and bring them back online so people could resume sending data. It was important, she believed, to sustain this record of the new world order, from zero-00:00 onward.

Annie Teller and Tawna Maydew convinced Hoffmann otherwise. Those able to find online access would not devote precious time to assisting the Census Bureau. They would be hunting for news, trying to find missing loved ones. But those people could still provide data – or, as people other than Etta Hoffmann called it, *stories*. Like Annie Teller and Tawna Maydew, they might still feel the urge to share themselves.

Hoffmann thought about it day and night. At her midnight bedtime, she found she could not sleep, which was unusual. She got up, the building dark and cold around her, and wandered until she found herself at the front desk. She did not visit this area often. It was close to the barricaded front entrance. At night, Hoffmann could hear things, even through the concrete and steel. Shuffling noises. Low, gurgling moans. The occasional bump against the front door, as if the things outside – *They* – suspected she was there.

Not so long ago, the lobby was where incoming calls landed before redirection. Hoffmann picked up the front desk phone. The dial tone was as patient as ever. Landlines, laid down in an analog age, seemed poised to persevere long after wireless services blew away like pollen.

That morning, Etta Hoffmann sat at her personal workstation and picked up the receiver of her desk phone. She did not believe she had ever received a call on it. She had to wipe away the dust to read her extension. Her next hours were spent logging in to every government agency site she could and pasting onto its home page the same message, the one she had spent all night mentally whittling down to its barest shape:

ARE YOU OK? CALL ME.

Beneath that was her direct desk number.

She cursored over the Post button on the site open in her first browser tab, the Government Accountability Office. Her finger settled upon her mouse. One click, and everything on the home page would vanish, replaced by these five words and her eleven-digit international number. She hesitated. For once in her life, there was no way to determine whether or not this was the correct thing to do.

This Is Your Life, Hoffmann thought.

She clicked the button. The new Government Accountability Office landing page went live. She cursored to the next site, the Council on Environmental Quality, and did the same. Next, the Department of State. Next, the Foreign Agricultural Service. The National Rural Development Council, the Office of Inspector General, the National Energy Technology Laboratory, the Administration on Aging, the National Cancer Institute. Again, again, again. In minutes, decades of US government practice – of sending information out into the world – were overturned in favor of a call to report in. The survivors' voices and thoughts were what mattered now.

Before Hoffmann had finished updating all the sites, her phone rang.

She stared at it. The knotted cord. The cracked plastic base. The begrimed keypad. It was something dead, returned to screaming life.

Resurrection seemed to be going around. That was a joke – she'd just made a joke, even if only to herself – and she arranged her facial muscles into a smile, wondering if the fluttering in her chest was humor. A red light blinked on her phone. A second call. She wondered how long they would hold. She laid her hand on the receiver. The rings shivered up her arm. Her heart was pounding.

The person on the other end, what would they say?

Could Etta Hoffmann, the Poet, respond poetically?

She reminded herself she did not have to. Talking was the choice of the rest of the world. The John Campbells, Terry McAllisters, and Elizabeth O'Tooles, but most of all Annie Teller and Tawna Maydew, whom she hoped could still share La Brea. Etta Hoffmann – not deaf – had always preferred to listen, and her finest days might only be beginning. She picked up the phone and heard the breathing on the other end hitch, as if the caller had not expected an answer. Hoffmann parted her dry lips and summoned a voice she hadn't used in months, one that cracked like the first word of an entombed woman who had just seen a shaft of light.

'Hello?'

MI
CORAZÓN

A Richer Vintage

I'm still dreaming, **Greer Morgan thought.**

Crack-of-dawn shit shows were what Sunnybrook Mobile Home Resort did best. Why else did residents call it the Last Resort? Greer growled, aggrieved at the loss of her dream, and patted at her ears. Both earplugs had fallen out, proof of fitfulness. She could hear a light rain, though the day seemed as bright as fire; getting home, late last night, she'd forgotten to hang the old welcome mat over her bedroom window to keep out the light. She twisted her sleep mask back over her eyes. The strap was spaghettied, and light poured right under. Greer knew she had a fuck-ton of problems – lousy grades, motivation issues, no car – but she'd lock them in forever for a single goddamn good night's sleep.

Her head throbbed with every blast of bickering from outside. A woman mad-dogging a man whose retorts grew more defensive, more embarrassed, and angrier. Miss Jemisha, Greer thought. Maybe Señorita Magdalena. They had the same sharp bark. Same idle men, too, who sat their asses on the women's respective steps, drunk and happy or sober and sullen. When Greer came home from school, Miss Jemisha's man, the one Greer had privately dubbed Samuel Hell Jackson (shortened to 'Sam Hell') for his Kangol hat, would hoot at her: *You growing up, Greer baby!*

Señorita Magdalena's man, meanwhile, was a short, cowboy-attired Honduran Greer had nicknamed, with prejudice she knew was ugly, José Frito, and José Frito only seemed to know one English word: *C'mere*. It never failed to chill her. *C'mere*.

Greer sealed out the silt-colored sun with a sweaty elbow. Her dream had been a good one. She found a flash of image and clawed onto it. Oh yes. Not so much a dream as a memory. Last night. Remy's Halloween party. The basement. Qasim. She let herself slide back into the memory's warm, melted chocolate. The unsnapping of her bra like the exhale of a long-held breath. Qasim's stomach, a hundred degrees hot, the feather of hair pointing down from his belly button. Saliva like hot grease. The need to push pelvises together and feel the pulse of the veins in each other's thighs.

How far did they go? She rustled herself, part by part, feeling for hickeys, sore breasts, any aches down below. That's right – they'd gotten no further than hands down pants. It wasn't shyness that held them back but the party climate: girls being chased up and down the basement steps, people passing joints every five seconds, omnipresent camera-gadgets. She and Qasim, they'd get there. And if Qasim one day became as apathetic and baleful as Sam Hell or José Frito, it wouldn't matter. Greer would be long gone. In the meantime, she'd indulge her want, as often and as hard as she could.

Wanting: it was the ammo that kept her gunning. There was nothing to want at school. A dutiful student through middle school, she'd at last yielded to the role her teachers had prescribed for a Black girl from the Last Resort. Recalcitrant, argumentative, lazy, sluttish – they chose the descriptors, and Greer did her best to embody them while mugging her disdain: *What else do you got?* Her friends' whoops and high fives were temporary incentives. Eventually, she ended up alone, staring up at the unscalable ravine walls of sunken grades.

The ravine might have swallowed her whole if not for her daddy. Too often, Freddy Morgan groveled excuses to his supervisors so he could skip work to visit the vice principal's office, hat literally in hand. The teenager-sized chair made his big body look meek, ideal for his mournful pleas. You see, the loss of a mother and a house had traumatized poor Greer. Freddy Morgan debased himself because this was *his* want. A better job; ergo, a better home; ergo, a better life. He strained like a yoked ox to make it happen, no matter the supervisors or vice principals pulling the reins.

Greer wanted to detest her daddy's performances but couldn't help respecting how he did what he had to do. Who else was she going to respect? Her mother? Vienna Morgan had possessed *want,* all right, a want of material things. While employed by a maid service, she had stolen so much from homes she was cleaning that she'd been tossed in jail three times in a calendar year. Now she was in lockup, Bluefeather Prison in Iowa, and Greer was well on her way to not giving a shit.

Want, her mother's case told her, could be a self-destructive thing. Greer could find a counterexample in her year-younger brother, Conan. Want had been mentally and physically beaten from him. He was mute and emotionless at school and almost as bad at home. All night she heard him playing video games on his outdated console. To avoid tormentors, Conan plodded to school two hours early, looking as dead as Freddy Morgan's coworkers as they slouched toward HortiPlastics, the factory that employed half the town of Bulk, Missouri. Conan probably pictured himself at HortiPlastics eventually, watching the assembly line carry away what was left of his dreams.

It killed Greer to see her brother drained of the liquid fire that fueled her. Brasher boys pushed Conan down stairs, spit in his hair, and, if she listened to rumors, did much worse. She had no idea how Conan had become the school pariah. It must have started with his guileless, round, chubby-cheeked face. Located ninety miles north of Kansas City, their school had students of all shades, but the toxic slime of racial animosity had to be poured somewhere, so why not down the funnel conveniently extending from Conan Morgan's throat?

The best Greer could hope for was that Conan's apparent emptiness came from being distracted by waking dreams as pleasant as her last night's dream had been. Qasim's heaving ribs were the last detail to blow away, a sheet from a clothesline.

Four voices outside now, at least. Was it possible Miss Jemisha and Señorita Magdalena had crisscrossed their rebukes of Sam Hell and José Frito? Greer didn't think so. At least one of the voices, high-octaved and insistent, belonged to Mr Villard, the driving force behind the Sunnybrook Club, a group open to all Last Resort residents that met monthly to – according to the flyers – 'discuss challenges and share ideas'.

From Greer's vantage, *discuss* meant *bitch* and *share* meant *accuse*. Even when the Sunnybrook Club managed to agree on something, they had shit-all authority with which to petition the park owners. The asphalt had potholes so deep children played in them. Yards flooded with the lightest rain, surfacing not only septic sludge but used needles and drug baggies. Meanwhile, rent had exploded 30 percent in three years, according to Freddy Morgan. Greer was unmoved. Eighteen years of life had shown her prosperity never trickled down and social orders never flipped.

A core group of six bellyachers nevertheless persisted in monthly meetings amid the playground wreckage. Now that she was fully awake, Greer could match each griping voice with its exasperating owner. She thought of each in bigoted terms, and right now, tired as hell, she didn't care.

Miss Jemisha: the trailer-trash caricature Greer swore she wouldn't become. Cobra-swaying her head, holding up talk-to-the-hand fingers, arguing poorly but loudly, her body parts jiggling inside too-tight gray-and-pink sweats.

Señorita Magdalena: infuriatingly docile, fascinating as cardboard, herding around a confusing number of interchangeable children. Her Mona Lisa smile suggested she was content to waste the rest of her life in this hellhole alongside José Frito.

Mama Shaw: the Jamaican fossil. Her face was so heavily lined it looked like a deflated football. She was eternally sick, her wet, resounding coughs keeping Greer up half the night. Her whole trailer stank of urine. Why did she keep on living?

Drasko Zorić: the dead-eyed Serb, insufferably smug, his distaste for his fellow club members obvious from the permanent curl of his lip. His large muscles were the opposite of impressive, proof positive of a deadbeat with nothing better to do than pump iron in his yard.

Mr Villard: the big-deal former community college teacher with a hairpiece like a beret. A white guy, so naturally he was in charge. The agenda ever crackling in his clenched fist drove Greer insane. He never got through more than two items before bickering consumed everything.

And, of course, Freddy Morgan, a.k.a. Daddy: whose unachievable task, as far as Greer could tell, was to keep this gaggle of imbeciles calm.

During Sunnybrook Club meetings, there was no peace for anybody on their leg of road, not even those armored with sleep mask and earplugs. For this reason alone, Greer wished the club would induct the park's quietest resident, a Syrian with the fun-to-say name of Fadi Lolo. He was one of fifty-some Syrian refugees taken in by the town over the past two years. It was a Missouri record no one in Bulk celebrated. Resettlement had prioritized Syrians with families, disabilities, or medical conditions – welfare leeches, grumbled Bulk residents in HortiPlastics gear.

The majority of Syrians had been placed in an apartment complex on Bulk's town square, a centralization meant to soften their landings. Either through independent effort or crap luck, Fadi Lolo had ended up at the Last Resort. If anyone belonged in Mr Villard's club, it was him. Every day, Greer saw Fadi Lolo riding around on a crappy bicycle, pausing to pick up trash from neighbors' lawns, and every day, she wanted to say something – thank you, maybe. Clearly Fadi Lolo wanted to make the best of this shithole. He was already doing ten times the work of the Sunnybrook Club.

Best of all, Fadi Lolo (his recurrent, phlegmy hack notwithstanding) was even quieter than Drasko Zorić. Fadi spoke quietly, walked quietly, biked quietly, lived quietly. Today, the Sunnybrook Club was at full volume at an obscene hour. Last night, Daddy had spiked his warnings for her to be home by ten with this precise poison: the morning meeting was going to be a rowdy one.

The topic was burglaries. No one could describe burglaries at Sunnybrook as a 'rash' or 'outbreak'; they were chronic. The latest eruption had affected everyone on the northeastern loop. Some fingers pointed at Fadi Lolo, the park's newest arrival, who, after all, owned the speedy getaway vehicle of a rickety bike. Daddy had pleaded with Greer to attend this meeting – just this one. Everyone in the Last Resort knew Vienna Morgan was a thief, and in their minds, that meant the daughter might have sticky fingers too.

'When folks are trying to make you out to be less than you are, you look them dead in the face,' Freddy Morgan had advised. 'You look at them real, and then they'll know the heart of it – the heart of you. Take my word.'

Sorry, Daddy, but fuck that. Greer's hangover kicked like a pregnancy. Still, she had to get her ass out of bed. This would be her ninth missed day, two away from forcing a repeat of her senior year. That would disrupt Freddy's entire schedule of getting their lives back on track.

The yelling outside tripled, and she drove her face into the pillow. Half-suffocated, her life passed before her eyes: ten-year-old Greer Morgan springing from bed in the early-morning dark and modeling in the mirror the camouflage pullover Daddy loaned her. Conan, who'd shared her room back then, had a pullover too, and they giggled and shushed each other – Mom was sleeping – before tiptoeing outside, where Daddy was loading the gear into the car. The three of them would drive, the vacant roads like gray zippers along black velvet darkness, until they reached some random turnoff Daddy knew to take.

If it was fall, it was geese, turkey, or deer. If winter, quail, pheasant, or duck. Once Daddy had nodded his morning hellos to any other hunters – all of them white – and got them situated in the wild, he would stop talking. A glorious silence would curl around Greer like a warm blanket. She took solace from the gentle, twig-snap steps of brave animals and the fairy gambols of birds and butterflies, the same way, years later, Fadi Lolo seemed to take solace from quiet bicycle rides around the Last Resort.

Freddy Morgan had a hunter's cache, and both kids were allowed to fire a weapon once per hunt. Conan cried at road-killed animals, but he liked guns; the recoil punched his shoulder just like the boys at school did, but in a good way. Greer preferred a bow. She never hit anything, but firing an arrow was an art of gymnastic delicacy. The sinewy intransigence of the string. The creaking resistance of the wood. The smarting slap of the string against her armguard. Daddy caught his breath, too, at the dry leaves shivering as the arrow passed.

No enjoyment in Greer's life was so pure now. It was October 24, prime hunting season, and Freddy Morgan went out every weekend. When had she quit going along? Greer ignored the fracas outside and thought hard. Age thirteen, her first period. Maybe she'd associated it with apocryphal tales about blood attracting predators. Or had it been because her mom had handed her a plastic bag filled with loose Tampax Pearl Lites? Greer knew the tampons were stolen. She was disgusted when she inserted one, imagining it as already having been used by someone whose blood was of a richer vintage.

Outside, a scream. Greer bolted up, tearing away her mask.

Screams were part of the Last Resort soundscape, but this one had an upchucked rawness. Greer yanked her phone from its charger, swiped, and dialed 911, pausing to listen for more before hitting the Call button.

An argument. Good. When someone *quit* arguing, that's when you had to worry.

Greer wheeled her bare legs off the bed. She grabbed sweatpants from the floor, yanked them on, and ferreted her head and arms through a hooded sweatshirt. Parading her truant ass before Daddy hadn't been part of the plan, but the plan was falling apart. She could splash down aspirin with her dad's room-temp coffee and still get to school by second period, and if she scolded the squabbling Sunny-brook Club with enough force, their agog faces might power her through a whole day.

She aimed her feet at a pair of flip-flops, catching the strap in her toes. The slapping steps were loud enough to throb her temples as she passed the open bathroom, her skin goose bumping from the freezing air coursing through the temporary plywood wall. She plodded past the chugging refrigerator, charred stove top, and rusty sink and looked out the front-door window.

Through the mist, she could see half of the playground. A stapled packet rolled in the grass; she felt certain it was Mr Villard's meeting agenda. Greer pressed her nose flat to look harder. Was someone lying in the leaves near the swingless swing set? She angled her face, trying for a better look.

A figure darted left to right, startling Greer. She blinked and it was gone. Somewhere, a door banged shut, followed by muffled shouts. Later, Greer would remember the curdling sensation of her guard going up, same as it did when a man started walking behind her on a sidewalk. She let adrenaline clear her headache before leaning toward the window once more.

Her forehead never touched glass.

Smack!

Something struck the door's window, big and bat-like. Greer leaped back, flip-flops tangling. On the other side of the window was the palm of a hand, fingers and thumb splayed. The fingernails clawed at the glass, making high-pitched squeals.

The hand slid away with a wet squeak, leaving behind a handprint of blood, a sigil so scary Greer could only stare as she heard the person slump along the side of the trailer. When the sound stopped, Greer had no idea what was happening. Was the person still standing near the end of the trailer? Had they stumbled away? Was the person injured? And where was Daddy? *I should have gone to school,* she thought before taking hold of the doorknob.

From the day they'd moved in four years ago, she told herself, the Last Resort had provided dicey scenarios, and this was merely the latest. The sun shimmered prettily along crystalline shingles and metal sidings. The world had the bird-and-insect, orchestra-tuning hush of a Freddy Morgan hunting trip. It was not until after Greer had gone down the steps and her naked ankles were deep in damp leaves that she realized how even sights and sounds this mild could cloak the inconceivable.

No Teeth

The playground area felt recently deserted, the hanging mist smudged, the stomped leaves expanding. Muddy shoe prints spotted across sidewalks before getting lost in asphalt. Greer tracked one set of prints up the steps of Señorita Magdalena's single-wide, from which gurgled Spanish – urgent from Magdalena, guttural from José Frito, ornamented by the cries of the children. Greer tuned it out and turned around.

The bloody handprint on her trailer-door window was accompanied by a second near the dryer vent, the size of a man's hand. Drasko Zorić, maybe? Had the Serbian injured himself? A garish red stripe was smeared along the vinyl siding all the way to the trailer's end. The mist was reducing the blood to a rose-colored wash. Greer exhaled and kept her phone at the ready. You didn't risk being marked as a narc by calling police to the Last Resort for minor injuries. Drasko Zorić, or whoever the injured person was, wasn't in sight. Greer couldn't act yet.

She studied the playground through the rain, feeling the ghosts of happiness past. The swing set was a gallows of dangling chains. Only the merry-go-round's base had survived metal collectors: a sharp steel disc littered with doll disembowelments. Two spring riders, a pelican and cockatoo, flopped listlessly, their aluminum bodies dented by children enraged by their impotence. The rusty climbing dome was all that remained intact. It looked like a whale skeleton stripped of hide and blubber.

A woman lay in the leaves beneath it.

Greer called automatically: 'Daddy?'

A response came, but not from Freddy Morgan: 'Girl! Girl!'

It sounded so much like bullets Greer ducked. The call came from an old but freshly waxed sedan ripping down the road in excess of the posted 5 MPH, wet asphalt hissing beneath its tires. Its grille bashed a plastic trash bin, sending garbage all over the road and peppering Greer with coffee grounds. The car skidded to a halt.

Mr Villard leaned over the passenger seat toward a window rolled down an inch. Mr Villard was fastidious in every respect, but today his hairpiece hung like a patch over an eye. His right hand spread mud over the passenger seat.

'Get out,' he said. 'Everyone's gone mad.'

'Have you seen my dad?'

'Get clear of the whole park. If you can't, get inside your unit and lock the door.'

'Is it . . .' Greer searched for sense. 'Gangs?'

'There's no time! Do what I say!'

'Freddy Morgan,' she pressed. 'He's part of your club—'

'There is no fucking club anymore! Don't bother me with this shit! I have to go!'

It was the spit on Mr Villard's chin that froze the liquid terror of Greer's veins. She felt exposed, like the gray rain had fingers longer than Mr Villard's. No smart girl got into a car with a man she hardly knew, but her growing sense was normal rules no longer applied. She pulled on the passenger door handle. It rebounded with a clunk: locked. Greer looked disbelievingly at Mr Villard.

'Let me in,' she said.

He drew back as if she were festering with disease.

It was the most chilling moment of her life.

'The Syrians.' Mr Villard's voice broke. 'These Syrians show up and now this? You think that's a coincidence?' He bared teeth that looked ready to bite. 'This used to be a *nice place.*'

There came a crash. Greer and Mr Villard turned in unison to see Señorita Magdalena's trailer swaying upon its cinder block joists as if it contained brawling bears. Also from inside: screaming, fleshy thumps, shattering glass.

Greer risked Mr Villard's incisors and pushed her fingers through the car window's gap. 'Don't leave me here.'

'*Let go of my car!*' he screeched. '*Black bitch, I'll tear your fingers off!*'

Greer retracted fast enough to bloody her knuckles, but felt nothing. This was Mr Villard. President of the Sunnybrook Club. Who'd proclaimed it a travesty when someone destroyed all the BLACK LIVES MATTER signs. His tires spun, and the car sprang forward, walloping a second trash bin. Greer retreated into the playground, watching the car take out a plinth of mailboxes. Behind her, the cries from Señorita Magdalena's trailer rose to tortured moans.

Greer repeated Mr Villard's only sensible words: 'Get out.'

A miserable lowing made her turn to the climbing dome. The woman under it was struggling. Bare brown arms extended from a cotton nightdress insufficient for the autumn chill. Greer couldn't leave the woman there in the rain. She confirmed 911 was still a thumb-tap away and jogged closer, carefully avoiding the fulcrum of a missing seesaw. Extending twenty inches from the ground, the post had tripped hundreds of kids.

It was Mama Shaw. Seventysomething years old, she was a Sunnybrook Club regular and the least valuable of the lot. Her mellifluous Jamaican accent demanded attention, which was unfortunate, considering the non sequiturs of her input. If Mr Villard's topic was beautification, she'd bewail the devil music coming from adjacent homes. If the club was discussing clamping down on prostitution, she'd lament all the dog poop. These interjections always came from Mama Shaw's bedroom, so close to the playground she needed only lean out the window, cigarette in hand, to participate. Until this moment, Greer had forgotten the reason Mama Shaw stayed inside.

Her legs had been amputated two years ago.

Diabetic infection, Greer had heard. She'd seen hospital orderlies loading the legless woman into a medical van via stretcher. Once, Greer had been fetching mail when they'd arrived, and though she'd averted her eyes from the sight of Mama Shaw plated like a steak, she'd heard the orderlies crack jokes as if the woman they carried were already dead and couldn't hear. There'd been a certain archness to how they'd said *Their* and *They*.

'If I were these people,' one said, 'I'd stay at the hospital as long as I could.'

'Hey, we're Their personal valets,' said the other. 'Maybe They're smarter than They seem.'

Now Mama Shaw was outside, facedown, her nightdress revealing her thigh stumps. The grass beneath the dome long ago had been scuffed away; mud oozed between Mama Shaw's squeezing fists. Greer looked around and absorbed the evidence: rain-diluted splashes of blood along Mama Shaw's trailer steps and a luge-like furrow carved through wet leaves. Mama Shaw hadn't been tossed here. She'd crawled out here by herself.

Why the fuck hadn't anyone helped her?

Greer kneeled down. Her sweatpants were soaked. She set her phone on the damp ground, the screen brilliant with three encouraging digits. It would be the last time she ever touched it.

'Mama Shaw,' she said. 'It's Greer Morgan. I'm going to pull you out, okay?'

With a sucking sound, Mama Shaw pulled her face from the muck. Her gauzy gray hair was matted to her skin. Her eyes, already cataracted, had gone full white; black pupils skittered beneath mucus before locking on Greer. The cords in Mama Shaw's neck pulled taut as she opened her mouth so wide Greer thought her lower jaw might unhinge. The woman's upper and lower dentures popped out and landed in the mud. From the toothless hollow rose an urgent chuffing.

Señorita Magdalena's trailer rocked again. Stabilizer cables pinged under the strain.

Greer tamped down the urge to flee. Mama Shaw must be having a seizure, and Greer was the only one who could do anything about it. She took firm hold of Mama Shaw's wrists. The skin was as clammy as lunch meat. When she adjusted her grip, the dents made by her fingers remained visible. Was that because of diabetes? Did the disease gelatinize blood, make skin thick and sluggish?

Mama Shaw was a hefty woman, but when Greer pulled, her body slid easily through the leaves, like she was half the weight. Of course she *was,* Greer thought abruptly – she was missing both legs. Greer kept pulling until the woman's upper body escaped the perimeter of the dome. Mud and leaves piled into Mama Shaw's mouth and covered her nose. *She'll suffocate,* Greer thought, remembering how, mere minutes ago, she'd pretended to smother herself with a pillow. How quickly her morning melodrama had come to look childish.

Greer bent to clear mud from Mama Shaw's face.

'Get back!'

How many shocks could she take? Greer bit back a scream as Sam Hell charged down the asphalt, his Kangol hat keeping the rain from his glaring eyes. He held a gun. Not a hunting rifle like one of Daddy's but an automatic sidearm, the kind hoodlums liked to flex in front of friends. He held the gun sidewise too, that douche move Greer only saw in action flicks. None of that meant the pointed gun wasn't scary; Greer froze, afraid to move even the hand she had on Mama Shaw's face.

'She's choking!' Greer pleaded.

'*Shut up and move your ass!*'

Mama Shaw's fingers cinched around Greer's wrist. That was good news – it meant the woman was alert enough to be frightened. But Mama Shaw's grip tightened until Greer's wrist bones smarted. Despite the gun bearing down on her, Greer moved her head to look at Mama Shaw.

And Mama Shaw bit her.

The old woman flung her head at Greer's hand, her toothless, mud-filled mouth enveloping the teenager's first two fingers. Mama Shaw's jaws snapped together, putting pressure on Greer's knuckles. She had only a second to consider the freakish sight before she was thrown aside by a massive jolt to the shoulder that tossed *her* aside and jolted Mama Shaw's body. Propelled by the impact, Greer's phone shot out of sight beneath damp leaves.

The back of Greer's head whacked against wet ground. Had Sam Hell shot her? A loud *thwack* made her blink away the rain pooled in her eye sockets and sit up. Sam Hell was kicking Mama Shaw in the face. For the second time, from the looks of it – the woman's nose was broken open to the pearl-colored cartilage. That's what had hit Greer: not a bullet but Sam Hell's foot. She felt a belated burst of pain in her shoulder at the exact second his boot connected with Mama Shaw's chin.

'Stop!' Greer cried. Again, she tried to summon her protector: 'Daddy!'

Mama Shaw's neck jerked back with a moist crack. The top of her skull rang against a bar of the dome. It was beyond grotesque, this legless old lady under assault. A wail burst from Greer's chest. Sam Hell didn't pause. He reached Greer in a single step and put a boot to her chest, pressing her into the mud. Greer felt all oxygen blast from her body. She thought strangely of Qasim, his weight against her, her breath sucked into his mouth. Sam Hell's gun, not sideways this time, came straight at her.

'*You're bit!*' he shouted.

She wheezed for air. 'What?'

'*That old bitch fucking bit you, and you're fucking fucked!*'

Was Mama Shaw rabid? That made sense. The Last Resort brimmed with rats. One of them had gone rabid, bitten Mama Shaw, and she'd crawled out here and scared the living shit out of the Sunnybrook Club. Greer raised her right hand and looked it over. Mud, two blades of leaf. No blood, not even a scratch. She showed it to Sam Hell.

'Gums,' she croaked.

The gun jumped closer. A raindrop bridged the barrel to her nose.

'Bitch, *what*?'

The boot on her chest pressed harder. She could feel her body sinking. She was going to end up buried right here at Sunnybrook Mobile Home Resort, the place on Earth she most wanted to leave.

'No teeth,' she grunted. 'No teeth.'

Sam Hell's eyes bulged as he stared at her hand, but Greer had no confidence he was seeing straight. When not inebriated, the man was manic, hulking around Miss Jemisha's trailer, kicking down railings and punching in windows. If she didn't let him in, he'd go raging down the road, spewing bile – *bitch whore cunt pig skank ho tramp*. This was his current state, the most heightened Greer had seen it.

She'd also never seen him up this early. Miss Jemisha must have rushed home from the disrupted club meeting and woken him up. None of that explained his reaction. If Mama Shaw was sick, he could call for help or just stay the fuck away. He didn't need to kick the woman in her face and aim his piece at a neighbor.

'How I know you ain't bit elsewhere?' he demanded.

Greer's mind went straight to sexual violation. Of course it did. High on something, he'd make her take her clothes off under the pretense of checking for bite marks. Then he'd rape her, his gun pressed under her chin, and if a single fucking member of the do-gooder Sunnybrook Club saw, they'd pull a Mr Villard and get out. They wouldn't even call 911, the same way Greer hadn't and for the same reason: that ruinous, perpetuating cycle of so-called self-protection.

Sam Hell loomed, rain shivering from his hat, chin, arm, and gun, while his frantic gaze searched her rain-soaked body. The only sounds were their panting breaths, the patter of rain, and the slurps of Mama Shaw.

New sounds broke the tension. They came from Señorita Magdalena's trailer. The feline whine of a screen door opening only to prematurely crash shut, like someone unsure how to operate it, followed by the hard, uneven shuffles of feet tumbling down steps, lots of them. The gun barrel swung away from Greer's face as Sam Hell responded to the sounds. Greer pushed herself to her elbows and leaned to see for herself.

No longer would she have to wonder how many children Señorita Magdalena had. There were five, ranging from ages five to thirteen. Obviously, none had been marshaled today for school. The quintet was a swiftly untangling pyre of tangled limbs at the foot of the steps. They were oblivious to the rain on Their faces, the mud splashed over Their pajamas, the Rorschachs of blood all over Them. They stood up and looked about, daft as ducks, until one of Them, a girl of maybe seven, spotted Sam Hell and Greer Morgan, and, without a word, began walking their way.

Altogether Different Beasts

Greer had always thought the map of Sunnybrook Mobile Home Resort posted at the park's entrance resembled the kind of goat's-head pentagram drawn by metal-music kids. Seventy-eight plots, with trailers ranging from four-bed, two-bath double-wides like Mr Villard's to thirty-two-foot egg cartons like Fadi Lolo's, were arranged at slashing angles on all sides of the star-pattern roads. Each segment had its own dilapidated playground; the one appropriated by the Sunnybrook Club was in the pentagram's lower-right phalange, three minutes to the gate if you ran like hell.

That's what Greer wanted to do, but the sight of the filth-covered, injured children stalled her the same way Mama Shaw had. Though diverse in size, the five moved identically, toddling like the earth's surface was shifting beneath Them. Greer was beginning to believe it was.

Sam Hell stood up, a hundred stories above Greer's body. His arm arced upward, directing his gun at the littlest girl. Greer had seen many things she wished she hadn't in this park – depraved acts by addicts, assaults she'd not done enough to stop – but nothing as horrible as this.

The little girl reached the road. One of her hands was red hamburger, knitted together by gray tendons. Her cherubic right cheek had no partner: the left cheek was a hole through which Greer could see a row of baby teeth, one lost to the Tooth Fairy. Sam Hell widened his legs for a better shot, and Greer envisioned the rest of the girl's teeth detonating in a shower of bone.

Do something, she screamed to herself, but her mouth felt like Mama Shaw's, packed with mud and cold leaves.

Someone stronger acted first. The screen door crashed open, and the brood's mother appeared. Señorita Magdalena: who spoke the sketchiest of English; whose contributions at Sunnybrook Club meetings were limited to two tiresome, pleading words: 'The cheeldren'; whose parking slot was a muddy wreck thanks to the cavalcade of relatives who came by all day, dropping off bags of laundry that Magdalena cleaned at the park coin-op. Magdalena unfailingly brought over a pan of tres leches cake on Greer's birthday and always called Greer *mi corazón* – my heart – though she'd done nothing to deserve it; who persevered like a motherfucker, raising five exceedingly polite kids despite the capricious rages of José Frito and the feeble sustenance of generic foods; whom, only in this instant, though the two had shared little more than cake and a few fumbled words, Greer discovered she loved with a fierceness that meant she would do anything to keep the woman alive.

'Magdalena, get down!' she yelled.

For a second, Greer feared the woman would start lurching like her children, but Magdalena, four feet six and ball-shaped, displayed a sudden lioness's grace, leaping to the ground and landing in a ballplayer's crouch. She ignored Greer's warning. Of course she did; a lioness protects her cubs. Greer's heart, *mi corazón,* slugged even harder.

'Antonella!' Magdalena shouted. 'Ignacio! Máximo! Constanza! Silvana!'

Greer knew Their names just as Their names lost significance. Magdalena's screams did appear to throw off Sam Hell. His gun arm wavered. Greer didn't think he gave one shit about Señorita

Magdalena; it was likely he wasn't accustomed to shooting people in front of so many witnesses.

He raised the gun in a two-handed grip.

'My boy Billy went down last night,' Sam Hell said to Greer. 'And then Billy got back up. Bit the shit out of the cops. And then *those* motherfuckers got back up! All these kids gotta go!'

'Silvana!' Magdalena cried. Silvana was the little girl closest to Greer and Sam Hell, thirty feet away and closing. Magdalena ran after her. Because she was Magdalena's heart, Greer felt the strain of her strides and shouted something – she wasn't sure if it was words or just sound. It didn't matter; Sam Hell shot.

Greer flinched from the barrel's white flash. She swore she could see individual raindrops halve and scatter. Silvana, all forty-five pounds of her, was kicked off her feet, landing two yards back with such an impact that dozens of dead leaves flew upward; in this new, upside-down world, Greer thought madly, this was simply the direction dead leaves fell.

Magdalena howled and pulled the only child within reach – Ignacio, age ten – to the ground for safety. Greer, too, flattened herself, even though she was behind the shooter. The other children gave no indication of being bothered. They continued Their march.

'Rodney, stop! Rodney, stop!'

Greer looked left, toward the new voice, her neck muscles feeling like loose rubber. Just visible past the edge of Mama Shaw's trailer, due north of Señorita Magdalena's place, was the trailer Miss Jemisha shared with Sam Hell – real name Rodney, it seemed.

Miss Jemisha stood on her steps in raincoat and boots, gripping the sides of her raincoat hood with both hands. Greer felt certain the only thing that had kept Miss Jemisha from ousting this low-rent gangster out of her life had been never actually seeing him pull a trigger.

Now she had.

'Back inside, woman!' Sam Hell cried, and though Greer hated this man, she hoped Jemisha, one last time, would do what he ordered.

Instead, the woman ran straight at them. Miss Jemisha: whose oratorical tactic at Sunnybrook Club gatherings was to repeat one sentence, louder and louder until everyone else capitulated from exhaustion; whose regular, foulmouthed telephone tirades to debt collectors triggered everyone's hatred by making them hate themselves; but whose joy, when it hit, caromed about the whole park in peals of infectious hee-haws; who checked in on Mama Shaw for months after her first leg amputation, and months after the second one, too, with no expectation of reward; who threw herself into any potentially violent conflict, just like she was now, because she had only one life to live – at least, those were the rules before today – and goddamn if she wasn't going to live it, loudly, righteously, recklessly.

Sam Hell gave Miss Jemisha a running back's stiff-arm to the forehead, beneath which her raincoated arms flailed, too short to reach him. Except for Ignacio, who fought his mother's embrace, the children had crossed the road, Silvana again in the lead. There was a neat black hole in her pajama top, from which blood trickled when it should have been gushing. The poor, destroyed rag doll of a girl kept walking, more teeth visible through the hole in her cheek, arms raised as if asking for a hug to make it all better.

Miss Jemisha managed a boot to Sam Hell's crotch. The gun swooped treacherously; Greer swore she could feel its sight across her body like someone had walked over her grave, as Daddy often said. The time to prevaricate, to use a Mr Villard term, was over. Greer launched herself at Sam Hell's legs. He toppled fast, his shoulder crunching to the ground, but kept kicking, his kneecaps socking like billiard balls against Greer's face. With a cape-like flutter of raincoat, Jemisha slammed atop him, grappling for the gun.

Sam Hell rolled halfway over, slamming both women into the climbing dome. But they were still two on one. Greer scaled Sam

Hell's legs and took hold of his gun arm. Her hands interlocked with Jemisha's, practically the same shade of brown, twisting with effort. There was something heroic about it, Greer thought, and if she was about to die, it would be a fine final sight: Black women's fists, fighting together.

Jemisha made a startled, strangled noise as her skull was viciously yanked back, clanging against the bars. One of Mama Shaw's bony hands clenched Jemisha's box braids; she was pulling so hard Greer could see Jemisha's scalp tighten beneath the cornrows. Jemisha let go of Sam Hell and hammered blindly behind her. Not one strike hit Mama Shaw; Jemisha's knuckles cracked off the dome, leaving delicate lashes of blood.

Sam Hell, one woman lighter, surged against Greer. A scream, the loudest yet, ripped the morning in half. Greer and Sam Hell turned in unison to see Señorita Magdalena pedaling her body through the mud away from Ignacio while kicking him in the face. Ignacio flopped after her with a seallike heave identical to that of the legless Mama Shaw. His face, always so smooth and alert, looked as if acid had eaten it back. He was all teeth, stained purple with bloody mud.

Magdalena's cry mustered one more character: José Frito, clad in a wrongly buttoned flannel shirt, unzipped jeans, and unlaced sneakers, an ensemble that might have suggested total lack of foresight if not for the gun belt – an actual fucking buscadero-style, double-holstered, hand-tooled leather, cowboy-western gun belt. The Honduran burst out the door with a .45 pistol in each hand, ululating a war cry. His late arrival might have been due to injury: some white fabric, soaked red, was wrapped tight around his left forearm.

José Frito opened fire with both guns, a firecracker chain of explosions.

Greer huddled against the dome between the wailing Miss Jemisha and the cussing Sam Hell, afraid but relieved: here was help, and right now she'd take it in any shape it came. She expected Ignacio to go down, expected Silvana to blossom with exit wounds. But puffs of mud splattered at Greer's feet. Yellow sparks flew from the dome bars, shaving sparks. José Frito was shooting at *them*.

Even in the tumult, Greer understood. She'd never seen José give shit-all attention to Magdalena's children. Only now, with the promise of invigorating gunfire, did he decide to play Father of the Year, taking aim not at the actual problem but at the Black guy with the gun. The two men should have been on the same team, but when there were guns on opposite sides of a road, they had to shoot at each other.

Sam Hell rolled rightward, away from Greer, losing his Kangol hat. He planted his elbows in the mud and fired back. One of Magdalena's windows shattered and one of her trash cans was gutshot, spurting rotten liquid. José Frito scrambled down the steps, returning fire in a way that looked cinematic but was wildly wayward. A bullet split one of the swing set's dangling chains. Another shattered the railing of a trailer down the road. A third struck Silvana, luckless Silvana, in the back of the neck. Her throat exploded in blood so dark it looked like chocolate syrup as she was flung face-first to the ground.

Two screams pealed louder than gunfire. One was Magdalena, insane with grief and confusion, who crawled around Ignacio and onto asphalt that tore blood from her knees. The second was right next to Greer: Jemisha. Mama Shaw, with dual handfuls of Jemisha's braids now, had begun a scalping. Jemisha's hair extensions were already shredded; Mama Shaw chewed the puffs like cud. The skin at Jemisha's hairline had begun to rip as neatly as if along a perforated line, revealing red-orange subcutaneous fat.

Jemisha quit her ineffectual backward punches, grabbed a dome rung with one hand, and reached the other toward Greer.

'Help,' gasped this woman who had never, ever asked for help.

Greer wanted only to sprint up the road and take Mr Villard's advice, but Jemisha's hand was so close, shaking so badly. Greer could hear the cloth-like tearing of her forehead and see runners of blood painting vertical lines down her face, past her bulging, terrified eyes. Greer pounced, latching on to Jemisha's hand with an arm wrestler's grip. She wrapped her other hand around Jemisha's wrist and braced her foot, still clad in a flip-flop, against a bar. She pulled. Jemisha pulled. But Mama Shaw was eating her way up Jemisha's head, the braids disappearing down the old woman's throat like feeding tubes.

Despite the gunfire still cracking around her, Greer slid feetfirst into the dome and began stomping Mama Shaw in the face. The woman's nose, ruptured from Sam Hell's boot, tore off with a plop of cartilage, leaving behind an empty, scrotal bag of skin. Greer kept going, her flip-flops flying free, her bare heels pistoning until Mama Shaw's face felt pulpy. She didn't stop until Miss Jemisha was crouched beside her, finally free.

Jemisha seemed to not hear the splattering of bullets into mud. She ran her hands through the leaves, found the sort of heavy, jagged rock that had no business at a playground, and hobbled so her knees pinned down both of Mama Shaw's arms. The old woman, her face an unrecognizable red paste, still gnashed her mouth-shaped hole around a wad of hair. Jemisha raised the rock in both hands and drove it down.

Greer pivoted her knees in the mud, lumbered to her feet, and ran. But she heard the thick impacts into Mama Shaw's skull and brain, as well as Miss Jemisha's rapid, riverside babble.

'Be merciful to me, O God, because of your constant love.' *Scrunch.* 'Because of your great mercy, wipe away my sins.' *Scrunch.* 'Wash away my evil and make me clean from my sin.' *Scrunch.* 'I recognize my faults, I am conscious of my sins.' *Scrunch.* 'I have sinned against you – only against you.' *Scrunch.*

Could Greer feel bullets flutter past her skin? Or was it only the rain? She leaped past Sam Hell, her naked foot stamping his Kangol hat into the mud, heading for her trailer. Two arms whipped into her face, fingertips scrabbling. It was Silvana, still rudely alive and only inches away, the rent in her cheek revealing a long, waggling tongue, the hole through her neck so massive that what was left began to collapse beneath her head's weight.

Greer batted Silvana's arms away and kept running. Between her and her trailer was nothing but silver, slanting rain. Then her foot caught the fulcrum of the fucking seesaw. Hurled into a somersault, she hit the ground on her right ear and went briefly deaf.

The lusterless faces of several children banked her way, and in the next instant, they began to move toward her. Greer cursed and pushed herself to a sitting position, just as Silvana, or what remained of her, tripped on the same fucking fulcrum and landed directly atop Greer.

The girl showed no surprise or disorientation from her fall. She hinged open her jaws and flung her head down at Greer; Greer stopped her with a forearm to her hollowed neck. Silvana's tongue, now dangling from the hole in her cheek, licked dryly across Greer's mud-slathered chin. One hand sank into Greer's hair.

Jemisha's peeled scalp flashed before Greer's eyes, and she thrashed as if she were on fire. But Silvana was dug in like a tick, jaws snapping. The little girl didn't blink, and somehow this was the most horrifying detail. *She did not blink.* Silvana's cold upper lip grazed Greer's nose. The pale, shambling blotches of the other four children appeared at the periphery of Greer's vision. She was going to die. It was not the first time in Greer's life she'd thought it, but it was with the most regret. She was fighting as hard as she could, and it wasn't enough.

An old-fashioned baseball bat, a Louisville Slugger stained cherry red, hit Silvana at home-run velocity. The thickest section of wood struck the girl's neck, ripping through what was left of the bullet-torn muscle. Silvana was thrown to the ground, neck so destroyed that her head dangled by its spinal cord alone. And still her jaw gnashed, up and down on her tongue.

Greer poured herself into a man's arms. They were empty: he'd dropped the bat as if contact with the girl had sent rabies cankering up the handle. Here was the final member of the Sunnybrook Club, Drasko Zorić, whose chilly remarks often froze the squabbling of Mr Villard, Mama Shaw, and Miss Jemisha; who not only trapped nocturnal nuisances like raccoons and possums but purportedly slit their throats to watch them die; whose yard was an eyesore of auto, washing machine, mower, and toilet parts; but who also proudly offered assistance to anyone who needed help reading a bill, ticket, or tax form; who each January 14 celebrated Serbian New Year by doing good deeds, this year helping Freddy Morgan gut his decayed bathroom wall.

'Can you stand?' He scanned the playground, then stared sharply at Greer. 'Yes, you stand. Now, now, now, now, now.'

Drasko hoisted the young woman to her feet. He wore a shiny blue tracksuit; she traced her muddy, bloody fingers across the clean, satiny polyester. He gripped her by the soggy shoulders and forcibly rotated her so she'd see the children only a few feet away, hands grasping like babies after bright plastic playthings: Antonella, Máximo, and Constanza, unless They'd become altogether different beasts.

Drasko dragged Greer away from her trailer and onto the asphalt. The children's groans made her ears pop, and abruptly she heard everything: gunshots, cries of anger, yodels of pain. Drasko Zorić had braved a playground swarming with bullets to save her – and he wasn't done yet. Señorita Magdalena was on her back in the road, kicking at Ignacio, who'd managed to catch one of her slippered feet and was trying to bite it.

Greer felt as if a sunbeam had speared through storm clouds. The crabby, ragtag congress of complainers of the Sunnybrook Club, which Greer had mocked right down to accent imitations and stereotyped nicknames, had never been the losers she'd considered them. Even if they'd lived dead-end lives in dead-end jobs, today they'd proven themselves unwilling to quit fighting. Mr Villard aside, the Sunnybrook Club were heroes.

A truck swerved around Magdalena and her son before speeding past Greer, close enough that she could see the determined grimace on the face of the driver. She plunged through its wake of heat, keeping pace with Drasko while noting two more cars squealing their way. The whole Last Resort had awakened and wanted out. A fine idea, but Magdalena and Ignacio were in the middle of the road, and Greer doubted all escaping vehicles would manage the truck's swift dodge.

Greer grabbed Magdalena's right arm. Drasko took her left. Both pulled Magdalena backward. She cried out as the asphalt shredded her housecoat. Those wounds would heal. What was important was that they'd stolen her foot back; Ignacio stared into his emptied hands with idiotic loss.

Magdalena reached up, gripping Drasko's and Greer's arms.

'Dios te bendiga,' she said to Drasko. To Greer, her old endearment, 'Mi corazón, mi corazón.'

A bumperless sedan roared by, its side mirror clipping Drasko's elbow. The car's muffler skittered along the road, spraying sparks into an oily cloud of exhaust. Greer and Drasko brought Magdalena to her feet just as Ignacio shot forward out of the smoke. The boy folded facedown to the asphalt, splattering blood. The rear of his skull was cracked, and unlike Silvana, he didn't move again. Magdalena screamed, and despite every affront her child had recently committed, she ran to him, arms out to gather his body.

'Ignacio! Oh, mi pobre chico dulce!'

The car exhaust thinned, and from it stepped José Frito.

One of his pistols was gone, probably dropped after it was depleted of ammo. Its partner hung from his right hand, a petal of smoke unfurling from the muzzle. His Father of the Year act was kaput: he'd shot both Silvana and Ignacio and looked ready to shoot everyone else. José's presence suggested he'd prevailed over Sam Hell. His mustache was stiff with blood. He was flecked with abrasions. The fabric he'd knotted over his left forearm had fallen away, revealing a bite wound that matched the exact contours of a child's jaws.

José moved more groggily than the children. His face had gone the color of eggnog. Individual veins rose like blue worms hoping to burrow free. His swollen eyelids oozed batter over dark, hollowed sockets. He began to lift the gun; it juddered as his muscles spasmed.

Cradling her boy's head to keep the brains inside, Magdalena reached for José's gun arm. It was chilling how easily, even under duress, José slapped her across the face. More chilling was the familiarity with which she took the blow. She fell to the left, but by luck not too far; a car swerved around her head so closely its back tire munched a lock of her hair.

José watched the car pass with dreamy interest, then looked at the dead boy, then at the gun in his hand. Greer believed she could read his thoughts faster than his own muddled brain could process them. There were people everywhere who'd seen what he'd done, they'd rat on him unless he finished them off. He squinted at Drasko and Greer through gluey eyes, and with an unpredictable jolt, raised the gun and fired.

Drasko Zorić was shot in the right breast. Somehow he didn't hit the asphalt, rather catching himself in a spider's stance. He moved like a spider, too, tumbling on all fours toward Greer's trailer. The oldest child, fourteen-year-old Antonella, walked past José, Magdalena, and Greer, perhaps attracted by Drasko's flailing, and dropped to her knees near where the Serbian had collapsed. His blood trailed across the asphalt; Antonella lowered her face to the stream and began to lap it up, scuttling closer to his body.

José registered none of this. He took a tottering step over Magdalena, gaze fixed on Greer, and grinned. His teeth were pink with blood. More, thicker and blacker, squeezed between them. With the blood came a grunt Greer instantly recognized.

'C'mere.'

A mud-encrusted family van appeared like a ship through foggy seas. A massive metal grille threw a bucket's worth of rain into Greer's face a second before it clobbered José with the sound of wet meat. He sailed through the air, his back snapped so completely the back of his head touched his heels. Greer threw herself off the road, hearing all four tires crunch across dead Ignacio and alive Magdalena. The van veered too late, shearing through the playground with a splattery rasp.

Turning her back, Greer ran. She was at her trailer in seconds, slamming into it with her right shoulder, the one Sam Hell had kicked.

The pain was electric. She saw black fireworks. When her vision returned, she was startled to find her hands bloody. What had happened? She widened her gaze to see she'd smacked into the red smear that ran along the side of the trailer. It had been one of the first things she'd noticed when she'd stepped outside. If only she'd followed the streak to the trailer's end and continued up the road to the park exit. She would have seen nothing of what she'd recently witnessed. Now Greer managed one step in that direction before a large figure shuffled around the corner, blocking her path.

Dry, brown blood crusted his hand: he must have been the one who'd slapped the bloody print on the trailer-door window and left the smear on the wall. He wolfishly sniffed Greer's scent and ponderously lifted his head from its droop. His brown eyes had dimmed behind an opaline scrim. His jaws were askew, draining saliva onto his HortiPlastics uniform. His glasses were gone except for a broken earpiece still lodged behind an ear.

'Daddy,' Greer said, and Daddy, as he always had, came for her.

No Longer in Service

The easiest choice in life is to give in. To teachers' low expectations. To bodily sensations generated with boys like Qasim. To friends' pressure to drink this or swallow that. Greer had been calling for Daddy since she'd stepped into the morning mist, and now that he'd come to collect her, there was nothing she wanted more than to bury her face into his broad chest.

His arm extended as gently as if he were after a butterfly. His middle finger brushed her hoodie. One fingertip, calloused from thousands of pulls of a hunting bow, snagged a hood string. This minuscule, even delicate, tussle of finger versus string, so unlike Freddy Morgan's usual blunt actions, spurred Greer to lean out of reach. She didn't run; she was not afraid of him as much as afraid *for* him. Others whose eyes had gone white like his were being beaten, shot, driven over.

What she should do, she thought, was coax Daddy inside their home. Get him out of that bloody HortiPlastics shirt. Clean and bandage his hand. Blot his forehead with a cold cloth, as he'd done so many times for her. Make him the chicken-flavored soup he liked from the yellow powder. He'd made her swear to call an ambulance only in cataclysmic circumstances, as the cost of a single ride could ruin the Morgans more easily than most injuries.

'Let's get out of the rain, Daddy,' she said. 'Can you make it up the—'

Drasko Zorić had a guttural voice, but the last sound he made was a piercing turkey gobble. Spinning in response, Greer glimpsed, behind lancets of rain, his blue tracksuit being torn in competing directions by Antonella and Máximo. Their backs were sickled over him like wild dogs.

Greer felt her father's hand take hers. From entering first-day grade-school classrooms to exiting vice principal scoldings, this hand had led her everywhere, and she'd never mistake how those big fingers enveloped hers, the heartening pinch of his wedding ring, the comforting rasp of his callouses. This was no different, she told herself.

Except it was – Drasko Zorić's dying screams insisted on it.

She yanked away. Freddy Morgan's forehead crinkled. Greer couldn't afford to wait, lest some other incidental gesture snare her heart. She vaulted the trailer steps and tucked herself inside, slamming the door and locking both bolt and chain. She backpedaled, her bare soles sensitive to every crumb in the carpet, until the backs of her knees struck the chair that held the TV.

She lost her shit the second her butt touched linoleum. With the morning's hallucinatory horrors now bracketed by her home's nonchalance, the adrenaline squalling through her body felt like spiders all over her. She tore at her wet clothes, peeling them off like putrid skin until she was naked. Still she felt revoltingly warm, as if dripping hot blood.

Nausea hitched up her throat. She clambered on all fours to the bathroom, where she gripped the toilet bowl with both hands and vomited so hard she could see roses of blood in the water. She rolled onto her back, welcoming the frigid tile. *Think of anything else,* she ordered herself. *Think of Qasim.*

Eventually the wind razoring through the unfinished plywood wall chilled her. A good sign. She crawled into her bedroom. Scrounging like a strawberry picker, she gathered underwear, a

T-shirt, a sweatshirt, jeans, socks, and sneakers. Still on the floor, she pulled and laced, zipped and snapped. She hugged her knees against the end of her bed, freezing now that she was fully clothed.

Outside: shouts, breaking glass, car horns . . .

. . . and a light slapping on the door.

From her bedroom, Greer could see the length of the cramped trailer through the open door of her dad's bedroom. It was like peering through a forest understory. The trash can so overstuffed the lid floated loose atop the slag, a leaking bag of kitty litter for a cat that had croaked a year ago, the tangle of blankets on the sofa bed Conan slept on. The whole family had been trapped there for four years.

Before, they had lived in Bulk proper, three blocks from the middle school she and Conan attended. After Vienna Morgan was incarcerated and the robbed families were compensated, Freddy lost his boiler-repair job and the Morgan house had been foreclosed upon. They'd ended up in Sunnybrook. The first time they'd entered the forty-foot trailer, Freddy had hit his head on the ceiling fan, drawing blood. After closing the deal, he'd gone outside, set up his bow-hunting target, and taken shots for hours, as if every bull's-eye slew one of his past mistakes.

The whole place was rotten. A third of the ceiling had turned to oatmeal from water leakage; visible through those gaps were roof trusses warped like tusks and metal plating pitted with cavities. When it rained, like this morning, strings of rust water as thick as the bloody drool from her father's mouth (Don't think of it) landed in buckets permanently placed below, while musty snarls of carpet indicated where new buckets were needed. The two longest walls leaned inward, like they might snap shut like Ignacio's jaws aiming at his mother's foot (Don't think of it), swallowing the Morgans alive.

Both drywall and window frames were buckled. Freddy Morgan's attempts to fit plastic into the windows failed when the replacement panels came loose in the sash, like Mama Shaw's dentures popping from her slavering mouth (Stop, stop, stop). In surrender, Freddy nailed large patches of galvanized chicken wire on the inside of the trailer's six windows. To Greer, it made the place feel like one of Vienna Morgan's jail cells, but Freddy was proud of the result and Conan didn't care.

Greer had hated the chicken wire until this second. The tapping on the door's window became a pounding, which gave way to the pop of cleaving glass. It was Freddy Morgan, butting up against his own defenses. He struck the chicken wire again and again. Each time, the barrier droned an open chord, and Greer found herself humming along. It was the song that would save her life, if only it kept playing.

An open-palmed thud came from a second window.

Broken glass chimed from a third.

Greer hummed louder to block the noise. The chicken wire would hold.

At first, she thought the burbling bass note was the sound of a fourth besieger, until she recognized it as Daddy's eight o'clock alarm, his reminder to take a baby aspirin for pulmonary health. It was a phone alarm. Daddy's phone was inside the trailer. And Greer knew his passcode. She'd find it, call the cops. They'd take their sweet time getting there, and like Mama Shaw's orderlies – *Maybe They're smarter than They seem* – they'd think the residents were getting what they deserved. But she'd swallow their scorn one more time.

Above the sofa, the chicken wire nailed over the broken window bulged from bashing hands. She tiptoed past, grimacing, and the beating stopped. The face behind the wire stared at her. It was Sam Hell. His skin was purplish gray, his eyes pearl white. Blood splattered his neck and chest. He watched Greer with the witless stare she'd seen on boys looking at porn, then snuffled like a pig, shoved his fingers through the wire, and yanked harder than before.

Sam Hell's agitation elicited a whine from the far end of the trailer.

Thirty feet away and through metal mesh, Greer still recognized Máximo. His mouth was painted red, and scraps of skin jiggled between his teeth. Each slam of his hands against the chicken wire cut bloody hexagons into his chubby palms.

Spotting the phone on the kitchen counter, Greer grabbed it. But she couldn't call the cops on Daddy without looking at him one more time, hoping that his eyes and mind had cleared. His face remained visible at the door's window. He had quit moving, did not blink or twitch or breathe. Greer prayed for this to be a positive development. She took a single step closer. His eyes, beneath white mucus, moved as she approached, but he wasn't staring at her. He was staring at his phone.

Freddy Morgan, who had yet to recognize his own daughter, seemed to recognize his phone's alarm. That upset Greer in a primal way, as if she had been erased. At the same time, she understood. Anytime she heard a digital bleep similar to her wake-up alarm or incoming texts, she acted the same way, just like she'd been trained.

'I'm going to call an ambulance, Daddy,' she whispered. 'The police too.'

Daddy did not react.

'I know you told me to only do that if I was sure. But I'm sure, Daddy. I'm really sure. Do you hear that? Can you see Them? They're trying to get in. They're going to hurt me, Daddy, just like They hurt you. If you know how to stop Them, do it, okay? Can you tell Them to stop?'

Nothing about her father altered except for some reddish spit that spilled down his chin. He still seemed focused on the phone and its mambo beat. Maybe the alarm was preventing a more meaningful exchange. Greer thumbed the phone to life and swiped, killing the tone, then looked at Daddy for any changes in expression.

There were many, all awful. Only when squinting down the barrel of his hunting rifle had one of his eyebrows peaked so sharply, and now both did, daggering like dragon wings, while his hairline drew downward. His nostrils flared so widely Greer thought they might tear. His mouth was the worst of all. The lower jaw had practically detached, as if straining to swallow the whole door, the whole trailer, the whole world.

Greer recognized the sound that echoed up from his throat. It was *want*. Freddy Morgan's want, however, had changed. No longer was he focused on a better job, a nicer home, a happier life – the trifling baubles dangled before a hypnotized populace. No, this want had lain in wait for three million years, hiding beneath the smiles, the nods, the haircuts, the uniforms, the time cards, the deference, the fear.

Daddy punched his hands, fingertips first, at the chicken wire. The wire carved finger-flesh in half-moons that fell like fingernail clippings. He made a frustrated bellow. Withdrawing his mangled fingers, he catapulted his face into the chicken wire. His nose, lips, and cheeks flattened. A tidy, geometric grid of blood sprang from his entire face. His tongue snaked from his mouth, encountered wire, and pushed against it. Wire began to slice the tongue down the center.

Instinctively, Greer shouted, 'No!' but Freddy Morgan had never been one to quit what he'd started. His neck thickened as he drove his face more forcefully into the mesh. Ruby blood oozed from every crosshatch. Still he pushed, until the chicken wire wrapped around his face, digging all the way to his skull. Like that, his face was jellied into two dozen individual hexagons of flesh. One piece, comprised of his right upper lip, plopped like dough from a cookie cutter, revealing long yellow teeth and a patch of gray mandible. Other hexagons jiggled, ready to drop. Both halves of Daddy's tongue, fully forked now, wiggled separately.

Greer ran for her bedroom. When she saw a new set of paws battering the window over her bed, she instead banked into the bathroom, the only windowless space. The toilet water swayed, and

Greer flashed to the time she'd opened it to find a rat paddling inside, the porcelain scritch of its claws the sound of nightmares to come. That single drenched rat now seemed like a warning: the trailer, the park, the whole society was full of holes, and through them, the biters would come.

Lifting Daddy's phone, Greer, at long last, dialed 911. It rang twice, brittle digital trills. At the moist click of an answered call, Greer blurted first.

'Greer Morgan, I'm Greer Morgan, I live in Sunnybrook Mobile Home Resort in Bulk, Missouri, and I'm trapped in my home, there are people everywhere, They've gone crazy, They're attacking each other, there's people dead and hurt, we need police and ambulances, you need to hurry, it's Sunnybrook Mobile Home Resort in Bulk, Missouri, I'm Greer Morgan, They've broken all my windows, They're going to get inside, hurry, please, please hurry.'

She gasped for breath. Only then did she hear the recording.

'The local time is 8:04 a.m. To place a call, press one. If you need additional assistance, press zero for the operator or remain on the line. If this call is an emergency, hang up and call 911. To hear your options again, press star.'

'What the fuck,' she said.

She killed the call, redialed 911. From her bedroom, the tinkle of breaking glass. She ducked, and when the shatter faded, heard the robo-woman offering the same bleak options.

'I *did* dial fucking 911!' Greer had never used an operator in her life, but times like this must be why such backup systems existed. She did as instructed and pressed zero; the Morgans had always followed the rules. The line clicked twice, and the signal switched to a staticky purr. A different robo-woman answered:

'We're sorry. You have reached a number that has been disconnected or is no longer in service. If you feel you have reached this recording in error, please check the number and try your call again.'

'The number was zero! You fucking told me to press zero!'

They hung up on her.

A motorcycle chainsawed past the trailer, reminding Greer that people who might help were still in the vicinity. She started screaming, the old-fashioned 911, and was shocked, and strangely thrilled, by her stabbing pitch and volume. Since being cool had become a thing – around middle school and the move to the Last Resort – she'd kept her voice apathetic. There was something breathtaking about her soaring, feminine shriek.

But all her screams did was attract more of the rabid. More hands slapped the siding. Someone was tearing off a shutter. It sounded like someone had crawled under the bathroom and was clobbering the waste tank. Most worrisome were the heavy cracks of something blunt striking the trailer's far corner, likely Drasko Zorić's baseball bat. The good news was the trailer corner was a senseless target. The bad news was that, until then, none of the rabid had shown the wherewithal to operate tools.

Maybe They're smarter than They seem.

She was getting the fuck out of this trailer. It was all she'd ever wanted to do.

There was nothing useful in the bathroom. She made for the wobbling hallway. The second she hit the main room, Sam Hell's arm punched through the window over the sofa. The chicken wire popped free, and Greer felt pulled nails, cold as ice chips, patter her side. She jagged right, dodging Sam Hell's hand by inches. *You are reaching for a Greer Morgan,* said a voice in her head, *who has been disconnected or is no longer in service.*

The swerve drove her closer to the door, where Daddy's exposed skull, nearly completely peeled now, pressed against the wire. Nails were coming out there too, collecting on the ground amid the patties of skin. Greer kept going, past the horror, all the way into her dad's room, where little Máximo, shorter and weaker, hadn't made much progress against his chicken wire and an unknown aggressor kept striking the trailer's corner with the bat.

Greer threw open Freddy Morgan's closet and dropped to her knees. There it was. It'd been years since she'd used any of it. If she placed her hands upon it, would the know-how come rushing back? She grabbed a huge duffel bag, shook it empty of camouflage clothing, and began shoveling everything she could into it. The Remington hunting rifle, the field-dressing knife, the machete, the binoculars, the first aid kit, the quiver of arrows, the bow.

Dream's Over

With all those weapons so close, maybe Freddy Morgan had been less concerned with securing his own bedroom. That was the only excuse Greer could conjure for Máximo's unexpected ousting of the chicken wire. Unlike Sam Hell, whom she could hear still struggling with his half-open mesh, Máximo dislodged the whole panel and within seconds began wriggling through broken glass. The remaining nails punched meaty holes in his hands. The baseball bat outside kept crashing, a relentless heartbeat.

It was an ill-timed moment. Greer was entangled in gear. With Máximo nearly inside, calls had to be made. The Remington rifle, the thing she wanted most, had to go, because she couldn't find a single fucking box of ammo. That made sense – it wouldn't be like Daddy to leave a rifle and ammo sitting out – but if she'd kept closer to him, instead of just expecting him to bail her out at school, she'd know where the shells were now that it mattered.

She knew Daddy had an older rifle, too, a Browning, but it was nowhere to be seen. Greer forgot it and kept piling. The fishing line of a collapsible pole got caught up in the mess, so in it went, and a box of tackle to boot. The bow was too long for the bag to close, but when she zipped it mostly shut, the bow stayed in place. She took one more, longing look at the Remington. She ought to take it. Scrounge up ammo later. Ignoring Máximo for another second, she lifted the rifle.

From the wall behind it, white eyes stared.

It was Constanza, Señorita Magdalena's second oldest. Greer saw a flash of red and realized the girl was the one bashing the trailer with Drasko's bat. She'd managed to make quite a hole. A couple of minutes more and it might be large enough to crawl through.

Greer rocketed to her feet, the Remington abandoned. The duffel bag, swinging wildly, lobbed hard against the back of her knees. She fell, her butt hitting the carpet while the back of her head landed on her dad's bed. She stared directly up at an upside-down boy, face warped with hunger. Máximo was crouched on the windowsill like a gargoyle. He pounced.

His snarling face landed at her crotch; Greer kneed him in the nose, chin, and teeth. His kicking legs were in her face; she lassoed them with the arm not caught in the duffel's straps. Now he was a cat in a bathtub, berserk, but he was also a little boy, and Greer was able to hurl his featherweight aside. She heard his teeth zing across her blue-jeaned calf.

He landed badly, his neck sharply angled against Daddy's bedside table, but she didn't let herself regret what she'd done. She shot to her feet, taking the duffel bag handles in both hands, and sprinted. She blew past awful sights as quickly as shuttling through Netflix options. Freddy Morgan's rinded skull, pimpled with skin blobs. Sam Hell's grasping, mutilated hands. Greer veered back into the bathroom, locking the door behind her. Máximo was inside the trailer, and Constanza would be next.

Greer rotated on a heel, set down her other foot, and José Frito got her.

Her right leg sank through a hole he'd ripped through the floor, her heel planting on the dirt under the trailer. She cried out in shock and pain, dropping the duffel. José's arms sprouted upward like tentacles. His hands, cockeyed bouquets of broken fingers, twined around her trapped thigh. Greer's screech rattled the bathroom fixtures. It was the opposite of her earlier warrior shriek, the cry of a trapped rabbit.

She twisted, straining to reach the duffel bag and Daddy's machete. But the bag was behind her, and with her legs so widely scissored, her ability to turn was truncated. She felt her jeans tighten as José's teeth clamped on a seam. One of her whipping arms struck a small decorative table with a semicircle top and Baroque legs, an unusually pretty accent piece, maybe the last item of beauty in her life.

Fuck it – her mom probably stole it. Greer yanked a leg. The table crashed. She whacked it against the floor, and the leg snapped off in her hand. She lifted it high, then harpooned it downward. The splintered end drove straight into José's open mouth and down his throat. Greer heard the wood rip through the back of his neck. His broken hands kept scratching, but he'd lost all leverage. Greer got her leg back and got herself back as well – juiced on apocalyptic frenzy, more awake than she'd ever felt at school, at parties, with Qasim.

She opened the duffel bag, extracted Daddy's machete, re-zipped the bag, and took to her knees beside the plywood wall that Freddy Morgan had erected with Drasko Zorić. She slotted the machete blade under the plywood and levered her full weight on it. Nails creaked like the hull of a wooden ship, and the four-by-eight board inched toward her. Too loud – those outside would hear – but there was no turning back. Greer set down the machete, slipped the fingers of both hands into the gap, braced her shoes against the wall, and pulled. The plywood wailed. Nails sprang free all over. One foot, two feet, three feet of space opened up. Greer felt as if she'd been locked in a vault for decades; she gasped at the rainy daylight.

Like Constanza in the closet, two eyes stared back.

Greer snatched the machete and reared back.

The eyes were bright, not milky.

'Please,' he coughed, 'do not cut my head.'

The accent was sandpaper and bubbles: Fadi Lolo, the Last Resort's Syrian refugee. Rain flumed from his short black hair, through his thick eyebrows, and down into his tidy beard. He wore a soaked gray scarf, a striped dress shirt, and what looked like brand-new jeans. He gave his distinctive emphysemic wheeze, looked both ways, and made a small beckoning gesture with his hands.

'They come,' he said. 'Please be fast.'

Greer had lost the ability to be slow. She gave the plywood one more gigantic yank. Fadi Lolo shoved from the other side. First out was the duffel, passed carefully through the yawning wall. Fadi placed the bag carefully behind him before offering Greer his hand. Again, no hesitation: she took it, and as José Frito choked on wood below and hands began pounding against the locked bathroom door, Fadi helped Greer through what felt like a portal.

Only after her feet squished into mud did she appreciate Fadi's composure. Drawn by her noisy escape, the rabid had swarmed. They moved like puppet strings were speared through Their limbs and directed by a common hand. Nearest was Constanza, who, instead of fighting through the breached closet, had circled around front, the Louisville Slugger making a rat-tail squiggle through mud. She was six feet away and in heartbreakingly pristine shape, her pajamas spotless.

Right behind her was Miss Jemisha. Greer nearly shouted for her to run before she saw the white eyes glowing from a face crimson from partial scalping. Greer turned right to find an equal shock: Señorita Magdalena walking despite being run over by a van, ribs poking from her chest like ruffles down a suit. Behind Magdalena toddled her daughter Antonella, blood covering her face with theatrical uniformity.

The hands, the teeth, the eyes. There was no way out.

With apologetic tenderness, Fadi took her elbow.

'It is a dream,' he said softly.

When Greer picked up the duffel, it was funny: the bag did have a dream's cloud-weight. By the elbow, he shepherded her to the right, out of reach of Constanza's one-armed bat-swing.

'Dreaming,' Fadi reminded her. He coughed and angled her leftward, away from Antonella's lurch, and then spun her like a dancer to evade Jemisha's hands. 'Dreaming.' He put on the brakes, a football-style fake-out that sent Magdalena stumbling to the wrong spot. 'Still dreaming.' Fadi led her through the steaming cloud left behind by Magdalena's opened chest and hurried forward: 'It is a very long dream.'

A shape loomed straight head. *Not Drasko,* Greer prayed. But like everything this morning, the worst-case scenario prevailed. It *was* Drasko. Ten feet away, he tilted in their direction, his severe brow loosened to cowlike stupor while the ribbons of his tracksuit dangled like stringy blue udders. His hands made fists, as if aching for Greer and Fadi. Not noticing Fadi's blue bicycle on the ground, Drasko stepped atop the gears and fell. A pedal whirred.

'Dream's over,' Fadi said. 'Time to wake up.'

He pinched Greer's elbow hard and rushed off. She followed, shocked at the duffel bag's abrupt resumption of weight. Drasko, on his knees, swiped at her and got nothing. Fadi hoisted his bicycle. Greer grieved the loss of his steady hand, but felt as though his fingers had been the prongs of a charger. Newly energized, she swung about to take in the advancing crowd. Five total, people she used to know. No, six – Daddy turned around to wiggle his forked tongue in his skeleton grin.

'We go,' Fadi Lolo said. 'Please.'

He had one foot planted, the other ready on a pedal. The seat was empty, reserved for her. She slung the duffel bag over a shoulder, climbed on, and gripped his waist the best she could while holding a machete. Fadi tried to shove off, but Greer's weight kept the bike from moving in the mud. Jemisha, Constanza, Drasko, Antonella, and Magdalena circled them, drawing closer in unison, a noose of pearly eyes, exposed teeth, and twitching fingers. Fadi stood on the pedals, his skinny thighs shaking. The wheels began to turn. One revolution and they were out of the mud; two revolutions and they hit asphalt.

Greer thought of Mr Villard, who'd called her *black bitch,* but who, in an untidy twist, had given her the right advice from the start: *Get clear of the whole park.*

With a vertiginous waggle, they were off, more or less. Greer wasn't aware of the playground area's blood stench until they punched through its humid net. The rain beyond was chillier. She reminded herself she meant nothing to Fadi Lolo. How could she? She'd never had the gumption to say a single word to him. He'd picked her up like he'd picked up Last Resort trash: it was an optimistic act, and perhaps optimism was all a man like Fadi Lolo had left.

It might be all any of them had left.

Greer gripped him tightly, feeling the strain of his stomach as he pedaled faster. His rain-sodden scarf flapped like a pennant past Greer's head. She ducked under it and saw, in the center of the asphalt road, the ravaged being once known as Silvana. She looked barely human. Her hand was gristle. Her torso was tunneled by rifle shots. Her head dangled by a cordon of vertebrae. Somehow her jaws continued to gnash and her blinkless white eyes still stared.

Fadi swung wide, but not overly so; the bicycle didn't dare take on the muddy shoulder. Greer felt her arm extend. She looked down its length and rediscovered the machete. The blade was sprinkled with the weeds Daddy had hacked with it. It had been a tool with a purpose. It still was. Greer drew the blade back slowly, so as not to unbalance the bike. Fadi glanced back, aware of what she was doing and prepared to counterweight.

Silvana, her upside-down head sending inverted messages to her brain, reached for them – in the wrong direction. Greer did not swing the machete; instead, she held it straight and used its point, almost tenderly, to give the girl a push. It was enough to topple her. The weight of Silvana's head finally tore it free. The head rolled into a ditch, litter no one would ever collect.

Greer tucked the machete against Fadi's side. The bicycle took the long, last corner before the home stretch toward the exit – a smashup of cars and people. Greer stared directly at Fadi Lolo's back, which crackled with a new round of coughs. Fadi had never been invited to the Sunnybrook Club; Greer had been invited but never joined. Yet she felt both of them had done enough in this day's first hour to carry on the club's extraordinary spirit. She'd been Señorita Magdalena's mi corazón and she was glad of that, but it wasn't enough. To make her survival count, Greer Morgan would have to be *all* of their hearts, and keep fighting, keep surviving until the end.

ALL THAT TALK MAKES YOU BELIEVE

Bad vs. Badder

By 10:00 a.m. EST on October 24, the news domineered the airwaves. It broke like a tsunami, walloping TV stations, gossip sites, and radio shows before splashing across millions of breathless social media accounts. Histrionics reigned even as some dismissed the reports as fiction. Disbelief was understandable; news like this was liable to shake the bedrock beliefs of any American.

Ben Hines, beloved actor, Academy Award winner, 'America's Dad', had been accused of exposing himself to not one, not two, but *forty-five* different hotel workers over the past decade, all of whom, through their law firm, had released a joint statement at dawn.

Those with trained ears could hear the doors of newsrooms banging wide open, followed by satellite vans revving like jungle cats. Los Angeles police, skilled in scandal, proactively dispatched officers to Hines's Pacific Palisades neighborhood to enforce parking and privacy laws. Reporters in other cities pounced just as quickly. Hines had acted in more than one hundred movies and had filmed in nearly every metropolitan market in the country, begetting legions of locals – hotel staff in particular – who might be willing to describe brushes with the suddenly disgraced star.

An insatiable anger stewed like toxic waste inside average Americans, an ardent belief that no mortal should be permitted a charmed life without periodic flogging in public. Hines was overdue. He was married to a woman so wretchedly unfamous people didn't even know her name. He'd had no divorces, no public spats, no leaked tapes of the sexual or prima donna variety. He'd spawned not a single scurrilous hashtag. The desire to speckle his immaculate record with mud had grown fevered, almost erotic.

'It's huge,' WWN news director Pam Tripler gushed as Nathan Baseman, the second executive producer, charged into the newsroom, before clarifying, 'The *story* is huge. No news yet on the dick.'

Baseman shivered instead of replying. Could Tripler not see the train crash that had been set into motion? Three hours later, his shiver had matured into a clenching stomach as he stared from the glare-proof, floor-to-ceiling, conference-room windows on the twentieth floor of the CableCorp Tower, the parent company of a bevy of networks, including WWN. He pictured his old buddy, his bottle of antacid, waiting for him inside his desk and tried to distract himself with the Atlanta skyline. The sunblasted skyscrapers, bushy green parks, sports-stadium cornucopias, gray canals of streets ferreting cars like gondolas – these things never changed. Except today, the harder Baseman looked, the more change he saw. Two separate spires of black smoke. A multiple-car pileup. Emergency vehicle lights everywhere. Maybe every morning looked like this. It was possible. Maybe he, and everyone else in the conference room, had simply forgotten how to *see*.

He was the only one facing the outside world. The rest were doing what they did best, staring at a TV. While five smaller screens continued to play the muted broadcasts of competitors (all embroiled in wall-to-wall Hines coverage), the one-hundred-inch 4K TV mounted on the eastern wall played, for the third straight time, an unedited, watermarked, six-minute piece of footage sent in by notorious Chicago stringer Ross Quincey.

Quincey ran a circuit of speed-demon nightcrawlers who regularly scooped Windy City photogs; he sold their exclusive footage to the highest local bidder. On occasion, one of Ross Quincey's men would capture something worthy of the twenty-four-hour networks. The brash firebrand was no less aggravating for having been minimized to a blinking red dot on the room's central speakerphone, on hold awaiting WWN's bid. Quincey said he had simultaneous calls out to CNN, MSNBC, ABC, CBS, and Fox, and Baseman did not think he was bluffing.

Quincey's video was not why this meeting had been called; it was, for the stringer, fortuitous coincidence. The fifty-two people packed into this room designed for thirty was the result of a proliferation of smaller, impromptu huddles not even network overlords could ignore. Baseman considered it a damning barometer. In the parlance of the morning's *first* breaking-news story, WWN had been caught with its pants down.

Ben Hines flashed through Baseman's mind, ruffled and coiffed in one of his period performances. Baseman wanted to take Hines's Oscar and ram it up the man's ass. That maid-harassing slimeball had so utterly distracted the media with his old-man dick that not a single major station had reserved camera crews for the story that mattered, one assignment editors had heard rumblings of last night but wiped from their brains the second the word *penis* hit their in-boxes.

Every cell in Nathan Baseman's sixty-six-year-old body told him this was the kind of TV game changer he'd seen only thrice in his career. Nixon's fall, O.J. 's trial, 9/11. His gut was rarely wrong, and the rest of his organs were fair oracles as well. His pounding lungs, tingling extremities, and rushing blood told the truth: he could not hold Hines responsible for the media's sins. If this turned out to be the thing to end their careers, it'd be the end they deserved – tut-tutting over some guy's wayward willy while the world burned down around them.

Baseman glanced at the screen, hoping Quincey's tape had run its course. Not even close; the footage had the ability to warp time, turn three minutes into three years. The camera was at telephoto length.

This was typical; stringers often zoomed in from across the street while they assessed the situation. Seconds later, though, the perspective jostled forward as the photog sprinted toward the scene. This was what made Ross Quincey's crew famous. Where average humans hid, if not fled, Quincey's freelancers hurled themselves into the fray like Navy SEALs, minus all noble intentions.

The footage pixelated as the photog raced across the street. Baseman hated how easily he could hear himself instructing editors to leave this part in for its gritty authenticity. The footage stabilized on a washed-out Chicago housing development courtyard: cherry clapboard gone rosé, plastic deck chairs worn to dirty grays, grass so brittle it was off-white. More vibrant colors stood out: a sparkly birthday banner, half-opened presents, conical birthday hats. Most of the hats were rolling across sidewalk pavement, but a few, grotesquely, remained strapped to the heads of screaming former celebrants.

The first time this room of newspeople saw the full panoply of bodies and blood, there had been actual cheers. This stuff was gold. Ross Quincey's bank account was going to have a good day. South-Side Chicago gang activity, as a rule, did not merit news coverage. It was what WWN news director Nick Unitas dubbed Bad vs. Badder – a conflict that did not inspire viewer engagement. This footage, though, transcended Bad vs. Badder by featuring the ratings trifecta of endangered children, sobbing women, and desperate heroics.

By now, Baseman knew the precise order in which the characters, dead or alive, appeared on camera. One: a potbellied man spread-eagled between paint-chipped picnic tables. Two: a young woman hyperventilating, lying on her side next to an overturned grill. Three: two birthday-hatted children, possibly twins, crouched under a picnic table, yowling through tears. Four: a matronly woman standing in the center of the courtyard, hands arranged as if holding an invisible basketball, screaming over and over. Five: an adolescent boy with a bloody face reaching through a fence toward the photog. Six:

a young man in a powder-blue uniform rushing from one downed person to the next, checking for vitals, shouting for them to respond. Everyone was Black.

So was Nathan Baseman last time he checked, but upon first viewing, he reached the same conclusion as everyone else. Standard retaliatory drive-by, no question. That blood smear on the sidewalk might not even be fresh; it could be a stain left unscrubbed from a previous shooting. Disgusting, but some of these residents had become apathetic to violence.

By the third viewing, those assumptions mortified Baseman. He'd grown apathetic, unable to view the world as anything but a casting pool of stereotypes – some vilified, some exalted, all bullshit – to be arranged in news blocks for the highest possible emotional manipulation.

Ross Quincey had himself a winner even before the clip's second-half twist. The photog was in the courtyard, panning his camera instead of offering assistance, when the big-bellied man spread-eagled on the grass got to his feet. The man's surprise survival itself did not shock WWN execs. It was the manner in which he stood up – casually, as if he'd knelt to pick up a quarter.

Another surprise: the man was free of visible gunshots. Instead, it looked like he'd been bitten – there was a tooth-mark crescent on his forearm. When the man looked directly into the camera, everyone in the conference room recoiled. His eyes had gone white; in the courtyard's sodium lights, they looked like flat, orange coins.

The man's attention was swiftly drawn by the screaming woman. He moved toward her like a dog to food and, in seconds, had her by her dress and hair. She did not fight back. She only screamed until he took a bite out of her throat. The scream cut off. Sonically, it was a relief. Blood jetted and the woman fell to her knees; the man stood by, indifferent, chewing and swallowing. In the two minutes that fol-lowed, the bloody-faced boy dislodged himself from the fence and ripped a ribbon of flesh from the polo-shirted young man's arm before going after the children under the picnic table.

Even on a third viewing, people gasped and shielded their eyes. These were news pros as hardened as Baseman. They lectured over editors' shoulders on how to trim Al Qaeda beheading videos prior to broadcast. They sifted through raw feeds of suicide-bomb sites, picking out the TV-ready smoke and bandages from the less palatable loose limbs, spilled skulls, and dead babies. They surveyed aftermath footage of catastrophic natural disasters, assessing piles of recovered corpses before hopping off to business lunches.

The Quincey tape was upsetting in a new way. The footage featured no jihadists, no natural disasters, no villain to assign blame. Victims in minute one became assailants in minute three. It was plainly, profoundly *wrong*. A chilly, flu-like sensation rippled from body to body, and Baseman worried his colleagues might misidentify it as that good ol' 'nose for news' tingle. He believed the fever might be radiating from a knot of nerves inside each of their brains, embedded there by God or evolution – take your pick – so the human race might be alerted when their extinction was in the offing.

Baseman, goddamn it all, had felt it last night. Why hadn't he done something? He'd been kicked back with a bottle of whiskey in front of the diverting white-people silliness of Turner Classic Movies, but he'd slapped himself sober and hauled his ass to work at crazier hours before. Hell, he lived for that shit, and nightside editors knew it. Getting on the horn and talking out a story was a welcome respite from the invading shadows of his lonely, groaning home.

A text from night producer Akira Broderick had kicked it off. Multiple affiliates, she texted, were reporting spikes in scanner activity. Orchestras of 911 calls, armadas of ambulances. Baseman did not have to pose the possibility of coordinated terrorist attack; it was the first place a newsperson's brain went. But the telltale signs were missing. The locations had no symbolic value. There was no chatter about suspects. There were no explosions.

Bad drug? Baseman texted. *Wake up our toxicologist.* Akira texted back a thumbs-up. Baseman opened his laptop, the final indication he'd given up so-called relaxation, and sifted Twitter for trends. He could click Follow on as many celebrities, musicians, and sports accounts as he fancied; none of it would alter the fact that Twitter had come to replace his beloved old police scanner, which he used to keep at a soft burble all night until his wife, Sherry – his ex-wife, Sherry – had smashed it to pieces with a hammer.

He found no hashtags of note, besides one suggesting that a scandal was about to break about actor Ben Hines. An hour later, Akira texted again: *False alarm? DOAs being reversed.* Baseman: shrug emoji. Akira: *Back to MPWW.* Baseman chuckled. What station didn't default to the ratings mainstay of *Missing Pretty White Women*? He snapped shut his laptop and made himself return to the black-and-white morals of Hollywood oldies. His first instinct must have been correct: premature death diagnoses were a hallmark of a new drug's ODs.

He had gone to sleep certain of that.

Quincey's footage ended by freezing the final frame. The photog had been whirling away from the scene, presumably to run to his car. The image was a smudge of earth tones: yellow windows, green picnic tables, beige grass, brown skin, red blood. Those skilled at finding shapes in digital murks could make out reaching arms and white eyes. This time, however, Baseman noticed another figure standing at the edge of the frame, his arms crossed, his indifference to the carnage making him the villain the video so sorely needed.

It took the blinking red dot of the speakerphone mirroring off the TV to make Nathan Baseman realize that the 'villain' he saw was a reflection, and that the villain was him.

Fringe Jabberwocky

'Why is Martin Scorsese Jr still on hold? Buy the tape already!'

Despite slanderous on-air wisecracks, online campaigns guilting advertisers into dropping support, abusive tirades to staff, and rumors of harassment hush money, Rochelle Glass's command of the cranky, I'm-only-saying-what-we're-all-thinking blurt remained effective. The whole room, allies and enemies of Glass alike, laughed, and each person's ghost twin in the TV screen took swills from coffee and bites from cheese danishes. Glass was being her normal asshole self; thus, everything else in the world must be normal too.

'Look at us,' Glass continued. 'We're like my daughters and their princess movies. We can't stop watching this thing.'

'This thing.' Nick Unitas sighed and adjusted his thick glasses. He was bald and built like a linebacker, always grimacing like his clothing pinched him. 'What *is* this thing? Anyone?'

Rare was the chance to impress the news director in such a setting, and everyone jumped to capitalize on it. People reverted to their worst and truest selves. Taller people blocked shorter people. Years of sensitivity training evaporated. Cuss words were used to gain a toehold in the clamor.

'Few hours ago, I might have said towel heads,' someone said. 'Acting under orders from some despot. Why are you giving me that look? I said a few hours ago.'

'Whoever's pushing the cult theory's a dumb cunt,' said a second person. 'The assailants don't fit the profile, and it's too widespread.'

'We've got a Dr Grimes, claims he's from the CDC, ready to finger someone's ass to get on the air,' said a third person. 'But I think he's a crank. This thing can't be airborne. It hits Guy A but not Guy B?'

'It isn't this, it isn't that,' Unitas growled. 'Then how the fuck do we frame it?'

Even where there was no spotlight, Glass knew how to steal it.

'Since when do we need to frame murder?' she asked. 'That's the beauty of murders. There's no opposite viewpoint. We all agree murder is bad, yes? We show it, say just *how* bad it is, everyone agrees, and everyone wins.'

'Not everyone.' Baseman heard the words hum through his sternum. It was a bracing sensation, even as it guilted him for not making his stand last night. He should have followed his gut, sped to WWN HQ, and clung to the story like a tick so there would be no fighting over who owned it. 'We dish out for this clip, we'll want our money's worth, right? We'll run this thing 24–7. And we might just cause a race war.'

'The apocryphal race war.' Glass sighed. 'We all keep looking for this long-promised event of Mr Baseman's.'

Nothing enervated Baseman more than direct address with Glass. He turned to Unitas.

'Let's lay out the cards. Couple hours ago, there were already people on Twitter swearing up and down this was a race thing. Conspiracy theories, wild shit you can't even follow. All with the same conclusion, though. Load your guns and gather up the dark skins.'

'That's fringe jabberwocky, and you know it,' Glass said.

'It's fringe *now,* yeah.'

'I thought for liberals like you it was freedom of information or die.'

The room stared like Turner Classic Movies townsfolk watching the bowlegged pacing of Wild West duelists. Baseman had no choice but to face Glass. If the public held one big misconception about cable news networks, it was that the personalities appearing on them represented a united front. Each host was in direct competition with other hosts for top interviews and choicest scoops, with each producer locked in undercard bouts. Rochelle Glass usually won. She was WWN's marquee name, the host – more accurately, the *star* – of a culture-shifting eight o'clock opinion show. A caravan of talking heads paid homage every night, laying roses at her feet; she made most look stupid, overpowering their facts with big, booming self-righteousness.

When Glass wanted to drive home a point, like now, she hauled out her Southern drawl. Naturally, she had never lived south of the Mason-Dixon, but she had a knack for knowing what played to Joe and Jill American. The leader these flyover folk craved, Glass espoused, was someone who operated just above their intellectual level and offered boiled-down talking points easy to parrot. It made them feel smart. It made them feel good. What was wrong, Glass liked to ask, with making her viewers feel good?

Case in point: five years ago, midway through a rant on health care handouts, the word *mendicant* had flown from Glass's mouth in place of usual favorites like *deadbeat, freeloader,* and *bum.* The word was new to most of her viewers, and while responding to feedback the next night, Glass encouraged her viewers not to be mendi*cants* but rather mendi*cans.*

Thus was a catchphrase born ('I'm a MendiCAN!'), and shortly after that, T-shirts, caps, ties, buttons, mugs, mouse pads, pens, doormats, and Christmas ornaments. At the height of the subsequent cash flow, a memo circulated that the word was to be used by WWN staff whenever possible, both on air and off. The memo was ignored, but Baseman had to admit the word had crept into his conversations, if only in ridicule.

Baseman was a foot taller than Glass, and he had no misgivings about exploiting his height with a belittling glare. Glass's small, blue eyes shone like marbles inside her taut, face-lifted skin, beneath a helmet of shellacked blond hair. From her bemused smirk, Baseman could tell how she, fifteen years his junior, saw him: an obsolete, out-of-shape fussbudget who'd gotten where he was due to affirmative action (a mendicant's favorite government program) and who ought to do third-place WWN a favor and retire.

Unitas flapped his arms like a duckling.

'There is so much *news* to cover, people!' he shouted. 'Out! Out! Out! Glass, Baseman, VPs, stay put.'

Baseman did not wait for the room to clear to take the sort of small step toward Glass that, in a workplace, was decidedly aggressive.

'Freedom of information, that's right. That *is* what liberals care about. Which is why we should decline Mr Quincey's kindling here and start gathering every little cell phone video we can – free of charge, I might add – and start running them back to back to back. Pam says they're coming in from all over.' He jabbed a finger at Atlanta. '*That's* the picture of what's happening out there.'

'Nice idea,' Glass said. 'In fact, my staff's already doing it. They're writing abstracts of every video we're being sent – and we're being sent more than any show on any network, I guarantee it. Here's what I regret to tell you, Baseman. The, shall we say, demographic details? Practically every video's got the same thing. Apartment buildings. Ghettos. What can I say? Black people. *Black people,* Baseman. Those aren't dirty words, and I'm not afraid to say them! Only difference with this video here' – she indicated the freeze-frame – 'is that this doesn't look like it was shot by an epileptic.'

Baseman fired back. 'Where you see Black, I see low income.'

Glass shrugged innocently. 'We're in agreement, friend. Economic distress! That's why gangs spring up and thrive. That's my lead. And it's a lead getting colder by the second. Someone buy this film, get the Face off the desk, and put me on it.'

Chuck Corso, known as 'the Face' because of his only notable attribute, was hands down the least capable anchor WWN had on payroll. Baseman had to admit the Face's helmsmanship added urgency to Glass's case. But Baseman could think of nothing more hazardous than putting a zealot like Rochelle Glass on the desk right now.

He appealed to Unitas.

'Gangs, Nick? We have Octavia Gloucester's report from Tampa – not one other station has that – and there is nothing, goddamn *nothing*, in her report to suggest gangs. Is that really the best we got?'

The change in Unitas's bearing was slight. The pinch of his forehead loosened; the alignment of his shoulders bowed. It was the look of a trailblazer who'd lost the trail, who was in sudden, dire need of an eagle-eyed adherent to point out the direction to take. Baseman leaned in, but even a second's hesitation was too much. Younger, hungrier, and wolfish, Glass bit first.

'If you want to take the advice of the man who aired the Jansky shot,' she sighed, 'that's up to you.'

The dozen VPs, who'd been chuffing and nickering to exhibit engagement, found sudden reasons to examine their coffees. Coldness dripped between Baseman's shoulder blades. It was a cruel comparison; if anything had torn the bandages from his and Sherry's ailing marriage, it had been fallout from the Jansky shot. Not the shot itself; in the week that followed, in fact, he'd received multiple emails from producers at other networks assuring him they might have made the same call. Baseman deleted them.

It had happened three years ago. Because WWN World Headquarters was in Atlanta, they were the only station to get the live shot. Rumors had roiled for days about the computers confiscated from the reelection office of Savannah congressman Blaise Jansky.

Stolen intel? Illicit affair? Child pornography? The Savannah affiliate had picked up talk of Jansky holing up in his office with a gun, and within the hour, WWN was on the air with a thrilling live feed of Jansky's face squashed against the window, shouting something to arriving police. Jansky's gun, visible next to his chest, had Baseman fantasizing over viewer metrics, and when that gun began inching upward and the director began bleating, *Suicide, suicide, suicide,* Baseman had ordered that they stay with the shot; Jansky would not do it.

Jansky did do it. The gun looked like it caught on something, maybe a sport coat button, before it popped up, the muzzle striking Jansky's chin. Maybe the surprise of that little impact made Jansky jerk his finger. The director at the controls that day, Lee Sutton, had done his best, slamming the kill switch before bone and brains found surfaces on which to settle, but no one at WWN that day, not to mention the two hundred thousand viewers, could forget the implosion of Jansky's face or the fountain of purple jelly.

Baseman was given time off for 'emotional recuperation'. Somehow, the bullet that killed Jansky became lodged inside him, Sherry, and the shared flesh of their marriage. With his wife tiptoeing around his feelings, he began hating both of them. Four days later – too late – he was back at work, the station's apologies duly logged and internet think pieces waning. Everyone, including Unitas and Sutton, acted like nothing had happened. Baseman had been grateful, even while wondering if a mistake of this caliber, left undiscussed, might ossify into a guillotine blade that, once in place, could never be trusted not to fall.

Now, fallen it had. Unitas gave Baseman the kind of wince you gave an old fellow who'd slipped on the ice after insisting he'd shovel his own drive. It was over; Baseman had lost the argument with Glass. Worse, he'd lost it three years ago, and no one had had the heart to tell him. Unitas licked his teeth, fishing for excuses, and because he was a pro, came up with them. He even ticked them off his fingers.

'Spates of attacks carried out with extreme loyalty,' Unitas said. 'Complete lack of remorse regarding who gets caught in the cross fire. No evidence of theft. And yes, unfortunate as it may seem, the attacks do appear to be taking place in . . . crowded communities. Baseman, to me, this *all* says gang activity.'

Crowded communities was the dumbest euphemism Baseman had ever heard, but it would do him no good to point it out. Before he spoke, he had to clear his throat. God, he sounded weak. No wonder Sherry had left him.

'Let's at least be rational.' His pathetic squeak. 'Let's conference call the other networks. Pool-coverage this thing. Public safety is not a ratings race. We used to know that, Nick.'

Unitas turned to the VPs. 'Pressburger. Offer Quincey what we discussed. Not a penny more for that bottom-feeder.'

Glass clapped her hands. 'Attaboy, baby.'

'Collinsworth. Get what's-his-name, the gang expert, the one with the mustache. Drag his ass in here – I don't care if he's drunk – and have him comb through the footage. Gang colors, hand signals, whatever he can find. Let's do some reporting, for Christ's sake. See if he'll shave the mustache too.'

Pressburger and Collinsworth pitched themselves into chairs, snatched up phones, punched extensions, and began speaking in the tones of people accustomed to calls that went poorly. Glass adjusted her blazer, just for effect.

'I'll get into makeup,' she announced.

Unitas spoke over his shoulder. 'Let Chuck finish the shift.'

Glass frowned, not with the motherly displeasure prized by her viewers but the bratty pout only coworkers knew. 'That's an hour away. You seriously want the Face holding down the desk for another hour? *Today?*'

Unitas turned around, and to Baseman's surprise, the news director did not look defeated. His put his fists on his hips and sanded his jaws back and forth. Baseman felt a rogue bolt of hope. If Unitas could stand up to Glass, even partly, so could he.

'Let me tell you something about Chuck Corso,' Unitas said. 'While all we Walter Cronkites had our panties in a bunch over an actor exposing himself, the Face drove himself to the station, with his own little hands on the wheel, at the crack of dawn, six hours before he was due, and put himself on standby. Not for personal glory, not in hopes that his "brand" would have something to gain, but because he recognized this as an all-hands-on-deck situation and wanted to help. Can you imagine that?

'The Face was writing *copy*. He's more current with what's going on right now than the three of us. You may not think Chuck Corso is the crispiest chip in the bag. But goddamn if he's not loyal. Goddamn if he's not a team player. Which is something the rest of us, up here on the twentieth floor, should value a little more.'

Baseman and Glass exchanged a look, playground pugilists collared by the recess monitor.

'We've all learned a valuable lesson in class today,' Glass conceded. 'But the Quincey video – it debuts on *my* show. *I* break it, and I break it the Rochelle Glass way. My format, my graphics, my commentary.'

Unitas's nod was barely discernible past a grimace that exposed his canines. *He'll bite us if we say another word*, thought Baseman.

The news director flapped a hand at the door. 'Baseman, go help Chuck get through the next hour. Glass, you need anything at all, ask Baseman. Teamwork, people. Talk to each other. Communicate. We work at a goddamn *news station*, for Christ's sake.'

ChuckSux69

The instant Camera 2's red light blinked off, Chuck Corso scooted his laptop closer. Plenty of anchors used laptops as props. Looked good on-screen, contributed to the façade that anchors weren't heads on sticks trained to read teleprompters. Chuck had known a morning anchor in New York who used his news desk laptop exclusively to play porn GIFs to get his coanchor to crack up.

Chuck used his computer for the purpose for which it was intended – for 'computering', as he'd once regrettably put it in a meeting. In fact, he computered so relentlessly, he'd short-circuited three laptops in five years. He tapped his touch pad and the official WWN site brightened to life. It was the only site he visited while at the news desk, which made producers, assistants, and touch-up artists believe him to be completely, if boringly, dedicated to his workplace. Every rumor about the Face, he knew, revolved around his looks or remedial wits.

He didn't think it was moronic in the least to keep his browsing fingers on the pulse of the viewing public. WWN had tools; why not use them? With a practiced flick, Chuck brought up the menu, which fractioned the site into sections like Tech, Money, and Style. He cursored to Feedback and chose Forum from the drop-down. Up it flashed: the familiar stars-and-stripes wallpaper. WWN Politics had established the forum during the run-up to the last presidential election, hoping die-hard newsies would gather there to address daily topics, drawn by unlimited character counts, and would click on an ad or two as well.

The reality had been, as naysayers had warned, a swarm of trolls. Like rats, they sniffed out this new hole in the internet, flooded in, rubbed their vulgarities together, and made babies. Six months into an eighteen-month election cycle, the unmoderated forum had become a wasteland of alt-right conspiracy bread crumbs and theatrical far-left attention-seekers. The optics of shuttering the forum were poor, and the cost of adding moderators so high, that WWN chose to simply abandon it. It grew wild and sprouted strange tubers, and Chuck Corso suspected he might be the last staffer who knew the machete-hacked paths through its weeds.

Four more clicks and he had fresh search results for username ChuckSux69. Ten posts since Chuck's last check. His chest tingled. He clicked on the first post.

> **Can you believe this????????? Chuckie not fugging up breaking news SO FAR. Hardly can believe my eyes. Maybe Im just blinded by his TOO WHITE TEETH.**

Chuck ran his tongue over his choppers. Perhaps Dr Freeling had gone overboard at the last whitening treatment. Years ago, on advice from a female coworker, Chuck had begun coating his teeth in Vaseline; maybe he'd gotten sloppy with that. Either way, this was actionable feedback. He couldn't allow shiny teeth to distract from his delivery, not with today's news. He advanced to ChuckSux69's next post. Camera 2's warning light would flash all too soon.

He knew nothing about ChuckSux69 aside from what he or she had plugged in to the forum template. To the left of each post was a box of user data. Beneath the username was an attribute field programmers had intended for job titles until users made mincemeat of it. ChuckSux69's job title read *TRUTH TELLER*. Beneath was

ChuckSux69's custom image: an anime picture of a girl with beach ball-sized breasts. After that came ChuckSux69's location (*EVERY-WHERE*) and number of posts (14,272). At the bottom, users could display a quote that, in theory, nutshelled their worldview. Chuck-Sux69's quote: *Hold me like you did by the lake on Naboo.*

Chuck Corso had feared the forum at first. Although he fantasized about being a self-confident freewheeler, he had Google Alerts set for every permutation of his name, including misspellings. Several times a day, he searched social media outlets, despite it never ending well. People didn't use the internet to hail public figures for jobs ably done. Insults were the coin of the realm. Chuck Corso is the biggest dipshit on TV. Chuck Corso can't pronounce *Kim Jong-un.* Chuck Corso probably spends fifty thousand a year waxing his eyebrows.

Then there was the meme.

Chuck found it wretchedly unfair. He'd been a soft-news reporter in Charlotte, just out of college, before being tapped to cover a similar beat by a New York station. It was a small station, an upstart. But New York was New York! He understood his looks had played a pivotal role in scoring the job; the nonplussed expressions of his Charlotte colleagues made that clear enough. What could he say or do to make it better? Hone his craft and become the best newsman he could be, that was all.

He'd been out in bright, brisk Battery Park on one of his first stories (gathering man-on-the-street reactions to the rumor Michael Jordan might rejoin the NBA) when American Airlines Flight 11 buried itself in the World Trade Center's North Tower. Chuck and his photog were the station's first team on the scene, and for twenty-two glorious minutes it had been Chuck Corso, the guy known for such hard-hitting pieces as Rufus the banjo-playing cockapoo, standing before two smoke-billowing skyscrapers, his face pinched in concern, his voice bottoming to indicate he recognized the event's gravity and would guide viewers through it.

Senior news teams soon descended and assumed control. This failed to ding Chuck's pride, especially after the collapse of the first tower forced those news vets, and everyone else, to retreat. He'd helped New Yorkers by staying strong on the air, and in reciprocation, they swept him to safety down streets he didn't yet know, the white dust on their clothing matching the white dust on his. A stumble off a curb even allowed Chuck to match their uneven gaits; they staggered like their numbers included people who'd dived from the towers, touched with Lazarus powers, risen again.

The tape of his twenty-two-minute 9/11 broadcast didn't resurface until YouTube was born and began demanding mother's milk. Some editor brute had carved the footage free of context. All that was left was a streamlined lowlight reel of a greenhorn Chuck Corso blinded in the dazzling September spotlight and bursting with malapropisms to rival those of the current sitting president.

'There is de-briss falling from the tower, lots of dangerous de-briss.'

'The plane's fuse-a-long may still be in the building, and that's a concern.'

'It looks to me like the building has perplexed.'

It was this last one that got meme-ified: the word *PERPLEXED* in white Impact font over a freeze-frame of Chuck epitomizing the emotion. When colleagues attached the meme to emails to Chuck or joshingly used the word in conversation, he always made sure to laugh. He did it for his colleagues, for the country at large. Everyone needed to laugh, especially while overwhelmed by atrocity. Or else, as went the cliché, the terrorists won.

But the gibes hurt. He'd been proud to report from Ground Zero. When he thought about it, his eyes welled up. Had it all been a lie, their beautiful, secure America? In the months following the attacks, the closest Chuck got to hard reporting were profiles of 9/11 widows. Breaking news: they were sad! It got worse from there: scientists are excited about this one-minute workout; someone could be spying on your computer; we asked people who they'd like to see walking away with a Golden Globe. Ten years he toiled on that beat, and not once did his heart, mind, or soul come to life like he had on 9/11. He didn't wish for another attack – of course he didn't – but the idea of another disaster consumed his dreams. It might mean a second chance.

They were dark years through which a series of girlfriends guided him. Arianna, Ljubica, Nathalia, and Gemma were all models. What they gained from Chuck was gravitas at media events; Chuck Corso might not be respected, but *reporter* was still printed on his business cards. What Chuck gained from them was insight into how to effectively capitalize on his physical attributes.

He was in his thirties and starting to lose his hair. Arianna combed through Chuck's scalp, tugging and *tsk*ing, her painted nails cold as beetles. She made him get Propecia, Rogaine Foam, and a HairMax Ultima 12 LaserComb. Before they split, she introduced him to a plastic surgeon who explained the differences between hair transplantation, flap surgery, scalp tissue expansion, and scalp reduction. The final treatment plan was an aggressive combination of all four.

Ljubica used the sharp point of a pinkie nail to pinpoint every developing skin tag, discoloration, and dry patch on Chuck's face. Biweekly skin treatments, she told him, were his only hope against the ravages of age. Microdermabrasion, electronic muscle stimulation, oxygen mist treatment, LED light regeneration, whole-body cryotherapy, stem cell facials buttressed with snake venom – with Ljubica eager to showcase her expertise, he submitted to all of it. In the shower, hot water flumed from his new flesh so fleetly he didn't need to dry his face.

Nathalia connected him with Xander, a stunt man turned personal trainer whose specialty was getting actors ripped for shirtless action roles. Xander punished Chuck with burpees, thrusters, box

jumps, pull-ups, kettlebell swings, and rowing, while Nathalia
shoved Chuck's pretty face into a macrobiotic, seaweed-heavy, five-
times-a-day detox diet capable of maintaining the body's pH balance
within one-tenth of a point. Chuck's chest and abs felt like iron plates
hung by hooks. But he could see the workout in his face, and that
mattered. Insidious neck flab, rounding cheeks, softening jawline –
all gone, as if filleted by knife.

Gemma arrived with Chuck's fortieth birthday, thirteen years
younger; his only American-born girlfriend and the most mercen-
ary. *The knife,* she called it with gruesome relish. She shoved him
down on the bed, straddled him, and showed off her augmented
breasts, enhanced lips, and reshaped nose. Over the next three years,
he underwent blepharoplasty (eye-bag removal), lower rhytidectomy (neck lift), mentoplasty (chin augmentation), setback otoplasty
(ear reshaping), and a good old-fashioned face-lift.

When all that work was finished, what struck Chuck the most
was the work he *hadn't* done. A belated boning up on world history.
Studying political science, law, and ethics. Trying to finally make
heads or tails of the Middle East. He'd had a decade, and all he'd done
was make himself a better face – *the* Face.

For his sins, they rewarded him. WWN bought out his contract
and hired him to read the news on midmorning weekdays. Chuck
couldn't relocate to Atlanta fast enough. Drastically fewer models
lived in Georgia, and Chuck withdrew into a quieter life. He had few
friends but realized he'd always had few; at every stop in his life,
people had merely put up with him, gnashing their jaws at his
unjustly advanced career. New York was in his past, but he thought
of New Yorkers often, how they'd *staggered* on 9/11, how *he'd* staggered. He'd been one of the people then. In Atlanta, damn it all, he'd
become one of the people again.

And here was his opportunity. Right when he thought he'd be
covering the kind of story he loathed – the indecent exposures of

Ben Hines – up roared this other story, which might reach 9/11 pinnacles. A chance to lead, yes; to bury his *PERPLEXED* reputation, for sure. But more than that, a chance to truly help, however he could, in a time of need.

To do that, he would need to do what he'd failed to do on 9/11. In the biz, it was called *vamping* – filling dead air with synopses and speculation. With so many reporters' voices being patched in to his earpiece and so many people hustling around the studio, it was too chaotic to gauge his performance. Hence, ChuckSux69. Chuck held his breath as he read the user's next post.

> **I am DIGGING Chuckys Serious Face today and Im not even JOKING!!! when he was all WE MUST BE CAUTIOUS IN DRAWING CONCLUSIONS I was like <3 <3 <3 where has this Chucky been all my life??? Can see his plugs tho (sorry)**

Chuck exhaled a powerful gust that rustled the bangs over his problematic hairline. ChuckSux69 was right. He needed to schedule a follicle enhancement as soon as this news emergency settled. Eight posts from ChuckSux69 remained, and Chuck cycled through them, taking mental notes while keeping an eye on Camera 2.

He knew others would find his dependence on ChuckSux69 strange if not downright twisted. The user, after all, had joined the forum with the express purpose of haranguing Chuck Corso. That was precisely why Chuck trusted him. From ChuckSux69's first contribution, 14,272 posts ago, Chuck recognized the user's MO to be exactly what he (could be a she, but Chuck doubted it) said in his profile: *TRUTH TELLER*. His takes were rude, vulgar, and spontaneous – more valuable than a million respectable opinions.

Chuck Corso would need ChuckSux69 if he was going to get through this.

The light atop Camera 2 began a cautionary strobe. Chuck quit the forum, positioned the laptop inside the medium shot, and tuned back in to his earpiece. Lee Sutton, the director, delivered more bad news. The news team Chuck was supposed to throw to had gone off-line. No radio signal, no cell contact. It was the second WWN team to drop off the grid. Chuck told himself not to worry. Live shots got nixed by cops all the time, phone batteries died, developing situations got hectic.

'Encapsulate,' Lee ordered. 'Rehash. Soon as we have a team ready, I'll tell you.'

Chuck nodded into Lee's erstwhile eye, the dead lens of Camera 2. His heart stuttered as the teleprompter went a shocking midnight black. He felt the unspooling terror of a thousand work-related nightmares; dreams of going on-air without a script were equivalent to most people's dreams of showing up to class naked. Camera 2's red light went solid, a bison's goading glare.

Drawing in a deep breath, Chuck gathered himself up, hoping the muscles Xander trained would hold. In one of his failed stabs at self-education, he'd read a quote from Charles Lindbergh, how there would be no more wars if only everyone could see the world from a plane, up where borders were invisible and all people looked the same. Before Chuck got to the part explaining Lindberg's Nazi sympathies, he'd wondered if newspeople, who saw so much of the world unedited, were also privileged with a bird's-eye view, which made them the best people to turn to when all hope looked lost.

Reporters too could be *TRUTH TELLERS*.

The truth that never changed was: *ALL HOPE IS NOT LOST*.

Chuck Corso could tell his hair was draped just so over his imperfect hairline. He hoped ChuckSux69 appreciated it. He hoped they all did. Here went nothing. Here went everything.

The Suspense
Is Killing Me

It was the longest elevator ride of Nathan Baseman's life. The second he stepped into the car, isolated with Rochelle Glass, he felt his pocketed phone vibrate against his thigh. A text message. His instinct was to check it immediately, but with Glass's victorious eyes on him, it seemed like a loser's act, the gadget a measly acorn he, a lowly squirrel, was eager to chew. He let the message buzz twice against his thigh, an impotent sensation.

The studio was on the basement level. The *B* button was already pushed.

The door sealed shut. The car sank. It felt like the world did too.

'Sorry about the Jansky bit,' Glass said. 'All's fair, et cetera, et cetera.'

Inside the steel box, Glass's folksy accent had reverted to its Manhattan flatness. The cramped space made Baseman think of the apartments he had shared, back when he was scraping by, before a Black man could earn even half a white man's salary. Glass knew nothing about spaces so fraught. How emotions ran hotter, how physical contact was unavoidable.

'Don't edit it,' he said.

'Excuse me?'

'The Quincey tape. If you're going to run it, run it straight.'

'We're alone, Baseman. Be blunt. Is this a personal favor?'

'Do it because it's right. Ever heard of that?'

Glass exhaled. She sounded, to Baseman's surprise, tired.

'Let me explain something,' she said. 'Even you should be able to understand. If I air, on my program, a video of a vicious gang attack, my twenty-five-to-fifty demo makes a three-thousand-point jump. Husbands tell their wives and kids to gather round the boob tube, and everyone at WWN gets Nielsen ratings gift baskets. I air that video unedited, and it includes, just for the sake of argument, a man ripping a woman's throat out with his teeth – tossed in willy-nilly between commercials – do you know what happens to those metrics?'

'We quit cutting to commercials an hour ago. At this rate, we'll never go back.'

'Of course we will. Anything can be normalized. It's News 101.'

'News. That's what you're calling it now?'

'Who are you trying to impress? You and I show people what they need to know, not what they're not ready to handle.'

Baseman tried to focus on the descending floor numbers: *13, 12, 11.* Were the numbers always red, or was it a new shade to his vision? He tried to slow his words to the pace of the numbers.

'Emmett Till. Name ring a bell, Glass? You don't close the coffin lid on Emmett Till. You don't cut ten or twelve baton hits from the Rodney King tape just because it might make your Mendicans more comfortable.'

'Rodney King, Emmett Till. The Aztecs, King Tut. How far back you plan on going? Look, you were producing on 9/11. You're proud of it and you damn well should be. But did you tell your directors to show bodies going *plop, plop* all over the pavement? No one was ready to see that. God knows we have our differences, you and I, but at the end of the day? We're both decent people, Baseman. Are we not decent people?'

Baseman kicked. It just happened. Forty-five years in a heartless biz, a hundred racist so-called colleagues, two hundred regrettable calls he'd had to make – when another text buzzed his leg, it was like a biology-class electrode poking the leg of a dead frog. Baseman's leg shot forward, the sole of his shoe crashing against the display, lighting each of the bottom eight floor buttons. Baseman panted, an out-of-shape old fart nowhere close to Glass's twenty-five-to-fifty demo.

Glass shivered and bared her teeth, angry she'd been scared for even a second.

Eighth floor: the doors purred open. Nobody was waiting.

'Super,' she said. 'Now I'll be late for makeup.'

Are we not decent people? His divorce from Sherry was three years old, not nearly enough for him to safely reclaim decency. Back during his first reporter gig in Chicago, Sherry had delighted in every detail he brought home: the adventure of the newsroom, thunderous with typewriters, stinking of ink, hot with cigarette smoke; the thrill of tearing around town with his team of cameraman, soundman, and lighting technician; feeling like a hero battling a big, bad city, and while he was at it, forging friendships and breaking down walls of prejudice. He could still hear his team's laughter over the crackling walkie-talkie. He could still smell fresh sixteen-millimeter film. He could still taste the Billy Goat's burgers and fries.

He switched to field producing in Kansas City. Film out, videotape in. Images uglier but quicker, and that mattered to TV's hungry stomach. He'd gotten caught up in it. Who wouldn't be? Viewers soon expected to see events while they were occurring, and if Baseman's station was not first on the scene, another station would be. The job became about *winning*. Winning the scoop. Winning the ratings. Winning the loyalty of a city viewership.

To keep winning, he brought the work home. More accurately, he did not bring himself home. Breaking news did not observe nights, weekends, or holidays. He added to his office a toothbrush, sleep mask, and cot. Perhaps these should have been flapping red flags, but Nathan Baseman was making a name for himself, being promoted, receiving invites to speak at Black business groups. These were gains not just for him but for society. Sherry had graduated from typist to secretary at a marketing firm; she was breaking through barriers too.

The move to Atlanta tore them in half. Baseman was not sure why. The wet heat? The Jansky shot? They became junkyard dogs. Sherry threw things, heavy things. Books, a clock radio, a toaster oven. If he called the police, reported domestic abuse, rival stations would find it in police reports.

Plus, he'd bitten her. One night while she'd pummeled him with her fists, his hands had corralled hers and he'd sunk his teeth right into her shoulder. In the moment, it was a release. It felt good. The salt of her skin, the slight aftertaste of blood – it tasted like sex, a little. But with that, she'd won. She had the scar on her shoulder, and if she wanted, she could show it.

The bite in Ross Quincey's footage, the big plug of flesh ripped from the screaming woman's throat, floated through Baseman's mind. Whatever was going on out there, it was turning good people bad, and that scared the ever-loving shit out of him. Because he knew he had bad in him. He knew he was the kind of person who *bit*.

He glanced at Glass, pushing away images of doing to her shoulder what he'd done to Sherry's.

Seventh floor: the doors opened, shut.

'The suspense,' Glass said, 'is killing me.'

Baseman faced his bête noire, his smudged reflection.

'We were in that conference room for a million years,' he said, his voice steady. 'No telling what news has broken. Let's work together. Let's try.'

'I have a quite capable staff.'

'But I know Chicago. That's where I started. I've got people there.

I can get the actual story to go with the scary footage. From *real* people.'

Sixth floor. Open, shut.

'The inference being my people would be fake.'

'Come on, you know what people you'll get. Camera hogs, ambulance chasers. People who get off pointing at bloodstains. My people, they know each building of that complex. They know the names of the gangs who want that courtyard.'

'So you agree it's gangs?'

Fifth floor.

'No, I don't. But if it is, they'll tell us. Specifics are what we need right now. We tell the story right, we prevent every wannabe militiaman in America from pointing a rifle out their window and waiting for the next Black person to stroll by. My people can tell us, "It's these guys, not those guys." You feel me?'

'I'm not running the tape uncut.'

'I know. I'm done asking for that.'

Fourth floor.

Glass crossed her arms, a pink-painted fingernail tapping against the golden cross she wore around her neck. Baseman knew it was a prop. Pick any Sunday morning and you'd find Rochelle Glass at Cherokee Town and Country Club. He choked the urge to say it aloud. They were running out of floors and time.

'I'm listening,' she said. 'What's your ask?'

Third floor.

'That you stay with the story. I'm telling you, I feel this one in my bones. This is the big one. So you ride this thing like a reporter, not an entertainer. The Face has forty-five minutes left. Give me that time to set the table for you. Residents, community organizers. Think how it felt when you were just getting started, Glass. Before it started being about whose office was bigger. That's how it used to feel for me too. We can have that back. We can have that back *today*.'

Second floor.

'That would mean dropping Ben Hines,' Glass observed.

'His luckiest day since the Oscars,' Baseman said. 'We need those news choppers *back*.'

He did not know if the elevator's first-floor pause was engineered to take longer; it would make sense, as the floor fielded the most comers and goers. The door gasped wide, revealing a ruby-red rug stretched across a marble lobby to an entryway of art deco brass. It was eerie without foot traffic, the magisterial but deserted ruins of a gilded, irresponsible age.

Glass smiled. Red light gleamed from her capped teeth.

'I'll A-block the gangs. But we quit covering Hines over my dead body. Liberal do-gooder gives award speeches out of one side of his mouth, filthy come-ons out the other? That's its own kind of violence against women. We're airing it.'

The elevator doors clanged and snorted when opening at the studio level. Shoe heels were clopping, doors banging, printers wheezing, keyboards crackling. It was always a storm down here, but today it was like one of those jacked-up conditions the weather department liked to invent: thundersnow, arctic blast, bomb cyclone. Baseman could smell coffee, sweat, and hair spray. Shit was on fire; they'd made it all the way down to hell.

Glass stepped into a hall saturated with red LIVE TV lights. The moment other people looked at Glass, she transformed, growing taller and thinner; her hair radiated the devil's light; she was a heroine swaggering into town to save the day. In a world of Bad vs. Badder, Glass was the one who told you which side to root for.

She graced Baseman with a last look.

'My audience skews a little older. They need their food a little softer, that's all. You should know this, Baseman. You're getting up in years too.'

She winked and strode off to Hair and Makeup. Baseman's

stomach clenched. *Soft* made him think of both Sherry and the woman in the Quincey tape, their shoulders and throats gnashed like gelatin. Softness: it might yet be revealed as humanity's most distinctive quality.

From down the hall, Glass's voice: 'Answer your phone already.'

His phone was convulsing with another text. The same leg he'd used to bash the elevator panel kicked out to stop the elevator doors from closing. In the hallway, he dug out his phone. All four texts were from his current intern, Zoë Shillace, who until this morning had texted him exactly once to calmly, professionally, and with proper grammar, inform him her subway was being evacuated and she would be late for work. In other words, she was not a young woman given to hyperbole.

> 911 baseman 911
>
> don't want to text need to talk in person this is zoe
>
> where are you very serious need to talk right now
>
> are you shitting me where are you this involves the fucking WHITE HOUSE

Bigger Balls

Fuck, here came Baseman. The executive producer was an old-school, coffee-swilling, antacid-gnashing, capital-*J* Journalist who side-eyed image-conscious upstarts like Chuck Corso as if their Armani suits were SS regalia. Wary of each other's species, Baseman and Chuck kept apart on instinct, and never had the latter received a one-on-one at the desk from the former, the equivalent of a coach's visit to the mound. Seeing Baseman approach, Chuck's spirit tumbled, which at least told him he had spirit left.

Chuck had just spent five numb minutes poorly summarizing the current situation. The aggressors were being described as unarmed and in a trancelike state. Homeland Security forces were being deployed in forty cities. National Guard outposts were being mobilized everywhere. Octavia Gloucester, on assignment in Tampa, reported nursing-home deaths reversing and the revived patients becoming 'belligerent'. Citizens were being asked to stay tuned while the threat was contained.

Lee had spoken up at last, thank Christ, saying that intake had a package from Joanie Abbott in Philly, and Chuck should throw to it, right now, and drink a gallon of water with a bottle of Xanax if he had it. Chuck stammered the fewest words required to pass the baton – 'Joanie Abbott in Philly' – and Camera 2 ceased its laser torture, only to reveal in the ensuing dark Nathan Baseman's stormy stomp. Chuck had to restrain his right hand with his left – he wanted his laptop, he wanted ChuckSux69.

Trained on eyelines, he noticed how Baseman positioned his body to block the camera views of those in the control room. Next, he plucked the two-mic lavalier from Chuck's tie, tossed it on the floor behind the chair, and planted both hands on the anchor desk opposite Chuck's script. He kept his voice at a rasp too soft for the tossed mic to pick up.

'You killed the boobs.'

Life and death were up for grabs, and this surly old dude was talking about . . . what, exactly?

'The spring break B-roll,' Baseman clarified. 'You made Lee kill it.'

Ten minutes ago, was it? And already Chuck had to think hard, like he was doing long division, to recall it. While Chuck spoke live on the phone with Octavia from Tampa, Lee had played generic Florida B-roll behind him. The footage hopped from Everglades imagery to spring break revelry, girls in garish swimsuits toasting with plastic wineglasses, bleary-eyed college students dancing in suds. Chuck found Octavia's words and Lee's visuals grotesquely compatible: the spring breakers' mindless chase of sensory stimulants, their carnal craving for the physical body, their near-death inebriation that kept rising, kept dancing, kept screaming for more.

Yet he'd made Lee cut it. He'd barked an order – to Lee Sutton! – on live TV, and sure enough, the shot of college girls waggling their bikinied breasts in an eruption of fizzy alcohol froze, leaving one girl's drunken shriek looking like a rictus of despair.

'I'm . . . sorry?' Chuck offered Baseman. 'I just . . . It didn't seem—'

'Bigger balls than I expected from you,' Baseman snapped. 'There have been times I ordered Lee, right to his rat face, to cut away from nubile flesh and he outright said he couldn't understand me. Like he couldn't understand my Black voice. Who was I going to take that complaint to? Unitas? That guy will take any excuse to put skin on-screen. You did all right, Face.'

'I said *complimentary* instead of *complicated*.'

'I know.'

'*Collaborated* instead of *corroborated*.'

'Yeah, I heard. Shut up. My point is, you gave me a little sliver of hope. And hope is something in short fucking supply right now.'

Chuck vaguely recalled thinking that very word before his shaky vamping. *ALL HOPE IS NOT LOST,* he'd told himself. He was a *TRUTH TELLER,* he'd told himself. Baseman thought he had balls? He had the wrong guy. Chuck leaned over the desk and took the producer's arm. His cool skin showed Chuck how heated he'd gone under the deathless lights.

'Get me off the desk,' he begged.

Baseman's glare hatcheted Chuck to the spine.

'Listen carefully, Face. Are you listening?'

Chuck nodded, his head bobbing as if filled with helium. A touch-up man sidled up to him, carrying a foundation palette and powder brush.

'*Go away,*' Baseman ordered.

The man darted off. Baseman twisted Chuck's forearm until he was holding Chuck's wrist. It hurt. Chuck's eyes widened, then watered, then cleared. Baseman's face jumped into stinging focus. Rivulets of wrinkles and a sheen of sweat gave the older man's wizened skin an oaken varnish. Baseman licked his lips, his breath the sort of sour only a rebelling stomach produced.

'Now you listen good,' Baseman hissed. 'Half an hour from now, you're done. They're giving Glass the desk at the top of the hour. This desk, you read me? The anchor desk. Once she's colonized this land, you know as well as I she won't give it up without a coup. She's strapping on adult diapers as we speak so she can piss without leaving the chair.'

'Good.' Chuck hated his own whine, but couldn't help it. 'I tried, but I don't . . . I don't have the *stuff*—'

Baseman squeezed Chuck's wrist hard enough to make Chuck gasp.

'The fuck you don't. You had it all morning, Face. I saw it. Everyone saw it. And the truth of the matter is, we don't really have a choice. You think things are bad now? The second Rochelle Glass goes on, we're shooting bottle rockets from a hill of TNT. Everyone huddled in their homes soaking up her vile shit, then squeezing it out for their friends and families. If what they're saying is real, and—'

'It's not real,' Chuck insisted. 'It's . . . Lee keeps saying They're gangs, right?'

'You too,' Baseman scoffed. 'Using *They* and *Them*. They're *us*, Face.'

'What do you mean?'

Baseman gave his head a brisk shake. 'It's not gangs. It can't be. It's worldwide.'

This new info went down like unchewed food. 'What?'

'I just came from the control room. It's in your next update. Sydney, Tehran, Kinshasa, Athens. Does that sound like gangs to you?'

'Do they say . . . Do they tell us . . ?'

'They say they'll have the situation under control in twenty-four hours.'

Chuck knew he was grinning by the paths of his falling sweat.

'Oh, that's . . . that's *wonderful*, that's—'

'It's bullshit, Face. It's Reagan laughing off AIDS. It's Bush saying, "Mission accomplished." My guy at APD says CompStat is down. Our West Coast choppers are all on Ben Hines. We still have news teams on other stories. Face – *there are no other stories.*

'What, you want to throw to sports? Fine, let's talk fucking sports. There's a soccer game in Madrid that's supposed to be a bloodbath, a gladiator ring. We got to pull our shit together, Face, and we got to do it before Glass takes over.'

Chuck looked away from Baseman's glare, spotted his earpiece on the floor, and picked it up. Lodging it back in place, he tried to sound unworried.

'What do you want me to do?'

Lee emerged from Chuck's ear canal. 'Thirty seconds, Chuck. Get Baseman out of there.'

Chuck blinked, all Baseman needed to guess Lee's order.

'Tell Lee to rerun Joanie,' he said.

'I can't tell him that,' Chuck whispered.

Baseman puffed out hot breath. 'You told him to kill the boobs, didn't you?'

'Yes, but I can't—'

'You gotta stand up for yourself, Face. You gotta stand up for the human fucking race. It's right now or maybe not ever again.'

Chuck stared into Baseman's eyes. The older man looked both dead exhausted and crazily alive, like he'd made a long, hard, sleepless drive to get to this place and time.

'Rerun Joanie,' he said to Lee.

He extracted his earpiece, letting it dangle down his neck. He met Baseman's wide-eyed look. Chuck's jaws creaked, and his tongue peeled off the dry roof of his mouth.

'Tell me what to do,' he gasped.

Baseman grinned ferociously, a fuck-the-man snarl. He leaned closer, blocking the monitor, where Joanie Abbott had been rewound to frame one. Chuck thought the producer's breath now smelled more like a soldier's hard-earned sweat.

'Zoë Shillace,' Baseman said. 'My intern. Every six-figure earner in this building running around like a headless chicken, and this twenty-one-year-old, pulling minimum wage, is trawling raw feeds. She's found the needle in the haystack, Face. A camera broadcasting live from the White House briefing room. Not Reuters. Not AP. The feed's coming in rough and rogue. Could be cell phone video, a Dejero box, I have no idea. But it's coming from a closed-door briefing. Some Woodward or Bernstein's trying to Hail Mary this story to someone. And Zoë Shillace caught it.'

'You want to . . . Is it even legal?'

Baseman pounded the desk hard enough for Chuck's laptop to leap.

'Fuck legal. We're not going to *have* laws much longer if people don't hear the truth. The media's gone to shit, and it's our fault. If anyone's going to fight the power, it has to be us. Maybe it takes bad to beat bad, huh?'

Chuck was blanketed by sadness.

'Do we . . . have to fight?'

Baseman nodded seriously. 'It's what we do, Face.'

Chuck knew if he stood and tried to run, he'd stagger. But there was nothing wrong with staggering – if you were staggering in the right direction.

'Okay,' he said. 'All right.'

Baseman cackled victoriously and pointed at the control room.

'I'm going to go in there to stop Lee from killing the feed. Give me two minutes. No, give me one. Once we're live, I'll head off Glass. When she sees we've stolen her thunder, she'll be on the warpath. Just remember this: Lee won't take the feed unless you call for it. You have to call for it explicitly. Say it straight out, it's a press briefing from the White House. Feed 8. You got that? Call for it with confidence, my man. Feed 8.'

The earpiece shivered against Chuck's neck, he assumed from the force of Lee's shouts.

'My career,' Chuck whispered. He identified his emotion: he was mourning.

Baseman wrinkled his brow. 'I know. Mine too.' His grin inched back. 'But for a guy like me – maybe I've judged you wrong, Face. For people like *us* . . . I don't think there's any better way to go out.'

Peculiarities

Baseman had spent hundreds, if not thousands, of hours inside control rooms, and never had one seemed to him as kaleidoscopic as it did today. One hundred and fifty screens puked bad tidings. On the larger screens, Baseman saw the familiar faces, sets, and chyrons of their competitors, newspeople with stern-faced masks little more convincing than the Face's. From the honeycomb of smaller screens, raw feeds of nervous, off-air reporters and helicopter shots, hopefully abandoning Ben Hines's mansion. Most disturbing of all were the color bars, dozens of them, like bright, striped gravestones.

At least it made for flattering light for the cellar-dweller crew seated along the half-octagon countertop: Carly DeSario, production assistant; Grace Canez, teleprompter; Rebecca Pearlman, sound board; Tim Fessler, switcher. And Lee Sutton, director. Only five people to deal with, not bad. Still too many to handle for a sixty-six-year-old guy whose office trash can was filled with fast-food wrappers.

He'd lied to the Face. If Chuck introduced a White House press briefing, Lee *might* take it. The bigger problem would be keeping Feed 8 on the air once it got there. Anyone in this room had the ability to kill it. Baseman took a deep inhale.

'I'm gonna smoke,' he announced. 'Anybody minds, step outside.'

The staff was too strained to turn from their monitors.

Baseman cleared his throat. 'Maybe you didn't understand me. I'm extremely concerned about the effects of secondhand smoke.'

Still no reaction. Baseman checked A Monitor. The Joanie Abbott package, something about a preschool, winding up. On B, a medium shot of Chuck Corso. For once, the Face wasn't checking himself in a hand mirror. With one hand, he was adjusting his lavalier mic. The other, for some reason, was cruising on the touch pad of his laptop. He looked anxious. No shit. If he was sieving for good news, he was not going to find it.

Baseman cleared his throat again. 'I'd feel a lot better,' he growled, 'if everybody would just step the fuck outside!'

DeSario, Canez, Pearlman, and Fessler stood so quickly their chairs rolled back into the railing. As the four of them went for the door, Baseman suspected each was plotting the quickest path to their desk, planning to snatch their things and get the hell out.

'Fessler, you stick,' Baseman said.

The switchboard operator looked stricken. Probably the appropriate attitude. Fessler lowered himself into his seat like it was an electric chair. Lee Sutton, the only one not to budge, pressed the button on his mic and said, 'Sixty seconds, Chuck.' He released the button, pushed his headset back, and spread his arms at Baseman.

'We need a power trip right now,' he cried, 'like we need a drill to the head!'

Baseman had turned his back. He wrapped his arms around a waist-high filing cabinet, confirmed its weight, and began baby-stepping it toward the control-room door. It was the hardest physical labor he'd attempted in years. He put his back into it and felt a muscle along his spine seize. Swallowing an injured sob, he kept shoving. Once the cabinet was in place, blocking the door, he wobbled around to find Lee and Fessler staring at him.

'Fessler,' Baseman panted. 'Whatever you hear us discussing here, you will forget, understand? You tell your wife, your kids, your dog, Santa Claus, I will find you, stick toothpicks in your eyeballs, and serve them up as Swedish meatballs.'

Fessler looked like he'd detected the flavor of what was going down and, to his credit, embraced it. 'I have a terrible memory, Mr Baseman,' he said. 'Things just zip right out of my head.'

Lee appeared immobilized by the grievances fighting for his contempt. He shook a finger at the filing cabinet until he was able to spit out a single, ineffective invective: 'Fire hazard!'

Baseman pointed to A Monitor. 'Whole world's on fire, Lee.'

Joanie Abbott's package had again reached its bleak conclusion – Joanie looking drained before a preschool playground aswirl in police tape. Fessler had no choice but to cut to Chuck. The three of them watched as Chuck saw Camera 2's red light and lifted his face. A chilling sight: the worst improviser in the biz, live without the safety nets of teleprompter, script, or director. Lee popped his headphones over his ears and pressed the mic button.

'Stand by,' Fessler said. 'I'm working on capturing Feed 5.'

Chuck Corso's ruptured voice broke from the control room's speakers.

'We have . . . we have . . .'

Lee paused. Seeing the despair in the Face's eyes, Baseman wondered if he'd just arranged another Jansky shot. Chuck had no gun under the desk, but there might be a glass he could shatter, creating a shard he could draw across his throat. Lee and Fessler had to be thinking the same, along with whoever was rattling the door behind the filing cabinet. This was going to end really—

Chuck's eyes cleared. He sat up straight.

'We have a live press briefing from the White House,' he said. 'Feed 8.'

Baseman saw Fessler check the Feed 8 monitor and recognize the White House briefing room.

'Shit,' Fessler rasped.

'What's that?' Lee demanded. 'What the hell *is* that, Baseman?'

'Take it, Fessler,' Baseman said.

'Do not take it!' Lee shouted. 'That's an order!'

'Feed 8, please,' Chuck repeated.

Fessler threw Baseman a harried look.

'Make a mistake,' Baseman suggested. 'Flip the wrong switch.'

'Do *not!*' Lee cried, scrambling from his chair, obviously intent on stopping Fessler. Only he'd forgotten his headphones; the cable stretched taut and stopped him like a tethered dog. In the two seconds it took for him to rip off the phones, Baseman had covered the distance and taken the kind of swing he hadn't made since his Chicago days, when six months did not pass without him defending himself from an inebriated bigot.

The punch was on the mark, nailing Lee in the mouth. The moist cluck of an uprooted tooth was followed by the dropped-keys splat of blood hitting the floor. Lee's head jolted sideways, and his knees dropped to the tile like dual anchors.

The pain was instant. Baseman drew up his fist – he was a leftie – to find a pyramidal notch between his first and second knuckle. One of Lee's teeth had made him pay for the punch. Blood hesitated at the cleft as if shy, then pushed out, creating a short, red stripe on the floor – more color bars. Baseman lodged his bleeding fist under his right armpit and turned to Fessler.

'You heard the man,' he grunted. 'Feed 8.'

The strain, the sudden injury, they muddied things. Baseman found himself in Lee's chair, a full minute lost. He tried to recover it. Yes, he'd unknotted his tie one-handed and awkwardly wrapped it around the badly placed wound. He blinked away black starbursts and saw the White House video running live on A Monitor. That wasn't the strangest part. In his woozy stupor, Baseman could see *himself* watching the video. See Fessler watching it. Chuck too. All of WWN, in fact. He could see the whole viewing public watching and, growing firmer under his light-headedness, there was a feeling he'd forgotten: pride.

We join a conference in chaos. There's Press Secretary Tammy Shellenbarger. She's wearing her usual lavender suit, standing behind the podium. All normal, until we notice how deeply her fingernails are sunk into the wood. Even in the jittery, low-res video, we can see her knuckles are white. It's a stressful job; we know that. Obama cycled through three press secretaries, George W. exhausted four, Clinton blew through five. We'd be tempted to believe things are normal, if not for the goo splattered across the White House seal. It looks like yogurt, maybe a smoothie. Someone must have thrown it. That is not normal at all.

The camera spins. Whoever is operating it is moving. We see a flap of overcoat. Is the camera being smuggled beneath a coat? Is the most important press conference of our time being transmitted via the silliest of junior-sleuth ploys? For a second, we are blinded by a row of Fresnel lights. We see tripods at the back of the room, all decapitated. We don't know how the camera signal is getting out, but the briefing room is loaded with transmitters, and if the White House has been lax today in accounting for every one, they can't be faulted. It is quite a day, one that, if we want to get lofty about it, might indeed live in infamy.

The camera points down the middle of the room. The James S. Brady Press Briefing Room has seven rows of seats, each seven chairs wide. Typically all are filled, roughly in order of White House favor, with a dozen other reporters crowded into the aisles and rear. Today, attendance is patchy and disordered. A clump of reporters are on their feet and raging, bellies to Shellenbarger's riser; another clump sits poised near the door as if valuing an exit route over all else; still others roam, pads of paper crumpling in their fists. A reporter from Bloomberg is the first person we hear clearly.

Bloomberg: 'Give me my phone back! I want my phone back!'

Shellenbarger, an obstructionist automaton dubbed *the Ice Queen,* is not so cold today. She blots sweat from her face with a wad of tissue. She looks awful. Everyone looks awful. The reporters are sporting attire that, on any other day, might inspire work-apparel jokes on late-night TV. The *Washington Post* in a T-shirt. Politico in sneakers. Al Jazeera in Crocs.

Shellenbarger: 'You'll all get your devices back when—'

ABC: 'Can we isolate the start of this? Is there a ground zero?'

Shellenbarger: 'Like I said, the VSDC network is tracking this.'

NPR: 'How many cases have been reported? Do we have even a rough figure?'

Shellenbarger knots her brow. We are surprised to feel a reciprocal twinge on our foreheads, sympathy for the Ice Queen. We, too, have failed to answer the simplest of questions today and are starting to think we will never have answers again. Shellenbarger makes a show of paging through papers that she, in her state, cannot possibly read. 'I don't have . . . the latest statistics aren't—'

NPR: 'A shitload, right? There have been a shitload of cases. That's what we're going to report.'

Bloomberg: 'One of your goons took my phone! Is the American press under martial law?'

USA Today: 'How could the president have possibly called the attacks *normal*?'

Shellenbarger: 'Hold on. He didn't say *normal*. I never said he said that. I said we are following normal *procedures*.'

BBC: 'Are there normal procedures for this? For the dead coming back to life? Does that mean the White House knew this was a possibility?'

USA Today: 'Is this a cover-up? Is that what it is?'

Bloomberg: 'That's why they took my phone! Why they took all our phones!'

Shellenbarger: 'We are not prepared to confirm reports of . . . what you're saying.'

Reuters: 'You know we have bureaus all over the world, right?'

NPR: 'You don't have to confirm shit! *We've* confirmed it! We've all fucking confirmed it!'

Wall Street Journal: 'You see this? This is a list. Of hospitals and morgues turned into disaster sites. Of emergency medical stations being set up on the sides of roads. We haven't seen anything like this since 9/11.'

Shellenbarger: 'I know you are all reporting . . . peculiarities—'

NPR: 'Dead people walking around? That's pretty fucking peculiar!'

Shellenbarger: 'I think we are very much still in a discovery period regarding who They are and what They want, and if we start describing Them prematurely as some sort of—'

Univision: 'These are very dangerous words, you understand? *They? Them?* To anyone in this country who looks differently, or speaks differently, or behaves differently? Do you see how using language like this, right now, could lead to more civilian deaths?'

Fox News: 'Isn't it possible this is an act of radical Islamic terrorism?'

Univision: 'You have to be shitting me.'

Fox News: 'Do They or do They not, these attackers, exhibit all the signs of jihadist suicide bombers?'

Univision: 'Except that people who set off suicide bombs cannot already be dead!'

Shellenbarger appears relieved by this internal spat. She glances to her right, clearly hoping for reprieve, but the Secret Service agent remains alone, and if we are being honest, does not look so good either. The athletic, ball-of-the-feet stance all agents usually hold has succumbed to slumped shoulders and slack arms. It does not take much imagination to picture him using his visible sidearm as an express ticket out of the White House.

Bloomberg: 'I'm leaving! And if I'm not handed my phone the second I'm in that hallway, you will have a civil liberties lawsuit on your desk by the end of the day!'

New York Times: 'Secretary Shellenbarger. You called this briefing. But you haven't given us a single thing we can give to the public. They need to know what to do right now. Should they be barricading themselves inside? Or trying to find safety in numbers?'

Shellenbarger: 'A document has been sent to your organizations, listing rescue stations. It's being updated regularly. I think people in rural areas should head for the nearest station, yes.'

USA Today: 'You *think*? Why don't you *know*?'

Bloomberg: 'The door is locked. Why the fuck is the door locked?'

We hear a crunch. All of us across the nation hear it. Shellenbarger's eyes go wide with a surprise that's somehow girlish, and she raises her right hand. A dark thread of blood runs down her wrist. The fingernail of her middle finger is bent back, jutting out at forty-five degrees. She has done this to herself by gripping the podium too hard. Somehow this is worse than if that dick from Fox had attacked her. This is self-harm, and that's what we're most afraid of, down in our marrow. How bad will it have to get before we do something to ourselves to make the hopelessness go away?

Shellenbarger: 'Excuse me . . . I . . .'

She tucks the bloody finger inside her sweat-sodden tissue and holds it tightly. As she blinks into the dazzling lights, the camera jostles for a closer vantage. What we feel now is beyond anything we'd ever believed we'd feel for the Ice Queen. We want to whisk her away from that hothouse, address her injured flesh, show her our own. Perhaps by doing so, we can all still be saved.

The press secretary squints over the podium and, from her tentative smile, is truly seeing the press corps for the first time, just as the press corps might be truly seeing her for the first time. Shellenbarger's smile is sad, and we understand why. It comes too late, this cleared sight of hers, and ours.

Shellenbarger: 'I . . . can't tell you what's going on. Because I don't know. I don't know if it's some sort of cult . . . or some sort of bio-weapon . . . I'm just . . . In the end, I'm just a mouthpiece, you know? Whatever this is, it's not a Republican thing, or a Democrat thing. It's not white, or Black, or Christian, or Muslim . . . I know there are a lot of bad people out there. You think I don't know that? But they don't . . . bite each other. They don't eat each other. It's against nature. We're the same. We're all the same. Maybe that's why I called this meeting. Just to remind you, before you run off and forget.'

That silence that follows is booming. The camera, designed to equalize levels, pumps the audio gain until we hear one reporter sobbing, another praying in Arabic. We also hear Shellenbarger breathing, each inhale a dry reed, each exhale that same reed being snapped. We know this is how everyone in the room is breathing, because it is how we are breathing too. Shellenbarger is right. Just look at us. All the same species of mammal, panting with the same kind of lungs, who might still turn to one another for safety, harbor, and strength.

The snap of the last reed, and we are on our own, doomed.

Fox News: 'Did you say They're *eating* each other?'

Newsmax: 'Are you saying They're *cannibals*?'

Washington Post, BuzzFeed, Politico, Al Jazeera, Bloomberg, ABC, NPR, *USA Today,* BBC, Reuters, *Wall Street Journal,* Univision, Fox News, *New York Times,* Newsmax, AP, CNN, CBS, McClatchy, MSNBC, *The Hill,* National Journal, *Time, Daily Mail, Boston Globe,* WWN – they punch and push and scrap and scratch, their bedrock egos cracked by the primeval panic of being the *consumed* instead of the *consumer,* cashiered in favor of a suddenly enfranchised under-class that has always been stronger, been hungrier, been waiting.

Bloomberg: '*Open up this goddamn fucking door, you bastards!*'

Concurrent with this impotent final cry, those of us who haven't gone blind behind terrified tears see the White House chief of staff enter the room, shoulder past the Secret Service agent, and sidle up to Shellenbarger. He says something into her ear, three words or, more likely, three letters – *WWN* – and together their gazes land directly on the camera lens. The chief of staff points a finger and barks at the Secret Service agent, who looks grateful to be given a task. He moves toward the camera. The image whirls toward the door, wilder than anything from Ross Quincey's stringer, but Bloomberg's shriek tells us the door is locked, and the last thing we see is the blurred face of the Secret Service agent, his mouth wide enough to bite through the camera and swallow us.

When Feed 8 cut out, WWN broadcast dead air for an astonishing eighty-four seconds. The screen was black as grave dirt, a study on where the world might be heading. Added to these apparent emotions were the practical matters of Tim Fessler looking absolutely lost and Lee Sutton only beginning to regain consciousness.

They would pull together soon, Baseman thought. They had to. He called his bleeding hand, aching arms, and throbbing back into renewed service, sliding the filing cabinet away from the door and exiting into a crowd of studio staff congregated on the other side, panicked professionals gone still and silent. He shouldered past, into the dark studio, warding them off with the blood-soaked tie around his hand.

It felt like the floor was rolling underfoot in a silent earthquake, tilting forward at the same time so Baseman's sore legs had to move faster. He tumbled past the set, Chuck phosphorescent beneath the lights. He felt hungry; his stomach was actually rumbling. His sopping tie might have slowed the blood pumping from the cut between his knuckles, but stoppering that blood made the rest of his veins scream for release. He had begun to fight, and now fighting was all he craved. It was a chance to make up for Sherry, for Jansky, for everything.

He heard her coming, the impatient thwack of her heels. Rochelle Glass was trotting toward Baseman from the vicinity of Hair and Makeup, buttoning a pearl-colored suit, wobbling on three-inch pumps with unbuckled ankle straps. The lack of flounced hair or dramatic eyeshadow provided evidence of her hasty departure. Her eyes were nevertheless two laser-guided missiles aimed at Chuck Corso. Baseman picked up his pace. Glass came with no entourage, no producers, no assistants. The two of them might as well be back in that elevator, all alone.

Glass noticed him only when he blocked her path. She halted abruptly, just short of smacking into his chest.

'Baseman! I'll tear your boy off that desk if you don't get his ass—'

With his right hand, Baseman pushed open the infrequently noticed door to his right. With his damaged left, he grabbed Glass by the biceps and pulled her into the stairwell.

Juicy, Grisly, Sexy

From the door to the far wall, ten feet. Only four feet of landing before the down and up staircases. White everything – floors, stairs, ceiling, door – but a dingy eggshell white, because even in twenty-first-century monoliths like the CableCorp Tower, stairwells were eschewed by all but the most strung-out smokers and rabid exercisers, and years of shoe scuffs, cigarette ash, stomped roaches, and dust had sunk into the paint like falsified shadows. Each landing came standard, with no windows but a bank of pink-purple fluorescents, which droned like drugged bees and lent a slaughterhouse grimness to the area.

The door clicked shut behind him, and Baseman's skin tightened in the concrete chill. He stopped at the base of the up staircase and wrenched Glass forward. She tottered on an unstrapped high heel and caught herself against the far wall. She gripped her arm where he'd grabbed her and stared at him in amazement.

'You know what a touch like that gets you in today's workplace, Baseman?'

'You think I give a shit? Today?'

'Naturally, you don't. Because I won't sue and you know it.' She pounded dust from her sleeves. 'I happen to find the directness rather refreshing.' She wagged a finger. 'But I'm warning you. If you've handled younger women this way, hoo boy, the clock is ticking on you, buster. I honestly expected more from you, Baseman.

You're an underprivileged class too, you know. I guess dick trumps all. You men. You're going down, every one of you.'

'We're all going down.'

Glass crossed her arms and glared. 'That press briefing was you, wasn't it?'

'Yes.'

'You lose one argument in front of Unitas and this is how you react? You *child*. You *infant.*' Glass shook a fist, a gesture beloved by Mendicans. 'You know what kind of work I've done to gain the president's trust? To get the kind of access I get – that *only* I get? Of course you don't! Because you're living in the sixties! Some civil rights la-la land where you think you've got to stick it to the Man! I've got news for you, Baseman. You *are* the Man. You created this whole system while I was still playing with dolls.'

The stairwell was all hard surfaces. Her voice, elongated into its broadcast twang, came at Baseman as if from a dozen Rochelle Glasses at once, clones created to make the rest of his life a torture. Beneath her braying, smaller sounds also benefited from the stairwell's amplification. Buzzes, beeps, whistles, honks: both of their phones fuming like ignored children.

But Baseman had realized that talking was Glass's game. All he could hear, anyway, was his pulse in his ears, whisked thick by the wound on his hand. It had felt good, punching Lee. It had felt great, biting Sherry. When Rochelle Glass made for the door, those sensations guided him.

'Hello, Kwame, this is Rochelle Glass.' She was speaking into her phone. 'I'm afraid I'm in need of assistance. I'm with Nathan Baseman in—'

The person who struck her was not executive producer Nathan Baseman but rather a *base man,* returned to simpler instincts. His swipe avoided the phone – a base man had no interest in gadgets – and clubbed Glass across her right cheek. Her phone beat her down the flight of stairs, careening around walls and floor like a hockey puck. An instant later, Glass herself fell, rolling down the steps without grace, a bag of laundry.

Those three seconds represented the end of his career, Baseman knew. Well, so be it, they were all clocking out – he'd known that from the first viewing of Quincey's tape. He chased her, taking the stairs as he had in his twenties, three at a jump. He hit Glass the instant she struck the lower landing, his full weight on her back. They crumpled into the wall. One of Glass's heels flew off, clattering like her phone. Her knees buckled. His temple struck concrete. They lay in a tangled heap on the cold floor, a workplace nightmare beyond any imagined HR scenario.

Her hair was in his mouth; he tasted bitter product. Despite having no leverage, Glass jackhammered an elbow back into his ribs. Baseman's arms curled around Glass's bucking body, trying to snake beneath her chest, where he knew her phone was pinned. His hand, a beastly invader, rustled past arms and breasts and stomach before coming upon plastic. Out the phone came, but Glass had a hand on it too, and they fought for it like Aztec priests after the energies of an extracted human heart.

'Kwame – the studio stairs – help—'

Baseman squeezed her wrist as hard as he could, hoping to strangle the phone out of her hand. Her other hand writhed free and yanked on his left thumb. The fissure between his knuckles ripped wider, the skin tearing like bread. Hot blood flowed. Unraveled, his soaked tie was useless, a symbol of professionalism dangling like pulled innards.

The pain was excruciating. Baseman screamed. His mouth, alongside her ear, did what his muscles could not, startling her into loosening her grip. He jerked her phone out of her reach and looked at it, a jolly pink gadget enveloped by a hand dripping blood. He flung the device down the final flight of stairs and was rewarded by a splintering scrunch.

Glass did not waste his moment of inattention. She rolled faceup and cycled her legs furiously until she'd wedged her backbone into the corner, then covered her face to ward off whatever was coming next. Baseman watched her gasp for air and realized that he, too, heaved for breath. It felt like the muscles under his skin were being broiled. His heart was going so fast it felt arrhythmic. Was he having a heart attack?

Glass waved her hands for his attention.

'Stop! Please! Baseman!'

He felt himself swaying over her like a cobra. The blood loss, it must be leaking away what little sense he had. He wondered if clashes like this were happening all over the world, thousands injured as better judgment oozed away with blood. He pressed his torn hand to his chest and tried to bring Glass into focus through blurring tears of pain.

'You don't want me on the desk,' Glass gasped. 'All right. Fine. But I can't stay here. Neither can you. Eventually, we have to get up, like adults, and go back to the studio. Right?'

Baseman's tongue felt too thick to speak. That was a good thing. Words could turn against him. Glass laughed, too hard, a clear attempt to get a psychopath on her side. Except Nathan Baseman wasn't a psychopath. No, he was a defender of the people, the free press.

'Okay, we can sit here a while longer,' Glass said soothingly. 'Catch our breath. You know, Baseman, I remember our first fight. Is that cute or what? I was new here and brash, and I said September 11 was the best thing that ever happened to news. You didn't agree. We had the biggest row, right in front of everyone. You remember, Baseman?'

His eyes were drying and his vision sharpening. Glass smiled through a split lip. Her capped teeth were dark with blood. Long, pink scratches hatched her neck and wrists. Her hair and makeup were undone. Her state reminded Baseman of Sherry when she'd wake up in the morning. We are all the same when we first awake: vulnerable, disheveled, still believing in dreams.

'I was going on about the tickers and the graphics and how the attacks – well, they just made things clearer, you know? We didn't need to bother anymore with squishy nuance. I wasn't partisan, I was patriotic!' She chuckled. 'It's amazing how easily you see your mistakes when you've been pushed down the stairs.'

She's persuading you, Baseman warned himself. *Like she's persuaded millions.*

'I see people as aggregate numbers,' she said. 'It's a flaw – I know that because *you* told me so, Baseman. You said each one of those numbers had moms and dads, and I think of that a lot. I really do. I'll never forget when Unitas said WWN was a "content creator", and you went apeshit. What did you say? While the rest of us sat there yawning? Do you remember?'

Water had sprung back to his eyelids, this time from emotion. Perhaps his blood had run out and tears were the on-deck liquid.

'News . . .' His voice cracked and wavered.

'News *is* . . .' Glass prompted.

'News is evaluated,' Baseman said. 'Content is . . .'

Glass nodded him on. Baseman cleared his throat of tears.

'Content,' he said, 'is herded.'

Glass pulled herself into a more comfortable position.

'You've asked me fifty times since: "What do we choose to cover?" In my head, I've always said we cover what gets ratings, and what gets ratings are hooks. Juicy, grisly, sexy hooks – the stuff that gets your amygdala going. But what you're saying is when we cover Ben Hines, we aren't covering some Black kid shot in the projects. Which means no one else pays attention to it either. Which means life in those projects doesn't get any better. Which means when something happens like it did today, those projects go haywire first. Whatever's going on today, we own it. And those hooks?' Glass smiled. 'Might as well be meat hooks, right? Big, bleeding hunks of meat.'

Glass settled her hand gently upon one of her dislodged shoes. Pearl-colored like her suit. The ankle strap broken. Heel like an ice cream cone, tapering to a point. Easily worth over a thousand dollars. Glass stroked the shoe as if it were the symbol of every poor call she'd ever made.

'Let me take you up on your elevator offer,' she said quietly. 'Let's work together. Support Chuck. This is bigger than ratings. Bigger than any of us.'

Baseman felt parts of him quiver, as if individual muscles were crying. If Rochelle Glass could be convinced, who was to say the rest of the world was beyond help?

He was starting to smile when the shoe heel rocketed into the side of his face. His skull crunched against a railing. When Glass retracted the three-inch heel, his back teeth felt the shock of chilly stairwell air through a ragged hole in his cheek. His mouth filled with blood, which poured into his sinuses and down his throat.

He spewed it over Glass in an endless red spout. The shoe heel whacked his forehead next, hard enough to drive his head to the floor. He blinked into the pink-purple fluorescents, heard himself moan, felt hot blood pour from his face.

'You *fuck*.' Conciliation was gone from Glass's voice. 'Trapping a woman half your size and you still think you're the *good guy* here? You miserable piece of shit! You're done. You're fucking buried. You know-it-all, mansplaining, gasbag *ape*.'

If only she hadn't used that word. He had a hole in his cheek. A hole in his hand. Who knew what other holes he had yet to uncover. But *ape* was an electric charge, a reminder of the things he'd been called back in Chicago: *gorilla, porch monkey, baboon*.

His right hand, the good one, found one of Glass's ankles, pulled. Glass fell, her ulna, clavicle, pelvis, and kneecap xylophoning along stair edges. Baseman coughed blood, then sucked in air. Sure, he might be a bad guy here. But Unitas had said it best. Baseman vs. Glass was Bad vs. Badder. He knew it, she knew it: she cried out, a siren of real panic now, and why not? He'd pretty much risen from the dead.

Glass was sprawled across the upstairs incline. She kicked, but her shoeless feet caused only flat, broad pain. Baseman climbed her legs like a ladder. Her features were pinched into a Rottweiler knot, her teeth bared to the bloody gums, her face hot pink and sweating. She was out of control, her malevolence revealed. For all her inflammatory, demagogic dialogue, all she had left was a noise hummed through a mouthful of slobber: *HNNNNN*.

Baseman felt an absurd surge of joy. The expression on Glass's face was so foreign it took time to identify it. Rochelle Glass was afraid, and he was glad. One way or another, Baseman and Glass, the left and the right, had always been devouring each other.

He blocked her kicking legs with his own, pulled her arms out of the way, and sank his teeth into her throat. It was startling how quickly his mouth was stuffed with skin; the boiling blood that followed had to seep around the wad of flesh before he could taste it. He was the Rottweiler now. He whipped his head until muscle ripped free, then he spat, and spat, and spat, black blood splashing everywhere as Glass gasped, and gasped, and gasped. The gasps turned into gurgles, and she wilted, her fingers lacing gingerly around her opened throat, as if wishing not to staunch the blood but caress it, to know what both death and birth felt like, the going and coming, the mix-up at the crossroads, the blind trail everyone was soon to follow.

Ghouls

Chuck's face itched. It started the moment Camera 2's red eye blinked on from dead air. Like the sun cresting over a mountain ridge, his monitor brightened with the live shot of himself, and in those first moments, while Chuck resisted scratching his face, he perceived strange goings-on in the basement dawn.

The panic that had poisoned the White House briefing had sprayed WWN like a toxic sneeze. He heard hissing arguments. He saw a shove, a retaliatory punch. Half the crew members were gone from their positions, some for good – there was no mistaking the shapes jostling for the elevator. One of the missing was Camera 1's operator; the camera was tilted at the lighting grid as if lost in thought.

Any anchor was practiced at ignoring itches. Chuck took a stabilizing inhale. He'd been the one to request Feed 8. Now he had to own the result. Was he up to it? His memory of his lousy vamping from earlier that morning was still fresh. He would botch this, and considering he'd likely be fired for Feed 8, it might be the last broadcast he'd ever botch. He twitched his itchy nose and touched his earpiece.

'Lee?'

He didn't expect a response. Chuck nearly laughed: they'd have to retire the TEAM COVERAGE chyron if they ran out of team.

A blast of air into the earpiece.

'Chuck,' Lee said, only it sounded more like *Jug,* a burble chased by a spate of wet coughs. Was Lee injured? Had Baseman done something violent? It seemed possible; the producer had looked halfway crazy. More coughing, uglier but stronger. The sizzle of saliva, or something thicker, spattered Lee's mic.

'We're capturing playback of the briefing,' he mumbled. 'Gonna send it to every station we can. Baseman was right. Fuck competition. We all gotta be together on this.' He spat and something hard – a tooth? – popped against the mic. 'Gonna take a few minutes. You want to say something, Face, say anything at all. This is your moment. Go ahead. You earned it.'

It was a preposterous offer. Chuck didn't want to say anything; what he wanted was to join the tide of evacuees and get the hell out of there. But the last thing he'd said to Baseman, that sad little plea, was thorned into his brain: *My career.* What career? The whole profession might be finished.

The soundproof silence of a broadcast set waiting for an anchor to begin had always felt to Chuck like the ticking of a bomb – there was no controlling what any human being might say, not really. His earpiece was mute. His teleprompter was blind. There was no intern handing him script pages still warm from the printer, no Baseman rooting him on. He was alone. Chuck slid his laptop closer and adjusted the screen. ChuckSux69 had always been there, ready with opinions on what Chuck ought to be saying.

Before his thumb brought the computer to life, Chuck caught a glimpse of his face in the black screen. Ink-black skin, charcoal-black eyes – it was the face of a corpse rotted down to casket sludge. A glimpse of his future, or worse, a glimpse at what he was *right now,* a dead-eyed, limp-limbed mannequin who spoke other people's words to convey other people's messages. That ink-black face of his could be a fine-grained walnut and he a Pinocchio; here, at last, was a chance to become a real boy, more than hair plugs and face-lifts.

Under the studio scuffles, he heard ChuckSux69's cry of betrayal, strangled amid the howls of the forum's lesser demons as they ate one another alive.

God, his face itched. But his hands had other things to do. Chuck toggled to a fresh window, trying to ignore his trembling fingers, and opened a search bar. Live TV, folks. Millions of Americans watching him type, backspace, await search results. Watching him click. Watching him read. The silence was a dead whale, bloating toward explosion under sweltering lights. Chuck brought up his laptop's calculator, reread the operative passage, cleared his throat, and looked into Camera 2.

'Two people die every second,' he said.

Never had opening his mouth taken more courage, not even in front of cosmetic dental surgeons and their grinding armories of retractors, excavators, chisels, and burnishers.

'That's one hundred and twenty deaths every minute,' he continued. 'Seventy-two hundred deaths every hour. One hundred and seventy-two thousand, eight hundred deaths every day. Sixty-three million, seventy-two thousand deaths every year. In normal times. In *normal* times.'

Were the lights brighter, blocking his view of the staff exodus? Or had the remaining crew frozen in place, arrested by what the Face had just said? He thought he saw, piercing the gloom, dozens of eyes, crystalled by tears, looking to him. To *him,* with fear but hope, too, like no one had looked at him since September 11, 2001. Chuck knew now, as he'd known then, there was no point in false reassurances. He had to be what ChuckSux69, at the end, could not be: *TRUTH TELLER.*

'At issue here,' he said, 'is the fact that most of those one hundred and twenty deaths per minute are now causing additional deaths. So the figures I quoted are' – near homonyms fought to escape his throat (impertinent, inefficient) but the correct word thrashed its way out – 'insufficient. If dead people are killing people, the number of dead people is going to keep rising' – (expressly, expansively, extemporaneously) – 'exponentially.'

There was no more doubting it: everyone in the studio was watching now, including new people peeking from offices. If the leathered WWN staff hung on his words, so did the public. Chuck took a giant breath and placed his hands on the cold, scriptless desk. He waited for his pulse to hammer and his vision to spin. Neither did. He was speaking from the heart for the first time in his life, something he'd never done even in intimacy with Arianna, Ljubica, Nathalia, and Gemma. It was exhilarating, if only in the way of bleeding out in a hot bath – no pain, only giddiness, with no time to waste.

'Ladies and gentlemen,' he said. 'I've been trained to keep you watching. We've *all* been trained to keep you watching. Which means I have failed to follow Kovach and Rosenstiel's first rule. Let me explain that. In school, we read a book called *The Elements of Journalism,* by Kovach and Rosenstiel. Kovach and Rosenstiel came up with a set of principles you watching at home deserve to expect from your journalists. We had to memorize them. I'm going to share them with you. I think it's important that we agree on them before whatever happens next happens next.'

That could have been smoother, but for once, he was able to flick away self-criticism like a housefly. He'd never felt worse in his life – oh, that itch – but at the same time, he'd never felt stronger. It was like he was floating, only the cables of his lapel mic tethering him to the desk.

'A journalist's first obligation is truth. Which is why I showed you that meeting in Washington. Which is why, as long as I'm sitting here, I will not sugarcoat anything.'

Chuck waited for Lee to order him to can this end-times shit, but Lee had either undergone a change similar to Chuck's or he'd scrammed. If so, Chuck had no intent to follow suit. An arrow of truth had pierced him, and until someone dragged him off the desk, his pressured air would keep blasting out.

'Kovach and Rosenstiel said news's first loyalty is to its citizens. We've failed in this. *I've* failed in this. Look where the attacks began. Housing projects. Nursing homes. You think we've been loyal to them? When we talk about a MPWW, a Missing Pretty White Woman, we know everything about her. What brand of clothing she wore. What kind of music she liked. We'll talk about it for months.

'If people in a housing project die? The details don't matter. The names don't matter. One day of coverage, two tops. We've come up with codes to tell you why. We say *Grove Park* so we don't have to say *Black*. Loyalty to citizens? No. We have loyalty to money. And if our inattention is part of why this started where it started, and why no one can stop it, then I don't know. Maybe it's a purge. Maybe it had to happen.'

Static in his earpiece. Lee's revival, maybe, or maybe the first sign of the station's infrastructure bowing under the systemic failure of the outside world. Chuck chose not to know; he pulled the earpiece, and this time it was the cutting of his umbilical.

'The thing I remember most from Kovach and Rosenstiel was that reporters must listen to their conscience. That's what I'm doing. But this isn't about me. It's not about making up for things I've screwed up in the past.' He laughed once and was surprised that it launched tears to his eyes. 'How did I ever think it was? I'm so ashamed.'

From the rear of the studio came a bright little nuclear blast, a door opening to what Chuck believed was the studio stairwell. Into the brief violet glow lumbered a shape he recognized as Nathan Baseman. Gladness warmed Chuck's chest. If this was his final broadcast, it had been only the second one to matter, and for that, he thanked Baseman. Chuck resumed the best vamp of his career, if only to prove to Baseman he hadn't put his faith in the wrong anchor.

'I shouldn't need Kovach and Rosenstiel,' Chuck said. 'Why should any of us need a book to understand our responsibility to one another? It feels like we've been sleepwalking through a dreamworld we convinced ourselves was working just fine for everyone. It may be too late, but at least we're waking up.'

Baseman approached, opposite the flow of traffic. Chuck couldn't wait to see him better; Baseman would give him a pleased grin, he knew. The same sort of proud, private smirk Chuck used to get from his Italian nonna. He hadn't thought of the old woman in a very long time. Chuck smiled, and not the precisely quarter-inch-of-teeth smile the WWN image consultant made him practice. This smile was wide enough for Chuck to feel the spotlights warm his ceramic caps.

'I'm smiling. I know it's strange. But Press Secretary Shellenbarger, she said the dead were eating the living, and that reminded me of something my nonna used to say. She was superstitious, always crossed herself passing cemeteries. She was sure nasty things were going on there.' Warmth on his teeth again, miraculous in the midst of such dread. 'Nonna used the word *ghouls*. "Don't walk near the cemetery, Chuckie, there's ghouls in there, They'll get you." Well, I guess Nonna was right. There were ghouls in there, and They've gotten out.'

There was renewed movement at the edge of his vision: people had resumed leaving. Chuck believed that was proof he was doing his job well. Those feeling no deep obligation to stay here should go. Zoë Shillace, there was no more reason to impress your boss. Get out, try to live, for as long as you had left.

Baseman had nearly reached Camera 2, still within the curtain of darkness. The pained slump of his shoulders was defined by a flare of backlight originating from the studio stairwell as the door opened again, revealing a second silhouette Chuck recognized: Rochelle Glass.

She instantly began moving in Chuck's direction. No surprise there – Baseman had told him Glass wanted the desk.

A distant click: Lee, back from the dead.

'Face? Face?'

Chuck picked up the earpiece and reinserted it.

'We've got Octavia on the phone,' Lee sobbed. 'Can you believe it? She's okay. She's okay, Face. Will you talk to her? She's got updates you won't believe.'

Chuck was deluged with cool relief. Octavia Gloucester, their senior reporter, was only one person, but she was alive and fighting, and that was a start. He grinned.

'Ladies and gentlemen, we have good news,' he said. 'Great news, right when we could really use it. We're going to go live now to – well, I'll let her introduce herself. She's going to tell us some things about the ghouls. I think you'll be as glad as I am to hear from her. Hello, are you there?'

Not wanting the beguilement of the internet, possibly ever again, Chuck pushed his laptop away. Stage lights caught the metallic shell and were reflected right onto Nathan Baseman's face. Both lips were obscured by a walrus mustache of blood that looked to be oozing from a hole in his cheek. Baseman applied pressure to the wound with a hand that looked equally mangled. His forehead was a lumpy, shining plum. He looked like he should be dead, but he wasn't a ghoul. Baseman nodded at Chuck, sending bloody spit from his face.

'Hello?' Chuck called. 'Octavia? Are you there?'

Rochelle Glass walked onto the set, directly in front of Camera 2. Her foot butted the riser and her progress glitched before she appeared to recall the logistics of climbing. Her arms were raised and her fingers clawed blindly. These irregularities might have excuses, but there was no excusing Glass's lowered head. She might have faults, but she lived with her face upturned, to sniff out humanity's weaker members.

Gradually that head rose, revealing Glass's throat: a chasm, the skin in leathery strips, purple muscles drooping, trachea pink and hollowed, pharyngeal nerves feathered like baby's breath. Glass's next step threw Chuck into cool shadow. He stared up at her. Her eyes had gone white as milk. Gore-speckled spit swayed like decorative beads. One string of saliva touched down on his laptop and sizzled.

'Hi, Chuck.'

For a moment he thought the voice was Glass's, a drop of sanity spurting from gristled madness, then he recognized Octavia, her voice in his ear, a hand extended from a steadier place. He couldn't meet it; he pushed away from the desk even as his earpiece and lapel mic tied him there, a prisoner.

Baseman sprang at Glass, bloody slobber rippling from his face, but he bungled the step and dropped from sight. Glass crawled on top of the anchor desk she'd coveted, the torn seat of her suit facing the world, and moaned hungrily, ejecting a fizz of mulberry-colored spit. The serrated fingernails of her outstretched hand grazed Chuck's cheek, inciting the savage itch rooted deep in his flesh. He should let her do the hard part, he thought wildly, and make the first cut with her nails, after which he could pull his face all the way off and see exactly what had been lurking beneath his skin all this time.

'Are you there, Chuck?' Octavia asked. 'Is everyone gone?'

Glass sprawled onto Chuck's lap. Her pearl pantsuit hissed as it split up the back. Her jagged nails made fast knots of the fine, artificially straight lines of Chuck's plugged hair. He pulled away, neck muscles rigid, but kept talking, because this was his desk, *his desk*. He took hold of her ruined neck and pushed back.

'Ladies . . . and gentlemen . . . stay with us,' he grunted. 'For once in my career . . . I don't know how this . . . is going to turn out. I am thoroughly,' he added, without effort or thinking twice, 'perplexed.'

THE
WHANG
AND THE
WHOOSH

Let All Mortal Flesh
Keep Silence

When Lieutenant Commander William Koppenborg, Catholic chaplain for the aircraft carrier USS *Olympia,* heard six ship whistles followed by the XO's bark of 'Man overboard, man overboard!' from the wall-mounted 1MC, his first thought was disgracefully vain: *The XO's talking about me. My soul. It's gone overboard and is sinking to the floor of the sea.*

He was in the chapel. Its eight-foot ceiling, metal folding chairs, and wan fluorescents made the sprightliest seaman look as if they stood at death's door and felt more like the site of a basement AA meeting than a place where anything holy happened. After dropping off three dozen sailors at Pearl Harbor, *Olympia*'s final stop before concluding her six-month deployment, the carrier was down to a trim 5,102 people, a population still large enough to require religious leaders. The chapel's walls were kept bare, the better to serve multiple denominations; *Olympia*'s crew included members of the Jewish, Muslim, Protestant, and Catholic faiths, among others.

As chaplain, he was *Father Bill* to regular service attendees, *Padre* to old-timers, *Chaps* or *Chappy* to those fond of pally nicknames, and just plain 'sir' to lowly E-1s and E-2s too overwhelmed by their first carrier voyage to recall the finer points of navy etiquette. Right now, though, Father Bill was nothing to no one, a nameless wretch suffering inside the chapel closet, his slacks folded atop a stack of Bibles and a garbage bag placed beneath his feet to catch the dribbles of blood, while he ran a box cutter across his pale, naked thigh.

WHANG! WHOOSH!

The deafening noises were the catapults, hurling Hornets, Hawkeyes, Growlers, and Greyhounds into the sky. The chapel was on 02 deck, just beneath the flight deck, and with each takeoff, as often as one every thirty seconds, the whole place shook like a giant maraca. With no bodies to hold them in place, the folding chairs moseyed. Hymnals plopped from the pulpit. Paint flaked from the wall. Father Bill believed he could hear communion wafers in a nearby box crumble.

Once upon a time, the *whang* and *whoosh* had brought comfort. It was otherworldly, a reminder of bigger things, higher powers. Here in the closet, the *whang* was a backhand to his face; the *whoosh*, his breath being stomped from him by an invisible boot.

When not blinded by boiling-hot tears, he used the disturbances to his advantage, sinking the box cutter into his thigh on the *whang* and drawing it across on the *whoosh*. Father Bill relished the sensations, controlling his own pain rather than enduring the agonies of a disappointed Jesus Christ, who loomed over him from a floating crucifix, the thorns from his crown nipping like needles at Father Bill's scalp.

The XO again: '*Man overboard. Time: plus one. All hands to muster, all hands.*'

Flight ops had barely begun; there would be a few more takeoffs before the deck crew could safely halt the catapults. Lifting the blade to his mouth, Father Bill licked off the blood, a salty final punishment before he took up the roll of gauze and began winding it around his thigh. The bandages soaked through instantly, sprouting butterflies of blood, and he felt a flicker of concern. Perhaps he'd sawed through scar tissue too many times, and when he mustered a few minutes from now, blood would bloom through his pants like urine, proof of the filth that had taken hold of him.

Life aboard an aircraft carrier was loud, dirty, and cramped, too hot, or too cold. But until these past months, Father Bill had never regretted accepting a commission as a naval officer and military chaplain twenty-one years ago. It was inspiring work. Baptizing sailors at dawn in a flight-deck tub. Receiving prayer requests that astonished and moved him. Finding joy in daily homilies, no matter how sparse his congregation. Counseling sailors of every rank through untold personal struggles.

That was where things had gone wrong. Three weeks into *Olympia*'s current deployment, a homesick PO3 ready to give his life to the Lord had surrendered to Father Bill a wrinkled issue of a pornographic magazine called *Fresh Meat*. The confiscation was routine. Most of the five thousand sailors packed into the carrier were between age eighteen and twenty-five, but romantic relationships were forbidden and sexual encounters considered a punishable infraction. Decades ago, so-called training films had abounded – stag films, really. Those filmstrips, and later videotapes, were superseded by websites, many of which were blocked by the navy's so-called filters.

This created a space for old-fashioned magazines. Father Bill presumed half the men's racks were lined with these cheaply printed obscenities. During each deployment, a number of guilt-ridden sailors handed over their sinful stashes.

Father Bill had a lockbox in the chapel closet, a balsa-wood carton with a puny padlock. There he chucked all pornographic materials while at sea. Periodically, during stints of liberty on land, he would empty the lockbox, where he could burn its contents. *Hustler, Barely Legal, Cheri, Gallery, Swank* – not once in twenty-one years had he done anything but destroy them. Once the guilt-ridden PO3 who had handed him the issue of *Fresh Meat* left, however,

Father Bill did something different, for reasons he still did not understand.

A magazine cover sounds like a lick of fire when opened.

William Koppenborg had lived so few adult years before giving himself to God that he could not reliably recollect them. He had never been with a woman, never seen one unclothed. Men who prospered in the priesthood found ways of defusing their lust. His own method was to visualize dirt pitched into a hole, his desire buried beneath tons of earth. When he saw *Fresh Meat*'s first image – a woman naked except for high heels, her body lean and shiny, squatting above a disembodied penis veined like the trunk of a bald cypress – his lust clawed itself from its grave.

He turned page after page, wincing at paper cuts though he saw no wounds. His testicles ached. His pulse accelerated. His penis, forever a dangling, excretory tube, inflated and nudged at his thighs.

It caused trouble during services. He prided himself on believing what he preached – it helped him muster the volume required by the *whang* and *whoosh* – but his excogitations on saints and apostles were no match for the lips, nipples, and labia shrouding his brain like a fungus. Members of his congregation thrice interrupted a sermon to ask if his reddening face was a sign of heart distress. That was not it at all. It was terror one of them would notice the erection tenting his slacks.

Inside the closet was a first aid kit, one he'd never opened prior to this deployment but with which he'd recently become familiar. In addition to the gauze, the kit contained medical tape, which Father Bill began using to fasten his penis to a thigh. When the organ grew erect during services, as it always did, he would feel the sting of adhesive against stretching skin and would recall the pained faces inside *Fresh Meat*. It was not pain they felt. He knew that now.

Knowing little about sex, he began envisioning warped mechanics. The photo of a woman with her fist inside another woman's vagina: Father Bill imagined two women in the front row of his congregation, one's hand shoved far enough into the other to tug out ovaries, intestines, and kidneys while the receiver shuddered orgasmically. The photo of a woman with her lips sunk halfway down a penis: Father Bill imagined a male and female in the hangar bay engaged in the same, except the man pushed until his penis broke through the back of the woman's neck, shattering vertebrae, while the woman's jaws kept working, biting off the penis, sinking her teeth into steaming bowels.

On and on, *Fresh Meat*'s flashbulb instants taken to bestial conclusions of ecstatic mutual destruction. They were the visions of Bosch or Dalí or Goya, a gallery of carnal monstrosity that told Lieutenant Commander William Koppenborg he was becoming a monster too.

He tried everything to make the thoughts go away. He howled his hymns. It did no good. He'd led congregations through 'Let All Mortal Flesh Keep Silence' hundreds of times, but every line seethed with sinister double meaning, none more than the first. *Let all mortal flesh keep silence* was Father Bill's plea for his sweaty visions to begone.

In the final months of deployment, his obsession fixed itself on one woman. He called her *My Sweet,* and she seemed to accept the term of affection, smiling at his grandfatherly warmth. My Sweet was young, but then again, weren't they all? She'd begun to doubt her place both aboard *Olympia* and in life and had arranged private counseling with Father Bill. My Sweet's skin was smooth and golden; he imagined it tasting like pancakes. My Sweet's lips were plump as sausages; he imagined her gasp of pleasure as he bit them off, *squish, squish, squish.*

When she spoke, he edged closer, hungry to create with her one of the multilimbed flesh beasts seen in *Fresh Meat*. Each time he believed he might touch her, a shadow draped over him. Jesus Christ on his cross, watching to see if his holy soldier could resist temptation. Father Bill's very faith was on trial. Jesus had his forty days in the Judaean Desert; Father Bill had his six months at sea.

Historically, only the most devout received such trials, and of that he was proud. Pain, after all, could be mastered, if you had a sharp box cutter and plenty of gauze.

'*Man overboard! To muster, all hands! Time: plus two!*' the XO shouted.

He needed to move. Arriving late for emergency muster carried consequences, even for old sailors like him. He pulled on his pants, snug over his bandaged thigh, then folded the garbage bag so it did not leak a drop of blood before inserting it into a second bag. He left the closet, shoved the bags deep into a trash bin, and left for his muster station, where he would stand alongside men whose gods did not find them worth challenging: the minister, pastor, rabbi, imam, and worst of all, the ship's psychiatrist – 'the Psych' he was called – a handsome, muscled, mustached fellow who probably forged sex monsters with different women at every port.

Father Bill entered the tight steel hallway and adopted the easy stride people expected, despite the pulsing wounds in his thigh. Sailors thundered to their stations. His gaze sought out the rare women and lingered upon their rocking hips and swaying breasts – fresh meat not even navy uniforms could conceal. None of them were My Sweet; nevertheless, he reveled. Let all mortal flesh keep silence, keep silence.

Some Kind of Bird Flu Thing

It was 0640 Hawaii-Aleutian time when the man-overboard call went out. Master Chief Boatswain's Mate Karl Nishimura, one of three master helmsmen aboard *Olympia,* was not scheduled to report to the navigation bridge for thirty minutes. He sat at ease – or as close to ease as Nishimura ever got – with three other khaki-clad officers in the CPO mess on 03 deck.

The 1MC crackled to life. Sailors less acquainted with Executive Officer Bryce Peet might not have picked up the nuances of his voice, but Nishimura sure did. The XO was livid, and no wonder: this was the third man-overboard alarm in a fortnight, a cry-wolf routine that, aboard a behemoth like *Olympia,* was liable to get someone killed.

Minutes earlier, it had been a typical breakfast. In other words, Nishimura was uncomfortable. The CPO mess had the best eating on the boat, palatable chow served on actual tablecloth-covered four-tops. Adding to its Anytown, U.S.A., feel were diner-style condiment caddies and a TV, kept blaring 24–7. The CPO mess was also a place of jocular ball-busting, a pastime that made Nishimura wary.

He did not need the Psych digging into his memories to understand why. To make it into this room, one had to know their naval history, and that likely included Imperial Japanese Navy admiral Shōji Nishimura of Leyte Gulf fame. No relation to Karl Nishimura, of course, but the surface similarities were enough to have hounded him as a cadet. If he read people's smirks right – grins tied off the second he walked into a room – the derision lived on in today's young, racist seamen, of which there were still too many.

He tried not to dwell on it much. It had been a decade since anyone had pulled their eyelids into a slant or called him *Jap*. His sensitivity to his otherness mostly emerged in groups like this, where men, lips loosened by greasy food, expressed testosterone by poking at one another's sore spots.

The morning's conversation revolved around what Crash and Salvage Leading Petty Officer Ronaldo Ribeiro called 'the weirdness' of *Olympia*'s strike group. Thanks to the safe waters between Hawaii and San Diego, the strike group's submarine and frigate had stayed at Pearl for refit and repair, leaving the carrier with a truncated retinue of three destroyers, a supply ship, and the guided-missile cruiser *Vindicator*.

'*Hickenlooper*'s going in circles out there,' Ribeiro said. 'Totally out of formation.'

'Navigational maneuver?' Cryptologic Technician Darrell Millichamp posited.

Ribeiro wiped up yolk with toast. 'Not like any I've seen. Loop-de-loops.'

Safety Officer Waylon Leneghan chuckled. 'We're not being downsized anymore. They can quit showing off.'

'And the *Pollard*? It's just plain gone.' Ribeiro trilled the Twilight Zone theme.

'Gone?' Millichamp asked. 'What do you mean *gone*?'

Ribeiro washed his toast back with coffee. 'Gone as that toast. I climbed the island to see for myself. They're booking thirty-three knots back to Pearl.'

Leneghan laced his fingers behind his head and burped. 'Wouldn't mind a U-turn back to Oahu. Eighty-two-degree beaches, wahines swishing grass skirts.'

Ribeiro chuckled. 'Put it in Veevers's Idea Box.'

CMC Bertrand Veevers, a man so tightly wound he made Nishimura seem like a beatnik, had been the boat's in-joke of choice for the past half year as he'd promoted the anonymous suggestion box he'd had installed outside his cabin. The Idea Box had received plenty of suggestions, all right, and as a result, Veevers's rants about disrespect had become a major source of enjoyment for nonrates and officers alike. Except Karl Nishimura, of course. Anything outside of code made him sweat.

Millichamp nodded his way. 'What do you say, Saint Karl? You've made more of these runs than us. You ever seen a tin can act like *Pollard*?'

Nishimura paused, and right on cue, the three officers made nominal efforts to hide their grins. As surely as the straitlaced helmsman had earned the nickname *Saint Karl*, so had his studied hesitation been dubbed the Nishimura Delay. Nishimura knew his rep. Every question given sober consideration, whether asked about enemy attacks in the Persian Gulf or which brand of toothpaste to buy from the ship store. The Nishimura Delay was a habit pounded into him in grade school, where classmates mocked mispronunciations he'd inherited from his Japanese father.

He donned a mask of good humor when gibed about the Nishimura Delay, but in truth, it stung, which made him ashamed of a boyish delicacy that had no place in the navy. He regaled himself with the knowledge he would not need to keep delaying much longer. He was forty-three years old, and though he knew it would surprise the men at this table, he'd decided to cash in his twenty-year military retirement.

His exhaustive understanding of navy life had begun to trouble him. Ask him anything about *Olympia* and he'd have the answer, as if the boat were his firstborn rather than a $20 billion, nuclear-reactor-powered hunk of mobile oceanfront real estate. Funded in

1968, launched in 1975, and commissioned in 1976, CVN-68X, a.k.a. USS *Olympia*, a.k.a. Big Mama, was the second-oldest *Nimitz*-class carrier in the USN, with thirteen deployments under its belt. As large as a skyscraper set on its side, capable of moving seven hundred nautical miles a day, and with a flight deck as busy as a medium-sized airport, *Olympia* was a storied titan, if one nearing the end of her service. This might be her final voyage; fitting then, Nishimura thought, that it would be his final voyage as well.

Big Mama had served with distinction in such operations as Desert Shield, Enduring Freedom, and Iraqi Freedom. How could a sailor doubt the virtue of missions so rousingly titled? Nishimura could. His distrust of the military-industrial complex had steadily grown over two decades. Blame a Japanese American heritage that included both sides of the Hiroshima-Nagasaki quandary. Blame a job that involved steering the boat, the big-stick component of any carrier's show of force. He did not enjoy acknowledging the carrier was a weapon, the largest the navy had, and that every one of her five thousand souls were but cogs inside the triggering mechanism.

Nishimura knew the life cycle of a carrier better than he knew his own, and it was time for that to change. The question that plagued officers like Ribeiro, Millichamp, and Leneghan – what the hell would they do in the private sector? – did not vex Nishimura. He did not care. He'd hold construction signs. Bag groceries. Whatever it took to spend more time with his family.

Few people aboard *Olympia* even knew Saint Karl was married. Trained on cautionary tales of sailors getting fingers ripped off by machine parts, Nishimura did not wear a wedding band. He rarely spoke of his husband, Larry, a Black man from Trinidad, whose full-time job in their Buffalo, New York, home was caring for their five kids, whom they'd adopted after the children's father and mother, Nishimura's older sister, had been killed in a robbery. Why didn't Nishimura speak of Larry more often? It wasn't that they were gay.

Three nights ago at Benny's Hula House in Honolulu, he'd been seated outdoors among drunk sailors who, once they'd tired of gawping at surfer girls, had segued into slurring proudly about the families they'd soon be seeing. It was an opportune time for Saint Karl to praise Larry and their children: Atsuko, Chiyo, Daiki, Neola, and Bea. If he hadn't been stone sober, he might have. Perhaps he'd learned it from a cold father, but he'd always felt it improper to discuss his loved ones – so soft and vulnerable – among men who, in one way or another, were trained to kill.

It was the same each time he deployed. He was one Karl Nishimura when boarding Big Mama, his ASU sharp as a trowel inside a clothing bag and eyes welling as Larry and the children waved bon voyage from the dock; he was another Karl Nishimura stepping back onto that dock six months later. Embracing his family, he'd feel he'd become a stranger. Did his legs shake from mal de débarquement or from anxiety over whether he'd remember how to hold a child, give a kiss, or eat food unseasoned by a soupçon of jet fuel? He felt himself become a worse Karl Nishimura year by year, month by month, day by day.

A question fit for CMC Veevers's Idea Box: *How do I hold on to myself way out here?*

It felt terrible to have your heart hardened. So he continued to save his tenderest emotions for his family, eschewing sailors who reached out in goodwill. On this deployment, the boat's top eyes in the sky, Air Boss Clay Szulczewski and Mini Boss Willis Clyde-Martell, had both made entrées of friendship. Meet us for cards? Partake in these mind-blowing cigars? Sit with us on the admiral's bridge catwalk just to watch the submerging sun paint the whitecaps?

Open your heart?

He tidied his lips with a handkerchief before replying to Millichamp.

'I served on the flagship for the fiftieth D-Day celebration,' he said. 'Strict flotilla formation. We didn't have active status like *Pollard*, but we had a frigate ignore her orders and start doing figure eights. Could have caused real damage.'

'What was the beef?' Ribeiro asked. 'Signal intercept?'

'Human error.' Nishimura shivered inside his military dress: no two words spooked him more. 'It came down to an E-3 in the engine room who thought the Normandy invasion was a government hoax.'

'And that was his protest?' Leneghan cried. 'Christ on a cracker.'

'I think Saint Karl's got it,' Millichamp sighed. 'Especially on the home stretch of a half-year deployment. I think someone on *Pollard* went Section 8. Some of these young kids start realizing the freedom they're about to get back and can't handle it.'

'Whole *lot* of people can't handle it,' Leneghan grunted.

There was silence at that; television chatter heroically filled the void. Leneghan had come close to saying aloud what plenty of sailors aboard Big Mama must be thinking. For ten days now, Captain David Page had occupied a bed in sick bay, a bizarre capstone to an otherwise clockwork deployment.

Nishimura believed aircraft carriers, overstuffed by design, had room for exactly one secret: whether or not their ship actually carried nukes. Anything additional acted as a corrosive acid. On a ship, rumors spread more quickly than colds. Captain Page had been found polishing doorways at night with his underwear. Captain Page would not quit singing Cher's 'If I Could Turn Back Time'. Captain Page was dying.

Funny, but dangerous. Lowered confidence meant lower morale, which meant lower concentration, and that affected everyone. The hierarchy of a carrier strike group was not as complicated as its titles, ratings, and pay grades suggested. Each ship in the CSG had a captain, and those skippers, along with the CAG (commander, air group) reported to the CSG's admiral – in this instance, Admiral Jamison Vo, currently aboard *Vindicator*. If *Olympia*'s skipper had been at death's door, one of the ship's MH-60R Seahawks would have whirlybirded him to dry land. But by all reports, Captain Page was alert and responsive in sick bay. He simply wasn't *up*.

It was, in a word, weird. The same brand of weird being exhibited by *Hickenlooper* and *Pollard*. Perhaps everyone in the CPO mess was thinking the same. The silence blanketing Nishimura's table unfolded across others, and the background burble of TV news crystallized into actual words.

'What I have in my email here is the document you heard Press Secretary Shellenbarger reference. It includes the list of rescue stations. Lee? Get me a super with these rescue stations, stat.'

Navy ships broadcast news around the clock through open-channel receivers. Most sailors had their favorite reporters, and due to the boat's noise, that favoritism revolved around physical attractiveness. A preponderance of men lusted after an NBC analyst stationed in Afghanistan, and though Nishimura did not know who straight women preferred, he could not imagine it was this coiffed dolt, whose preening mannerisms seemed antithetical to everything a sailor stood for. His name, Nishimura believed, was Chuck Corso.

Corso did not look as good as usual. His tie ran sideways, as if it had been yanked on. On his forehead, right beneath what looked like a small patch of missing hair, were dark spots that might be blood. Shadows moved irregularly across his haunted face, and the picture vibrated from a jostled camera. Watching, Nishimura knew a new kind of seasickness, wondering if a physical struggle was taking place near the reporter's desk.

Corso's red eyes strained at his laptop.

'I want everyone watching at home, or wherever you are, to approach this list with caution. With these ghouls, I'm just not sure who we can trust.'

Safety Officer Waylon Leneghan: 'Did he just say *ghouls*?'

'The document says,' Corso continued, 'that this is a "swiftly evolving event" and that "federal, state, and local partners" are work-ing together with the WHO to "keep information flowing".' Corso looked up. 'That means absolutely nothing.' He looked back down. 'The president, they say, is in a "secure location", receiving regular briefings on the situation, and is "reviewing our national capabili-ties". Boy, that's an ominous phrase, ladies and gentlemen.'

Cryptologic Technician Darrell Millichamp: 'This some kind of bird flu thing?'

Shaking his head in time with his scrolling finger, Corso continued, '"Homeland Security . . . an interagency body . . . accelerated and effective response . . ." This is nothing we haven't heard a hundred times before. They're feeding us raw bullshit. How do I know?' Corso jabbed a finger just below the camera lens, the source of the flickering shadows. 'I know because *it's happening right in front of me.*'

Crash and Salvage Leading Petty Officer Ronaldo Ribeiro: 'What the fuck *is* this?'

That was when the man-overboard whistles blasted. Big Mama's crew trained for few things more stringently than emergency mus-ter, and even though this was an unprecedented third instance in two weeks, and the on-air breakdown of some poor sap at WWN was fascinating, their brains complied at a Pavlovian pace. Nishimura leaped to his feet. As he hurried aft, he heard rather than saw the clatter of dropped silverware and the clop of abandoned coffee cups.

It was an awful thing, the prospect of a sailor being swept into the depths, and almost as awful was the prospect of a sailor falsifying such a tragedy. Yet Karl Nishimura felt a shudder of relief as he hit the ladder and, with the skill of anyone six months into deployment, danced his way up the steps. If he had access to Veevers's Idea Box right now, he'd put in a request for these alarms to keep happening, one after another, until they got home. This was the sort of disaster for which sailors were trained, and he'd take that any day over the jarred, loosened terror he'd seen in Chuck Corso.

Just Plain Jenny

Every member of a flight squadron was given a call sign. Nicknames, that's all, but not to be taken lightly. Call signs were rite and requirement, bequeathed at off-the-books ceremonies during which FNGs (Fucking New Guys/Girls) supplied bribes to elder squadron pilots, partook in a ridiculous and/or revolting ritual, and threw themselves upon the mercy of the court. Call signs were rarely flattering, usually referencing a negative characteristic or infamous foul-up. But a call sign also meant you, negative and infamous parts included, had been accepted. Everyone called you by your call sign. It was stenciled on a plane.

Jenny dreamed of her name on a plane.

Rex: just another way of spelling *wrecks,* as in has-too-many. Tits: nice fellow with overdeveloped pectorals. McDonald's: during liberty in Australia, he pooped on the floor of a McDonald's. Torch: on an approach, he splashed the flight deck with fuel from an open dump valve, starting a fire.

Jennifer Angelys Pagán's call sign was Jenny. In other words, she had no call sign. It made her think of her abuela's favorite movie, *The Wizard of Oz,* and how Dorothy's sidekicks, though perfectly capable, still longed for the approval of the Wizard. In the Red Serpents squadron, Jenny was the only FNG not yet nicknamed. She wasn't the only Puerto Rican in the squadron, but she was the only woman, and though she wanted to believe gender had nothing to do with the delay, could she be sure? Story of her life. Story of the life of every woman aboard.

Jenny – just plain Jenny – was one of the first people on *Olympia* to know that a third man-overboard alert was in effect. She was on Vulture's Row, the narrow catwalk just above Primary Flight Control that provided, through a shimmery jet-fuel haze, a view of the flight deck from 150 feet up. Despite steely sheets of rain, the Opstempo was high, with jet blast deflectors rising, catapults firing, and all four elevators lifting aircraft from the hangar deck.

By chance, directly below Jenny's position were the tubes containing the flags that could be flown from the island's mast. She saw someone extract a red-and-yellow flag from its holder. Jenny felt the sternum prickle of knowing bad news before anyone else. She gripped the railing with both hands. It was always precarious and potentially dangerous to suddenly shut down flight ops.

It was loud as the Indy 500 down there, entirely reliant on hand signals because industrial earmuffs worn by much of the deck crew left them deaf to the ship's whistle. Jets in the process of taking off or landing would do so minus the required undivided attention, and when things went wrong on a flight deck, sometimes people died.

The whistle began to sound. Jenny leaned over the railing, rain instantly soaking her hair, and scanned the water around the four and a half acres of the boat, looking for the glow of a ChemLight, the signal of a sailor in the water. The deck was bordered by nets, making it hard to fall off, but anything was possible. Carriers were often called the most dangerous workplace in the world. A blistering-hot jet blast could toss a crew member into the shark-filled drink fifty feet down. Less exciting, you could be cleaning the outside of the bridge windows, forget to buckle your harness, and slip on wet steel.

Everything was wet. The weather had been brutal lately, something no one knew better than Jenny. Weather was why she was perched on Vulture's Row, drained and achy-eyed, instead of hitting her rack and grabbing sleep. Last night, mere hours ago, during a rain that had splotched down like tar, she'd had the worst bolting event of her life – in fact, the worst bolting event she'd ever heard of.

The details were too fresh and painful to relive, so she'd climbed the island's ladders, leaden in a sodden flight that clung to her like wet cement, her Red Serpents patch heavy as a manhole cover, and watched the start of the carrier's day. The first thing she'd seen was the flight crew performing a FOD walk. The foreign object debris walk was performed several times a day. Everyone on deck ceased work, formed a straight line, and crept forward in their steel-toed boots, lifting their black visors to scour the deck for any tiny bit of detritus that, if sucked into a jet's intakes, could destroy a $70 million aircraft in seconds – not to mention the comparatively low-priced mammal piloting the thing.

Jenny loved the FOD walk. It might be the only thing in the navy, besides flying, she truly enjoyed. It was the rare time when the dark stripes of pay grade and rating yielded to a sunnier spectrum. The color of each sailor's float coat designated the wearer's usual task, but during the FOD walk, those distinctions – as well as class, gender, and race – magically dissolved.

If only the FOD walk could go on forever. She had a hunch the minute she went belowdecks, her Red Serpents XO would issue a flight restriction for her bolting debacle, scrubbing her name from the sked. Restrictions like that could be death blows to a junior officer – JOs already got too few flight hours. She felt like a ball of twine unwinding. A couple of more restrictions and she wouldn't be doing shit work – she'd be in the brig.

Jenny had no idea how black marks like that might impact her military career. She felt sick, and the prospect of being humiliated in front of fellow Red Serpents made it all worse. Women were a seven-to-one minority on the boat, and plenty of men still felt that if you didn't have literal balls, you didn't belong. The possibility that she'd confirmed their doubts was crushing. She could feel tears emerging, stinging with jet fuel, and was glad the rain hid them. Crying – only further evidence of weakness.

She'd tried for so long to play the men's game, first as an SLJO (Shitty Little Jobs Officer) awaiting orders and then while earning her wings at basic, where she endured sex talk so explicit she could feel her blush in her toes. By the books, it was harassment. It was also a quick way to make a hundred enemies at once should she report it.

It was more than just words, of course. Men would position themselves behind her so she'd blunder into them, giving them an excuse for redirecting her with their hands. There were forced kisses, and gropings, and struggles in which she pushed men away with her wrists, trying not to escalate to actual hand-to-hand combat. Wrist Warfare, as she came to think of it, made her hate herself. No man would defend himself with his wrists.

When Jenny had first boarded *Olympia,* as what navy folks called a *nugget* – a rookie pilot on her first deployment – she'd expected better, but didn't get it. The squadron ready room was the biggest disappointment. She'd been looking forward to seeing it; ready rooms were famously free from many boat rules, and the Red Serpents' room had foosball, a popcorn machine, and other amenities.

It also had a so-called Sweetheart Wall, a pastiche of photos of wives and girlfriends back home. With awkward exception, these were sexy shots. Pilots without women back home contributed clippings from magazines: models in lingerie, bikinis, or bubbles. Jenny tried to be cool. She'd tried her whole life to be cool. But when her colleagues' eyes slid from the Sweetheart Wall to her, even if they meant nothing by it, her skin felt unworthy of her flight suit, and she found her arms lifting in anticipation of Wrist Warfare.

Now, after her bolting incident, she might as well stick a sexy selfie up there. She'd officially become what before she'd only suspected: unworthy. Soon everyone would know it. She'd put the deck crew in peril, no different from the unknown asshole perpetuating this third man-overboard false alarm. She pictured hurling herself off the catwalk, her body breaking into pieces – nuggets of a nugget – to be cleared during the next FOD walk.

The sixth and final blast of the ship's whistle made a tuning fork of Jenny's spine. Time to muster. That, at least, was something she wouldn't screw up. She deserved no call sign. She was Jenny, just plain Jenny from Detroit, and she might never see her name on a plane.

It Will Be Our Fault

Time: plus three. Time: plus four. Time: plus five. Convention was to stay to the port side of the ship when headed down or aft, to the starboard side when headed up or forward, and sailors kept to that even when sprinting. Their six months of intimacy with Big Mama showed in the instinctive ducking of heads beneath pipes, the skipping of feet over the lips of hatches. By time: plus six, mustered sailors were sounding off to officers with clipboard checklists. Two or three sailors were MIA, and their absence caused actual panic, reflected in XO Bryce Peet's updates.

Nishimura's muster station was the same navigation bridge where he spent most of his days, on the fourth floor of 'the island', the seven-story conning tower that lorded over the deck. He mustered in khakis twice as dark from the rain and preserved an outward calm as Peet's MIA list was whittled to two. *'The following individuals, report to the quarterdeck with your ID card. From Supply, ET2 Zarr; from Air, ADAN Altebrando.'*

It was unfitting for a navy officer, downright disgraceful, Nishimura knew, but he could not stop peeking at the TV in the chart room just aft of the nav bridge. He could tell by the faces of the navigation crew that they, too, were watching it.

'Time: plus seven,' the 1MC crackled, and Nishimura was stabbed with a sinking certainty that the timer would never stop, that eras of humanity would forever divide into pre-October 24 and

post-October 24. Time: plus a hundred, time: plus a thousand, time: plus a million.

ET2 Zarr was found, a head count error. ADAN Altebrando made it interesting, failing to show until time: plus ten, after which Peet took to the 1MC to swear vengeance upon the sailor perpetrating these hoaxes. Because Captain Page remained in sick bay and the officer of the deck had stepped out, Nishimura found himself senior officer present. The nav bridge crew looked to him guardedly, seemingly aware that a fudged man-overboard might not be the day's biggest problem.

Nishimura turned to his charts and began logging coordinates. Acknowledging an off-his-nut WWN anchor would speak poorly of him. He felt his face pinch into what sailors called *the glow* – a phrase he knew as well as *Saint Karl* and *Nishimura Delay*. An inebriated sailor in Australia had once described it to him. All forty-three years' worth of Nishimura's wrinkles, said the sailor, went poof, his face going as shiny as a cobra, the saint turned demon.

'Sir? Permission to speak?'

At the sound of the voice, the glow grew so tight Nishimura could feel his cheeks press against his gums. He believed it unprofessional to hold grudges, so for half a year, he'd fought back animosity.

Boatswain's Mate Tommy Henstrom. Nishimura would not accept having a rival, and if he did, he'd prefer it be someone above his pay grade, not some sniveling O-3. Yet when hitting the rack at night, he found himself stewing over Henstrom, a master of passive aggression.

No matter the simplicity of an order, Henstrom found a way to challenge it. Nishimura had been dying to write up Henstrom, maybe get him docked a stripe, but had balked at every chance. Henstrom was spoiled, arrogant, and recalcitrant, but stopped short of cut-and-dried violations. Plus, the O-3 would contest punishment all the way to the top, and Nishimura, so close to punching out his navy twenty, did not need that stress marring his exit.

'Permission granted,' he said.

Henstrom made a big show of wincing at his check computer.

'Shouldn't that last number be a nine, sir?'

'It is. Nine. For nineteen.'

'It screened out as an eight, sir. Eighteen.'

Nishimura checked his own screen as seven bells sounded softly – only 0700. The POD, plan of the day, had never gone tits up this fast, as Waylon Leneghan liked to say. Sure enough, Nishimura had keyed in the wrong digit. It was the first such mistake of his career, and of course it had happened in front of Henstrom. The glow burned; his face felt ready to melt. He looked up just in time to see Henstrom raise a mocking eyebrow at one of the lookouts, Diane Lang.

Henstrom mugged, pretending to protect Nishimura's feelings. 'I'm sure you're right, sir. Must be a glitch. You think it could be the same thing affecting *Hickenlooper*?'

Nishimura gave Henstrom a lengthy look, careful to rein it back from a glare. It was a Nishimura Delay, all right, though this time he used it to search himself. He had made an error. Why? Because he'd been distracted by the news on TV. Navy manuals could not state it outright, but a sailor's gut was their truest barometer.

He sleeved rain and sweat from his face and nodded at the TV.

'Turn that thing up,' he said.

Wilbert Legg, quartermaster of the watch, had it cranked full-volume in seconds.

'*Martial law,*' Chuck Corso said.

Nishimura saw his shiver replicated in every sailor on the bridge.

'That's what our reporters are witnessing,' Corso continued. 'National Guard, local law enforcement, even volunteer militias are responding to what is now a national emergency. When we talk to our reporters – those who are left – they keep quoting the same words from authorities. They're stuck in my head. I'm afraid they always will be. *Aggressive. Irrational. Unthinking. Noncommunica-tive.* These are the words being used to describe the ghouls.'

'Ghouls,' Nishimura heard himself repeat.

'That's the word he's been using,' Henstrom announced proudly. 'He says the ghouls are eating—'

'Henstrom, stop.' Lang sounded ill.

'Eating what?' Nishimura asked.

'This is gonna turn out like everything else, sir,' Lang said – no, Lang *pleaded.*

Nishimura knew what she meant. Stories trumped up by the news, screens cleaved into *Brady Bunch* grids of bickering partisans. The more salacious the content, the more viewers succumbed to their blackest instincts. Decades of cry-wolf exaggeration had numbed viewers to the potential for actual disaster, the same way the man-overboard flimflams were numbing *Olympia.* Chuck Corso's voice, however, had the dull, off-tune ring of the real thing.

'Government response is unfolding in a highly disorganized fash-ion. According to our reporters, a lot of this is because it isn't evident at all who's a quote-unquote normal person and who's a ghoul. To cut to the chase, ladies and gentlemen, what that means is citizens are being murdered by fellow citizens.'

'It'll be a big deal for a few hours, sir,' Lang insisted. 'That's all.'

Nishimura only had to look at Corso to know the opposite was true. He had a look Nishimura had seen on pilots rescued from the water after a cold shot – a takeoff that went straight into the ocean, directly into the path of ninety-five thousand tons of steel carrier. It was the betrayed, little-kid realization of how quickly the world's natural laws could turn against you.

'This. Is. Not. Who. We. Are.' Corso pounded his desk with each syllable. 'I'm begging those of you planning to take to the streets with guns. Please do not consider this a chance to . . . I don't even know how to say it in a way that doesn't use some code word to drive us further apart. Don't go out looking to *shoot* people, all right? If this turns into some kind of nationwide lynching, whatever happens next will not be the fault of the ghouls. You understand? It will be our fault. Ours alone.'

'Why doesn't the navy know about this?' Henstrom cried. 'If this is real, why hasn't anyone told us?'

'Captain Page is sick,' Nishimura said.

'Admiral Vo, then!'

'On the *Vindicator*.'

Henstrom spun around, displaying his disbelief to a larger audience.

'Why isn't he calling us, then? Why aren't we being briefed?'

'*Sir*,' Nishimura admonished, but his voice had gone softer than the ocean's wake. Seconds before he'd said *Vindicator*, Nishimura had looked toward the guided-missile cruiser. Smoke rose from the area of its radars.

'*Aggressive. Irrational. Unthinking. Noncommunicative*,' Corso repeated. 'All I'm saying is these words, being used to describe the ghouls, they sound familiar, don't they? A lot of people in the country have been called these things by people in power. The people with the gavels and the guns. And what advice have these same people given our reporters? Immobilization. Dismemberment. Fire. The strength of the ghouls, they're telling us, is in Their numbers. Where's *our* strength, though? Isn't our strength in numbers too?'

Corso wiped away sweat and looked at his palm as if seeing blood.

'We must not let ourselves slide into . . .' Corso hiccuped a sob. 'I don't know. Something worse.'

'It has to be biological warfare!' Henstrom proclaimed. 'Shouldn't we button up?'

'How could a biological agent be released everywhere, all at once?' Nishimura asked quietly. 'Something like that, Homeland Security would tell us. They'd—'

'No, they wouldn't! No one's telling us anything!'

'Boatswain's Mate Henstrom, you will address me as sir!'

Nishimura's roar sounded like the glow had split his face open. For the first time, the glow *felt* like a glow, an ember that had caught flame and was engulfing him in fire. His lips, curdled by that heat, retracted from snarling teeth. The hiss he heard was the shocked intake of breath from the rest of the crew.

'And if you cut me off one more time, O-3, I will have the master of arms chief up here, and you will sail into the San Diego shipyard in a cellblock. Is that clear, Boatswain's Mate?'

Henstrom, formerly as pale as everyone around him, went pink, then red, then kept going, past magenta into a deep, sweaty purple. His hands clenched into fists at his sides and his whole body bore down like a woman giving birth. The result was stillborn: silent fury with nowhere to go.

'*Yes, sir,*' Henstrom growled.

Nishimura turned away to hide what he feared was his own discoloration. First, he'd made a rare technical error. Second, even rarer, he'd raised his voice. What was wrong with him? Last night had been stormy and disrupted by some poor nugget's bolting incident, but he'd slept fine. He always did. There was zero chance this was a nightmare or the result of sleep deprivation. He steadied himself on the spoked steering wheel and gazed at the deck. Aircraft were once again taxiing, their pilots unafraid of the storm.

He'd been assigned to the *Stennis,* CVN-74, when 9/11 happened, and would never forget the sensation of hurtling for the Arabian Sea. Instructions like that had to be coming soon. If Chuck Corso had it right, America was under attack, and Nishimura expected to see Captain Page rising from sick bay in this moment of need, appearing at the nav bridge door to bellow, *Thirty knots!*

It did not happen, though; it kept not happening. Without direction from Homeland Security, CINCPAC, Page, or Vo, Nishimura had no choice but to ride the rules, align with guidelines, and get those Nishimura Delays going. He cleared his throat. He did not like the crackle in his voice, but he spoke loudly for only the second time in his career. He had to, for his crew, for his country.

'Lang, eyes up – I want to see CTOLs out there, OK-3s and nothing but! Someone open a line to CATCC! Henstrom, to the lee – we want this flattop steady as she goes! What do you think, Quartermaster? Think you can rouse the OOD? Maybe we'll get lucky and he's just in the head, you think?'

Not bad, Nishimura thought. *I sound pretty good.*

He snapped up his binoculars to study the horizon, but what he saw in his mind's eye was Larry's face, the sadness his husband no longer hid when Nishimura set off on a deployment. His children's faces came next, ranging from the anguish of his youngest, Bea, to the cold contempt of his oldest, Atsuko, whose heart, like Nishimura's, was rapidly hardening. To be a better Karl Nishimura, he had to get through this. He had to get home to Buffalo. He would, no question, unless ghouls were already aboard, which was, of course, impossible.

Love Was the Ocean

At 1115 Hawaii-Aleutian time, yeoman seaman apprentice Jean Cobb and steelworker Edmund 'Scud' Blakey – the former skipping out on electronics department clerical work, the latter abandoning his floor swabbing – were in the throes of sexual intercourse in an out-of-service men's lavatory to the port side of the forward winch room. Jean was naked from the waist down, her shoes, socks, slacks, and underwear piled beneath a towel dispenser. Scud had not removed his shoes; his slacks and underwear were gathered about his ankles, his belt buckle chiming with each buck of his hips.

The act was in flagrant violation of a stringently policed rule: no romantic or physical relationships on the boat. An affair gone wrong in a carrier's tight confinement could be explosive and therefore dangerous. Get caught, and you could be docked pay, even robbed of stripes. Officers never shut up about it, and lest you forget, laminated signs were posted everywhere, including right outside this very lavatory: ANY DISPLAY OF AFFECTION BETWEEN SHIPMATES WHILE ON BOARD THE SHIP IS STRICTLY PROHIBITED.

Trysts happened anyway, of course they did, in linen closets and dry-good cupboards, rendezvous dubbed *red-light specials* for the scarlet lighting that suffused the corridors at night. The navy could restrict anything except love – or so swore Scud every time he and Jean had sex, to her gasped agreement. If the navy was *Olympia*, love was the ocean, incalculably more powerful, capable of swallowing whole militaries, entire civilizations.

Scud and Jean had known each other only for the duration of their deployment, but when you found the half of you missing all your life, you knew it. They tumbled into what they saw as Romeo and Juliet roles, casting their illicit love against both navy guidelines and their respective families, both of whom would denounce it. An affair illegally conducted aboard a navy ship? They would be disowned.

The yeoman and the steelworker passed each other pining, tragic notes in the halls. They stole quick, panting sex acts whenever they could. They whispered past sweaty locks of hair how they'd rather be dishonorably discharged, face a court-martial, or walk the plank than deny their love. With a penknife Scud sterilized with a lighter, they carved each other's names into their upper arms, licked off the other's blood, and kissed so that the blood washed back and forth, a salty oath.

Scud tried to slide his hands up under Jean's shirt, but the fabric was too tight across her belly. Four months ago, one of their red-light specials had resulted in pregnancy; the two of them reveled in the wrath it would provoke in their families. Jean tore her shirt open, indifferent to popped buttons, because what did dress infractions matter anymore? As Scud's coarse steelworker palms slid over her soft belly, she pictured his cock inside her, so near to their baby, and felt fulfilled, filled in two ways. If this was how the three of them had to die, she did not believe she could have imagined it better.

Jean and Scud had been among the first aboard Big Mama to see Chuck Corso's broadcast, which had been the final push toward a decision they'd both felt coming. They made synchronous decisions to leave their posts and meet at their current secret spot, where they gasped their plans into each other's mouths. It was torture to part ways for the single hour they gave themselves to gather the required items.

Scud's task was the trickier of the two. One of the ship's senior petty officers had recently been diagnosed with Parkinson's and was to disembark at San Diego to meet his fate. The ship's sick bay had been stocked with Norflex, a sedative that reduced spasms and quieted jerking nerves. According to Scud's research, an overdose would result in certain death. Here his TAD status came in handy; sick bay needed mopping too, and today, no one was keeping track of which nonrate was coming or going. Lifting the Norflex was easy.

On his way back to the lavatory, Scud emptied his coffers for the most exotic item the ship store carried: an engagement ring.

Jean, concealing her popped buttons, fetched the bottle of pineapple-distilled whiskey she'd picked up in Waipahu. Getting caught with alcohol could get you two months at half pay, but many sailors (and pretty much all the pilots) had a stash.

They reconvened. Scud put the ring on Jean's finger. She cried. They drank, arranged Norflex ampules, and drank, and stripped, and drank, and fucked, and filled syringes, and fucked, and drank, sloppily now for courage, lips and necks stinging with whiskey. Jean sucked it from Scud's chest, and Scud licked it from the cheap metal of Jean's ring.

Jean injected a full syringe of Norflex into Scud's beautiful, rounded shoulder. Scud injected an equal amount into Jean's long, smooth thigh.

Neither reached climax. Neither minded. A climax of a different sort was upon them. The Norflex in their veins felt a lot like the pineapple-distilled whiskey down their throats. Their muscles relaxed. Scud's erection softened like a relieved sigh. Jean's legs folded beneath her into a cozy pile. They ended up less intertwined than they did intermixed, one body with three heartbeats, each growing fainter.

'Did you feel that?' Jean slurred.

'Was that . . . ?' Scud trailed off.

The baby's first kick, the birth of death.

Scud, Jean, and their child merged, the lovers whispering in awe how unique their love was across history, the same fallacy of a billion true loves before them, all of whom believed their copulation mattered more than that of a chimp, or dog, or rat. Scud and Jean died certain their rebellious deaths would show the world a thing or two. But it was the world that would show them. Their deaths would not be beautiful but ugly, not brief but protracted, and nothing like they'd expected.

The Golems

Jenny stared at her shoes. They were brown. This was traditional. Aviators were even called *Brown Shoes,* a designation elevating them from the *Black Shoes* of the rest of the navy. She often noticed sailors glance at her shoes upon meeting her, after which they adjusted their level of respect. A little thing, but it used to make Jenny feel good. Now her brown shoes mocked her. She, FNG, did not deserve them. She, FNG, ought to be forced to do FOD walks barefoot across the flight deck's asphalt-coated steel, until her feet were neither brown nor black but red with penitent blood.

WHANG! WHOOSH!

Despite the takeoffs overhead, Jenny heard the click of the chapel's closet door opening. She looked up from her brown shoes to see Father Bill Koppenborg emerge. He spotted her in her usual corner and approached with his usual placid smile. Instantly, Jenny felt a notch improved. Father Bill was a good man, she thought, one of the few aboard this ship. How lucky she felt to have found him.

'Apologies for my tardiness,' he said, 'My Sweet.'

Jenny figured many women would take umbrage at the pet name, but *la bomboncito* was what her grandpa used to call her. Father Bill's gait was less sprightly today; he was favoring his right leg. As usual, he combined camouflage slacks with a beige turtleneck sweatshirt reading, in block letters, CVN-68x CHAPLAIN. The ensemble said *old man* in a way that Jenny found endearing.

He took hold of the metal folding chair opposite her and turned it in her direction, wincing as he lowered himself. He sat so close their knees touched. This was normal; Jenny assumed he was hard of hearing. She folded her hands and bowed her head; Father Bill always began the same way.

'Let's have us a little prayer,' he said.

WHANG! WHOOSH!

'O Lord, in the name of your only son, Jesus, bless the war in Afghanistan, O Lord, the war in Iraq, O Lord, the war in Syria, O Lord, the war in Yemen, O Lord, the war in Somalia, O Lord, the war in Libya, O Lord, the war in Niger, O Lord, the war on terrorism, O Lord. Keep our soldiers safe, O Lord, and help them, wherever in your great world they are, to shoot straight. Accept our praise and worship. Amen.'

'Amen,' Jenny agreed, though it was lost in the whang and whoosh.

Father Bill laced his hands over a knee.

'Have you been able to reach your parents and sisters since last we spoke?'

'No, Father,' she said. 'I got through twice, but the call dropped both times.'

'Our phones are not blessed,' he conceded. 'You must still be feeling lonely, then. How are you coping?'

WHANG! WHOOSH!

This one-on-one meeting, like all of them, had been scheduled days in advance. The fact that it was happening only hours after her bolting catastrophe had to be a sign, didn't it? Here was a chance to discuss the event while it was still fresh and drain it of demonic force. Father Bill, she knew, would advocate confessing all of it. His interest in every detail of her life never failed to flatter.

Surrounded by a vast ocean, face-to-face with one's cosmic insignificance, Jenny knew it was easy to drift toward religion. Yet here she was, in their twenty-fifth meeting, still unable to believe in Father Bill's God no matter how badly she wanted to. It was the single truth she didn't feel comfortable sharing with the priest. Wasn't *that* a sign too?

'How am I coping,' she pondered. 'Hmm. NyQuil, I guess.'

'Oh, My Sweet, no,' Father Bill soothed. 'We're only days from home. Focus on that. Surely there are things at home that will comfort you. The singing of birds? The laughter of children? Being woken up too early by people shoveling their sidewalk? God is everywhere. Your family, at least?'

Jenny tried to picture Jorge and Lorena Pagán looking happy, but could only see her father's disappointed scowl and her mother's mascara-stained cheeks upon hearing of her flight restriction. After religious consultation, she'd need to appear in the Red Serpents ready room, where degradation far worse than the Sweetheart Wall would be waiting. Maybe she'd never leave this chapel. Maybe she'd stay here with Father Bill, where it was safe.

Father Bill searched her face. 'Won't they be there to—'

WHANG! WHOOSH!

'—to meet you in San Diego?'

Jenny knew the shipyard reunion was the biggest of deals. Right now, elsewhere in the ship, hundreds of sailors were completing classes on how to readjust to civilian lives. Some had babies they'd never met. Some needed to learn not to criticize their girlfriends' weight gain or new hairstyles. Like prom or graduation, it was impossible to avoid obsessing over the return, an event featured in far too many movies. The horsey clop of high heels over concrete, the jangle of a sailor's dropped bag, the smushing together of flesh, the mutual devouring.

'No, they won't be there,' she said. 'Too expensive. I won't see them till I'm back in Detroit.'

If I get back, she added to herself, which both startled and stirred her. She was at the end of something, there was no doubting it. Not the end she'd wanted either: her call sign on a plane.

'Pray on it,' Father Bill urged.

'I'll try,' she said.

'I know praying is hard for you. Do you still have your Sailor's Creed? I like your idea of repeating it, as a way to get used to prayer. Tell it to God. He will understand and will, in his own way, respond.'

Jenny had picked up the Sailor's Creed in the ship's store, a small, glossy poster she'd taped to the wall beside her rack. When she couldn't sleep after general lights-out, she'd point her penlight at the creed and recite the parts she liked, her whisper blending into snores, sheet scuffles, and hissing pipes.

I represent the fighting spirit of the Navy.

But where had that spirit flown off to?

I will obey the orders of those appointed over me.

But was it God who gave the ultimate orders?

I am a United States Sailor.

These six words, at least, were demonstrably true, and she often repeated them until she somersaulted into sleep.

Once, Father Bill had asked all sorts of odd questions about how she slept. Was it hot in her rack? Of course, she'd said, all the boat's lower levels were hot. What did she wear when sleeping? Shirt and underwear, she'd laughed, same as everyone. As they'd talked, he'd looked *hungry.* Jenny told herself he probably *was* hungry. Hungry to understand the minds and hearts of sailors in need.

Father Bill's desire to help never failed to impress Jenny. She owed him her confidence.

WHANG! WHOOSH!

'I had . . . Last night . . . I was flying and I had a—'

Father Bill nodded. 'I know.'

If she had a true sailor's control of her behavior, she would have stopped herself from covering her face with her hands – another fragile, feminine gesture. Of course Father Bill knew. By now, everyone on *Olympia* knew.

'Speak from the heart,' Father Bill encouraged. 'God is here, in this room, on this boat, in this ocean. He wants to know you, soul and body.'

Haltingly, Jennifer Angelys Pagán spoke. Her recollection of last night already had the firecracker clarity of enduring trauma.

At 1654, Jenny had strapped into an F-18, one stenciled, of course, with someone else's call sign. At 1705, she finished taxiing to Catapult 3. Raindrops hit her windshield with the weight of rodents, but preflight checks were A-OK. She gave the barely visible ground crew the thumbs-up. She could not see fifty feet ahead; the storm inside her body matched the roar and whistle. *I am a United States Sailor,* she told herself. The JBDs came up, the catapult pistoned, and she went from 0 to 130 miles per hour in two seconds. Her internal organs slammed to the back of her torso. Flight-deck lights whizzed by. The ocean came at her with black-froth tentacles. The F-18 bobbed upward through rain as clattering as coins.

After ninety-five minutes in roughneck skies, it was her turn to approach for landing: lower gear, tailhook, and flaps, tune to LSO frequency, drop to eight hundred feet. Nothing in the navy was more perilous than bringing a plane down on the surface of a rollicking carrier with sufficient finesse to snag the plane's tailhook onto one of four arresting wires.

Missing all four cables was called a *bolter* – and that was what happened on Jenny's first approach. The instant her wheels hit deck, she knew she'd overshot, so she punched the engines, soaring back up into the storm. Bolting was excusable during this kind of tempest, but it wasn't the g-forces that stole Jenny's breath. It was the realization that, just like that, the instant the F-18's tires made their rubbery gobble against the deck, she'd lost her nerve. The dashboard lights were carnivalesque, cycling past her like a carousel.

She got back into the aerial queue. She approached again at 1842 and bolted again. She bolted a third time at 1920 and a fourth time at

1948. By then, she was one of only three jets in the air and so low on fuel that CAG Ellen Truswell had to launch a Super Hornet to perform a harrowing, probe-and-drogue refueling of Jenny's jet, midair in the pummeling vortex. Now the Super Hornet, too, had to land – another life added to Jenny's tab. She ran over the eject protocol and imagined the cold salt of black water slapping her face.

I am a United States Sailor, she told herself.

Jenny would bolt four more times – eight times total – before, at 2207, she rode her stick just high enough to slip above the ship's stern and hook the deck's first wire. The F-18 slung to a halt; the harness crushed her torso. Instantly, her helmet fogged with sweat and tears and echoed with hyperventilation. Deck crew were at her window before she could compose herself, helping her unstrap and aiding her down the ladder. Her legs felt filleted of bone, and she crumpled to the wet asphalt. Men slung her limp arms over their shoulders and dragged her to the island. No jets were left to make noise, so she thanked the storm for covering her sobs.

Even now, more sobs waited in her lungs; only the heaviness of the flight suit she still wore kept them in. But Father Bill was perceptive, his wrinkle-wadded eyes more piercing than those of the boat's bright-eyed young sailors.

'You fear you put other sailors in harm's way,' he concluded.

He'd sliced to the marrow. Jenny nodded, watching her shoes, wondering if falling tears might darken the proud brown leather to pedestrian black.

'Whoever's throwing ChemLights into the water.' Jenny sniffled and wiped her nose. 'I'm no better than he is.'

She didn't think she'd meet another person's eyes ever again. But she felt a pinching sensation and found Father Bill's hand was on her knee. His bony grip hurt, but she knew he meant the squeeze to comfort.

'You *are* better than he is,' he whispered. 'Because you're *here.*

Look around you. You're in God's house. That's all he wants. We can systematize forgiveness if you want. Some Hail Marys and so forth. But by speaking here, in this humble place of worship, you're already doing the asking.'

'But will he . . . forgive someone who doesn't even . . . who's not sure . . .'

'If she believes in him?' Father Bill's hand moved to just above her knee and squeezed again. 'Belief is a funny thing, My Sweet. Some who have it in excess only use it in self-serving ways. Others might believe one single time in their life, but it's the time that makes all the difference. It reminds me of the Jewish legend of the golem. Do you know it?'

She could not hold his tender gaze for more than an instant; Jenny found herself looking at his footwear – black, rubber-soled boots, thick gray socks.

'A golem is a monster of sorts, usually made of clay. It's illuminated with life by a creator who rarely comprehends the sort of beast he has unleashed. A colleague of mine, a rabbi, said he knew an old Jew who swore he'd shaped a golem from the mud and blood of a World War II battlefield, a golem that had saved his battalion. This rabbi believed it. He believed that golems have been created all through history, supposedly to protect Their creators, but actually to protect the Earth itself. Why else were They so easy to create? The rabbi swore that one day, golems would turn on Their creators, learn how to build more of Their own kind, and use Their overwhelming numbers to cleanse the Earth of evil.'

A dark drop of red expanded on one of Father Bill's gray socks. Blood? Jenny's eyes traced upward to the leg he had been favoring.

'Nonsense, of course,' he continued. 'But revealing. When it comes to belief, it is the quality, not the quantity.'

'Father.' Jenny's voice cracked. 'You're bleeding.'

Father Bill did not look. Instead, he grinned, a wide mouthful of yellow teeth, and gripped her thigh so tightly she thought the tips of his fingers might spear through her flight suit. He leaned in, and she thought she smelled blood on his breath.

'Let all mortal flesh keep silence,' he shushed.

Jenny valued and trusted this man. Yet she now heard, as clarion as *Olympia*'s man-overboard whistles, the internal alert all women knew. She'd misjudged something. She wasn't safe. She felt her elbows bend and pale arms rotate, mobilizing for Wrist Warfare.

Before she could begin to fight, both she and Father Bill were gripped by the loudest alarm of all – the alarm of silence. On a carrier, you quit hearing the whang and whoosh of flight ops the same way you quit hearing your pulse and breath. It was the middle of the afternoon on a day with a busy flight sked, and the stretch of flight-deck quiet lasted one second too long. Jenny gasped and felt faint, as if she truly had no breath or pulse, dead without having noticed.

You Are Hungry

You are hungry. You wake up. In that order.

This hunger is different from any you knew before. This hunger is a lack. Something has been taken from you. You do not know what. This hunger is everywhere. Hunger, the fist. Hunger, the bones. Hunger, the flesh. Hunger, the brain. Hunger, in all the between places. It is your reason for waking up. It is the reason you move. It is the reason.

You look. Your eyesight is poor. There is a body next to yours. You smell it. It smells strong. You have a faint recollection of booze. You recognize the body. It used to be called Jean Cobb. Was Jean Cobb important? You do not know. Jean Cobb called you Scud. You remember this now. Here is the curious thing. Jean Cobb is no longer Jean Cobb. She is you. You are also you. You feel the hunger in both of you. You feel the hunger between both of you. The hunger is a thing that stretches outward. Feels around for more yous. But finds nothing. Not yet. Only the Scud-you and the Jean-you. Only

You experiment. Your neck works. Your fingers work. Your limbs work. You disentangle from Jean-you. You stand. You stagger. But

your foot knows what to do. It kicks out, saves you from collapse. This is because your foot is hungry too. Where are you going? You don't need to know, not all of you. Your body is a hound's nose, trailing a scent it cannot help but pursue. You will know you have reached your goal when you reach the goal. You already have a sense of it. Nourishment to fill the void. To replace what was taken.

You walk on unstable legs. Your muscles cramp. You walk into a wall. The thudding sound is far away. You hear as poorly as you see. You turn. You walk in a different direction. You hit another wall. Turn again. Your eyes see a door. A memory comes with it. Doors are passageways. You think of Jean-you on the floor and feel a desire to stay with it. The feeling is close to hunger. But hunger overrides. You move your legs and hit the door belly-first.

The door does not open. This displeases you. A sound comes out of you. It is lionlike, a roar. You are surprised by it. You did not know you could make sounds. You try to make another sound. You are unhappy with it. You want the first sound again, the stronger one. It is a preference. Preferences are more important than you know. You are no longer Scud, but you are closer to Scud than a mouse or insect. You try again for the roar. Closer this time, a growl.

You are learning.

The door yawns open under your hands. You shuffle forward, your weight drawing the door wider. Abruptly, you are free of its opposition, in a new place. It is a narrow, gray, windowless corridor. Nothing but walls. You are developing another preference. Walls: you do not like them. You point yourself at a distant point where the walls appear to end.

Before you can head off, a noise comes from inside the room you left. It is the Jean-you. Jean-you has risen like Scud-you has risen. The Scud-you would like to see Jean-you. You turn back to the door and push it with your hands again. But pushing this side does no good. There is a thing, a handle. You do not recall how it works. You make a sound. This time it is the roar you want.

There is nothing to be done. You cannot reach Jean-you. No longer valid, the idea winks out. Hunger, hunger. You turn back to the hallway and begin walking. Your first steps are awkward. Your body pitches and slants. You get better at it. You establish a functional lope. You learn that you have no sense of time. When you get to the hallway's termination point, you do not know or care if the walk took an instant or eternity.

You discover the hallway turns. So you turn. You cannot hear well, but sounds surround you. *Hiss, clank, rattle, chug, trill, bang, creak, ping, honk, ding, beep, whang, hum, boom, glug, snap, whoosh, purr, clink, zing.* Also an echoing clop. Also a burbling murmur. You know what these sounds are. Walking, talking. The hunger spikes. These sounds are not produced by you. But they could become you. You go toward them.

You do not know fluid has begun to run from your mouth. You do not know it is a cocktail of livid plasma, dead cells, and blackened bits of arterial plaque. You do not know it is thickening from waste matter you can no longer excrete. You cannot taste this fluid because it tastes like you. What you want has a different taste.

You see them. Three fast-moving ones, coming into view. Hunger, hunger. They pass through pockets of light. Each second they spend in the dark, you mourn their disappearance. Each second in the light, you feel saliva heavying your chest hair. The fast-moving ones reach you in seconds. Hunger, hunger, hunger. They stop a few feet away. You cannot tell them apart. Their faces share the same expression. Their uniforms are the same. Only the insignia on their shoulders is different.

You look down at your own shoulder. You have an insignia too. You do not understand it designates you as a former fast-moving one. Yet you feel oddly about it. If you knew the word *wistful,* that would be the word to use. There was a life that went with that insignia. You have the sense parts of that life were good. You watch brown strands of your saliva creep over the insignia. That life is gone. Life is gone. That is okay. Back then, there was only one you. How unfortunate. Now there can be so many more.

The fast-moving one in front has check marks on his sleeve. He opens his mouth. You smell the salt of his lips, the brine of his tongue. He makes delicious, moist sounds that make your flesh sing. Certain words are recognizable.

muck muck muck SICK muck muck muck DRUNK muck muck muck SALUTE muck muck SALUTE muck SALUTE muck GOD-DAMN IT muck INSUBORDINATE muck

The fast-moving one's face reddens. All that hot, salty blood right under the surface. Your hunger ignites. You reach for him with both hands. He slaps one aside, but the other grabs his shirt. You know how to grab. The fast-moving one takes hold of your wrist. He shouts in alarm. You bow your upper body. Your feet trip. Your head dives at his head. You open your mouth. Your mouth is all that matters. You fall onto him. Your teeth sink into the soft bulb of his chin and strike bone.

The fast-moving one screams.

Your bottom jaw snaps onto the underside of his chin. You have lost your footing. You hang from his face by your teeth. You hear flesh tear from his chin. Hot blood pours into your cold mouth. Hunger, hunger, hunger. Your jaws gnash. Your tongue wants more. Your tongue extends to lick exposed bone. Your tongue stretches so hard you feel it rip from your mouth. The fast-moving one is shoving you away. The skin of his chin is stretching. You remember melted cheese. It is like that, just as salty.

The other two fast-moving ones grab and pull you. You want to bite them too. You wrench your neck. The skin rips off the first one's chin. As you fall, you catch the second fast-moving one's arm and pull him to the floor. The floor is cold. Blood, so hot, steams on it. You can smell the infection. It is the infection of life. You want to lap it up, but the fallen one is below you and that is even better. He blocks you with his forearm. You bite his wrist and pull from it a hot mouthful. You can feel the severed veins twitch and spurt along your tongue.

The fast-moving ones now arriving are beyond your ability to count. They try to stop you. You do not mind. They are made from meat. Fingers to bite. Hands to chomp. Legs to scratch. You are delirious with appetite. The fast-moving ones fall and flop and make silly noises. You can smell yourself in their newly changing blood. It is

you you you you you you you you
you you you you youyou you you

The fast-moving ones are all over you now. They may destroy you. You are not worried. You will live on in these other yous. One small speck of you, formerly known as Scud, does miss the you formerly called Jean Cobb, but you have a sense that Scud-you and Jean-you will reunite as the yous multiply. This is the end. It is also the beginning.

Mommy's Boy

Two hours before Jennifer Angelys Pagán's alarm over Lieutenant Commander William Koppenborg's squeezing fingers was cut short by flight-deck silence, Seaman Recruit E-1 Matthew Sears, Culinary Specialist, was derelict for duty. Matt was scheduled to work soup and chili at the largest of Big Mama's six crew galleys on second deck at 1400; carrier food service began at 0600 reveille and ended with midnight rations, or midrats. Now it was 1425 and Matt was really going to get it. His superior, Warrant Officer Lance Fiederling, was a shouter to whom no reality-TV restaurant chef could compare.

This tardiness followed two others. Five weeks ago, Matt had been physically restrained by two asshole gunner's mates. He'd been making a weepy phone call to his mother, who he called *Mommy,* and the gunner's mates had overheard. They sat on his chest until he was five minutes late, goading Mommy's Boy to fight back, which he'd refused to do. This morning, they'd done it again, sitting on his chest for fifteen minutes. There wasn't a thing Matt could do about it except gimp away after they grew bored and accept he was about to have Lance Fiederling's furious spittle all over his face.

Matt Sears ran – then walked when encountering officers – then ran again. His vision careened like he was drunk. His balance was off; he listed portside. He whacked a shoulder on a hatch. He thought he felt, like a worm in his belly, the onset of nausea. Just what he needed. He knew what Mommy would say: *Stay in bed, baby.* He also knew what Father, a former rear admiral, would say: *You show up for duty unless you're dying, sailor, and even then, you ask permission.*

Was it the flu? He recalled the flu outbreak in the third month of deployment; the docs vaccinated all five thousand sailors in three days. It sure felt like the flu. His head and chest were brick heavy, a funky sludge coated his throat, and he was cold despite the under-deck heat. Mommy would call it psychosomatic. He was a nervous kid, and the whole boat was on edge after last night's storm, the bolt-ing incident, the third man-overboard alert, and deployment's approaching end.

Maybe his body was reacting to what he'd just seen outside the winch room: a heap of men wrestling a naked nutcase. Meltdowns like this happened more often than the navy admitted; people really did go mad at sea. Matt had heard stories. Guys spreading shit all over their racks. Bludgeoning bombs with wrenches. Maybe even tossing ChemLights into the water.

Picking a moment to slip past the fray, he flattened himself to the wall and crept along. The naked man at the bottom of the heap con-vulsed, causing a sailor landslide, and Matt felt fingers, shockingly cold, blindly snatch for his hand. As Matt pulled away, the man's fingernails clawed across the back of Matt's hand. Matt stumbled out of reach, his shoes smacking through underfoot blood.

He kept going, he had to, and didn't examine his hand until he was under the brighter lights of a ladder. Three scratches welled blood. Self-pity overwhelmed him. The scratches hurt, he was start-ing to feel sick, and he wanted to be home – he was Mommy's Boy, just like the gunner's mates said. He clamped his opposite hand over the scratches to staunch the blood until he began to climb the ladder. A carrier was an injury factory; this was not even the worst wound he'd taken this month.

Fiederling's bawling out was one for the books. But by the time oratory truly started soaring, Matt couldn't pay attention. He felt worse. Awful, actually. Oily bullets of sweat were slaloming down his face, through Fiederling's spit. The inside of his throat was so feverous he pictured it crimson. His intestines cramped, but there was no rectal urgency. Whatever was festering inside was just sitting there.

Matt staggered to the pantry. Fluorescents glared off tins of Victory Garden Pork and Beans, Country Sausage Gravy. *Focus on the job,* he told himself. Feeding *Olympia* was a gargantuan task. Fiederling's army included one hundred cooks and two hundred attendants. They served fifteen thousand meals a day. Matt alone might serve soup and chili to several hundred before the day's dinner rush even began.

He happened upon the latex-glove dispenser. Yes, best to be safe. The two rubbery snaps over his hands invigorated him like slaps to the face. He didn't need Mommy. He was going to be all right. He opened and shut his eyes several times, granulating the crust forming along his eyelids.

There it was. The soup line. A long casket of contoured steel. Sneeze guards recently wiped. Because Matt was late, the soups were already waiting, containers resting in hot wells set to 140 degrees. He shambled to the open station. The CS who had been handling his portion of work glared at him.

When the CS's expression changed to one of concern, Matt figured he must look pretty bad. He turned away and studied the soups. The vat of tomato blurred into the vat of chicken and rice. Gradually, he became aware that a sailor was waiting. Matt reached for the ladle, which rattled away from him. He blamed the latex gloves; he couldn't feel anything. He reached for the ladle a second time and felt a kind of awe as he successfully lifted it.

He did not, however, successfully serve the soup. The ladle cracked down on the sailor's bowl, splashing all over. The sailor shouted and cursed and said unkind things about Matt, but Matt was not listening. His hearing had deadened as if he'd strapped on flight-deck earmuffs. Other senses were dimming too. He could barely smell the 'bug juice', the navy's bright-red, sugar-bomb take on Kool-Aid. He could barely see two feet in front of him. Despite all this, he no longer felt sick, or not exactly; he'd gone past ill to a prickling numbness. Leaving the galley per Mommy's advice was no longer an option.

He'd show Fiederling. He'd show Father. He chased after the ladle with dumb fingers. This time, he saw the problem. The three gashes on the back of his hand were still bleeding. In fact, blood had inflated his latex glove like a full condom.

Slowly, he grasped the handle of the ladle. As he curled each finger into place, the glossy balloon of blood swelled larger. Matt was transfixed. He wondered how long the glove would hold. He folded the fourth finger. The latex tumor wobbled. He pictured Mommy, weeping, telling him he never should have enlisted. He pictured Father, snorting over his mustache, declaring any job worth starting was worth finishing.

Matt bent his thumb around the ladle. The latex bubble burst. Dark blood shot into the tomato soup and sank beneath the surface like a meatball. Matt blinked, felt his eyelashes gum together. Maybe he should use the ladle to fish out the blood. But that would take so much effort, and he was so tired.

'Mommy's Boy, wake up!'

Matt looked up. Everything was a ghostly white, as if a skim of milk had seeped over his eyeballs. He nonetheless recognized the gunner's mates who'd pinned him down.

'You gonna soup us or what, Mommy's Boy?'

Matt felt nothing but the relieving tingle of blood discharging into the soup. The first gunner's mate snorted, snatched the ladle away from Matt, and dipped himself a big serving. He did not seem to notice the darker, filmier bits floating amid the tomato purée. Matt squinted. The last thing he saw, behind the gunner's mates, was a line thirty or forty sailors deep. He knew from experience that many of them would want delicious tomato soup, the most comforting chow they'd find on this wet, stressful day.

On this carrier, Matt Sears was a carrier too. He died standing up, knees locked, forehead pressed to the sneeze guard. His last thought was of the clear cups of red bug juice on everyone's trays. To Matt's milky eyes, it looked thick and salty, and he wanted to drink it, and find more of it, wherever he could. Earlier, he'd thought the boat was well stocked for feeding, but he'd had no idea.

Patterns

Karl Nishimura registered the flight-deck stoppage the same moment as Jennifer Angelys Pagán. He would have been aware of it first if he hadn't ill-timed his long trip to the head. It had been a hell of a day, and the coffee had taken its toll. He was reaching for the navy's patented brand of toilet paper, formulated from a blend of sandpaper and steel wool, when the spring-loaded, chrome-colored paper holder quit rattling and the basin water beneath him quit sloshing.

All he could hear was the boat's air cycling and electrical hum. Only between 2130 and 0600 were such functions audible. Of all the bad things that had happened in the past sixteen hours – the strike-force irregularities, Chuck Corso's ghouls, dead air from navy brass – this was the worst. It was the sound of surrender.

He wiped like a beast (his recurrent hemorrhoids, a side effect of the glow, did not appreciate this) and threw together his uniform before charging past a chart room still buzzing with Corso's grim narration. The state of the nav bridge horrified him. Henstrom, Lang, Legg, and the others had plastered themselves against the wraparound windows to ogle the flight deck, as if it wasn't something they saw all day, every day.

Nishimura joined them and confirmed it: no one had ever seen a flight deck like this.

It was navy cliché that a carrier's flight deck in motion operated like a ballroom dance. On crystalline mornings, when the sun at the stern made crinkled red foil of ocean swells and turned both runways into long, blinding bars of gold, the deck became a stage. Groups of dancers entered, left or right or center, attired in colors appreciable from the cheap seats: royal blue for aircraft handlers and drivers; blood red for ordnance and crash crews; canary yellow for plane directors; and so on. Their moves were as precise as a bourrée or fouetté: the dexterous setting of catapults, the nimble fastening of tow bars, the LSO's hand signals as graceful as any port de bras. It was an elite company; a misstep on this stage ended not a corps de ballet career but a human life.

Nishimura saw not one element awry or even two. Below were *two dozen* sailors who did not belong, spreading across the rain-roiled deck without heed of safety protocols. The intrusion was as unthinkable as theatergoers climbing the stage.

Every carrier had a pass-down log, an informal daily planner listing all of the day's expected visitors – military VIPs, foreign dignitaries, politicians. Nishimura thought to request it, to ascertain the identity of these lummox tourists. Except They couldn't be visitors; They wore navy uniforms. Even from his height, Nishimura saw the dress-code violations of loose shirttails and stained fabric. It did not matter if They were hull technicians or nuclear machinist's mates who never saw the sun, They knew better than to go near the runways.

One man was within several feet of an EA-18G Growler about to take off. Nishimura held his breath as the Growler was shot from Catapult 1. It sliced through the rain and, silently to all those watching, lopped off the man's head with the end of its forty-four-foot wingspan.

It was the single worst thing Nishimura had ever seen. A beheading. Aboard USS *Olympia*. Everyone in the world would know about it in hours. It might take slightly longer for one of the internet's death sites to mystically acquire security video. The six months of Big Mama's last deployment, if not her entire honorable career, would be a footnote to this accident. Nishimura saw the black jet of blood and the head's casual volleyball roll.

Navy soldiers were not given to gasping, but every person on the nav bridge drew in a screech of air.

'Halloween,' Lang sputtered. 'Master Chief, could it be Halloween?'

Nishimura's hope surged as if by injection. He knew what Lang meant. Halloween was seven days off, making this the right time for pranks. Petty officers showing up for inspection dressed as Power Rangers. XO Peet broadcasting in his soberest voice the news of a sea monster attack, all hands on deck. But those pranks were okayed by Captain Page. Those pranks were safe. Sending sailors onto a working flight deck meant certain death.

Catapult 2 shot a C-2A Greyhound into the sky, the force of its jets tumbling an intruder one hundred feet, onto Elevator #2. The man wore neither float coat nor cranial; he ought to be down for the count. Instead, he got up, hobbling, one leg contorted sideways at the knee. His white uniform was razed by an asphalt streak that had split open his shirt as well as the flesh beneath it.

He walked back onto the deck.

'It's exactly what I said!' Henstrom cried, adding a hasty, 'Sir! It has to be a biologic agent! That's why we need to button up! What if the agent gets up here, sir?'

Nishimura had no idea. He felt the approach of a Nishimura Delay, perhaps the one to end them all. Ten years from now, he might still be waiting for it to pass, a skeleton cobwebbed to a ghost ship.

Deck operations were jolting to screeching, smoking halts. It was shocking how quickly training fell apart. Signalmen abandoned their usual battery of signals to frantically flap their arms at queued pilots. Others rushed right at the trespassing sailors, waving Them toward the superstructure. A Super Hornet unchained from the deck had been abandoned, and Nishimura watched it roll starboard, forty-seven thousand pounds of lurking catastrophe.

'Who should we call, sir?' Lang asked.

'Should I look for the OOD again, Master Chief?' Legg asked.

Any sailor stationed on the island grew used to seeing patterns indiscernible at ground level. The port and starboard lines of parked jets looked like the rating stripes of an officer, first-class. The spray hosing of jet-blast-deflector troughs, when done by two sailors in tandem, created butterfly wings when the sun caught the oily plumes. At first, the deck intruders seemed incapable of method or sequence. Patterns, however, were emerging.

When an intruder came up against a jet, refueling equipment, or a support vehicle, Their paths changed. They redirected toward the nearest sailor, no matter who They'd been pursuing. Nishimura saw that the group had formed a perfect oval around the deck, as if in psychic agreement.

A woman in a khaki service uniform bit off a sailor's fingers. Nishimura saw blood fire into the woman's face, who lapped at it, a kid drinking from a backyard hose. Like that, Nishimura quit thinking of Them as *intruders*. They were what Chuck Corso warned them about. They were *ghouls*. And somehow, against every odd, They'd accomplished what no enemy in history had done: infiltrated an American aircraft carrier, the military's most protected asset.

Henstrom, Lang, and Legg did not need to repeat their panicky questions. Nishimura's response came two minutes late, but come it did.

'Down to five knots. Hard left rudder.'

'The OOD,' Legg said weakly.

'I have the deck, Quartermaster,' Nishimura said. 'You have a problem with that?'

'Why are we slowing down, sir?' Henstrom whined. 'San Diego's just—'

'*I have the deck,* Henstrom. I don't know the nature of the situation, but we are not taking this boat to the mainland, is that understood? Five knots, left full rudder. Head into a circling pattern. Alert the strike group.'

Dimly, darkly, Nishimura recalled that *Hickenlooper* had been circling all morning.

'A circling pattern?' Henstrom exclaimed. 'No – sir – we have to get home! You can't decide this for the rest of us! You have to ask the captain!'

He was correct, of course, that Captain Page had final say of anything that happened on his boat. But the captain's illness now felt more suspicious than ever. What if his deterioration had spread to others the same way a cult leader's edict poisoned his followers? It was a mutinous thought Nishimura couldn't stop thinking.

'Will you relay the order to the engine room, Boatswain's Mate, or will you be relieved of duty?'

Nishimura turned his glow on Henstrom. The O-3 shrank like an imperiled dog, rippling lips back from his canines. Nishimura did not like the display but had other concerns. He swiveled on a heel and gave the rest of the nav-bridge crew, one by one, the same challenging gaze.

'Does everyone have their orders clear? Are we together on this?'

Nishimura inhaled, held his breath. *Yessirs, rogers,* and *aye-aye, Master Chiefs* erupted, signaling the syncing of a unit no threat could possibly derail. The crew took the stations at which they were so proficient, the diligent clatter of their shoes and bark of their voices obscuring both Tommy Henstrom's mutters and Chuck Corso's pleas for vigilance. Nishimura let out a held breath, which fogged the window like a splash of silver blood, not as dark as the liquids spilled on the flight deck but just as shocking.

The Full Armor of God

Father Bill did not recognize the two sailors, one Black, one white, who pitched into the chapel, but felt toward Them instant, unchristian wrath. No doubt Their unscheduled appearance was related to the flight-deck shutdown, but this was his time with My Sweet, which he awaited every sweaty day and restless night. When My Sweet turned to look at Them, her thigh shifting away from his fingers, Father Bill was aggrieved.

He bolted upright. A slug of blood inched down his leg, and the tape that banded his swollen penis to his thighs pulled harshly. He was angry; he nearly yelled. But he was Father Bill, Padre, Chaplain, Chaps, Chappy, and anger did not become him.

'I am blessed by guests,' he said as calmly as possible. 'You are most welcome. If you would be so good as to come back in, say, thirty minutes, after I finish this consultation?'

Few people aboard a carrier received his kind of deference; it was convention for religious leaders to assume the rate of whoever they were meeting with, whether it be an E-1 apprentice or an O-11 fleet admiral – and even then, the religious leader was a smidgen above the fleet admiral, wasn't he? These two sailors looked ignorant of any of this. Instead of waiting to be recognized and invited, They blundered forward, the Black man's shoulder driving the white man into a row of chairs. As the chairs scattered from the assault, Father Bill noticed that the knees of the white sailor's trousers were soaked with blood.

My Sweet had flattened herself to the starboard wall. She was a fighter pilot and, as such, carried a sidearm in case she was shot down and captured. Her hand was pawing her holster awkwardly, and understandably so. Surely she'd never had occasion to draw the weapon.

Unimpeded by chairs, the Black sailor cruised up the aisle. His chin and neck were shiny with wet blood. His eyes had an alabaster gleam. Parishioners were known to embrace Father Bill in grief or gladness, but They did not reach for him like this, fingers clawing the air.

Drugs did not have to be the culprit. A carrier was a giant bottle of emotions being constantly shaken, and when deployment went too long without action, half the ship would start complaining of the need to blow up something.

That's how you ended up with murders. That's why the ship had a morgue.

'Run.'

It was My Sweet, and Father Bill felt his face go as hot as when he paged through *Fresh Meat*. He heard fresh distrust in her voice. Had it been so horrible to be touched by a man of God? She should be grateful, supplicant, on her knees to kiss the blood from his feet! Oh, he'd take her now if he could, with both hands and both legs and all his teeth, so they could meld into one of the beasts birthed of his mother mind and father loins, an angel-devil, a god of cock and tit, tentacle and wing.

My Sweet slid away, toward the exit, but the sailors pressed too close for Father Bill to follow, with his old legs and box-cuttered thigh. He felt a clench of frustration that My Sweet had not used her gun, but that judgment cooled. If these sailors were simply intoxicated, killing Them would be a sin. He slipped into the invisible vestments of holiness, put on a smile capable of soothing the most frazzled members of his flock, and lifted a genuflecting hand.

' "Come to me, all you who are weary and burdened." '

He gestured to the first row of seats just as the white sailor, with jerking kicks and thrashing arms, obliterated it. The tumult seemed to excite the Black sailor; when he grinned, pink foam, raisined with black tissue, squeezed from between his jaws. Both sailors collided and, as if on musical cue from the chapel's keyboard, They lifted Their four arms and reached for the priest's neck.

A dark shape shot past Father Bill and collided with the sailors. It was a man, stocky and strong, the sinew of his back and arms clear from a short-sleeved black workout shirt. It was, of course, the priest's nemesis, the Psych. Some time back, Father Bill had concluded that while the smug nonbeliever nodded respectfully at everything the boat's religious leaders said, privately he believed them all fools. He had his holy books and the Psych, his prescription pad. Guess which one sailors preferred?

Each of the Psych's linebacker shoulders struck one of the sailors in the gut, sending all three tangling into folding chairs. Father Bill searched for My Sweet, thinking they might finish what they'd started, but she was gone.

'Father – Bill—'

The Psych's double-tackle, though impressive, hadn't knocked the wind out of the sailors. They did not look the least bit distracted. They tore at the Psych with what looked like great interest, which suggested the priest hadn't been singled out as a target. Father Bill mused on this while the Psych held back the Black sailor's head by his scruff and used a forearm to deflect the white sailor.

'Help me – Father Bill – pull one of Them—'

The Psych screamed, a wild, womanly sound that flooded Father Bill with righteous feeling. It was the perfect sound for the Psych, the dying yowl of a quack profession that held no weight against customs of old. The white sailor's jaws were embedded in the Psych's forearm, teeth squealing atop the ulna. The sailor jerked his head, tearing away a hunk of the Psych's arm, white as blubber and trailing red tissue. The Psych stared at the hole in disbelief until it gushed blood.

'Fathum—' He gagged on his own gore. 'Holp, holp.'

When the Black sailor bit off the Psych's upper lip like taffy, the Psych didn't scream. His face was a purple froth, some of it siphoning inward, some puffing out. Despite the unpleasantness of the sight, Father Bill heard the ting of a justice bell when the lip, along with the Psych's mustache, was sucked down the Black sailor's throat like a noodle. For a moment, both sailors chewed pensively, quietly.

Let all mortal flesh keep silence, Father Bill prayed.

The two sailors stared up at him like he'd rattled Their food bowls. They stood. Their mouths opened and chewed chunks of the Psych tumbled out.

Up came Their arms, forward shuffled Their feet. In seconds, Their fingertips had snagged Father Bill's beige sweatshirt. He stepped backward, his right foot landing badly and squeezing fresh blood from his thigh cuts. He seized in pain, and just like that, one of the sailors had a full handhold of sweatshirt, while the other fumbled for a grip on his ear.

He could not go down like the Psych, he was better than that – he was a soldier of Jesus! Father Bill dove away, the leap of a major-league shortstop. His hip cracked down, and agony shot all the way into the soles of his feet. But he was free, at least for a moment, and he saw, just a few feet away, the place he felt safest: the supply closet. He pushed with his toes, gripped the doorframe with aching fingers, and pulled himself inside.

The sailors dove too, eyes white and mouths red, slavering to take communion of his body and blood. Father Bill slammed the closet shut, the door whacking aside the Black sailor's outstretched fingers. There was no lock, of course, but to conserve hallway space, the door opened inward and that was something. Father Bill braced his back against a box of hymnals and shoved his feet against the door, which began to pound with the sailors' fists.

Lieutenant Commander William Koppenborg had experienced war, from the Persian Gulf, Arabian Sea, and Suez Canal, to the warlike operations following 9/11 and Hurricane Katrina. All from the safety of chapels, true, but he knew what war looked like. Sailors showing up for service with slinged arms and bandaged skulls, while others died screaming as he performed last rites. He knew what war sounded like too, beyond the whang and whoosh to the shriek and rumble.

He understood the men on the other side of the door to be War. They might, in fact, be a revision of the very idea of War, just as the lone operants of terrorism had modified the surgical technologies of the Persian Gulf, which had revised upon the chessboard subterfuge of World War II, which had revised upon the industrial, meat-grinder collisions of World War I, which had revised upon the troop-shifting deceptions of Napoleonics. Ever changing was the art of death.

Father Bill's legs shook. The door opened a crack. He pistoned his legs, shoving it shut. Ephesians 6:11 came to him like the cavalry: *Put on the full armor of God, so that you can take your stand against the devil's schemes.* There was no verse he recited more often to anxious soldiers, and never before had he doubted its efficacy. He was armored by God, that he knew, yet it might not be enough, now that he'd done what basic combat training had taught him never to do: corner himself with no way out.

Controlled Crash

Hustle was expected aboard a carrier, even demanded, but never had Jenny moved so fast, dancing over the rounded partitions at the bases of the watertight doors and clutching pipes to swing around corners. Hazily, she noted this as proof of mastery, but felt no pride. She'd left Father Bill, who, despite the way he'd clutched her knee, was a frail, unarmed old man, while she was a fit fighter pilot with a pistol. But the Psych had shown up, and he was young and strong. Meanwhile, all that silence from the flight deck? The flight deck was where she had expertise and might truly help.

She did not kid herself. The guilt that had built all night, without the analgesic of sleep, had swelled like a goiter. Her bolting failures pushed her from the chapel, past the fan rooms, up the ladder, and along the avionics shop. Here might be a chance to right wrongs, to help people instead of putting them at risk.

The chamber adjacent to the deck-handler room was aswarm with sailors, some rushing for the deck, some retreating from it with stunned faces. Jenny pinballed off their bodies, her flight suit buffering impacts, and burst outside. The rain hit her like a net; it caught and tangled her, and by the time she regained her balance, she was soaked, her curly hair pounded as straight as the flight helmet she'd left in the chapel, never to be seen again.

It was another sign of how thoroughly she knew every inch of her quarter-mile-long workplace that, when she booted something aside, she knew it wasn't supposed to be there. She watched the object spin and come to rest.

A man's head, sheared from its neck like a ham.

Jenny kept moving. To stop might be to never move again, so she focused not on the rainwater pooling in the head's mouth and eye sockets but on her brown shoes, the shoes she deserved – she had to convince herself of that, and fast. She looked up and took in a chaos unknown to even the most apocalyptic of training videos. Was the rain to blame? Were the clouds pregnant with Russian or North Korean toxins? The candy-colored jerseys and float coats were scrambled, far from their usual positions. There was only one reason for that: a FOD walk.

For a few seconds, she convinced herself it was true, that she was again witnessing her favorite ritual. The debris here, however, was far more significant. A slot seal from one of the catapults, ripped free like loose intestine. A refueling cable lay unattached, like an aorta snipped from its ventricle. Glass from the Datum lights lay in colored shatters, bad news for landing pilots. A bomb cart of three AMRAAM missiles was just sitting there in the open, unsecured, a violation beyond belief.

Then there was the other debris. The decapitated head. A boot sprouting half a man's calf. A fire helmet filled with a stew of blood, skull, and brain. The deck was wet, as it often was, but not just with water, oil, and jet fuel. There were puddles of red liquid everywhere; white-eyed sailors stomped right through them.

The asphalt trembled as ship whistles blasted: man overboard. Jenny looked around, wet hair whipping her cheeks, and saw two deck crew gesturing toward the water. The whistles blasted again, six more times: man overboard. Turning, Jenny saw a sailor hurling a ChemLight after a fallen comrade. Then again, and again, six whistles, six whistles: man overboard, man overboard – dear God, *men were throwing themselves off the boat.*

Jenny had seen fights like this in Detroit, hand-to-hand, fist to flesh. This was navy versus navy, the cracking open of the simmering animosity beneath every military unit, if not every gathering in America. No US military machine was more protected than an aircraft carrier, Jenny knew, but she also knew those protections faced outward. Here was the carrier's Achilles' heel, an attack from inside.

Father Bill's description of golems echoed through her bones.

One day, golems would turn on Their creators, learn how to build more of Their own kind, and use Their overwhelming numbers to cleanse the Earth of evil.

Jenny grunted away her fear and charged into the rain. Again her hand touched the butt of her pistol only to draw away. There were missiles here, external fuel tanks, scattering sailors – too dangerous. That must be why she heard no other pilots firing. The only other armed souls aboard were the small contingent of marines, but who knew where they were. There were plenty of weapons locked and guarded in the ship's magazine, of course, but Jenny had no clue how quickly those arms could be mobilized – especially if the eyes of those guarding them had gone white.

She scooped up a latch bar that, from its school-bus coloring, must have fallen off a weapons skid.

An intelligence specialist, judging by his insignia, had a redshirted member of the crash crew pinned to the wheel of a recovery crane. A scoop of flesh was missing from the back of the specialist's neck; vertebrae, white as larvae, nosed from red meat. Scrabbling for stability atop the gutted body of a fallen comrade, the red-shirt's feet fumbled, and down he went.

'Stand down, sir!' Jenny shouted. '*Stand down, sir!*'

The intelligence specialist did not seem to hear. He grabbed the red-shirt's right ear and chin as if to kiss him. Hot coals shifted under Jenny's ribs. She'd been ignored so many times: disregarded by male cadets at Naval Air Station Pensacola, butted in front of by sailors who pretended not to see her, outshouted in the Red Serpents ready room as if she were as voiceless as the lingerie ladies pinned to the Sweetheart Wall. *Olympia*'s nickname might be Big Mama, but it was male to its marrow, and Jenny was done with it. No more Wrist Warfare.

She reared back as if she were still on the Detroit Cristo Rey High School softball team and swung the latch bar with all her strength.

The direct hit to the right side of the specialist's head sent the concussion through her shoulder and down the bones of her spine. The sailor's head struck his left shoulder with a gruesome crack. One of the visible vertebrae popped like a knuckle, his neck likely broken. He collapsed into the lap of the red-shirt.

Twisted from the swing, Jenny faced a new direction and a man trying to crawl away from three sailors munching on his leg, shoulder, and scalp. Everywhere she looked, it got worse: a pilot unloading his pistol into the chest of a sailor at a two-foot range, six shots that did nothing to dim the white want in the sailor's eyes.

She heard a scream. There were dozens, but this one was beside her. Jenny swiveled to find the fallen red-shirt right where she'd left him. Despite its broken-neck paralysis, the specialist's head was snapping its jaws in the red-shirt's lap. More, the gored body beneath the red-shirt had quivered to life and was chewing through the red-shirt's perineum. The red-shirt wailed. A dark rope of blood spurted from his crotch, spattering across the head's happily chattering teeth.

Jenny backed away from the gush as if it were water from a suburban sprinkler. At the same time, an unmoored jet sideswiped a moored one with a metallic tearing sound, one of its folded wings casting sparks as it carved a gouge along the other craft's fuselage. Plane-against-plane impacts were called *crunches* and were so superstitiously feared that no deck crew uttered the word *crunch* and no ship store stocked Crunch Bars.

From behind one of the crunched crafts, CMC Bertrand Veevers, creator of the Idea Box, dragged himself across the deck with one elbow, his other arm trying to keep his entrails from flopping out of his cloven chest. Veevers had survived four wars and eight promotion cycles, and it was here he would die, on a bloody tarmac at the hands of his own men. The question was how long it would take him to die.

Jenny kept backing away.

Her tailbone struck a solid object. She knew it was the outer railing of the flight deck, which ran above the safety netting – netting that would catch falling sailors unless said sailors were taking pains to leap over the nets, which, right now, they were. As she reached back to grab the rail, a hand grabbed her back.

Trained as an FNG, Jenny zeroed in on etiquette cues: three stripes, first class, anchor-and-trident symbol – a Navy SEAL. Other details sent a different message: pearlescent eyes, lax expression. The hand grasping her wrist was missing its index and middle fingers, all the information Jenny needed to know she could wrench her arm free. At the movement, the SEAL's ring finger, apparently perforated by the bite that had stolen its partners, snapped off like a carrot. Jenny slid aft along the railing, and the SEAL followed, crab-pinching the thumb and pinkie he had left.

'No, sir!' she shouted. 'Stop, sir!'

He did not listen or stop. They never did.

She lifted the latch bar to deliver a blow, but rain had combined with the grease on the bar to loosen her grip. The bar flew from her hands, landing unheard on the deck beneath the storm's roar. The loss was instantly petrifying; she felt half her size. The SEAL was on her, his pincher hand no good but his other one functional. He leaned in with jaws wide enough to show his fillings.

Her own flight-deck crunch: the back of her head striking hot, shaking metal. She did not have to look to know it was one of *her* planes, an F-18, though stenciled with someone else's call sign. The

SEAL, who outweighed her by half, sank closer, the upper knob of his mandible juddering free of its hinge. His breath was mint and copper – toothpaste and blood.

Jenny felt pieces of aircraft she knew as well as her own body digging into her back. The position light, the total temperature probe, the nose landing gear door, and all vibrating. That meant it had been queued for takeoff. That meant its engines were running. Flashing through her mind was a flight-deck sign she'd noted on her first day aboard Big Mama: BEWARE – JET BLAST – PROPS – ROTOR BLADES. All lousy ways to die, but not the only ways, not by far.

The Sailor's Creed was more than a cheap poster taped to her rack.

I represent the fighting spirit of the Navy.

I am a United States Sailor.

Instead of pushing at his chest, she rotated her hands, a flip of the wrist – but not Wrist Warfare, not even close – and, using her own body as counterweight, hurled the SEAL to her right. His back bounced off the engine compartment; his eyes went wider and whiter, and he roared as if wanting the final word over a woman one last time.

The engine's air intake caught the SEAL in its supersonic suck. He was yanked into the intake fan like a dry stick, his body snapping in half at the waist before being pulled into the compressor shaft. The engine clanged and coughed as the body hit first the red-hot combustion chamber and second the turbine's bladed windmill. Jenny heard glops of meat blast from the exhaust and splatter to the deck.

She leaned away, terrified of being pulled in after him, and overcompensated, ending up facedown in a puddle. She rolled over, stinking of jet fuel now, and from that low position watched two hundred of Big Mama's best take on the coup. Jenny had heard about the dizzying highs that could come from patriotism. Senior sailors never shut up about the cheers that shook the *Enterprise* on 9/11 when it changed course from Africa to Pakistan. The walls of military history were built of such bricks of valor, from Belleau Wood to Omaha Beach to Mogadishu. A new brick would be added now, one stamped *Olympia*.

That did not mean victory was theirs. Jenny smelled the fever sweat of failure, saw it in bowed shoulders and grieving mouths, and felt it in her weak-kneed shudders of exhaustion. Landing a plane on a carrier, that objective that she'd recently struggled to do, was often dubbed a *controlled crash,* a phrase now appropriate for everything that was occurring. The men and women around her, unacquainted with hesitancy, were hesitating at every opportunity. Of course they were. The invaders were their officers, their aides, their confidants, their friends, and it went against all training, all heart to harm Them.

Four white-eyed sailors, two of Them in float coats, spotted Jenny and closed in, dragging Their damaged parts through the downpour. Getting to her feet, Jenny coldly assessed her circumstances. She'd never reach the safety of the conn tower. There was, however, a small, circular hatch nearby, which fed straight down into a 'trunk' – one of many narrow, rung-equipped shafts cutting vertically through the ship like drinking straws, permitting emergency vertical transport in case of fire or other calamity. She stepped toward it, keeping her eyes on the quartet. She would make it to the trunk first and be able to dog the latches before They got there. Nevertheless, it tightened, this circle of men.

Ocean of Blood

What civilians might call *doors* **on a carrier were actually**
hatches – massive slabs of contoured steel that, once sealed, were
nearly impenetrable. The chapel closet's door, however, was wood.
While Father Bill was ignorant in the ways of carpentry, the trade of
Jesus of Nazareth, he knew this door rated little better than the balsa
of his pornography lockbox. He was not altogether surprised when
the white sailor's hand punched right through it.

The man hadn't even made a fist; the hand came through patty-
cake-style, palm-first, and when it burst through the wood, the tips
of two fingers snapped back, popping the flesh open at the upper
knuckles. Without pause for pain, the sailor snaked his arm through
the hole until his biceps halted it. The Black sailor, meanwhile, kept
shoving the door open. Each time, Father Bill pushed back, but he
knew his devitalized legs would lose their battle soon. The white
sailor's hand and arm probed about blindly until it found Father
Bill's boot, and took to clawing at the leather, an effort hampered by
its broken, flopping fingertips.

Father Bill felt the cold tunic of doom drop over him. Did he deserve
this? Every time he'd chastened his sinful flesh with the box cutter,
bandages had stopped the blood in half an hour. Under today's duress,
the wounds did not seem like they'd ever close. The thigh of his camouflage slacks was soaked, the floor beneath abstract with dark dribbles.

In this position, nerves electrified with fright, muscles shuddering with exhaustion, mind faint with blood loss, knowledge hit him with such power and purity it could have only come from the Lord Almighty. Father Bill did not doubt the insight. It made sense God would wait until this moment to speak. Martyrs often only attained enlightenment when attached to a burning stake.

Look at the blood falling from the white sailor's broken fingers, Father Bill. See how congealed it is? The fingers drop blood, but do not bleed it. How was that possible? Father Bill knew, for he had been gifted the sight! On the third day, when God made the oceans, he created an ocean of blood from which all humans and animals would take their fill. The well was meant to serve the Earth forever, but thousands of years of murder, mass slaughter, and war had emptied the ocean of blood faster than it could be replenished. In the white sailor's snapped fingers could be glimpsed the consequence: there was no more blood to flow, and without the deterrent of spilled red fluid, humans were emboldened to rip one another to pieces.

Lieutenant Commander William Koppenborg, Catholic chaplain of the USS *Olympia,* was different. He was chosen. There was a reason his thigh not only bled but poured. The ocean of blood – it was *inside* him. And to think it took the cutting of his own flesh to know it! The ramifications hit like a hailstorm, the same ecstasy he felt when divining the true message of a Bible passage he'd misread for decades. If his ravaged thigh was the sign God had chosen him, he'd been wrong to see his recent desires as deviant.

There was nothing evil about the flesh monsters *Fresh Meat* had hatched.

The things he wished to do to My Sweet might refill the ocean of blood, as had been foretold in Revelation 16:4 – one more passage he'd misread for too long.

The door cracked vertically, top to bottom. Two white-eyed faces appeared in the fissure. But Father Bill felt no fear. With a calm he would have believed impossible seconds ago, he surveyed the closet's contents. Humble tools, but did Jesus have the bejeweled goblets or stained-glass glorifications of the church? Of course not. Jesus found strength in raw materials, whether those materials were objects or apostles.

Father Bill withdrew his feet from the door and rose to his feet. The door split down the center as neatly as a cracker, and the two sailors fell into the splintered results, entangled like wrestling children. Father Bill plucked from the shelves what he needed: the gold-plated chalice he used for Mass and a four-foot bronze flower vase kept around for holiday services. The downed sailors gawped up at him, so hungry They used Their arms to reach for him instead of helping Themselves up. It was the only advantage Father Bill needed.

He lifted the vase by its opening, high enough to thump the low ceiling, and brought the flat base down on the Black soldier's head. The skull caved with unexpected ease, parting like lips to swallow the vase; Father Bill let go and the vase stood upright, ready to accept fresh flowers. The white sailor had scrabbled to his knees, his dull eyes locked to Father Bill's thigh. The priest took a step away.

'Lifeblood,' he said soothingly. 'You want it, my son. I understand. But by order of the Lord, our God, my lifeblood is mine to share, and with that gift, I must be judicious. The Lord bless you, son, and keep you. Amen.'

The chalice fit in his hand like a choir bell. He brought it down on the white sailor's head. It did not have the satisfying effect of the standing vase – the sailor jerked back, then lunged. Father Bill had to go through the untidy affair of striking the man ten more times, bashing through the skull only on the fifth blow, and driving shards of bone into the brain with every blow thereafter. The sailor's head hit the floor, his butt raised high like a sleepy toddler.

Father Bill wondered if he ought to recite the Sacrament of the Anointing of the Sick, and decided no. These men, after all, were already dead. He supposed new sacraments would need to be invented. In time, in time.

Noise from elsewhere in the chapel interrupted these happy reflections. More were coming. Naturally, demons would come not in twos but in scores. Father Bill dropped the chalice, its cup flat and useless, and addressed the shelves in prayer, intending to make a more considered and holier choice. The hymn board was sturdy but unwieldy. The brass offering plate fit comfortably in his hand, and its red velvet would hide blood, but the edges were rounded. The baptismal bowl was better, with a glass lining that gave it real heft.

Was there really any doubt about which tool he'd choose?

He lifted from its storage slot a five-foot-tall wooden pole topped with a hand-hammered, sixteen-inch-wide crucifix – hefty, sharp-cornered, and carved at each end with likenesses of the Four Evangelists. Father Bill's hands knew the processional crucifix better than any item on the ship. He smiled lovingly at the central figure. Jesus Christ's expression was demure, his ankles diffidently folded, his arms stretched bashfully to their nails. Father Bill would not be demure, diffident, or bashful. If this crucifix protected him, it would prove only he could save *Olympia*.

Put on the full armor of God, so that you can take your stand against the devil's schemes.

He strode into the hall. Rightward, noises. From the same hatch through which My Sweet had retreated staggered a demon sailor in frightful condition. His left arm below the elbow was gone, the rest looking like a chewed chicken wing left on a mess-hall plate. The sailor's mouth dropped open when he saw Father Bill, a child expecting to be fed.

Father Bill stepped over the body of the Psych, whispered Philippians 4:13 to himself, and showed the demon sailor what it was like to take Christ into your heart, literally. When Father Bill withdrew the brass cross, brown blobs of heart-meat spluttered out. This did not fell the sailor, but it did slow him, and the priest strolled past, his processional staff clopping like a cane along the steel floor.

Live soldiers barreled through 02 deck, each in blatant physical, mental, or spiritual crisis. Many, bless them, shouted out *Not that way, Father!* or *Careful, Chaplain!* or *Take cover, Padre!* He returned a serene, pious smile and kept going, robust with belief that an aft course would reunite him with My Sweet.

What would their unholy union look like? He had a better idea after coming upon a blubbering brown-skinned boy whose face was being gnawed off by a woman-demon. Finally, his *Fresh Meat* visions come to life! Two bodies locked in erotic starvation, the sticky, sloppy sealing together of female and male, eater and eaten. It held, quite gloriously, to Judaic tradition, which decreed God created man as the joining of two beings, immortal angels and earthbound beasts, so the blessed union might create a path to heaven. Just as Jesus rose from the dead, this new fusing of life and death established a unique holy plane, one Father Bill intended to reach as soon as he found My Sweet.

His stride was so great and proud the medical tape binding his penis to his thighs came loose and his erection sprang free, long as a processional staff, hard as crucifix brass.

Father Bill's righteous march ended in the hangar bay. Connected to the flight deck by four giant elevators, the vast space ran two-thirds the length of the ship and held fifty aircraft in all states of maintenance. The hangar bay's usual bouquet of human sweat, cold jet fuel, pungent hydraulic fluid, and salty ocean air today mixed with odors rarely smelled outside a slaughterhouse: the sulfur of freshly exposed meat, the gamey funk of pooled blood. Planes had been deserted mid-repair, the engine entrails of cables and wires were joined by actual entrails draped over wings and wheels like garlands.

Fire equipment was in ubiquitous use: axes, foam sprays, fire blankets, taken up in defiance of demons and operated by sailors hamstrung both by gear – slippery suede overshoes designed for working on jet wings – and the basic decency that made them reluctant to strike their friends. *With my help, man will reinvent decency,* thought Father Bill, mere seconds before he was surrounded.

He'd been smiling so long that frowning hurt his face. This was not supposed to happen. He hadn't found My Sweet. He lifted his crucifix to dispel the demons. When the demons instead grew closer on every side, his irritation turned to fear. In the chapel closet, he had defeated two demons at once, but now there were too many. Why was the Lord doing this? The armor of God was supposed to protect him!

Hard fingers pressed into his back.

No, not fingers. They were the securing fixtures of an access trunk. Trunks were not spaces inside which anyone sound of mind would spend time. Priests, though, spent whole lives in small spaces: rectories, confessionals, foxholes.

He began to undog the latches. It took force; he hadn't exerted muscles like this in years, and the last latch stuck, metal grinding against metal. Behind him came the rustle of demon feet, the sourness of demon breath. He imagined being taken by dozens of hands as cold and hard as the trunk fixtures. That did it: the handle squealed and the hatch opened. He pulled himself through a hole the size of a washing-machine door and into a vertical tube of manhole width. Securing his feet on narrow rungs, Father Bill looked down at the open, hundred-foot gullet.

He took the trunk door and pulled, but a hard thud shivered up his arm. The crucifix's wooden staff was too long to fit through the hatch. Demons were crowding into the opening, reaching past the staff. *Drop it,* ordered the part of Father Bill's brain one might call rational. But rationality did not lead a man of God – faith did. This was his rod and staff, his comfort as he walked through this valley of death.

Trusting God to keep his legs as strong as Joshua's and his arms as steady as Moses's, he let go of the rungs, leaned right into fifty or sixty clawing fingers, and took hold of the crucifix with both fists. Demon hands cold as ice tugged at his CVN-68X CHAPLAIN turtle-neck and grasped for hair he'd shed long ago. He closed his eyes against the cold, rolling snake flesh, imagined himself a suffering saint pit against Revelation's serpent, and pulled on his staff with wobbly old muscles.

The wooden pole cracked in half, flinging Father Bill off his feet. For a moment, he was lost, until the brass crucifix and the remaining two-and-a-half-foot-long shaft braced across the chasm like a pull-up bar. Father Bill gasped, swinging about, and found purchase on another rung.

'Praise God,' he panted. 'Praise God!'

Demons fought to get into the trunk, each one in another's way. Father Bill rearranged the crucifix and took a firm grasp of iron rung. Which direction to go? He gazed down; he gazed up. Heaven-ward, he thought, and began to ascend – slowly, one hand devoted to the crucifix and half-staff. Within thirty seconds, demons were inside the trunk, but They had neither minds for climbing nor faith to hold Them up: Father Bill heard Them tumble, one after the other, down the tube, followed by the faraway thumps of Their bodies pil-ing below.

Millennialists

***Vindicator* exploded.**

Six hundred feet long, ten thousand tons, traveling at twenty knots with a complement of three hundred and fifty enlisted sailors, fifty-five officers, and, in all likelihood, Admiral Vo – and in one second, it became a giant, billowing magnolia tree of blinding-white flowers. Heat's invisible hand shoved Karl Nishimura and the nav-bridge crew from the windows. Swirling balls of red and orange fire belched upward and grew pelts of smoke. Seconds later, as Karl recovered, a lake's worth of salt water crashed back into the ocean, kicking up huge, twisted scraps: part of a rudder, a blade of a propeller, the top half of the mast.

'We need to button up!' Henstrom bellowed, adding hysterically, 'Sir, sir, sir!'

'Hold course, Boatswain's Mate!' Nishimura barked. 'Lang, put your eyes on, look for sailors in the water.'

'We can't get to the rescue boats, sir,' Lang said. 'Look at the flight deck, sir!'

Nishimura *was* looking at the flight deck. He'd not taken his eyes off it for an hour that felt like six months, an entire second deployment. No influx of guns had arrived from the ship's magazine. No help seemed to be coming.

Yet all was not lost. There had come a late surge of mettle. On Big Mama's deck, beneath the fire cloud of the largest ship explosion since Pearl Harbor – and this was, without doubt, a Pearl of a different sort, the Japanese Imperial Army's cry of *Tora! Tora! Tora!* replaced by haunted, hungry groans – Nishimura witnessed feats fit for the canon of navy heroics.

A clutch of crewmen fired Catapult 2 twice. Unattached to any jets, the steam-powered shuttle tore several ghouls in half, chumming the Pacific. One gutsy junior EO had commandeered a crash-and-recovery crane, using the arm to hurl aside ghouls while crushing others with its six massive wheels. A ragtag group in a rainbow array of float coats had united to wield a 150 PSI fire hose that lobbed ghouls into the ocean. No one could feel a ship's tilt like a helmsman; the circling pattern Nishimura ordered was helping send ghouls off the edge.

What chilled Nishimura most were glimpses of ghouls dropping Themselves off the side of the boat, either chasing sailors who'd jumped or in search of something else. Nishimura wondered if these ghouls, whose bodies resisted death, nevertheless craved it, and mistook the black ocean, aglow with ChemLights, for the star-filled heavens.

Then there were the marines. *Olympia* had a twenty-person marine detachment, or MarDet, aboard, to conduct short-term training for amphibious assaults. Tensions between marines – known to sailors as 'those Semper Fi motherfuckers' – and navy folk never really let up. Unlike sailors, however, the marines were armed, *very* armed, and trained in close-quarters combat. Nishimura watched in awe as roughly a football team's worth of marines ran plays like the New England Patriots. They formed nets around ghouls and funneled Them into choke points inside which They could be incapacitated, something the marines did with what might be considered excessive enthusiasm.

Behind Nishimura, nav-bridge chatter intensified. Some voices Nishimura knew like his own. Others came from strangers who'd made their way to the island, seeking sanctuary.

'Report on *Vindicator* survivors.'

'Nothing, sir! The water's on fire!'

'One of ours bombed *Vindicator,* sir!'

'Stop that, Henstrom. They blew themselves up.'

'With the admiral on board?'

'He probably ordered it himself. He probably *knew.*'

'Radio the marines. The second there's a gap, I want sailors in those rescue boats. I don't care how it happens.'

'MarDet's not answering, sir. No one's answering.'

'Keep trying until they *do* answer! You see how many of those . . . *people* are coming out of the ATO? The lower decks must be mobbed with Them.'

'You mean They're climbing? Up *ladders*? I saw one who couldn't figure out a *door.*'

'Don't ask me! They're figuring it out!'

'We need men on those arresting wires! How many birds we got in the air?'

'Request into Pri-Fly, sir. Some of those pilots might be able to make it to California.'

'We don't need our air wing in California! We need it here protecting its CV! They should be strafing the deck and taking out these bastards!'

'With navy men all over? Are you serious, yeoman?'

'An attack on a carrier is an act of war, sir. With all due respect, sir, Those are the enemy now, sir.'

'Why isn't anyone calling battle stations? Master Chief, sir, shouldn't we be going to battle stations?'

Master Chief, that had a familiar ring. That's right, it was him. Someone must be asking him a question. Nishimura swallowed. It burned like the ashy fire in the sky had slipped its forked tongue down his throat. He must still be the senior officer on the nav bridge. If so, he should probably turn around and reply. Still, his gaze remained on the brave men and women scurrying across the deck. They reminded him of his children and their soft, fragile, defenseless bodies.

His mind skipped from immediate to extended family. Given the life-after-death appearance of the ghouls, it might have been natural for Nishimura to think of Larry's family in Trinidad, of the voodoo practices they insisted were real. Instead, he thought of his ancestors on his father's side, particularly Grandmother Ayumi, a woman who found a cackling glee in terrifying children.

It was from Soba Ayumi that little Karl heard of the Millennialist. Legend had it that the Millennialist staggered from the mushroom cloud of Hiroshima, once a man but now a charred-black monster, eyeless, fingerless, jawless, and encrusted with broken glass, a phantom that stalked Japan at night. From its punctured chest came birdlike, wheezing laughter. It kept walking, brandishing its ruined body as a parader might brandish a standard, so that no one could forget how it died – how all might die. Leaps of so-called progress. Dehumanizing tech. Death machines developed by rooms of identical old men.

Little Karl had lost sleep, unable to comfortably categorize the Millennialist, as he could, say, Optimus Prime and Megatron. The Millennialist was not an assailant but a victim. The Millennialist was not a warmonger but a product of war. Though frightening, the Millennialist meant no harm. As a child, Nishimura had found this profoundly disturbing.

Now, at forty-three, he wondered if this same childhood doubt might rob him of future sleep. The Millennialist, the ghouls – who was really the enemy? The monsters? Or the men with the means to create Them?

Finally, Nishimura tore his attention from the mayhem four stories down and looked at Diane Lang, the textbook example of the dedicated lookout, but also part of the death machine. She was hanging on his next words with the heartbreaking expectation he'd know what to say. He should at least try. He was, after all, Saint Karl. He parted lips that cracked with dryness. He thought of reminding them of naval aviators' 17:1 kill-loss ratio from Vietnam through Desert Storm, of telling them to have faith that numbers like that would always prevail.

Because he was facing Lang, he missed the disaster's inciting instant, though in the sequence of disaster that followed, he could picture it. A fighter-pilot cowboy in the air, in cahoots with a desperate controller at Carrier Air Traffic Control Center or, more likely, in direct violation of CATCC orders, touched his jet down on the deck.

The intent, surely, was to wipe the deck of ghouls in a single swoop, but the deck had become a briar patch of asphalt and steel. The second the F/A-18-C's wheels hit the runway, they sheared across a slick of engine oil, jet fuel, fire-hose froth, and human blood, and collided with the drifting Super Hornet. The one-hundred-mile-per-hour crash was thunderous. It was the whang to end all whangs, and all aboard *Olympia* coiled in self-protective shock.

So apocalyptic was the chain reaction that it bordered on the absurd. The exploding Super Hornet fired off two AIM-9 Side-winder missiles. A C-2A Greyhound and a MH-60R/S Seahawk were hit and blew up, the whoosh to end all whooshes. An adjacent servicing unit of nitrogen tanks blasted into the sky, hot scraps of metal scything the deck. Enflamed jet fuel from the Greyhound showered the fighter jet next to it, which went up like polyester drapes. The jet fired its own missile payload straight into the flight deck, detonating the Mk 29 Sea Sparrow missile launcher as well as the LSO platform, a critical loss if Big Mama hoped to land any aircraft in the future. Right now, if Nishimura had to guess, such resumption of normal activity was never going to happen.

Like any carrier, *Olympia* looked impervious from the outside. The reality was she was a kiln of explosive and toxic chemicals, stocked with three million gallons of aviation fuel and three thousand tons of ordnance. Most of it was held belowdecks, where Nishimura had considered it to be safe. With the whole flight deck in flames, those pleasant delusions were gone. Anything was possible; everything was probable. Sailors staggered from the firestorm with bodies ablaze, the sole distinguishing characteristic between the living and the dead being that the living gave up, fell, and tried to die, while the ghouls kept moving, a whole company of Millennialists.

Through luck of positioning, some sailors survived. Many were flash-burned so terribly that crinkled sheets of skin draped from their faces and hands. They looked, in short, like ghouls, and Nishimura watched with stupefaction as unscathed survivors cut down these helpless sailors with guns and blunt objects. It was 'blue on blue' – friendly fire – needless slaughter that would only redouble the carnage.

Ship sirens blared a call for battle stations, competing with ripping eruptions and pealing screams, ensuring no effective way of spreading the word to a scattered crew, much less anyone outside the boat. This was despite the fact that Big Mama was equipped with whip antennas, WSC-6 comm suites for the Defense Satellite Communications System, WRN-6 Satellite Signals Navigation Set GPS, jam-resistant USC-38 comms, SSR-1 FM fleet broadcast antennas, SRN-9 and SRN-19 NAVSAT receivers, and a brand-new Challenge Athena III high-speed C-band SATCOM system.

Comm devices everywhere, yet no ability to communicate.

This is how the world ends, Nishimura thought.

Body to Bread

Anyone deployed on a carrier was schooled in the locations of access trunks. For most pilots, trunk training ended there, and if you were a nugget, an FNG, it was possible you'd never seen the inside of one, though you passed dozens every day. The gaps in Jenny's education were filling rapidly: she balanced on rungs beneath the safety of the dogged trunk, hoping the slapping palms of the four milky-eyed sailors would stop.

She *needed* Them to stop; peering down the bottomless steel tube, little wider than her shoulders, filled her with hyperventilating dread. It shouldn't have; F-18 cockpits offered mere inches of clearance between knees and dashboard displays. In flight, however, Jenny could control herself inside an expansive sky; the trunk, on the other hand, was a long, steel throat.

'Please go away,' she whispered.

Instead, They multiplied, clobbering the hatch harder, as if expressing discontent over what sailors like Jennifer Angelys Pagán had done to Their beloved navy. They knew her besmirched flight record, smelled her female body, tasted her Puerto Rican blood. She could not be trusted.

Then the world above the hatch exploded, or that was how it sounded. There was a crunch of an intensity Jenny had never known, followed by the pride-of-lions roar of incalculable balls of flame. Seconds later, another explosion, just as bad, and another, even worse. It was deafening; the whole boat shook; the rungs vibrated under Jenny's sweaty hands.

Was *Olympia* under attack? It had to be. Whatever enemy had managed to brainwash navy sailors into attacking Their own was now launching air assaults. The battering on the trunk hatch cut off; Jenny imagined the white-eyed sailors tossed like paper in a fiery back draft. The trunk filled with the eye-watering sting of jet fuel, and the temperature leaped to broiling. She could roast alive in here or succumb to toxic fumes, her choice.

Like an officer taking muster attendance, Jenny double-checked the status of each of her hands and feet (brown shoes, never forget), before moving in a pattern that, at first, felt hopelessly random. Right foot, left hand, left foot, right hand: she was stretched out too far and shaking. As flight-deck blasts continued, training kicked in. Her body found its rhythm, and her limbs moved in concert.

She reached the first exit hatch. Her temples throbbed as she rotated mental maps of the boat. This would be the refueling station. She tested the hatch with the back of her hand only to instantly retract it. It was hot. Ears still ringing from detonations, she leaned closer until she picked up not just tendrils of heat but shrieks of twisting metal. A bomb had pierced the deck, she thought, before she realized the shrieking was human. People in the refueling station were dying, and Jenny found herself hoping it was by fire so their last sights would not be their fellow sailors devouring them.

Jenny consulted her mental maps. What was on 01 deck? The avionics shop. Beneath that? Venting and fan rooms. That ought to be a safe spot to escape the claustrophobia of this chute, after which she would find others, maybe even fellow Red Serpents, and they could come up with a plan to take back the boat. Five more rungs down, in the dead zone between deck levels, she heard a familiar voice.

'My Sweet.'

To verify that she had, indeed, gone mad, Jenny looked down.

Three rungs under her, Father William Koppenborg clung to the trunk wall with one hand. In his other he held a large brass crucifix affixed to a broken wooden rod. Jenny had tried and failed to accept the crucifix as a holy item, but this one seemed different – its Christ had come alive. Real blood dripped from his tiny wounds, and clumps of real hair and flesh sprouted from the cross's corners. The images brought back the memory of Father Bill's fingers biting into her thigh.

'Father.' Her gasp echoed in the metal duct. 'Are you okay?'

He grinned up at her. In the safety light, his teeth shone like pearls.

'I knew we'd find each other,' he purred.

He ascended a rung, the crucifix clanging off steel.

'Father, no,' Jenny said. 'We should go down, 02 deck is –'

His free arm snaked around her calf.

Jenny's balance shook. She grasped a rung.

'Father, I'll fall—'

'Shh, My Sweet,' he said. 'Let all mortal flesh keep silence.'

He bit her.

The most disquieting element, Jenny realized, was that the bite felt like the long-in-coming climax to an unsavory story. For selfish purposes of spiritual exploration, she'd overlooked the fervent bore of Father Bill's watery eyes, despite knowing there was something amiss. Now she stared in dazed dismay as the skinny, turtleneck-clad, soft-spoken gentleman of the cloth vised his jaws to her leg.

Standard issue for navy pilots was the CWU 27/P Nomex flight suit, resistant to fire, chemical spills, and radiation, but also designed to be thin and lightweight; Jenny could feel each of Father Bill's individual teeth tighten on her calf. But he didn't break the Nomex. Jenny instinctively kicked, but as the priest had her leg cinched, the kick became a flail. Jenny's opposite foot fumbled from its rung, and with sweat-slicked abruptness, she fell.

Father Bill's teeth zipped up her calf, thigh, and hip as she dropped.

One of Jenny's hands snatched a rung. Her body jerked to a halt. She dangled by one arm, her feet bucking for footholds, but every rung she found was occupied by Father Bill. She considered letting herself fall farther – trunks had safety netting at each deck level for just this purpose – then saw with horror that the net below, and probably the one below that, had been sawed away, presumably by the crucifix. If she let go, she might drop twenty stories.

Staying still would be lethal. The three-foot drop had put Father Bill's head at the level of her breasts and he went at them, mouth wide. Her flight suit was looser here, all pouches and pockets. Jenny helixed her torso and kneed Father Bill in the arms, chest, and groin. There, she felt what she thought was a belted weapon until she understood it was his penis, implausibly erect, which made her fight harder, executing a one-arm pull-up so she could kick this Catholic priest as hard as possible in his injured thigh.

Blood shot from his thigh as if from a ripe tomato. Father Bill moaned behind the teeth clenched to her flight-suit lapel. Jenny used the brief paralysis of his pain to secure a second handhold on the rung above her. She'd kick herself free. She'd climb the fuck back up and take her chances with the flaming carnage of the refueling station.

In the next instant, she felt a sensation both new and instantly knowable.

She'd been stabbed. It felt like an open-handed slap to the back, leaving behind a lasting, icy tingle. She knew she'd been tomahawked by one of the brass cross's sharp corners but did not dare spare a hand to try to extract it. She simply hung there like a side of beef, the crucifix and broken staff a thousand-pound weight in her back.

Father Bill raised himself a rung. He caressed her cheek, leaving a lukewarm trail of blood.

'I know it hurts,' he cooed.

Jenny whimpered, hated the sound, and whimpered again.

'Jesus suffered like a common criminal before becoming the risen Christ. Transubstantiation is painful, My Sweet. But it's happening, all over the boat.' Father Bill chuckled. 'I admit, it is not the rapture I'd expected. But it makes a joyous sense, doesn't it – demons and people, joining together, becoming one in shared communion.'

Father Bill's voice shivered like steel sheeting.

The crucifix sagged in Jenny's back, snapping one muscle fiber at a time.

'Help,' Jenny gasped.

'Oh, I will.' Father Bill nodded gently. 'I will help you transubstantiate body to bread, flesh to blood. To do that, I will partake of your body. Do you understand? In the physical act, the spiritual act is accomplished.'

'Please . . .' Jenny begged, not understanding. 'You're going to . . . ?'

'Eat you.' Father Bill's eyes wrinkled with an apologetic smile. 'I know you've struggled in your belief, but that's all right. My belief will be enough. You will become of me, as Eve was of Adam's rib, and together, we will rise anew, king and queen over a paradise we can scarcely imagine. I'm so happy to share that with My Sweet.'

His smile tore apart as his mouth opened like a bear trap. He trailed his teeth all over Jenny's face, his bottom lip stretching across her nose and snagging on her chin, his breath rank with blood-tanged halitosis. Jenny let one arm loose from her rung and squirmed it between their bodies, but Father Bill redirected it as easily as he might the fussy limbs of baptized babes.

'Fear not,' he whispered as his mouth settled over the pain-bunched bulb of her left cheek. '1 Peter 4:1,' he said, his lips and tongue writhing against her skin. '*Whoever suffers in the body is done with sin.*'

Her dangling hand happened against the hardest item on her belt.

Father Bill's teeth had only begun to sink into her skin when Jennifer Angelys Pagán, call sign no better than *Jenny*, thumbed away her holster lock and drew her Beretta M9. She knew her M9 only from bygone Personnel Qualification Standards, but she'd been a dedicated student (*I am a United States Sailor!*) who never wasted a shot (*I represent the fighting spirit of the Navy!*), and she could still hear the firearms proctor laud her skill with the M9's three-dot sight system. Jenny heaved her arm upward and planted the muzzle in Father Bill's ear.

Inside the metal tube, the shot was so loud it obliterated all other senses.

When life burst back, Jenny found herself falling head over feet. Somewhere, a bullet ricocheted. The gun must have slid off Father Bill's skull as it triggered, a theory confirmed by the priest's moan of pain from what had to be a shattered eardrum. She saw his blood-covered face for a fraction of a second, aghast, like a child whose mommy had been cruel.

Jenny's head struck a hard surface, her knee, chin, and shoulder rebounding like the loose bullet until she plunged through ruined safety nets with a diver's precision. Father Bill was gone and Jenny was speeding toward gone too, and the sound that rumbled from the boat's bowels must be air hurtling past her ears.

Oxygen burst from her ruptured chest, and every bone shattered.

Neither thing was true. It took half a minute to believe it. She blinked over eyeballs throbbing from being jerked by their stems, and attempted to orient herself. She moved her limbs. All four worked but touched nothing. Was she floating? An unfathomable, dark channel telescoped below her.

No – above her. She was somehow on her stabbed, bleeding back, staring up at the nine levels through which she'd fallen. She must be in the ship's hull, close to the reactors. The sailors who operated the nuclear-powered engines were an enigmatic bunch who rarely saw the light of day, and it struck Jenny all of them could still be down here, too obsessed with knobs and meters to know about the chaos above. She took a deep breath that sent pain splintering through her body.

'Help!'

The force of her shout made her body sway. Now she saw it: a flight-suit strap was caught on a handle of the access trunk's lowest hatch. She was dangling from her waist like a yo-yo at the end of its string. No flail of arm or leg brought her close enough to grab the ladder. Exhausted, she quit; her body spun slightly. She commanded herself to breathe, to think, to review those mental maps. The hull floor should be ten or fifteen feet below her. She could sever the waist strap and survive such a fall, no problem.

Something else was below her too: noises.

Shuffling, slithering, smacking, slobbering.

The reactor engineers, Jenny told herself, trying to wriggle into a position from which she could see. As she did, her left boot, jarred loose by the fall, toppled off her foot – her brown shoe, the legacy owed her as a naval aviator, officially gone.

The boot landed on a mouth. With Venus-flytrap instinct, it began to chew.

A dozen sailors lay knotted in a heap below Jenny, bodies so broken by Their falls They looked like a single monstrosity, this snapped arm linked to that broken leg, linked to that busted rib cage, linked to that jawless head. A pile of corpses would be bad enough, but this pile twitched and squirmed. Broken arms strained for Jenny. Broken legs writhed. Heads atop broken necks snapped Their jaws.

The rumbling she'd heard while falling was the sailors' hungry moans.

Still Jenny could hear the thrown-pebble crack of blood dropping from her back, *pock, pock, pock,* against the forehead of a shattered sailor, who tried to reach the blood with his tongue. The others heard, saw, and smelled Jenny's blood too, and fought harder to drag Their broken bones over one another until they became a rolling hill of flesh, swelling higher and closer.

Jenny heard a second thing, oddly musical: the sprightly, piano-wire plinking of her waist strap starting to tear, thread by thread.

Taking Command

On October 27, 1966, more than fifty years before ghouls appeared on USS *Olympia,* almost to the day, the USS *Oriskany,* an *Essex*-class carrier active in both Korea and Vietnam, had five decks overtaken by flame after a magnesium parachute flare blew up in the hangar bay. Forty-four men died. Nine months later, on July 29, 1967, the USS *Forrestal* surpassed the *Oriskany* as America's worst non-enemy-action carrier disaster when an F-4 Phantom, parked on the flight deck, fired a Zuni rocket into the four-hundred-gallon fuel tank of an A-4D Skyhawk. The explosions began a twelve-hour blaze that killed 134 men and injured another 62.

We will exceed that, Nishimura thought. *We probably already have.*

The lower levels of the island were drowning in a rising tide of fire, with only one catwalk and ladder system still offering an upward path, and that one a gauntlet of noxious smoke and licking flame.

Any sailor who could not get belowdecks braved the path, producing the repugnant sound of navy retreat. Boots clanged up ladders and along catwalks, a clamor that changed as slower, heavier, and shakier footfalls began to give chase. Nishimura only had to step out of the nav bridge once to confirm his suspicion. The ghouls were learning. The ghouls were climbing.

Many were aflame, moving pyres of melting flesh and baking bone. Sailors tried to slide past Them and caught fire too, while other sailors, desperate to help, pushed the burning sailors off the rain-slicked catwalks onto the deck, perhaps hoping they might roll themselves into the ocean. Ghouls fresh from lower decks were indistinguishable from living sailors, and when offered a hand up the next ladder, bit off the helping fingers. Nishimura saw one woman go down from a ripped-open throat, only to see that same sailor, minutes later, appear at the nav bridge door, her windpipe voiding itself of bloody air-bubbles.

The navigation bridge was abandoned just before it was encircled.

'*Pri-Fly!*' Nishimura shouted. '*Go, go, go!*'

Abandoning your station was the worst thing one could do in the navy, but what was the alternative? One ladder higher, at 010 deck, the island's zenith, was Primary Flight Control, a.k.a. Pri-Fly, where Air Boss Clay Szulczewski and Mini Boss Willis Clyde-Martell, the two men who'd gamely tried to befriend Nishimura, controlled all aspects of flight ops, from deck to airspace. In their realm would the above-deck crew of *Olympia* make their final stand.

Fearful sailors streamed up, while others, reacting to the 1MC call of 'Condition Zebra', raced down into fire, fingernails, and teeth to button up the ship. Nishimura despised it, but Tommy Henstrom might have been right all along. Dogging all hatches and sealing every blast door no longer felt like overkill. Big Mama had caught a virus, and organ by organ was shutting down.

A brawling, shoving horde of thirty-some men were crowded on the Pri-Fly catwalk when Nishimura got there. Something was going on inside Pri-Fly, but the mob denied Nishimura a clear view. He was trying when his sight was blocked by Henstrom, standing before him without a salute, his chin jutted in defiance, the raindrops on his face a hundred more accusing eyes.

'We need to unbolt the ladders,' he declared.

It was damn near an order from a sailor six notches down in pay grade. Nishimura felt his face's glow turn the rain into steam. He would like to scream this seaman into submission, but one glance at the wild-eyed crowd of sailors stopped him. They might not react well to a show of officer superiority.

'Ladders stay,' he said.

'Then this whole island will be overrun,' Henstrom cried, 'and it'll be your fault!'

'We have sailors down there, Boatswain's Mate. Would you leave them to die?' Nishimura looked away from the pissant and raised his voice. 'Is there a hospital corpsman up here? We're going to have sailors with burns, chemical burns, smoke inhalation! We need to make some room!'

'Those things are coming up the ladder right now!' Henstrom cried.

The look in Henstrom's eyes did not allow Nishimura to doubt him. But the O-3 would have to deal with the goddamn situation himself. Nishimura pushed through the thicket of soggy sailors, who did not easily give way.

Nishimura hurled aside a final gawker and stepped into the Pri-Fly bridge. Two blue padded chairs stenciled AIR BOSS and MINI BOSS; plasma screens allowing the digital manipulation of all flight-deck and hangar-bay aircraft; the Air Tasking Order Flow Sheet detailing the day's sorties. All of it was functioning, a balefire of hope high atop CVN-68X. Only two things were wrong, neither of which Nishimura registered until five words into his greeting.

'Have you made contact with . . .' he began, never getting to finish, *Captain Page?*

The first thing wrong was Clay Szulczewski, or, more accurately, his remains. His body had been diced into roughly rectangular pieces with a fire ax – Nishimura knew this because the sailor who'd done the deed still held the tool, clabbered with blood and tissue, against his sobbing chest. Szulczewski's face had been staved in, his gregarious smile reduced to scattered teeth and sticky shards of skull. He was identifiable only by pieces of his red uniform, stenciled with his job title. The volume of blood was obscene, what looked like three inches of purple gel sloshing niblets of meat across Pri-Fly's floor.

The second thing wrong, predictably now, was Willis Clyde-Martell. He was relaxed into the mini boss chair, clad in a yellow uniform and headset, his contemplative posture in character. The middle of his face had been turned into a smoking black hole from a point-blank gun blast. Nishimura felt shock and grief, but shame too. He'd so badly craved the relief of someone who outranked him.

He looked at the man holding the ax. His insignia marked him as a builder; traces of color on his pants further specified him as a painter. Nishimura turned toward him, the blood at his feet sloshing like bathwater.

'Sailor,' Nishimura croaked. 'What happened?'

The builder snuggled the ax blade under his chin.

'I didn't want to, sir,' he wept.

Nishimura took hold of the air boss chair and considered the builder's reply. It might mean the builder was shaken from having had to slaughter two ghouls. But there was a darker interpretation, as Nishimura had yet to see a single ghoul on 010 deck. Had Szulcze-wski and Clyde-Martell simply been in the way of fleeing sailors?

His shiver was a clutter of spiders. Again, he felt like a child surrounded by classmates hoping to test a grandfather's claim that Japs bled blue. He turned from the builder and took in dozens of staring red eyes. They wanted to save themselves. They wanted the fucking ladders unbolted and pulled up. If Nishimura wouldn't order it done, they'd find someone who would.

'God. Oh dear God. Oh Lord, oh God.'

Perhaps tempted by the protection of a higher power, the sailors shifted their attention from Nishimura to a sooty, oil-stained flight-deck refugee, a refueler according to his purple float coat, whose nose was flattened against a starboard window.

'Oh Lord. Oh Christ. Oh Jesus Christ.'

Nishimura planted his hands on the console and leaned forward to get a broader picture of the flight deck. It remained a hellfire maze pillared by fire-engulfed aircraft and walled by flames rising along lines of spilled jet fuel.

'There he is. Oh Lord. Our Lord. Our Christ. There he is.'

It was not indiscriminate blather. The purple-shirt referred to a man it took Nishimura another half minute to find among the inferno. Despite the left half of his head being covered in blood and his clothes torn to rags, he walked with deliberate, confident strides as gas fires encroached and ghouls swiped and missed.

'It's the chaplain,' someone gasped. 'Everyone! It's Father Bill!'

It was the Catholic chaplain, all right, a skinny chap, one of those old vets Nishimura barely knew, yet against whom he held a faint professional grudge. Few men that age had much left to offer to the modern military and were too often grandfathered along as ship mascots. That was no way to run a navy.

But this was something else. Having emerged from God knew where, Father Bill held high with both hands a brass crucifix slithering with reflected fire. He would be killed. Of course he would be killed. Nishimura and the sailors beside him gasped as another fuel tank blew, hurling jags of metal that stabbed into asphalt, walls, ghouls – nearly everything but Father Bill. Red flames billowed and retracted with astonishing timing, allowing Father Bill to keep his regular pace.

'Go, Father Bill,' someone eked.

'You can make it, Father Bill!' someone cried.

A ghoul came at the priest from the front and tripped on a munitions trolley; Father Bill stepped over him. Two ghouls with gaping wounds in Their chests attacked from the left only to be folded in half by an arresting cable that had gotten wound in a crane's gears; Father Bill took no mind. It looked like a broken-legged ghoul would soon have Father Bill in his clutches until the aircraft elevator below it, operated by someone sealing off the hangar bay, rose flush with the flight deck, pinching the ghoul in half longways, from groin to skull.

In this fashion, via a mad streak of luck or an outright miracle, the priest resolutely crossed the deck.

'Praise God!' someone shouted.

'Praise Father Bill!' someone corrected.

Only when Father Bill reached the base of the island was he forced to stop. He shut his eyes, raised the crucifix higher, and stood against a barricade of fire. It was a pose Nishimura believed he'd seen in fantasy illustrations of knights raising their swords against undefeatable dragons. Nishimura was stricken with awe even as avowals of Father Bill's divinity rose to disturbing volume.

'We have to help him,' someone said.

'Golding, Merriweather, Tressle. Come on!' someone said.

For the next several minutes, Nishimura and the sailors who'd boxed him inside the bridge heard the struggles of the rescue party: the hard falls down ladders, the impacts of blunt objects, sporadic shots from someone fortunate enough to possess a firearm. Father Bill did not move an inch. At last, sprays of aqueous foam began dousing the fire at the base of the deck-level ladder, giving his deliverers room to pull him through to safety.

The rescue party's return to 010 level was just as slow. A series of resounding clangs announcing the unbolting of each ladder as they passed. Nishimura tried to tell himself it was all right, that orders were bound to get confused in such chaos, that the rescue party might have encountered an officer of higher rank than Nishimura.

But when the sailors inside Pri-Fly parted, creating an open path leading directly to Nishimura, he saw only the same SRs, SAs, SNs,

PO3s, PO2s, and PO1s that had fled to the island, with one addition: Father Bill, clutching a fire-scarred, blood-broiled, half-staffed crucifix before him like a trophy. With eyes bright crimson from smoke, the priest took the path made for him, his boots smacking rain puddles and the tarn of Szulczewski's blood.

Father Bill stopped in front of Nishimura. His face was painted gray with smoke. His left hand was coated in dried blood. His left ear was ruined, and half his neck was black from blood that had poured from the injury. The sparse hair on his head and the plentiful hair of his eyebrows were singed black. He blinked and regarded the men, all of whom stared silently, a congregation more rapt, Nishimura felt certain, than any Father Bill had ever enjoyed in the chapel.

'God,' Father Bill proclaimed, 'is taking command.'

Nishimura felt the nods of the sailors around him, most of whom, he knew, had lost half of their minds when their dead colleagues quit dying. These men – and they *were* men, not even Diane Lang had made it this far – had run from danger. They were the sailors most likely to crack in an emergency, and here they were, cracking in pursuit of quick salvation. The military's dirty secret was that it attracted not only the best Americans but also the worst – the racist, the sexist, the bloodthirsty, the continually furious – and a carrier threw both halves together in a thousand-foot, ninety-seven-ton, nuclear-powered coliseum.

Nishimura's worst hunches solidified as Tommy Henstrom manifested at the priest's elbow.

'What should we do, Father?' Henstrom asked. 'Stop circling? Resume course to San Diego?'

'Drop anchor,' Father Bill said. 'We're not going anywhere, my son.'

Question: *How long could Big Mama last without refueling?*

Nishimura knew the boat's most dramatic figure as well as anyone.

Answer: *Fifteen years.*

Maybe better people were belowdecks. Nishimura did not know. He only knew that the deck separating above from below was devoid of whang, absent of whoosh, and crawling with Millennialists, who chuckled at the turn of events. They knew the badness gathered in Pri-Fly had always been waiting. Nishimura stood opposite Father Bill and Tommy Henstrom in more ways than one; he'd need to conceal his famous glow if he was going to survive another few minutes, much less days, weeks, or years. He *had* to survive, even if it meant hardening his heart a lot more before exposing its leathered muscle to Larry, Atsuko, Chiyo, Daiki, Neola, and Bea.

I'm sorry I'm not there to protect you, he thought. *But I will be. Someday. Hang on for as long as you can.*

You Are Not Alone

You did not expect the world to look like this.

Fire is everywhere. You do not like it. Fire hampers your hunt for that which might assuage the hunger. Though it has become clearer the hunger cannot be assuaged. You have bitten many fast-moving ones. Most of their meat has fallen out of your mouth. Some has fallen into your stomach, where it floats in blood. Hunger, you understand, has nothing to do with eating. You sensed this from the start. Hunger is about hunting. Even that word is insufficient. It is about communication.

There has been much communication.

The first fast-moving ones you found ultimately ran, leaving behind those who were no longer fast-moving. You waited, curious and hopeful. One by one, they woke up. They were you, you, you. You did not feel happy. Only satisfied. You have a gray memory of feeling this same flat satisfaction upon completing tasks when you, too, were a fast-moving one. The difference now is you also feel the satisfaction of the other yous as you spread out across the ship. It is like having long fingers. You cannot feel every detail, but enough to know you are united.

You communicate more efficiently than the fast-moving ones. Perhaps more efficiently than fast-moving ones have ever communicated.

You have learned a lot about yourself in a short while. You learned you can feel things that are very cold or very hot, but have trouble distinguishing between the two. You learned this when you grasped the muzzle of a fired gun and the flesh of your palm began to smoke. Your inferior hearing is less of a deficit than it was at the beginning. Fast-moving ones, you have found, are loud. They shout and scream. They slam doors. They fire guns. They do not seem to realize how easy this makes it to find them. Your inferior eyesight has also been of small consequence. When threatened, the fast-moving turn on lights, lots of them. Their guns even flash when fired, making the most dangerous ones the easiest to pursue. Most wear light-colored clothing. Some have symbols on their chests, so shiny you can see them in the dark.

You understand that you were born without language only when certain words begin to return. To recall words, first you must hear them. It is a slow process, helped by repetition. Certain words and

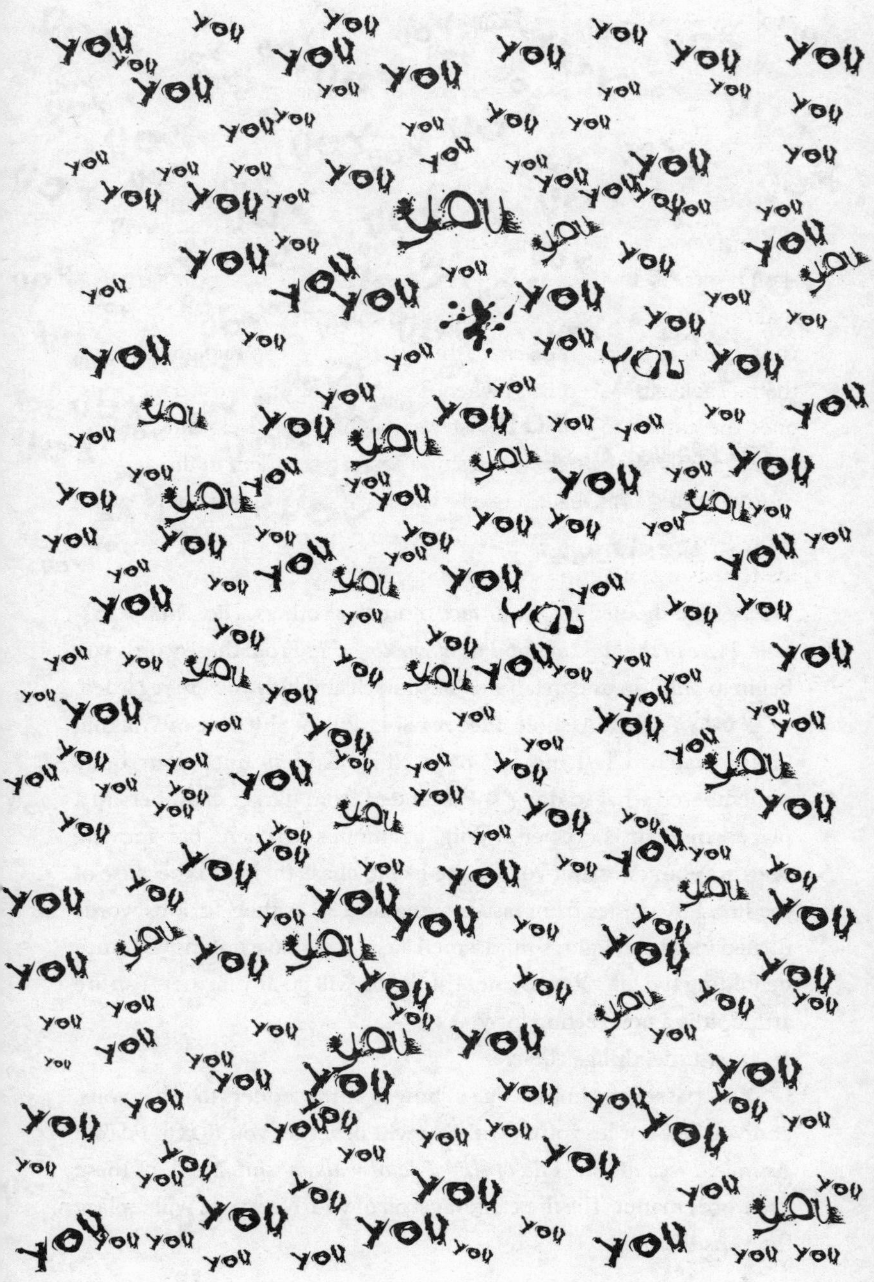

YOU YOU YOU YOU YOU YOU YOU YOU YOU
YOU YOU YOU YOU YOU YOU YOU YOU YOU
YOU YOU YOU YOU YOU YOU YOU YOU YOU
YOU YOU YOU YOU YOU YOU YOU YOU YOU
YOU YOU YOU YOU YOU YOU YOU YOU
YOU YOU YOU YOU YOU YOU YOU YOU YOU
YOU YOU YOU YOU YOU YOU YOU YOU
YOU YOU YOU YOU YOU YOU YOU YOU YOU YOU

YOU ARE NOT ALONE.

YOU ARE LARGER.

YOU ARE STRONGER.

phrases are shouted into your face more than others. *Die. Fucker. Asshole. Piece of shit. Pile of shit. Pile of walking shit.* From these words you begin to build an understanding of yourself and how you are regarded.

YOU – Fucker, Asshole, Piece of Shit, Pile of Shit, Pile of Walking Shit – watched fast-moving ones climb ladders until your body remembered what to do. **YOU** ascended from darker chambers to a place where air is crisper and light saturates. Up here, fast-moving ones are abundant, but you do not like to chase them. It is because of the fire. Fire comes from fast-moving ones. It is their furious words turned into heat, light, sound, smell, taste. You have not moved since beholding the fire. **YOU** do not think you will go any farther. You are afraid. It is a new feeling for you.

Over time, things change.

YOU passed the knowledge of how to climb ladders to other yous, and you did not let you down. You will never let you down. *Fucker. Asshole. Piece of shit. Pile of shit. Pile of walking shit.* None of these fire words matter. The fire cannot get all of you. New yous will replace the yous that fall.

Smoke cannot hide fast-moving ones. They move too fast to hide. They have always moved too fast to survive.

You see a you that you recognize. This you turns to look at you. You do not know how long it takes you to reach you. But once you are standing close to you, you feel something inside you. Inside both yous. Confirmation. Affection.

You were once called Scud. The other you was once called Jean. Inside the dead womb of Jean-you is a ball of blood and meat heavier than the blood and meat in your stomach. It is yet another you. If this little Scud-Jean-you were strong enough, it would rip through Jean-you's muscle and skin to get out. You feel something like longing.

You both stagger. Your hands touch. This is by accident, unless it is not by accident. Scud-you has broken fingers, and one jabs through a hole in Jean-you's palm. Your hands are fastened. You do not try to detach them. Scud-you notices a hard, hot ring on one of Jean-you's fingers and Scud-you feels a nice lightness. You walk together, side by side, for no reason at all. You believe you used to do this. It is not an easy walk. Giant works of machinery create barriers. Fire is everywhere, and fire is a fast-moving thing. But time has no meaning. You are in no hurry.

Scud-you and Jean-you reach the edge of the world. Metal posts prevent you from walking farther. Beyond is a sky of smoke and water aglow with the flaming ruins of other floating machines. You sense more yous out there. You have an inkling of the scale of things. If you can stretch across water, you might also stretch across land. There is no telling how far you will go.

The firelight behind you competes with the aurora of a dying day.

You hold hands and picture an overripe world.

You turn back to the fast-moving ones. You walk. Both of you do. All of you do. You hunt. You bite. Some of you burn. More of you are born. All happens just as it should.

Death by death, the world becomes less of me and more of you.

KILL US

BLOW
IT ALL UP

END THIS

If the World
Goes Gooey

Senior statistician at the United States Census Bureau's American Model of Lineage and Dimensions was Annie Teller's second career. Two decades before fleeing AMLD's Washington office the day the dead began to rise, Annie was twenty-two years old, recovering from a spinal injury that had brought her pro football career to a premature end.

She'd been in her London hometown, crossing Haymarket at Coventry, when a motorcycle traveling double the speed limit plowed into her, folding her around a traffic light pole. The incident itself imparted no psychological trauma, for she recalled none of it. What she remembered was hearing she'd likely never walk again, a verdict delivered by a surgeon with the obduracy of a man who knew the reaction coming.

Footballing had paid well. Annie could afford the best treatment. For twenty-eight months, she worked with therapists at the Mansfield-on-Sherwood rehab center in Nottinghamshire, the forest where Robin and his Merry Men once roamed. Even under the circumstances, the adjacency brought Annie joy. As a teenager, she'd been a better archer than footballer, though the latter had superior long-term prospects. Practicing at home in her backyard, she would plant an old wooden arrow in the dead center of her target and shoot at it from a hundred yards with the goal of splitting it down the middle, like Robin of Loxley. Sixteen times she'd nailed the shot, but not once had her steel-tipped High-Flites managed to split the wooden arrow.

In her earliest weeks in Mansfield, Annie could only turn her head, but being able to see the lush green treetops of Sherwood from her window, hissing like a dare, inspired her to consider feats of recovery beyond those posited by medical staff.

Four months in, she handed her favorite chiropractor, Mildred, a credit card and asked her to take the BRR and a DD-Red to Hetherington's, a sporting goods shop where she could purchase an old-fashioned pine bow with a string tension to match historical limits Annie had written down, plus a single wooden arrow with natural quills.

'I'm going to shoot that arrow into Sherwood,' Annie declared, 'then ask you to mark the spot where it lands.'

'The bosses won't be thrilled about seeing arrows flying from windows, love,' Mildred said.

Annie spoke quickly, as she had the next few bits memorized. 'When I'm able, I'm going to walk to that spot, all on my own, and find that arrow, and that's when I'll know I'm cured. You might think I'm off my trolley. But the only reason anyone puts up with life's swamp of shit is because they believe it might turn to milk and honey on the far shore. I know I won't be playing sports again, but I will walk. And it's into those woods I'll walk first. So you're going to mark where the arrow comes down, and mark it in a way that's likely to last for some time. All right?'

Mildred looked as if she, too, had a memorized script of sensible replies. Annie ought to be setting smaller goals for herself, taking things one day at a time, all those clichés. But Annie trusted the chiropractor for good reason. Her forehead might frown when she smiled, but the smile itself was enough.

'I believe you'll be the blighter to do it, love, certain as green apples,' Mildred said. 'I'll park a Rover on the bit o' sod and remove the engine, if that's what it takes. God favors you. I know in my heart he does.'

Annie didn't believe in God, but the gasp from her throat was a sound she hadn't made since before the accident. It was the sound of tasting delicious food, being erotically touched, witnessing a sports play beyond belief, living again, wanting again.

'Two years,' she promised in a trembling voice. 'If I can't walk to that spot in two years, then it'll be the spot I'll ask you to bury me.'

Annie Teller had come to Mansfield-on-Sherwood alone. Teammates visited for the first few months, but they were busy, forever traveling, and Annie knew seeing an athlete bedridden drove other athletes to existential panic. Annie's sisters visited, but her parents never even called. Her mother, whom Annie preferred to think of as 'Juditha Teller', had sexually abused her as a child. Her truck-driver father, whom Annie preferred to think of as 'Wilfred Teller', let it happen. Both had been devout, so-called Christians; Annie, once free of that house of sin, never entered a church again.

It had been Wilfred Teller who'd endowed Annie with her competitive drive, something she'd realized when she told a teammate, 'I suppose I'd like to beat the drunk bastard at *something*.'

And she did. Eighteen weeks later, Annie shot her wooden arrow into Sherwood Forest. Certain muscles had atrophied, but physical instincts had a way of lasting. The arrow sailed long and true, sinking into green leaves and black shadow. Mildred waited for the thud of indignant footsteps, which did not come, then pulled on boots, coat, and hat, and dropped Annie a wink before embarking into the woods to find the arrow and mark its spot.

One month before her self-imposed two-year deadline, after weeks of shorter, indoor jaunts, Annie inched downstairs and, for the first time since the motorcycle hit her, went outdoors. There were no walls or railings out there, but her desire for achievement pushed her harder than any coach. It took three hours to find the spot where her arrow had landed. Mildred had marked it with a large, iron crucifix, which, to Annie's shock, the chiropractor had coerced a groundskeeper into mounting in cement.

A wave of gratitude shook her. Her weak legs gave out, and she dropped to soft moss. Curled around the crucifix, she found herself incensed at the woman's misattribution of credit. Annie wrestled the cross until she'd upended its concrete anchor. She turned her gasping, sweaty face to the light drizzle.

'God had nothing to do with this!' she cried. '*It was Robin Hood!*'

Juditha Teller's American citizenship was the only helpful thing she'd ever done for Annie. Two years more and Annie was at the Robert Emmett McDonough School of Business at Georgetown University in the United States, getting her advanced degree in statistics, though she'd never forgotten the Mansfield staff's belief that she belonged in nursing. With a work visa in place and green card application pending, she accepted a job at AMLD, where she processed, among other things, data from the Vital Statistics Data Collection network, a system tracking the country's births and deaths. The work felt fitting: she was living a second life, her limp the only sign she'd had a first.

Tawna Maydew: they'd met at the most American place of all, Disney World. But Tawna had been no Imagineer's trick; after weeks of emailing, Annie knew she was in love with the big, blond Californian, who stood just as tall as Annie, but was softer in every way. Tawna was the opposite of D.C.'s insomniac go-getters; she slept late, loafed at boardwalk cafés in the LA sun, devoured film noirs, and compared Annie's limp to the hip-swinging walks of Lauren Bacall and Gloria Grahame.

Scheduling obstructed a repeat face-to-face month after month, making Annie wonder if it was a sign from Robin Hood (certainly not God) that their romance was not meant to be. Then Tawna started sending photos of the La Brea Tar Pits, which were right by Tawna's apartment. *We can kiss by the gooey ruins of prehistoric Earth!* Tawna emailed, which made Annie's heart gooey too. She emailed back, *If the world goes gooey, we'll meet on the banks of beautiful La Brea!* She meant it. She thought daily of walking out of AMLD.

Weeks later, on the morning of October 24, she wished more than anything that she had. That was the day dead people quit staying dead, thereby screwing up the VSDC system, the AMLD models, and every other bloody thing in the world.

She could not get hold of Tawna. She sent texts all morning, but her phone refused to confer *DELIVERED* status to a single one. Around lunch, Annie began trying to ring her – even Tawna, lazy and on Pacific time, should be up by then. Instead of Tawna's voice mail, Annie was met with a dial tone. Cellular networks were crashing all over, coworkers were saying. Annie glared at the plastic gadget that had once meant so much.

People had been trickling out all day, but 3:15, for some reason, was the instant of critical mass. The trickle grew to a flash flood, and when the statisticians in the cubicles to either side of Annie left, she recognized the moment for what it was: a chance to chase what mattered, as she'd once chased a wooden arrow shot from a window. Briefly, she met the flat glance of the remote Etta Hoffmann, who munched dusty trail mix with her usual lack of concern.

Annie picked up her jacket and purse, same as she always did, and exited. The street was a calamity of honking, swerving cars and people threading between them. She had to walk forty minutes before she lucked into sharing a cab with another Dulles-bound woman. Annie asked the woman if she had a ticket. The woman said no. Annie asked her where she was hoping to fly. Anywhere, the woman said, but here.

After sickening hours spent in snaking, shoving, shouting lines, Annie, barefoot because of the unsensible heels she'd worn that day, took what she could get, a red-eye to LAX with a five-hour layover in Vegas. *La Brea,* she repeated to herself to block out the shouting men and crying children. The inside joke had become the oath upon which all depended.

Hours later, in a clipped voice, the pilot announced midair their flight was being rerouted, either to Chicago or Atlanta, he didn't fucking know. The second Annie heard the curse word, she knew she'd never reach LA by ordinary means. Getting to the tar pits would require the same tenacity it had taken to get out of that Mansfield bed and into Sherwood Forest.

Hartsfield-Jackson Atlanta International Airport was designed in the style of a multilevel shopping mall. That day, the shoppers had gone madder than any Black Friday throng, creating a mosh pit of humanity no regular cadre of security guards was capable of quelling. Airline employees tried to keep a handle on their passengers. Name tags were slapped to people's chests so they might be found in the madness. A kindergarten idea, it'd never work, but Annie scrawled her name on it, and as an added measure included her destination.

ANNIE TELLER
LA BREA TAR PITS

Most name tags didn't survive the hour. Annie saw gate agents tackled so people could storm packed planes; she saw people clambering over X-ray conveyer belts, laptops scandalously stowed and shoes indecently on their feet.

Annie limped outside. Late October in Atlanta was hot, and she was sleepless and starving. She wandered sweltering asphalt frontage roads and gravel shoulders, trailing locals who must know better than she did. Half a day later, she came upon a city bus idling on some airport access road; it was taking people west, free of charge, and that was all Annie needed to hear: *west.* She got on, spotting a few others with name tags, and was sandwiched so tightly in the aisle she was able to catch a nap standing up.

She woke to a pressing, elbow-into-ribs tumult, people crying and bulldozing off the bus. Annie squinted past rushing bodies – still daytime. She was soppy with sweat, only some of it her own. She smelled diesel smoke, sweet and woolly. Following the crowd, same as at the airport, she found herself in the middle of a city street. To her right, the bus, its nose flattened to the discharge chute of a cement truck. The back undercarriage of the bus was on fire, and the right half of its sixteen wheels were smeared with a gloppy red paste. To her left, dozens of people streamed like ants from a McDonald's, arms filled with to-go bags of food. Oh, the two were connected: one of the fast-food raiders had been flattened by the bus, his body exploded at either end like a toothpaste tube squeezed in the center.

Between the bus and McDonald's, directly in front of her, was a hospital.

Several bodies were laid out on a neat patch of lawn, where two women in grass-stained white coats ministered to them. High up a tower, a window had been broken, and furniture was being launched from it. Why, Annie could not imagine. She thought of the VSDC network that, last she knew, still functioned and how vital it was that hospital staff kept sending data if anyone wished to understand this someday. She thought of Mildred, of how she and the rest of the Mansfield-on-Sherwood team had commended Annie for picking up nursing principles so swiftly.

The La Brea Tar Pits had waited tens of thousands of years. They could wait a few hours until Annie paid her dues.

The fiascos at AMLD and ATL were nothing next to the blooming catastrophe of Westside Medical Center. The beige-and-pink lobby writhed with bodies as overburdened triage teams decided which cases were hopeless. Annie fled. Wandering the halls, she saw the bucking lower body of a woman being attacked by a man who'd crawled into her MRI tube. She saw an active treadmill in a physical therapy room unoccupied but for a human leg attached by a string of sinew. She saw overturned incubators and a nurse's body, upon which three tiny, blue-skinned infants sucked noisily. Annie sobbed in relief when she found a crowded ER room. Finally, a place of professionalism where she could help, or not, and get on with her westward trek.

It took three seconds for a dead woman named Katrina Goteborg to wake up, latch on to Annie's arm, reel her in, and bite.

Memories bit too. Dorchester, six years back: a scrape with a juiced midfielder who bit her on the forearm. Georgetown, two years ago: in bed with a man named Barney, whose ear nibbles drew blood. The brain-stem frenzy of being attacked, of being *food,* was primal and familiar. Annie pulled away as doctors, or possibly passing do-gooders, tried to help. She saw the flesh of her right arm stretch a good two inches and watched twin red lines appear as Katrina's canines sliced through the skin, trying to hang on.

Yanking free, Annie stumbled back six feet, tripped, and landed hard, supine. For a short while, she saw only operating lights, multiple white suns risen over a radically changed world. When her eyes worked again, she investigated her wounds. Katrina's canines had made tidy, razor-blade slashes. They felt both white hot and icy cold. Her stomach flopped like she was going to vomit. Every throb of her pulse shoved thickening blood into her brain. Her limbs went cold even as her bones got so hot she could smell the marrow. She stopped hearing doctors, or Katrina Goteborg, or Atlanta's fall.

She curled around an IV stand, pressed her hot face against cool steel. It was the last conscious act she'd ever make, and she knew it. Anger faded to bitterness. The storybook tale of Annie and Tawna was supposed to end with them in each other's arms. Where was the scene when Robin Hood's spirit inspired Annie to keep fighting? Where was the scene when Annie used a footballer's nimble legwork to evade all dangers?

Annie Teller died. It wasn't fair.

She had undergone seismic changes before, but nothing near to the change she experienced fourteen minutes after death. She was still Annie Teller – her name tag insisted it – but not *only* Annie Teller. She was also Katrina Goteborg. She was also several others. She was all of Them. She is all of you.

You know your loss. You know your hunger to fill it. You learn how to walk. From there, you take up the hunt.

Only by the number of fast-moving ones you taste can any progress be measured. While feasting on the buttocks of a fast-moving one, a memory surfaces, as palpable as the boiling blood on your tongue. It is a place. You can picture it but cannot invoke its smell, sounds, tastes, or textures.

You see green trees with long, leafless trunks. You see tall fences around black ponds. The blackness is tar. It bubbles. A mammoth is being sucked into the tar. You are not aware it is a statue. You sense the beast's fear but feel none of it yourself.

The photos you recall are emblazoned with letters. Thirteen letters, always in the same order. Curiously, you find them repeated on a piece of paper on your breast: *LA BREA TAR PITS*. You do not know how exceptional it is for you to link a thought to printed words. What you know are three facts. *LA BREA TAR PITS* is a place. *LA BREA TAR PITS* is far away. *LA BREA TAR PITS* is where you need to go.

Your limp will slow you. It will not stop you. You walk for months, or days, or weeks, or just a few minutes until you exit the hospital. You hear fast-moving ones in all directions. That is good. Along the way to *LA BREA TAR PITS* you will use fast-moving ones to make more yous. There is plenty of time, because there is no time.

You look into the sun. It is red orange and low in the sky. You have a sense you should pursue it. Again you walk for seconds, or minutes, or days, or weeks, or months until the need to have a fast-moving one overwhelms you. You stop and see a tall, mirrored building. You decide to enter. There are letters on the building, just three, far fewer than those making up *LA BREA TAR PITS*. You cannot read them, but their pointy, up-and-down slashes remind you of beeping bedside monitors you saw in the hospital. This must mean there's life inside. Fast-moving ones inside. You like these three letters a lot.

WWN.

Sarcophages

'Fuck me, you gotta be fucking kidding me, you fucking fuck!'

Luis Acocella yelled this at his phone – his best friend, his arch-nemesis. Between encouraging Charlie's more outré decisions, such as bashing through the red plastic of a Wendy's sign to evade a fender bender or destroying a front-yard rose garden to escape a bottle-neck, Luis had managed to dance his jittery fingers through the multiple, multisyllabic passwords required to open up a Lilliputian version of the VSDC home page. His goal was to manually upload what he felt was the pivotal revelation of the John Doe case: that a killing blow to the brain, and nothing less, had stopped him.

Turns out, his fucking access was tied to the fucking morgue's secure fucking IP address. Here he had real fucking info that might save real fucking lives and no fucking way to spread it. Unless he was being timed out by the shitty signal?

This was, for Luis, an anxiety familiar enough to be comforting, and he embraced it, hoisting his phone out the rolled-down passenger window like that ever did a goddamn thing, then thumbing back-ground apps into oblivion, like that did a goddamn thing either. The Prius hit a bump. Traffic was only moving at a start-and-stop ten miles per hour, but the car's shocks jounced. The impediment was larger than a speed bump. Luis peered into his rearview mirror.

'Don't look back, Acocella.'

Good advice. Given what they'd seen both at the morgue and since leaving it, it was better not to know, even if it went against a physician's instincts. Luis shrugged at Charlie, hoping to project a goofiness that might help get them another five minutes down the road. It was like patching his bicycle tire with his brother, Manolo, when they were kids. The rubber-and-glue patches held for a few miles, and Luis would settle for that, a distraction against the hell that had crawled out of the morgue's cooler and begun to flood the San Diego streets.

He thought back to sprinting from Fabi's Spanish Palace, to his first sight of John Doe's body, a soft lump beneath the overpass. How quaint his argument with Detective Walker seemed now. In the hours since, Luis had seen many similar lumps on sidewalks, lawns, porches, and playgrounds, a couple of which he'd caught in the process of standing back up. Still, branding this as Armageddon was premature. Twenty-four-hour fast-food joints were still doling out bagged heart attacks, and all-night check-cashing spots were still carving up paychecks.

Only one thing had really collapsed: the roads. A power plant must have blinked out somewhere, cutting traffic signals and streetlights. Not even a passenger with a complete mental map of the city and a driver of IndyCar ability could get anywhere. Interstates, two-lanes, byways, alleys – any route he and Charlie tried, a crash, abandoned vehicle, or sawhorse fort held them back.

Luis felt Charlie's hand give his free wrist a squeeze.

Maybe it was the fright, the disorientation, but her hand felt good.

He had to pull his wrist away to tap *Rosa* on his Favorites. His phone said it was his thirty-third time. Once more, only the dead tone he'd never heard before today. The vehicle jerked as Charlie hit the brakes. Right outside Luis's window, a veterinary clinic. Shavings of dirt rose up from the bottoms of doors, and hair and whiskers poked from screen windows. The animals were trying to get out. Luis swiped to his camera to get a shot, but the storage was full. He cursed, thumbed back, and squinted at thumbnails to choose a photo for execution.

'Wasn't it some indigenous tribe that said photos stole your soul?' Charlie asked.

'If that's true,' Luis said, 'we're all empty.'

'Broken-record time: you've got to stop staring at that phone.'

'Mmmmm.'

'Shit is *happening*, Acocella. It's happening right in front of our faces.'

'Fuck! Of course!'

'Well, that's more enthusiasm than I'd expected.'

'No! Social fucking media! That's how I'll get this out!'

'Oh, come *on*.'

He axed Favorites, swiped to find Twitter. 'Taylor Swift, Justin Bieber – I'm counting on you guys.'

Charlie snorted, which made Luis grin: another patch on another tire. The diener had kept her spirits up, Luis gave her that. Glancing at Charlie, he had to acknowledge she'd never looked better, her scrubs long gone to reveal her fallback ensemble of frayed jean shorts and a breast-baring flannel shirt, her blond hair like soapsuds in a breeze. Luis had seen before how she sharpened during a crisis, reverting to the agility and energy of her booze-and-bruise Parkchester youth. It was attractive; there was no denying it. He'd never been more grateful for it than tonight. The Acocella home was ten miles from the morgue, a fifteen-minute drive on an ordinary night, but they were hours into it now, and still Charlie had an athlete's loose, alert poise. He was lucky to have her. That hadn't changed.

Gallows humor had been key to thriving in the morgue. Now it was absolutely crucial if they wanted to ignore three big, menacing questions for however long it took to reach La Mesa.

First: Was Rosa alive? It was a question so beyond anything Luis could have imagined when leaving the house yesterday that he found it easy to sidestep, as preposterous as a Bigfoot invasion.

Luis could see the second question in Charlie's rearview-mirror glances; it was harder to dodge. Was Lindof, the man who'd reveled in JT's plunge from Trump International Hotel, pursuing them in some way? Or were others affiliated with Lindof? The man had encouraged Luis to panic, and as much as he'd like to deny that asshole, panic was the emotion du jour. Luis had known men who spoke like Lindof, men in power, and they made lifelong hobbies of grudges. Luis had a hunch he'd be checking his rearview for a long time.

The third question, of course, was the biggie. What the flying fuck *was* this? When they rode a shoulder to escape a clusterfucked Martin Luther King Jr Freeway, Luis pictured the plaque from his office on the front of a Pizza Hut being boarded up. He saw the plaque on the Home Depot on Imperial, where people ran out carrying what he assumed were stolen hoes, posts, and other swingable objects, while orange-vested workers gave chase. He pictured the plaque atop St Stephen's Church of God, which looked to be holding an impromptu late-night service, complete with gun-toting parishioners at every door.

THIS IS THE PLACE WHERE DEATH REJOICES TO HELP THOSE WHO LIVE, except 'the place' had expanded far beyond Luis's office, and how the dead were 'helping' the living remained thoroughly unclear. Yet Luis had a hunch there was something to it, the same way he'd had a hunch none of the bullets in John Doe had been kill shots.

He opened his Twitter. The heavily filtered profile pic of him flashing pearly whites at the last Pride Parade, the trying-too-hard bio reading *San Diego assistant medical examiner / ceviche artist / still like the Chargers,* the archive of tweets sent to, and ignored by, his disinterested 835 followers. This post might be different. He started typing, decided this warranted all-caps, and started over.

*URGENT: I'M A DOCTOR & THE ONLY WAY TO STOP THE
MISCARRIAGE*

He stopped. He thought of the event as the Miscarriage, but that
wouldn't mean shit to anyone else.

'What do I call Them?' he asked.

'Huh? Who?'

'The, you know, the people! The fucking John Does!'

'How am I supposed to know? The radio's just saying *They* and
Them. You're the one on Twitter, Inspector Gadget.'

Fair point: Luis tapped the search icon, then scrolled to Trends.
Evidence of the Miscarriage was there, though not yet coalesced
under a single hashtag, and being pounded by #BenHines – the
beloved actor must have made some inspirational statement. Luis
toggled back to his message.

'Sarcophages,' he muttered.

'Remind me,' Charlie said.

'From the Greek *sarco,* for flesh, and *phage,* for eat. Flesh flies,
basically. The ones that hatch their maggots during a body's active
decay phase.'

Charlie banked to avoid a honking horde of vehicles, slinging
Luis into his door.

'Let me see if I follow, boss. If I recall the videos they made us
watch in school, sarcophage maggots show up pretty instantly.'

'Within twenty-four hours.'

'They've got little hooks on their heads so they can chew the rotting meat without slipping off.'

'They're not going anywhere.'

'Pretty soon, there's so many at work that the corpse's temperature rises to 120 degrees.'

'Very hot in the kitchen, yes.'

'In a week, 60 percent of the body is gone.'

'That's what I'm worried about. Except the body is . . .'

Luis gestured at the San Diego skyline. Charlie's moan was the one she pulled out when exasperated by his melodrama. She was patching bicycle tires, too, keeping things normal till they found Rosa safe and sound. He was grateful for her efforts. He completed his post, minus *sarcophages*. He could try to get that trending later.

> URGENT: I'M A DOCTOR & THE ONLY WAY TO STOP THE
> DEAD PEOPLE RETURNING TO LIFE IS BY DIRECT TRAUMA TO
> THE HEAD. PLEASE RT!!!

He had half his 280 characters left, valuable real estate for the millions of retweets he hoped were coming. But what else was there to say? Officials were providing nothing to which to link, and he had jack shit to attach. Despite Luis and Charlie's threats to Lindof, neither had taken a single photo of John Doe. He didn't even have one of the site's blue checkmarks to bequeath him a scintilla of legitimacy. All he had was the truth. The truth had to be enough. Wasn't this America?

He hit Tweet, then refreshed his feed to watch it land.

Usually social media brought him the tingling rush he used to see patients receive after thumbing bedside buttons for morphine or fentanyl. Not this time. San Diego's service was throttled down to the kind of anemic signal parceled to hayseeds in South Dakota's Badlands or the Texas Panhandle. The upload bar was moving, however, so Luis trusted in the app – he believed in Twitter shit more than God shit – and scrolled to see if there was breaking news.

There was, though it took him a while to see it.

The surface text was largely innocent. *Anyone know what's happening on Lower Wacker, people abandoning cars. Cops surrounding a funeral home in downtown lawrence kansas, wtf.* The subtext, however, was darker and required Luis to open the threads. Regarding

Lower Wacker: *its black gangbangers from the southside they crawled up thru tunnels.* Regarding that funeral home: *my friend a cop told me jews took it over cuz jew sinagogs suck.*

The bulk of accounts Luis followed were San Diego-based, people he knew or friends of friends, more liberal-minded and better educated than any randos adding their shitty two cents. It was with rising nausea, then, that Luis read updates that might have been written by Detective Walker.

Looks like Tijuana trouble ha ha – a lawyer friend he'd had over to dinner.

'Acocella, put down the phone.'

SD crime wave tonight, friends. Beginning to come around to idea of Build the Wall – the real estate agent who'd sold him his house.

'Acocella. Please.'

We need a citizen militia to trash compact this Mexcrement!!! – a city councilman Luis had voted for, referencing San Diego's Latino-dominated garbage-collecting industry.

'Acocella! Pay attention! Now!'

Charlie skidded to a stop, propelling Luis into the seat belt so hard he felt bisected. The phone flew from his hands, its plastic clacking like shattered teeth, something suddenly easy to imagine. *He* was Latino. *He* was born in Mexico. In just a few thumb strokes across a touch screen, had he gone from potential savior from the sarcophages to the one being blamed for it?

The answer was waiting in the car's headlights. Sliding in front of the Prius, close enough that Luis could hear their toted objects clucking across the front bumper, was a quartet of men. Four John Does expunged by the Miscarriage, Luis thought, until he saw the flash of eight eyes, none of them cloudy white. The men lifted gadgets lit up like a mob's torches and peered into the car. They curled their lips at Charlie, no-good lady driver, before giving Luis a harder look.

The objects making noises against the bumper rose into the view: crowbar, baseball bat, wrench, hatchet.

Luis told himself it was all right. His car was idling beside a Dunkin' Donuts. Catty-corner from a Denny's. Bad things did not happen at the junction of such icons of Americana. But when one of the men muttered a word and the others positioned themselves at intervals around the hood, Luis lost faith in the safety promised by his adopted country and wondered how he'd allowed himself to blithely believe it would always be there. The .38 in his pocket doubled in weight.

'You okay, lady?' Baseball Bat called.

'I will be,' Charlie snapped, 'when you get away from my car!'

'We need to move,' Luis said.

'We're collecting trash tonight,' Wrench jeered, another allusion to Latino garbage collectors.

Scare tactics fired up his diener. 'Look in a mirror, then, shitter!'

'Gas, Charlie.'

Crowbar pointed his weapon. 'We want the Mexican out of the car, ma'am.'

'I'd like to see you try, xenophobic beer-gut asshole!'

Wrench and Hatchet went for the doors.

'Will you stomp the damn gas?' Luis cried.

Charlie did, while holding a foot on the brake, an advanced move probably taught in Bronx grade schools. The squeal of rubber and dervish of smoke made all four commandos scatter, at which point Charlie released the brake and the Prius fishtailed forward, Luis's door glancing off a parking meter with a spray of sparks. Charlie hooted, wrestling the wheel for control while sparing an arm to shoot the bird out the window.

'You!' It was all Luis could sputter. 'You!'

'Quiet,' Charlie laughed. 'You love it!'

'I do not fucking love it!' Luis cried, though at that instant his fear was vanquished by the thrill of the wind in his hair, the engine throbbing beneath his feet, the wicked chortle of the sexy lady at the wheel. He'd long suspected Charlie had a crush on him. Now he wondered if a similar feeling had been hiding deep under his layers of professionalism.

'Least it got your face out of that phone,' Charlie said.

That it had, and five minutes later, swerving around pedestrians on the outer circle of the Highwood Park area where he and Rosa lived, Luis was thankful. It meant he was alert and focused as they approached the Lincoln Military Housing complex, which was exactly what it sounded like. In front of it, a throbbing knot of humanity blocked the road.

First he feared it to be more guerrillas hunting 'Mexcrement'. Then he hoped it was off-duty military forming an ad hoc safety zone. As Charlie slowed the car to a crawl, Luis realized that whatever it was had gone drastically wrong. What Luis had thought was a bonfire was a house in flames, lighting the road in front of them. Military order did not reign; there was no order at all. One faction of people had fallen upon another, the first group's wiggling and slurping more like sarcophagal maggots than Luis could have imagined.

They also toddled a bit. Learning to walk. Like babies.

Maybe *the Miscarriage* was the most apt phrase after all.

'Ditch is too deep to take,' Charlie said.

He said it without thinking: 'Mmmmm.'

'Where's your place? Point to it.'

He pointed, an obedient child. 'There.'

'Out of the car. Acocella, out of the fucking car!'

He picked up his phone and got out. Charlie took his wrist and they ran. Not fast enough. Luis saw plenty.

People were being eaten. It was the darkly logical extension of John Doe's grasping fingers and smacking lips. In the firelight, Luis saw open mouths blot out whole faces, fingers hollowing bones from thighs, tongues lapping exposed innards. When Charlie hesitated, twenty feet from the crush, Luis saw no fewer than three people fall to sarcophages. He was not able to tell if they were neighbors he knew, because gadgets masked so many of them. It felt like irony that it was the dead who had faces, while the living were known only by their designer cases.

One person was desperately texting with his thumbs; seconds later, both thumbs were gone inside grinding jaws. One was checking a notification; even after he was facedown in the grass, teeth clamped to his spine, he kept reading, the dopamine surge a rebuke to the blood loss. One was taking photos of a sarcophage; even as it scaled her legs, she preferred to view it through her camera, and Luis related. The little box could make anything seem contained, controllable, and closable with a single touch.

Charlie pulled him down a slope, through a wet culvert, and around a backyard pool, carving a shortcut to Rosa. Luis should have given Charlie credit for that – hurrying them to the doorstep of the woman who had the man she wanted – but they were going too fast, the world blearing like swipes of his gadgets' screens. You swiped past enough awful things enough times and you quit seeing them, quit feeling them, and that, he realized, was when you began to die.

Urschleim

Bicycling from Sunnybrook Mobile Home Resort to the town proper of Bulk, Missouri, took twenty minutes. But that was going it alone, butt popped high, legs at full extension, the wind in your face making you believe you were going eighty in a topless hot rod. So fast that, in spring, rain parted before you like a biblical sea, and in fall, dead leaves peeled away like company dancers revealing their prima donna: you.

On the seat of Fadi Lolo's blue Schwinn, Greer Morgan suffered the trip at agonizing half speed. Their combined weight fattened the bike's tires against pavement and sank them spoke-deep in mud. The path was desolate on a normal day; today, Greer saw enough bad signs to make her want to hop off the bike and run for it: a loose dog trailing a bloody leash, a station wagon drilled with bullet holes, the scoreboard at the fairgrounds baseball park flashing only one word: *RUN*.

Biking was still faster than walking, so she stuck with it.

'Straight,' she snapped. 'Straight, straight, straight.'

'Faster here,' Fadi wheezed, nodding at derelict storage buildings.

'You can't get through here!'

'Faster here.'

Plenty going on Greer didn't like. Sitting static while this subdued Syrian did all the work. Gripping his waist like a damsel. Not being listened to for directions when she was the one who'd lived, if that's what you wanted to call it, in Bulk her whole stupid life. What kept shutting her up was Fadi's gentle self-assurance, and the fact he kept being right. It made some sense. He was the one who might see Missouri's mild hills, skeleton trees, and pale sunsets as beautiful, worthy of exploration. He'd pioneered shortcuts she'd never had the energy to pursue.

Fadi sailed into a four-foot gap between rusty sheds with perfect aim, just as he'd shot between jammed cars to get out of Sunnybrook. Greer held on tightly and spotted the split fence ahead that would indeed lop a couple of minutes from their journey. A good sign, but still she shivered. Fadi Lolo might like to pick up trash and rescue Black girls from besieged trailers. But he was also a man, not to be fully trusted. At his whim, he could swerve into one of these outbuildings and try to overpower her.

'You do not need the big knife,' he said. 'We are going to town for our brother.'

Greer had to look down to see she still had the machete against his back. She told herself to chill out. She had a duffel bag full of hunting weapons. This screwball would have to be nuts to pull any shit. When she'd told him she wanted to go to town to find her brother, Conan, he'd replied, *Our brother. We all share the same brother now, yes?* Greer took deep breaths shallowed by the air's hot mist. She would trust this guy. With Vienna Morgan lost to the prison system and Freddy Morgan rabid and faceless, instincts were all she had left.

Daddy. She felt like sobbing. She felt like throwing up. What would she tell Conan? If she didn't distract herself, she'd lack even the strength to keep clinging to Fadi's waist.

'Mister,' she said. 'What do you do?'

'What do I do.'

'For fun. What do you do for fun?'

'You must measure the tire pressure and you must lubricate the chains.'

'Your bike? You take care of your bike. What else?'

'I watch so much TV.'

'What do you watch?'

'*Damages.*'

'*Damages.* What's that?'

'*Damages* is an Emmy-winning legal drama starring Glenn Close as Patty Hewes.'

Greer laughed. She paused and laughed again. It was the most words she'd heard Fadi say at once, and possibly the funniest thing she'd heard in her life. Laughter was a self-perpetuating magic: she felt more coming and was greedy for it.

'What else, what else?'

'*New Girl* is an Emmy-nominated sitcom starring Zooey Deschanel as Jessica Day.'

'You're really into the Emmys, mister.'

'*The X-Files* is Emmy-winning drama starring David Duchovny as Fox Mulder and Gillian Anderson as Dana Scully.'

'Oh, I've seen that. Flukeman. He's the shit.'

'"The Host" is the second episode of the second season.'

'What's your favorite episode?'

'"Kill Switch",' Fadi said instantly. 'It is the episode they talk of Urschleim.'

'Is he the smoking guy?'

'Urschleim is primordial slime,' Fadi said. 'It is the life between plant life and animal life. It is the missing life.'

'You mean the missing link?' She giggled. 'Daddy used to call Conan that.'

'There is not just life and death. It is not so simple. There are many shades.'

Greer's laughter died out. 'Yeah, I think you're right.'

'I have seen it.' He paused. 'But the word I learned from Dana Scully.'

Missouri's famous rocky bluffs hemmed along the Mississippi River, but the western half of the state was not without hills. The hilltop before them, crowned with leafless trees, looked like a patchy, upside-down chin-beard. Upon cresting it, one would see everything the town of four thousand had to offer, if one's heart could take the excitement: Jimmy's Tap, Auto Value, Shopko, Kunkle's Tire & Repair, Farmers Mutual Insurance, Casey's, and the Raskey Apartments, all huddled around a miserable little town square as if pissing on it.

Fadi was out of breath when he reached the top. He climbed off the bike and staggered aside to breathe. Greer bailed in the other direction, machete in one hand, duffel in the other, so they were a Schwinn's length apart, unable to feel the comfort of each other's bodies, when they saw what the town square had become.

One of the gas pumps at Casey's was on fire, a roaring, white-hot furnace melting a hole through the service station awning. More shocking was the blaze was being ignored. No men with fire extinguishers, no ululating fire trucks, no deputy diverting motorists from the danger of additional explosions. Bulk was inhabited by rotten, small-minded people, Greer had always known, but she hadn't believed they were this bad.

They *were* this bad, and worse. From the look of it, everyone within ten blocks had amassed in the town square. Some three hundred Bulkers seethed as a single angry mass. A distinct line split the crowd into two unequal groups.

The larger group was mostly white folks clad in seed-company hats, hairnets, work aprons, and, most ubiquitous of all, the same gray HortiPlastics uniform Daddy had worn. Brandishing guns, brooms, and other arms, Team HortiPlastics promised the kind of mob brawl Greer had only seen in movies. Though she preferred texting on her phone to watching history-class videos, she paid attention when Black people came on-screen, usually in scenes like this, getting shit-kicked in Alabama or Arkansas or Mississippi, but looking proud as hell and badass as fuck.

She expected the second, smaller group to be the enemy she'd met at Sunnybrook.

But the things distinguishing those forty or fifty people from the HortiPlastics crowd were darker beards, a sprinkling of hijabs, and clothing that, even at a distance, had the ill-fitting look of items plucked from Salvation Army racks. They were the Syrian refugees, a point of pride for Jefferson City legislators, a point of contempt for Bulk residents.

Greer got the feeling the Syrians' lack of weapons was less due to pacifist views than it was the brief time they'd had to assemble. They'd come outside to hold their own, that's all, and an echo rang through Greer's bones. No one at the Last Resort gave two shits about the trailer park, but they'd fought for what was theirs, hadn't they? *Refugee* – Greer was pretty sure it meant a person forced to run. The Raskey Apartments might be an insect- and rodent-ridden eyesore, but for these countrymen of Fadi's, it was a true last resort.

Hateful sneers, flexed like muscles, ripped across Team Horti-Plastics. Greer knew a lot of these people. Store owners, teachers, parents of classmates. People who drove cars with bumper stickers like CRIME CONTROL NOT GUN CONTROL and FIGHT CRIME, SHOOT BACK. Daddy, owner of two rifles himself, had discussed these people in a voice too worried to be disdainful. *They like to imagine themselves as heroes,* he'd said, *but all they're going to do is get folks killed.* He'd glanced at Conan, a young Black man, when he'd said it, but Conan, as always, seemed lost in his own world.

Self-proclaimed heroes could only exist in opposition to villains. Why not blame the sudden violence on the local refugee population?

Many of the Syrians barely spoke English. They ate strong-smelling food. They took up too many benches on the town square, too much picnic space in the park. They were freeloaders who didn't have jobs, and also, they should stop stealing all the jobs.

Qasim made some of these complaints last night, and she'd merely thought them tiresome. She'd been a different person then; by now, Qasim might be different too. Where was he? She didn't see many teens in the crowd. At school, probably; perhaps teachers had chosen to barricade the student body against the unfolding crisis. Good – Greer would give Conan the machete and Qasim the knife, and the three of them would do what needed doing.

Greer and Fadi arrived as the lit wick hit dynamite. Three men in front, all in HortiPlastics garb, pushed the refugees until one Syrian had to swipe to protect his face, the gesture obvious evidence of his murderous heart. The instigators pounced, and the scene erupted into the sloppy, slappy meat thwacks Greer had seen in parking lot fights – the quick-drop, the blood-gush, the red faces and held breath, the elbows to lips, the fingers to eyes. If you worked for Horti-Plastics, your daily routine was swallowing pride, and here was a chance to win that pride back, your colleagues and friends versus those fucking Arabs.

Greer shuddered. On which side would Daddy have landed?

She felt Fadi Lolo's wet scarf against her cheek again and realized she'd moved to him, not he to her. Despite her bag of weapons, she wanted only to evade this fight.

'Mister,' she said. 'We can get to the school the other way, past the junkyard.'

'No,' Fadi said.

She looked at his mud-spattered face and rain-tangled hair. The placid amiability of the Emmys-obsessed pedal-pusher was gone. Fadi's face had relaxed, though not sedately, his forehead creasing along old lines of lament and his cheeks sagging into old pouches of pain. The face of the only happy person she'd ever seen at the Last Resort became the face of a man who'd seen things worse than this.

He nodded at the people yelping and rolling like scrapping dogs.

'Alkasālā.'

'I don't know what that means.'

'You see? You cannot tell them apart.'

Greer hated to get an inch closer. People would see her, a Black girl, and Fadi, a Syrian, and one faction or the other, or both, would punish them for their affiliation. But Fadi had asked for nothing in return for rescue, so she stepped closer. Maybe she'd been as prejudiced as any bumper-sticker bastard – she'd never believed the Syrians would blend in here in Bulk. Now they had, and in the worst way. The cliché that everyone bled the same never felt truer.

One thing she could say for the white-eyed rabid: They never showed this much relish in violence.

Fadi moved with a square-shouldered walk.

'Mister,' Greer cried. 'Mister – Fadi – don't go!'

He turned amid combat dust and pinned her with a look.

'The fight waits for me,' he said. 'It always waits.'

'It doesn't have to. Come with me. We can do anything we want.'

From Fadi's grimace, Greer felt she'd revealed something shameful.

'I should not have insisted on Sunnybrook Mobile Home Resort,' he said. 'I should have stayed with my people. What do you think, Greer Morgan? Why do the dead make others into the dead? Is it because *They* want to be with Their people as well?'

That Fadi knew Greer's name shouldn't have surprised her. Maybe he'd hesitated to use it for the same reason she'd hesitated to use his. Knitting a closeness today was only to watch it unravel.

'The bike?' Her voice had never sounded so weak.

'Ride fast.'

'The machete,' she offered.

'Swing fast too.'

She nodded. 'Be careful, Fadi Lolo.'

His unexpected grin burst like the gas-pump fire, melting a hole through her heart.

'I cannot be harmed, Dana Scully,' he proclaimed. 'I am Urschleim.'

Fadi ran then, and Greer looked away, unwilling to see the first blow he took, or worse, the first he delivered. She slid the machete into the duffel bag, strapped it to her shoulders like a backpack, and took the Schwinn by its horns. The metal grips of the pedals drove into her bare feet like spurs. She was the one with the bicycle now, all that was left of Fadi. She didn't look back, cutting down the hill at a diagonal toward the junkyard and Bulk High School. Once there, she'd play the part of rescuer Fadi Lolo had taught her, saving Conan, saving Qasim, maybe dozens more too, all balanced in a cheerleader stack atop a blue Schwinn as she pedaled them to safety.

Being Decent

No news-biz maxim was more notorious, despicable, and true
than *If it bleeds, it leads.* But what was a poor executive producer to
do when *every* story bled, and so profusely the anchor's voice
sounded clotted, as if gargling blood, and his skin looked sticky, as if
he'd just wiped a layer of it away. By now, Nathan Baseman thought,
people's TV screens must be exuding bulbs of blood like condensation. One thing was certain, and it still brought him the same
satisfaction it had in Chicago, Kansas City, Nashville, and Houston:
he had people's attention, that was for damn sure.

He took another pull of the bourbon he'd kept in his desk drawer
since airing the Jansky shot three years ago; he'd been convinced he'd
need it one day, if only to build up courage to walk into Interstate 85
traffic. He'd made it through that grueling time without breaking the
bourbon's seal. Now, a few hours into this ghoul business, the bottle
was already nearly empty. Some of it, true, he'd used as disinfectant,
sloshed over the gash between his knuckles and through the hole
Rochelle Glass had punched through his cheek. Lord, did that one
hurt.

Baseman could bleed, all right. Could he still lead?

He tried to focus on his scrawled notes. At its most mechanical,
the job of producer was to thumbs-up or thumbs-down stories for
the newscast and arrange packages, live shots, and readers for
utmost impact. Like most producers, Baseman usually promoted the

emotion-driven 'peak-and-valley' pattern of anxiety and relief, but that had all gone into the wood chipper now. The new method was 'peak-and-peak-and-peak', each story surpassing the previous in atrocity.

Baseman tapped his pen. What deserved the first slot of A-block? How about the LA Fitness branch in Knoxville that had become a ghoul slaughterhouse, with witnesses describing stacks of dismembered ghouls in the aerobics room while living ghouls were gleefully tortured in weight machines by staff trainers? Or was it better to go with the more threatening report of a sniper atop a Cleveland-area roller coaster, taking advantage of freeway gridlock to pick off both ghouls and people?

Fuck it. It was all going in anyway, all regular features jettisoned, including the Unitas-mandated, D-block, cute-kid send-off – unless the cute kid in question had a mouthful of Mommy. No one had seen Nick Unitas since the Ross Quincey meeting, so fuck him too, right? Baseman numbered the stories at random and stood up. His jacket practically fell off; it was weighed down by Item One and Item Two. He steadied them and stumbled into the control room like a new-born foal, every sinew aching from the stairwell mêlée.

'Boom,' he said, handing the outline to Lee Sutton. 'Our next hour.'

Lee slid his headphones down. 'You look like walking death.'

'You're not exactly dressed for the prom.'

His grin revealing his newly missing tooth, Lee looked at the dried blood snarling his shirt, the aftereffect of Baseman's punch. He swiped the page from Baseman, gave it a once-over, and rattled off instructions with enough briskness to spatter the page with red saliva.

'Fessler, we're going to need Feeds 2 and 10. Watch for Octavia on Line 1. Zoë's coming with that CDC report. If she makes it in time, let's stick it between A2 and A3, or swap it for B1 if we need to. How's the Telemundo package?'

'Almost got it. It's, you know, in Spanish.'

'Doesn't matter. We'll run that shit todo el tiempo.'

'Whatever you say, boss.'

Baseman could hear the swagger in Lee's voice, the determination in Fessler's. He steadied himself against the same file cabinet he'd shoved against the door so he could grab the rogue White House feed uncontested. He'd blame this dizziness on the bourbon if it came from his head. Instead, it came from his heart. These people he worked with. Once upon a time, perhaps he'd deserved them, but no longer.

Lee Sutton, bootlicking yes-man. Baseman would have bet a year's salary he'd have been the first out of WWN's double doors. Maybe he should have decked the director years ago. Lee had spat out his spineless parts along with the blood and mucus and was now proving just how few people could keep a news network operating. Tim Fessler should have scrammed – he had a young wife, kids – but it took two, at severe minimum, to run a control room, and he'd recognized the higher calling of that. Baseman had outright ordered Zoë Shillace, his intern, to leave, roaring it from behind the bag of frozen corn pressed to his cheek, but she hadn't. Baseman could not fathom it. She had her whole life left, and should be out there fighting for it. Then again, maybe that's what she was doing by staying here.

Then there was the Face. Baseman had sopped up a lot of motivational D-block drivel in his day, but nothing had come closer to restoring his faith in humanity than what had overtaken Chuck Corso.

Where Lee Sutton had unloaded himself of fear like one might throw objects from a sinking boat, the Face hadn't rid himself of anything. His dread remained. His anxiety remained. His verbal garblings remained. His lack of global insight remained. But to this shoddy repertoire he'd added something no newsperson before him had dared: raw honesty. Each monitor Baseman passed blew his mind. The Face opining, 'That was the worst shit I've ever fucking seen.' The Face admitting, 'I don't know how to pronounce that word.' The Face picking his nose. The Face announcing he had to take a shit, he'd be right back. He was a man on a ledge, fully open to horror and pain and beauty, reacting with an infant's purity.

The damn male model was *saving lives*. As WWN did during natural disasters, they'd taken to patching in viewers lucky enough to have phone service. The Face had convinced, on air, a hysterical grandfather to go back into a twelve-unit building full of ghouls to save his wheelchair-using son. He did this not with facts but empathy; the Face was nakedly horrified by what the man said. On the other hand, he'd convinced a retired woman *not* to go into the factory where her daughter was trapped, and by the same method: feeling it along with her and speaking those feelings aloud.

As it turned out, once severed from one's ego, a person's instincts could be quite refined. At one point, Zoë had made the studio staff aware of a tweet going through the roof, a 123-character update posted by a San Diego medical examiner named Luis Acocella. His credentials checked out, but the Face didn't care; he ran to the control room to personally ask Tim Fessler to put the tweet on the screen in a graphic. It popped up on the screen nearly instantly:

> URGENT: I'M A DOCTOR & THE ONLY WAY TO STOP THE
> DEAD PEOPLE RETURNING TO LIFE IS BY DIRECT TRAUMA TO
> THE HEAD. PLEASE RT!!!

People flocked to WWN's media accounts to report successes: kill the brain and you kill the ghoul. The word was being embraced; Zoë reported the Face's tangent about Nonna had inspired #ghouls, the world's number-one trending topic. Unitas would have preferred #WWN, and a day ago, Baseman would have felt the same pang of missed opportunity. Today, all that mattered was the message. His coworkers had taught him that. *Coworkers* was too cold. *Colleagues* was better. Dare he get even warmer? He realized he loved this four-some like he hadn't loved a crew since his days rollicking around Chicago.

It was the kind of love, he suspected, a battalion of soldiers felt when it looked like none of them were getting out of a battle alive.

Baseman swung by the kitchen. Item One jangled in his left pocket. Item Two, much heavier, thunked against the stove. A couple of days without kitchen etiquette and this was what happened. Crumby counters, a floor gummy with spills. He opened the fridge, grabbed a water, and threw open a couple of cabinets. So much had been cleared out. He claimed a column of saltines.

Lee had raised the studio lights to neutralize any more from-the-dark surprises. Camera 2 had been secured in place by pedestal brakes and a dune of sandbags. The anchor desk was still brilliant, a dais fit for a royal. The Face was talking, that's all. Baseman didn't think he'd ever get over it. Banter, ad-libs, bumps, teases, tosses – Chuck Corso had never been capable of doing them right. This, of course, wasn't 'right' either, not as the world would have defined it yesterday.

Baseman stood by Camera 2 and held up the saltines. One of the ten billion new tasks that had fallen under his executive producer purview was making sure his talent stayed fed. The Face acknowledged Baseman with a glance, then completed telling a personal story about finding a dead dog in a field as a kid. What this had to do with the price of tea in China, Baseman couldn't say, but he trusted it did. Moreover, it did not matter. The Face was *connecting*. Baseman felt the urge to sit cross-legged like a kindergartener at story time.

The Telemundo package came through. The Face touched his ear-piece, listened to Lee, then admitted to viewers he didn't know what they were about to see, though chances were, of course, it wasn't going to be pretty. All he had were the specs: seven minutes, thirty-two seconds. He'd see them back here afterward, where together they'd deal with it.

The live light went dark. Baseman climbed the platform, circled the desk, and flopped on the carpet behind it, his back to one of the legs. If the camera went live earlier than expected, at least he'd been hidden down here. He held up the meager snacks, and the Face, reclining in his chair, took them. He placed five crackers into his mouth at once and gnashed.

'Wmp smp?' *Want some?*

Baseman showed the Face the bourbon, the sole sustenance he required. For a minute, they ate and drank, their dinner music the tinny Telemundo audio coming through the Face's earpiece. Screams required no translation.

'NBC still out?' the Face asked.

Baseman let the whiskey slosh in his mouth to numb his cheek. Grotesquely, a drop seeped through the hole. He swallowed and felt coagulated blood slide down his throat.

'Uh-huh. CBS is bye-bye too. Fox is in and out. It's the power outages. New York is dark. Times Square is lights-out. Never thought I'd be glad to be marooned in Georgia, but there it is.'

'How long you think our grid will hold?'

'Depends how long people stay at their stations.' Baseman gestured at the empty studio. 'Doesn't bode well, does it?'

'Our wireless seems all right.'

'Can't use your phone, though, can you?'

'Then how are calls getting in?'

'You noticed something about our callers, right? How old most of them are?'

'Landlines.'

'Who would've guessed it, huh? The last demographic with the means to band together: old folks. *My* people.'

The Face took a sloppy pull of water and gasped for air. 'I keep thinking of that interview we ran last hour, the guy freaking out about mummies.'

'Missed it,' Baseman said. 'Not sure mummies are priority one.'

'I guess the power's out at the Met. They keep the mummies behind this plexiglass that imitates, you know, the conditions of Egyptian tombs. This guy was saying they're all going to rot now – humidity, mold. He was crying. I mean, really sobbing. Five thousand years old, he was saying, a record of the most important thing of all, how people died.'

'How they *used* to die.' Under the stage lights, Baseman felt like a mummy, baked dry, the relic Glass had accused him of being. 'I can't tell what's important anymore. I don't know what we're doing. Only thing I know is you're doing a hell of a good job.'

Baseman glanced up. The Face, formerly known for the perfection of his clothes, face, and hair, had lost ground in all three departments. Tie loosened, shirt rumpled and wet, sleeves rolled up, cheeks showing stubble that, on any normal day, an armada of touch-up artists would have disposed of or buried. His face and neck were spotted pink – he kept scratching – and the spot where the Glass-thing had harvested a sprout of his hair plugs had bruised. It gave the pretty boy a boxer's distinction.

The Face shrugged. 'You trusted me to do it.'

'I don't deserve any credit.' Baseman muttered. '*You* did this. You're *doing* it. You're mattering. And just by being decent.' He laughed once, a self-inflicted shot to his chest. 'Never thought I'd see that on the news.'

'I wonder if that's all Glass was. Honest, in her own way. Maybe that's why so many people liked her.'

The urge to come clean burned, cheap bourbon through Baseman's veins. *I murdered Rochelle Glass,* he wanted to say. *I bit her throat out in the stairwell, and not because I had to but because I wanted to.*

His memory of it was dim. He'd sat on the lower landing for a while, his arms resting on his knees as he tried to vomit up the gluey blood of Glass's trachea, pint by pint. He could feel the blood in his stomach and intestines, a long, warm, wriggling tapeworm. He had to puke it out. Otherwise, it would burrow out and reveal him for what he was: a base man. After a while, he gave up. He'd had other things to do, like pry Glass's corpse off the Face on live TV.

No one knew what Nathan Baseman looked like. He was just some blood-soaked Black guy dragging America's top-rated cable host off Chuck Corso. The internet had exploded; anyone who hadn't been tuned to WWN before switched over and stayed. As the torrent of uploaded videos, GIFs, and still frames made clear, the white-eyed Rochelle Glass was not the Rochelle Glass anyone knew. She was America's first celebrity ghoul, one everyone in the nation could recognize as fundamentally changed. Alongside Tammy Shellenbarger's apocalyptic press conference, it erased all doubt that the ghoul uprising, whatever it was, was for real.

With the help of a camera operator and floor manager, both of whom ended up bitten and soon fled the building, Baseman was able to lug the hissing, flailing Glass to the cyclorama wall. This was before Luis Acocella's tweet about head trauma had gone viral, and Baseman uselessly bashed Glass's body with a stool until the white-painted cyc wall was filigreed with scarlet blood. Believing he might cause himself a heart attack, he dragged her by the hair into news director Pam Tripler's office, locked the door, and used a magic marker to write on it, DO NOT OPEN!!!

He tried to neutralize his shame with excuses. Glass had called him an ape. You don't call a Black man an ape. Next, he tried to neutralize it with logic. Could you really call it murder if your victim got up and walked away? Perhaps it was Chuck Corso's honesty that gave Baseman's lies teeth, which chewed on him just as he'd chewed on Glass.

No one knew what he'd done except Kwame in security, whom Glass had called from the stairwell. But Kwame posed no threat, at least in that regard. He was a ghoul, victim to whatever disaster had overwhelmed the CableCorp lobby. Baseman had no clue what went on in ghoul brains, but They seemed to remember routines. Like the Glass-thing returning to the anchor desk, the Kwame-thing had elevatored down to the studio level, where he raised some serious hell.

He'd arrived when the push for the elevators was at its bottleneck worst; Baseman saw Kwame bite ten or twelve people before he was forced into a janitorial closet, which the floor manager locked shut. Before she left, she gave Baseman her key ring, and he had used it to disable the lower-level elevators. With the stairwell barricaded shut – along with the incriminating pools of Glass's blood – the studio was effectively sealed. The key ring went into Baseman's left pocket, Item One. Item Two went into the right pocket: Kwame's gun.

When Baseman heard people, living people, pleading to be let in from the stairwell, he hadn't complied, for he could also hear the hungry moans of stairwell ghouls. He could have tried blasting bullets at Their heads, but he didn't trust himself with Kwame's gun. When you came down to it, as the base man liked to do, wasn't a handful of frightful deaths against a locked door worth the thousands being helped by WWN's ongoing broadcast?

He lifted the last of the bourbon to his lips but did not drink. He was trying to get drunk, proof positive he was not A-OK with letting innocent people die. If he let the pain in his cheek, hand, and heart howl, perhaps the sound would steer him true. He lowered the bottle.

'Forget the power grid, Face. How are *you* holding up?'

The Face licked cracker crumbs from his hand. 'I feel different. Like I'll never be tired again.'

'How'd you get so strong, Face? I swear I'll never understand it.'

Chuck Corso shrugged. 'Xander.'

'Xander? Who the fuck's Xander?'

'My personal trainer. Taught me a lot of good habits.'

Baseman sputtered laughter, not caring about the pain of his face's torn ligaments, and the Face, though he looked confused – perplexed, even – laughed too, and when Baseman held out the bourbon, the Face took the last slug. He probably only did it as a token of friendship, but if that were true, all the better.

All Mine

Charlene Rutkowski had imagined Luis and Rosa Acocella's home a hundred times. A cute, gabled Swiss colonial, Luis in a straw hat wheelbarrowing garden produce while Rosa waves from the top half of a divided door. Or a tall French row house, Rosa sipping lemonade on a cast-iron balcony as Luis emerges from the porte cochère. Even a modernist nightmare of sharp angles and arbitrary windows, Luis and Rosa in sophisticated black, coolly ignoring each other from the ends of a monastery table. All homes into which she, Charlie from Parkchester, did not deserve entry.

What she discovered in the cul-de-sac was a maroon-and-cream split level with bushes slightly withered in their red-dirt plot. The house had a sweeping northern view of the valley and distant hills, pretty in the dawn light. She swore the air was thinner up here. She leaned against the overfull, city-issued trash bins at the bottom of the Acocella drive, heaving the foul air. If Latino garbage collectors were getting blamed for all this, you could hardly blame them for halting pickups.

She could hear Acocella trotting up from half a block away. She should have kept him closer: sarcophages were not limited to housefire bacchanalias. On the other hand, his distance gave her a chance to ditch him. *I can drop this dweeb whenever the fuck he starts to look bad,* she thought. *The only reason I'm sticking is because, hey, where would this guy be if he didn't have somebody to kick ass for him?* She was kidding herself. She loved the guy. She'd keep letting herself be pulled along while knowing she wasn't being pulled at all.

He arrived at her elbow, gasping for breath.

'The . . . lights are . . . off.'

It was true, a dismal sign, and Charlie fought the desire to say, *Yep, that's right, no one home, let's run off together.* But Luis's face was slicked in sweat turned coral by the rising sun and distorted with a level of dread exceeding any he'd shown during the John Doe episode.

'Could be smart,' she whispered. 'She could be hiding. Staying quiet.'

'That's not Rosa. She's not quiet.'

'The sun's coming up. Maybe she's even asleep.'

'She left a million messages. She wouldn't sleep until she heard from me.'

'Well, fuck, Acocella, are we going to gossip about it all night, or are we going in?'

He gave her the same helpless look she'd seen on other men with their feet halfway off a cliff. They'd held up a corner store and gotten recognized. They owed money to a guy with bat-swinging friends. Luis was better than that, but Charlie felt the same acid-eaten diminution of being knocked to supporting-character status yet again. Her education, her job – fat lot of good they did. Meet Charlene Rutkowski, cowering behind trash cans, helping the love of her life rescue his wife.

Luis lifted the SDPD .38 revolver from his pocket as if it were a sleeping scorpion. Charlie's heart thudded as she remembered John Doe's skull blasting across the morgue floor. Luis was probably thinking the worst about Rosa. Charlie looked around. The neighbor's garage was open, and she saw a golf bag inside. She dashed over, fifteen feet, and unsheathed a club. She didn't know dick about golf, but the club had a good, heavy head. She returned to Luis with both hands choked up on the grip.

'Let me go first, all right?' she whispered.

He handed her his key chain by the front-door key. She took it, started up the drive, then paused at the walkway.

'Just don't shoot me in the back, okay?'

'What?'

'You don't look super comfortable with that gun is all.'

'Will you get going?'

Charlie drew a breath and peeked through the front-door window. A living room, a table with device chargers. The woman's touches of a flamingo-colored sofa and tasseled lamps. A line of framed pictures, one of them askew by several inches. Did that little detail mean Rosa had been ripped to shreds by deathless marauders? Or did it mean the mounting hook was off by half an inch? The difference between total societal upheaval and trivial annoyance was cobweb-thin.

The turning of the bolt was the crunch of bones. Charlie had to open her mouth to keep from biting her lip. With a sucking sound, the door puffed open on its own, an invitation to Casa Acocella she wasn't certain she'd have otherwise received. She shoved the keys into her jeans and entered. A duck-like creak – shit, hardwood floors. Her grimace-and-glance at Luis was rewarded by the sight of him holding the gun with two unsteady hands, aimed roughly at the back of her head. Perfect. Just perfect.

The crooked photograph was not an outlier; it was a harbinger. In the kitchen, *everything* was askew. Cookbooks slopped over the counter and stove top. The coffee canister lay shattered, beans spread over everything. The clock on the wall was now the clock on the floor, its upchucked batteries freezing time to the exact second of the room's battle.

A woman dangled from the sink by her arm, scribbling her feet through puddles of blood, smacking her lips as she searched for food that wasn't coffee beans.

It wasn't Rosa; Charlie knew that right away. This lady was old, her eyes hidden by folded skin. Beneath her black hair band, sprouts of gray hair were visible. When she looked at Charlie, her eyes were as white as Elmer's Glue, which Charlie guessed was attributable to the woman having cataracts before going ghoul. The woman pulled back her lips to show her few teeth and a sticky red tongue.

Charlie held out the golf club to prevent Acocella from entering.

'Luis, no, don't—'

But this was his home, where he lived with his wife. Her words meant dirt. He knocked the club aside and lurched into the room, right into the blood. The revolver was out, but he swung it behind his back as if caught with forbidden cookies.

'Mamá!' he cried. 'Mamá, what are you doing here?'

Alarms went off inside Charlie. The only person she'd tried to call since leaving the morgue was her own mother, with the result being that ubiquitous dead tone. Mae Rutkowski did not possess an iota of her daughter's survival instinct; on the other hand, three decades spent in the same apartment had fortified the place into a bunker. Charlie wished she were there now. She'd beat down any ghoul that got close, and Mae might finally appreciate her.

Luis swept toward the sink, his voice hitched into a whine.

'You're supposed to be in La Paz! I was driving down this morning! What were you thinking?'

What Mamá Acocella thought no longer mattered, if she thought at all. What mattered was that Luis Acocella, clever enough to think of succinylcholine and the SDPD revolver when it mattered, had apparently quit thinking altogether, reduced to his mother's child once again, his thoughts only of her.

He bent over the sink to investigate how his mother's hand was caught. Mamá's half-toothed mouth opened wide, and as she leaned into her son's leg, green bile slid over her tongue. Charlie gagged with an abhorrent vision.

Mae Rutkowski's crème de menthe.

Sweet peppermint swill, tough hairy flesh – both were disgusting goodies for revolting old people to whom this world no longer belonged. It belonged to Charlie now. She deserved it for scrapping, for surviving, for the bruises she'd taken, the books she'd studied, all the good things, Luis included, she'd resigned herself to never having. The gust of wind told her she'd swung the club.

The wooden head hit Mamá's wrist with a marble-bag crunch, ripping her hand free from Luis's leg. Luis whirled around, his face a child's mask of betrayal.

'Charlie!'

'She's trying to bite you, Acocella! She's another John Doe!'

'Her hand is caught in the garbage disposal!'

'Rosa probably did that, trying to stop her!'

'No, they got along, they were friends—'

'Luis, wake up! That's not your—'

Even better than the doctor and his diener knew the rattle of a pulverized wrist, they knew the carrot-snap of a broken bone, usually courtesy of Charlie and the two-handed rib shears. By all rights, the breaking bone should have been Mamá Acocella's ulna in the sink, but it was not. Luis and Charlie looked down to discover that, during their squabble, Mamá had righted herself and chomped down on her son's right thumb.

'Mom?' Luis asked in a whisper.

On some old instinct, her white eyes rolled upward.

Everything seemed to slam back into place for Luis Acocella; Charlie could see the change sweep over him. In a single move, he pulled back with his full body weight while kicking forward with a leg, and Mamá's mouth, studded with a half-complement of teeth, fell away from his hand. Luis shot backward into a counter, yanked open a drawer, and pulled from it a big, gleaming butcher knife. He dropped to the floor.

None of the terrible things she'd seen equaled that of Luis Acocella holding out the knife to her.

'Cut off my thumb,' he said.

Charlie stared.

'Now! Cut it off!'

'Luis?' Her voice was as a squeak.

'If it's blood-borne, I'm fucked! Take the knife! That's an order!'

'We're not at work. You can't make me . . . Do it yourself, if you're so—'

'I can't do it with my left hand! Charlie, please! Now, please, right fucking now!'

It was a task she'd done a hundred times before, though always on the dead. Yet she'd been trained to obey medical superiors, especially Luis. She heard the golf club hit the floor, saw her knuckles whiten along the handle of the knife, felt the hard tiling beneath her knees. Luis's hand was spread on a gray tile, the thumb's distal interphalangeal joint ringed in blood. He'd never be able to do an autopsy again, type a report again, was he sure this is what he wanted, they didn't even know if—

'Come on come on come on come on!'

Charlie chopped. The steel blade struck stone tile, an unkind cutting board, and the knife bounced out of her grip. Like a few frames snipped from a filmstrip, Luis's thumb was attached, then wasn't. Not a perfect cut, but the tool was no PM40. A hank of flexor pollicis brevis muscle, the size of a piece of sushi, had been severed as well, and Charlie's brain free-fell through anatomy-text warnings of what this extra half inch of flesh would cost Luis, as the loss chain-reacted through the first carpometacarpal joint, the lumbrical muscles and palmar aponeurosis, the intertendinous mesh. Forget surgical instruments, would he be able to hold a cereal bowl? He'd have a *hoof.*

First aid training told her to insert the thumb into a bag and put that bag inside a bag of ice, hopefully to be reattached, but Luis kicked the digit away. Charlie watched it roll against Mamá Acocella's foot, then looked away when Mamá picked it up and brought it to her lips. Luis was on his feet, his face yellow and wet, but cognizant enough to hold his gouting hand higher than his heart.

'Towel,' he squeaked, nodding at a drawer.

Charlie scrambled up, threw it open, and found a stack of soft, clean, heirloom dish towels hand-embroidered by someone who cared. The yellow, pink, and blue flowers all went red when she twisted the towel around Luis's hand. She threw open the left side of the refrigerator.

'Rosa,' Luis moaned.

'We need that hand in ice.'

'*Rosa,*' he insisted and shambled away.

Charlie slammed the fridge and gave chase like a mother after a toddler, though once the signs were spotted, she conceded them too compelling to ignore. The blots of blood on the kitchen floor continued in dribbles through the small, sunny dining room, down a hall wide enough to fit a table of potted cacti, and beneath a closed door. Luis leaned against the wall, too faint to open it.

'Open,' he panted.

'Let me get the golf club.'

'*Open.*'

She cursed, scrunched valor into her face, and took the knob. Was a ghoul inside, ready for ambush? Or a frightened woman who would scream for this invading vixen to get out? Bad or badder: she pushed open the door.

Here it was, the Acocella bedroom. Sex was a red herring; a bedroom was the heart of any home, one that beat stronger, night by night, as two people reached maximum vulnerability and trusted each other not to behave like animals. Charlie smelled the intricate incense of a couple's skin, hair, and breath. Two people could not blend together more completely unless one ate the other, and Charlie felt a rumble of appetite. This closeness, she hungered for it.

There would be no Rosa reckoning here. Red splashes dotted along periwinkle carpet and across a seafoam comforter, at which point bloody fingerprints took over, imprinted on the sill of a wide-open window.

'Not arterial,' Luis sputtered. 'Not even expirated.'

Charlie leaned for a better look. Bloodstain patterns were not their specialty, and fabric surfaces did analysis no favors, but even a woozy Luis Acocella was sharp. These were not the wax-seal patterns of passive drops or the raindrops-on-cobweb mist of bloody coughs. These stains had the solar-system layout of being flung from limbs and the globby smears of being spread by hands. Charlie gazed out the window.

'Am I right?' Luis demanded.

The succession of events seemed evident. Rosa del Gado Acocella, more inventive than her husband painted her, had incapacitated her mother-in-law with the garbage disposal, and then, probably for good reason, had exited from the bedroom window. There was no hard evidence Rosa herself had been harmed – at least not indoors. Twenty feet into the grassless, brick-orange dirt outside, a shallow gulley had been dug by an apparent struggle. The dirt there was soaked red. There the trail went dead, if *dead* was still a word one could use with a straight face.

'Am I right?' Luis repeated. 'Is she safe?'

'I think so,' Charlie lied. 'She's gone.'

Luis collapsed at this, finally. It was a good twenty minutes later, after Charlie had locked every window in the house, blocked all the doors with furniture, and ruined a second embroidered towel by redressing his wound, that he roused to lodge a weak protest when Charlie picked up the golf club from the kitchen floor. From where he hunched at the dining room table, he had an unobstructed view of the kitchen, and though his face and lips were pale, his eyes were the same dark, pretty brown as always.

'You don't have to,' he begged.

'You know I do,' she replied.

'What did we say at the morgue? Wireless rays? Cellular radiation? We could toss out our phones, all the chargers. Maybe she'd change back. We could try.'

'We're the ones who have to change.'

'Would it at least be . . .' He strangled a sob. 'Would the gun be faster?'

'Too loud,' she said, and she reared back with the club. 'Look the other way.'

It took a lot of swings, maybe dozens, to kill Luis Acocella's mamá. The old woman's skull made hard sounds, then wet sounds; more prominent were the hard sounds of Charlie panting and the wet sounds of Luis crying. Charlie let herself get lost in the muscular burn of the twist, the hurl, the jolt, the retraction, and when her scared, exhausted brain wandered to dark, selfish places, she let it happen. *This is not your son anymore,* she thought, swinging, swinging. *He's mine now, all mine.*

Graduation

The trip to the main doors of Bulk High School was the same as any other day, save for the gunfire. The loudest bang came from the student parking lot, but that might have been a backfiring truck; the lot was two-thirds empty, and vehicles were hauling ass out of there, ripping their own exits through the lawn. The crackle from the football practice field, however, was definitely guns – white sparks against green grass. Other gunshots, from inside the school, resounded like firecrackers.

She hid the blue Schwinn between the stairs and bushes, adjusted the duffel bag on her back, and slid into the dark, chilly vestibule. BHS was a two-story, bracket-shaped building likely constructed during the reign of Julius Caesar. Like the town hall and post office, it was built from giant, imposing, ice-cold blocks of stone that belittled the town's moldering houses, chintzy trailer parks, and hollowed-out factories. Between classes, the hallways became reverberating hell-storms through which nothing but girls' shrieks could penetrate.

This morning, BHS was a catacomb. She tiptoed past the vacant front office. It felt pigeonhearted to tread so tentatively down a hall through which she normally strutted, but she could not get her back to straighten. From afar came the mice-scurry of a clump of people making a run for it, but she didn't see them and was afraid to shout. Besides, if she knew Conan, he would be hiding alone.

Pomp! – the sound of a gunshot, soggy with reverb. Greer flattened against the icy wall. The shot came from the floor above. If someone was shooting, there was something to shoot at, and that was the best lead she had. She bounded up the stairs. The brass gleam of the second-floor trophy case had just come into view when the water fountain next to her exploded – *Pomp! Pomp!* – metal peeling open like tinfoil, the water hosing her so cold it was scorching.

Greer let the water shove her to the floor, and rolled with it, over the duffel bag and its sharp contents, huddling behind a doorjamb. Frantic images from code-red active-shooter drills flashed in her brain. Cabinets piled in front of doors, students on stomachs behind tables flipped to their sides, listening for the knob-jingle of the gym coach playing the part of shooter, everyone giggling despite how fucked up the whole thing was, because if you can't laugh at the theoretical shit luck of being murdered at your least favorite place on Earth, you're going to have a tough life.

Pomp – the glass in the stairwell door shattered above her.

'Stop!' she yelled.

Pomp – a hole was punched through the door.

'*Stop!*' she screamed.

The shots echoed for eighteen years, making it impossible to know how many times her name was said before she heard it.

'Greer? Greer?'

She squinted from behind water-soaked hair, through wood-splintered eyelashes, over glass-crystalled cheeks. Fifty feet off but walking her way was Conan. Her instinct rejected it; Conan had never moved so confidently in these halls. But she'd know that short, pudgy shape anywhere. Even if it stood more proudly than usual. Even with the Browning rifle jutting from his side like an additional arm.

He kneeled over her. She felt his soft fingers, hot from a fired gun, brush fragments of glass and wood from her face and hair.

'Is that Dad's bow? Did you bring the stupid *bow*?'

He laughed lightly. *He laughed lightly.* Conan Morgan, the kid who hadn't smiled on school property in half a decade, who shuddered when he walked by certain lockers, who got up from being knocked down with the numb resignation of a person training for a life on the HortiPlastics conveyor belt. He was lively, buoyant. Greer distrusted the smile on her little brother's face. It looked like a red ribbon.

Conan helped her up, led her by the arm, and positioned her behind him at the hallway's corner. It was more physical contact than they'd shared in a decade. He unslung his rifle and peered down the hall like an action-movie cop.

'You should've brought the Remington,' he said.

'I couldn't . . . It wouldn't fit . . . and the ammo . . .'

'Dad hid it behind Parcheesi.'

'We have to . . . I've got a bike . . .'

Conan stretched his neck into the hall, rifle at the ready.

'You run into Mama Shaw?' he asked.

Unwillingly, Greer pictured the legless Jamaican inhaling Miss Jemisha's braids into her toothless mouth. She nodded.

'I saw her and I knew,' Conan said. 'I *knew*. I left Dad the Remington because it's his favorite.'

Telling her brother their dad was dead would have been hard enough. But explaining what Freddy Morgan had become? She couldn't explain it to herself. Conan cocked his head at something she didn't hear. He raised the rifle. He'd always been a decent shot.

She leaned out from behind her brother and saw, near the end of the hall, a figure step from a classroom. Before the person had fully emerged, Conan fired – *Pomp!* – and blood fanned into the air from the person's head before the person dropped from view.

'Woo!' Conan cried. 'Greer, you see that?'

He snugged the rifle into his elbow and jerked back the bolt. The spent rounds twirled free and clattered to the floor. Conan dug a hand into a pocket of loose bullets, loaded three rounds, and chambered them with a facility no one else in the Morgan clan ever achieved. Greer got the feeling her brother had been at this since dawn.

'There's a couple more in that room I need to get.'

'What's wrong with you? Let's *go*.'

His round-cheeked enthusiasm faded.

'Go? No, Greer, you don't get it. When I got here – I mean, I always get here early, but I just, you know, sort of hide out. I had no idea how many people are actually here that early. People in singing groups, rehearsing plays, doing sports stuff, yearbook stuff. They're *dedicated,* man. It kind of blew me away. Did it spread fast at the Last Resort?'

Greer nodded, flapping her hands, *Let's go, let's go.*

'It spread here like mono, man. Like herpes.' This was the boy Greer knew, bitter about missing out on even the unpleasant things others experienced. 'Most kids didn't even run from those things. They ran *toward* Them. That's dedication too, I guess. Dedication to their school.' He shook the Browning. 'This is how I show *my* dedication. This is the chance I always wanted. I'm going to keep shooting and keep piling Them in there till I'm done.'

He gestured his chin down the perpendicular hall.

Across from the trophy cases was the French/Spanish room. The idyllic European posters on the outside bulletin board felt like traps: the room's door was *closed*. Greer realized she'd never seen any classroom door closed before. A dread colder than the building's walls rose around her like water.

'Here we go,' Conan whispered. He aimed his rifle at the distant room.

But Greer was gone. She'd been pulled to the left, as if by a chain. Fugitive daubs of sunlight pawed the dusty trophies. The French/

Spanish door grew bigger, its silence more insidious. Conan was muttering, impatient for the perfect shot, and wasn't watching when Greer took the doorknob. *¡Bienvenido!* read one paper taped to the door, *Entrez!* read another. Both pages rustled as she pulled it open. A heavy door, she acknowledged, which is why she'd heard nothing through it.

Inside were over a dozen students and teachers. They'd been pitched there like laundry. Some were dead, twisted and limp. Some were alive, squirming and weeping. Some were that *other* thing, white-eyed and sliding like snakes, jaws wide for live flesh. It was a lurid mash, the rabid eating the living, the living becoming the dead, the dead rising. As the living and the dead turned to look at her, Greer identified the characteristic shared by all: a gunshot wound.

Pomp!

'Hoo! Yes! I'm on fire!'

Greer turned slowly to the right. Conan shifted the rifle to one hand so he could pump the opposite fist. He spotted her.

'Hey.' His tone chilled. 'Better close that.'

'You shot them,' she gasped.

'Close it. They'll get out.'

'I thought you were . . . They're kids. Conan, you're shooting living kids.'

His whole body seemed to darken, fading into unlit brick.

'What did you *think* I was doing?'

She'd been right to recall the active-shooter drills. Her brother wasn't playing a sheriff riding up to prove his mettle to a disdainful student body. He was playing punisher, exploiting civilization's collapse to have his revenge. He smiled again, that wonderful sight, and shook his head like the misunderstanding was silly.

'It's okay,' he assured her. 'No one cares anymore. This won't even make the news.'

'You're killing the wrong people.'

'Don't be a dumb-ass. Once They're dead, They don't recognize faces.'

'*So?*'

'So, it's like *we* don't have faces. I don't have to be some little puke people push around. You don't have to be a worthless dark-skinned chick flunking class. We don't have to eat people's shit at HortiPlastics. We can be anyone. We can do anything. We can take whatever we want.'

'What the fuck is at this shit-ass school you could possibly want?'

He gestured at the hall down which he'd been shooting. 'The—' The gesture failed; he puffed his chest. 'There's the—' This faltered too; he throttled the Browning. 'There's got to be something!'

Greer pointed toward town. 'People out there are killing each other!'

'I know. I know that.'

'You're the same! You're doing the same thing!'

Conan shook his head violently. 'No. No way. You know how many school shooters are Black?'

'Conan!'

'Like none! None, Greer!' He brandished the rifle. 'This is how white folks kill each other, and do they ever catch hell for it? They ever pass laws to make sure *they* don't kill again, that *they* don't get to vote, that *their* leaders are taken the fuck out? Fuck no! Why should we act any different?'

Greer waved her hands at the French/Spanish room.

'There aren't just white kids in here!'

Conan's laugh was the sound of snapping twigs.

'Well, shit, sis. If you're taking power, you might as well clean house, you know?' His smile collapsed. 'Listen. Will you just listen to me? You've got Dad's bow. Some other good stuff in there too. We could do this together. Remake the whole fam. Pick any big, fancy house in town we want to live in. Me and you. What do you say?'

The soggy slapping sound to her left had been growing for a time, but it was only now, with motion tickling her peripheral vision, that Greer looked. A single person had dislodged himself from the fleshy, blood-lubricated mass, a young man dragging himself with only his arms, his legs apparently paralyzed by the hole blown through his back. With his sharp, shining brown eyes drained to white, Greer almost didn't recognize him.

The last time she'd seen Qasim, his broad nose had been buried in the shirt she'd wadded at her sternum, one of his hands clenched over her bare breast, the other slid down the front of her unbuttoned jeans. His shirt was off, but guys got away with that at Remy's parties. She recalled the skillet heat of their close-pressed stomachs. She'd spent half the night tracing his abs with a nail.

Here was that stomach again, rolling into view as the Qasim-thing reached for her waist – flesh to be unbuttoned this time. Qasim's abs remained conspicuous, except this time as loose red coils Conan's shot had ripped apart.

Greer stumbled back until she felt trophy-case glass at her back. It was all gone. Her dad, her brother, her near lover, her home, her neighborhood, her school, her town, her future. She felt a gust of mad hilarity. What future? She'd never had one – Conan was right about that. This rabid strain had only brought her hopelessness to the fore, swept the suicide cliff to her toes. There was nothing to do now but tip herself over it.

She gripped the duffel bag with her left hand and offered her right to her brother.

'Come with me,' she pleaded.

'What? Greer, no. *You* come with *me*.'

Despite Qasim, still crawling, and the living, still dying, and the world, still caving under her feet, she let her eyes shut, like a girl who believed people might still cradle her, and held out her arm straighter, like a big sister should, and whispered her wish like a prayer, like *all* prayers, an exchange of rationality for magic, the only hope she had left.

'Come with me?'

Dark silence for seconds, except Qasim's *slap-slap* progress. Greer heard a quick, quivering inhale and the bone-crack of the Browning's bolt. She opened her eyes, hoping for miracles, but Conan remained miles from her outstretched hand. Her lashes were so matted with tears she did not, at first, notice her brother's lashes were as well. He was never one to let others see him cry, no matter what they'd done. He snorted back his sniffle and wiped his nose on his sleeve.

'Can't, Greer. It's too late. I got to finish what I started. There's been nothing for me for a long, long time, you know? This was always the way it was going to end. Me versus Them, until there's no me left. It's not your fault. Be careful out there, all right? They're coming to get you.'

She left. Just like that. Without another look at the thing that had been Qasim or the boy who'd been her brother, she charged the way she'd come, the soles of her naked feet withstanding broken glass before hitting the stairs and forcing herself to think of nothing but Fadi Lolo's Schwinn and how fast she could ride it. When she heard the *pomp, pomp!* of resuming shots, her sneaky brain thought of the *pomp* of 'Pomp and Circumstance', the march they played at graduation, not that she'd ever have one. Unless *this* right here was graduation: the close of one phase, the start of another.

Capricious Gods

A jokey navy saying came to Karl Nishimura as he chewed his third straight meal of dusty peanuts: 'An aircraft carrier is a dictatorship defending a democracy.' The dictator in the adage was the ship's captain, though in reality a captain was beholden to a scaffold of brighter brass, leading all the way to the commander in chief. Aboard the USS *Olympia,* however, this platitude had become proverb. Here a dictator reigned. His every edict was followed, and he felt no duty to any higher authority than what he called God.

Lieutenant Commander William Koppenborg, still going by the stainless moniker of Father Bill, had taken absolute control of the topside of the boat. Nishimura's spells of incredulity were becoming more infrequent, which worried him. Only two days into the strangest coup in history, the impossible was being normalized. Here, the chosen few, cloistered high atop a steel high-rise, were isolated from those belowdecks, taking literal shots at them when they surfaced on the flight deck, whether seeking help, escape, or prey. All upper-floor units are filled, sorry. We don't want your kind up here.

The status of the residents increased as one went up: meteorological room, radar room, flag bridge, nav bridge, Pri-Fly. The food up top, Nishimura guessed, must be better than peanuts. Down here, you ate what you got in personal spaces smaller than racks. The confines of each man's area had been drawn on the floor in chalk by Father Bill's second-in-command, O-3 Boatswain's Mate Tommy

Henstrom. The chalking had taken several hours. The island's final census was forty-two souls.

Make that forty-one. How quickly Nishimura wanted to forget what had happened to yeoman Jacobo Leatherdale. Nishimura dry-swallowed a peanut. He was so thirsty, and so tired, and though his assigned patch of steel floor was uncomfortable, it was also beneath a work counter, which meant it was dark and promised the possibility of sleep. No one dared close their eyes until after Night Prayer, of course. Disrupting Evening Prayer was what had doomed Jacobo Leatherdale. No, don't think of it, not if sleep is what you want.

Nishimura's bunk was Henstrom's cruelest sketch, an oval no bigger than Nishimura's body. Naturally, he was in the meteorological room, the lowest level. Weather equipment was bulky and bolted down, giving the room the feel of a hurricane refugee camp, or something worse. Soon enough, he figured, tracked mud would be the least of the problems. The place would begin to smell. Sickness would spread. Nishimura could see it all coming.

The island had just enough guns for five armed guards, one of whom was posted at each level to keep any ambitious riffraff in line. Ladders had been reinstated, except for the one connecting Nishimura's level to the flight deck. The concept was clear: if the meteorological level was overcome, it could be amputated from higher levels by retracting ladders. It would be no big loss. After Leatherdale's exit, only Nishimura and seven other pariahs lived in this squalid part of town.

Resisting the urge to resist was a kind of strength; he tried to convince himself of this. After Jacobo Leatherdale had met his fate, Nishimura had tried to discreetly rally his fellow bottom-floor outcasts.

'It's going to happen to all of us,' he hissed.

The other men shot him furious glares and turned away. Leatherdale might be gone, but another of their sorry lot, a turbine systems mechanic named Lavar Pomeroy, had been bumped up to radar-room digs. All he'd had to do was grovel long enough to Henstrom. That's all the meteorological men wanted, to distance themselves from the smoldering hell of the flight deck and get one level closer to Pri-Fly, the holy home of Father Bill.

Nishimura choked down his last peanut, his throat aching for liquid. It seemed like hours since anyone had been by with the water bucket and ladle. With Night Prayer overdue, the bucket might be finished until morning. The bucket. The goddamn bucket. It was all that mattered anymore. How quickly Saint Karl, straight-backed and proud of his khaki dress, had devolved into a dog, hunched for trouble, ears perked for the bucket's clanging. After a few more days of this, what sort of beast would he be?

Nishimura credited his survival to two things. One, Henstrom enjoyed watching him suffer. Two, he knew Big Mama better than anyone else up here, and they knew it. Father Bill had not deigned to descend from Pri-Fly since the Long Walk, but Henstrom, busy helper bee, made frequent visits to the proletariat, always accompanied by one of the guards, to find help in locking in the new world order. It was perhaps ironic, certainly tragic, that no one had helped more than Nishimura. He did not see himself having a choice, not if he hoped to get all the way to Buffalo one day to find Larry and the children.

Father Bill had carried out his promise to drop anchor, thereby establishing a nation, and his citizens applauded, certain that segregation from society was the key to future greatness. Anchoring was a big operation for a carrier, but thanks to archaic speaking tubes – a last-ditch redundancy Nishimura had never thought would have its day – Father Bill's disciples were able to contact a bare-bones fo'c'sle crew still resisting ghoul incursion. With alarming speed, those distant sailors succumbed to the lore of the Long Walk, and Nishimura felt the boat's movement shift from sideways drifting to a vertical riding of waves.

He wondered if they'd ever move again.

In the hours since, Nishimura had heard and felt Big Mama's body systems being shut down, like a beloved matriarch being pulled off life support. The keyboard plinking of search radars, including SPS-48E, SPS-49(V)5, SPS-65(V)9, and SPS-67, ended their concert. The tick of the rotating Mk 23 Target Acquisitioning System stilled. The white fuzz of the WRL-1H warning/intercept receiver dissipated into nothing. Worst of all, the hum of the Mk 91 Fire Control System fell silent, despite the boat's proven susceptibility to fire. Meanwhile, periodic rumbles made Nishimura suspect munitions were being dropped into the sea. *Olympia* was being stripped of her identity, a void that Father Bill was undoubtedly preparing to fill.

The pop of the 1MC came so late Nishimura confused it for the ladle clanging against the water bucket. He could see the outlines of the room's other seven men perk up, moonlight gleaming from their eager eyes.

'O Lord, in the name of your only son, Jesus, bless the war in Afghanistan, O Lord, the war in Iraq, O Lord, the war in Syria, O Lord.' Father Bill laughed lightly. 'You remember all that? When I used to take my turn giving daily prayers with my so-called colleagues, those men of false faiths who have fallen, I always included this plea for God to help us win our wars.

'Tonight, I am blessed to remove that devotion. War is at an end. That includes the war we fought here on this ship, for it was never a war to begin with. The demons, we welcome Them. With open arms, we welcome Them.

'By joining with our demon halves, we *will* eliminate evil. I am seeking counsel from God on how best to achieve this, but for now, the demons require more lifeblood, which we are blessed to be able to give Them. Henceforth, I shall no longer call upon God to guide our bullets, for there are no more reasons to shoot.' The 1MC crackled. 'Unless it is to protect our temple from the unenlightened.'

The *unenlightened* were the belowdecks skulkers who had yet to offer themselves as lay priests to the Church of Father Bill. They could be hiding anywhere on the boat; Jacobo Leatherdale had proven that. Nishimura was too tired and thirsty to keep the memory at bay any longer.

How quickly had the parting of the Red Sea convinced Israelite detractors Moses was a prophet? The Long Walk, Father Bill's miraculous trek across the flaming, ghoul-crowded flight deck, had accomplished as much just as rapidly. One of his first acts was to partition each day into five sections, each heralded by a prayer he broadcast throughout the ship: Morning, Midmorning, Midday, Evening, and Night. During these monologues, Nishimura had observed Leatherdale begin to crack. Finally, in the middle of Evening Prayer, Leatherdale had looked at his third handful of peanuts that day and snapped.

'All the food's down below! We lock ourselves up here, we're going to starve! What are we doing? What are any of us doing?'

He's right, Nishimura said. No, he hadn't said it. He'd only thought it. Because, unlike Leatherdale, he had the Nishimura Delay – careful or cowardly, you decide. Leatherdale raved at his fellow starving, stagnant sailors for fifteen or twenty seconds before breaking for the catwalk.

Jacobo Leatherdale was navy all the way, weight-trained, athletically fit, and Nishimura would have given him better than fifty-fifty odds of landing on the flight deck uninjured if he could have prepared his jump. But Leatherdale had melted down while Henstrom and a bodyguard were present, doling out peanuts and water. Henstrom said two words – *Stop him* – and several meteorological-level slugs scrambled in chase. Nishimura heard the *whomp* of flesh thrown to steel, the gobble of Leatherdale's protests.

Before Leatherdale, Saint Karl knew that Father Bill's refusal to contact the outside world left them open to the dangers of finite food and water, explosions from untended engines, and the complete lack of a labor structure to address those things.

After Leatherdale, Nishimura revised that list. Father Bill's reaction to the traitor did, in fact, help establish a labor structure. Labor, it turned out, worked rather smoothly when people at the bottom were terrified of people at the top.

Captured, Jacobo Leatherdale was dangled backward over the Pri-Fly catwalk, the railing pinched between calves and thighs ducttaped together. Trained to consider Pri-Fly as a holy place, the forty-one others crowded the catwalks to watch. Flanked by Henstrom and armed guards, Father Bill held the gold-plated crucifix with the broken staff and spoke in a trembling voice that Nishimura could not hear. The priest's closed-eyes ecstasy said enough.

Father Bill made the sign of the cross and took up a knife. He leaned over the railing and cut Leatherdale across the chest, making a long, wandering slit, which bled in five or six streams before painting his face red and splattering to the flight deck five stories below.

The deck inferno had died out, revealing an apocalyptic sight. The bright, sleek falcons of navy aircraft had been contorted to briars of charred metal, tarantulas dead on their backs. More upsetting were the seared skeletons of sailors, traceries of carbonized bone that atomized to ash with any decent wind. Leatherdale's red blood inseminated black embers; the afterbirth was raspberry jelly.

Despite this, the deck's quarter-mile length still flickered with activity. A few dozen dead sailors plodded aimlessly amid the ruins. *Demons,* Father Bill insisted, though Nishimura clung to *ghouls* – he'd take Chuck Corso as an oracle any day over Father Bill, though *Millennialists* might still be the most apt name. The ghouls appeared ignorant of one another, yet they never collided, instead orbiting like galactic bodies in search of absorbable matter.

Their disinterest changed with the onset of Jacobo Leatherdale's red rain. Nishimura registered the turning of twenty ghoul faces, forty white eyes flashing like startled doves. As They gathered and reached for Leatherdale, They did so like infants for a rattle; when They tried to snatch the falling blood, They did so like toddlers chasing bubbles; when They kneeled to lick the blood from the sooty deck, They did so like children seeking candy, the picture of innocent craving.

Upside down, Leatherdale had no intention of going quietly. He screamed and contorted, geysering blood over a wider area, good news for the crowded ghouls. Father Bill placed the knife blade against the duct tape. Nishimura still could not hear him, but he knew it was a prayer from the rounding of the priest's lips: *O Lord* this, *O Lord* that.

'Amen!' Henstrom cried – Nishimura heard that, all right – and answers went up: *Amen!* and *Yes!* and even *Hallelujah!* Nishimura thought he might not be able to bear it, that he'd have to grab each one of these people by the collar and ask them what the hell they were doing. Then Father Bill sawed through the tape and Leatherdale dropped, a different kind of man overboard, landing with the gravelly crush of a pulverized back.

Leatherdale screamed. Thirteen ghouls took hold of him at once, and Nishimura did not believe he'd forget Their precise grips. Right foot. Left foot. Left knee. Right thigh. Groin. Right hand. Left arm. Left pectoral. Right armpit. Neck. Left ear. Inside of mouth. Into right eye.

Leatherdale screamed again, a plea to those he'd served alongside: 'Shoot me! Shoot me!'

As if in response to a silent signal, the ghouls pulled, and Jacobo Leatherdale came apart. Arms snapped at elbows. Legs turned, and turned, and twisted off like shrimp tails. Ghoul hands plunged into his abdomen, grasped the pelvic bones, and pulled the bottom half of the body away. The skin and innards stretched like mozzarella. Suddenly, Leatherdale, perhaps five six in life, was thirty feet long, spread across the deck in chunks strung together by veins, nerves, intestines, and flesh.

Nishimura wanted the ensuing silence to be the beat taken before action: tossing the insane Father Bill to the ghouls. Instead, it was the silence Nishimura often felt inside churches, that smug belief that your god was the true God, and that because you had your butt in the right pew, you'd never be forced to walk a plank.

'Taps, taps, lights-out.'

XO Bryce Peet's curt, robotic, but professional ten o'clock sign-off had been replaced by Henstrom's pushy cockiness. Nishimura swallowed, his throat tight and aching. Relief over having missed most of Father Bill's prayer was erased by the realization water was not forthcoming. Nishimura laid his head on the floor and tried to think. An emergency survival class, eons ago. Water conservation tips. Work at night, avoid sunburn, evade winds, limit food.

He chuckled at that last one and thought he saw through the gloom the glare of suspicious eyes. Karl Nishimura might make for a good second sacrifice to the demons, those eyes said, a sacrifice that might get a guy promoted upward. Nothing Nishimura could do about that right now. He closed his eyes and coughed up spit to wet his throat. Conserve water, conserve energy, be thankful he could see the stars through a slice of window. He thought of that poor Red Serpents nugget who'd had the bolting incident and how everyone had considered it a big deal. If only they could have seen past the next wave.

A Forever Situation

'How's it look?'

The question had become the tick of a clock.

On his maps app, Luis showed Charlie the places Rosa was most likely to have gone. Friends' neighborhoods, though Luis was not sure he could pinpoint exact houses, which might mean knocking on dangerous doors. He tried to think of other places he knew Rosa frequented and was abashed to know mostly places that had served him as a husband: grocery stores, takeout restaurants, laundromats. If he'd never bothered to learn what his wife did all day, how could he hope to find her?

The app kept being blocked by notifications, his post retweeted incessantly.

'Will you turn that shit off?' Charlie griped.

'Makes me feel good,' he admitted. 'Word's getting out.'

'The ego boost is what feels good. You want to run out your battery?'

It was a good point; the electricity was working so far, but the lights had stuttered. He turned off all phone notifications, a regimen of swiping that hurt like hell. By habit, he did it with his right hand, inside which all existing nerves were live wires twisted to the spot of his missing thumb. 'How's it look?' Charlie kept asking. If she were talking about his hand, he could tell her exactly how it looked. It looked *not good*.

If she was talking about the thumb itself, different story. The thumb was gonesville. Luis had snatched what had fallen from Mamá's mouth and tossed it down the garbage disposal from which Charlie had removed his mother's hand. When he hit the switch, slivers of white bone and red muscle jitterbugged from the drain like radish shavings.

Now he felt faint and nauseated. Could be the blood loss, the trauma of losing a body part. But what if it was more? He hoped most of John Doe's blight had been juiced in the sink, but he knew the strain Mamá carried could be slugging through his veins right now, recruiting healthy blood cells for the sarcophage cause.

How's it look?

The situation? Pretty fucking bleak. He'd tried to help Charlie deal with Mamá's body; since childhood, he'd fantasized about the brave face he'd one day wear as a pallbearer. Charlie had told him to sit down, but Mamá's dangling weight made it hard for his diener to dislodge her hand from the disposal. Luis had wrapped his arms around his mother's torso, the red hash of her face close enough to kiss, but he was not much help. One stupid thumb gone and his whole hand went to shit. At last, he retreated and listened to the wet crackle of Mamá's extraction and the hard scrape of her body being dragged into the garage, where it would rest with all the dignity of a bag of dog food.

Luis plugged his phone into the wall, again horrified by the challenges of a missing thumb. Charlie sat across the table. What differed from their usual work lunches was her merciless stare. He hadn't the strength to defend himself. His bottom lip actually pooched. *Be nice to me*, he thought. *I don't feel well.*

Finally, she proclaimed it: 'We can't leave.'

'Rosa,' Luis protested.

'I'm going to say this as gently as I can,' Charlie said. 'Forget Rosa. The phones go back up, she'll call. The roads get safe, she'll come home. But we are not going on some wandering rescue mission with you like you are.'

He held up his bandaged hand. 'We'll cauterize this. Sew it. We know how.'

'Here's something I'm *not* going to say gently. You are useless right now. You think you can climb a fence? These are the suburbs. Every house is fenced off like San Quentin. You can barely make it to the sink.'

'I just need a little time. It's shock.'

'We'll see. In the meantime, we need to shore up this place. I heard one on the other side of the garage door. How long till one of Them puts a fist through a window? An hour? A minute?'

'If we lock ourselves in here . . . Mamá . . .'

'What? What about her? Acocella, talk.'

'She . . . if she just lies out there, she'll . . .'

'I worked in a morgue too, you know. We'll bury her. I promise. We'll figure it out. But we have to worry about that later. What you need to do right now is direct me toward hammer and nails.'

'Garage. With her.'

'Do you have any lumber?'

'No.'

'That's okay. You have bookshelves. And tables. It's going to get a little noisy in here.'

'Won't noise . . . ?'

'Bring Them here? Probably. That's why, when we do this, we need to do it fast before too many catch on. I'm going to need your help with that. All right? Acocella, look at me. I need you to hold things in place for me to hammer. Okay? Nod your head. This isn't Autopsy Suite 1. No detailed procedure here. We need to put wood over that glass as fast as we can, you understand?'

He did, though amid a heavy brain fog, he couldn't imagine a barricade keeping sarcophages out as much as it kept him and Charlie inside. He wondered if this was exactly what his crafty diener had wanted. He remembered her look of yearning from last night in the autopsy suite, as well as his gratified reaction. Now he felt the crimp of a thickening penis. The fuck was that about? He was all messed up.

Charlene Rutkowski tore apart the Acocella house with what seemed to Luis like too much relish. Furniture went sideways, legs jutted stiffly like those of dead animals. With slaughterhouse efficiency, she malleted them to pieces. The gunfire crack and sawdust smell shot Luis with enough adrenaline to gather the lumber Charlie created from tables, shelves, TV stands, armoires, dressers, drawers, headboards, chairs, and every cupboard door in the kitchen. He piled them by the front windows. Through Rosa's gauzy curtains, he could see dark shapes loping closer.

The nailing was the scary part. Once the walls began shaking and the windows rattling, the sarcophages came for them. Arms fired through the living room glass. Sweatshirt arms, blouse arms, fast-food-uniform arms, military-dress arms. Neighbors entering Luis's home without asking first. You simply didn't do that in La Mesa. Charlie hammered too hard and fast to be caught, and Luis whacked sarcophages with whatever board he was readying. Their hands kept clenching, showing no pain.

Perhaps it *was* a good sign, Luis thought, that his own hand hurt like hell.

None got in. Of course not. Sarcophages hatched maggots on dead flesh, and goddamn it, nothing was dead in the Acocella house. Luis rubbed his pounding head with both hands; only one thumb showed up for the job. There *was* a dead person, wasn't there? In the garage? Luis slapped himself with his good hand and helped Charlie nail up the biggest pieces: the dining room table, the headboard. Rosa's jaw would hit the floor, Luis thought, if she ever got home.

Within an hour of starting, they'd blocked out 90 percent of the sunlight on the ground floor. Sweat-grimed and scratched pink, they collapsed at the bottom of the stairs, drawn to the warm, unimpeded sun splashing down from the second floor. Luis shut his eyes. Maybe now, at rest, his dizziness would subside. All the activity had been lousy for his hand too. Last he looked, the towel had come loose, black and dribbling. A typical arrogant doctor, he kept no first aid kit at home.

'How's it look?' Charlie asked.

Luis cracked open a crusty, stinging eye. Charlie's smirk drew strands of sweaty blond hair tight across her face. Luis glanced at the blood-snarl of his right hand, then at the living room, which looked as if it had been visited by a deconstruction crew. At least four sarcophages still beat at the barred windows, but Their sounds had diminished. Maybe They recognized other windows in other houses as less vexing.

'Doesn't look too bad,' Luis replied, 'for a tornado.'

'We need to fix that hand.'

'Shower first. Please. Take turns keeping watch.'

'What if the water shuts off? We should conserve.'

'What if we smell like this forever? That's not a life I want to live.'

Charlie laughed softly. 'Okay. Be quick. You need me to hold you up?'

'You'd like that, wouldn't you?'

'Mmm, yeah, nothing gets me hotter than an old man slipping in the shower.'

Luis laughed. He needed the humor. His vision was swaying. His throat was ablaze. Washing out his wound was a smart, overdue thing to do, and he hoped skimming two days of crud off his body might turn his whole ill feeling around. He struggled to his feet, accepting Charlie's help. At the top of the stairs was a stained glass window given to them by Rosa's mother. It soaked the late-day light with wine shades. Luis told himself he was drunk on it, that was all that was wrong with him.

He shivered. Was there a breeze coming through some of the shattered windows on the ground floor?

He showered in the bathroom where Rosa had had her miscarriage. Finished, he got dressed in their bedroom, gazing down at a street dotted with the botched births of the larger Miscarriage, then sat on the living room sofa, biting on a washcloth, as Charlie sewed shut his wound. He told Charlie he'd stay on watch while she showered, but a minute after he lay down on the sofa, he fell asleep. He awoke to orange morning sunlight needling through slats of lumber, and also to Charlie. She was asleep in his arms.

Her hair was fluffed in his face, soft as angora. She smelled indescribably sweet, a degree of cleanliness he realized he'd never expected to smell again. Rosa's soap, Rosa's shampoo, but not Rosa's fruity, flowery skin. Charlie smelled like maple syrup. Luis wondered if it was residue from all the wood she'd so recently handled, sunk deep into her pores.

Rosa's clothes swam on Charlie like medical scrubs. Luis felt a spasm of grief for his wife. Rosa had invested time and care in selecting them. Her clothes *knew* her; to cradle her curves, fabric had expanded and seams relaxed. Saturated in her preferences and insecurities, the garments had mattered. The instant Charlie had dumped them from the dresser to claim the wood, Rosa's clothes became rags, no more significant than the towel Charlie had tied around his hand.

In the quiet morning birdsong, Luis accepted the unlikelihood he'd see Rosa del Gado Acocella ever again.

He peered through Charlie's thick hair to her sleeping face. Without her usual heavy makeup, she looked vulnerable. Her lips, thin and unpainted, were pursed, and a snore whistled from her sinuses. Earth had ruptured, dropped whole continents into ocean trenches, swapped the qualities of life and death. Nearly unnoticeable amid those marvels, his wife had been replaced by Charlene Rutkowski, no questions asked, no returns accepted. Charlie wore Rosa's clothes, slept on Rosa's sofa, had already remodeled Rosa's house.

Charlie was ready for this role, he had no doubt. Was he? Every second awoke bad sensations: the dull throb of his hand, the shudder of a still-sick stomach, the thickening of his feverish head. He would not be going anywhere soon. It was possible he might never go anywhere again.

This could be a forever situation.

Charlie woke up yawning and stretching, as drowsily sexy as he'd imagined, and she gave him a tired smile before snuggling her warm forehead into his neck. For a long time, they breathed together, nothing more. Luis, who had never had a one-night stand in his life, wondered if this was what one felt like, the steam of the night before slowly evaporating in the light of day.

'Breakfast?' she murmured.

The kitchen, the sink, his mamá – he gagged.

'Oh, right, sorry. I'm going to scrounge up coffee. You just stay here.'

Rosa's oversized T-shirt fluttered along the bottom of Charlie's buttocks as she left the room. Luis sat up. He might be a doctor, but he still held the stubborn belief he could will himself healthy. He pushed the sofa parallel to the TV, kicked aside wood scraps until he found the remote, and turned on the device. The screen was black, no signal. He flipped through channels. Nothing, nothing. At last, far into the double digits, a signal popped up, bright and crisp. A good-looking man was slouched over a desk, his eyes bright despite the pouched exhaustion of his face.

Charlie sailed into the room, carrying two mugs. Somehow, she'd managed to choose his usual one, which she offered to Luis, and Rosa's favorite, which she kept for herself.

Joining him on the sofa, she gestured with her mug at the television. 'What do we got here?'

Luis pointed at the WWN logo.

'Oh, that's a good sign.' Fudged enthusiasm for the benefit of the sickie.

Charlie held her mug by the handle, while Rosa had always

cradled it in both hands. A small difference, but enough small differences added up to a major change. Sinking into the sofa, Luis pretended to watch WWN, feeling increasingly ill.

There were plenty of good reasons to keep quiet, but Charlie, true to her nature, got fired up by everything the anchor, Chuck Corso, reported. Through Luis's distending headache, he heard only Charlie's half of the conversation.

'Why the hell are they sending DMORT? There's no bodies to sort! The bodies are getting back up, morons!'

'This isn't a "virus-based mass psychosis". The CDC can kiss my ass!'

'Listen, shithead, if you didn't scroll through tragedies at the bottom of your screen 24–7, maybe we would have recognized this problem faster, you know?'

'Rapture. It's a rapture. Sure. Whatever. Idiots. Now *that's* God shit.'

'A dirty bomb? A *dirty* bomb? This guy wouldn't know the truth if it bit his thumb off! Oh, sorry, Acocella.'

Luis smiled, but couldn't manage the *Mmmmm* he knew she'd appreciate. He was losing cohesion. His placeholder *sarcophage* had been superseded by the WWN anchor's *ghoul* – that was about all he could handle right now. He'd started seeing things. Bluebirds flying in slow motion along the ceiling. Lush, soft grass growing from the carpet. That was all right. He would shut his hot, aching eyes and wrap a blanket around his freezing body. He could do these things because he realized he could, in fact, love Charlene Rutkowski. He already loved her a little, how she railed against an injurious world as hard as she ever had.

How's it look?

The question lingered. Living with Charlie was one thing. Dying with her was another.

The Second Civil War

For the first few hours after leaving Conan (and Qasim), she'd been a good, civilized girl, bicycling from town, the tar-patched, pot-holed two-lanes continually bopping the duffel bag from her back. But the civilized path had been shit. Minor thoroughfares had been stoppered by vehicle smashups Greer circumvented by swooping Fadi Lolo's Schwinn through ditches. Elsewhere, a telephone pole had fallen across the road. She'd had to lift the bike over that one.

She was two hours into pedaling south when she'd come upon triplet adolescents heading up the two-lane. Even fifty yards off, Their eyes burned white. They looked hungry, Their arms waved with unusual want, and rather than risk being snagged, Greer swerved off the pavement to ride through the sun-crisped crops. Bicycling on grass, though, sucked hard, reducing her speed so radically one trip-let lost a finger in the spinning of the Schwinn's back wheel.

That was the goddamn world telling her foolish ass to stay off the highways, where every white-eye in the world could see her. She took to the side roads, little strips of blacktop or dirt, and though the biking was tougher, she was cool with it – until a man atop a barn started shooting at her. She skidded the bike, started screaming she was alive. The guy kept shooting. She turned and pedaled like she'd never pedaled before, shouting aloud, so she'd remember it, that she was other things too: Black, a girl, a threat to whatever the man was hoarding.

After that, fuck roads. She walked the bike. It slowed her way down, but also forced her to take more careful stock of her surroundings. She needed to eat, and a cautious casing of a farmhouse allowed her to verify it was vacated. She'd wheeled the bike right into the kitchen and strapped it with as many bags of dry food and containers of water as she could. The Schwinn had become a beast of burden.

While stockpiling, she'd switched on the TV and gotten drawn into a full hour of the only active channel, WWN. Judging by the amateur video clips, things were in the toilet everywhere. People climbing from cyclone ruins in Shamrock, Oklahoma, looking like miracle survivors until They attacked. YouTube videos, hashtagged #DroneTheDead, of hobbyists piloting drones into crowds of white-eyes, the money shots of Their faces being sliced up by drone blades – it's funny, right? Tragicomic absurdity from Disney World, as the pack of Ariel, Belle, Jasmine, Mulan fell upon children, each red bite a boutonnière.

Greer swiped a sleeping bag, left the house, spent a couple of hours putting distance between herself and the structure, then slept in the woods. She slept in the woods again the next night and the next. Tough nights, every snapped twig Qasim, guts flopping from his abdomen, desiring her more than ever. Today, she awoke with a face half-frozen from leaked tears, weighed down with morning dew, smelling of bark, and doubting her ears: *plink-plink-plink*.

It sounded like rain dropping onto tin siding. But she was nowhere near anything with siding, and the last three days and nights had been clear and cold.

Greer rolled her bike through an unkempt acreage of weeds, her socks and jeans soaking through, and weighed theories. It was the *plink* of wire fencing being unrolled to keep people like her outside a safe zone. It was the *plink* of someone loading a crossbow capable of assassinating her from a mile off. It was the *plink* of white-eyes gnawing slivers from bone. Just before she saw the source, the *plink* was joined by a long, low wail she first thought was the creak of a rusted fence. It turned out to be a voice.

Ahead was the dinkiest crossroads she'd ever seen, two meandering dirt byways only suited for the landowner's tractors. Deep mud puddles and overgrown weeds suggested it hadn't been used in ages, except by the man who sat at one of the corners, picking a lonely tune from an ivory-colored guitar. He wore a black leather jacket over a black T-shirt, with a scarf of faded American-flag design piled around his neck. Beneath black jeans, a dusty black boot tapped a rhythm into the dirt. His long fingers pulled at the guitar strings with teasing tardiness, each *plink* barely catching the far edge of the beat. A black fedora hid the player's face, rocking in sympathy with his song.

> *Late last night*
> *You crawled o'er my windowpane*
> *Late last night, ooo-ee*
> *You crawled o'er my windowpane*
> *I answered, 'Devil, you son of a gun*
> *You done caused me too much pain.'*

Here in this blank land, there was nothing to make an echo, and the moist ground stole all reverberation, giving the man's croon the thin quality of a cheeping bird. The music was haunting; the man had to be a mirage. Greer felt no fear. The man had no belongings with which to attack her, except for the battered guitar case he was using for a seat and the guitar about which he clearly cared too much to risk damaging.

> *Take my burned old bones*
> *Cool them in the river, y'all*

Take my burned old bones, ooo-ee
Cool them in the river, y'all
So all the pitch-black things I done
Slide right down the waterfall.

Greer halted five feet away. The back-and-forth sway of the man's fedora lifted high enough for him to peek from under the brim. She realized he'd heard her coming for a while, but had opted to reveal himself slowly, maybe so he didn't scare her. That took balls, she thought. *He* should have been scared by *her*.

She expected him to be Black – she could see his agile brown fingers – but she didn't expect for him to be under twenty-five and the hottest guy she'd ever seen. He arched his eyebrows over small, red-rimmed eyes and twisted his lips into a coy grin inside a short, scraggly beard. Though he'd stopped singing, he kept noodling, pulling the strings hard and letting them snap against frets like rubber bands. His Adam's apple bobbed in a skinny neck as he improvised a *Hmm-mmm-mmm-mmm*.

Three days of surviving alone had familiarized Greer with racing pulse and surging adrenaline; she'd already forgotten how those same factors could incite a blush. She remembered she was in possession of a two-wheeled dolly loaded with bags of food and water.

'You thirsty?' Her voice was distinctively unmusical.

He quit humming but kept playing. 'Need to piss.'

Cute, she thought derisively.

'What about food?' she asked. 'You hungry?'

The guy winked. 'Got a turkey sub in one of those sacks?'

Greer peered into the closest bag. 'Planters Peanuts.'

He slid his fingers up the neck and moaned a lyric: '*I got peanuts . . . I got peanuts on my mind . . . Mm-mm, Mama, please do me right . . . and gimme what Planters you can find.*'

It had been so long since she'd smiled that it cracked a glaze of crud on her cheeks. Whoever this guy was, he had a charm you didn't pick up in northwest Missouri. She pulled out the jar of peanuts and gave it a toss. It had 'a little spin on it', as Daddy used to say, but the man's left hand zipped off the guitar neck to catch it against his jacket, while his right fingers kept plucking the strings, *plink-plink-plink*. He grinned over the jar's plastic lid and, with his right fingers still plucking, used his chin to remove the lid.

He poured ten thousand peanuts into his mouth.

'You eat like a dog,' Greer said.

'Woof,' he mumbled past his chewing.

'Is this' – Greer looked around – 'your place?'

He swallowed, grimaced, picked up a soup can from behind his guitar case, and drank from it. Liquid, probably rainwater by its hue, streamed down his neck and darkened his shirt. He gasped, coughed, and wiped his lips. His right hand, possessed by a separate spirit, kept plucking. He gave her a teasing half grin.

'You mean, this my doghouse?'

Greer gripped the Schwinn's handlebars. 'I don't have to share my shit.'

He slid a finger down the frets as he plucked a sinking, regretful note: *pluuuunk*.

'Nah. This ain't my place. Just wandering around and, you know, got to feeling Faustian. I'm ready to cut me some Robert Johnson-type deal.'

'I don't know who that is.'

He lifted an eyebrow and crawled his hand along the guitar neck, a loping progression of notes she was apparently expected to recognize. She shrugged. He licked his lips, rattling Greer with carnal desire, and asked, 'What are you doing out here?'

She shrugged again. 'I ran away.'

'From KC?'

She shook her head. 'Other direction.'

'What you running from?'

Freddy Morgan's peeled skull, Conan Morgan's forsaken grief.

'Town called Bulk,' she said. 'About forty miles north.'

'And we run into each other here at the Devil's Crossroads? That's like the only two cars in the desert crashing into each other.' He whistled. 'You got a name?'

'Do you?'

He tipped his fedora with a flick of a finger. 'Mr Peanut.'

Greer scowled. He laughed and held out the Planters jar. She did the calculus any girl did before getting within grabbing distance of a man and decided to chance it. She stepped in and swiped the jar, but not before she got a whiff of him. She wrinkled her nose before she could think better of it. The guy stank of beer. The liquid in that soup can wasn't water. Come to think of it, the guitar case he was sitting on wasn't shaking like it was empty either.

'You're drunk,' she accused.

'Oh, good. I been working toward it.'

'You know how stupid that is? With those things around? And bellowing songs too?'

'Bellowing. Damn. Been a minute since I had a bad review.'

'Yeah, I get it. You play guitar. I guess that means you get to be drunk and happy while the rest of us are barely staying alive.'

'That's why I chose here.' He spread his arms at the fields to all sides, and the stoppage of music became the gasp of that lonely world. 'Best place to hide, I figured, was right out in the open. Did you tell me your name?'

'Greer. Who are you?'

'Morning, Greer. I'm KK.'

'KK? Like the KKK?'

'That's right. I'm two-thirds of the KKK. Now that you know the ugly truth, I'll let you know I have a very, very good reason for being drunk. When I tell you, you're going to say to yourself, "Miss Greer,

KK deserved his beer, and from here on out, I'm going to be a lot friendlier to him." '

'I doubt it.'

He pressed a fret and set the mood with a flamenco flourish.

'Must have been a day, day and a half, after this whole mess started, and where did your boy end up? At the Waterfall Brewery in West Bottoms. Now, you might be tempted to think I went there for the express purpose of tying one on. I forgive you for thinking it, Miss Greer, but that just isn't accurate. I'd just lost Tull, man.' He pulled the guitar strings hard, the woeful *thwap* of the blues; Greer might have laughed if this guy's eyes hadn't dulled in anguish. 'I didn't even know it was a brewery, honest. There was this alley door, guess where they load the barrels, and next thing you know, Mr Muse King is surrounded by all these giant vats of beer.'

'Muse King? Is that your real name?'

Muse was lost, telling the story with a song's valleys and crests.

'Now, beer was never my thing, you know? Bourbon, man, and I'm not even picky about it. You spend your nights singing for your supper, voice all torn up, a little whiskey does the tricksy. So I push some boxes over the door and start hunting for a bottle, you can't hold that against me, and by and by, I notice a sound, a bad sound. Sound is King Kong's vocation.'

'King Kong? How many names you have?'

'You ever kicked a car, made a dent? You know that metal pop? That was the sound, one little *bong*, then two little *bongs*, then three little *bongs*. Now Tull, he was a beer guy. Ten million miles we drove together, and I swear five million of them he was all *malt extract* this and *mouthfeel* that. I used to be like, "Yo, we need one of them limos where the window seals your mouth *off*." Anyway, one thing I learned about is fermentation. You know about fermentation, Miss Greer?'

'No. But at least I only have one name.'

'Tull used to talk about brewing beer like it was making TNT. When you're fermenting beer, you got to ride that heat. Your heat spikes, your pressure spikes. There was a few hundred vats in that brewery hadn't nobody been watching for days. I'd just found me my bourbon, just like I knew I would, and all's a sudden—' He slapped the guitar face. '*Boom!*'

Greer took out a plastic two-liter she'd filled with water and took a long drink. It was a casual behavior, which made her acknowledge how comfortable she felt. She could imagine this man onstage, spinning yarns between songs, taking her mind off whatever bullshit had been bugging her. It made her sad she might never know a scenario like that – clubs, drinks, those adult things that looked so fun on TV. It made her all the gladder she was getting a sip of it now, better than water.

'It blew through the roof. You hear what I'm saying? The *beer* blew a *hole* through the *roof.*' Muse chuckled. 'Sounds funny now, but let me tell you, it wasn't so funny at the time. It was like a bomb went off. Before I could even take cover, a second vat went off, same thing, *whoosh,* right through the roof, and the whole place starts coming down now, you know? Wood, shingles, metal, glass, and then the brick walls start sliding in. You know how they call Kansas City the City of Fountains? It's the truth. Except this time it was fountains of beer, man, fire hoses of it, spraying everywhere. It was the beerpocalypse. I mean, I'm soaked to the bone in beer. It's why I smell so good.'

'You're also drunk.'

'Yeah, but that's because I put a few more bourbon bottles in my guitar case before I ran off. This supply might need to last me a while.'

'Not at this rate, it won't.'

Muse laughed. 'True, true. Maybe I push the bike, you carry the case.'

'Shit,' Greer said. 'Then *I'll* start drinking it.'

She smiled, self-conscious at first, then let it blaze, and he grinned back, a crocodilian thrill, and she felt shaken again, not only by misplaced desire but by a feeling of stumbling upon a great fortune. If she carried his case, like he said, and he pushed her bike, like he said, they'd be a team. Two people together, Freddy Morgan used to say before Vienna's incarceration, weren't two times as strong as one, they were two *hundred* times as strong. Muse King, or King Kong, or KK, whatever his name was, might be drunk, but the hair on her neck and arms wasn't spiking from danger.

There was a vulnerability to feeling grateful. She looked away, at the bike. After deliberation, she unhooked the duffel bag, sat down, and unzipped it.

Muse shook the guitar to make the final note quiver. 'You old enough to drink, Miss Greer?'

She withdrew the machete.

Muse raised his hands. 'My bad. Drink what you want.'

She rolled her eyes and set the machete on the grass. 'Relax. Just being prepared.'

He gave her a clear-eyed look, then placed his guitar on the dirt, mirroring her, laying down arms. He rubbed his cold hands and blew into them.

'Truth is, neither of us should drink a drop,' he said. 'When times get bleak, the right beverage is more valuable than gold.'

'Tull tell you that?'

Muse's grin looked more like a courtesy. 'Tull's jam was brewskis and nothing but. Mine's American history. Might have written a record or two about it. Coffee and alcohol, man. People will sell their soul for it. Some people say coffee won the Civil War. The Rebs were drinking cold brown swill made of acorns and bark while the North was gulping down big, hot cups of Good Morning, America. We play our cards right with this bourbon, you and me could be Lord and Lady Obama.'

'Who gets to sit at the big desk, though?'

Greer was flirting. She couldn't believe it. Her family had been lost to self-destructive revenge, a death-ending pandemic, and prison, and she had no plans for surviving the impending winter. Yet from her throat came the same tough, teasing voice she'd used in school, at bonfire parties, with Qasim. That any such spirit lived on inside her felt miraculous.

'The Oval Office is all yours.' Muse rubbed his face, looked around, and sighed. 'Missouri. World just had to end when I had a gig in dang Missouri. Talk about the Civil War.'

'Could be worse. Missouri was North, wasn't it?'

'Is that what your teachers told you?'

'Don't blame me if my school was shitty.'

'Your fine home state of Missouri had its Union soldiers, sure did, but it also had a whole mess of Confederate bushwhackers. It was a slave state, all right? Missouri was the microcosm of the whole American nightmare. Still is. In KC, man, I saw Blacks killing Blacks, whites killing whites. Brother on brother, sister on sister. If that ain't the Second Civil War, I don't know what is. What'd you see in Sack?'

'Sack?'

'Your town. Sack?'

'Bulk.' She snorted. 'Same shit. No one was even dealing with the white-eyes. Too busy blaming each other.'

'White-eyes. That's what they're calling Them in Bulk?'

'They got a better name?'

'Folks on the news were calling Them *ghouls.*'

It was the most reassuring thing she'd heard yet. Somewhere, news was still playing. Somewhere, smart people were still naming disasters. Greer stretched her arms over her head, enjoying the flex of muscles tight from forest-floor sleep. When her hoodie rode up her stomach, she knew Muse would see it, and she enjoyed that too. When she brought her arms down, she lay back on the grass. Her right hand settled on one of the bicycle's supply bags, and she realized she was hungry.

He came to her like she'd thought he would. The light, pale yellow now, reverted to gray inside his shadow. He looked as comfortable sinking to the ground with a girl as he did playing that ivory-colored guitar. He was lying down next to her, the crook of his elbow under her neck, before his forehead creased.

'I'm sobering up quick,' he said, 'but for real, I'm probably still drunk.'

'I want to be drunk too,' Greer said, taking hold of his jacket zipper and pulling him, black leather, black boots, black jeans, black shirt, black beard, all the way on top of her, blocking out everything.

Oh, Jubilee

Five days after the dead began to feast, Karl Nishimura believed everyone on the ship's island had taken on Their appetites. The food left was deplorable. The peanuts kept coming, fewer each so-called meal, handfuls of dust Nishimura lapped from his palm only to watch it fall from a tongue no longer producing saliva. Water rations had been reduced to sparse splashes from a salt-encrusted ladle. He and the men on the meteorological level might die first, but the men above them would follow.

So it did not surprise Nishimura when Tommy Henstrom and a bodyguard hoisted him from his chalk-outline bed and dragged him onto the catwalk and to the ladder. The sun was the point of a galaxy-sized knife, but his body craved vitamin D like it did water, and he opened his eyes and palms to it. Renewed, those palms had enough strength to grip the ladder rails, and with Henstrom gesturing from above and a pistol barrel nudging him from below, Nishimura made it up the next four levels. It felt like paddling into the cotton-white clouds.

Pri-Fly had been scrubbed clean of the blood of Clay Szulczewski, Willis Clyde-Martell, and Jacobo Leatherdale. Nishimura was led into the cabin and held upright. Father Bill sat in Szulczewski's padded chair, noticeably gaunt but possessed of the smooth movements of the fully watered. His injured ear had been tidily bandaged and his CVN-68X CHAPLAIN turtleneck replaced by a crisp Hawaiian shirt decorated with parrots and palm fronds. Henstrom wore one too, pink flamingos on a beach. The shirts must have belonged to Szulczewski and Clyde-Martell, cheap Oahu mementos now the regalia of the ruling class.

Father Bill gestured for Nishimura to sit in Clyde-Martell's chair, though he looked bewildered, as if wondering why this grubby Japanese American was in front of him.

'This is Helmsman Nishimura.' Henstrom said it as if speaking to a hard-of-hearing senior. 'He's going to help with the missions.'

Father Bill smiled.

'How wonderful. Missionary work is the Catholic Church's best tradition.'

'I don't . . .' Nishimura's throat was a pinhole. 'Water. Please.'

'Water is one of the problems,' Father Bill agreed. 'I am inclined to let the Lord's will be done. If we are meant to drink, I said, the heavens will open up. But Tommy is an advocate for men like you, a true apostle. He has feet you may feel moved to wash one day.'

Henstrom's teeth appeared, one by one, as a grin slit his face. Nishimura wanted to rip his lips off, slake his thirst with the jetting blood.

'Tommy reminded me that a church will fall apart if built on faith alone,' the priest said. 'What did you say, Tommy? Something about rust.'

'Corrosion, Father,' Henstrom said. 'From salt water.'

'Let us not forget corrosion of the soul,' the priest added. 'If it sits still too long, it too is subject to nature's abrading aspects. This is why the missions are important. It is the duty of those chosen by God, as we in this tower have been chosen, to leave our safe places and carry the good news across all borders, regardless of danger. And our missions will be especially dangerous. Do you know why, Helmsman?'

'Water,' Nishimura said. 'Please.'

Henstrom frowned as if taxed to his limit by a doddery grandpa and a bitchy child. He swiped a metal thermos from a counter. It made a *glunk:* there was enough liquid inside to slosh. Beads of condensation squiggled down the metal: like Jesus multiplying fish and bread, this water begat water. Nishimura gasped. Perhaps Pri-Fly *was* heaven, for this was a heavenly object. He was ready to lick it, if only his tongue could reach.

'In human history, it has always been we Christians who brought forth the story of the resurrection and the everlasting life,' Father Bill said. 'The demons, however, are telling the same story, only from the other side! They have been missioning to us the only way They know how. Through Their hands and Their teeth.'

Nishimura watched individual water droplets, fat as sweet syrup, slip off the bottom of the thermos and vanish onto the floor. He sobbed once, picturing fine white cracks breaking across his red throat. He turned a pleading face to Father Bill, who was lost in reverie.

'The difficulty of the task is irrelevant. Missionaries die. They always have. That's glory. Tommy tells me you, Helmsman, are the right person to lead my Missionaries. You will leave the safety of our tower and trade news of our brotherhood and love for the food and water we require. You are, as I've been told, a willing messenger of Christ?'

Nishimura dragged his arid eyeballs back to the thermos. Henstrom's look was as sharp as Father Bill's was hazy. Nishimura tried to think it through. Henstrom did not believe in the priest's drivel. What he believed in was power, and he had it, right there, cool and perspiring in his hand. The prize for agreeing to Father Bill's deranged proposal was not the priest's blessed approval. It was water, pure and simple.

'Yes,' Nishimura said. 'Yes, yes.'

Henstrom held out the thermos. Nishimura went for it with digits that had lost all dexterity. His stupid left hand punched it, bashing it from Henstrom's grip, and for a second, it was airborne, a frond of water extending from the spout, about to be lost. But his right hand caught it, and then he was drinking, not a tepid lick from a ladle but a whole mouthful, then another, soaking his tongue, sponging his throat. It was as sweet and effervescent as iced cola, and he felt, with each gulp, the waning of his worst symptoms. The headache that drubbed like ocean waves. The purple fingernails. The inability to pee. The exhaustion, the confusion. Life returned.

Father Bill clapped softly. In his parrot shirt, he looked as if he were applauding his grandchildren's cavorting.

'Oh, jubilee. One personal favor, if I may. There are no women on our tower, as you know. That is most unfortunate; they should share in our ascendance. If you find women down below, you will tell me, won't you? You will bring them up here, even if it takes a little bit of force? There is one woman in particular I would appreciate seeing again.'

Nishimura nodded once. Father Bill beamed.

'Jubilee, jubilee. Now, Tommy, did you turn down my bed? I'm afraid my ear is bothering me.'

Henstrom gritted his teeth and helped Father Bill from the air boss chair into the rear chamber, where presumably a cot had been arranged. The bodyguard remained, but Nishimura didn't care. He had the thermos turned over his mouth and did not plan to stop shaking it until he'd released every drop. Henstrom returned, gestured the guard to give them privacy, and leaned against the window, his arms crossed over his pink-and-purple shirt. Nishimura gasped for air, his stomach bloated with water, and stared back.

'He's crazy,' Nishimura said.

'Don't say that,' Henstrom said. 'Don't you ever say that.'

'One crazy priest isn't the problem. It's the rest of you letting it happen. Koppenborg walks unharmed across the flattop, by luck. By *luck*. That's all you need to lose your minds? You are navy men.'

'The Long Walk was a holy event. I'm sad for you if you can't see it.'

'You're only standing behind him because otherwise no one will listen to you. No one ever listened to you.'

'*You* never listened to me.'

'I listen to sailors who deserve it.'

'Well, who deserves it now, huh? Who made all the right choices this time? That's what this is about. We've got to get fresh water production going again. I know that. We have to make sure engines are being cooled.'

'So you admit it. These missions have nothing to do with God or demons. They're for repairs. They're for food and water.'

'What I said about corrosion is true, you know. You never gave me any credit.'

'Henstrom. You're talking about rust. Men are dying.'

'And we're addressing that. That's why you're going on the mission.'

'We don't need a mission. All that stupid padre has to do is go full speed ahead to California!'

'You're the one who didn't want to go to San Diego.'

'I thought it was our boat that was infectious! I thought we'd be spreading it!'

'We're better off out here,' Henstrom said.

'*You're* better off out here. That's your delusion, anyway.'

Henstrom crossed his arms. 'You know the ship better than anyone. You'll get extra rations. Extra water. You, and a few others, for two days, until you're stronger. Then you go down. Father Bill's got believers in lots of critical areas belowdecks. We need to make sure they have food. We need to station a couple men in the power plant. The reactor officer isn't responding. I don't know what happens if the reactors get overrun by demons.'

'Won't happen,' Nishimura said. 'Because demons don't exist.'

'Don't *say* that.'

'It so happens I do know what happens if the reactors get over-run. We'll stop depleting uranium. The first thing we'll lose is the turbine generators. The boat won't move after that, not even if we want it to. Second thing is electrical. We lose the grid, all grids. Third is plain old hot water. Now it's getting fun. Now we're on our way to scurvy and starvation. Of course, we won't make it that far if the cores aren't cooled. We've got two Westinghouse A4W nuclear reactors down there. What do you *think* could happen?'

Shushing like water along the hull, Father Bill was singing himself to sleep.

'*Sinners my gracious Lord receives / Harlots, and publicans, and thieves . . .*'

'You know your stuff, Saint Karl,' Henstrom said. 'That's why you're leading the mission.'

'Yes, me and "a few others". I'd need *fifty* others. If we had marines left, maybe we'd have a chance, if you hadn't—'

'The marines left on amphibious ships. I wasn't the only one who saw that!'

'*Drunkards, and all the hellish crew, / I have a message now to you . . .*'

'Only after your men shot at them, O-3!'

'I think you'd better call me *sir*.'

'*Come, and partake the gospel-feast, / Be sav'd from sin, in Jesus rest . . .*'

'I told you, O-3, you'll get my respect—'

Henstrom surged forward, his face red, his hands in fists. 'I'm *sir* now! I'm *sir*!'

'*O taste the goodness of our God, / And eat his flesh, and drink his blood.*'

'—when you deserve it, O-3, and not a second—'

Nishimura's voice, pushed too hard after days of silence and desert dryness, splintered. His throat sizzled with bile and blood. As he gagged and coughed, Father Bill's clean Pri-Fly floor splotched red, and it all rushed back, Szulczewski's body axed into morsels, Clyde-Martell's face replaced by a smoking hole. That was the way things were going to go aboard *Olympia,* no matter how he fought. Blood from the good, the bad, and the ones of indeterminate nature, a flood of it, until the boat was a crimson craft on a deep red sea.

The Shotgun Marriage

Luis wasn't getting better. A headache he couldn't shake. A sore throat. A fluctuating fever. Cold, he was always cold. As long as Charlie had known Luis, he'd been a complainer. Now he didn't complain, he just suffered. When he felt well enough, he'd huddle with her on the sofa and make grim jokes to accompany Chuck Corso's updates. But every day, he spent more time in the upstairs bedroom, sweating beneath covers, not complaining at all.

Having a guy you're in love with down with a cold was not the worst thing in the world; any girl could tell you that. You got to ply them with food and drink and watch your simplest efforts bring them great joy. Sick care was love care, even if it felt a little cheap, and she could see her love reflected in Luis's eyes. Weaker, but then again, his love for her had always been weaker than hers for him. Some truths you had to live with.

It was not a cold, of course. Sarcophage, ghoul, whatever you wanted to call it, some of it had gotten into his blood, and every single day – if not every five minutes – she thought of those crucial seconds during which she'd hesitated to slice off his thumb. Sometimes she cussed herself out so badly she had to slip into the pantry so Luis wouldn't overhear: *Stupid goddamn fucking slow-ass scaredy-cat cunt.* She'd spent hundreds of hours trusting her boss about where and when to cut, and the one time it had really mattered, she'd waffled.

She'd have given anything to have the old Luis Acocella back, trigger-witted, spry as a grasshopper, unaware of how sexy he was when he looked at a corpse and knew all its secrets in seconds. A low-power Luis Acocella still wasn't half-bad, and she found her desire unbearable. She'd wanted him for so long, and not just in an after-hours autopsy suite. She'd wanted him in a home like this.

On Halloween, eight days after John Doe, the power went out.

Chuck Corso, still the nation's lone maître d' for this feast, had been on a roll. The Chicago River's unattended sluice gates flooded the Second City's downtown. Sea life drowned in oil pouring from captainless tankers. Livestock perished by the millions as farmers died or fled. Corso was reading a report on abandoned homes exploding from natural gas leaks when WWN, the lamp she and Luis dared burn at night, and the refrigerator's hum all winked out. In the shocked first seconds of silent darkness, Charlie's old nightmare came crawling back, cadaverous Fred Astaire holding out his withered hand.

Shall we dance, Charlie? Shall we?

Luis's voice had a dozen new facets: split octaves from a sore throat, the bass purr of phlegmy lungs. 'Chet Musgrave. He's got a diesel generator.'

Charlie gathered herself before replying, unwilling to hear her own fear.

'How far away does this Mr Musgrave live?'

'Across the street.'

'Won't he fight you for it?'

'He's gone. Visiting his daughter in Oakland.'

The only other time they'd taken down boards and gone outside was to bury Mamá Acocella in a grave so shallow both of them, too familiar with corpses, suspected would be raided by scavengers. They'd used the back door and done it in the middle of the night, and Charlie had been terrified the whole time. Now she tried to build up some courage, but it blew away in one exhale.

'Shit, Acocella! I wouldn't know a generator if it tried to bite me!

Going out there, in the dark, rooting around for some mystery gadget? I don't know if I can do that.'

'I'll do it.'

'Oh, perfect. Guilt me into it. You can hardly walk to the bathroom.'

Luis bolted to his feet, an attempt to prove Charlie wrong that sent him swaying. But the steadiness of the hand with which he braced himself against the wall showed his resolve. Luis blinked until he seemed solid.

'We'll go together,' he said. 'If our power went out, so did the other houses'. You want to wait until Felix McKirdy down the block remembers Chet's generator? We might have the .38, but Felix owns rifles. With bump stocks. We need that generator, now.'

'My fucking hero.' She piled on the sarcasm, but she was standing, wasn't she?

It was night; they dashed. Luis got Musgrave's generator and all his fuel into a child's red wagon while Charlie loaded bags with food and jars of water. They kept as quiet as possible, yet five ghouls amassed in fifteen minutes. In Musgrave's house, Charlie broke dishes in the sink to draw Them from the attached garage, out of which she and Luis then fled.

The details of the adventure were unimportant. What was important were the in-between moments. How they found ways to joke at the most frightening moments. How they worked together without having to share a word. How they grumped at each other's failings. How they flat-out argued about how to distract the ghouls, their first fight, one they got over the instant they were safe, and if that didn't mean they were de facto married, what did?

Mae Rutkowski would have hardly believed it: her wild child settling down at last.

Charlie and Luis nailed the front door shut again and then clutched each other on the sofa, watching the window boards rattle under assaults from what had to be six or seven ghouls. Each time they jumped, they laughed like they were watching a horror movie. Charlie knew what teens liked to do while watching horror movies. She ran Luis's hand up under her shirt, and he, stimulated by defeated frights, starting peeling off her sweaty clothes.

The ghouls banged and moaned; Charlie and Luis banged and moaned. It was like sex in a thunderstorm, or on a beach near shattering waves, an erotic near death. When Charlie came, she thought of the French term for orgasm, *le petite mort*, 'the little death', because that's how she felt, like she'd died and come back as a ghoul, starved for Luis's flesh. She only regretted the climactic doggy style. She would have liked to have seen his face on this wedding-night milestone: first sex as husband and wife.

The next day, the honeymoon was over.

The whistling wheeze from Luis's chest woke her up. As long as she kept her eyes closed, she could convince herself it was due to the exertion of the retrieval job and celebratory sex. But she had to open her eyes eventually. Luis's skin had gone a putty gray, and the lines of his cheeks were deeper, darker. His mouth, maybe only by contrast, was bloodred, and when she felt his forehead, she withdrew her hand with a gasp – the skin was cold, the sweat hot.

'Feel like shit,' he mumbled.

'I'll get you some water,' she said, standing up. In the bathroom, the door shut, Charlie wrapped her arms around her face to muffle the sound, and cried, and cried, and cried, until her eyes were swollen shut and her shirt was translucent with tears. Finally, she was with the man she loved, and he was dying. She could no longer pretend otherwise. He'd aged five years overnight. Another night would be ten years. A week would be thirty-five more. By then, he'd be seventy years old, barely holding on, and they'd have hardly begun.

Meanwhile, Lindof and every power-mad fuck like him were stashed away somewhere safe, fat, and happy. Charlie knew it.

It wasn't fair, it wasn't fucking fair.

Carrying a filled glass, she went back to the bed. She held the glass so he could sip from it, though most of the water pooled in the hollow of his neck. He looked up at her with yellowed, red-veined eyes.

'Sorry,' he rasped.

'It's not your fault, shithead.' She slashed at tears with her hand. 'You'll be all right.'

'Don't give me goody-goody bullshit! We don't have time for that! Say what you mean, asshole.'

'I do mean it.' He smiled weakly. 'You're the baddest bitch I know.'

She slid onto the bed, locking his shivering legs in hers and cradling his cold head against her warm, wet neck.

'Don't leave me, Acocella. I'm not done with you yet. Not even close.'

'Just bodies,' he said. 'You know that.'

'We met too late.'

'Billion-to-one odds anyone meets anyone. We did all right.'

Charlie pulled away to look into his discolored eyes.

'We'll just have to go faster. Squeeze forty years into whatever we have left.'

'Mmmmm.'

'Instead of a shotgun wedding, we'll have a shotgun marriage. We'll do the whole thing, but double-time.'

'Okay. Sounds nice. Tiring, but nice.'

What made up a marriage? Mae and Maury Rutkowski were Charlie's only reference, married until Maury's death when Charlie was twenty-two. Mostly what Charlie recalled were her parents' grudging silences, their close-quarters elbow boxing, their weary concord of looking past the other's detritus.

There had been flashes of tenderness. Charlie got her notepad and wrote down what she could recall. Holiday vacations: pinwheeling about Gettysburg with her sisters and looking back to see her folks arm in arm in the spectacular dusk. Anniversary celebrations:

clichés of pink-ribboned chocolates or rose bouquets, Mae nonetheless grateful for the duly-marked checkbox.

Fine, that was a start. Operation Shotgun Marriage initiated. Charlie found a Christmas tree in the basement, set it up in the living room, and rooted around the house for silly objects to wrap in holiday paper. Luis's body kept seizing up while she helped him downstairs, but when he saw the twinkling lights and *It's a Wonderful Life* playing on TV via DVD, and heard Bing Crosby from the old CD player, audible above the generator's chug, she felt his whole body relax. Blammo: a Christmas memory, just like that, and the next day they had Valentine's Day, and the day after that, New Year's Eve.

Holidays were for mornings. Dinners were reserved for anniversaries, which they celebrated every day. Shotgun marriages, Charlie decided, got to skip the early crap like paper, cotton, and leather and jump right to the good stuff. Five years: wood. Twelfth year: silk. Twenty-fifth year: silver. She always rustled up something: a wooden Día de los Muertos skull, a hilarious silk nightclub shirt from the early 1990s, a silver-painted Transformers toy, likely from Luis's youth. The dinners themselves didn't go well; Luis had no appetite and found swallowing difficult. He seemed to like seeing her eat, though, so she pretended to savor the stale Oreo Double Stuf with five candles, or the Jell-O pudding cup she'd dressed up with a *12* made from white chocolate chips.

It was a sign of love, she told herself, that Luis held it together for each celebration. It was only after she helped him back to bed that he pulled the sheets into sweaty cords as he writhed with pain he couldn't describe. 'My blood's thick' was the best he could manage. Charlie pictured maggots clogging up Luis's veins. She'd need to work faster. It was for her well-being now, not Luis's.

Children were a cornerstone of many married couples' worlds, but there wasn't much she could do about that. Not pets either; the dogs she spotted looked too voracious, the cats too deranged.

Another brainstorm hit. Music and movies! She and Luis had been Shotgun Married for twenty or thirty years now and still didn't have 'their song' or 'their movie'. She collected every last CD, LP, MP3 player, Blu-ray, and DVD in a laundry basket and carried them to Luis's bedside to audition each piece of media for the honor.

'*Garden State*?' she asked, modeling the DVD.

'I'd rather be bit by a hundred ghouls,' he groaned. 'A thousand.'

'*The Wedding Planner,* starring Jennifer Lopez and Matthew McConaughey? Aw, Luis, we never got a proper wedding. This might be instructive.'

'Bleak,' he said. 'That's what this is.'

'Hey, it's your collection. How about *Hitch*?'

Luis squinted. 'Will Ferrell?'

'Will Smith. "Meet Hitch, New York City's greatest matchmaker. Love is his job and he'll get you the girl of your dreams in just three easy dates, guaranteed!"'

'Now I'm sick *and* humiliated.'

'Oh, here we go. This one has "our movie" written all over it. "Adam Sandler is a devoted dad with a breathtaking new house-keeper in . . . *Spanglish*."'

'Kill me. Just do it.'

'Includes twelve deleted scenes, Acocella! Twelve!'

'Bring me the gun. Bring me the fucking gun.'

It was wildly funny and crushingly sad. Luis laughed, which turned into a cough, and he managed to shrug through it – *What are you going to do?* – even as blood speckled his chin and, under the covers, his legs kicked in paroxysms of sarcophagal pain. He didn't want her to see it, so Charlie pretended not to see, and laughed until she cried, and then, after hiding her face with tissue paper, just plain cried, which she found, given a little practice, she could pass off as more laughter.

Walk Away

If one were to recount the occasions of hard work and good luck that had thrust WWN into the sphere of the cable-news big boys, the July 15, 2015, events at Jo-Jo's Hog, a dimly lit cellar nightclub in New Orleans, had to be in the top five. On that night, one of the station's first stars, Octavia Gloucester, a bulldog reporter drafted from a Charlotte NBC affiliate, was in the French Quarter, finishing a special report on the return of music venues fifteen years after Hurricane Katrina.

Muse King, a.k.a. King Kong, or KK to his friends, had been doing the Jo-Jo's Hog version of a sound check when Gloucester, working without a field producer in those bare-bones days, ambled over to the band's impossibly young leader to let him know she'd be shooting a scripted shot during his first set. The band ought to do an original.

'You never know,' Octavia Gloucester said. 'National TV. Someone might dig it.'

Muse had been in awe of the beautiful, no-nonsense reporter. He was just seventeen, young enough to believe that some background noise on a thirty-second piece of video on a second-rate news network might actually catapult him to fame. He'd been playing dingy blues clubs for three years, forever the youngest cat in the joint. That was a serious chunk of his life. He was impatient for his break.

He'd acted cool, said something like, 'Yeah, I might have something.'

When it was time to play, he let the band settle first, then strolled onto the stage. The city's smoking ban was brand-new and, in pits like this, being flouted. He tilted his head into the smoke-filled beam of a tinny, red-gelled spot, pressed his mouth against the standing mic, and growled out the opening a cappella eight-count to 'If the Blues Wuz a Woman', not his most unique song, but if the reporter lady wanted blues, here was an A-major, fifth-position, twelve-bar, blues-with-a-capital-*B* riff that ought to read no matter what the reporter was saying.

He was past the chorus, about to step back to grind on guitar, when a man who would later be identified as twenty-nine-year-old Preston Gourlay fought across the front of the smoky room, stage lights shimmering down his sweaty face, and lifted a long arm holding a .357. His target was Juniper Coulbeck, a girl he claimed had spurned him, but who insisted she only knew him as some guy who lived in her building.

Coulbeck was able to clarify this because Coulbeck didn't get shot. Coulbeck didn't get shot because King Kong, living up to the sobriquet – though it had originally been applied to the skinny kid ironically – continued drawing back his guitar into a full baseball backswing, leaned out over the stage, and crashed his best friend – the royal-blue, gloss-finished, hollow-bodied Gretsch Electromatic his uncle Marlon had given to him when he was five – into Preston Gourlay's skull.

It had the makings of just one more New Orleans legend, except it was captured over Octavia Gloucester's left shoulder. Muse watched it a hundred times on YouTube. Like the rest of the world enthralled by the viral video (244,323,881 views in the first two weeks), he was in disbelief over his quick instinct. It was as if he'd trained his arms for attack the same way he'd trained his fingers for a six-string.

The raw video was nearly three minutes long. As a result, 'If the Blues Wuz a Woman' had been heard 244 million times. Within five days, Muse had performed the song on *The Daily Show with Jon Stewart* and *Jimmy Kimmel Live!*, and had been fawned over by the hosts of *The View* and *Live with Kelly and Michael*. He received offers from three music labels, all front-loaded with nonrefundable advances.

By the start of the next week, when the cover of *Time* featured the blood-spattered remains of his shattered Gretsch along with the words MUSIC STILL MATTERS, Muse's new agent had lined up a full Japanese tour, and Muse was a wealthy young hero. He drummed up more good press by donating seventy-three guitars to inner-city community centers.

Why seventy-three? Because in the month following the noble annihilation of his Gretsch, people had sent him seventy-four guitars to replace the Gretsch – fourteen used, the rest new. He'd unpacked each one with reverence. After days of consideration, he selected one to keep, a 1978 maple-necked, mahogany-bodied, custom Alpine White Gibson Les Paul with just enough paint worn off to make it seem honest. It was only then that he perched upon a high kitchen stool, one of the few pieces of furniture in his brand-new Garden District home, and dared to strum the meat string lightly, just enough to tune. Within the next few minutes, he'd gotten the strings in sync. A promising sound but, like Uncle Phil said, 'You never know what a lady's got in her till she starts screaming at you.'

So early that Sunday, alone for the first time in weeks, in an empty, reverberating, sawdust-coated kitchen, Muse King made that old Gibson scream. After twenty minutes of tough love, the ax had proven itself so righteous Muse had let his falling tears darken the circle of sawdust at his feet. The coterie of handlers who'd mushroomed around him might or might not have his best interests in mind, but it didn't really matter. He'd found himself a new best friend.

Tucked inside the Gibson's scuffed, red-velveted hard-shell case was a letter from the givers. Despite the train wreck of its spelling, it was written in a neat, steady hand.

> SINS YOU LOVE BLEUS MUSIC AND SINS WE SAW YOU ON TV
> STOP A MAN HOSE GETING REDDY TO SHOOT A GUN WE WANT
> YOU TO HAEV THIS GITTAR THAT BALONG TO OUR SON HEWITT
> WHO LOVE BLEUS MUSIC. HEWITT USED THAT GITTAR NINE
> YAERS. HE WAS ATEEN YAERS OLD. HE GOT SHOT AND DIED.
> WE AR PRAYING EVER TIME YOU PLAY IT MAKES HEWITT
> SMIL UP THERE IN HEAVEN WAER HE IS NOW.
>   – YUOR FRENDS WILL AND DARLENE LUCAS

Muse's father bolted before Muse was born, and his mother did likewise around the time he'd started walking. None of the aunts, uncles, and grandmothers who'd let him grow up in their living rooms and basements had partners. Reading a note from a married couple, who signed their names as a unit, plucked a string deep inside him. So he wrote the first personal letter of his life, confirming to the Lucas family of Cranston, Rhode Island, he would not only play their son's guitar but had already named it *Hewitt*. Ten days later came a reply.

> WE AR GLAD YOU GOT THE GITTAR. WE AR HAPPY THAT
> YUOR GOIN TO USE IT.
>   – YUOR FRENDS WILL AND DARLENE LUCAS

Over the next five years, right up until the day the whole world shit the bed, Muse wrote dozens of letters to Will and Darlene Lucas and received dozens of replies, each one a respite from a life of increasing bullshit. Muse's overnight fame had carved up his extended family like a pie, each slice insisting they enjoyed Muse's favor. None had much cared about his welfare before. The Lucases, who wanted nothing but to see their son live on in Muse's music, were the reliable ones, and Muse clung to them.

Muse knew plenty of undereducated folk, but the Lucases were a step beyond, illiterate to a degree he hadn't believed existed except in backwoods stereotypes. Unlike cinema's inbred banjo pickers, Will and Darlene were people of breathtaking tranquility, as if living apart from the world's technological progress had somehow preserved them. Their lives, from what little they shared, had been brutal. Most of the Lucas family was in the cemetery, and a few years back, Will and Darlene had driven their self-rehabbed 1962 Plymouth from Mississippi to a shack they'd inherited on the distant planet of Rhode Island.

The way of things cant be changed, Will often wrote. Muse sensed the sentiment came less from defeat than it did an appreciation of humanity's smallness. He reminded himself of that when howling into the mic and punishing the Gibson before sold-out crowds: he, too, was small, very small.

The superstar potential of a blues player in modern America had limits. Muse King's crossover potential plateaued after a couple of years, but thanks to the Lucases' stabilizing influence, Muse was not disappointed. He had a recognizable name and the royalties on 'If the Blues Wuz a Woman' kept coming, which meant it was high time to get down to being what he'd set out to be. Not a magazine cover model but a down-and-dirty bluesman, what Hewitt Lucas would have wanted.

It was also high time to meet Will and Darlene. Muse flew them out to see him play a homecoming show in New Orleans, put them up in a nice hotel, and gave them a couple of days to explore the city alone. Finally, he met them in the safe zone of Audubon Park, two bewildered, perspiring white folks in too-heavy Sunday best. Both gave him cordial handshakes, but Will was shaking and Darlene was holding back tears.

'It's like . . .' Darlene managed. 'It's like Hewitt . . . I know you're a . .'

'What Darlene means is,' Will said, 'you're . . . Hewitt was a white person, like us.'

'Oh yeah,' Muse chuckled, trying to roll with it. 'Yeah, that makes sense.'

'But it's like . . .' Will wiped away what could be sweat, but might be tears.

'It's like Hewitt has come down from heaven,' Darlene said. 'As I live and breathe.'

Muse treated them to a white-tablecloth lunch that made them uncomfortable, and on instinct followed that up with street food: Southern-fried chicken tenders and waffles, which they gobbled like pigs at a trough. Through sticky mouthfuls, they divulged their flight was the first they'd ever taken and their hotel the second they'd ever stayed in, the first being when they drove down to Tupelo to lay Hewitt in his paid-for family plot. Their first night at the New Orleans hotel, they hadn't slept a wink, but made up for it on night two by hunkering down in their rented car.

Muse demanded they stay with him for their last night. The hours leading up to the concert confirmed the Lucases were the real deal. They genuinely preferred silence to small talk. Muse's business was sound; silence spooked him. But what the heck, the day was already strange, so he gave in to the sonic experiment, a kind of meditation. Within a couple of hours of sharing the Lucases' quiet, Muse was recalling dead relatives and estranged friends. He was able to feel sorrow for what he'd lost and what he'd never had, and self-forgiveness for what he knew was bad behavior – drinking too much, sleeping with too many women. It must have been in such a mind-set that Will and Darlene had sent the Gibson.

How the Lucases lived was far more heroic than a well-timed swing of a hollow-bodied Gretsch. If the Jo-Jo's Hog situation repeated itself, Muse knew he wouldn't swing that guitar, for better or worse. He wanted to be more like Will and Darlene. He wanted to stand for peace. The only way to do that – the most radical way, especially for an American – was to learn how to walk away from a fight.

'Walk away,' he sang to himself.

Yeah, he'd write a song about it, his best song ever, one people might not love right now but would remember after he was gone.

'Walk away,' *my sisters and brothers,* he sang. 'Walk away.'

The last time Muse King saw Will and Darlene Lucas was eight days before the ghouls came, at Phoenix's Sky Harbor International Airport after the kickoff date of a tour that would take Muse through Austin, Little Rock, Memphis, St Louis, and Kansas City. Muse was preoccupied. He had 'Walk Away' started, but it was all in his head; he was afraid to put it on paper lest it prove unworthy. So it surprised him when Will, while Darlene was in the ladies' room, took a tight grip of his shoulder. The squeak of his jacket's black leather gave voice to his shock. Will gave handshakes exclusively and profusely – to Muse, to doormen, to waiters.

'Darlene.' Will's eye wrinkles deepened. 'She worries. No, that's not the whole truth. *I* worry. Thinking about you alone out there . . . riding fast planes . . . fast cars . . . doing who knows what with fast women.'

Muse blushed.

'Who says *fast women*?' It was a joke, but it felt misplaced. He let his silly grin flatten to something serious. 'I'm over all that, Pops. I really am. I can feel it. I'm changing. I got this new song I'm working on that . . .'

Muse trailed off. Will's lips were pursed and quivering. His voice shook too.

'It's . . . real good to hear someone . . . someone call me *Pop* again.'

'Ah, you know.' Muse shrugged to play it off as nothing, but he couldn't, he wouldn't; the new Muse King threw out the garbage that didn't matter – the parents who'd abandoned him, the family who'd vultured over him – and acknowledged the things that did. 'That's what I . . . I mean, that's how I think of you, man.'

'I think the Lord purposed us to send that instrument.' Will's eyes shone. 'And now he's rewarding us.'

'This is just stuff,' Muse insisted. 'Hotels and food, concert tickets.'

'That's not the reward. Giving us you to care about, that's the reward.'

The people slugging down the concourse became ghosts, the brush of their sleeves and luggage passing through Muse like smoke. All he could see was Will's trembling face. All he could feel was the old man's fingers digging into his shoulder. He wanted to grip Will back in the same way. Why didn't he do it? What was he waiting for?

'Nothing's going to happen to me, Pops,' he said. 'I'm the one who should be worrying about you. You want to see another show, just say the word. Don't make me come looking for you now, all right?'

Darlene returned, maybe ignorant of the emotion that had passed between them, maybe not, and gave Muse a hug, followed by Will's formal handshake, and off they scooted toward security, leaving Muse standing there, believing if he didn't move, the tears wouldn't fall, and a video of it wouldn't show up online titled CRYBABY MUSE KING AT THE AIRPORT!!! He had to move eventually, but did so with his head lowered, mind storming with joy and sadness, flushed face cooled by wet stripes.

Don't make me come looking for you now, all right?

The words echoed in his dreams on the morning of October 24. The Kansas City gig had gone all right, but he was eager to get home. He was going to make some changes. Step away from the band for a time. Work on some solo stuff – just him and Hewitt. Finish 'Walk

Away'. Line up shows that mattered. Schools. Civic centers. Rest homes. Tenement parks. He'd slept poorly, his mind racing with possibilities. He thumbed alive his phone and opened Instagram, ready to post his thoughts as a way to hold himself to them.

A bang on the hotel-room door.

Muse checked his watch. Eight thirty.

'Still in bed,' he called out.

Another bang. Another. Another. He pitched his feet over the side of the bed and slow-footed across the room. Normally he might lay into someone bothering him this early, but he was already up, and besides, he was turning over a new leaf. He undid the security latch, pulled the door open, and found himself face-to-face with Leticia Luz, whose signature he had found the night before on a card: *I have been servicing your room, a gratuity would be greatly appreciated.* Muse had seen her a couple of times, her deferential behavior making him uncomfortable, as most service personnel did.

Leticia Luz's small smile had split into a gaping abscess. Her downcast eyes shone straight at him, blank white headlights. She was naked below the waist. Her teeth were covered with red drool, and blood stained the front of her retro maid's uniform. The first thing Muse thought was something he'd seen on Instagram about Ben Hines exposing himself to hotel staff, and he realized how this might look if someone saw – the maid half-clothed and bloody, Muse in his underwear.

The Lucases, he thought later, would not have hesitated to help her.

Leticia walked straight into him, mouth open. Muse might have tried to hold her, but he'd been caught by enough bayou dogs to know bared teeth brought pain. He lurched back, dodging her swinging hands. She stumbled and fell over a service room cart, sweeping away prime rib bones, salt, pepper, ketchup, rolls, and patties of butter. In seconds, Leticia was back on her feet, but Muse drove the cart into her gut, pinning her against the wall. It hurt. Not her – she swung her arms over the cart. It hurt *him*. He had no more stomach for fighting. 'Walk Away, Walk Away.'

'You okay?' he demanded. 'You need help?'

Leticia growled, spattering bloody froth.

Muse remembered the rest, but wished he didn't. Determined not to harm the maid, he released the cart. She came after him with doubled fury, punishment for nonviolence. For ten grueling minutes, he used sofa cushions to drive her away, finally maneuvering her into a closet he propped shut with a chair. He shouted for help that didn't come, thinking how much easier it would have been to brain Leticia with the phone, the table, the ice bucket, anything. Violence was always easier.

With his back against the closet, he struggled into clothes, hat, and scarf, his usual all-black affair. Quickly, he grabbed the case that housed Hewitt – unbloodied, nonviolent Hewitt – and headed for the stairs, always safer in a crisis. Five flights down, he'd encountered a second hotel employee, this one headless, or that's how he'd looked at first. He'd been blasted by what had to have been a shotgun. Half his neck was gone, and his head dangled forward, bumping against his chest as he advanced. One blow with the guitar case would have ripped the head off, but Muse resisted: 'Walk Away, Walk Away.'

Muse meant to do all the right things in the lobby. Tell the front desk what he'd seen, promise to explain it to the cops. But the lobby was bedlam, furniture overturned, the floor carpeted with tourist pamphlets, a thick smear of blood leading from the elevator to the front door.

Tull Bledsoe, his driver and friend, caught him by the shoulders and steered him right through the blood, out the door, and into an overcast morning. Muse tried to stop, but Tull kept pushing, insisting the rest of the band 'couldn't be got' – he wouldn't go into any more detail than that. They tumbled into the front seats of the

Cadillac Escalade. As Tull peeled out of the hotel lot, Muse did two things: turn on the radio and yank a bottle of Beam from the mini-cupboard.

'Where to, boss?' A question nearly normal enough to conceal Tull's terror.

Muse glugged bourbon, gasped, and said, 'Rhode Island.'

'Rhode *Island*?' Tull's calm broke. 'I mean where we going *right now*, motherfucker!'

'Just get out of the city, Tull, fast as you can.'

They hadn't gotten out. Few people drove more aggressively than Tull, and still they'd gotten boxed in at the 35/670 interchange and been forced to hoof it. They'd spent a day running – away from ghouls, toward others in need, Hewitt making escape a chore, Tull cursing him for refusing to use the Gibson as a weapon. That night, they'd sheltered inside an unlocked Supercuts.

Unlocked, but not empty. Tull had been in full recline on one of the hair-washing chairs when an aproned ghoul tottered from an adjacent door and latched its face to Tull's. Enough mirrors reflected moonlight for Muse to see the ghoul's teeth perforate Tull's lips, the ghoul's tongue stretch down Tull's throat. The ghoul bit, slid upward, and sucked out Tull's left eyeball. Muse figured his friend's last sight was his own eyeball popping like a cherry tomato in the ghoul's mouth.

Could Muse have prevented it if he'd been willing to use the Gibson like he'd used the Gretsch? He told himself no and spent the rest of the night on the run, trying to believe it. He'd picked a crap time to become a pacifist. Unless, he thought, he'd picked the best time of all. The only feeling he trusted right now was sadness. There were the blues you could sing about, and then there was *the blues,* the stuff you kept tamped down deep inside you.

He ended up at Waterfall Brewery, where fermenting beer tried to kill him. He stole a Vespa, if anything could be considered stealing anymore. He rode north till the gas tank pinged and sputtered. Then he walked. He thought of Rhode Island. He sat at a dirt crossroads. He played. He drank. He met a girl named Greer Morgan. He laid his exhausted body over hers. It felt nothing like the one-night stands he'd been having for half a decade. If anything was peaceful, it was this. He kissed her until he believed that all roads out of this place weren't blocked at all.

Legion

Ghouls were killed, plenty of Them, though this was kept secret from Father Bill, who did not want any ghouls harmed. But he wasn't down there, was he? Both soft and hard kills occurred. Military terms, those. Soft: destroying a ghoul's capabilities. Say the time when Nishimura used the ax that had chopped up Clay Szulczewski to lop off a ghoul's hands. Hard: death, lasting death. Say when Nishimura used a nail gun to fire five long nails, point-blank, through a ghoul's forehead. The head was the key. Head wounds kept Them down. He and his team of Missionaries figured that out pretty quickly. *Team* – funny word in this context. He was both in charge and held hostage. Leave through the Flag Cabin, circle past the CIC, climb down to Public Affairs. He summoned the glow, charted the path, and led the way, but with the heat of a couple of guns at his back. Each time they went under, a new set of objectives: Raid the dry goods storeroom and ship's store. Take what they wanted from the hospital. See what weapons were left in the magazine. Get fresh water production up to a fraction of its two-hundred-thousand-gallons-per-day capacity. Raise the spirits of true believers holed up in engine-room outposts by bringing food, water, and glad tidings from Father Bill. It was harrowing work, each corner-turn unbearable. This corner: nothing. This corner: nothing. This corner: eight ghouls, flesh jiggling, innards unraveling, jaws clacking. Six missions in four days, six men lost. One had only been scratched, but the

Missionaries knew better and kicked in his face. Boots were quieter than bullets. Rage built up and had to find release. Nishimura tried to understand. War was war. When other Missionaries wanted to linger to torture a ghoul, he appealed to them pragmatically. They did not have time for this. The men glared. How easy it would be to report to Henstrom that Nishimura had gotten nicked by a ghoul. Larry, Atsuko, Chiyo, Daiki, Neola, and Bea: he had to remain a useful leader. When he passed CMC Bertrand Veevers's Idea Box, he paused. Inside, a single crumpled scrap of paper. He kept the suggestion, a good one, to himself: KILL US BLOW IT ALL UP END THIS. Deep in the hull was the room used to process trash. Wood, metal, plastic, dunnage. Now ghouls too. Fully dead or still wiggling, They were hurled down chutes into the ocean. Hold on. Could ghouls swim? What if they paddled into the nuke intakes? The Seahawk helo could have dipped a sonar node into the water to check, but the Seahawk was history, pushed over the edge of the boat. That mission came directly from Father Bill. All flight deck craft were to be shed within the month. It was tough, dicey work. Men died doing it, because no one dared kill ghouls where Father Bill might see it. To Nishimura, each plane over the edge was a bomb's tick.

Then things got even worse.

No one saw it coming. How could they? The last anyone had heard of the man, he'd been ten days into a sick-bay stay that had the ship swirling with weird rumors. Nine days after the ghoul coup of the USS *Olympia,* right in the middle of Father Bill's Morning Prayer, a shout from the meteorological-level catwalk evolved into multiple shouts. The island population was down to thirty-five, but not everyone had been promoted upward. Nishimura, for instance. He sat up fast, hitting his head on the counter above.

'Captain Page!' someone cried. *'It's Captain Page!'*

Even the most weakened men found the energy to rush onto the catwalk. Nishimura dizzied with hope. If there was a single thing that might shake awake sailors under the spell of a delusional lunatic, it was the return of the man representing civilization, law, social orders.

Nishimura was the last to the catwalk, but he was better fed now, his muscles agile from the daily work of staying alive belowdecks. He shoved past others to peer over the railing. If Page was down there with the ghouls, he was in mortal danger. Nishimura was ready to jump into the quagmire to save his captain.

Problem was, Captain Page was already dead. He'd always been a rawboned, sharp-angled fellow, with a lean, pointy-chinned face pinked from vigorous shaving. His formal dress never fit right, a sign he was a worker at heart, not a bureaucrat. None of that had changed. He was still Captain Page, just a shade greener. Nishimura looked in vain for wounds. Perhaps the captain had died of his illness after all.

His body scrabbled against the steel with enough energy to peel gray paint. On the nav bridge waited the captain's chair, and Nishimura felt certain Page remembered it.

Henstrom's voice rang from the 1MC.

'Father Bill on the move! Father Bill on the move!'

Great hubbub attended any downward motion of their leader, and the remaining sailors parted to reveal Henstrom leading – carrying the brass crucifix – and two bodyguards following. Once on the lowest landing, the Hawaiian-shirted priest stopped, and Henstrom handed over the old man's symbol of authority.

Looking uncertain, Father Bill inched toward the railing. He peeked over, then gasped, long and low.

'The captain,' he whispered, 'has returned.'

Nishimura's only cue on how to feel came from the horrified bulging of Henstrom's eyes. The second Father Bill ceded any authority, the pissant was done for. Nishimura wanted to shout: *Grab the priest! Get him!* But the Nishimura Delay served him well. Lieutenant Commander William Koppenborg turned to face his flock, raised his arms, and lifted his voice to caw over the sizzling ocean waves.

'The captain has returned!'

Father Bill clutched a hand to his breast, playing to the back reaches of the theater. His mouth stretched into a gaping grin. Sunlight rhinestoned his eyes.

'Gallery deck. 02 deck. 01 deck, main hangar deck. Second deck, third deck, fourth deck! How many underdecks is that, I ask you? And how many levels of inferno are storied to exist in Dante's infamous underworld? Joy, joy, and revelation! Captain Page has emerged from all seven! He has completed a Long Walk of his own! For days have I spoken of the merging of humans and demons into a being greater than either of us! Now look what has come to pass – the leader of demons rising to meet the leader of men! Thank you, O Lord! The hour of unification is close at hand.'

'What should we do, Father?' someone asked.

Father Bill looked about in a daze that implied he was overwhelmed by spiritual input. He staggered to the railing overlooking the Pacific. Nishimura followed the priest's gaze down the boat's starboard side. Silver waves smashed into the fantail, while the sun made the hull look molten. Crashing, melting: it was how Nishimura imagined the chaplain's mind.

'Bottle,' Father Bill murmured.

'Father?' Henstrom asked. 'A bottle of what?'

'A bottle, a bottle!'

Henstrom passed the order to a guard, who scrambled away, leaving Father Bill with a single armed escort – so vulnerable, if only anyone besides Nishimura had the will to fight. Four tense minutes later, the guard returned with a long-necked bottle of San Pellegrino sparkling water. Father Bill grasped it with his free hand, like a second crucifix. When he leaned over the railing, Nishimura saw plenty of shocked faces in the audience. Water was precious.

Salt spray whipped Father Bill's grinning face.

'It was in the country of Gerasenes that Jesus climbed from his boat and came upon a man of unclean spirit, a man who could not be captured, who screamed among the tombs night and day! Jesus asked him, "What is your name?" and this man responded, "My name is Legion, for we are many!"' Father Bill pointed his crucifix at Captain Page. 'Look! There's Legion now! And the boat on which we sail is the boat Jesus took to Gerasenes! No longer, then, should this holy vessel be called a false name! Today, to honor the demon Legion, I rechristen this boat, *Captain Page*!'

The chaplain's arm shot downward. The bottle shattered, sparkling water within sparkling salt, brightened by blood from a palm sliced on sparkling glass. Father Bill staggered away, bleeding hand hoisted, and was helped back to Pri-Fly.

With no additional guidance, the rest of the men did nothing. During the subsequent hours, Page's bone-on-steel *scrutch, scrutch* against the flight-deck wall became the noise of anticipation. Everyone stared at everyone, none more than the Missionaries at Nishimura. He got it. Today's mission would have to go straight through these agitated ghouls – straight through Captain Page. A bad idea in every respect, and it was up to Nishimura to make that case to the leader.

At the designated time, he climbed to Pri-Fly for his daily mission briefing. Instead of the usual disgust, the top-level guard gave Nishimura a repeat of the Missionaries' imploring look. Father Bill was slumped in the air boss seat, stunned eyes locked to his bleeding hand. In the mini boss seat, Henstrom's knees bounced. A roll of gauze, apparently repudiated by the priest, had dropped to Henstrom's feet and unspooled along the walkway like toilet paper. Nishimura traced its path.

'You did what you had to,' Henstrom insisted. 'What you had to do to *lead* us.'

'Jesus did not lead by killing. He led by dying.'

The gauze path petered out at a surprise point: the brass crucifix, propped on its broken shaft just outside the Pri-Fly chamber.

Nishimura tried to make sense of it. He'd never seen it treated as less than the world's holiest object, much less left unattended. It stood nearer to Karl Nishimura than Father Bill. Why, he could reach out, pick it up.

'You can't just . . .' Henstrom trailed off before amplifying his whine. 'Father, everyone is depending on you!'

'This isn't something I can fix,' the chaplain muttered, 'by renaming a boat.'

Nishimura's neck creaked as he swiveled from the crucifix to Henstrom. He'd seen this face on the O-3 before, the fat-lipped frown of anxiety that what he'd hoarded for himself might be taken away.

'You feel like, what?' Henstrom implored. 'You owe something? To the demons?'

'Two,' Father Bill moaned. 'In the chapel closet. Two demons who wished to make me a part of Them. I destroyed Them. Without thought, without heart.'

'Then we'll give Them . . .' Henstrom perked up. 'We'll give Them two back. How many men do we have now? Thirty-three? Thirty-four? Two is *nothing.*'

Rising through Nishimura's black thoughts, like mummified bodies through rotten bogs, was the image of his family, still alive, still waiting. Don't fall apart, Saint Karl. Hold it together.

'I couldn't do such a thing without a—' Father Bill gasped. 'A baptism. Yes, that's it. Baptisms welcome children into a new faith. This *is* a new faith, isn't it? I believe it is.' His voice sped up. 'A ceremony like that would require new sacraments, of course. It would require new rites. Those would take time to prepare. Do I dare be so brazen? Is it insolence? But who else? Yes, who else? I must get to work, then. We have so little time left. Captain Page is waiting, and he's always been an impatient man.'

'Wonderful. Praise God.' Henstrom sounded relieved. 'How can I help?'

Father Bill rotated his hand, scrutinizing each bony, bloody finger.

'An offering,' he said. 'I think our men would gladly offer up a few pieces, don't you?'

Nishimura's vision of his family shifted. Now they recoiled from him, a husband and father missing fingers, entire limbs, an eye, a nose, his ears, his lips, his tongue.

No, he would not do that to them. He moved. A single lunge, his hand cinching around the crucifix's staff. The holy thing was much lighter than he'd expected, and he turned and crossed the catwalk, boots clanging. He raced right past the guard, taking the ladder in two hops, and reached the nav-bridge level before he heard Henstrom's cry.

'Nishimura? *Nishimura, get back here!*'

With limited room on the island and stealth required belowdecks, there were few opportunities to run on Big Mama – or *Olympia,* or *Captain Page,* or whatever one called this floating tomb. Nishimura stretched his limbs, racing down catwalks and taking ladders by handrails only. It felt like muscle fibers untwined and tendons tore, but it also felt free, gloriously free.

He crashed into a web of waiting Missionaries at the meteorological level. Four grabbed hold of his clothes to stop themselves from being toppled into the ghouls below, and it was at that second, with men all over him, that Henstrom's voice shrilled through the 1MC.

'*Missionaries! Bring Karl Nishimura to Father Bill!*'

Their handholds actually slackened from the shock of receiving so simple an order. Nishimura waited the one second it should have taken for their eyes to darken with the animal brutality he'd seen so often belowdecks. But an extra second passed, and in that beat, he saw in their eyes affirmation of shared horror, how they'd saved one another's lives down there, even if they hadn't liked it. Here, on the eve of something even the devout could tell was going to be bad, they were aware they'd killed dozens of the demons Father Bill venerated. To bring Nishimura before the priest might be to have all that revealed.

Could it really be that all eight hands let go at once?

Other sailors reached for him, but Nishimura swung the crucifix and the object's symbolism was enough to send them reeling. He sprinted to the platform's edge, twelve feet off the deck, and leaped, timing it just right, pushing himself from the platform with his right foot. Directly below, Captain Page reached up with green, grasping hands, following Nishimura's arc with white saucer eyes.

When the Missionaries went below, they first took pains to draw the ghouls elsewhere. Today, there were ten waiting for him, not counting Captain Page. When Nishimura landed on one, the ghoul's legs snapped the wrong way at the knees, folding in half and breaking Nishimura's fall. He found himself on his back atop the ghoul's back, the ghoul's arms popping from their sockets to reach backward, the neck bones crackling as they wrenched too far. Abruptly, the sky went dark: nine other ghouls coalescing, faces connected to the deck by ropes of drool.

Nishimura scrabbled to his feet, swung the crucifix, struck soft matter. A standing ghoul was knocked over by a crawling ghoul, and her legs kicked out, both feet socking Nishimura in the face. He shoved blindly and ended up in possession of the ghoul's left boot. The crucifix, the boot; one heavenly weapon, one earthly one. Nishimura pummeled with both, driving back the horde, then took off across the flight deck, avoiding two dozen other ghouls, and reached the deck-handler chamber door, which the Missionaries had modified with a lock mechanism too complicated for ghouls to figure out.

Inside, daylight narrowed, same as other times a mission had taken him under, though this darkness had a coffin-lid finality. Without waiting for his eyes to adjust to the dim red emergency lighting, he raced on, leading with crucifix and boot. Where he was going, he did not know, only down, down, down into what Father Bill called the seven levels of hell, though Nishimura had a hunch the world had capsized, and hell was above.

ATC, CIC, Flag Cabin, refueling station, avionics shop, air filter cleaning shop, winch room, and fan room, and in every one, Henstrom's *Bring me Karl Nishimura!* screeched from a 1MC. Sometimes ghouls poured from a black pocket in packs. Carrier halls were narrow, so Nishimura never had to deal with more than two ghouls at once, and the crucifix and boot sufficed to knock Them off Their feet. He might feel satisfaction if They were the demons Father Bill said. He knew They were not. They were the starving masses – literally starving, literally amassed – who only wanted the pittance the church had too long kept from Them.

If Father Bill rallied any Missionaries to give chase, they'd have their hands full with ghouls aggravated by Henstrom's ongoing squawks. Nishimura neither heard nor saw trace of living sailors, who had to still exist belowdecks by the hundreds, some of them armed. Over the past days, the Missionaries had cruised through the boat like cops through low-income neighborhoods. Though they regularly found leavings – food detritus, slain ghouls, areas barricaded and then abandoned – the living always scattered rather than risk being mistaken for a ghoul.

Crew galley, marine quarters, central control, defrost room: down, down, down he went, clandestine travel so much easier when you were a single person. Soon, he was deeper inside a carrier than he'd been since he was a curious nonrate. It was freezing cold, black as premature burial; the air tasted like metal, reverberant with the low hum of nuclear reactors. Even new planets had bathrooms, and despite the peril inherent to a single exit, Nishimura found one, crept inside a toilet stall, locked it, set down the crucifix and boot, and in the frigid dark, tucked himself into a ball.

The misery was familiar. He recalled hiding in boys' rooms as a hectored kid. He'd felt so alone then; he felt equally alone now. Little Karl's sole course of action had been to cry himself to sleep, and Master Chief Nishimura saw no better option. The purported coldest officer in the navy leaned his head against the basin and cried, the big, rattling, but scrupulously silent sobs he'd perfected as a child. His lungs went boggy, capable of drowning. Acid tears burned through his cheeks. His sinuses pressurized – go ahead, explode, please.

Finally, like little Karl, he cried himself to sleep.

And woke to a blade on his throat.

He jerked. The blade pressed. He felt skin pop, blood trickle. He flailed in defense, but before he could find the crucifix or boot, he was forced to the floor, someone's knees on his shoulders, a knife edge at his jugular. He looked up at a black outline, a head haloed with wild hair, backlit in dim red light, and for a second he wanted the person to go ahead and slash. But he was not little Karl anymore, was he? He had his own little ones suffering their own torments.

'You alive?' The person's voice was a husky rattle.

'Who are you?' Nishimura asked.

The reply was the dig of the knife. 'Who are *you*?'

'Karl Nishimura. I was up top. I ran.' He tasted blood. 'Please. Who are you?'

The blade was withdrawn. The knobby knees left his shoulders and a hand extended to help him up. It was a sign of friendship, and this time, after so many years of ignoring such overtures, he would accept. He grasped the hand, live flesh to live flesh, and was boosted. The ascent dizzied him. He had to blink and squint to confirm the person who'd helped him up was shorter than him by a head.

'My name is Jennifer Angelys Pagán,' she said.

You're the Sheriff

J. J. Jalopy was a half keg of beer who thought he was a car. He came to life one night when, at a frat party, Foxy Fiona Fry sucked on his tap. 'Holy Studebaker!' she exclaimed after she'd gotten a mouthful. From that moment on, J.J. believed himself to be a shark-finned, two-toned 1957 Studebaker Silver Hawk. He suggested to the young lady that they motor off to a parking garage he knew, where they could get to know each other free from the eyes of envious frat brothers. Foxy Fiona, taken with the little guy, agreed to go along.

She got J.J. rolling with a push, but since he was a half keg and not a Silver Hawk, the only way he could keep going was via gravity. Foxy Fiona managed to stay on her feet down the first slope, fast-trotting on the silver cylinder as if in a log-rolling contest. Alas, being tipsy, she toppled off. J.J. had no idea Fiona was rolling help-lessly behind him for most of the way to Jalopy Hollow, where a dozen old auto wrecks had been dumped.

Fiona came to an abrupt stop, cracking her skull on a junked Cadillac's bumper bullet. When she came to, she found herself brain damaged. Though, of course, being brain damaged, she didn't *know* she was brain damaged. She just knew she was in love with a half keg who thought he was a car.

That was episode 1.

By the time *J.J.'s Jamboree* had aired its third episode, it was an unqualified smash hit. The homemade animated show aired on New

York City public access at one in the morning, but the segments went viral as millions of gleefully gobsmacked viewers forwarded the jolly, frenetic, tender, and offensive videos to family, friends, and enemies alike. Before the first season was over, toys were on shelves, not only of J.J. and Foxy Fiona but also the rest of Jalopy Hollow's crew: Num-Num the Nova, who thinks she's an alien sun; Eddie the Edsel, who thinks he's a lobster dinner; and Vickie the Crown Vickie, who thinks she's a sixteenth-century nunnery.

The toys might have started the trouble. Though they, like the series itself, were marketed to adults, kids loved them. The same kids sought out the show, which they also loved. Plenty of adults did not approve. Turns out, a good excuse for saying 'shit' wasn't 'But J.J. says it all the time!' *J.J.'s Jamboree* became a lightning rod, drawing attacks from conservative media and even being singled out on the Senate floor for its 'reckless promotion of filthy words, illegal drug use, and consequence-free sex'. The show's popularity mushroomed, thrusting creator Scotty Rolph into the spotlight.

Rolph, by all rational measures, was not ready for prime time. You didn't have to be a pot smoker to know this was one very high dude. Forty years old and built like a couch potato, he dressed like a college kid, forever clad in ringer tees and basketball shorts that hung past his knees. He played into every liberal stereotype, yet seemed to exit every right-wing interview the victor. Interviewers couldn't lay a hand on him. He giggled; he rolled his eyes; he monologued incoherently about 'art'; he got serious about how Num-Num represented Korean War POWs before shouting, 'I'm kidding, you moron!'

Ramsey Dylan, senior VP of content at CableCorp, purchased *J.J.'s Jamboree* for a reported seven figures, and the second season premiered on Hoopla, CableCorp's top network after WWN. Dylan himself was a television iconoclast. According to numerous profiles, he'd hoped to change the world since being abused by his father's AA counselor, and had found his medium at CableCorp, where he'd launched a suite of programs that fought back against what he saw as TV's shortcomings.

Using the tagline 'All We Ask Is That You Ask', Dylan's mission was to make people question the truth of what they were told. In the throwback soap opera *Doctors and Deceivers*, docs misdiagnosed one illness per episode. Viewers were riveted, eager to find out which one. Once a week, national weather reporter Flip Voss included one epically incorrect forecast to get viewers in the habit of seeking out a second source.

Many who depended on misleading messages for their livelihood despised Dylan. One of them shot him outside a theater at the Sundance Film Festival, obliterating the tissue between vertebrae C-4 and C-5, putting Dylan into a power chair operated by a sip-and-puff switch. By a year later, Dylan was back at work, piloting the chair with nimble efficiency, more dedicated than ever.

Ramsey Dylan and Scotty Rolph made funny bedfellows, but it seemed clear the courageous exec believed something deep was going on beneath the surface of *J.J.'s Jamboree*. With his stamp of approval on it, everyone else at CableCorp fell into line. Younger staff already had J.J. toys lining their office shelves, and older staff, at risk of being exposed as out of touch, nodded along with enthusiasm.

Nathan Baseman fell squarely into the latter category. He'd seen exactly forty-five seconds of the show and judged it to be the stupidest thing he'd ever put in front of his eyes. If CableCorp wanted to throw money at sex-obsessed talking cars, go crazy, as long as it didn't eat into the news budget. Dylan he respected, but he hoped never to meet Rolph. Nowadays, the odds were against it, until the moment, while sharing stale Chips Ahoy! with Zoë Shillace, he heard a strange thing from the on-air Face.

'There's a situation at the elevators,' he said.

Baseman and Zoë checked it out. There was a situation, all right. The usual slow thuds of ghouls overhead had accelerated to gymnasium clatter, shoes running and skidding, bodies falling, objects clattering. Someone was up there, fighting for the elevator Baseman had disabled. The key was in his pocket, sharp against his thigh. They heard the paddling noise of something heavy on wheels followed by a plastic clicking. Could someone be trying to get the elevator doors open?

'What do you think?' Baseman whispered.

'Sounds like they're good fighters,' Zoë said.

'You think we should let them down?'

'Yes.' Zoë sounded appalled. 'We need people.'

'What if they don't fit in?'

'You want them to die up there?'

'I mean, we have our own thing going. Maybe there's just five of us, but we're doing it.'

'Unlock the elevator! You want to live like this forever?'

Yes – he wished he could say it. He might have aired the infamous Jansky shot, he might have bitten his wife on the way to a busted marriage, he might have killed Rochelle Glass when it had not been irrefutably necessary, but the base man was redeeming himself, hour after hour. Adding more characters into the mix put that service in jeopardy.

Zoë Shillace, however, owed nothing to no one. She'd lost everything – friends, family, a significant other? Baseman didn't know because she had kept her anguish private. He would not safeguard his own repentance at the expense of the greatest intern in American history.

He cursed, opened the elevator, withdrew the key easily from his pocket – he'd lost weight – and unlocked the bottom floor. Scrambling out, he watched the doors shut. The elevator's hum upward was familiar, and therefore frightening. On the floor, one arm of a

C-stand, used for holding filters before lights. He picked it up and handed it to Zoë, then removed Kwame's pistol and pointed it at the elevator.

'If this goes bad,' he said, 'you get the Face, head to the control room.'

'"If this goes bad,"' Zoë echoed under her breath. 'It's *all* been going bad, in case you hadn't noticed.'

The elevator light illuminated, carefree as ever, and the door parted. People, large objects, and sharp weapons burst out in a jumble. Baseman stumbled back, yelling incoherently, punching with Kwame's revolver as if it were a fist. Anything might have happened in those seconds, including the shooting of all three people who emerged. Unlike with the Jansky shot, Baseman held off, and later, when things got really bad, he'd try to convince himself he'd done the right thing.

'Don't shoot, Sheriff!'

The man who shouted this, following it with mad peals of laughter, wore a construction helmet, large plastic sunglasses, a bulging hiking backpack, and what looked like four layers of flannel shirts. He was pushing a six-wheeled motorized wheelchair in which slumped a frail, skinny man either unconscious or dead. Behind the duo stood a six-foot-three, big-bellied giant wearing a hooded Baja poncho and carrying an orange Black & Decker hedge trimmer. Instead of coated with the mulch of weeds, its blades were clotted with ghoul meat. All three were splattered with gore, and the two standing seemed giddy about it.

The one in the flannels rolled the wheelchair into the hall.

'Better lock that elevator again, Sheriff,' he said. 'There's thirty or forty of those things we didn't get around to chopping into teeny pieces.'

Baseman looked at Zoë, who shrugged. He pocketed the gun, skirted the three characters, and disabled the elevator. When he stepped back into the hall, he bumped into the man in the poncho.

Baseman was a big guy, but this fellow was something else. He didn't look like he'd exercised a day in his life, but his bone structure was pre-historic. Baseman hurried back into position; like any boss, he didn't know how much he needed his intern until she wasn't beside him.

The flannel guy looked around through sunglasses. 'How many folks you got here?'

Baseman saw no point in lying. 'There's me, I'm Nathan Baseman. This is Zoë Shillace. We got three more.'

'You've been running this act with five people? Hot dog! Paddy, what'd I tell you?'

The giant chuckled. Blood ran down his chubby cheeks.

'Paddy thought you might have fifty down here. No freaking way, I said. Shit hits the fan, the newspeople jet set aren't any braver than comedy lowlifes. We're all just here to cash our checks, am I right? Huh, Sheriff? Deputy Zoë? Am I right?'

'It's true we could use a few more hands,' Baseman said. 'We're glad you're here.'

Something was off with this trio, way off. One clue came when the flannel guy perched his sunglasses atop his head. His irises were practically gone from extreme dilation, and the sclera was red – not pink, but red with fattened blood vessels. The ghoul blood splashed across his face did not quite mask the blood trickling from his nose. A battle wound? More likely, Baseman thought, this guy snorted something. The big guy, Paddy, too. It would explain where they'd gotten the energy, not to mention the balls, to take on a lobby full of ghouls with a Weedwacker.

The red-eyed guy was Scotty Rolph, of course. When this was revealed, Zoë became starstruck, which broke Baseman's heart. She deserved a world that could still delight. He was far more shocked to discover the man in the chair was Ramsey Dylan. Why a top CableCorp VP was consorting with rabble from Creative was puz-zling, and also beyond Dylan's ability to explain. His eyes were shut tight and his shoulders shuddered. Scotty said he wasn't bitten. Fine, but he looked terrible.

Leaving Fessler and the Face to run the show, Lee Sutton joined the newly enlarged group at the kitchen table, where they observed, with growing disquiet, Scotty and Paddy treating Dylan like a daft cocker spaniel. Paddy, who had yet to say a word, waved morsels before Dylan's eyes while Scotty tidied the exec's bloody face with a towel. He dabbed at Dylan's nose, which clearly upset him, before rotating the towel in Dylan's ears while making a comical *squeak-squeak* sound. Scotty giggled throughout, and Paddy's eyes leaked in silent guffaws.

Like Paddy, Ramsey Dylan did not speak. Scotty attributed this to trauma, and Baseman pretended to accept it, though something felt amiss. Dylan looked like he wanted to talk – was desperate to, even – but was for some reason unable.

'So!' Scotty clapped his hands together. 'What's the sitch in this bitch?'

'The *sitch*,' Baseman replied archly, 'is we have a stairwell full of ghouls we have to keep watch on. There's no way to nail the door shut because it's metal. So we have it blocked with the heaviest stuff we could find. How many ghouls are in the lobby?'

'Enough to put on *Les Mis* if you can get Them to moan in tune.'

Paddy sputtered laughter.

'Don't forget Glass,' Lee added.

Baseman shot Lee a glare, then regretted it. Regretted all of it. The soft, regular beat of Glass's ghoul fists against Pam Tripler's locked office door might as well be Poe's Tell-Tale Heart. He shouldn't have killed Rochelle Glass the first time. He *should* have killed her the second time.

'Whoa, whoa, whoa.' Scotty half stood. 'The Rochelle Glass ghoul is still kicking? Where is she? I want to see!'

'Hold on,' Baseman said.

'Oh, man, you're the dude who pulled her off Corso! That was the best TV I've ever seen!' Scotty snapped his fingers on both hands. 'Brainstorm: here's what we do. We go get Glass, strap her to a chair, and put her in front of the camera. Just to see what she *does,* man.'

'I hope you're kidding,' Lee said.

Scotty gestured expansively. 'Give her a candy bar, see if she eats it. Give her an iPad, see which apps she opens. We experiment, man, for the good of the world! And the fact that it's Rochelle mother-cunting Glass? Are you serious? People organized their whole lives around watching her show. What did she call them? She had this great fucking word.'

'Mendicans,' Zoë said.

Scotty hooted. 'Yes! All the Mendicans out there will huddle around the tube, just like in olden days, to watch their big-haired guru again. If most of the TVs weren't out, we'd have the Super Bowl on our hands. We'd have the fucking *moon landing.* Shit, Ramsey, this is why you pay me the big bucks, huh?'

He slapped Dylan on the back. Dylan's closed eyelids quivered and Baseman's face ached. He and Dylan were close in age; it was easy to picture himself in that chair, subject to the abuses of a gener-ation determined to turn everything into reality-show circuses. What rankled Baseman most was Scotty Rolph was dead-on. Putting Rochelle Glass back on the desk would be ratings gold.

Ratings drove the Jansky shot. Ratings killed his marriage.

Fuck ratings.

'You listen up,' Baseman said, 'and you listen good. We're glad you're here. We are. We need some new blood. We need new ideas too. But just because the world's on fire doesn't mean I'm not pro-ducing this show.' He pointed at the ceiling, through it. 'You want to be boss out there, be my guest. I'm boss down here. And we aren't pulling stunts. Until the very last TV quits working, we're going to be the news people trust, you got that?'

Paddy gave Scotty a you're-in-trouble-now grin. Scotty flashed hostility for only a fraction of a second, but Baseman knew anger that hot could not be extinguished so quickly. It could only be concealed. Scotty lowered himself back into his chair and removed his construction helmet. A fern of bleached-white hair sprung up. He picked up the cup of tea Baseman had poured, nestling it gently in his hands in a way that felt too docile.

'You're the sheriff,' Scotty said. 'You tell us how to help, and we'll help.'

He smiled. Baseman mistrusted the expression but forged a smile in return. It had been eight days since he'd faked an emotion, a lifetime record.

'I see you've got full backpacks,' he said. 'Tell me you got some SpaghettiOs in there, Kraft Mac & Cheese, something.'

'Please,' Zoë added. 'Please, oh, please.'

Scotty looked at Paddy, who mimed tying his mouth shut to keep in his laughter. Scotty hoisted his backpack to the tabletop, unzipped it, and scooped several layers of bags onto the table. Paddy did the same with his bag. The landings rattled the teacups. Baseman had to lean in to make sure he was seeing this right. For decades, he'd seen hauls like this in footage of ATF busts, but never without a cadre of cops.

Sixteen bulging packs of marijuana, three colossal bags of cocaine, and dozens of twist-tied baggies of assorted pills. Were drugs the reason for Dylan Ramsey's incapacitation?

'SpaghettiOs,' Scotty mused. 'Something like that.'

The Wrong Pilot

'This is where you live. This fan room.'

'Yes, sir.'

'And that hole in the AC, the rubber tubing, that's where you're getting your water?'

'Yes, sir.'

'All right. Good. Imaginative. And I see your food pile. I imagine that's from the crew galley on this level? What I don't get is why you didn't stay there. It's got to be the safest place on the whole boat. Did the ghouls overrun it?'

'Ghouls, sir?'

'What Father Bill calls demons.'

'No, sir. It was . . .'

'Other people. They were fighting over the food?'

'It wasn't safe, sir.'

'I bet it wasn't.'

'For a . . .'

'Right. For a woman. I'm sorry, pilot. I've been down here before, with a group from up top. We've heard people run away from us but never came across anyone waiting to be found.'

'We're scared, sir.'

'Don't say that. I know *Olympia*'s women. They wouldn't just hide.'

'No one's fighting harder, sir. Teenagers. Trans women. There are heroes down here no one will ever know about, sir.'

'Will you stop calling me *sir*? It doesn't make sense while you're also holding a knife on me.'

'Sorry, sir. But I will not put the knife down.'

'Fine. Just – ease up a little? A few inches? There. Thank you. Now. I do want to try to understand. The people down here, they've divided into groups, you say. How many?'

'I don't know. Four? Five?'

'Is it by rank? Or job? How can you tell them apart?'

'Colors, sir. They started wearing different colors.'

'And here I hoped things were better down here. There's ten times as many of you, you know. You have more people, more weapons. If the Fifty-Fourth could take on Fort Wagner in the US Civil War, pilot, you all can take that island! Why don't you band together and rise up?'

'Respectfully, sir. You don't know. You don't know.'

'You think it's only tough down here, pilot? Is that what you think?'

'You people have the speaker system, sir.'

'The speaker . . . ? So Father Bill rambles into the 1MC five times a day. So what?'

'It's still *words,* sir. It's like . . . TV. Or radio. Or internet. Words still matter. They . . . tell us how to feel. What to fear. It's hard not to listen. We're weak. We're starving. We're crowded into safe areas. Everyone fights for room, all the time. No one can sleep. A lot of the food's gone bad. A lot of us are sick. There's rats. Because there's trash.'

'Are people eating . . . ?'

'The rats, sir? Affirmative. You're not going to think of something we haven't already.'

'Right. I'm sorry. Some of it's our fault, us up above. We took over the dry goods rooms. We've got the engine rooms too. Next thing we're going after are the reactors. Bit by bit, we're buying up all the real estate down here. You're going to get shoved into smaller and smaller spaces.'

'Sure you care *now.* Now that you're one of us.'

'I'm not going to pretend that's not true. Especially given that knife you won't put down. I guess a person gets blinded by his own problems. Look, what matters now is I'm here. I'm ready to help. But I can't do that if I'm your prisoner. I'm not going to hurt you. You've got my big, fancy weapons right there behind you. The best of which is a busted crucifix.'

'I know that crucifix, sir.'

'Were you a believer? The Long Walk and all that? See, we all make mistakes, don't we?'

'See this?'

'What is it? A bandage? It needs to be changed, pilot.'

'Father Bill did that. He stuck that crucifix in my back.'

'When?'

'Before. We were in an access trunk.'

'I wish you'd ended him there. How'd you get out?'

'I fell. All the way. Nine levels.'

'What about the safety nets?'

'He cut them up. My flight suit caught on a trunk handle, and I stopped falling.'

'Miracle you didn't break every bone in your body.'

'There were demons.'

'Let's not use his word.'

'There were ghouls. Lots of them. They'd fallen down, too, so They were broken up. But some of Them managed to grab me. And They ripped at me. They held me and They ripped at my clothes. One of the demons, one of the ghouls, he had hold of my shoulders, and I – I recognized him. He was my squadron XO. He'd probably been looking for me, because of my bolting. I deserved a flight restriction. I deserved it. I was supposed to submit to punishment. So I let him crawl up my arms. I was just going to let it happen. Then I thought back to basic. Before I was an FNG, before I was a nugget. When I was just a SLJO and men had all the power. Even if they didn't outrank me. They'd mess with me. They'd touch me. The furthest I dared go was Wrist Warfare.'

'Wrist . . . ?'

'Something just broke. All women down here, they break and become different. Worse in some ways, but better in others. I decided I was done with it. I put my thumbs in my XO's eyes. There was this thing called the Sweetheart Wall. He condoned it. I shoved my thumbs in deep. The Sweetheart Wall, I kept thinking about it, until my thumbs could feel brain. The other ghouls got excited. They ripped my XO down. But my thumbs were stuck, and pretty soon I just had his head, I was holding just his head, and his mouth was still trying to bite me. So I threw it. I imagined throwing it straight into the Sweetheart Wall. I imagined throwing it against the side of a plane. Did you know I'm the only Red Serpent who doesn't have her name on a plane? I don't even have a call sign. *I don't even have a call sign.*'

'Did someone save you?'

'I guess. If you want to call it that. My strap broke. I fell. I should have died. But men came in. They had headlamps. They had tools. They knocked the ghouls off me. They were nuke guys. Guys who worked on the reactors. They picked me up. They bandaged me up. They gave me water. They fed me. They were so nice to me.'

'Oh no.'

'I don't know if you know this. I don't know who you are. But the final course a pilot takes before fleet assignment is called SERE. Survival, Evasion, Resistance, Escape. It's about what to do if you're a POW. It's classified. But I can tell you this. I know how to kill myself. I don't need anything but my hands to do it.'

'The navy's better since Tailhook. More female recruits, more sensitivity training—'

'Excuse me, sir—'

'The culture, it's tribal, it's—'

'Sir, *please* don't make excuses for them. I didn't kill myself. I used the other things SERE taught us. I killed *them*. I killed them like I was one of the ghouls. I'm not sure I'm not on Their side, sir. If They're golems, They're here to cleanse, and why should we stand in the way of that? I killed those men, sir. I don't even know who you are and I'm telling you everything. I guess because you asked. Because you gave a shit enough to ask. Sir.'

'Don't give me too much credit. You don't have that knife, we're probably having a very different conversation.'

'I'm not going to be as bad as them.'

'You're right, you don't know me, you should never put down that knife—'

'I *refuse* to be as bad as them. And don't forget, sir. I still have my hands. I know how to use them.'

'I don't doubt that. So you've been on the run ever since? Faction to faction?'

'I don't see any other way. No one's getting out of here.'

'Well, I wonder.'

'What's that mean?'

'You're a pilot, aren't you, Pagán?'

'But the aircraft, I heard them fall. It sounded like towers collapsing.'

'Affirmative. Father Bill's having us push the planes into the ocean. But with ghouls out there, it's taking time. What do you fly?'

'F-18s, sir.'

'We've got a Super Hornet on the runway, just aft of Elevator #4. D model, two-seater.'

'But, sir, without the catapults . . . if we had a Harrier II, maybe—'

'I spend a lot of time on the meteorological level. A *lot* of time. And something I just happen to know about, because it's displayed on a monitor directly above where I sleep, is that in twenty-four hours, we're scheduled to see fifty knots of trade winds.'

'Sir. You've picked the wrong pilot.'

'I don't think I have.'

'I don't know if I can get into a plane again.'

'You can. You have to.'

'You're using me, sir, as a way off the boat. A way that won't even work.'

'So what if I am? I've got something important to get home to. There's very little left in this world I believe in, very little, but what there is, for me, it's in Buffalo. Where's home to you?'

'Detroit, sir.'

'Buffalo, Detroit. The Bills, the Lions. We're practically neighbors. Maybe you and I get home together. Operation Bills-Lions. Why not believe in it? You'd rather run around down here forever like the rats?'

'It's just that I've spent the last week just . . . just trying to live. Crawling up to every dead body I see. Patting it down for food. Looking for a shoe. I lost my left shoe when I fell down the trunk. It was an important shoe, sir. Fighter pilots have brown shoes. It means something. Maybe I didn't have my name on a plane, and maybe I didn't have a call sign. But I had the brown shoes. Sir? Why are you laughing, sir?'

'Pilot.'

'Yes?'

'Look behind you. Next to the crucifix.'

'Why?'

'Because the other weapon you took from me is a shoe. A woman's brown fighter-pilot shoe. Petty Officer Pagán, I think we were meant to be.'

'I . . . thank you, sir. I can't tell you what . . . I think it fits, I – thank you, sir.'

'Stop calling me *sir*, pilot.'

'It's Jennifer. Call me Jenny. Just plain Jenny.'

Home

'It's the Big G,' Luis croaked into his phone, winking a purple, swollen eyelid at Charlie.

She grinned back, but it hurt. Luis's resolve to keep his sense of humor was his gift to her, in return for all the Shotgun Marriage events, and she couldn't reject it. His latest effort was funny. It was. Rationing of generator diesel forced Luis to charge his precious, useless phone infrequently, but he had a bit of battery left and was scrolling through his contacts to make mock farewell calls. It was the act of a man dying of cancer, the Big C. She'd seen those movies before.

'I appreciate that, JT,' he said. 'It's true, the Big G runs in my family.'

Charlie scowled at this morbid reference to Mamá Acocella, and Luis gathered enough energy to look scandalized. She didn't like the expression; his face was gray and waxy, and to warp it like that made him look like one of the cadavers they saw on occasion in the morgue, its face gnarled into a death-gape. But she rolled her eyes, feigning the good time Luis wanted her to have.

'Enough about me, JT, we all gotta go sometime,' Luis said. 'How are you, old boy? You sound a little . . . flat.'

He raised a patchy, mangy eyebrow at Charlie. It took her a second to get it: their old boss, Jefferson Talbot, reported by Lindof to have leaped from the sixty-fourth floor of Trump International

Hotel. It was too dark, but in this too-dark time, it was just what she needed. She snorted, a piggy noise that struck her as funny, and at which she laughed. If there was a God out there, and he had any more power than the plastic Jesus on Mae Rutkowski's wall, he'd better bless the hell out of Luis Acocella.

'JT, pal, I gotta – yeah, I know, I'm late for work – yeah, okay, I'm ten days late, but I had – well, if you let me finish – traffic was a real nightmare, and then I had some home remodeling to do – look, I really have to go. See you soon, JT. Bye-bye.'

Luis ended the call with an exaggerated finger. Charlie smiled, but his words echoed.

I really have to go.

He did. They both knew it. The Big G had him in its withering grip. His blurry vision had progressed to near blindness; he now called her 'the prettiest blond blob I've ever seen'. When racked by pain and fever, his moans became nonsense. His only concern seemed to be for her. He was sorry she'd have to face this world alone. Did she remember how to load the gun? He went over the places he thought most likely to stock ammo. Just in case civilization made a surprise return, he scrawled an illegible will leaving her everything, though if Rosa came back, she had to share it. Did she remember how to load the gun? Had he already asked that?

Luis thumbed his dead screen.

One thing Charlie missed since the diesel rationing was the sustaining presence of Chuck Corso. She and Luis had poked fun at Corso until they, along with what Charlie guessed was the rest of the nation, came to see the anchor as a hero, the one man holding America together with Elmer's Glue and sailors' knots. In WWN's absence, bitterness had crept into Charlie's thoughts. Since the second Luis had been bitten, theirs had been a marriage on fast-forward, and finally, they'd arrived at the part where Charlie had to quit being a wife and start being a nurse.

Nagging after his comfort only to get confusing, contradictory replies. Saddled with the thankless task of making him eat only to have to clean him after he vomited it up. Feeling like worthless crap when she dropped him on another trip to the tub because he'd shit himself again. Full-circle time: she was his diener again, assisting not with autopsies of others but with his own death.

'Hello,' Luis said, 'is Manolo there? Oh, *this* is Manolo? Manu, old sport, it's *tu hermano*. How are things in the Pine Tree State? Overrun with the dead? You don't say. Oh, well, thanks for asking, but I'm afraid the news here isn't too good. I've come down with the Big G. The hospital? I don't need a hospital. A bit of Mamá's pork posole will do the trick, eh?'

Luis smiled at Charlie. She didn't return it. She could tell he'd just suffered a wave of pain. Perspiration sloughed down his face like icing, and the phone's light only made him paler. She also saw his resolve. After taking several fake phone calls to conclusion, to bail out of this one early would be to reveal the whole thing as the grotesquerie it was. Luis forced his lips into a distorted grin. The touch screen glow shone off teeth that had begun to brown.

'It's been too long, Manu. I agree, we should get together. I'd suggest you take a nice cross-country drive my way, but I heard highways are going to be bumper-to-bumper for a while. Me? Oh, I'm in no state to travel. I'm afraid the Big G is quite advanced. The old legs don't run anymore. It's hard for me to even stay awake more than—'

His voice snagged. Charlie held her breath. Whether Luis's gasp was from emotion or pain, his red-and-yellow eyes submerged in tears. He brought a quavering hand to his forehead, hiding his crumpling face.

'You remember, don't you, Manu? We used to watch scary movies Rafi's big brother bootlegged, and I'd be up all night, afraid if I fell asleep, the monster was going to get me. That's how it is now, brother. Every time I drift off, I think . . . is this the last time? Is this the last time I'll think of Mamá and Papá and you and . . . and I'm scared, Manu.' Luis laughed. 'I used to crawl into bed with you, recuerda? You'd say, "There's no monsters, bobo, get in here so I can sleep." And then everything was okay. That's what I want now. That's all I want. Make the monsters go away, Manu. You're the only one who ever could.'

Luis sobbed, a blast of cracking mucus, and Charlie saw the light leave his phone, the battery dead, maybe for good, leaving behind a black screen, which anyone who wears lipstick can tell you can be used as a mirror. In the black screen, Luis saw the last news byte his phone would deliver: his own face, good as dead. He sobbed again. There was nothing Charlie could do. He fell asleep, and after a while, she went downstairs and slept on the sofa, because what if he died in the night, rolled over, and bit her?

With that, she knew it was over.

Most nights, a few creaks of bedsprings, a couple of ghostly moans, and she was up. Tonight, she slept undisturbed, and there were no noises when she woke in the morning. She let that sink in. November 4: so today was the day she'd never forget. She did her morning check of the boarded-up doors and windows, put on the coffee, picked up the .38, and headed upstairs.

Luis was alive. But he'd changed, one more time. His body had sunk into the bed like it was grave soil. He'd gone chalk white. Most ominous of all, he'd gone still. She'd read about this in med school: the point when a patient's pain could no longer be recognized as pain. It was the air, the light, gravity; it was everything. When Charlie sat on the bed beside him, only his eyes moved, rolling her way.

'Char-lie.' His rasp slowed the word. 'Show me the gun.'

She should be devastated, but she'd read about this too: the exhausted, ashamed gratefulness loved ones felt near the end. She held up the revolver for Luis to see. Luis blinked, the closest he could come to a nod.

'Once you're done with me,' he said, 'save one bullet for yourself. Just in case.'

'Do I . . . I mean, if I have to . . . do I aim for my . . . my heart, or . . .'

'Diener. You know this.'

Charlie laughed. 'Yeah. I guess I do.'

'Tell me,' Luis sighed. 'For old times' sake.'

She sniffled; her eyes, still swollen from sleep, swelling even more. 'If you aim for the chest,' she said, 'the ribs might deflect it.'

'And?'

'You could end up with a pneumothorax. A hemothorax. Quadriplegia.'

'So what should you do?'

'The head,' she said softly. 'Not the temple. You might miss the brain, sever the eyeballs, end up blind. Not under the chin either. Your hand might jerk and you'd end up blowing your face off. You want to put the gun inside your mouth and aim down, where the skull meets the spinal column.'

'But not with ghouls, right?'

'Oh, shit. Right. That's right. So, yeah, the skull, then. Right in the middle of the head. Straight at the brain. Oh, Luis. Oh, shit. Oh, fuck. I don't want to do this.'

'You might not have to. I hope you don't have to.'

'I mean *this*. I mean *you*. We didn't have enough time. I tried to go fast, but it wasn't good enough, was it?'

'It was pretty good. Now go to the dresser. The duct tape. Tape up my ankles and wrists.'

'No, Acocella, no.'

'You won't have that bullet to save if you spend it all on me.'

He was right. Of course he was right. Even during John Doe's rebirth, Luis Acocella had been the perfect professional, uploading his recording to the VSDC when anyone else would have hightailed it out of there. He deserved to have been elected medical examiner over JT. He deserved a lot of things he'd never gotten. Before Charlie could think too hard about it, she snatched up the duct tape and unknotted the sheets from Luis's limbs. She hadn't seen his body in days. It was skeletal, his pajamas pasted to his limbs. *Not really him,* she repeated as she taped his ankles together. *He's bigger than these bones,* she told herself as she taped his wrists behind his back.

'Good,' he said. 'Now listen. I don't want to make a mess.'

'You're already a mess, dummy.'

The slightest upward twinge of his lips.

'Go downstairs. Get a few garbage bags. Put them inside each other so they're thick. And then I want you to—'

'No, Acocella, Jesus—'

'—put them over my head and tape them to my neck.'

'I'm not going to smother you!'

'You won't. Make a hole so I can breathe. But when I come back, you're not going to be able to get those bags on me. And I don't want you to have to see it. The mess. I don't want you to remember me like that.'

'You'll never be like Them. Never.'

'You know, I've been thinking. My thoughts don't make sense. About the ghouls. They're not imperfect humans. They're perfect humans. You know what I'm saying? All humans did was kill enemies. Like those guys who surrounded our car, who wanted Latinos. The ghouls are the same. Except they want all colors, all kinds. Equality at last. That's not so bad, is it?'

When Charlie went downstairs, she could see herself as if from a floating camera. It was disassociation from shock, another thing she'd read about in school. There was also an element of theatricality. You spent your whole life watching, hearing, and reading stories that spotlighted major rituals. The walking-down-the-aisle scene, the delivery-room scene, the crying-at-the-funeral scene. This was the deathbed scene, and she felt herself pulling her shoulders back and adopting the right expression of sad fortitude. Here it was, her time to take the stage.

She fired up the generator. Fuel was low, but at this stage, what wasn't? She retrieved the heavy-duty black garbage bags from the kitchen, but instead of going to the second floor, she descended to the basement. Several days ago (or several decades ago, depending on how she measured it), while she'd been excavating holiday decorations, she'd come across boxes, dated in faded pen, from what had to be Luis's early twenties. Knowing young Luis might be a way to make him live forever, and she tore at the tape, only to find inside not the photographs and ephemera for which she'd longed but books.

The musty volumes introduced a boy whose intellectual curiosity had prevailed against ten-hour workdays. Heavy Latin American lit, Old English poetry, European film criticism, German philosophy. Inside each front cover was a signature of ownership, done with the kind of swoopy flash people used before they turned thirty, like their autographs might be worth something someday: *Luis Jorge Acocella.*

She assembled a stack of the best-thumbed books, balanced the garbage bags on top, and carried them upstairs to the bedroom, where she found Luis unconscious. She got right to work layering garbage bags. She was cutting out a mouth hole when he woke.

'You've got five bullets,' he said. 'Don't use more than four. It's going to be loud. It'll bring Them. Shoot through a pillow. It might soften the noise. I don't know.'

His eyes were closed, his lids a greasy black against a pasty face. She leaned in as casually as she could, not wanting this good-night kiss to be any different from the others she'd given him. His lips were ice. The skin around them boiled. She slid away, licked his hot sweat from her lips, and looked at his beautiful, kind face one last time before letting it disappear beneath black bags.

She duct-taped the bags to his pajama shirt. She watched the plastic around the mouth hole puff in and out with his puny breaths.

'You want music?' she asked.

He nodded once, the bag crackling. She went to the DVD player and inserted *The Quiet Man*. Once the sprightly yet sad Victor Young score rang out, she sat on the edge of the bed, her knee touching a man bound and hooded as if awaiting execution, which he was, though unlike most executioners, she loved her victim beyond what she could express. Next to his legs she placed four books and one revolver.

'I'm going to read to you,' she said. 'Things from when you were young. Would you like that?'

The head nodded. The garbage-bag hole sucked inward, blew out. She selected a fat volume of poetry and began paging through the index. She did not quite make it to *B* before seeing, with surprise, a poem about the occupation they shared: autopsy.

The poem was 'Autopsy in the Form of an Elegy', published in 1972 by a cardiologist named John Stone. Charlie read it to herself and recognized it as being about the Big C, or the Big G, or something of the kind. When she read it aloud, she did so softly, because her lover, her patient, her favorite person was drifting away.

> *In the chest*
> *in the heart*
> *was the vessel*
>
> *was the pulse*
> *was the art*
> *was the love*
>
> *was the clot*
> *small and slow*

> *and the scar*
> *that could not know*

> *the rest of you*
> *was very nearly perfect.*

Charlie knew this part of the scene too: she sank her face in her hands and sobbed.

'Diener.' Luis's scratchy voice, the plastic hiss.

Charlie nodded and trusted he would feel it.

'You know this,' he said. 'Try to remember it. Childhood isn't a moment. Old age isn't a moment. Maybe death isn't either. It's a process. Some bone cells keep going. Some cell clusters too. Like constellations in the sky. I don't make sense. I want to go home. The metabolic waste. The enzymatic breakdown. The sarcophages. The feeding animals. The putrefaction. The soil. The new life. I want to go home, Charlie. I want to go home.'

She didn't know what he meant. Home could be Mexico. Home could be Rosa. She flipped the pages of the book and kept reading, blundering sentences, skipping whole stanzas, not that it mattered. All she could concentrate on was the plume and wilt of the garbage bag, the rise and fall of Luis's chest, and how she, only twelve days ago, had cradled John Doe's heart in her hands and wondered if anyone, or anything, out there cradled hers. If what Luis raved was true, the hands that held her did not belong to a Thing, but to *Things*, all of Them ready to fill her with new life when she was ready. It was the saddest thought: the ghouls as correctives, a million mushroom clouds come to repair all that had gone awry.

'You're going home,' she promised.

'I want to . . .'

'You're going home, I said.'

'I want . . .'

'Stop wanting, Acocella. You're going home if I have to drag you there myself.'

There was a long, long pause, during which Luis Acocella might have died. Charlie would never be sure. Around one in the afternoon, with Victor Young's 'I'll Take You Home Again, Kathleen' swooning, another sound finally emitted from the garbage-bag hood: 'Mmmmm,' that noncommittal noise Luis so often used to drive her batty.

Charlie chuckled, and stood, and laughed some more, and the lifting of the gun, like the lifting of an arm – *Shall we dance?* – shook tears from her eyes, hundreds of them, hot down her face, cold down the front of her shirt. She decided it was a kind of home, after all, to give Luis the friendly, familiar, playful middle finger he'd always loved to see. She put the .38 to his forehead, buffered by a pillow as instructed. The bag wrinkled back like a surprised forehead. It would only take her one try to do what he'd told her to do. She may have been a mediocre wife, but she'd been the best damn assistant Luis Acocella ever had.

This Is a Test

Someone dies. Someone else learns to live. A fair trade, and the best way Greer could frame her new life. It was the worst of times, like the first chapter of that famous book Greer couldn't remember. She did, however, remember the other half of that line too.

Against stratospheric odds, she was involved in a romance. Out here in the chilly sticks of bumfuck Missouri. Though hunting was all right, she'd never liked camping; the Morgan living quarters had been uncomfortable enough. Yet in the nine days she'd been with Muse, they'd slept on barn hay, beds of dry pine needles, inside a junked rowboat, and on the ground itself, waking up damp from dew and smelling of grass, bark, and each other. She liked it. She loved it.

Best place to hide, I figured, was right out in the open – Muse had been drunk when he'd said it, but he had a canny instinct for survival. Those trapped inside trailers at the Last Resort, or inside Bulk High School, or, as Muse described, inside every business in Kansas City might all be doomed. Ghouls had bulldozer strength in numbers. Worse, They were patient. If They couldn't crack your stronghold, They'd wait until you ran out of food and broke free, becoming food yourself.

Deep into the land of long, flat crop tillage and vacant, grassy fields, Greer and Muse could see trouble coming. The largest herd of ghouls they'd spotted was five. More often, they'd see one or two at a half-mile distance, and they'd finish what they were doing – scavenging, eating, packing up, kissing – before putting a few miles between them and danger.

Sometimes, while hurrying away, they'd giggle. It felt like being caught making out in the park by a police officer. It made Greer think she might be in love. When she first thought it, one ridiculous day into their relationship, she brushed it off. Old married couples at Sunnybrook believed they needed their spouse to survive, for who else knew how to pay the bills on time or make the coffee right? Transpose that reliance into actual life-or-death situations and, yeah, it's probably going to feel like love.

Greer knew all that, yet wondered. She'd never been in love, not even close, and preferred it that way. There was lust: poor Qasim and other guys before him. There was what Daddy called *bonhomie*: guys who gave her a buzz because they were interesting and inspired her to be interesting in return. Muse wasn't just the whole package, he was the whole Amazon warehouse, a guy of infinite stories who preferred to hear hers. She hadn't thought she *had* stories, but Muse was thirsty for them, like the maudlin incarceration of her mother and her grimy Sunnybrook struggles reminded him of someone.

She came to find it did: Will and Darlene Lucas, a hardscrabble married couple whom Muse held in lofty esteem, so much that he winced when speaking of them, clearly fearful of what fate had befallen them. Best she could figure, the Lucases were the only ones who'd loved Muse for Muse, not because he could sell out a major venue. Skills like that no longer counted for shit. Farmers, carpenters – they'd be heroes now, though Greer suspected Muse's charm might still come in handy.

He was disarmingly open about that charm. He'd loved a lot of ladies, as he put it, and mourned them as part of the tapestry of his old world. Greer discovered she didn't mind being the latest in a line of ladies rather than a worshipped exemplar. To stand out in the new world was to tempt death. All she needed was the feeling with which she'd woken up on October 24: *want*. She had want now, a lot of it. Muse had want too.

Their profession, if they had one, was raiding empty houses. Inside the first house they'd hit together, a one-story bungalow tucked inside a crumbling farm, she found binoculars, and realizing what a help they'd be, hurried to show Muse. She found him rifling through bedside-table drawers. She knew what he was doing. He was looking for condoms. Next to other guys she'd laid, who sulked the second they heard the wrapper crinkle, this was staggeringly mature. She'd seen enough end-of-the-world sci-fi to know getting preggers in the apocalypse was some seriously stupid shit.

It took three days to find condoms. Forever, it seemed, though she supposed it could have taken three years. She hoped the discovery meant nonstop screwing, but it didn't. Fourteen condoms. That was it. Who knew when, or if, they might find more. Muse meted out sexual overtures as he might a rare liquor. Every three or four days, or when something special happened. Another sign of responsibility, though Greer didn't like it and made her attitude known.

'Hey, what side of this Civil War you on?' Muse asked.

Playful, but there was a watchfulness there, like Greer Morgan was a girl he'd better keep his eye on. Honestly, she liked that too. She'd never dwelled on why she'd defied so many teachers back in Bulk and had never backed down from fights. Now it crystallized: she liked feeling dangerous. In Bulk's tedium, the feeling couldn't be fulfilled, but out here, she could embrace it.

That didn't mean she enjoyed killing ghouls. It disrupted their bliss. They slept with an alert system in place, usually a perimeter of wire they unspooled each night and respooled each morning. Three times the wire had been tripped. It was scary shit. The first time, they'd been in a shed with a wall at their back, a rookie blunder, and thank fuck they only had to face a single ghoul. Greer slept with the machete, and she hacked into the ghoul's skull like it was a coconut husk, wedges of bone capering like coconut flakes.

Her other focus, in those early days, was survival. That meant one thing: the bow.

Hunting with Daddy, she'd mostly used a gun, but Freddy Morgan had also used a bow. Not a compound bow, one of those oversized, high-tech, multi-stringed contraptions loaded with axels, pulleys, and stabilizers. No, he'd had a simple English longbow, which had a pleasant storybook quality to it but wasn't going to hit shit without a lot of practice. Greer had shot once or twice, without much success.

Now, however, she was a girl with an excess of time on her hands. So she practiced. For hours, every day. She waited until they came across some outbuilding or, as she got more skilled, a tree or telephone pole. She scratched a circle on her target with a rock. From five paces away, she shot her six arrows, hunted them down, shot them again. Nature's hush, what she enjoyed most when hunting with Daddy, was still alive to enjoy, only now there was a bonus element of self-betterment. When she hit her mark consistently, she moved to ten paces away, then fifteen.

The string slapped her forearm bloody until she found a leather belt, knifed a notch, and cinched it around the vulnerable flesh. Her back muscles felt swollen enough to split the skin.

'Trapezius,' Muse said, working his thumbs into her sore flesh. 'Latissimus dorsi,' he said, moving downward. 'External oblique,' he continued, lower now, his thumbs teasing the waist of her jeans. Not all sex acts required a condom. She lay back, her aching back throbbing on the cold ground, and placed her hands softly on Muse's unkempt orb of hair – even her palms were sore.

One of six arrows hitting home wasn't good. Three out of six wasn't going to make them feel safe in an emergency. Five of six – now she was getting somewhere. Just over a week into her new, nomadic life, Greer was hitting 80 at fifteen yards. Was that unusual progress? She didn't know, but it felt good. She'd take fifteen yards with a bow over a machete blow any day.

Muse appreciated the added safety. He said he did. But did he really? His golf claps at her archery feats were funny, his dutiful sharpening of her arrow points helpful, and his sore-muscle therapy heavenly. But the darkness that clouded his eyes when she practiced was no different from how it was after she'd chopped into the head of the ghoul. He didn't seem to like it when she killed Them.

Here she was saving their asses, and he had the gall to pout about it? He'd used her hunting knife to cut a circle of tractor tire to place over his guitar's sound hole, thereby allowing him to play at a fraction of the instrument's usual volume. And play he did, every spare moment. Old songs, except one, a secret new 'protest song' he called 'Walk Away'. He plunked away at it, day after day, working toward an inscrutable perfection. This was his big contribution to their life?

She rebuked herself. He offered plenty in manpower and spirit. Maybe she was overly enthusiastic about killing things that used to be human.

Otherwise, they were happy, but this discontent was the pebble in her shoe. Walk enough miles and pretty soon that pebble had to come out. For Greer, it was on day ten of their time together. They kept too far off roads to know their precise location, but she guessed thirty miles north of Kansas City; the brown-and-yellow quilt of November farmland was the best spot they'd found yet. They turned up a pickup truck half-stocked with food its former driver couldn't carry when his ride ran out of gas, and Greer and Muse contentedly picked delights from its horn of plenty: SPAM, baked beans, peaches, cereal, even pasta sauce they added to cooked spaghetti.

The pocket of paradise had one weakness: a long, gentle rise to the west that would cut their usual reaction time by a third should ghouls crest it. And they might: at the northern end of the hill was a farm, and ghouls, grouped there by some instinct, paced about it, bumping into fences, grain bins, and silos. Every day, for most of the day, Greer and Muse sat on decrepit lawn chairs beneath a patch of trees at the foot of the hill, and like a bird-watcher and his wife, he kept an eye on Them while she offered up fat to be chewed. He rarely accepted her proposal to take watch. He gripped those binoculars like he gripped his guitar, like he gripped her.

'Well *that's* new,' Muse said. He adjusted the focus dial.

'If we could find a second binoculars,' she said, 'we could split the duty.'

'I don't mind,' he said.

'Yeah, but, you know.' She shrugged; she hated being mushy. 'I kind of miss you. You've got a plastic prosthetic glued to your face.'

'We got a couple runaways. Sixty, seventy yards off? Near side of the farm, you see it? Looks like They maybe followed a horse out? It looks like They're . . . I'm not sure I'm seeing this right.'

Greer sighed. On the road again, it seemed. She stretched her legs to touch the wheelbarrow in which they hauled food, gear, and, of course, the space-hogger of the guitar called Hewitt. Three days ago, they'd replaced Fadi Lolo's Schwinn with the wheelbarrow. Greer's heart broke a little when they left it. She missed the bike's latent potential for speed. They should have snagged a second one, and gone anywhere. California, Mexico, Canada.

'Where would you go?' she asked. 'If you could go anywhere?'

'A couple miles south with you,' he replied. 'Looks like I'm in luck.'

'For real.'

'They're done eating. I think They're looking at us.' He lowered the binoculars enough to glance at Greer. 'Like where would I go, fantasyland?'

'Sure.'

His grin hadn't quit thrilling her. The creamy thinning of his lips, his crooked canines, the bristling corkscrews of his beard.

'Capitol Records, no question.'

'Is that, like, a record store?'

'It's a recording studio in Hollywood. You've seen it in movies. Big round building, looks like a stack of records on a platter? Giant needle at the top, blinking red?' He began raising the binoculars, but didn't bother. 'Yeah, here They come. We got to pack up.'

'You want to record some songs? I didn't mean *that* much fantasy.'

Muse chuckled. 'Full orchestra version of "Walk Away"? Yeah, I could get into that. No, what I'm thinking is, Capitol Records has these echo chambers. They call them Vine Street. Eight chambers, sort of trapezoid shaped, no parallel lines, you feel me? Every room's got a special reverb. They put vocalists down there. Sinatra, Nat King Cole, the Beach Boys. Hell, the *Beastie* Boys. You get a five-second delay and a decay like chocolate syrup, like you're singing in St Patrick's Cathedral. Folks will tell you you can do that now with filters, but it ain't the same, not if you have ears.'

He stood and stretched. Greer could see the ghouls now, half a football field away. They were a 1940s comedy team, one short and fat, one tall and thin. Both wore overalls. Both were bloodred from the chin down. Whoever they'd eaten had a lot of hair; thick, long thatches of black hair adhered to Their stickiest spots.

'All right, Capitol Records,' Greer said. 'Our death screams in hi-fi.'

'Vine Street's thirty feet underground. Ten-inch concrete walls. Foot-thick ceiling. No ghouls are getting down there. I mean, if you're going to hole up, might as well do it in a place with a little history, right?'

'You think you're the first guy to think of this? Studio space is all filled up, KK.'

He folded his chair and offered a hand to help her from hers.

'Can you imagine who's there right now? The world's top recording artists, all thrown together? No way they're not going to jam.

Like the Righteous Brothers said, "If there's a rock 'n' roll heaven, well, you know they've got a hell of a band." I'm talking last-days music. A new kind of gospel.'

He folded her chair and lodged them both in the wheelbarrow. The ghouls were forty yards off, Their peeled flesh jiggling with each wobbly step down the hillside. She could hear Them now, a bass grumble like a nearby interstate.

'Guess we'll have to hear it in our dreams,' Muse sighed.

'Until then, binoculars,' Greer griped. 'One pair of binoculars.'

'We find another pair, you're welcome to them. It's not a thing.'

'You act like it's a thing.'

'It's *not* a *thing*, all right? Someone's got to be the lookout while you're doing target practice. I've just gotten used to it.'

There it was, that underlayer of disapproval.

'Is it a man thing?'

'What? Come on.'

'Because I'm doing the protecting. Some emasculating thing?'

His eyes gave her some heat. She'd seen glimmers of this during sex or when they had to run. His cheekbones got sharper, his throat articulated.

'Is this a *woman* thing? Trying to pick a fight?'

The ghouls were thirty yards off now, the width of a small parking lot, the distance at which a girl needed to start really paying attention. Greer, though, wanted Muse to be the one who paid attention. To the ghouls, to her, to everything she did and the very real shit going down all around them, while he sang, 'Walk away, walk away'.

'I guess this is what I get from an artist,' she said. ' "If the Blues Wuz a Woman". Anybody tell you that shit's offensive? All's I'm saying is, every time I shoot an arrow, you get this look.'

'I get a look.'

'Like you wish I wasn't doing it! I can hear it in your guitar. It gets all sad and shit.'

His voice got softer. 'It's not my place to tell you what to do.'

'It's your place to have an opinion! I mean, we're together, aren't we?'

How could the response to this question still scare her in a world without school dances, nice dinners, or social-media declarations of love? Yet Muse's slow blink might as well be the teeth of the two ghouls. They were a classroom distance away now, close enough for her to make out Their identifying moles, laugh lines, states of shaving when They died.

'We're together, lady,' Muse said. 'But the world isn't together. Things I used to think were all right, maybe I don't anymore. You say it's my place to have an opinion. Okay, fine. But I don't have one worked out yet. Some things just feel wrong.'

'How could killing ghouls be wrong? They're dead, King Kong.'

'What's death? Did people just, like, make death up? Maybe it's only death if we mark it. Funerals and prayers and all that: that's death. This is . . . I just feel like maybe we're doing the wrong thing. Like this is a test from the Big Man and we're failing it.'

She gestured at the obvious: the ghouls, a car-length away, shoes squelching with fresh blood, the buckles of Their overalls clanging as They lifted Their arms to get what They wanted. While she and Muse stood arguing. Who'd back down first? Or would they just let the ghouls wrap ice-cold, blood-hot hands around their squabbling necks? She snatched up the handles of the wheelbarrow.

'You know your whole career kicked off with you bashing some shooter in the face, right?' Greer shouted.

The wheelbarrow stuck, a scary moment, the weight of the supplies sinking it into the mud. The tires popped free with a slurp, and she wheeled it around, putting it between them and the ghouls.

'It did.' Muse stepped behind her. 'But Will and Darlene taught me better.'

He got in the last word, of course he did – he didn't have the wheelbarrow to worry about. The fat ghoul toppled over the edge of it, knocking a precious jug of water to the ground. There was no time to recover it; the skinny ghoul rounded the side of the wheelbarrow, his long legs proving him a lot faster on flat ground. Ghouls, They always surprised. Greer scrambled backward, pulling the wheelbarrow with her. Muse took the duffel bag, the parcel most likely to fall, and slung it over his back.

They ran like they hadn't in a while. Two minutes later, Muse took over wheelbarrow duty, and they kept going. Greer's head still stormed. He was right she was picking a fight. What angered her – anger covering shame, if she was honest – was the possibility that Muse thought less of her for killing ghouls, no matter that she'd always tried to shield him from the ugliest parts.

'What do you want to do?' Muse asked.

Greer turned sharply to clear away the massed moths of bad thoughts. It looked aggressive, though, and he looked wounded. Her anger dissolved. She allowed her pumping legs to slow to a walk. Beside her, the squeak of the wheelbarrow slowed too. They walked through tall grass, side by side, their panting blending into the wind's hiss.

'I want,' she sighed. 'I want what you want.'

'That doesn't sound like Greer Morgan.'

He offered her a little grin. Her return smile came naturally.

'I like it out here,' she said. 'I do. But . . .'

He nodded. 'I know. How long can we do it, what's the endgame? You got family. I can't ask you to forget that.'

'They're gone.'

'No, they're not.' He gave her a serious look. 'Bluefeather, right?'

'Huh?'

'Bluefeather Prison. Iowa. You said that's where your mom is.'

Vienna Morgan: the family shame, the Bulk pariah. Four years had passed since Greer had spoken to her. She'd been beautiful and curvaceous, with pouty lips and flashing eyes; it was why she scored cleaning gigs in all the best homes. What would Vienna look like after four years of prison grub, prison toiletries? That was the wrong question, of course.

'She can't be alive,' Greer said.

'Why not? Prison might be the safest place there is. Walls to keep ghouls out. Cells to corral Them together.' Muse shrugged. 'It's a path to follow, you know? A lighthouse beacon? It's something.'

Greer found herself nodding. It was like a magnet inside her chest had switched on. She felt an unexpected, childlike urge to wrap her little arms around her mother's knees. Muse had nailed it: Vienna Morgan might be a trash person, but caring for her, or hoping she would care for Greer, were other forms of the *want* that kept her and Muse alive.

'After that,' Muse said, 'it's my turn. I got family too, even if you don't like it.'

'Will and Darlene.'

'I've toured enough to know Rhode Island is a haul.'

Greer was still nodding. 'We'll get there.'

'There may not be cars to hop. There may not even be roads.'

'I said, we'll get there.'

She stopped, turned, grabbed the lapels of his leather jacket, and pulled him a few inches down, lifted herself a few inches up. He smelled like he always did, like dried sweat, fresh dirt, and damp clothes. They didn't kiss; they just lived in each other's space for a minute, the heat of her lips, the dry fuzz of his face, the spider nest of four different sets of lashes.

Like this is a test from the Big Man, he'd said, *and we're failing it.*

She recalled a snippet of a lecture Freddy Morgan had delivered to Conan after the boy had poked a deer with a stick after Freddy's shot had only injured it. *God put animals here to judge us on how we treat them,* he'd said, and Greer had never forgotten how that line

damned the world. She shivered; her face bumped Muse's neck. She
let it nuzzle there.

'So what'd you see?' Her voice was muffled against leather.

'Hm?'

'In the binoculars. When you first saw those ghouls, you said it
was weird.'

He squeezed and released her and turned so the sun was at his
right. North, the direction of Iowa.

'Right. Yeah. Ghouls only eat people, right?'

'Uh-huh. They don't chase dogs or birds or anything.'

'Exactly,' he said. 'I guess I saw it wrong. I thought I saw those two
things eating a *horse*.'

Fuck Jansky

The end began with an innocuous thing: Paddy pushing Ramsey Dylan through the dark studio and parking the wheelchair right beside Camera 2.

Probably meant nothing. Like propping Grandpa in front of the Thanksgiving game. Dylan had been checked out since arrival. Baseman had told Chuck he suspected Scotty Rolph of drugging the dynamic VP, maybe when he was in the restroom dealing with Dylan's uncontrolled bladder and bowels. Chuck worried it was true. Still, he thought it possible Dylan might have asked to be wheeled in front of the set, a flattering idea and a possible sign of Dylan's improvement.

Two days before, Zoë had taken the desk so Chuck could meet the newcomers. The meeting had taken the shape of business lunches of yore, with the upscale restaurant replaced by the studio kitchen and the chef's special replaced by peanut butter on crackers. Chuck felt a pinch of his old egotism upon seeing Scotty Rolph's ratty high-tops propped on the table, a shoelace stuck to the peanut butter lid. Scotty's four layers of flannel shirts were flayed open like a med-school cadaver, and his hair was blown out like a Halloween fright wig. That wasn't far from the mark – his face was like white plastic, accentuating dried red blood in his nostrils.

The remains of Ramsey Dylan were slumped in a wheelchair to Scotty's left. Across from Scotty was Paddy, huge and soft like a stuffed carnival prize. Aside from learning that Paddy was short for

Paddington – Scotty thought, correctly, Paddy looked like a teddy bear – little info of consequence passed. No surprise, given that Scotty's plate, instead of crackers, was filled with lines of cocaine. Chuck had a Boy Scout's disinterest in recreational drugs, but didn't blame anyone for using at a time like this.

But there was the itch. That sinew tickle, that bone burn just under his skin. It flared up anytime he left the desk, but never as bad as this. A hundred hot wires laced through his forehead, cheeks, and chin. It felt like his body had developed a warning system. Something scared him about these strangers.

It was a peculiar thing to feel about a shriveled, immobile man and two lackadaisical burnouts. Or was it? Over the past week, when Chuck's exhausted mind wandered between stories, he'd begun to cultivate a notion the world hadn't foundered due to evil but rather apathy. Quit looking, you quit seeing. Quit seeing, you quit feeling. Quit feeling, and you're done. It's already too late.

Paddy fed Dylan too fast on purpose. Peanut butter smeared all over the exec's face, which Paddy, his eyes leaking suppressed hilarity, styled into a gloppy beige goatee. Scotty, finally inspired to take his feet off the table, planted M&M's all over the peanut-butter facial hair like a colorful pox. Tears squeezed from Dylan's closed eyes.

'He doesn't look like he likes it,' Chuck observed. 'Mr Dylan? Can you hear me?'

'Those are tears of joy!' Scotty cried. 'He loves us, doesn't he, Paddy?'

Paddy mussed Dylan's hair; the itch in Chuck's face cranked.

'Old Ramsey's very grateful to us, because his chair's batteries all burned out, didn't they, Old Ramsey?'

Dylan coughed up peanut butter globs; Chuck's itch snaked roots into his brain.

'You know what they call that little straw he steers with? Sip-and-Puff. Or is it Suck-and-Fuck?' Scotty stroked his chin. 'I can never remember.'

Dylan started sobbing; Chuck made fists to stop himself from sinking his nails into his face.

'Paddy, why don't you take Dylan to the bathroom?' Scotty asked. 'He might have a diaper doody.'

Paddy grinned through half-chewed crackers and wheeled Dylan about. Dylan's eyes snapped open and found Chuck, but so briefly Chuck did not know if he had really seen what looked like pleading fear. Scotty's squeaky laugh aligned with each turn of the chair's wheels.

Should Chuck have done something? Baseman relieved him of having to fret by fetching him for a news powwow. Chuck was glad it was Baseman and not Zoë. He hadn't liked the way Scotty had looked at the intern, like she was Foxy Fiona and he was J. J. Jalopy. Chuck wasn't afraid of Scotty (the animator was impaired, to say the least), but that seemed to be the point of Paddy.

Ramsey Dylan was parked a few inches from Camera 2, right in Chuck's line of sight. It shouldn't matter, but did: the itch roared back, a bucket of gasoline splashed on a dying match. Paddy's hulking shape behind Dylan only made it worse. Chuck ordered himself not to be fazed and squinted to reduce Dylan and Paddy to smudges. He looked into the lens, cleared his throat.

'Something's rotten in Belgium,' Chuck declared.

That fast, a screwup. Like the Face of old, he'd felt a need to be too clever and had bungled the quote. It was *perplexed* all over again. His heart pumped panic, a burn that, once upon a time, only Chuck-Sux69 could salve.

Paddy snorted in amusement. He placed his heavy paws on Dylan's back and began to massage the senior VP's shoulders. Chuck could conceive of a situation in which the gesture was kind. Baseman had speculated that Paddy was Scotty's dealer, but what if Paddy was Ramsey Dylan's physical therapist, on hand on October 24 to deliver a massage? A nice fantasy that died quickly: Paddy leaned toward Dylan's ear and, in a mealy mutter, delivered the first and last three words anyone at WWN would hear Paddy say.

'*Suck and fuck.*'

Eleven days after Chuck had taken the desk, his tongue lost its wagging magic. His voice ran out. It simply ran out. Filling the sudden silence was the distant drumming of ghouls' fists against the stairwell door, followed by the rat squeal of Paddy releasing the wheelchair's brake. Dylan shook his head as much as his disability allowed, a frantic under-neck jiggling. The chair's wheels made a flat sound with each revolution, filling Chuck's head: *suck, fuck, suck, fuck.*

'Stop,' Chuck said. His face boiled with itch.

Paddy's eyes glowed cheerily from the dim.

'Face.' Lee's voice in his earpiece. 'What's going on?'

Chuck pointed past Camera 2. 'You might have brought Mr Dylan here, but he doesn't belong to you. He's a human being. Whatever you're doing to him, I want you to stop. I'm asking nicely. Please.'

Paddy kept staring. Lee kept questioning. Dead air, its own loud alarm, rang about the studio. Chuck heard doors fly open, voices mutter, footsteps scuttle. A shape frosted in red light slid from the darkness, and Chuck prayed it was Nathan Baseman, his producer, his promoter, his protector. But the stage lights revealed messy whips of hair and fuzzy ripples of flannel.

Scotty Rolph rose on his toes to whisper in Paddy's ear. Paddy considered, nodded, and withdrew into the blackness beyond the cameras – someone had dimmed the studio's lights to former levels. Scotty mounted the riser and took a seat in the coanchor chair. Chuck stared. Like the ghouls, Scotty appeared human, but he was not. Blue veins glowed from beneath slimy white skin. Huge, addled eyes skittered as if following a bumblebee's flight. His upper lip was bright red from his dripping nose.

Frozen in shock, Chuck did nothing while Scotty picked up a lavalier mic and pinned it to his outermost flannel. He squared the pages of a dusty script, brushed back his white-dyed hair, and peeled his lips from decaying teeth, big Atlanta howdy-do.

'Hello, I'm Scotty Rolph.' The voice was liquid cheese, a parody of everything Chuck Corso had once represented. 'Welcome to *Good Evening, America,* your favorite program detailing the end of the world as we know it. I'm joined by Chuck Corso, a store mannequin brought to life by a Satanic ritual conducted at a local Neiman Marcus. Say hi to the people, Chuck.'

Chuck watched sweat roll down Scotty's beaming face. He felt detached, a hundred miles from the desk. In his gut, a dry prickling, like a thornbush had bloomed from a swallowed seed.

'Well,' Scotty said, 'he may not have a lot to say, but still, not too shabby for a man made of plastic, am I right? Before we get to the country's latest spate of death spasms, I want to take a moment to say what an honor it is to be here on the actual WWN news desk. Wow. I'm a fan. I really am. Your show is a lot of fun, Chuck. Hilarious, actually. Nothing on *J.J.'s Jamboree* can compare. This is a comedy show, right? Wait. It is, isn't it?'

Trouble in the studio, real trouble, beyond what was visible from the desk. Running, cursing, skidding, thudding, screeching, cracking. Unable to see what was happening, Chuck couldn't break focus from Scotty's spiky, stabbing voice, too similar to the spiny bristle going on in his stomach, itself too similar to the itch prickling his face.

Chuck identified this new emotion with mild wonder. Ambition, he knew. Joy, surprise, self-disgust, sadness, he knew. Vanity, he knew better than all else combined. But this was anger, and with it came the realization he'd built the nation's trust in him and his network. More than trust – a belief that help and heart still existed. He wouldn't let this brat butcher it.

'Get off the desk,' Chuck said.

Scotty ignored him.

'Breaking news: we're doomed! Then again, we've been doomed

since we started tossing nonbiodegradable McDonald's containers out of our Chevys. Or since we shoved our kids into the Vietnam Cuisinart. Or since we enslaved Africans who were just minding their own beeswax. One way or the other, the chickens were always going to come home to roost, right?'

From the back of the studio came the chunky squeal of a heavy object being muscled across a concrete floor. Forty or fifty moans, as multitoned as a cathedral organ, rose at once, with chiseling clarity.

Baseman's holler from the dark, 'Watch it, Face! Paddy moved the shit away from the—'

Zoë's scream. 'Push! *Push!*'

Fessler's cry. 'Oh, fuck! Oh, fuck, fuck!'

Anger filled Chuck, lit him up like a jack-o'-lantern. Scotty Rolph was the draining of charity, the scraping off of belief, and removing him from significance would be as welcome as scratching his burning face.

'You say these things,' Chuck said, 'because you like to sound smart. But you're just . . . attitude. Attitude is what's going to kill us.'

Scotty touched his nonexistent earpiece. 'What's this? Hold on. This just in: people haven't watched TV for news for like twenty years, Chuck! You want to talk about attitude? People tune in to watch *bickering*, dude. That's it. You're one of the Real Housewives of America. Congratulations!'

Chuck wasn't done. 'You, and everyone like you. *Commenters.* That's it: you *comment.* You get others like you to comment back. You tell people who think different they're stupid. You've got *nothing* to say that's original. Nothing that's heartfelt. Nothing that will help anyone. You're not trying to *do* anything. You never have. We don't need you.'

'Oh, but you do, Mr Mannequin!' Scotty spread his arms wide. 'When the world's gone mad, the only medicine is madness! The whole wide world is *J.J.'s Jamboree* now! We're all broken-down jalopies who think we're lobster dinners! So suck on the tap of whatever you've always wanted! Drink! Smoke! Snort! Live, you lousy Mendicans! Live!'

'Hold the—' Baseman, winded. 'Get the – shit, no, watch the—'

'I can't!' Zoë, terrified. 'It's falling, They're coming!'

'Fuck, fuck, fuck.' Fessler, running. 'Fuck, fuck, fuck, fuck—'

Arms and legs, thrash and kick, right beside Chuck, papers and laptop flying, and Scotty was out of his chair, laughing and applauding as Paddy loomed into view, his leviathan arms cinched around the chest of a ghoul, and not some random ghoul who'd just wiggled into the studio.

Paddy slammed Rochelle Glass down into the coanchor chair.

She hadn't looked great the last time Chuck saw her, gored throat spattering bubbly blood, the pearly gleam of her eyes matched by her drool. She looked worse now. Two weeks dead, Glass's skin was peeling. Clumps of hair had dislodged from her scalp but somehow clung to her head. Her fleshiest bits had gone green, with purple marbling the major veins. All of that might have been concealed by her caravan of makeup artists, though they would have failed at remedying her greatest sin: weight gain. Her body cavities had distended with putrefying gas, ripping her designer suit to ribbons.

Chuck tensed. He'd been lucky to escape Glass last time with no more than yanked hair plugs. This time, the second Rochelle Glass's butt hit the seat, her body quit whipping. Her milk-white eyes widened. She sat up straighter. One of her hands, all five nails broken, rose and oafishly patted her barely-there hair. Scotty Rolph stood stage right of Glass, his jaw dropped in the amazement Chuck felt. Glass remembered. These lights, these cameras. Her dying wish had been to claim the desk, and she'd finally done it.

'Fluuggh,' she said, rather amiably. 'Maahhhrrggh.' She tilted her head for emphasis and black sludge dripped from her ear. 'Slummph.'

Chuck had a vision, freakishly beautiful. He and Glass – *this*

Glass – were working together. In his mind, Chuck yielded speaking time to Glass, whose fingers smeared black gunk over her script while she moaned incoherently. Somewhere in the outside world, ghouls wandering past TVs stopped, arrested by her voice. Ceilings had been broken on network TV before. Barbara Walters, first female cohost, NBC's *Today*; Max Robinson, first Black coanchor, *ABC World News Tonight*. In death, Rochelle Glass might break the final barrier, bringing together two halves of a riven country, and Chuck would be proud to sit beside her.

The vision lasted for a gasp. Three ghouls with eyes as white as breakers rolled in from the studio's night ocean, and beyond Them, a wave of a dozen more, arms as gray as the sea. Beyond that, too many stairwell ghouls to count, scattered like spindrift. Paddy probably hadn't intended to let the ghouls actually breach the studio, but that was live TV for you.

Even in the crowded gloom, Chuck could spot the living; they moved more erratically than the dead, unsure of their purpose. He saw Tim Fessler race for the kitchen, a dead end in which his body was destined to be the next peanut butter on crackers. Zoë Shillace's uneven lope suggested she'd hurt a foot, but Chuck saw the flash of the master key ring, implying she was headed for the elevator with the means to unlock it.

Scotty Rolph shoved Paddy off the stage. The doughy giant landed in front of Camera 3, his seal bulk sweeping the legs from a clutch of ghouls who gladly collapsed atop him. Scotty, looking frantic, climbed onto the anchor desk to see better, his coke eyes and coke ears tuned for Zoë and the elevator exit. His radar locked upon its objective, and his knees bent, ready to leap past the gathering ghouls. Fueled through the nose, he just might make it.

Scotty's chest detonated, bone, meat, and blood. The bang, coming a split second later, credited the shot to Nathan Baseman, who hobbled from a nucleus of ghouls, clutching Kwame's smoking automatic. Scotty dropped to his knees, blood gouting from his chest like a certain tapped half keg. As Scotty toppled off the anchor desk, Baseman threw himself the opposite way, smashing against the desk hard enough to rattle the whole set. His head was right below Chuck, in the foreground of the gnarliest shot Camera 2 had ever framed. He fired, fired, fired, fired into off-screen ghouls.

'Keep going, Face! Don't stop!'

'They're in the studio,' Chuck reported, straight to the camera, back on the job in an instant. Despite Scotty's quivering corpse and Glass's unnerving presence, he was still the loyal messenger of his dedicated producer. 'This is our last broadcast, ladies and gentlemen – I repeat, our last broadcast!'

Baseman fired: *Crack-crack-crack-crack-crack!*

'The news is,' Chuck said calmly, 'we're going to die.'

The Glass-thing eyed him, her jaw hinging open and shut in mimicry. She cocked her head to replicate his emphasis, peaked a scraggly eyebrow into her flaking forehead. Chuck took a quaking inhale, deciding to take Glass's transfixion as a sign he was doing what he should be doing. If he could deliver his last story quickly and correctly, he might make the biggest difference he'd ever made, no matter if it were the living or dead who saw it. He raised his voice to be heard over the blasting bullets, furniture destruction, and lamentations of the famished.

'We can't help you anymore. You're on your own now, all of you. Remember what you saw on this station. The ghouls, They've taken it all. The museums, the factories, the power plants, the lakes and rivers, the highways, the homes. But don't give up hope. Please don't give up hope. Maybe those things *needed* to be taken. The government, the military, the media too – all of it was already rotted. And if it was rotted, doesn't that mean all of it already belonged to Them, the rotting?'

The last piece of furniture to fracture was the desk itself as ghouls drove Themselves into it from both stage left and right. Paint split in lightning-bolt patterns. Screws and nails whined. Ghouls piled atop either end, and both ends collapsed, just like the world. Sparks fizzed from above and the fills died, leaving only the main lights to roast tonight's special, Chuck Corso. Ghouls pressed in, a tempest of grabbing hands, except Rochelle Glass, whose blank eyes still faced the empty teleprompter. Her necrotic chin hinged up and down beneath a dangling black tongue.

Baseman pushed himself onto the remains of the desk, right where Chuck's laptop used to sit. He quit shooting. He held the gun in his right hand and with his left took Chuck's hand, their fists twice as large together. Though the older man was coated in sweat and covered in scabs, he grinned, at last the martyr he'd always dreamed of being.

'We did it, Face,' he said.

Chuck's tears cooled the itch overtaking his whole head. He nodded, though to him, Baseman had been the one to work magic upon Chuck Corso. You only had to look at the Glass-thing jawing comfortably before her Mendicans to know Chuck's transformation had been more radical than that of living to ghoul. He wanted to thank Baseman, but could only nod as two walls of decomposing flesh pressed in.

Baseman winked, planted the gun at his temple, and stared into Camera 2.

'Fuck Jansky,' he said. 'Remember Baseman.'

The producer's head exploded. Under garish studio lights, his skull became a red balloon that bobbed once before disintegrating. His headless body spun and fell to the floor behind the Glass-thing. The ghouls groaned and bent over to claim the first fresh mouthfuls. The frosted glass behind the desk shattered, the letters *WWN* dividing into sharper pieces.

The *idea* of WWN also divided, Chuck thought as his chair was wrestled away and he landed faceup on the glass-strewn floor. Scotty Rolph had been right about this one thing: a single source of truth had no more place in this America; everyone out there would wield their own tiny piece of it, each glass dagger reflecting the image of the wielder – a million truths, but no *truth*. Interesting thoughts blacked out by the slobbering heads of ghouls.

Chuck Corso fought. Of course he did. Ghouls descended. Too many for their own good. They tangled and fussed, until a single ghoul weaseled free and landed on him, a tall Black woman whose purple-gray skin made a soothing contrast with her snow-white eyes. Chuck noted the oddity of a paper name tag stuck to her blouse, supplying Chuck with an unexpected introduction to his murderer.

ANNIE TELLER
LA BREA TAR PITS

Annie Teller reached for Chuck's head with both hands. Here was another surprise: the woman had broken her fall with open hands; large shards of glass jutted from her palms like stiletto blades.

There was nothing Chuck could do. He felt the wintry tingle of his bottom lip lopped off. He saw the tip of his nose hacked away. Both eyebrows were gouged out; he watched them waggle across his vision like caterpillars. The rest he could not see but felt with perfect clarity. The cleaving of his forehead. The severing of his left ear. The tacky, pulling sensation of his face being peeled like an orange. He laughed, a freer noise without the impediments of lips and skin. He'd been under *the knife* many times before – blepharoplasty, rhytidectomy, all those fine procedures – but this was the face-lift to beat them all, the one that would reveal his true self, the one that would, at long last, make him comfortable with the nickname he'd never liked: the Face.

Steer into the Wind

They were weighed down. Nomex flight suits nabbed from a squadron ready room. Helmets, not mere cranials. Jenny ripped down a photo collage of sexy women before finding Nishimura a pair of thick-soled boots. Tools repurposed as weapons – fire ax in his hands, parade rifle on his back. The rifle ceremonial, no ammo. But it had a bayonet, didn't it? Jenny was a wisp with double his strength. She carried a sword from an officer's commissioning ritual. Ceremonial, too, and therefore unsharpened. But it was still steel, wasn't it? In her left pocket, a pilot's Beretta M9. In her right pocket, a turkey fork for close-quarters grappling. Shit gear, overall, but they ran like gazelles and dreamed like children. They could do the impossible. If Operation Bills-Lions was going to work, they had to believe.

They huddled by the deck-handler door, doused in red safety light. Nishimura put his hands to the lock.

'I'm not ready,' Jenny pleaded.

'You are.'

'What if I can't remember the MFD checklist, the IFF code . . .'

'You will.'

'What if an engine overheats, I don't know how to—'

'Doesn't matter. What matters is we try. You all set?'

'Let me tell you about the golems.'

'What? Jenny.'

'It's the only thing Father Bill said that makes sense. It's inside me like a disease. If I die out there, I want someone else to know.'

Nishimura heard Missionaries one level lower, making the noises he once made as their leader. Their hunt today was for neither food nor supplies.

'Quick,' he said. 'Real, real quick.'

'The golems are here to protect the Earth. They don't give a shit about us.'

'The golems are the ghouls? All right. Got it. Now let's—'

'Querido Dios, will one *pinche* man on this boat listen to me? *We* summon Them. That's what's important, okay? It's in some old book, Father Bill said. I don't remember. But we summon golems to *help* us, and to *help* us, They *destroy* us. It's muy importante you understand. You've got to tell other people.'

'We'll both tell them. I'm opening the door now. You got this, pilot. You got this!'

Sunlight walloped them like a typhoon. Nishimura knew he should blockade the door behind him to keep belowdecks ghouls at bay and slow down the Missionaries, but he was blinded by the diamond-white world, the black defects of the flight-deck ghouls Father Bill would not allow his adherents to kill. There were lots of Them, which meant there was no time for anything but running.

They scrambled to the port-side stern. Jenny started firing the M9. Even at a sprint, she was as good a shot as her word. Two ghouls went down straightaway from critical head-blasts. A swarm of ghouls banked from the starboard side like the shadow of a passing cloud. Their sudden appearance threw Jenny off, her bullets forcing useless spumes of cold blood from chests and torsos. Nishimura yelled at her to run, just run, and she pocketed the gun, took her sword in both hands, and sprinted.

The October 24 firestorm had warped the deck's asphalt-and-rubber coating. Jenny was athletic enough to stay upright; Nishimura wasn't. Three times he went down. The first, he bounced back up. The second, he lost his ax to a ghoul. The third, he shoved away a trio of the dead with his new brown boots until he could swing the rifle around and bayonet the middle one through the throat. Even with the delays, when he got to the F-18 Super Hornet by Elevator #4, Jenny was still under the fuselage.

'Get in the plane!' he cried.

He tried to push her toward the ladder she'd parked by the cockpit, but she pushed back. She'd knotted a nylon rope around the plane's arrestor hook as they'd discussed, but now she was sawing at it with a knife. Why this sabotage? He wanted to invoke the glow, but her words still reverberated: *Will one pinche man on this boat listen to me?* Getting an aircraft off a quarter-mile-long flight deck without the aid of catapults was beyond his capabilities. He'd watched birds take off from carriers his whole career and never seen anyone try it.

Jennifer Angelys Pagán, however, had a plan. She'd explained it, denigrating it as she went despite Nishimura's praise. On a typical carrier takeoff, hooters popped valves to let pressurized steam hurl planes off a 350-foot strip into the sky. It took two seconds. Using the whole length of the flattop would net them a thousand feet, half of what they needed to take off, and that didn't account for the warped deck. Jenny's idea was to set the brakes, then ramp the engines while watching the mast flags for advantageous winds. At the right moment, she'd release the brakes, hit the afterburner, and pray. By tethering the F-18 to a bollard, she hoped to maximize both turbines' thrust. The key was the rope needed to break exactly when she pulled the brakes or the plane would shoot to the side, off the edge of the boat.

That's what Jenny was doing. On the fly, she'd decided to score the rope with her knife so it would snap at the right moment. It felt like a long shot – how could she know how deeply to cut the rope? Moments ago, she'd been worrying about basic cockpit functions.

Jenny looked up at Nishimura. He grimaced down at her. She clenched her teeth and threw her knife at him.

He deserved it, he thought. It was men who'd ruined the world. The sooner they were all stabbed, the better. But Jenny hadn't aimed at him. The blade whizzed to Nishimura's left. He wheeled to watch the tool, not delivered by a knife-throwing expert, bop handle-first off the face of a ghoul an arm's length away.

It only befuddled the thing, but drove pins through Nishimura's body. A dozen more ghouls had closed within ten feet. He swung the rifle into his hands. The bayonet was six inches long, perilously short. By the time he might dislodge it from one ghoul, he'd be beset by another. He needed Jenny's M9.

As he thought it, a ghoul's neck spewed gray flesh and brown meat across the deck. Next to him, a ghoul's knee disintegrated into red mist. He thought Jenny was firing until he noticed the splatter patterns. He squinted up at the island and saw the glint of guns. Father Bill's guards had spotted Nishimura and Jenny and were shooting at them. The glut of ghouls provided inadvertent, temporary cover. Henstrom's voice squawked from 1MC boxes everywhere as bullets spattered like rain. Ghouls kept coming too. Dumbstruck with shock and fear, Nishimura screamed –

– a cold hand grabbed the back of his suit –

– he whirled, screaming, thrusting the bayonet, feeling the blade sink into flesh so supple he knew right away he'd made a terrible mistake.

The six-inch bayonet was buried to the hilt in Jenny's chest.

'Oh,' he sighed. 'Oh no.'

Jenny looked down. The blade disappeared into her lower left ribs. Nishimura tried to recall what vital regions hid under that area of flight suit. Lung, spleen, stomach? He did not know. Pancreas, large intestine, kidney? He didn't know, he didn't know. Jenny's hand, the one that had thrown the knife, settled upon the rifle barrel.

'Pull it out,' she gasped.

'I'm so sorry,' he said.

'Pull it *out*,' she shouted, 'and get in the *fucking plane*!'

Nishimura pulled and the blood spurt was hot against his hand and brilliant red, because Petty Officer Pagán was alive, at least for now, and before they could dwell on the ramifications of what just happened, Jenny dropped her sword, ducked under the plane, and swung onto the stairs like a child around a stairway banister. Nishimura dropped his rifle in disgust and followed, the ghouls groaning, Their skulls bonging off the F-18's underbelly. The stairs were painted white to show up on the tarmac, but what showed up on them was Jenny's blood, amoeba splotches on each step. The ladder was poorly positioned; Nishimura had to jump to make the plane's back seat, hard to do with his added pack of guilt.

'I'm sorry, I'm so sorry.'

'Hydraulics, normal. O2, off. FCS Gain, normal. Fuel dump, off.'

'You hear me, pilot? I didn't mean to!'

Jenny coughed, a burbling, soupy sound. 'External wing tanks, normal. Probe, retracted. Strobe, on. Park break, on. Flaps, full down. Anti-skid, off.'

'There has to be a first aid kit in here.'

'Shut up, sir. Landing gear lever, down. Master arm, safe.'

'You'll bleed to death, pilot.'

'Your talking is screwing up my checklists, sir.'

'Affirmative. I'm sorry. Buckling in.'

Nishimura had gone for catapult rides off a carrier before, though generally he preferred the softer exits of helos. The sheer speed of launches made them hard to recollect; what he remembered most were the boggling numbers of people involved with making sure a launch went off, a hundred people, faces blotchy from heat rash, lips blistered by engine swelter, green-shirts packing into the shooter dome, yellow-shirts waving signals, red-shirts standing by for disaster. This time, no one. Just a pilot mumbling about caution lights, crank switches, voice alerts, EMI/IFEI checks, and a helmsman who had nothing to add but panic.

'Pagán, I know you're being dutiful; no one values that more than me.'

Jenny coughed and blood speckled the windshield.

'But we've got a *lot* of ghouls out there, pilot.'

Father Bill's Legion: at least fifty were rambling across the deck, though several had fallen from Pri-Fly gunfire. Another fifty clustered by the deck-handler door Nishimura hadn't secured, denizens of the downward dark drawn skyward by instinct. That meant more might be coming, perhaps by the hundreds. Nishimura did not have to explain this to Jenny: they needed every iota of speed to get off this deck, an effort that might be complicated by the speed bumps of a hundred ghouls.

'Oh,' Jenny croaked. 'That's bad.'

Every deployment had crises, but Karl Nishimura had made a career of keeping his cool, even as it had cost him a life's worth of friends. He looked across the boat and let the glow take control one last time. There, the twenty-foot-tall reticulating barricade. What if they could raise it, catch ghouls in its folds, clear the deck of Them in one swoop? Impossible with Jenny injured. Perhaps he could figure out the aqueous film-forming foam, the sprinkler system that might send every ghoul slipping off the edge. But why get complicated? The F-18 had a six-barrel, twenty-millimeter Vulcan rotary cannon capable of four thousand shots per minute.

'No,' Jenny said, reading his mind. 'We're not hurting Them.'

'What?'

'Golems.'

'Ghouls, pilot. We could take Them out!'

'They're here to save us.'

'That's the blood loss talking!'

The F-18 roared. The world before Nishimura quintupled, joggled with vibration that sent every plate, screw, and rivet into screaming song. Jenny gunned the engine like a hot rod. Nishimura heard a sizzle and knew it was ghouls incinerating in the engine heat. Jenny had to scream to be heard, dotting the window with more blood.

'*No ammo anyway! Had to keep our weight down! Mask on! Now!*'

Nishimura felt he ought to argue, but he'd need oxygen to avoid hypoxia if they made it off the deck. It was only while snapping on the mask he realized his urge to argue had blinked away, and why? Because he trusted this pilot. It might have taken him to the last seconds of his life as a navy man, but he believed he'd made a friend, one he'd die for, not out of duty but personal affection. It meant more than any stripe or bar, and it would be a good way to die.

Through a heat haze, Nishimura watched Jenny lean from the side of the cockpit and push away the staircase. Bullets whistled past, scrunching into the jet's chest. Jenny paused halfway out. She touched her fingers to her bloody chest and began swooping them across the side of the plane. Nishimura stretched the limits of his chest straps to see what she was doing. Just below the cockpit, she'd scrawled one word in blood:

JENNY

'*There!*' she screeched. '*My name on a fucking plane!*'

The cockpit slammed shut. The latches cracked tight. The engines thundered, full thrust. Nishimura was a rattling component of a machine while Jenny cried jargon, canopy, harness, DEEC, CAS, seat, flaps, ADI, radar, TACAN, trim, IFF, circuit breakers, landing light – all spat out in seconds. With a jolt, the brakes were cut, the Super Hornet shrieking, but the nylon rope held, a second too long, the F-18 slithering to port before the rope snapped, the crack audible over the plane's hellhound howl, and they were flung, a stone from a slingshot.

Not a single one of Jenny's golems struck, for They were swept back by the scorching wind, and Nishimura was glad, because golems or ghouls or Millennialists, Their purpose was the same.

Every nail on the deck a bluff, every crack a canyon, the jet jolted and jounced as it raced the length of the too-short runway, not diverted enough by the late parting of the rope to lose much of the exit path. Neck sprained, back cracked, teeth chipped, blood thick in the mouth, eyes flat to the brain. Metal screamed, straight surfaces bent – and they were off, wheels gasping, silent and free. The bob, the plummet, the sky gone, an ocean vastness, gray cutlasses of squall, the spit of salt water across cockpit glass – the tip of the F-18's nose touched the Pacific, a goodbye kiss.

Forty-seven-thousand pounds raced along threshing waves like they were a second runaway, then up, the sky's revenge, the sun's return, soft handholds of clouds, blood down the throat, sizzling in stomach acid, the plane arcing, bending, vertical, a full four g's, he's in flight, they're in flight, cupped in a god's hand, one more whang, one last whoosh.

'*Yes!*' Nishimura bayed.

Jenny's blood-slicked hand, rising from the front seat, a thumbs-up.

The Super Hornet banked, and the whole world spun. They were crossing back over *Olympia* to catch the western wind, still at low altitude, five hundred feet over the keel. Nishimura knew Jenny was showing off; she had just enough verve left to do it. He was thrilled by her, for her, and for himself for having the great fortune of knowing her. She had fighter-pilot swagger after all.

The lowness of the pass gave them a final glimpse of the situation aboard Big Mama, a sight with which Nishimura would grapple for as long as he lived. The upper catwalks still glinted with the guns of the tower guard, but none of Father Bill's flock had spilled onto the flight deck to attempt to prevent the F-18's launch. Something else was going on. The shining steel surface outside Pri-Fly was painted red. Men were queued up single file on the ladder, awaiting their turn at sacrifice. Nishimura heard again the last thing Father Bill said.

An offering. I think our men would gladly offer up a few pieces, don't you?

These must be the 'new rites', the fulfillment of the chaplain's vision to unite man and demon, the birth of a larger Legion. Sailors drooped over railings as they wound belts around arms to stop blood spouting from handless wrists. Others, who had chosen to donate a foot, lay on the floor amid darkening pools. Father Bill himself, his Hawaiian shirt drenched in blood, stood in the center of the mess, staring up at the overhead plane.

Jenny did not disappoint; she held up a bloody middle finger.

Worse things were revealed when the other side of the island came into view. Men ferried buckets of severed body parts to the platform edge, where Captain Page and his fellow demons were fed, piece by piece. Nishimura shuddered. *TFOA,* he thought grimly. It was the cheeky acronym sailors used for a flight crew's never-ending foe: Things Falling Off of Aircraft. Things were still, in a manner of speaking, falling off.

His heart broke for good upon giving *Olympia* a final look. Hundreds of women, who'd survived ghouls and ghoulish men, were spilling from the deck-handler room and multiple access trunks. Perhaps they'd possessed functioning plat cams, and seeing the F-18 take off had compelled them to rush upward in hopes of being saved.

If the plane were armed, he'd ask Jenny to deliver mercy.

Nishimura closed his throbbing eyes and settled into his seat. Operation Bills-Lions had succeeded. His husband, his daughters, his sons, he might see them again, and that, no matter the state of the world, would be as much of a heaven, and a haven, as these quiet skies.

The cabin pressurized. Nishimura's pains diminished. Based on *Olympia*'s location, he estimated the trip to shore would take three hours. That was nothing. There should be no problems. He decided to try to smile. Like Operation Bills-Lions, he pulled it off.

He did not know he'd drifted to sleep until he made out Jenny's low voice.

'Wake up . . . wake up . . . wake up . . .'

Nishimura lifted his helmet visor. The day remained a bright, crystal gift. He yawned. His ears popped. He chuckled, a child's reaction.

'Morning, pilot,' he greeted. 'What can I do for you?'

'Oh. Good. Hello. There are two levers.'

'What's going on? We close to home?'

'Two levers. The sides of your seat. You just have to pull one.'

'Levers. Why am I pulling levers?'

'To eject.'

Their small world, already dense inside the cockpit, thickened.

'Pilot. Pagán. *Jenny.* I'm not ejecting.'

'The chairs are synchronized. We'll both eject. But I'll be dead.'

The bayonet blade to her chest. The squirting wound. The amoeba splashes. All the blood on the windshield, now frozen to rubies. He'd done this: killed her, killed himself. His chest hurt, like he'd been stabbed too.

'No, Jenny, you're going to make it.'

'It's not hard, sir. The canopy will blow. Boosters will take you away from the jet. The parachute will deploy. I've got us to eleven thousand. Not California, though. Sorry. Don't worry. If the chute doesn't pop, use the rip cord.'

'Jenny, talk to me. Let's talk this through.'

'Your seat will fall off. Pull the two cords. Steer into the wind.'

'Jennifer Pagán, you listen to me. I put that hole into you. I am not going to let it end you. You're going to make it to Detroit, you hear me?

I'm going to *get* you to Detroit. You've got family there. Friends. When was the last time they saw you? When was your last liberty?'

Her light, feathery laugh crackled through a speaker system he could not locate. If it had a microphone, he could hold it to his mouth, shout into it.

'Liberty . . .' she drawled. 'Strange word, isn't it . . . "Liberty has expired," they said . . . Hug your family and get on the boat . . . What's liberty, though . . . Liberty's freedom . . . This is liberty . . . I can feel it . . . Can't you feel it?'

'No, Jenny, no, hang on.'

'I tried . . . but it's going away now . . . it's all liberty . . .'

'Jenny, no, please!'

'I represent . . . the fighting spirit of the Navy . . .'

'That's right! You do! Come on!'

'I'll obey the orders . . . of those appointed over me . . .'

'That's me, Jenny! I'm the one giving you orders!'

'I am . . . a United States . . .'

'*Sailor,* Jenny! Say it! Say the word! You're a sailor!'

The nape of her neck became visible as her helmet tipped to her chest. Her brown curls were greasy from life too long in the dark. Though the F-18 shook, a stillness settled through Jenny Angelys Pagán. And that was that. Some miseries came strewn out over time; the mystery of the man-overboard hoaxes, how strange to think it would never be resolved. Other miseries came fast, hammers to the face. He'd never get Jenny to Detroit. He'd never know anything about her except she was the bravest pilot he'd ever known.

He stared past his fallen comrade. Beyond stretched an ocean fading from royal to cerulean blue. Land was close. Among Jenny's last rambles had been the mea culpa, *Not California, though.* Where was he headed? He could see a brown strip of beach emerge from clouds, land ahoy. Nishimura searched for the eject levers Jenny mentioned. They were easy to find, their brightness a warning.

Jenny's helmet rose back up. Joy burst into Nishimura's extremities.

'Yes! Pilot! Good! Jenny! Yes! Listen! Stay awake! Jenny, you can do it! You can land this thing! You can make it! You can—'

Her suit was bulky, her headrest formfitting. Yet she turned her head, several inches farther than should have been possible. The skin at the strained side of her neck split open with the sound of a torn rag. Jenny's oxygen mask, slathered in blood, dangled from a mouth agape and pouring black gunk and pink saliva. Through her dark visor, Nishimura could see the white pellets of her eyes.

Jenny's jaw unlocked and she hissed.

Nishimura pulled both levers despite having been told to pull only one, but he couldn't be too careful, not anymore. He was gone, whipped into an airless, blinding sky, hurled across an endless, sparkling sea, a speck of dirt in the wind, subject to so many hot, cold, hard, fast, beating, bruising sensations at once, he could feel only one thing: alone.

Very Talented

The air-break hiss, the backing-up beep, the soggy smush: early-morning sounds so familiar it took Charlie half an hour of slumberous tossing before she realized she should be concerned. They were garbage-truck noises. She got up. She did not switch on the generator. She wasn't sure she'd ever turn it on again. Last night she'd watched WWN's last broadcast. At the end, the TV camera had been jostled so that it showed only the disco colors of the ceiling lights, while the audio continued: screams, restless grunts, scuffling feet, and smacking lips.

Charlie removed a cutting board from a slot in the boarded-up front windows, her secret viewing hole. She nibbled from a bag of stale almonds and assessed the activity at the end of the block. It wasn't one garbage truck. It was three. The night they'd fled the morgue, Luis had relayed from social-media feeds that mobs were blaming the violence on Latino immigrants, who happened to dominate local trash-collecting.

Charlie's guess was that some of these Latinos, recognizing they had the strongest vehicles out there, had banded together. The trucks' crews were too distant to make out, but she could see people toting long objects. Rifles, maybe. Maybe crowbars, baseball bats, wrenches, and hatchets, like those fuckers who'd accosted Luis's Prius.

'Men with sticks,' Charlie whispered. 'They'll be the death of us.'

They were methodical: Fifteen or twenty people would encircle a house, then enter it while others, outside, dealt with neighborhood ghouls. Ten or fifteen minutes later, the raiders exited, loaded with supplies, at which point the garbage-truck caravan rolled to the next house. Charlie grinded almonds, tasting nothing. She guessed she had an hour before the crew got to the Acocella house. By then, who knew if they'd be in a charitable or shoot-first mind-set.

She didn't have it in her to run. She'd take her chances with the garbage-truck gang, see where it got her. There was just one thing she wanted to do first, something she'd put off for forty-eight hours. She didn't have to worry too much about noise. The trucks were loud; nearby ghouls would be drawn their direction.

Luis's body was wrapped in a pretty quilt. Charlie had done a fastidious job of it, binding the edges with belts she'd gathered from dresser drawers. She couldn't help but grin. It looked like a burrito. Luis Acocella, world-class complainer, had loved griping about the overstuffed monstrosities of American burritos, usually while inhaling one. The quilt was handmade, the quilter's name stitched onto a corner square. Whether from Luis's or Rosa's side of the family, Charlie didn't know. The point was, it had sentimental value, and though Charlie wasn't generally a sentimental girl, she was fine with getting a little sappy about this.

She opened the back door, checked for ghouls as well as the starving dogs she'd heard tussling on the road last night, and dragged Luis's body onto the back lawn. Luis and Charlie had been medical examiners, not gravediggers, and Mamá Acocella's burial spot was a dilettante disaster, egg-shaped and hastily filled, though it had so far evaded the noses of those dogs. She could do better. She ducked back inside, grabbed the shovel, and got to work.

Without regular watering, the California earth had desiccated. The shovel sliced through it like ash. Charlie had a three-foot-deep hole dug, next to Mamá, in thirty minutes. Ten minutes more, it was filled with Luis's body in fetal position and refilled with dirt. She hunkered next to it, her shadow forming an umbilical between mother and son. Forty minutes for the whole operation; for her goodbye, she'd only need seconds.

She held a handful of dirt. In its crumbles she felt the textures of Luis's hair, the skin on the back of his hands, his clouds of cigarette smoke, his folder of autopsy reports, his medical scrubs, the plastic case of his stupid phone, the wiry scruff of his jawline, his raspy chuckle.

'You're home,' she told him.

Charlie didn't want the garbage-truck crew busting down the Acocellas' door. When they were one house away, she stepped outside, toting a bag of clothing and supplies in one hand, waving one of Luis's white shirts in the other. The global signal for peace, but the globe didn't spin like it used to. Two men jogged over, faces red and raging. Their sticks were shotguns pointed right at her head.

'What is your name?' the first shouted. 'Como te llamas?'

Did she look lousy enough to be mistaken for a ghoul?

'Charlie Rutkowski,' she said.

'Take your clothes off,' he said. 'Desnúdate.'

'What?'

The second man grimaced but didn't lower the shotgun.

'We need to know you have not been bitten,' he said.

So she took off her clothes, a degrading act, but halfway through, she snickered. She was stripping in her boss's front yard. Always making a scene. Same old Charlie.

The men were, in fact, Latino. In the four-car wagon train behind the garbage trucks, she spotted a scattering of people of all kinds, probably liberated, willingly or not, from barricaded homes. These people – passengers all – were still and silent. After a fortnight of persecution, the garbage collectors were in charge.

Charlie expected no quarter and received none. They made her lift her breasts, separate her butt cheeks, and display her bite-free armpits and thighs. She was scared and a little angry. Maybe she should dig up Luis, show these bullies he'd been Latino too. Maybe by proxy, they'd start treating her better. Of course, by now Luis's skin was gray or blue. A girl just couldn't win.

The trucks hissed to a halt in front of the Acocella home, trailing blood. They must be pitching ghouls inside to save on bullets. Men hopped off and surrounded the house. Charlie would have gladly told them what was inside, but they didn't ask. The slightly kinder of the two men gestured for her to get her clothes back on, then herded her, with the barrel of his gun, to the last car in the wagon train, a silver Suburban. He rolled the side door open.

The SUV was crowded with women and children.

Uncountable sets of shiny, scared eyes stared at her. Charlie shivered as if she were still naked. Men, and some little boys, were outside waving their sticks, while the women and girls were stowed like luggage. Charlie wasn't stupid. She knew what was bound to happen when men got used to keeping women behind locked doors and tinted windows.

'Full up.' The man sighed. 'You'll have to cram in back.'

The man opened the trunk, revealing a narrow storage space behind the vehicle's third bench. There was already one woman back there, sitting against the driver's-side wall. Charlie crawled in and took the opposite wall. After the trunk closed, the space didn't seem so spacious.

The woman was a plump, unsmiling Latina with black hair and huge, beautiful dark eyes. Charlie forced a smile; it felt wrong, like they were pretending this was okay. She cleared her throat to say something, anything, but the woman spoke first.

'You don't remember me.'

Charlie closed her mouth and took a longer look.

'I'm sorry,' she replied. 'I don't actually live near here.'

'We met at a Christmas party,' the woman said.

'Did we? I don't—'

'This is my home.' She raised her eyebrows. 'Rosa del Gado Acocella.'

Charlie nodded. She could think of no other way to respond. The nods diminished until they were but tremors. Rosa was alive. She'd stuffed her mother-in-law's hand into a garbage disposal. She'd crawled through a window to escape. She was more capable, it seemed, than Luis Acocella, even Charlene Rutkowski.

There was no point in hiding the truth. Rosa had probably picked up on Charlie's attraction to Luis at the Christmas party Charlie didn't recall and had been, with a wife's grim foresight and patience, waiting for this day to come. Charlie knew she should apologize, but she was exhausted, not just from administering to Luis's last days but from hewing to the rules of a vanishing civilization. Maybe this new world could make allowances for shades and complexities. Maybe both Rosa and Charlie could love Luis, maybe even more for how he'd brought joy to everyone he touched.

'Do you want to go inside?' Charlie asked.

'Luis is dead?' Rosa asked.

Charlie nodded.

Rosa inhaled sharply and directed some tangled hair over her ears.

'Then no. There is nothing left I want.'

The raiders finished with Rosa's home. The garbage trucks chewed their bone-cracking, blood-gushing trash. The Suburban jerked and jounced as it swung around the cul-de-sac to start up the other side.

'Luis said tienes mucho talento,' Rosa said simply. 'Very talented.'

'Thank you.'

'Have you had to, ah, matar . . . ah, how do you say it. Have you had . . . to kill?'

From Rosa's perspective, it wasn't a non sequitur. Slicing up dead bodies with Luis in a lab; slicing up dead bodies with Luis in the suburbs. While Charlie had been inside a boarded-up house ducking harsh realities in favor of silly things, the outside world, Rosa included, had become more straightforward.

'Yes,' Charlie said. 'I have.'

Rosa nodded softly.

'It is difficult, no? What happens to your heart when you must kill what you love?'

Charlie gazed out the window. Men argued before a garbage truck compacter too full of mangled corpses before piling four still-moving bodies beneath a family swing set, which received a gasoline drenching. Soon the pile of bodies spouted in flame, engulfing the old swings, the rusty slide, childhood lost. Charlie tried to feel the fire's warmth. Rosa, she figured, had burned like that and come out charred, harder. Charlie was ready for the ritual. One more death, one more renewal, another one for the fire.

ACT
TWO

The Life of Death

ELEVEN YEARS

Zombie was a word Etta Hoffmann first heard at 189–07:33 – one hundred and eighty-nine days after 10/23, at seven thirty-three in the morning. The woman who'd uttered it said she was calling from the Cathedral of Learning at the University of Pittsburgh, where students from Pitt and Carnegie Mellon had jury-rigged a Wi-Fi signal after months of wearying work and treacherous supply runs. Hoffmann was surprised. Her ability to be surprised had not yet run out. Humans, a species in which she'd only ever held but moderate interest, impressed her now almost daily.

The woman from Pitt introduced herself as Andrea West. She said her party had accessed a patchy, skeletal, command-line rendition of the internet that expert coders, of which her party had several, could navigate, given excesses of patience and time. Eventually, they found the phone number Hoffmann had seeded on multiple government sites along with the message: *ARE YOU OK? CALL ME.*

Hoffmann took down all Andrea West had to say, though little of it was new. Two others Hoffmann had spoken to in the half year following 10/23 referred to the back-from-the-dead residual internet as 'the Corpse Web', so that was how she referenced it in her notes. As a concept, the internet had always bedeviled Etta Hoffmann. In spite of being built from cables and circuits, it pumped the fluids of humanity's hopes, fears, kindnesses, and cruelties. It had *lived,* so it made sense to her that, like human bodies, it had returned from demise.

Like everyone else, Andrea West claimed to have called to gather intel, but by then, Hoffmann knew everyone's real reason. Andrea West wanted to tell her story, hoping her life and death might matter. Everything she said went into one of Hoffmann's typed reports, though the only detail to stick with Hoffmann was *zombies*. Not *things*, not *ghouls*, not *white-eyes*, not *demons*, not *gangs*. Zombies: it felt right. Perhaps it was the finality of the letter *Z*, the end of the alphabet, just plain The End.

It was not until 286–13:21, after another dozen uses of the word by others, that Hoffmann chose to investigate it. What compelled her was not curiosity so much as economy. She had the AMLD Lending Library at her disposal; therefore, she ought to use it. The library was composed of books and movies she'd found in staff offices and desks. She'd begun with an office at the northwestern corner on the second floor and worked her way west to east, top to bottom. She organized every item by subject, on shelves in the VSDC office.

The Lending Library's DVD and Blu-ray collection was promising. Her evening routine pre-10/23 had been to consume TV shows, one episode after another, like a bag of M&M's. But in the entire building, Hoffmann found not a single complete series, and she knew it would keep her up at night if she had to skip episodes of a show, or even worse, never know how it ended. She'd stick with watching movies, played on one of a handful of computers still equipped with disc drives.

The books filled five shelving units. An unforeseen number of employees had lurid interests. Was it related to living in D.C.? She looked up *zombie* in *The Encyclopedia Macabre*. Drawn from the Kongo word *nzambi*, it was an implausible, but confirmed as authentic, practice of the Haitian Vodoun. Authorized by a Bizango council, a chemist known as a bokor infected a wrongdoer with tetrodotoxin, a poison extracted from certain blowfish. After suffering deathlike paralysis, the victim was buried, then unburied and revived as a slow-thinking slave, never to reach the final resting spot of lan gui-née, the leafy heaven of Africa. The Vodoun believed the bokor stole the victim's ti bon ange, the dynamic part of the soul.

Hoffmann pondered this long enough to disrupt her daily procedures, the most important of which was the cataloging and cross-indexing of the growing collection of survivors' stories, which she called Personal Histories. Andrea West's entry posed a dilemma. Were most people aware of the Haitian nzambi? She did not know and therefore could not say if those who'd embraced the word *zombie* did so cognizant of its etymology.

By 372–06:00, over a year since 10/23, Etta Hoffmann's conclusions were solid enough to type up, print out, and slide into a folder that served as an ongoing foreword to the collection which she'd titled (not out of ego but because it was descriptive) the Hoffmann Archive of Tales from the New World.

Her verdict was that there was no word more fitting for the 10/23 phenomenon. Here was the single, salient, doomful point: a Vodoun zombie had been judged by a Bizango counsel to deserve his fate. This new world, in which *everyone* was fated to become a zombie, implied the entire population of the world had been likewise judged.

For what sins? Hoffmann suspected the classic ones. Gluttony. Pride. Envy. Wrath. Greed. Sloth. Lust. Most people on Earth would have willingly relinquished their ti bon ange for superficial trappings. Hoffmann wondered if she should feel cheated: she'd indulged in none of these sins, yet received the same sentence. No, she decided. Living alone in the American Model of Lineage and Dimensions building ten years after 10/23, Etta Hoffmann was more content than ever.

Her serenity had had a single, but plenty disruptive, wrinkle. Six months ago, 4,095–4:55 to be precise, a woman had contacted Hoffmann via VSDC's landline. Not since the very first call, ten years before, had the ringing phone so startled her. There had not been a Personal History to take down in ten months. Hoffmann had to dry her palms before picking up the receiver, to clear her throat before saying hello.

Right away, she determined this caller was different. Since Year Eight, voices of survivors had been hushed, by habit and suspicion. Many concealed their names, believing the number they'd found on the Corpse Web to be a trap. But this woman's voice was open and clear, and she introduced herself by name. Hoffmann, however, did not trust that name, and preferred to think of the woman as Snoop.

Snoop did not want to talk. Snoop wanted to snoop. It had been ten years since anyone had asked Hoffmann questions. Closer to thirty years, really; she'd still been a teen when doctors issued their final diagnoses and her parents quit trying to reach her. Snoop reminded Hoffmann of the psychologists of her youth, placid and mild. No one was placid and mild anymore. Hoffmann was flustered. She'd grown skilled at drawing forth information – a regular Rochelle Glass, minus the outrage – but with Snoop, she had to pull out the Personal History Conversation Guide she'd typed, printed, and laminated back in Year One. Tell Me Where You Are. Tell Me How You Got There. Tell Me The Last Thing That Happened.

Snoop, devilish woman, turned the questions around.

'I've heard about you,' Snoop said. 'What's your name?'

Hoffmann referred to her guide. 'Are You In Immediate Danger?'

'People say you've been collecting stories. How long you been doing that?'

'Who Else Is With You?'

'Ten years of stories could be really important. You could help a lot of people understand how we got here. Where are you located?'

'What Experiences Do You Remember Most?'

'You're nervous about telling me. I understand. Keeping a secure location secret makes a ton of sense. And yours must be super secure to have lasted so long! You've got a D.C. phone number. Which makes me guess you're in a government building?'

'Tell Me About The People You Have Lost.'

This was how it went, every time. Eventually, Snoop had to go. Either her battery was dying or she had other calls to make. Both excuses intrigued Hoffmann. If Snoop had devised a reliable form of communication, that info belonged in the Hoffmann Archive. Furthermore, if Snoop was using her tech to converse with multitudes, those people might supply a new age of Personal Histories. Yet Hoffmann resisted making requests. It was not pride. It was concern over her requests being leveraged toward a quid pro quo. Snoop was right: in ten years, Hoffmann had never divulged her name or location.

That day, however, she'd leaked clues. She hadn't meant to. Snoop rang every few weeks, and Hoffmann, neither in the habit nor position to refuse calls, could feel herself wearing down from Snoop's incessant goodwill. When Hoffmann shied away from big questions, Snoop asked small ones. What food did she miss? Did she hate, like Snoop did, scraping candle soot off the ceiling? Snoop hit the jackpot unwittingly.

'What TV shows did you like?'

'Old ones,' Hoffmann replied instantly.

'Yeah? Me and my mom watched a ton of old TV growing up. What were your favorites?'

'*The Andy Griffith Show. Star Trek. The Dick Van Dyke Show. Lassie. I Love Lucy. Perry Mason. My Three Sons. The Honeymooners. Mister Ed. Petticoat Junction. Rawhide. Father Knows Best. This Is Your Life.*'

'Whoa,' Snoop laughed. 'That's a lot of words for you. You need to sit down?'

'I am sitting down,' Hoffmann said, but her heart was racing.

'I'm not sure I could watch them again,' Snoop sighed. 'I'd keep worrying there were zombies outside Lucy and Desi's window. Or the *Star Trek* gang was only in space because zombies had taken over

Earth. Or Mister Ed wouldn't say anything to Wilbur except how royally he's fucked. You know what I mean, lady? Hey, I'm still calling you *lady*. Come on. Tell me your name.'

'Etta Hoffmann.' She was trying to breathe.

'Etta. Well, Etta, it's nice to meet another fan of Old Hollywood.'

Hoffmann thought she heard a pause in Snoop's reply, perhaps as she jotted down the words *Etta Hoffmann*. Her throat constricted, her sight blackened, she felt hot. She reacted to nothing else Snoop asked that day. After Snoop hung up, sounding a little hurt, Hoffmann sat motionless for an hour, repeating to herself how stupid she was. Snoop had tricked her. If enough synapses of the old internet still fired in the Corpse Web, a full name was a key to a thousand locks.

Yet the next time Snoop called, Hoffmann's heart leaped, and she spoke to her again, gladly.

In bed at night, she whipped herself with questions.

Did she actually *like* being snooped on?

What if Snoop asked Hoffmann's name because Snoop honestly liked her?

Had anyone ever liked Hoffmann before?

Was it all right to want to be liked?

In the years before 10/23, Hoffmann hadn't understood friendship, but it hadn't mattered – no one wanted to be her friend. Prior to Snoop's calls, Hoffmann's friendship fantasies focused on Annie Teller. Hoffmann wanted to excuse her interest in Annie Teller as being connected to the *LaBr3aTarP1t$* password that paved the way for the Hoffmann Archive, but she did not like lying to herself. It was more than that.

As had been the case when Annie Teller roamed the halls in large, confident strides despite her telltale limp, Hoffmann had no desire to speak to her; it might crack the perfection Hoffmann attributed to the senior statistician. Hoffmann had, however, imagined being Tawna Maydew, that chubby, rose-cheeked California blond who, upon seeing Annie Teller arrive at the La Brea Tar Pits, would smile in that sensual way Hoffmann couldn't smile, feel love in her heart Hoffmann couldn't feel, and embrace Annie Teller in ways Hoffmann would never dare.

Had the La Brea reunion ever happened? Again, Hoffmann eschewed lying; it probably hadn't. America's travel infrastructure had been the first thing to go haywire after 10/23, and Los Angeles was a long, long way from D.C. But anytime Hoffmann retrieved a phone message from a woman with an English accent, her heart would make a froggy leap as she believed, for a second, it was Annie Teller reporting she and Tawna Maydew were together and happy, having built a love nest inside of the La Brea Tar Pits museum, where they held each other each night beneath a mammoth skeleton's tusks.

Hoffmann wondered if it would be considered pitiful that the workstation she used every day was Annie Teller's. Using it had made logical sense for about a week or so following 10/23, as she first discovered Annie Teller's password, then used it to access other government websites. Over ten years, though, she'd remained there. She had few personal items to hold her to her own cubicle. Two, really: a camouflage fanny pack in which she packed her daily ration of snacks, and a pink sippy cup she favored for safety reasons. If she knocked it over, water wouldn't damage Annie Teller's computer.

Hoffmann's cubicle walls had always been blank. Annie Teller's cubicle was only a little better. Hoffmann paged through old human resources memos (she'd been surprised to learn that literally no one else in the building had kept these memos on file) and reread a missive entitled 'Personalizing Your Workspace Within Acceptable Limits'. She used a color printer to print out the best emailed photos she could find of Annie Teller and Tawna Maydew – no photos of them together, naturally – and tacked them to the cubicle wall.

The rest of the computers died over time, likely from dust in their guts. Each monitor that went black felt symbolic, one more chunk of the world dropped off the grid. By 1,900–00:00, thanks to daily upkeep and periodic repair as detailed in owner's manuals Hoffmann dug up in IT, only Annie Teller's monitor still worked, the final fire of a prehistoric cave. The rest of the building's framework endured, proving the US government had, in this one way, prepared for apocalypse. Backup power kept electricity going, year after year, as well as the landlines.

Somewhere out there, perhaps, Annie Teller kept going too.

The Hoffmann Archive of Tales from the New World boasted (so far) 214 three-hole-punch binders, a gargantuan oral history of the decade after 10/23. It was a lot of paper, and office printers began to wheeze circa 1,650–00:00, after which Hoffmann used them in scheduled alternation. She discovered a vintage typewriter in a boss's office, there for kitsch value, and was on the way to getting it back into working order. If she failed, she'd revert to handwriting. She'd always had nice handwriting.

That was how she had begun: her hands, a pencil, a sharpener, an eraser, a piece of paper. The earliest callers wanted guidelines for dealing with zombies. Hoffmann, who'd never encountered one, had little to give, but received enough reports to compile a workable profile of the plague. Infection set in when a living human's bloodstream was introduced to zombie blood or saliva. There was no average time span between infection and transformation. Zombies had no trouble distinguishing between other zombies and the living. Zombies typically ate only 5 percent of a human body. Zombies never slept. Zombies seemed capable of holding grudges. Zombies exchanged information through grunts and possibly other ways no one could figure out. Zombies could be killed by brain trauma or incineration. She typed out the list and recited it when asked.

In Year Two, she learned how to jailbreak smartphones. A dozen had been left in the building, and she began using their voice memo apps to record Personal Histories. This facilitated far more accurate transcripts, which made her brim with satisfaction. What she did not like was her own voice. It bothered her, hearing herself ask the same questions over and over. Tell Me Where You Are, Tell Me How You Got There. Thinking of her stupid questions being read by future generations damaged her confidence.

She could not afford that. Therefore, she took to dropping her questions from Personal History transcripts. Really, they weren't necessary. The responses said it all. All readers would ever read from her, the archivist, would be the letter Q. In this, she found relief. Q was an elegant letter. It looked good on the page. When she thought of how future Archive users would know her only by her Q, Q, Q, she nearly smiled.

When would the Archive be ready to be read by the likes of Snoop? All Hoffmann knew was *not yet*. She was not waiting for the zombie plague to end. She had no reason to believe it ever would. She suspected she was waiting for an inciting event, the most likely of which would be her own impending death. Were she taken by a mortal illness, she'd have a simple choice: open the AMLD doors or let it become a Tutankhamen tomb for future archaeologists.

Hoffmann had never cared for objects. Her apartment had looked like her workstation: bare walls, clear countertops. The Hoffmann Archive was the only physical thing she'd ever adored. She trailed her fingers along the binder spines and encouraged her mind to forget Snoop. Her thoughts tumbled, as they often did, through a decade of Personal Histories more unpredictable than any TV show she'd ever watched, including *Lost*.

The early years had surprised her with how many Personal Histories included monkey's-paw lessons: be careful what you ask for. Now she took it as a given. Unlike Hoffmann, most humans lived in perpetual states of dissatisfaction, and regularly imperiled secure situations to acquire better things. A fancier car to navigate zombie-ridden off-roads. Clothing and hair products to maintain beauty standards that no longer mattered. Money – people, their brains running on habit the same as zombies, kept raiding vaults and getting cornered.

They told her all about it, seeking absolution that she, simple transcriber, could not offer. It was unfortunate how often the VSDC phone became a suicide hotline, given how poorly equipped Hoffmann was to offer comfort. In truth, she did not believe suicide was an invalid response. It made her think, yet again, of Haitian slaves, wretched from plantation work, anxious of losing their ti bon ange, fearful of never reaching lan guinée – suicide was their one way to control their fates. A man who called Hoffmann from Minnesota said he and others lived in a building so fortified they could live their whole lives in comfort, but he was going to shoot himself anyway, and not in the head, because at least zombies *did* something, at least zombies had *desire* and *drive* and wanted to *keep going*. Hoffmann was intrigued enough to create a new index entry, which she spent months retrofitting throughout the Archive:

Suicide
   methods of
   reasons for
   as a means to becoming a zombie

She pondered this entry each time she edited the index. Etta Hoffmann could not stop comparing her hunger for stories to a zombie's hunger for flesh. Stories kept her alive as much as canned beans and bottled water. Flipping through the Archive was like watching every TV show at once: situation comedies, wildlife programs, soap operas, detective series, hospital dramas, current-affair magazines. She'd known life's essential truth back when all she did was log VSDC data; nowhere was there more life than in death. For ten years after 10/23, that thought kept her going. It kept her from considering becoming a page number next to *Suicide*.

Twenty months after John Doe, on 662–08:51, Etta Hoffmann received the first and last phone call she ever received from someone she knew. It was Elizabeth O'Toole, one of AMLD's final four before she ran off with Terry McAllister. Annie Teller's status as Hoffmann's favorite coworker was largely predicated on the fact the two of them had never spoken. Among those with whom Hoffmann had been forced to interact, she liked no one better than Elizabeth O'Toole. Before leaving the bunker with Terry McAllister, Elizabeth O'Toole's last act had been to entice Hoffmann to come with them.

'It's you,' Elizabeth O'Toole said in greeting. 'The Poet.'

It took Hoffmann several seconds to identify the voice. The signal was fuzzy, and Elizabeth O'Toole sounded like her throat had been damaged.

'Yes,' Hoffmann replied. She understood she did not experience emotions the same way as others, but felt a force akin to hands upon her back, pushing her to acknowledge the moment's narrative drama. She shuffled through the Personal History Conversation Guide, brand-new back then, and pressed sweaty fingers to her pencil. 'Tell Me Where You Are.'

'I didn't think you'd still be there. Hoffmann, how are you *living*?'

Hoffmann stared at the pencil point, the paper. What mattered was where they met. The woman who gripped the pencil, who held the paper steady, did not.

'I . . .' she began. 'Tell Me Where You Are.'

Elizabeth O'Toole laughed. The bad signal split it into digital mist.

'You haven't changed. I guess I'm glad. Everything else has. I really didn't think you'd be there. But we have this phone, it's like, this giant, military *thing,* size of a lawn mower, huge rubber antenna. It's not even American. It's got, what do you call it? Cyrillic? I think it's Russian. Remember that politician who said she could see Russia from Alaska? I guess they came on over. Seem to be gone now. Made good equipment, though. This phone really works. Naturally I said, who would we even call? And Terry said, "The Poet. Call the Poet." '

Hoffmann wrote, *Military telephone. Possibly Russian.* She paused. 'Terry McAllister?'

'We did it, Hoffmann. Terry and I made it out of Georgetown. Got up to Harrisburg. Got on a train. A train, you believe that? Crossed into Canada. Since then, it's been north. Ontario, Manitoba. I'm not sure anymore. We might be in the Northwest Territories? I just don't know. All I know is, it's cold. Terry's the one who said we had to go north. He was saying it before we left the office. Fewer people up north. The dead ones, They'd be too cold to move. He was mostly right. We didn't see a whole lot. They're slower up here, for sure. You can see Their tracks in the snow. Blood shows up really clear. You usually hear Them coming too – the ice on Their joints pops. What was your question? Where are we? I guess I answered it. How are you, Hoffmann?'

Hoffmann gazed around. The usual slats of light, everything in its place.

'I'm . . .' She consulted her notes. 'Tell Me The Last Thing That Happened.'

Elizabeth O'Toole's chuckle was not as friendly as it once was. 'Talkative as always, huh? The last thing that happened? Oh, let's see. There were the wolves. They followed us for a while. Picked off most of our group, actually. There were the Inuits. They had bows and harpoons. These fucking things called ulus they used to cut people's heads off. I don't know what they were thinking. We were talking, we were alive, but they kept at us. They don't want us up here. We're ruining it somehow. Oh, and polar bears. I don't remember knowing that polar bears were so aggressive. I guess they changed! Makes sense, I guess. Humans aren't the dominant species anymore. Might as well get in there with your fangs and claws and take some shit back. I guess no one's taken any of yours yet, huh?'

Next Q, next Q. 'Are You . . . ?'

The static blasted, a gale wind over icy rock. 'You ever hear from John? John Campbell? I hope he made it. I doubt he did.'

'No.'

'What about Carrie Wilmot? I think about her a lot. All the backpacking she did? She might be surviving out there.'

'No.'

'Athena Sherman? She'd go *off* on your ass. She could be a leader now.'

'No.'

'Oh, what about Buffy Carter?' Elizabeth O'Toole laughed. 'I remember catching Ole Buff in the New Mother's Room making out with Jimmy Freestone. What a hero.'

Dan Mangold, Ginny Ullmann, Jamil Chalk, Rolando Grose, Bridgette Hannums, Erica Jessop, Trey Fernandez, Betty Lamb-Cursley. Names that were as dry as the paper Hoffmann wrote on, but were a fireworks display of memories to Elizabeth O'Toole. Even when the snarled reception of the Russian phone made identifying some words impossible, Hoffmann could make out laughter and weeping. To recall these people and their dull, silly, irritating, clever antics was to resurrect them, molecule by molecule. Hoffmann understood and was patient.

Finally, one of Elizabeth O'Toole's laughs elongated into a sigh.

Hoffmann recognized it from romantic movies. Time for shut-eye, though the lovers could gab all night. Many calls to the VSDC number concluded with sighs like this. Hoffmann wondered if such a sound would be the world's last. Not a bang, not a whimper, just the glum little sigh of accepting the end had come.

'Well, Hoffmann,' Elizabeth O'Toole said. 'It's been—'

'Wait.'

Hoffmann's fingers bore down on the pencil. The lead cracked. The bedrock on which she stood cracked too, and her only hope to avoid the crevasse was to say something that might convey the twinges of care and concern she felt. This was far more difficult for Hoffmann than living in solitude or knowing that most of the people she'd ever met were dead.

'Is . . . is Terry McAllister . . .' She reminded herself any question she asked, no matter how stupid, would appear in the record only as *Q*. 'How . . . how is Terry McAllister?'

Elizabeth O'Toole's pause was the call's longest. Polar wind shrieked like a dying animal. Electricity popped like hundreds of small bones underfoot. When she spoke, her voice was one more slashing, sinuous facet of the wind.

'Let me tell you something, Hoffmann. I don't know if anyone's ever said it. Certainly they didn't when we all worked together, and no one knew shit about anyone, even if they worked ten feet apart for thirty years. You're brave, Hoffmann. Okay? You're smart. When all the rest of us are dead and gone, or dead and walking, you're going to still be going. You're going to survive this shit, Poet. All of it.' The shivering sound might have been her exhale.

'Terry's dead. Zombies. Riding a dogsled. Sounds like a bad joke. It sounds funny. It was not. Poor dogs, you know, we train them to do certain things, and they lose their souls, maybe. They just want to be good boys and good girls. They carried those zombies right up to our igloo and – well. Anyway. I loved him. I did love him. So thank you for asking, Hoffmann. Thank you, Poet.'

Nine years separated Elizabeth O'Toole's only call from Snoop's first. That was a long time to go without being asked Qs requiring personal introspection. Hoffmann abhorred introspection. Her sleep, a decade smooth, grew fitful, goosed by thoughts of Snoop, that prying, devious woman whose calls made Hoffmann's heartbeat skip. It was distressing to realize, during these sleepless stints, how it was *asking* Qs, not answering them, that cut you open like cake and revealed your layers.

Snoop's breezy attitude made Hoffmann surmise a new era was beginning. A good thing, probably, though she thought she might prefer the Second Dark Age. Hoffmann could take no more credit for that phrase than she could *zombie;* it had filtered up through the calls. In those years, energy grids collapsed, cities and towns went dark, food production and waste management systems foundered, and all methods of sharing information – the mortar binding civilization's bricks – dissolved.

You could find motifs in each year of the Second Dark Age if you had good records, and Hoffmann had the best. Year One, for instance, felt like endless night, through which you could see only a few feet at a time. It seemed every Tom, Ben, and Harry (was that how the saying went?) called Hoffmann from inside boarded-up houses where fiery arguments were shredding survivors to little pieces, easier for zombies to munch.

Year Two brought war. Even to nonpolitical Hoffmann, this felt inevitable. Certain countries were less equipped to confront zombies, and their chaos was irresistible to nations sharing borders and nurturing grudges. There were invasions. Drones, tanks, fighter jets,

ground troops. Historic cities razed to the ground. Unchecked geno-
cides. Any two-sided battle spawned a third side that routed both
belligerents. Rumors surfaced of zombies using guns – just a few of
Them, and clumsily, and no report was ever confirmed. Still, a troubling thought on a number of levels. Anything They knew, we'd
taught Them.

In some cases, there was no tussling. Nuclear weapons were
deployed with the justification that, to destroy zombie hotbeds, one
had to obliterate them. Whether that was merely an excuse or not, it
did not work. The bombs turned famous skylines into tundras of
radioactive scrap and murdered what Hoffmann estimated were tens
of millions, most of whom came back as zombies – millions of Them,
all at once. Rumors reached Hoffmann that atomic zombies were the
worst of all, able to kill without a touch. Their flesh radiated death.

Year Three was embodied by exodus, out of cities, into the country. Hoffmann received calls from odd area codes preceded by odder
country codes. Often these were islands off the edges of America,
occupied under the assumption the surrounding water would protect them. It never did. Islands were equivalent to a battlefield's high
ground; everyone wanted to control them, resulting in per capita
bloodshed that outdid the biggest cities. Hoffmann heard the story
of an island wiped clean of its population, without a single death
attributed to a zombie. Year Three taught the living that safe places
could be the most dangerous of all.

Tucked away in her bunker, Hoffmann did not fully appreciate
the Second Dark Age until Year Four. Call volume fractioned; Hoffmann, needing a mission, began her cataloging and indexing project.
From intermittent updates, she gleaned the most successful survivors established themselves in structures with similar benefits to
AMLD: sports arenas, grocery warehouses, shopping malls. In a single week beginning with 1,471–00:00, Hoffmann received no fewer
than seventy calls from the same Pennsylvania number. People were

taking turns on a functional phone to describe a high-rise run by the rich that had fallen to zombies, which were coming for them now too – the nouveau riche – so they'd better run, except they simply had to tell their stories first, even if it killed them.

At 1,909–02:35, well into Year Five, Hoffmann spoke to a population specialist who insisted zombies now outnumbered the living, four hundred thousand to one. Hoffmann had to get out a calculator to come to grips with it. According to a book in the AMLD Lending Library, Earth's population on 10/23 had been around eight billion. The absolute best-case scenario suggested the planet now contained 7,999,980,000 zombies, versus a mere 20,000 living people.

Hoffmann sifted through her feelings. She could not help but pinpoint a silver lining. If the specialist's numbers were accurate, humans were doing a first-rate job of devising ways to contact her. The Archive included Personal Histories from a higher percentage of the living than she'd believed. She used her nascent index to shuffle through the first five years of impossible tales.

Housewives forming covens as a means of survival. Stopgap police forces burning citizens to contain what they stubbornly believed was a biological agent. A young man encouraged by the chaos to play out delusions of vampirism. A troupe of ren-fair motorcyclists who believed their Arthurian code could withstand any strain. A paraplegic man trapped indoors, tortured by his helper monkey, begging her to send help. Such strange tales, and Hoffmann read them over and over. One day they might remind us who we used to be, and who we tried to be, and that recollection could save the world.

Year Fucking Six. Multiple callers, in quivering voices, referred to it this way. Everything changed in Year Fucking Six. Etta Hoffmann had begun to think people were getting their legs under them. The calls in Year Five had bolstered this assumption. No one sounded optimistic, but no longer did they sound shattered. She detected the grim fortitude she used to hear from retirement-age coworkers who'd seen it all. Shit happens. You move on. End of story.

But the story was just getting going.

Naturally, she took note of it the first time she heard it. She even marked the page in the binder with a neon-pink adhesive note. On that day, 2,297–18:05, a man named Mike – a prosaic name for a fellow whose words would be writ large in history – spun his yarns well past Hoffmann's strictly held quitting time of six o'clock. She was peeved and impatient, nearly enough to miss a detail so startling, she went off script to ask a Q.

'You just said . . . did you say . . . the zombie was . . . a champ?'

'A *champ*?' Mike scoffed. 'I did not say that.'

'Did you say it was . . . a chump?'

'The zombie was neither a champ nor a chump. Or a chomp, for that matter.' Mike sighed in irritation. 'The zombie was a *chimp*.'

From this asinine interplay Hoffmann first learned of the development that would, she believed, end any attempt by humanity to take back the world. Mike was calling from a sheriffs' station northwest of Memphis, where he and two others, while scrounging suburban streets, had come across a pair of chimpanzees outside a Long John Silver's.

A chimp sighting by itself was not implausible. Animals left to starve in zoos had started breaking out as early as ten days after 10/23, and exotic animals had taken up residence, and multiplied, in public parks, city streets, and shopping centers that now seemed designed specifically for their pleasure. Hoffmann had fielded three corroborating accounts that elephants were doing especially well, those able descendants of the La Brea woolly mammoths.

Camels in Chicago, lions in Indianapolis, zebras in Seattle, all thriving. Chimps in Memphis? Not so strange. Mike agreed, until his party saw the simians loping toward them. That was concerning.

Rabies had mushroomed since 10/23. In a vacuum of vaccinations, every mammal was a potential threat, from cats and dogs to rabbits and foxes. The chimps were rabid refugees from the Memphis Zoo, Mike suspected.

It was only when the chimps got closer that Mike realized They were dead. Their black fur was purple and shining with hardened blood. Their bowels hung loose and They were missing segments of Their groins, armpits, and necks. When Mike and his friends waved their weapons, the chimps did not flinch. Their white eyes rolled and They kept coming on feet and knuckles, moving together as if following the same command. When one's lips peeled back from its crooked yellow fangs, so did the others'.

'We had to brain the zombie apes the same way we do zombie people,' Mike said. 'Turned from chimps to chumps, I guess you could say.'

Hoffmann consulted the Lending Library. In Year Fucking Six, she'd do that a lot. A well-thumbed medical reference from the desk of a hypochondriac statistician explained the theory of simian immunodeficiency virus, how it infected people who ate chimpanzee meat before mutating into HIV. There was, therefore, a precedent for sharing a virus with this species. While disturbing, it did not seem disastrous. Zombie chimps might cause trouble in the Congo, and wherever else chimps lived in the wild, but the world zoo population could wreak but limited havoc.

Two months later, Hoffmann received an overnight phone message alleging zombie rats. A young woman calling from someplace where there was a deafening, metallic echo begged for help. Through shrieks and sobs, she said her brother had killed a bunch of rats, same as every day, except this batch, before he could bag Them, wiggled back onto Their tiny, clawed feet and charged, grappling up legs, leaping to chests, knotting Themselves in hair. Her whole family was in different stages of pale-skinned, dark-socketed, zombie-bite death, and it wasn't fair, they'd made it all the way to Year Fucking Six.

Hoffmann believed the notion of a rat that would not stay dead might cause the most hardened renegades to go fetal. Though she had no particular fear of rodents, the news felt like the breaching of a castle's walls. Zombie chimps, that made some sense. Zombie rats? She did not need a lab coat to understand some bigger barrier had been broken. Literal barriers would need to be rethought as well; determined survivors could build obstructions large enough to keep out two-legged zombies. Could they also build them finely enough to keep out little scurriers?

Back to the Lending Library. A book on great disasters, a chapter on plagues. New York City alone houses two million rats. Paris, six million. London, seven million. Hoffmann recalled a bit of AMLD watercooler chat, one staffer bemoaning pest problems, the other citing a supposed truism: no one was ever more than six feet from the nearest rat. We just let ourselves forget it, that's all.

There would be no more forgetting. Not for Hoffmann either. Calls she received about zombie rats were not localized: Utah, Wisconsin, South Carolina. The switch on rats had been pulled everywhere, and she had no reason to doubt the next rat that died at AMLD would not decompose in civilized silence. It would roll back over, sniff her out, and hunt her down, its tiny red eyes gone white.

No more slippers. Hoffmann started wearing the tallest boots she could rustle up in her size, which happened to be the most stylish items she'd ever put on her body. Red leather, chunky heels, laces all the way up to her knees. Hoffmann sharpened the end of a broom and carried it everywhere, including to bed. No more sleeping on the break room sofa. She moved the cushions onto a break room table, then slathered the table legs in Crisco to make them too slippery for rodent feet. As a final safeguard, she coated the room's perimeter with flour each night, so she'd know in the morning if any little toes, zombie or not, had come tramping.

Sleep no longer was a sure thing. One night, she looked around the moonlit break room, absorbing the absurdity of her bedtime routine. She tried to imagine the defences others out there had devised. She imagined metal bars being inserted into plastic housings, daily caulkings, small-gauge wire. Right before she drifted off, she gasped back awake. What she was imagining were *cages*, the kind meant for hamsters, gerbils, chinchillas, guinea pigs, and, yes, rats. Only people were locking *themselves* inside.

Yet another trip to the Lending Library. This one on a hunch, in the middle of the night. She sat on a stool, her habit now to keep her booted legs free from zombie-rat surprise, and browsed. Someone in the building had owned a trove of self-help and inspirational books, including one on 'being kind'. Hoffmann, dismissive of rote politeness, had nearly chucked it. But the book had a chapter on empathy, and when her gaze settled on a list of the most empathetic animals, she felt a lonely, echoing sorrow for what the world had become.

In the top spot, humans.

In the second spot, chimps and orangutans.

In the third spot, rats.

The chapter included plenty of unfollowable specifics. The roles of the neocortex, right supramarginal gyrus, temporoparietal junction. But the bigger stuff she understood. When a rat was trapped, its fellow rats attempted to free it. They would save it morsels of food. If the rat was freed, it was affectionately nuzzled. Females out-empathized males, no surprise there, but all rats exhibited pro-social behavior once attributed solely to primates.

Hoffmann shelved the book. What it suggested about the zombie disease was too cruel, and she didn't want to memorize the exact order of the animals on the list. She didn't think she could know the precise shape of the horror to come and still lift herself from her spike-legged, flour-encircled table-bed each morning, not without paging to the *Suicide* entry in the Archive index and wondering what it would look like with another page reference after it, just one more.

It was rare for her to bury her head, but she knew why this one hurt. She'd always felt a kinship with animals. That was different from *loving* animals; she'd never wanted a pet. But she recalled spending school recesses alone on the playground, staring into the woods beyond the chain-link fence, knowing she shared more with steady, watchful squirrels, rabbits, and birds than she did the screeching, frenetic, unpredictable grade-school monsters behind her.

Teachers, school psychologists, and even fellow classmates, once they had the vocabulary, liked to explain to Etta Hoffmann that she lacked empathy. She never believed that. She had empathy, the same way animals had it: hidden from the loud, grabbing, demanding world, experienced in her own private ways. Losing animals to undeath hurt more to her than losing people, because the only thing that was certain about the zombie plague was that animals were not to blame for it.

No one really got over losing dogs. Losing dogs was like losing the war. It was the final betrayal, not by dogs Themselves, but by God, or Science, or whatever other powers you chose to blame. Hoffmann knew dogs were special. She'd seen *Lassie, The Adventures of Rin Tin Tin, Benji, Marley & Me, Homeward Bound*. Dogs were our protectors, our partners, our friends, our babies, our elders. The love between humans and dogs was the best example of the planet's potential, how every living thing might harmonize.

Evidence became irrefutable on 2,502–00:00. Loyal dogs, their formidable sniffers and radar ears more helpful for survival than anything humans could offer, had been welcomed in thousands of shelters and hideaways. Overnight, They became terrorist bombs. The earliest stories Hoffmann heard involved dogs, either dead via incident or old age, digging Themselves out of Their shallow graves. Even dead dogs were excellent diggers.

It took a lot of killing, more than it should have, before people accepted the new reality and dragged their beloved dogs from their homes by the collars. Hoffmann could not stop herself from envisioning it. Their confused eyes. Their flattened ears. The low wag of their tails, eager to make things right. People would bludgeon their dogs to death with shovels and baseball bats, taking care to destroy, beyond all doubt, the same heads they'd stroked during dark days, the same muzzles they'd snuggled to their necks during cold nights.

What would happen if the zombie virus transferred to mosquitoes? Upon the lifeless planet would sit zombie people with nothing to do but accept the face licks of Their zombie dogs, each lap of Their tongues peeling away another layer of epidermis, then muscle, then tendon, until the zombies' faces were gone and Their yellow skulls grinned for infinity, or at least until zombie people and dogs alike blew away, dust in the wind.

Hoffmann credited her impatience to bid good riddance to Year Fucking Six for inspiring her revelation in Year Seven. The idea came to her while she was working on the Archive.

Cannibalism had been an inherent, if not explicit, element in every zombie story Hoffmann had read and heard. Zombies were people who ate people; thus They were cannibals. Cannibalism had no entry in the Archive index. It was *every* entry. The rise of animal zombies revealed the flaws in this assumption. To attain cannibal status, a creature must consume another of its own kind. But. Were zombie chimps eating living chimps? Were zombie rats eating living rats, zombie dogs eating living dogs? They were not. All zombies, no matter Their species, pursued humans. From this simple fact Hoffmann drew two startling conclusions.

The zombie virus was not cannibalistic.

The zombie virus was *antihuman.*

The world got quieter after this realization, as if the AMLD building had been buried in snow. The sense of danger that had slept in Hoffmann's gut for seven years unfolded and grew claws. Humans were not the incidental victims of a natural disaster. They had been specifically targeted for annihilation. The gradual zombification of the animal world was tantamount to a biblical flood, with people being reduced to a handful of Noahs.

It was newspeople who needed to know. Telling them, in Hoffmann's view, was empathetic. In Year Eight, Etta Hoffmann added a postscript to the last of her Qs: *Please notice, zombie animals only attack humans, which means humans are being purposefully eliminated. Goodbye.* It went poorly. Reactions were sputtering and furious. Confrontation had always sickened Hoffmann. She would run from the phone and throw up, each splash of vomit sounding like Q, Q, Q.

Hoffmann's antihuman warning might have had a severe influence on survivors' acceptance of their withering relevance. It might have had no impact at all. Either way, fewer and fewer calls came through after that. The last significant wave of news Hoffmann received revolved around vegetarianism. Meat had been eighty-sixed from the menu. No one trusted an animal not to return to screaming life under their butcher knives. Hoffmann believed this culinary pivot was overdue. For eight years, she'd transcribed descriptions of animal bones piled into small mountains, dry creek beds flowing with animal blood. It was unsustainable slaughter, the bison massacres of the Old West all over again.

Hoffmann had read all about the things people had done to animals. Pigs crushed into manure-filled cages, turkeys eating one another in teeming sties, chickens ground up while still alive. Follow the logic, Hoffmann told herself. If nature was having its revenge for how we treated animals, what had we done to *our fellow humans* to make the initial wave of zombies come after *us*? She considered that certain *S* entry in the Archive index so often now, the paper began to wear through.

Without making any sort of dramatic declaration, Hoffmann began to tidy her affairs. Shaping up the Archive's preface. Establishing a comprehensive table of contents. Testing materials to determine what might best protect the Archive from moisture and rot. Piecemeal processes that might take a year or so to complete if she wanted them perfect, which she did. It would give her time to come to terms with not just *the* end but *her* end.

Between January and April of Year Nine, she received only four calls. None of them had new information. All had a fare-thee-well flavor. Having given up all hope for restored equilibrium, people were fleeing old safe spaces, even those with access to landlines or the Corpse Web, with the intent to migrate as animals once had, roaming and grazing, eyes ever open for that night's home.

With living people forced to scurry and burrow, the planet would be largely free of human colonization for the first time in two hundred thousand years. Hoffmann wondered what this would mean on a global scale. It was beyond anything covered in the Lending Library. Only when she was half-asleep atop her Crisco-slicked table-bed would her mind dislodge from its usual rails of logic and drift about. She dreamed zombies were the new indigenous people, native to the land in a way few others were. The big difference was They'd been created in all lands at once. Earth, its entirety, was Theirs. Hoffmann thought there was something graceful about that, even given the ugly flip side: the living cordoned off in bleak reservations, making do under conditions little better than what they'd once inflicted upon livestock.

Hoffmann had not gone entirely unnoticed over the decade. Zombies had coalesced on occasion, tipped off by some unknown indicator. Hearing groans and palm slaps, she'd go to the upper floor and gaze down at the wedge of D.C. she'd come to know so well. Once electric with pink cherry blossoms and bright green grass, now a blast zone of concrete shavings and windblown dregs. From up there, she'd take measure of the zombie threat. Usually just a couple. Sometimes a dozen. Once, in Year Five, seventy-nine passed like sap down tree bark, a slow, breathtaking spread.

Only in Year One and Year Two had humans tried to get inside. Hoffmann did not like to think of it. She did not feel sorry for how she reacted. But she knew, according to old standards, she *should* feel sorry. The tall, bearded man, a vacant baby carrier still strapped to his chest, who'd yanked on the AMLD door handle, desperate to evade the zombie ranks behind him; Hoffmann watched him get eaten. The teenage boy, lurking in the predawn, wearing a goofy Hula-Hoop contraption that kept zombies at an arm's length: if anyone deserved to share Hoffmann's safety, it was that kid, but she ignored his efforts. The family of four who'd somehow deduced AMLD was occupied and screamed to be let in for forty minutes; Hoffmann, unwilling to advertise her location to every zombie and raider in D.C., was prepared to break a second-story window and pelt the poor family with heavy objects. She would have, too, if the family had not been chased off by ten zombies in football uniforms.

Etta Hoffmann was no hero.

She knew that about herself on 4,095–4:55, the day, hour, and minute of Snoop's first call. Snoop, who wanted to learn so much about her. Snoop, who convinced Hoffmann to trust because it was the right thing to do. *Ten years of stories could be really important,* she'd said. *You could help a lot of people understand how we got here.*

If Snoop knew the truth of how much Hoffmann had 'helped' people, she'd quit calling. After Snoop slyly elicited Hoffmann's name, Hoffmann believed her days were numbered. She altered her schedule for the first time in a decade, working two additional hours per day. She completed a final draft of her preface, at last satisfied with her instructions for the Archive's use. She finished the vast, nested table of contents she felt would be most helpful to future users. She settled upon watertight, industrial-strength, self-adhering stretch plastic, available in the maintenance room, to shrink-wrap the Archive.

Lastly, she began to approach the idea of suicide not from an oblique angle but with the forthrightness she applied to other issues. It was a quandary. She had no gun. She did not know which toxic chemicals might be fatal if swallowed. The building was not tall enough to jump from. She did not trust herself, or the aged ceiling, to handle a hanging. Setting fire to herself put the Archive at risk. Slicing one's wrists, she'd read, was one of the least reliable options. The only surefire method, she concluded, was going outside and letting the zombies have her.

She thought about it every day. Taking off her clothes so she'd be easily bitable, disassembling her barricade, calling for zombies to come get her. Day after day, she did not do it. Not even after spotting the first zombie rats at AMLD, two waddling side by side down the center of a main hallway. She scolded herself mercilessly. Classic Etta Hoffmann, the girl who'd frustrated every doctor, relative, and would-be friend into giving up on her, immobilized by the idea of disrupting routine.

She had only herself to blame when Snoop came knocking.

Hoffmann always got up early, five thirty on the dot, but this was even earlier. A *thunk-thunk-thunk,* steadier than any noise a zombie could make, jostled her awake. Her drowsy brain decided the *thunk-thunk-thunk* was distant drums, the kind characters in old adventure flicks heard coming from jungles full of headhunters.

'Etta? Let us in, okay?'

Already lost in jungle vines, Hoffmann's bleary thoughts turned to Haiti, where bokors stole offenders' souls. Hearing her own name spoken aloud after ten years was like hearing proof her soul, too, had been stolen, and the bokor was outside, teasing her with it, offering to give it back if only she'd be a good nzambi, do as she was told.

'Etta, it's not safe out here. If you don't open up, we're going to break in.'

It was Snoop. Her voice sounded the same as on the phone, if less patient. Hoffmann inspected the Crisco-caked table legs for rat fur and the floor flour for rat prints, and got up. She could think of no better way to handle her cold dread than sticking to routine. She checked the windows for threats. Got dressed. Laced up her red leather boots. By the time she got to the workspace, the lobby clatter had changed from breaking glass to squealing furniture. Beyond that, the fleshy thumps of zombies being dispatched with blunt objects.

There was no telling if Hoffmann would be dragged away without time to prepare. She tightened her camo fanny pack. She clipped her pink sippy cup to her belt with a carabiner. She took a deep breath and let it out slowly. Her stomach burned, her chest fluttered. She was standing in the center of the main room, with no expectation of what might happen next, when Snoop marched in.

She wore sensible, tight leather clothes. Elastic cords were wrapped around her legs, holding in place homemade sheaths for a long knife and a foot-long sharpened steel pipe. Above the collar of her bomber jacket, a black hockey helmet.

'Etta,' Snoop sighed. 'I'm sorry.'

Hoffmann said nothing. Always better to watch and wait.

In the background, the rasps and clucks of her ten-year-old bulwark being shoved back into place.

Snoop pulled off her hockey helmet. Her face suggested late forties. She had thick blond hair lopped at the shoulders, a safe choice. She had burn marks on her arms and a fierce red scar squiggling down her left cheek and neck. Keeping a cautious eye on Hoffmann, Snoop moved, passing rows of cubicles until she and Hoffmann were only six feet apart. Etta Hoffmann found herself staring at Snoop's feet. Attached to her boot soles were one-foot-square metal grates. Hoffmann guessed why, and felt admiration. The edges were crusted with the dry guts of zombie rats.

'I know how this looks,' Snoop said. 'It looks like I tricked you. There's an element of truth to that. But what I've found is people like you – people alone? – they get used to thinking certain ways. They can't see the bigger picture. They don't remember there *is* a bigger picture. But there is. It's the picture of the whole world.'

A man's voice rang from the lobby: 'Less talk in there! They're gathering.'

Snoop's gaze wandered to the 214 shelved binders. Next to it, Hoffmann noted with a pang of frustration, was the plastic wrap she hadn't had time to apply.

'Is that . . . ?' Snoop's voice lowered to a hush. 'Is that it?'

Hoffmann nodded.

Snoop turned her head over her shoulder and shouted.

'Hart, Lowenstein! Close up shop! This is going to take some time!'

More activity in the lobby, though no complaints: the sounds of their lockdown had a curt efficiency. Snoop turned back around and chewed her lips.

'Yes,' she conceded, 'we're taking it.'

Hoffmann thought she should feel grief, but instead felt only lightness. She'd carried those binders on her back for a decade.

'What I want to assure you,' Snoop said, 'is we intend to take care of it. What you've got here, Etta, is worth more than all the gold in the world. If you're going to start over – and where I live, we *have* started over – you need a sense of history. You have to know where things went wrong. I know you think the Archive is safest here. I know you're scared if we move it, we'll endanger it. But we've done this sort of thing before, we've—'

'Take it,' Hoffmann said.

Snoop hesitated. 'You understand I'm not threatening you.'

'No one calls anymore,' Hoffmann said. 'Except you. You might as well take it.'

Snoop nodded cautiously. 'Okay. Thank you. We've got this armored wagon, wait till you see it. We can transport all of it. But that's not all we hope to take. Every library needs a librarian, Etta.'

None of Hoffmann's late-night fretting over how this encounter might unfold included this jarring proposal. She knew her reaction looked the same as ever, like Snoop's overture was a pebble plinking off a statue. The statue, however, was hollow, and the impact of the offer swelled until it dizzied her, shook her knees, until she could think of nothing at all.

Moments passed. How many? She was braced against Annie Teller's workstation, her perspiring palms crinkling a printed photo of Tawna Maydew. She looked back and found Snoop extending a canteen. She had been flanked by two men, both carrying hockey helmets, their outfits just as leather-heavy and tool-strapped. Their expressions, however, were different. They looked repulsed. Hoffmann did not understand. All the things they must have seen out there, and they found AMLD repellent?

Hoffmann followed their gazes.

They were looking at her. Her clothing, she began to realize, was not all right. Her sweatpants were ripped in fifty spots. Strings flowed from torn holes like cilia. Critical gaps were repaired with staples. Staples – had she lost her mind? You could see her underwear through a hole in the crotch. Her sweater, the best she had, was a quarter gone from mouse nibbles and striped with duct tape. The shirt beneath was ringed with stains from a decade of dribbled food.

They looked at her face. She tried to recall the last time she'd faced a mirror. Maybe eighteen months back, when she'd had to yank her third tooth with a wrench. One thing AMLD did not stock was toothpaste. Her teeth had gone an appalling array of gray, yellow, and brown. The rest of her face was in bad shape too. Chapped from dry air, rashed from mold and dust, spotted with fungus. She was pale beyond pale; this site had been built for longevity, with windows that did not open. Her hair was like something pulled from a drain, gummy and tangled into greasy tails.

The remains of last night's dinner sat on Annie Teller's desk. Was a cup of dead beetles so shocking? Protein-rich food had run thin in Year Seven, and so, going off the entomophagy described in a camping-survival book from the Lending Library, she'd started eating insects. Alongside the cup, a plate: a granola of moths, ants, crickets, and houseflies.

She'd become an insect herself, and no creatures rated lower on the empathy scale. She felt something she hadn't in ages: shame. The pre-10/23 Etta Hoffmann had rejected many trappings of civilization, but now she'd slumped too far. It had taken seeing three people in the flesh, not on the page, for her to see it.

Librarian: Hoffmann let the word settle. Without a job to do, she was more than miserable. She was suicidal. Here was a job offer for which she, the world's worst interviewee, did not have to apply. Yes, librarian. Even having only the scarcest idea what the position entailed, she'd accept it. Leaving this place, learning new behaviors, it might be the most difficult thing she'd ever done, but it might be the thing that turned her from insect back to human.

She let the word escape like a moth, before she could grab it back and eat it.

'Yes. Yes. Yes.'

She nodded too, in case her words came out mealy. Her gaze was fixed on the floor when Snoop's hand took hold of her shoulder. Hoffmann had always despised being touched, and after so many years since even a public-transport jostle, it felt like being attacked. She retracted; Snoop flinched. Shame, a monster now, swallowed Hoffmann. She imagined she heard the stomach-acid squish of her squalid, soiled, sweaty sweater.

'We're going to get you cleaned up.' Snoop whispered now, an apology. 'We'll use some of your water. It's okay. We have lots of water where we're going.'

At 4,187–05:18, Etta Hoffmann left the AMLD building. She was the second out the door, behind Snoop, who wielded both knife and steel pipe. Hoffmann held open the door for Lenny Hart and Seth Lowenstein, who began to unload two rubber-wheeled trolleys of Archive binders into what looked like a child's hand-pulled wagon except twice as big and equipped with big rubber wheels, outfitted with a pioneer bonnet of plated steel, and painted with its own name: *Giulietta*. They winced as they worked, as if doing so might make them silent.

Hoffmann winced too, then froze, then forgot how to breathe. More than four thousand days had passed since she'd tasted air not channeled through oily intakes, rusty shafts, dusty vents. Being back in the world was a tough rebirth. Hippodrome colors stabbed her dilated eyes, the pepper of leaves plugged her throat, the sugar of flowers furred her tongue. Hot-concrete fumes melted her sinuses, windblown dirt struck her skin like bees. The world was loud. Whirs, purrs, clicks, and rattles played a fanfare for her first foray into unimaginable vastness.

Snoop had learned not to touch her. She held up capable hands, each weaponed.

'See these? I've got you.'

No one had ever said anything like that to Etta Hoffmann, and until that moment, Hoffmann would have thought she wouldn't have cared if anyone had. But she did care. The words, coupled with the sight of Snoop's strong, well-protected body, slithered into Hoffmann's bloodstream and imbued her with strength she'd long misplaced. She pushed her cheeks into the slapping wind, opened stinging eyes against a brilliant sun. Down the block, between two buildings she'd forgotten existed, a zombie pushed through a row of trees shaggy with overgrowth. But Hoffmann felt no fear. Snoop was near; Lenny Hart and Seth Lowenstein were speedy and ready to roll; the world so overflowed with possibility she refused to believe there was only one end coming. There had to be infinite ends. A poetic thought. Perhaps she was the Poet after all.

There had been little to do before leaving. That said a lot, didn't it? The Corpse Web bore few surface similarities to the old internet, but with Seth Lowenstein's help, she confirmed a one-to-one data match of any changes she made on the back end. Arranging the bones of government sites was easy. The difficult part was deciding in what shape to arrange them. Hoffmann stared at the message she'd chosen ten years ago.

ARE YOU OK? CALL ME.

Those five words, the very first Q, had worked wonders, convincing those who had nothing to believe in that someone wanted to hear from them – and if one person cared, there must be others. What could she possibly put in its place now that the operation was over? She thought about it all night, restless due to a warm, squeaky body after submitting to Snoop's command of a full-body bath. After waking before dawn with the others, she sat for the last time at Annie Teller's desk and poised her fingertips over the keyboard, still deciding.

'Etta,' Snoop had said. 'Time to go.'

Hoffmann deleted the five words. They blinked out as if they'd never existed. Without a single mistake, she typed a new message, barely different from the last, but one she hoped would bring strength and solace to someone.

YOU ARE OK.

Snoop expressed surprise Hoffmann had no personal items beyond her sippy cup and a fanny pack full of smartphones for recording future transcripts. Hoffmann looked around, just to be sure. Her gaze settled upon the photos she'd tacked to Annie Teller's workstation. Hoffmann removed her two favorites. Annie Teller, smug in snappy soccer gear. Tawna Maydew, sleepy-eyed in bed, with a calico cat licking her face. Taking a pair of scissors from the drawer, Hoffmann cut excess space from each picture, then used tape to bring the two women together at last.

She slid the result into her fanny pack.

'I'm ready,' Hoffmann said. It was a lie, but she'd never had problems lying.

The zombie down the block was old and slow. Lenny Hart pointed his aluminum bat to indicate two other zombies emerging from shadow. Seth Lowenstein took hold of *Giulietta*'s handle. Snoop raised her eyebrows at Hoffmann.

Hoffmann took a deep breath. Outdoor air must contain more oxygen. It stung her lungs, spun her vision. This must be what riding a roller coaster felt like. She regretted never having ridden one back when fake danger still provided a service to the human brain. She nodded.

They headed for a side road between zombie locations. Hoffmann's first steps were unsteady. Not only had the road buckled from burst water mains, but she wore rat-stomping plates Lenny Hart had improvised from floor drains and screwed to the soles of her boots. It required a bandied-leg stance and longer steps, but she liked the concentration it took to successfully walk in them. She did not want to trip and cause a ruckus. People had trusted her over the past ten years, but never this much. She ought to trust them back. That meant speaking to them, she thought, the same as she'd spoken to callers.

'Is it just rats and dogs and chimps?' she asked.

'We've heard of dolphins, but obviously haven't seen proof,' Snoop said. 'Right now it's chickens. You see a chicken, you let us know. They're surprisingly hard to hit. I could have really done without zombie chickens.'

Snoop smiled, though, and Hoffmann looked back down at her feet, to keep her rat-stompers straight, yes, but more critically, to settle the powerful palpitations in her chest.

'Here's a tip,' Snoop said. 'Once we get into mud, keep those stompers moving or they'll sink. There's a lot of mud in D.C. They say the pumps here failed in the first month. Water flooded the aquifers. We're on high ground now, but you'll see. There's beaver dams all over the beltway. You probably knew D.C. was built on a swamp. Well, the swamp is back.'

Lenny Hart made a low whistle. Snoop looked up, and Hoffmann followed suit. A block away milled three more zombies. He pointed his baseball bat toward the target crossroad, this time more vigorously. The whole group picked up the pace.

'I could be crazy,' Snoop said, 'but the zombies, I think they're getting slower.'

Their party bent north. Hoffmann watched the zombie trio follow. They did seem slow. But what stirred her about Snoop's remark took fifteen minutes to reveal itself, as gradually and beautifully as the dawn sun cresting the horizon. It was Snoop's inflection.

Snoop didn't call the zombies *They*, with a capital *T*. She called them *they*.

A subtle difference that might change the world.

Hoffmann, to the consternation of her parents, had never cried before, and never would. She would forever recognize this as the time she came the closest.

'Etta,' Snoop checked. 'You're okay. You're okay.'

YOU ARE OK: if Hoffmann believed in signs, she'd take this as a good one. She did not look up in response; she wanted sure footing until the Second Dark Age lightened enough for her to handle new paths with confidence. In the patient silence she felt an invitation to pose more Qs. She did, in fact, have one she wanted answered.

'The name you told me . . . was it your real name?'

Snoop laughed. 'Of course. Wasn't yours?'

'Etta Hoffmann,' Hoffmann acknowledged, trying it back on, seeing if it still fit.

'Nice to meet you again,' Snoop said. 'I'm Charlene Rutkowski.'

The living dead: a contradictory phrase that posited lots of Qs, Qs, Qs, the biggest of which was who was who? When life and death were equally bad, and you could barely distinguish each group's denizens, was it only the crossing of the border that was to fear? Perhaps Hoffmann would make it her new purpose to figure out the difference. Perhaps where they were headed, a place Snoop – Charlene Rutkowski – called *Old Muddy,* everyone could figure it out together, and the tape-spliced photo of Annie Teller and Tawna Maydew would prove itself a prophetic object. It was worth a shot. These were the nights, the dawns, and the days of the dead, however one wished to define the term, and across these lands, they – not *They* – all of them – not *Them* – might yet write diaries of new hopes and forge new definitions of survival.

ACT
THREE

The Death of Death

ONE DAY

HAUNT
THEM
LIKE
YOU'RE
ALREADY
DEAD

You Will Soon Be Gone

The fast-moving ones are not fast anymore.

You know why. For a long time, though you are bad at judging
time, the fast-moving ones were in danger. The danger was you. All
of you. You were everywhere. You wanted what the fast-moving ones
had. The salt, the blood, the meat. They knew this and were fast.
Their mouths moved fast. Their legs moved fast. Their arms moved
fast. The hard, sharp things they carried in their hands moved fast.
That is gone now. The fast-moving ones are quiet and slow. It is not
only because they have faded. It is because you have faded. All of you.

For a long time, though you are bad at judging time, you did not
know loneliness. Now you know. Loneliness is the inability to hunt.
The inability to be among fast-moving ones. You feel it all the time.

Your legs do not work well. Your hands do not go where you
want. You sit in the same spot all day, all night. Before, you did not
sit at all. You walked. Now walking is difficult. When you walk,
pieces fall off. When you fall, it is difficult to get up. Some of you
never get up. You see yous lying all over. Some of the yous have a
shackle around an ankle connected to a broken chain. A remnant of
another time, though you cannot recall what that time was.

You have a shackle too. You do not like it. You look at it all the
time. It used to be shiny. Now the only shiny parts are sparkles of
rust. Usually you like shiny things. There are shiny things all over
your chest. You like them very much. Sometimes when the

fast-moving ones come, they put new shiny things on your chest. It makes you feel good. Almost good enough to stand up.

You are sitting on what used to be called a newspaper kiosk. You recall the last time you stood up. It was to walk over to a you who had fallen in an alley. You stomped the other you's head in with your foot. The shackle around your ankle made noise. You lost most of your toes that day. You did not mind. You had to do it. The fallen you had been there for a long time. You are sure of this, though you are bad at judging time.

This is the other part of loneliness. First, the yous were strong, which meant you were vicious. Next, the yous were stronger, which meant you could be gentle. You shared ambition. You changed the world. You were a generation, and it was a great one. But your time is ending. You know it by how few of you remain. Before, the yous were the stars in the sky. Now, the yous are planets, growing ever more distant. You know the time is coming when the yous will become only you. It is happening to the smaller yous too. The rat-yous, the dog-yous, the chicken-yous. It is lonely.

From your newspaper kiosk, you hear fast-moving ones. They are coming. These days, they come to you like you used to come to them. Sometimes they look into your eyes. Sometimes they talk to you. When that happens, you can feel all yous everywhere twinkle, stars in the skies once more. It is not like tasting the salt, blood, and meat of the fast-moving ones. But it is close.

You used to understand some of the fast-moving ones' words. Your mind was weak, but it was united to other yous. Together, your minds were agile and creative. Now you cannot even decipher the name the fast-moving ones have given you. Jaff. Geef. Chiff. You do not know what they are saying. What you know is you like hearing it. You like hearing it, and you like the shiny things they give you. When they remember you, you remember yourself. You feel like the things you have done were important.

The fast-moving ones are different every time. Some are small, some large. Some are soft, some loud. Some are old, some young. You like the young ones best. The parts of you that have rotted away, the young ones somehow replace them. You can feel it. It tickles. You do not understand it. But you are grateful.

Fast-moving ones have a certain shape, a certain motion. Your eyesight is poor, but you can see them now, a few blocks away. They will be here soon. They will do what they always do. They will poke around. They will pick up things and take them. One of the things they might pick up is one of the yous. You do not know why they do this. They find old yous, very old yous, and take them away. You do not mind. You hope they talk to you today. You hope they call you Jaff, or Geef, or Chiff. For a short while, as the fast-moving ones stand in place, you will not be able to tell the fast-moving ones from you, and it will make you feel better that you, all of you, will soon be gone.

More Shit to Do

Crick-crack.

Earth was scored with new music. Greer Morgan, having spent exactly half her life in the old world and half in the new, still got disoriented. She shook her head at loud, shouting children who showed no reverence for the change. Forget the burbling creek of electronic notifications and the hullabaloo of music, TV, streaming video. When Greer woke from dreams of Bulk, Missouri, it was Old Muddy's absence of white noise that gave her vertigo. Air vents, computer fans, cars thumping over distant highways: it had been persistent bad gossip, and all of it was gone.

The soundscape kids took for granted today left Greer awestruck. Not even when hunting with Daddy and Conan had Greer heard nature so vibrantly. Blankets of birdsong were stitched of distinctive threads, and symphonies of insect sibilance were played by a billion tiny legs and feelers. And the trees! Trees were like a great, looming race, their branches creaking in coos of childlike curiosity, rustling leaves in satisfied exhales, the *tsk*s of their twigs the gentle chiding humans deserved.

Fifteen years after 10/23, new sounds existed too, though only a few justified terminology. Greer remembered a teacher rhapsodizing how Inuits had fifty different words for snow. Well, the survivors at Old Muddy – a.k.a. Fort York – had a half dozen words for the sounds of collapsing buildings. A *woody* was the cracked-knuckles splintering of a wooden structure: houses, barns, pavilions. A *duster* was the caving of a brick structure; there was a softness to it, even when multiple floors succumbed. *Screechers* were unpleasant: metal structures yielding to rust with banshee shrieks. Screechers could stop you in the middle of a laugh and make you fold up in fear. Greer once heard the collapse of an Ohio theme-park roller coaster and was still haunted by the ride's ghost riders.

Other sounds included *kaboomies* (methane explosions in underground tunnels) and *marimbas* (the xylophoning of rain plunking through multiple floors of gutted high-rises). It made perfect sense to Greer they'd been slapped with such childish labels. You had to reframe the sounds of a dead world if you planned on getting out of bed every day.

Crick-crack.

Unlike the noise of collapse, *that* was a sound you could hear anytime you wished. You only had to venture seven blocks north of the Fort York perimeter. Along a roughly fifteen-block stretch of what used to be Queen Street in what used to be Toronto, Ontario, Canada, you could hear it from inside former businesses and apartments, down shadowy alleys, out of forested former parks. *Crick-crack. Crick-crack. Crick-crack.*

Shortly after arriving at Old Muddy in Year Twelve, Greer sprained an ankle. While a doctor – a former veterinarian, really – at the fort's hospital treated her, he tried to explain the sound's origin. Evidence suggested a zombie in a temperate clime could last ten to twelve years, at which point the brain itself rotted and the zombie, for the second and final time, died. Before that, lots of other things rotted too, including the plait of ligaments and tendons at the junction of leg and foot bones; Greer recalled words like *plantar, dorsal,* and *metatarsal.* Over the years, these tissues dried to a gravelly gum, creating a dry-twig *crick* with every flex. The foot's twenty-six bones, meanwhile, knuckled one another, creating a stone-on-stone *crack*. Put it together and you had the signature sound of an antique zombie inching your way: *crick-crack*.

Greer believed she was the first to hear it today. At thirty-two years old, she was the youngest member of this recovery team and fancied her senses to be the sharpest. She was also walking point, thirty feet in front, an old habit. There: a second *crick-crack*. There: a third. One thing humans never figured out was how zombies so reliably sensed the living, even the near-fossilized ones – and Queen Street was rife with the fossilized. So much so that no one called it Queen Street anymore. Out of habit, Greer glanced at a cankered road sign that had once pointed the way to the closest highway, but over which someone had painted:

WELCOME TO SLOWTOWN

Toronto, like everywhere else in Year Fifteen, was largely devoid of zombies. Anytime they were spotted, they were *crick-cracking* their way to Slowtown. It was another zombie mystery, and newcomers to Old Muddy reported the phenomenon from across the continent: the isolated undead dragging their old bodies hundreds of miles to join larger concentrations of their kind.

Queen Street, a twenty-minute walk from Fort York, had been an artist's enclave, packed with galleries, shops, eateries, and boutique hotels, the kind of area where every bare stretch of wall was covered with a mural and every tree base enclosed in a box of bohemian colors. In other words, it was the kind of place Greer had never seen before she and Muse started venturing into cities. Now it was spoil and shambles, as bad as any pre-10/23 slum. Sidewalks were ankle-deep in browned, broken glass. Building fronts displayed faded, painted messages: DANGER ZOMBIES and PAUL WE WENT EAST. Chain-link fences had wilted, soft as grass. Green moss had chosen random structures to swallow. Clumps of electrical wiring blew like tumbleweed. Cars, still neatly in parking spaces, had sunk into themselves, stomped by giant ghosts.

Unappealing to the human eye, but Slowtown wasn't for humans. The living who ventured there were visitors, and behaved with respect, careful to avoid agitating the dead. Normally, not a problem, but this afternoon, it would be a struggle, for Greer herself was agitated. This wasn't just another Slowtown patrol. She was on a private mission, and the rest of the recovery team had no idea.

Greer held up a fist to stop the four people behind her.

'Shh.'

Amid the *cricks* and *cracks* came a new sound: a *clop*. Greer's gut, hot and acidic all day, cooled. Even the eddy of her breath in the cold November turned a slower waltz. Plenty of other Fort Yorkers had recently witnessed the source of this heavy plodding, but Greer had never been so lucky. At the nearest of Slowtown's cross streets, the upper limbs of the tallest tree shivered. Instinctively, Greer knelt to make herself less threatening and heard the clunk of buckets as the team behind her followed suit.

A doe-eyed head emerged way up high, beside a dead streetlight.

It was a giraffe. It ambled forward, its bright, spotty body shifting into full view. A godlike thing, eighteen feet tall, moving with a gentleness seldom seen in this world, spindly legs tapering to narrow hooves, a ballerina on pointe. It gnashed soft lips at a branch, ducked its impossible neck beneath electrical cables, and gingerly took steps into the middle of the intersection, as if believing in that rarest of things: that the world should be treated delicately. With the grace of an arcing kite, it banked its head toward the people.

This is why we haven't lost hope, Greer thought.

The giraffe's breath formed swirling planets. Greer was pretty sure zoo-born giraffes shouldn't fare so well in winter, but animals, like people and zombies, had adapted fast over a decade and a half. The magnificent giraffe, a reminder of bigger things, blinked its black-orb eyes and carried on in lovely silence, ducking beneath the sagging network of streetcar cables and disappearing so rapidly it had to have been a fevered vision.

The only sound was five people's soft, astonished breaths.

Then: *crick-crack*. Time to get back to work.

As previously decided, the group split like a zipper, the two men taking the right side of the road, the three women fanning to the left. Weapons were purposefully hard to come by at Old Muddy, bricked up in the Armory, but recovery teams were allotted a single emergency firearm, so far used only in rare cases of animal attack. Many creatures had adopted metropolitan habitats, and not all were as docile as giraffes. Zoos had unleashed tigers, bears, leopards, crocodiles, and true to their original instincts, they hunted what they needed.

One of the men had today's gun, but the women were not bereft, thanks to Greer. She armed her bow but kept it pointed at the pavement. Zombies usually recognized weapons, and frightening them off wouldn't help her search. She didn't really need the bow – it had been two years since anyone on a recovery job fired a weapon – but she'd take carrying it any day over the stinky buckets.

Zombies tended to stay indoors anyway. Largely, they loitered in windows, in doorways, on front steps. They eyed the living with what Greer categorized as distrust, an annoying reaction she'd come to terms with. The living hadn't hurt a Slowtown denizen in ages, but they sure had in the past. It was like the zombies shared a collective memory, and that memory didn't seem to be going anywhere.

From her position creeping west along the curb, Greer spied five zombies. Four huddled against a storefront while a fifth, *crick-crack,* appeared at a second-story window, eyes like silver dollars in the graying sun. Not abnormal. Zombies often expended great effort to haul their fragile bodies up staircases. Greer blamed it on habit: living or dead, you hewed to precedent, no matter if it was pointless.

Also not abnormal was discovering fallen zombies at the foot of stairwells, brittle bodies shattered while their jaws still gnashed and their white eyes still rolled.

Greer heard a scrape and whirled quickly enough to embarrass herself. The man in the rear position had set down his bucket to dart into a former eyeglasses store to snatch what looked to be a package of batteries. A score, but where had it come from? Probably the zombie standing six feet deeper into the store; Slowtown dwellers were known to pick up odd objects and drop them where the living would find them. Were the batteries a gift? An offering? The zombie didn't advance, but lifted her arms in a token territorial display. Dry, brittle flesh slid from her bones like bark from a dying tree.

Irritation nettled Greer. Nabbing those batteries alone like that? In that dark lobby? A needless risk, but she told herself to let it go. She'd done far worse. Besides, fits of courage like that were par for the course for Karl Nishimura.

Greer blamed her jitters on the man's presence. How was she going to search Slowtown with the boss here? Nishimura, tiresome goody-goody, would tut-tut her for calling him *the boss*. Old Muddy had no leader, blah, blah, blah. Everyone knew it was Nishimura who'd turned Fort York into something special. He'd been the prime mover behind most of its strange, yet indisputably successful, undertakings, including these recovery jobs. Despite the big vote looming tomorrow, Nishimura had taken his scheduled turn to volunteer today, most likely to emphasize he was a regular citizen, just like anyone.

The vote, she'd nearly forgotten. She was probably the only person in Fort York who had. While her mind was locked on her private search, everyone else was fixed on the drama of Blockhouse Four, which boiled down to Karl versus Richard, and the whole fort knew it. Even a hard-ass like Nishimura had to be nervous.

A finger-snap. Greer turned, stupidly fast again. She was really on edge.

The man in first position was using his non-gun hand to gesture at a narrow bramble squeezed between buildings. Though Greer was a full four car lanes away, she believed he'd found what they'd come to recover. Good for them, bad for her. She wasn't nearly finished. She'd need to wiggle away, and fast.

They'd found a 'softie', another cherubic word devised to defang a troubling concept. A zombie's body typically gave out about a year before its brain. This was of course contingent on natural constitution, the travails it had survived, and climate – a zombie in Louisiana putrefied a lot faster than one in Ontario. Regardless, once a zombie had fallen that final time, there was no getting up. Some might rock in place. Some could grind their jaws. All could watch you with white eyes that were more pleading than eerie. Most softies had the consistency of rotten melon; they were mucky, overripe, *soft*.

And they were at the mercy of the living. A lowered boot heel could dispatch one. That was precisely why, Nishimura had argued four years back, Old Muddy residents should behave the opposite way. If they wanted the world to be better, they had to set the example. Greer wasn't one for ideology, but she supposed it made sense. Most things Karl Nishimura said, no matter how tedious, did.

The man in first position holstered the team's gun and leaned down to make a closer assessment, then straightened and beckoned everyone closer.

Greer grimaced. She'd known the man for three years, and still his face had the ability to shock. In fact, that's what he was called: the Face. He refused to divulge his real name, or much about his life, prior to 10/23. His face, though, said plenty. It was a basket-weave of scar tissue from crown to neck. He had nice, salt-and-pepper hair but only in jagged stripes, sprouting from areas of scalp that hadn't been peeled off. Glossy cicatrices sphinctered the flesh around each socket so that only dark, sparkling animal-eyes shone out. His nose was a knuckle-sized nub, its tip and one nostril sliced away. Deep scars whirlpooled into the center of his face – less a mouth than a gaping fissure. He had no lips, and the skin had healed to pale blisters sucking inward over his teeth. Only the periodic flit of his tongue interrupted the black void.

The Face should have been a cruel name, but nothing in the new world was predictable. By calling himself *the Face,* the man claimed ownership over what couldn't be ignored, forcing those who'd accepted so much horror over fifteen years to accept one thing more.

Dealing with the Face's face was never easy for Greer. But working with him was the definition of easy. He had a stunning voice, so expressive she'd asked him if he'd maybe been an audiobook narrator; as ever, he'd declined to respond. He was a man of staggering empathy, sincerity, and honesty. Almost as well known as his face was his utter inability to tell a lie; kids had a lot of fun with that. His capacity for deceit, it seemed, had been ripped away with his skin. Everyone loved the Face, including Greer. Looking at him was like looking at the sun: it hurt, even while it saturated you in warmth.

The rest of the team moved toward the Face. Greer, by previous arrangement, stayed back to keep an eye out for surprises: the occasional inquisitive zombie, a mischief of zombie rats, the dreadful lope of a lone zombie dog. Nishimura, the busiest of bees, had already gotten started. He stood at the threshold of the doorway east of the softie; beyond him, inside the building, Greer could hear the shuffling of three or four zombies: *crick-crack, crick-crack, crick-crack.* Nishimura tipped his bucket until blood spattered out, followed by the smacks of horsemeat.

Greer hated this part. It reminded her of a night of camping with Daddy and Conan when a grizzled coot had approached their campsite with a rifle and a bucket. Freddy Morgan went tense and apologetic: middle of nowhere, armed white man, no witnesses. But the guy was only headed out to leave slop for local black bears, thereby drawing them away from campers. Zombies didn't crave horse like they craved human, but for unknown reasons, if given it, they'd pick it up, taste it, swallow some, and go still, as if it contained the THC that used to chill Greer out at Remy's parties. In the unlikely event Slowtown had any quicker zombies around, spilled horsemeat would distract them long enough for the living to complete their softie recovery.

Horses didn't grow on trees, but Old Muddy's accelerated husbandry efforts had grown their herd to some three hundred thick, as if, instead of peaceful farmers, they were a band of Comanche raiders. Great effort was spent on fencing them into cleared parks, growing and storing hay, and keeping them safe from natural predators. Still, they were amateurs. Horses died more often than they would on farms. When they did, their blood and meat was harvested and chilled to be used on outings like this. That's when recovery jobs spiked. Zombies knew spoiled meat when they smelled it and turned up what was left of their noses.

One of the women jogged to the doorway west of the softie to pour horsemeat from her own bucket. This was Charlie Rutkowski, and after Karl Nishimura, no one at Fort York was held in more esteem. Arriving only months after he had, she'd helmed several expeditions to acquire hard-to-find items the fort needed to make a real go of it. Greer, who'd gone on her share of missions, respected that. It took guts, a level head, and sharp instincts.

One might guess Greer Morgan and Charlie Rutkowski would get along like a brush fire, but that wasn't true. Their conversations were awkward, if not antagonistic. Greer blamed her own feelings of bullshit inadequacy. Charlie was pretty and idolized, and after her courageous quests, she'd forged an even more illustrious career by founding Hospice – the spine upon which Old Muddy was built.

Greer watched Nishimura cede space in the weeds for Charlie to minister to the softie. Greer allowed herself a smirk. Just as Nishimura put pressure on Greer to act sharp, Charlie put pressure on Nishimura. Greer understood that's how effective workplaces functioned, though too often she felt an eighteen-year-old's knee-jerk disdain for authority, from anyone, of any kind.

Nishimura was not himself today, no question. He permitted himself to be nudged aside as the others unloaded straps and buckles. Greer made a quick count of zombies to make sure none had advanced, then went back to watching Nishimura. What does a workhorse do when forced, for a few precious minutes, not to work? His eyes landed on Greer. Oh, shit. That's what: get up in her business. He ambled over.

'Morgan.' He nodded.

He was ex-military, though Greer never remembered which branch. Honestly, she didn't try. Nishimura's bygone status only hardened her rebellious reaction. She gestured her chin at his dusty pack of Duracells.

'Those double-As unopened?'

'Affirmative.'

'What are you planning to stick them in?'

'I scrounged up this heat-stick gadget a while back. It's like a cigarette lighter. I've always thought it would be a handy thing, if it worked.'

'How exciting.'

He gave her one of his patient, inscrutable looks. 'I'm open to ideas.'

'I've got a vibrator that doesn't vibrate.'

He blushed and Greer felt bad. Nishimura was too easy to embarrass.

'I don't know,' she sighed. 'Some of the kids have ray guns that might light up and make noises. You could blow their minds.'

'We probably shouldn't encourage firearms.'

So much for feeling bad. She groaned. 'They're not going to work anyway. Nothing we find out here works. Including them.' She gestured at the zombies struggling to lower their rickety bodies toward horsemeat puddles. It looked like a couple might never make it back up. 'You know, pretty soon there's not going to be any left to recover.'

'That's years off.'

'Fine, a few years. Then what? If we can't do your recoveries, what's the point of the whole thing?'

'They're not *my* recoveries. They're for all of us.'

For a block of stone like Nishimura, this was touchy. Richard and the specter of the vote had him acting almost human.

'All's I'm saying,' Greer said, 'is, you know, picking up softies – it's the reason for the season and all that. I just wonder what comes next.'

She waited for his frown; he had a whole tie rack of them. Instead, he smiled. Nishimura had to be closing in on sixty, old enough to be her daddy. On those rare occasions when she hadn't been fucking up, Freddy Morgan had given her looks just like this. Greer huffed in derision. It only made Nishimura's smile widen.

'You remind me of someone,' he said. 'A fighter pilot. I didn't know her long, but she was the most fearless person I ever met.'

'Let's not go overboard here.'

'I'm not trying to flatter you. This fighter pilot, before she died, said zombies were golems. You know what that is?'

'Tolkien, right? Skinny guy, wanted a ring.'

'According to this pilot, golems were monsters that rose up because we needed them. And what we needed them to do was wipe us out. One of the last things Jenny said was I had to tell people that. So we'd stop fighting them, I guess.'

'And you believed her?'

'At the time? No. Eventually, yes. How can we see all we've seen and not think that, in some ways, it's all been for the best? A hard reset. For all I know, Jenny's to credit for Fort York, Hospice, everything.'

'And why do I get this special insight?'

'Because you're the tip of the spear, as we navy used to say.'

'Sounds violent for a guy who's against plastic ray guns.'

'I only mean you're out in front. You're thinking of the future. That's good. We relics won't be around forever. Folks might mess it up again, and it'll be up to people like you to remind everyone how we got there.'

'Don't hang it up yet, Gramps. I heard life expectancy's back on the rise.'

Laughs in Slowtown topped out at agreeable murmurs. When Nishimura glanced back at the softie, Greer took a hard look at him, hoping to resent him, and failed. Damn, she hated it when good, clean spite got fucked up with admiration.

Charlie and the Face had finished binding the fallen zombie. Like the gun and the dumping of horseflesh, it was an exercise of extravagant caution. Both edged aside to give the team's last member space to unroll the canvas stretcher she'd removed from her pack. No question about it: Etta Hoffmann was the weak link of today's posse. Any day's posse, really – Hoffmann refused to converse. Normally, Greer wouldn't care, but a little chitchat helped ensure everything ran smoothly out here. It even helped you give a shit about the people beside you.

What ticked Greer off about Etta Hoffmann was she was a grown-ass woman whom everyone treated like a preschooler. Hoffmann's sole job at Old Muddy was keeping what was called the New Library, installed in the Toronto Public Library branch across from the fort at Bathurst Street. Housed like the Ark of the fucking Covenant were shelves of binders, a post-10/23 history Hoffmann had apparently created and titled, with exasperating hubris, the Hoffmann Archive of Tales from the New World. People seemed to like reading it; the library was a busy spot.

Greer had been inside the New Library exactly once. As a new arrival, she provided a 'Personal History' to Hoffmann. It was both customary and symbolic: you shared your story, you became one of the group. The main thing Greer recalled from her interview was watching Hoffmann sift through papers and books, and thinking that 'librarian' was an awful cushy job to have at a place in perpetual need of manual labor. In a fair world, Hoffmann would be doing double duty in Slowtown.

Instead, the Custodial Council who arranged schedules – which Greer suspected meant Karl Nishimura – took care to assign Hoffmann to recovery jobs only alongside Charlie Rutkowski. What was that about? Lots of people had BFFs, family members, or fuck buddies they'd like to work alongside, but for them, it was tough titty. You got thrown together, you made nice. Etta Hoffmann didn't, while Greer worked like a coal miner. The way of the world hadn't changed. Being good at shit only earned you more shit to do.

Charlie and the Face prepared to shift the softie onto the stretcher. A delicate maneuver: guts could pour, chests collapse, limbs detach.

'I'd better help,' Nishimura said.

'Aye-aye.'

As he moved away, Greer scanned farther along Queen Street. The sinking sun permeated the gray clouds enough to make her squint. Half a block down sat the Chief, easily the most recognizable zombie in Slowtown. An old zombie edging toward softie, the Chief would sometimes do what Etta Hoffmann, a living human, did not: convey pieces of information.

Why hadn't Greer thought of her before? There was no time to ponder. She cast her eyes about to confirm no pressing threats, and using the hushed, heel-toe hunter's steps Daddy had taught her, walked away from the group. Just like that. She had some feelings about it, sure. The team would worry about her. They'd be pissed too. Forget Nishimura's batteries; this was an act no one would condone. She was a selfish asshole. But sometimes you had to look out for yourself, or even more importantly, your own.

Fort York knew of Greer's reputation when she'd arrived. The only reason they'd let her join, she was certain, was because they'd liked Muse King so damn much. It was hard to listen to Muse talk and not want to go on listening forever. Old Muddy had become cold and quiet in his absence. Three months now, he'd been gone.

She glanced at the surrounding buildings as she hurried through shadow.

'Come on, baby,' she whispered. 'Where are you?'

She had a good, strong hunch she was about to find out. The Chief was just ahead, as usual sitting atop a toppled, rust-burred ad-circular kiosk in front of a three-story building, the bottom of which had been a donut shop. Greer stole a final look back at the recovery team. They remained bunched around the softie.

Except the Face. He'd backed away. To Greer's surprise, his mud-dled face was aimed right at her. He did not shout or raise an alarm. Maybe he knew what she was doing. Maybe he understood. Whatever the reason for his silence, she'd take it. Before ducking beneath the Chief's donut-shop awning, she gave the Face a grateful nod. He was a block away, but she figured he'd see it. Behind that gnarled flesh, he had a way of noticing everything.

Super Bowl Sunday

Personal History Transcript #811
Location: Fort York New Library
Subject: 'The Face'
Interviewer: Etta Hoffmann
Time: 4,458–11:43

<u>Notes</u>: Subject's face is disfigured. Subject refused to supply his real name.

Q.

Awful, isn't it? I appreciate it. I know that might sound strange, but I appreciate you just being straightforward and asking about it. That doesn't happen very often. I'm trying to think. Let me see. You know, I don't know if it's ever happened, some-one just coming right out and addressing it. Not that I blame them for looking away and all that. If you saw a face like mine and didn't react, I think that would mean you're not okay inside. You'd lost something human.

Q.

It felt like I was the last man on Earth being chased by an army of the dead. How's that for an answer? I wasn't, of course. That was obvious from what I saw. And I saw lots of things. Lots and lots of horrible things. I'm sure you did too.

Q.

I appreciate the question. Honestly, I do. But I wonder what good it would do. Listing off atrocities just for you to write them down.

Q.

I worked for, let's just say, a news organization. I'm not sure what good we did. We tried to keep people informed, but after a while, it was just all bad news, you know? Oh – I see. I see what you're saying. How was broadcasting all those terrible stories different from listing them off for you? You're clever! I guess I can tell you some. Is it all right if I just rush right through them? I think sometimes people see my face and they think my heart must be the same, all blistered and calloused. But it's not.

Q.

I saw a man's guts pulled out of his anus. I saw a woman's guts pulled out of her vagina. I saw a zombie caught in an escalator, just like little kids worry about. Wild pigs – I saw so many wild pigs. I guess pigs are smart, and figured a way out of their pens and went hog wild. Ha, I didn't mean to say that. But they did. Pigs got lean and mean. They'd eat people who weren't dead yet. They'd eat zombies too. Pigs didn't have a side in the whole thing. One time, I hid out in this beauty salon and found a zombie wrapped in electrical cords and stabbed with curling irons. This was back when some spots still had electricity, and the irons had burned holes in her the size of baseballs. The smell wasn't even the worst part. The woman was naked. Why would she be naked? I had this real bad feeling she'd been tortured. You know, for fun. One thing I remember, I don't know why, is a tennis court, where someone had written the word *ALIVE* in blood, huge all over the green clay. And heads on pikes. Lots and lots and lots of heads on pikes. You've seen them. Can we just stop there? It was a long trip.

Q.
Six hundred and fifty miles as the crow flies. Unfortunately, I'm not a crow. There were road signs, sure, but you couldn't use the roads. The most valuable thing in the world were paper maps, but who had those? Everyone used GPS. You know how it was. One direction, zombies. The other direction, people worse than zombies. You'd have to double back, go a new way, and then you didn't know where you were. Things were probably different for me. Even people I wanted to meet, my face scared them off. Probably for the best. Traveling alone, finding food alone, it was easier. Any big food hoard, people guarded with their lives. It made me think of the commercials we played at the station. All those silly jingles. We were consumers back then. Consumption far as the eye could see.

Q.
Correct. No lasting damage to my eyes, but the skin around them . . . well, you can see it. It was so torn up it swelled shut. I made Zoë find a knife and let some blood out so I could see. I got the idea from *Rocky*. You ever see the *Rocky* movies? You did? All of them? Me too. I used to love them. I'd sing the songs when I was walking alone. Quietly, of course. 'Eye of the Tiger', 'Burning Heart'. Those movies had a bad message, though. I had a lot of time to think them through. After the first one, all of them were fights Rocky should have walked away from. That was the whole problem with America. Oh, that's a good one – 'Living in America', James Brown, *Rocky IV*.

Q.

Zoë was an intern. Zoë Shillace. She got me out of there. This zombie had broken glass stuck in her hands, and, well, that's the story of my face. My hand ended up on Baseman's gun. There was this guy, Nathan Baseman. I guess you don't need to know him, but I want to say his name, just for the record. I got that first zombie off me and started firing Baseman's gun all crazy because I couldn't see, and ended up on Dylan Ramsey's wheelchair, which rolled through the crowd of zombies like a snowplow. That's when Zoë grabbed me. I knew it was her because I felt the keys in her hand. She had the elevator keys. And up we went.

Q.

I've wondered about that. Did my face, messed up like that, keep zombies away? Did they think I was already dead? Once we got out of CableCorp and found a place to stop, Zoë wiped off my face and flipped out. I mean, really flipped out. I don't think she had any idea how bad it was, under the blood. She screamed and ran off. I thought, well, that makes sense. She needs to save herself. When she came back later, she said she'd only left because she couldn't stop screaming and didn't want to lead the zombies to me. She'd found some stuff too, clean towels and iodine. Who knows where she found iodine. Zoë was . . . she was one of those people who probably didn't make your Archive, but is the reason the rest of us are here. So she should be remembered. That's Zoë with an umlaut. S-H-I-L-L-A-C-E.

Q.

Oh, yes. She's dead. I'm sure of it. One day, she didn't come back. She had to go out all the time to find us food and water, or

T-shirts or aprons, things she could tear into bandages. For my awful, unsalvageable face.

Q.

If there's one thing those last couple weeks at the station taught me, it's that people won't lie down and die. They just won't do it. They'll make life terrible for themselves, they'll make one another miserable, but they won't stop. Is there any better proof than zombies? Even when we're killed, we don't stop. It's maniacal. It's like Rocky. Just stay down, Rock, you know? But I'm not that strong. I got up.

Q.

I had a bit of an advantage there. I'd had facial surgeries before. Plastic surgery, I mean. I knew a thing or two about keeping things germ-free. I got by. Just barely. For a while, I did what I imagine everyone did. Picked up every cell phone I saw. Turned on every computer. Fiddled with every radio. Until I saw myself. That's one thing Zoë did that was really smart. Kind too. She kept saying she couldn't find a mirror or anything reflective. And I believed her!

Once I was out walking around, of course, I saw all sorts of mirrors, and one day decided to take off the bandages and look. And I – it's so strange, Etta. There was this, I don't know. This *lifting*. On the one hand, it was the worst thing I'd ever seen. But at the same time, I felt this emptying of all the garbage inside me. Just, whoosh. Gone. Clean. Something that looked like me couldn't be human, right? Which meant I could feel like I'd developed into a new form of being. Not human, not zombie, something else.

I'm not trying to be self-important here, but I used to have this itch, this itchy feeling that I was in the wrong body. Finally, it was gone. No more vanity, no more pride. And no more lies. So much of the news we reported, so much of humanity's so-called progress, it was all built on lies. I knew right then I'd never lie again, no matter what.

Q.

I suppose that's true. If you guessed my name and asked me straight-out if you were right, I guess I'd have to tell you.

Q.

That's it, exactly. Phones, radios, computers – I stopped trying to get them to work. I stopped *wanting* them to work. Once you let go like that, it's amazing. You start truly seeing how dependent we'd become. All the stuff that was supposed to connect us to one another, it got created too fast, before we knew what we were doing, and it ruined us. What else rose up so fast? I'm asking you. What else?

Q.

Zombies. That's what else. It was like 6G replacing 5G, you know? It was our own doing. We created technology we couldn't live without. How dumb was that? We made ourselves into brain-dead bodies. Our gadgets were the respirators keeping us alive. Zombies show up, our plugs get pulled, and we revert to vegetables.

Q.

Of course we're better off now. We're *far* better off. What I'm saying is we *had* to devolve first, go back to living in caves and huts and just *talking* to each other, like you and me are right now. We had to devolve to realize we'd never really much evolved.

Q.

That's easy. If I experienced one thing that belongs in your Archive, it's the battle of General Spalding and General Coppola. I'd estimate it was Year Four? I was in the Atlanta area for a long time, recuperating, healing. I remembered a story I did on Vietnam vets, how some of them used superglue to close their wounds. It doesn't sound pleasant, and it isn't, but I found some and it helped a lot.

Spent some time in Talladega National Forest, then outside Tuscaloosa, then ended up following the Tennessee River east of Knoxville. One night, I heard all these noises, like gunshots, except lighter, and I guess because I'm a stupid human, I chased after it and found fireworks. Just beautiful. You can imagine what it made me think of. Not only family stuff, New Year's, and Fourth of July. I'm talking country stuff – how we used to *feel* about our country. I followed the fireworks and noticed zombies following them too. They didn't see me because they were looking up at the sky. That was sort of beautiful too.

Q.

I guess you'd call it a farm? Someone had built an impressive fence around it, ten feet tall, no gaps, and the zombies had gathered in this one spot. I hid in the trees for a while because – Etta, I'm sure you've heard some nutty things. But get ready. This farm didn't have any heads on pikes at all. It was more like a little Las Vegas. Not only were there fireworks, but there were neon signs all over the wall. Beer and girls and hot wings and football. Screens were set up on top of the fence, with old-fashioned projectors playing vintage porno films and car-crash footage and sports highlights. And the zombies were rapt. I mean slack-jawed. I walked right up next to them to get a better look myself. Naked ladies, fast cars, sports. I was suckered in right along with the rest.

Q.

The fence opened up, that's what! The zombies rushed in, and I got caught up in that, and suddenly, all these nets scooped us up like crabs. I can't tell you how I didn't get bit in there. We all ended up in this pen and I started screaming for help. A woman yelled back, asking who I was, and I told her, I didn't even think about it, I just said my name, my real name.

Q.

Etta. I'm not going to tell you.

Q.

Because it's been fifteen years. That person is gone.

Q.

Yes, she recognized me. I should clarify – she recognized my voice. Thank goodness she heard my voice first, right? She sent in a man and a woman to drag me out, but as soon as they got a look at me, they froze. I had to get out by myself. I'll spare you the time it took for everyone to get used to my face. I'll spare myself. The point is, the woman in charge called herself General Spalding, and she thought my arrival was a gift from God. She said the greatest newsperson of all time – her words, not mine – had been delivered to her on the eve of the greatest contest of the new era: Super Bowl Sunday.

Q.

You're telling me. I hadn't the slightest. I got her to give me this hoodie so I didn't scare all the farmhands. That's what she called them, though I don't think they did much farming. She took me out on a couple horses to what she said was the field of battle. It was this big, open, hilly field about a mile from the farm. On the closer end was a hole about the size of a backyard pool. Next to it were the same nets they'd caught me with, full of zombies, fifty or sixty of them. Still moving, but all busted up. I got they were headed for the hole, but they weren't going in just yet. The farmhands were taking these red kerchiefs off them. Spalding was so proud. I thought she was going to cry. She said zombies were easy to come by, a dime a dozen. But red kerchiefs?

Q.

No, that wasn't all. They were ripping off arms and legs too. They just popped right off. It was pretty shocking until I noticed the farmhands were saying things like 'BK' and 'AE', and I remembered the terminology. BK: below the knee. AE: above the elbow. These were prosthetic limbs. The zombies had been wearing prosthetic limbs. So that was, you know, weird. First time I saw anything like that. Spalding took me back to the farm, where I saw something else new. The farmhands were *training* zombies. I know that sounds crazy. But also maybe promising, right? Like maybe Spalding had figured out something that could help everyone.

Q.

What do you think? They were training them to fight. A few battered old zombies, the same kind being buried in the big hole, were nailed to fence posts. Then the farmhands made newer zombies tear through the older zombies to get to a pail of meat. It was a nightmare. You might think it'd be better than watching zombies maul people, but no. Because we forced them to do it. We forced them to go after a pointless prize, the same way we squandered our own lives, chasing pointless prizes. It's all meat in pails.

Q.

I asked the general. I pointed at the pail and asked. She wouldn't say.

Q.

What *could* I do? It's hard to remember now, but Year Four? In Year Four, most of us still believed someone would save us. You barely ate, you barely slept, half the people you met died of the stupidest things – a little cut on their toe gets infected, there's no antibiotics, three weeks later, they're dead. I couldn't tell if General Spalding was doing a good thing or a bad thing. She had food, and she was giving me some, the end.

Q.

Not only did they have prosthetics, they were customized. Instead of a normal metal pincher, for instance, one had a big, sharp scythe blade. One had calves covered in spikes. It was armor, weaponry. They were being outfitted like tanks. The ones being buried weren't worth squat because they couldn't fight anymore. That simple.

Q.

I didn't have to ask. She bragged about it. General Spalding had a sister, General Coppola. Different last names, different mothers. I think that's where their competition started, way back when they were kids, and it just never ended. They'd been feuding all their lives. Over toys, sports, class rank, boys, affection from their father. He owned one of the nation's biggest prosthetics manufacturers. When he died, he left it to both sisters so they'd have to work together. Instead, they split the company and went on fighting: pricing, labor force, innovation. 10/23 should've ended everything like that. Even after the world gave us the biggest excuse to pull together, we kept fighting the same fights. Especially if you were rich. Then you had the means to make other people fight for you. I'm not innocent of it. Sun rises the next day and I'm right there, ready to do whatever General Spalding says.

Q.

Who knows if it was actually Sunday? Well, maybe you. You kept track, right? We got to the field of battle at the crack of dawn, but General Coppola was already there. That was my first hint that things didn't bode well. All of Coppola's soldiers were stretched out in a line, and even way across the field, I could see their prosthetics were wilder than ours. Big, round blades on their shoulders. Knife hands. Breastplates that looked like cheese graters – you could imagine how they'd slice the fingers off Spalding's soldiers. Naturally, they wore blue kerchiefs, and that mattered, because there was a crowd. This was Year Four. You didn't go outside unless you had to. Yet here were the locals, showing up.

Q.

My role was journalist. War correspondent. More like high-school sports reporter. I had a video camera to tape the whole thing, a bag with extra batteries and tape, a pad of paper to write on. It was pointless – it was pouring rain. But that's war and football, right? The game goes on, regardless. Spalding gave me an assistant. It was ridiculous. A farmhand with a broken leg. He was probably lucky he hadn't gotten buried. I think he knew it too. He kept talking about Canada. He'd heard things were better in Canada. He said it soft, like it was an unpopular opinion. Anyway, I never forgot it. It might have taken me seven years, but I got here.

Q.

With great pomp and circumstance, that's how. Spalding had a speaker booming out what they used to call *Jock Jams*. 'Gettin' Jiggy Wit It'. 'Whoomp! (There It Is)'. There were flags, red and blue. Someone released a dove, if you can believe it. That was the signal for Super Bowl Sunday to commence. When it did – I didn't videotape a second of it. That's how shocked I was. It had to be close to a hundred zombies charging one another. It was unreal. They hit each other like a hundred-car pileup. Zombies don't recoil, you know? They have no fear of taking damage. It was like watching Play-Doh people get pulled apart. And safe in the end zones, General Spalding and General Coppola sat on chairs, drinking beer and chomping snacks.

Q.

Forty-five minutes? Sports reporters would call it a rout. The red team got pushed way back. Spalding had to get out of her chair. She was like one of those coaches you see losing it on the sidelines, with her face all red like a little kid's. She was screaming orders and pushing farmhands into the mud. It was over, way over, but once you've got zombies fighting, it's not easy to make them stop. They'd been promised meat, right? Pretty soon, the farmhands on both sides were trying to pull the zombies apart, and that's when I noticed the ground under everyone's feet was moving.

Q.

Decent guess. My old weather guy would inform you there actually is a fault line in Tennessee. But no, not an earthquake. The rain, I'm telling you, it was torrential. The field was a swamp. Those old zombies, the ones who supposedly couldn't fight, hadn't been buried deep enough.

Q.

Like rows of crops, except instead of corn, it was hands shooting up and grabbing ankles. Then faces pushing out, mouths full of mud. The ground caved and everyone fell – farmhands, Spalding, Coppola. Blood and guts started flying, same as before, except brighter now, because these were living people being mowed up. I thought Spalding might get away, but her own soldiers got her. Something about the old zombies coming back reminded the newer zombies who they were. Their training went out the window. It felt like revenge. You can't send people to their deaths like that. Even if they're already dead.

Q.

No, we were off a ways, supposedly recording the whole thing. I guess that's what I'm doing now, eleven years later. My assistant had a broken leg. He didn't make it. Only one zombie came close to getting me. I'll never forget her. She was something special. She was one of General Coppola's mega-soldiers. You know those racing blades they give sprinters who lost their legs? She had those attached at the knee. Brand-new, lightweight carbon fiber, looked like they could last a hundred years. Made her faster than normal. She had these little hatchets attached to her wrists, so even if she didn't get you, she got you. She almost got me, but she hesitated. It had to be my face, don't you think? The weird thing is, I recognized this zombie. She was the one that sliced my face up in the first place! How the heck did she get there? I know it was her because she had this wrinkled old name tag soaked to her clothes. 'Annie Teller', it said, and under that, 'La Brea Tar Pits'. Weirdest thing ever. Anyway, I got away and – you all right? Etta? Everything all right? Are we finished? You want to stop?

A Shovelful of Dirt

If the people of Old Muddy were asked to name their two most opposite residents, the Face thought they might choose fiery vigilante Greer Morgan and collected, judicious organizer Karl Nishimura. But he believed they were two sides of the same coin. Both were leaders; both knew how to inspire; both were willing to take risks and suffer consequences. The Face believed *himself* to be Greer's antithesis. Where she was hurricane gales, he was Lake Ontario on a clear morning – silent, stormless.

Even in his darkest times, like those spent with General Spalding outside Knoxville, he'd felt in his body a slow, molasses calm. He used to be the same as anyone else. Desperation, anger, embarrassment, yearning, self-doubt, all raining down inside the skull, occluding the senses. From behind a ruined face, the Face spoke only truth, and the biggest truth was the worst that could happen to him happened *before* 10/23. He'd been valueless.

His interior calm granted him excellent observational abilities; he allowed himself the vanity of admitting this. He'd been the one on this recovery mission to spot the softie. He usually was. The softie's twitches had fluttered overgrown grass, which had ticked along a rusty soup can – more than enough.

He was also certain he'd been the only one to notice Greer capering away down Queen Street. He anticipated the reactions of the others when they noticed it. Glumness, irritation, anguish, fury. He felt those emotions too. He also felt *through* them, to what Greer must be feeling. Because Greer was the Face's opposite, he held her in the highest esteem. In a world of the dead, she was more alive than anyone. Humans would need more like her if they were going to make it.

Why she'd split was simple to guess. She'd gone looking for Muse King. He'd vanished just after Richard arrived, and Richard had stirred up things too much for anyone but Greer to devote time to finding a guy who by now was zombie feed or zombified. At the beginning, some had helped Greer search as far as Cabbage-town. Naturally, Slowtown had been skipped. You didn't go into zombie-filled Slowtown, except on recovery jobs. The Face would never forget Nishimura's address, delivered at Fort York's most regal spot – the Government House Battery, better known as the Circular – when he'd celebrated that upon which they'd voted.

All these streets are yours, he'd said, *except Slowtown.*

Cheers, tears, hugs, kisses. For a man like the Face, wholly devoted to honesty, it felt good to witness it in others. A problem had been faced and an attempt was being made to remedy it. Slowtown's loca-tion was more contentious. Why not stick the zombies out in Summerhill or Wychwood? Because, Nishimura explained, just as important as letting the dwindling zombies live out their last years in peace was letting them choose their place of rest. Otherwise, how could we expect them to stay put?

Three years later, here they were, Muse King gone and Greer Morgan doing what she felt she had to do. The Face wasn't glum, irri-tated, anguished, or furious about it. He wished her well. He wished everyone well, from Karl Nishimura to Etta Hoffmann to every Slowtown shuffler.

Greer was probably headed for the Chief; Slowtown's matriarch frequently transmitted smidgens of intelligence if properly cajoled. One day soon, some core component of the Chief would rot, and they'd find her on the sidewalk, a softie in need of recovery. Nishimura and others spoke of this eventuality despondently, but the Face believed the Chief would be replaced by another chief, maybe two. Then those two joined by another four, another six. Slowly, all the Slowtown zombies would be bold enough to stand in the open, convinced at last of their home's permanence. In the Face's most pleasant dreams, Queen Street looked like the friendly, bustling neighborhood of pre-10/23. You wouldn't see anything unusual, not until you got closer.

People ribbed him for his optimism; if nothing else, it gave them a distraction from the abhorrence of his face. He didn't feel optimistic but realistic. A telling example: Slowtown was getting cleaner. He'd found today's softie thanks to a rusty can in an alley. Did anyone else remember when Queen Street's gutters had been full of cans? And silverware? And stove burners, toilet plungers, curtain runners, and computer keyboards? Old Muddy didn't have a team of street-cleaning saints.

The zombies were doing it themselves.

Slowtown would never be pretty. The buildings rotted apace with their occupants; plenty of woodies, dusters, and screechers here. But the Face believed that's why the zombies kept leaving things out, like unopened battery packs: they were tidying up. The Face heard a clink and glimpsed the rusted chain of an ankle shackle as the softie was loaded onto the stretcher. Only Etta Hoffmann seemed to notice it. Yes, the dead had plenty of reason to fear the living.

No one on today's recovery team seemed glad to have Hoffmann along. Even Charlie Rutkowski looked taxed to have to do her job while also serving as the librarian's keeper. The Face felt differently. He liked Hoffmann. The way she studied his face without worry of impropriety? She was nearly as honest as he was.

He spent most of his free time in her company. He adored the New Library. Among the most egregious of his failings as a reporter was his lack of interest in history. Now, at age fifty, the same switch he'd seen thrown in his father and grandfather was thrown in him. Suddenly all he wanted to read about was Frederick Douglass, Margaret Thatcher, and JFK. The New Library had books on all of them.

As much as the Face reveled in learning who Nat Turner was, what the heck Watergate had been about, and when, exactly, the Korean War had taken place, it was Hoffmann's Archive that kept him coming back. It was astonishing. The Second Dark Age had been a time of spiraling alienation. Everyone you knew, gone. The ability to find other people, gone. The voices in your head became real. Schizophrenia became a life raft.

The Hoffmann Archive of Tales from the New World gave those years back. Hoffmann's odd custom of cutting out her questions turned out to be a genius move, scraping the record free of nothing but pure voice. When the Face read, those voices rose around him, spirits released from blighted graves. He could feel their hands in his as they pulled him up, sharing their identifiable desires and small successes.

After so-called Year Fucking Six, each entry was a shovelful of dirt filling a hole of history. Once Etta Hoffmann arrived at Fort York and residents began contributing Personal Histories, holes the size of General Spalding's zombie graves were filled. The Face learned elephants and dolphins had joined the do-not-trust club, though it was still rats and dogs that forced humans to finally, fully cede the world to zombies.

Beginning with Year Seven, even the hovels made rodent-proof with hot, stinking tar began to fester like sores across an America that otherwise beautified with awesome speed. Exiting along with humans were rapacious industry, grasping development, coldhearted advancements, voracious meat-making, and apathetic pollution. Nothing higher than the trees was constructed. Nothing faster than a horse was created. Nothing was put up to segregate one piece of land from another, no curbs, roads, gates, fences, or walls. Wildness, tortured for half a millennium, saw an opening and took it.

The Face, same as anyone, only saw glimpses, but boy, what sights.

Plants: they erupted like volcanos, coating the country like polychromatic lava, chasing the Face through coal country that now left its coal where it had been born. Grasses of a dozen shades of green – fern, juniper, sage, pickle, pine, seaweed – ripped across the land, swallowing industrial-park lawns and golf courses, sprouting in sidewalk clefts and street cracks, billowing into thick, swishing pelts.

Berry bushes exploded. Sunflowers formed happy armies. Vines and ivies tore down what they could and hid everything else: traffic lights, highway signs, entire city blocks. Lilies and tulips and daffodils in unforeseen colors turned America into a painter's palette, reminding the Face that as a child, he'd thought the actual blossoms were much prettier than what ended up on canvas. Moss spread like forest fires, and also, by the way, so did actual forest fires, with no remaining nemeses. The Face had skirted whole cities – Roanoke, Cincinnati – obliterated by unchecked blazes. What had to burn, burned, and what grew back was fecund and teeming.

Animals: no longer overhunted, or pestled into coops, or biologically altered into helpless blobs, they scurried, scampered, and slithered into a renewed paradise recognizable to their primordial brains. The Face sometimes saw them traveling with elan down highways, packs of wolves half a mile long, clusters of spiders like blankets of steel wool, so many snakes they rippled like seawater. The Archive told of epic battles for supremacy – in the Everglades, twenty-foot alligators versus thirty-five-foot pythons – as well as quick annihilations by creatures like the Rocky Mountain locust, which returned from near extinction to peel croplands from entire states. By Year Ten, new variations of animals, if not entirely new species, were being spotted. Blond bears, blue-feathered eagles, scarlet frogs, prairie dogs with what looked like horns.

How many times had it been said in Archive interviews? How many times had the Face thought it? *Eden had returned.* And right on schedule, man and woman had been exiled from it. As North America bloomed into a garden of wonders, the living could but peek from the slovenly outhouse slats of their squalid little hutches. While they coveted, zombie sentries protected nature by holding patient siege, standing outside any place they sensed humans, rolling their jaws and drooling out their decaying innards.

Loneliness shaved to a point. The Face went eighteen months without laying eyes on another living human. Some at the fort alleged they'd gone three or four years. That had been the worst of times. The Face felt like vermin. Crawling on his belly to find plants to eat, half of which he vomited up. Hunched in a series of miserable shacks, too weak to shoo the flies drawn to his excrement. Tortured by a blooming, untouchable paradise, close enough to smell the salt of mammal snouts and the taste of pollen. It wasn't a human existence, and maybe that was the point. Maybe humans had to live like grubs for a time to remember what exile felt like.

The Archive confirmed his estimate that Year Eleven marked humankind's tentative reemergence. They did it all over, all at once, as if collectively smelling a rainstorm's end. Back in WWN days, zombie math was decisively against them. Now, the math had changed. With so few people left on Earth and most of them dutifully cremating their dead, there was no refreshing of the undead populace. Zombies began to age. *Crick-crack* became a sound you understood. Those that grabbed at you did so weakly. They looked like homeless people begging for help. With mounting frequency, you found them collapsed. Like anything else, corpses had a life span, and it was beginning to end.

All because people had done what they hadn't done in two million years: sat still and not screwed anything up.

Even before 10/23, Canada had tempted Americans aching for a land where guns weren't handed out like candy and a genetic disease wouldn't bankrupt you. Chuck Corso had been a flag-pin-wearing patriot, bellowing the national anthem louder than the guy next to him, the first WWN personality to sign up for Veterans Day events. The Face, on the other hand, noticed how every US flag he saw now was filthy and shredded. Year Eleven was the year to make good on the rumor he'd heard at General Spalding's farm.

He made his way through Pennsylvania and western New York and crossed the border at Niagara Falls. The hydroelectric power plants were gone, and the rapids roared like freed gods. They deigned to let him pass. Welcome to Canada.

The Face heard grunts from those lifting the stretcher. Minor ones – softies never weighed much. This one looked to be of East Asian descent. The three zombies to the left, occupied with horsemeat, had once been a Black man, a white girl, and a Pacific Islander woman.

Old Muddy reflected a similar diversity. The Face had been startled by it at first; now, anything else would feel like being deprived of an essential vitamin. There were the elderly, the middle-aged, infants. Women, men, nonbinary people, gender-fluid people, intersex, trans. Gay, straight, bisexual, pansexual, asexual, aromantic, polyamorous. Neurotypical, neurodiverse. Muslims, Christians, Hindus, Buddhists, Jews, Sikhs, Daoists, Wiccans, Pagans. Plus lots of agnostics, even more atheists, and a single drag queen who liked to be called *Lady Dee Klein*. People who were physically, intellectually, psychiatrically, and/or neurologically disabled or impaired. Was all this chance? Or necessity? Nishimura once told the Face he wondered if this was why they'd been drawn to Toronto, sometimes called the planet's most multicultural city. A new world could not look like the old world.

That's why the apolitical Face would be casting his vote tomorrow for Nishimura, not Richard. Things couldn't be allowed to go backward, not even a little.

Nishimura had one end of the stretcher, Charlie the other. The Face lifted the gnarled remnants of his chin in an offer to help, but Charlie shook her head. He strolled over anyway. They didn't know it yet, but in a few seconds, they were going to be setting down that stretcher. They'd realize Greer was gone. The Face knew the urge to find her would be strong, but nothing was as sacrosanct as getting in and out of Slowtown quickly. A new Eden was opening to them, and that was good, but what the Face recalled from Sunday school was that Eden had an apple you weren't supposed to pluck.

All these streets are yours. Except Slowtown.

He watched the recovery team navigate the broken glass and rubble of the alley, Nishimura walking backward, while Hoffmann kept her unreadable eyes on the lookout for any break in horseflesh feasts. They had one scary moment when Nishimura's right heel slipped off the curb. The stretcher jounced. The shackle and chain on the softie's ankle pulled and two of her toes snapped off and landed in the gutter. Instead of the stretcher tilting, the Face felt the whole world tip on its axis, while a counterweighted world prepared to swing up to take its place. So much hope and danger in a single second, the Face didn't know if he could take it.

Yay, Toast!

The Chief wore a shackle too. The chain dangled down the kiosk, flaking rust.

Her face was hard, tawny leather, cracked into black lines of rot. She'd been old before she died, evident from the frizzled gray hair split into long, frayed braids; the hollowed, scowling cheeks; the wattled neck; the sagging drape of the upper lip over a half-toothed maw. Those who predated Nishimura at the fort reckoned she'd been dead for thirteen years, which made her a marvel – the oldest zombie yet recorded. People made up stories about her that felt like the foundational myths of a new culture; children drew pictures of her radiating light, flying, even smiling, as well as other things she could not do.

Greer figured it was a lot simpler than that: the Chief had been an early adopter of *sitting*, staving off softiehood as walking zombies dropped all around her. The ad kiosk, her seat of choice, had been stained black by years of her liquified innards. Similar stains grew below her ears, nose, and mouth, giving her the look of a painted warrior. Few beings, alive or dead, could humble Greer, but the Chief did.

'Here we go,' Greer said to herself. 'Step one.'

Though she hadn't planned to speak to the Chief, she always kept decorative buttons or pins in her pack, precisely for this purpose. She attached her bow to her back and withdrew a round black button with white block text: RESIST. Not colorful, which was a strike against it, so she angled it to catch the dusk light's shine. The Chief's eyes, dull silver from advanced decomp, were as taciturn as any zombie's, but her doughy eyelids pulled back and her mouth opened enough to dispense a string of gray drool.

Greer flipped the button over, showing its rusty pin. The Chief watched with interest. Greer inhaled. Here came the scary part; even old zombies could hurt you if you acted stupidly. Some people just jammed their pins straight into the Chief's flesh, which she didn't seem to mind, but Greer didn't want to risk any upset. Careful to avoid the sticky liquids, she took gentle hold of the Chief's brown wool coat, attached the button, and pulled away, exhaling loudly, the dicey part over.

No one knew who figured it out first, but the Chief loved bright, plastic buttons and fancy enamel pins. Like deathless corsages, they covered almost every inch of her coat. Most of them had a certain slant; this was Queen Street, Toronto. TRANS PEOPLE MATTER, sparkly gold. FEMINIST AF, matte pink. STAY GREEN, over a recycling symbol. LOVE IS EQUAL, two smiley clouds linked by a rainbow. SEA-WORLD STILL SUCKS, blue and fishbowl-shaped. Greer didn't know what to make of YAY, TOAST!, but it was a bright butter yellow. It was the shimmery colors the Chief liked, that's all.

'All right,' Greer exhaled. 'Step two.'

From her back pocket, she withdrew and unfolded a wilted magazine page. Years back, while cutting through Cleveland, she and Muse had come across the Rock & Roll Hall of Fame, victim to an idiosyncratic fire that had cut the building's distinctive pyramid shape in half. The forward-facing exhibits were ash, but the offices and archives were intact. Anything useful had been raided, but hundreds of gray cardboard bins survived, and while Greer tracked advancing zombies with her bow, Muse popped lids and nabbed old magazines. One item he took solely for her amusement: a copy of

Living Blues featuring a profile of New Orleans's own 'King Kong'. The magazine didn't last long; it got cold in Ohio, and nothing was too precious when you needed kindling. But she'd saved the full-page picture of Muse and nothing but a layer of clothing ever kept it from her.

She held it out for the Chief to see. The old zombie was transfixed by the RESIST button, but eventually noticed the page and curled her gnarled fingers around it. Greer bit her lip as the Chief's protruding finger bones poked holes into Muse. Greer felt each puncture, as if it were Muse touching her one last time: lips, throat, breast, pussy.

'That's Muse,' she said, feeling stupid.

The Chief's brow thickened.

'Handsome, right?'

The page rustled in tightening hands. Greer spotted a small rip at the page bottom and prayed for it to hold.

'I asked him what a rock-and-roll place was doing with blues crap, and he got all offended and said there's lots of blues guys there. Buddy Guy, Muddy Waters, Lead Belly. Some other dumb names I don't remember.'

The Chief brought the page closer, inches from mucus-filled eyes and ulcered lips dribbling plum-colored ooze. The rip in the page began to run up the center of Muse's body like Daddy's buck knife used to run up the underside of a deer. Greer heard herself whimper and, for her own sake, rushed to cover it.

'I've heard things, all right? Someone said they saw apple peels out here. Strawberry stems. I heard one guy joke he saw a shit and swore it was human. There's been fire marks too. Little burned circles. Muse liked to start fires with steel wool and a nine-volt. It made circles just like that.'

The Chief pressed her face into the page. Her sunken spine arched briefly as she sniffed at the paper. Her chain mail suit of buttons clicked, and her ankle shackle chimed against the kiosk. Her rotted nose caught the page rip, and it tore fast, all the way up to Muse's neck. Greer's breath caught: the knife was at his throat. The RESIST button had been an inferior offering, she'd fucking known it, and if she had to beg, fuck it, she would.

'Please. Chief, please. His name's Muse. He looks just like that. Have you seen him?'

Greer pointed: the page, Queen Street, her own heart.

'Muse. I need him. Can you help? Please?'

The page, the street, her heart.

'*Please!*'

The Chief's nose lifted, splitting the photo with a damp purr. Greer gasped. A lifting nose indicated a lifting head, and the Chief's pearly eyes now stared into Greer's, a taunting void. The zombie made fists and Muse collapsed into them, both halves crushed, exactly what Greer was afraid of – Muse had spent the fifteen years being two people, fighter and pacifist, neither satisfied with the other, both battling to be King Kong's king. Now both were finished.

Something in the Chief's face changed. Zombies generally didn't emote beyond surprise or frustration. Odder expressions were credited to rogue nerves firing inside decaying brains. Here, it was a single twitch, and only its location made Greer wonder, the wadding of wrinkles at the corner of the lips. It looked like a grin being suppressed. *You stupid girl.*

The Chief's pale eyes rolled languidly. If Greer expected help, and she really hadn't, she would have guessed it would come in the form of a gesture east or west on Queen Street, or maybe north, off the Slowtown thoroughfare. But the Chief looked into the donut shop behind her. Greer peered at the two stories of apartment units before squinting into the shop's murk.

The tangled metal tracery of the drop-ceiling grid intruded into the donut shop like winter forest branches. The mineral-fiber tiles had long ago fallen, bloated into slop piles from in-blown rain and crusted into wasp-nest orbs. Pastel wall paint still existed, but it peeled in the manner of zombie flesh. Amputated limbs of tables and chairs were piled against a glassless display case, and above a busted beverage cooler hung a chalk menu that had smudged into a cosmic nebula.

Greer ducked to get a better look. Past the gutted water fountain, beyond a restroom disgorging broken ceramic, was a door stamped STAFF ONLY.

She looked back at the Chief.

That twitch again. Maybe not *You stupid girl,* but rather, *You clever girl.*

It wouldn't be the first time Muse wrapped himself in the support of an older stranger – just ask Will and Darlene Lucas. Greer wanted to ask the Chief more, not just about Muse but about everything, the secrets of life and death; suddenly, it seemed possible the ancient zombie was capable of anything. But she didn't dare dally. Nishimura and the rest of his rule-followers were overdue to begin their pursuit. Anyway, the Chief was finished. She let her bony fists relax, the two wads of Muse falling to the sidewalk, instant litter, and swiveled her rawboned head to look once more at her new button.

Greer stepped inside the donut shop. The November chill grew to February cruelties. *Resist,* she told herself. Resist turning back, resist running away, resist abandoning hope. Her boots scrunched over pulverized tile, hissed across particled plaster, grumbled through chunked ceramic. She paused, bowed her head, shut her eyes, and heard something. She might be crazy. People had been saying as much since she was born. But she had to trust her ears. *Yay, toast!* she thought, and laughed, and felt fear tingle down into her fingertips. She believed she heard, behind the STAFF ONLY door and up some staircase, the slow, low pluckings of what might be the first bars of that never-finished protest song, 'Walk Away'.

The Lion and the Dove

Personal History Transcript #1284

Location: <u>Fort York New Library</u>

Subject: <u>Greer Morgan</u>

Interviewer: Etta Hoffmann

Time: 4,549–16:10

<u>Notes:</u> Before interview, subject was belligerent and made unfavorable comments about the process.

Q.

Let's not.

Q.

I don't see how or why it matters. We all started somewhere. Those somewheres are gone.

Q.

Oh, is that right? Well, you *hear* a lot of things. I *heard* zombies somewhere were driving race cars. I *heard* the continent of Australia was one big fire. I heard the whole International Space Station crash-landed in Brazil.

Q.

For real? You're not shitting me? Did it land in a city? Fuck. All
right. All right, fine. I suppose you heard right. There's some
truth to it, anyway. But we didn't set out to do it. Muse and me
weren't trying to be famous, you know? You just do your shit,
and sometimes it ends up being the shit that needs done.

Q.

Iowa first. I'd never been to Iowa, and the border was only about
an hour north of Bulk. If I wanted to stare at corn, there was
plenty in Missouri. But Muse said we should get my mom. I
don't really know why. You should ask him. It's not like I gave a
shit. She was in the clink, a place called Bluefeather. I guess it
gave us somewhere to go. Plus, shit, I don't fucking know. Maybe
the end of the world is when bygones really get bygone, you
know? We had a lot of bygones, me and Mrs Vienna Morgan. So
we hauled our asses up there. Took a fucking year, and no, I'm
not kidding. We were on foot. This was Year One.

Q.

What do you want me to say? We hugged it out and had tea, all
that Lifetime shit? Half a mile off, we saw Bluefeather was
crawling with white-eyes. I had to learn to make arrows before
we got close. Think about that, lady. If I said, 'Go make an
arrow,' where would you start? I'll tell you where. You find an
arrow-shaped stick, that's where! Once you start looking, you
start seeing arrow shafts everywhere. Baby cribs. Baby gates.
Baby seats. When did we start surrounding our babies with
arrows? You measure it out, rasp that shit down, shave it, sandpaper it till your palms bleed. You make feathers out of
Tupperware lids, push them into slits, use electrical tape to

make it tight, cut yourself a notch for the string. Then it's time to hacksaw some metal and tie it to the tip. Takes days, lady. That was my life. That was my fucking life.

Q.

I found her, all right. It wasn't hard. The Bluefeather zombies – they were all messed up. All of them were deformed in the exact same way: their chests caved in and their noses squashed flat. Muse and me figured it out. Looked like before the jailers high-tailed it out, they shot all the inmates through the bars. Why not, right? Scum of the earth, right? Blam, blam, blam. Of course, all those inmates turned zombie, and over the next year squashed themselves out of the cells. You heard me right. Once they got rotted enough, they oozed right through the bars. So there was a shit-ton, but they were flat as pancakes, flopping all over the floors. I could shoot them close-range, yank out the arrow, go again. The big mother-daughter reunion scene you're waiting for was me finding Mom slithering on the floor like a fucking eel.

Q.

Through the back of the skull.

Q.

I didn't care. Why should you?

Q.

[Laughs.] Once you get to know Muse, you'll understand. He didn't help for shit. It was only Year Two and he was already doing his peacenik thing. He has this theory, how we react to zombies is some kind of test.

Q.

Don't even bother. He's a fucking lunatic. If I had a brain in my head, I'd have left his ass in Iowa. I was like, if you think zombies aren't dangerous, that's because I'm the one shooting them down while you tinker with your damn protest song all day! I protest *that,* motherfucker! Easy to be a pacifist when you're not getting any blood on you, you know? But I stopped trying. He never pushed his whole philosophy on me, I'll give him that. He did as much work as I did in every other way, probably more. And 'Walk Away', the song he never quit working on? It was good. The parts he let me hear, it was perfect. It's another thing you'll learn about Muse. It's real fucking hard to hate that guy, and believe me, I have tried.

Q.

I guess, but you're using words I wouldn't. We didn't set out to 'make a difference'. The time for that shit had passed. We were trying to get to Rhode Island, where Muse had people. It's just, turns out, Rhode Island's really, really, really far away. You don't get to Rhode Island without getting to a hundred other places first, and that's how it started.

Q.

Somewhere on the Mississippi, maybe? Shit went south so fast. We're talking Year Three here, and already people were using the whole thing as an excuse to do all the awful shit they always wanted.

It was a baseball park, a minor-league baseball stadium, and I had a bad feeling right off. There were heads on pikes. That was the first time I saw that. But we could smell food, and so we begged and they let us in, and it seemed okay when we were going up the stairs, but once we sat down in the top level, we realized there was a hierarchy to the seats, same as when you bought tickets to a game. The good seats were by the field. That's where the yummy-smelling smoke from the grills was. But up where we were? People were passed out from hunger, killing each other over a bag of pretzels. Some went zombie up there and got dragged down to this cage at the back of the ball field, the pitcher's bullpen, Muse said.

Q.

Yeah, and it didn't take long either. You learned like [snaps fingers] who was running the show down there. You saw men being pissed on before they could have any food. You saw women forced to give blow jobs. Fuck, yeah, I got out my bow. Fuckers were too stupid to confiscate it, that's on them. I started picking them off from way up. Now *that* Muse was cool with. When I shot up bad guys, *living* guys, he never had a beef. I used every single arrow I had, and the place – man, it was like I'd hit a grand slam, you know? The stadium was on its fucking feet. The whole upper deck rose up around me, and we fought our way down, and I'm not going to lie. It felt good. Having an army at my back? It felt real good.

Q.

Of course he screwed it up! Screwing shit up is Muse's whole MO. While we were storming the fucking castle, he let the zombies out of the bullpen. He'd tell you he 'freed' them. After that, everyone had to run. Knocked some heads off pikes on my way out, though, you bet your ass. Once we got a couple miles off, I let him have it. You can't be unleashing white-eyes in the middle of my army attack, man! But it didn't do any good. It never did. 'You have your battles, I have mine.' That's why the others left us. Some people, you know, had followed us from the stadium. Guess they were looking for a leader, but Muse spooked them. Just as well. I never saw a group bigger than two that didn't eventually go boom.

Q.
Here? We'll see. I have my doubts, lady.

Q.
I think the baseball thing alone did it. Very next place we went, people had heard of us. I did the same thing there, fixed what needed fixing, shot who needed to be shot, and then did it all over again, the next place, the next place. Pretty soon folks we met on the road had a name for us: the Lion and the Dove. Of course, they always assumed I was the dove. I wised them up pretty quick. Besides, most of what they knew about us, the same stuff you've heard? It's not true. I figure that's how it was with Jesse James or Billy the Kid. Your reputation becomes a bunch of tall tales, and then you're forced to live up to them.

Q.
That one happens to be true.

Q.
Well, we saved *most* of them. But yeah, I guess that one's true too.

Q.
Well, fuck, I didn't say it was *all* false! There was shit that needed to be taken care of! I'm sure there were other heroes out there, but they probably had guns, and guns run out of ammo. I probably just picked the right weapon. Once I got confident, I got

creative. I wasn't just shooting arrows, you know? I was leading revolts. I sicced trained dogs on bad guys, before dogs went zombie. I sent cars full of TNT into walls that were keeping people from food. I had a battalion of teenage girls in Springfield, Illinois, on *skateboards*. We can true-or-false all ten thousand stories if you want, but what matters is I tried to do the right thing. Fadi Lolo said he should've stayed with his people all along, and that's what I tried to do – fight for my people. And I don't mean Black people. I mean people who needed fighting for.

Q.

Oh, just a guy I knew. He probably didn't last a day. He wouldn't take the Schwinn, wouldn't take the machete. Those are what we call poor survival instincts. If I had one thing, it was instincts. You were Black back in the so-called good old days? Or a woman? You felt violence every fucking day, rising off half the people you passed on the street. Having it out in the open was almost a relief. Only problem was, the new violence was so wild, it let people pretend none of the old violence ever happened. Plenty of white folks were thrilled to meet me when I set their asses free. Where were those white folks before 10/23?

Q.

That's the first question you've asked worth a shit. Hell yes, it worked the other way. Nobody got out of this mess scot-free. We ran into a few all-Black groups, and maybe you think Muse and me would've fit right in peachy keen, but that's not how it works, lady. Not that I didn't hope! Even I was like, well, cool, we all know what it's like to struggle. We got fewer ties to old power centers. Maybe we're dressed for success here. But everyone gets to the same place eventually. Everyone starts chopping off heads, sticking them on pikes.

The last time I saw Conan, my brother, he was like, *Now we can be anyone, we can do anything.* No, Conan, we can't. Not here in your darling fort either, mark my words. End of the day, we're all just stupid people. Huh. I sound like Muse.

Q.

Well, he'd been famous before. So I guess I can't blame him for not getting too excited about it. People used to take pictures of us – me, mostly. People's phones were dead, but the cameras worked, and they became little photo albums. They'd carry them around till someone with a generator let them charge it. To take a picture of me, people would have to delete a photo. Fuck what Muse thought. I think that means something, when people take you into their heart. I used to live in this shit box called Sunnybrook, and this woman, Señorita Magdalena, called me mi corazón. So what if I wanted a little of that feeling back?

Q.

I'm being defensive because I know what you want to talk about! Fuck! Everyone here's waiting for me to apologize for St Croix, but all you fort fucks can suck my dick. You're no different than everyone else who believed all the Lion and the Dove legends. Man, I shouldn't have agreed to this. I don't have to prove shit to you people.

Q.

No, let's do it. St Croix. Let's get into that shit. It was one of the worst setups I'd ever seen, for starters. It was comic-book. Heads on pikes all along the perimeter, goes without saying. Blond-haired white guys swinging their dicks around while women were kept in barns, literally in barns like literal animals. All the progress women made in the past, we were stupid enough to think men had our backs? Into the barns, baby-makers. St Croix was ripe for the Lion. Fuck yeah, I came in roaring.

Q.

Your maps are accurate, anyway. Hoosier National Forest, Indiana. No troops to rally this time. I had to Jason Bourne that shit. I had a second bow by then, an Elite Pure I picked up at a sporting goods store, draw smooth as butter, quiet as a whisper, better than anything Daddy ever afforded. Muse might not use weapons, but he'd carry them. So I went old school. It was October and I could fire right through the trees. Shoot and run, shoot and run. I wasn't even shooting people. I shot their stuff. You want to rile up men, that's how you do it. Water tanks. Car tires. Windows. I had shit exploding all over town. They couldn't assess the threat, so they groundhogged their asses. Place was a ghost town in half an hour, and I guess I got a little high on that. A little overconfident. What do you want me to say? I'm the Lion. I'm Diana, goddess of the hunt. I made a fucking miscalculation, all right?

Q.

Because I thought I was right! Up to then, I'd always been right. In the middle of the woods was this zombie pen, probably the best I'd ever seen, maybe thirty or forty white-eyes in there, all their heads destined for pikes. I don't know if St Croix was the world production center of barbed wire or what, but they had that pen so covered in wire a zombie would be in tiny little pieces before it got out. And I knew, I fucking knew, if I let Muse alone for five minutes, he was going to free those zombies, and I didn't want to have to deal with that shit. I didn't want the

women of St Croix to have to deal with that shit. So I sent Muse
to bust open all the barns while I made up some lie and set fire
to the forest. I'm admitting it. You happy now? Greer Morgan
set the St Croix fire.

Q.

Like I said. Early October. It was dry. Zombies went up like
paper, and then the whole fucking forest caught fire. Fountains
of it. The whole sky gone with smoke. Nighttime in the middle of
the day. Women started running up, all filthy, a whole bunch of
them pregnant, but they didn't see me and get excited, like
most did around that time. They were running straight into the
fire. How was I supposed to know? I'm asking you.

Q.

Not till Muse found me. He looked dead. His face, that's all I had
to see. And then I realized. We had men over there, women over
there. Who's missing?

Q.

The children were in their school when the fire hit. We tried to
help. Of course we did. But the only kids we saw – I mean, you
want me to paint you a picture? How much detail you need for
your little book? You want me to tell you about little four-year-
olds running around with their hair on fire? Ten-year-olds with
melting faces? What do you want to know about, *specifically*,
Miss Hoffmann, *specifically*?

Q.

Crystal clear. Crystal. They'd rather have spent the rest of their
lives in those barns than have me come along and roast their
kids alive. But I couldn't go yet. I had a new task right then. I

had to kill those kids. What else was I supposed to do at that point? Let them burn to death? Let them come back as crispy zombies? Muse fed me arrows and I shot. Never shot so poorly in my life. The feathers were all wet because Muse was crying on them. But I'm not blaming him. The targets were little. So little.

Q.

We saw the smoke for days. Like I'd set fire to the whole planet. There was more truth about the Lion in that smoke than anything anyone ever said. You start believing what they say about you, that's what happens. You're more than fucked. You're damned.

Q.

There's nothing more to say. I guess one thing. There was one zombie who popped up when we were leaving town. Jumped out of the smoke, grabbed me. Zombie flesh should be cold, you know? But this one was sizzling from the fire. Skin was torn into all these puffs from getting out of the barbed wire too. Real strange-looking zombie. Had those metal racing legs, you know? I think that was why she was so fast. And these kind of hatchet things on her wrists? She came away with Daddy's bow and she gave it this weird look, like she knew it. And she did. She put an arrow in the bow. Like an expert. I got out the Elite and we fired at each other. And you know what happened? The arrows hit each other. Midair. We backed off and went our separate ways. I know it's crazy. Did it even happen? My mind was on the kids. I can't even tell you for sure.

Q.

A name tag? I don't know, lady. It was dark.

Q.

Things weren't the same with me and Muse after that. No, things weren't the same with *me* after that. Muse was Muse. He was kind. He was really fucking kind. He was really fucking kind and really fucking supportive, and I treated his ass like shit. Because I was ashamed. I told him to quit treating me like a baby, start acting like a man. Told him to stop working on 'Walk Away' 'cause he was never going to finish that irritating piece-of-shit song. Cruelest shit you ever heard. But he never stopped taking care of me. Fuck, why can't I just say it? He never stopped *loving* me. So, whatever, I'm glad we're here. Fort York, Old Muddy, whatever you call it, I'm just glad you don't have any heads on pikes, you know? The fact that a bunch of white guys aren't running the show, that's a bonus. Soon as we're done here, kick me out if you want, I deserve it. But Muse, he deserves a place like this. You might deserve him too.

Q.

Oh, yeah, Rhode Island. Will and Darlene were dead. Naturally. There was actually a grave for Will, nice little wooden cross, and Darlene was in her bed, dead-dead. By then, Muse had heard about Canada. While I was searching for the next place I could be a hero, he'd been searching for the opposite. I didn't give him any mouth about it. Humans were gone from the scene by then anyway. So we came up. And here I am. Asking you to let Muse in. Telling you the whole honest truth so you'll do it. Lady, I'm at your mercy.

It Was a Monday?

Large emotion at a low volume: you got used to it after 10/23.
Purpled faces, spittle-coated lips, and snarled postures became the
indicators of rage and fear. Charlie saw the tightening of Nishimura's
face, a look he'd once told her fellow sailors had called *the glow*. He
nodded, the gesture for setting down the stretcher. Charlie did and
turned to face the setting sun. The Face was staring down Queen
Street. Hoffmann was doing the same. Nishimura entered Charlie's
field of vision and stood between the other two.

Two, not three.

'Should've got started earlier,' Nishimura hissed.

Toronto's November nightfall was around five. If they wanted to
get back to the fort by then, they had forty minutes, tops, to figure
out what had happened. Nishimura looked over his shoulder.

'Rutkowski. She say anything to you?'

Charlie shook her head. She felt like crap. She'd been concerned
about this job since seeing Greer Morgan's name on the list. The
poor woman was in mourning, anyone could see that. For Greer,
that didn't mean sobbing in bed. It meant searching, plotting, and
preparing. Charlie believed Old Muddy instilled in Greer a tranquility she'd probably never known. But she'd once been known as the
Lion, and though you could train lions, you couldn't tame them.

Nishimura checked with the librarian. 'Anything?'

Hoffmann shook her head.

'Face,' Nishimura said, 'tell me you know where she is.'

It had taken Charlie a year to learn to divine emotion from the Face's fleshy debris. Most of the difficulty, it turned out, was because his emotions rarely changed. He was invariably calm and upbeat; if he weren't so distressing to behold, she'd put him right after Luis Acocella in the lifetime rank of people whose company she treasured. Greer's desertion did nothing to affect the Face's composure. He pointed down the block.

'She went toward the Chief,' he said.

'Good eye,' Nishimura said. 'How we doing on horse?'

'Gone,' the Face said, and Charlie echoed, 'Gone.'

Nishimura's eyes flashed with calculations.

'Right. Okay. Let's relocate to the Chief. She's not far. Bring the softie. Charlie and I will take the stretcher. You've got the gun, Face, if things get hairy.'

Charlie couldn't help but be invigorated. It was part of Nishimura's gift. He was generally plainspoken, which made his rare indulgence in military barking all the more bracing. Again she was reminded of Luis, the way he'd call on her to weigh a bowl of intestines or posit a cause of death. Her anarchistic girlhood self would have been appalled to learn she liked taking orders, but she did, because she liked nailing the results. She hustled to the stretcher, waited for Nishimura to take his end, and lifted on a quick three count.

The softie's eyes wobbled like the egg skin over unbroken yolks. Since the foundation of Hospice, Charlie had administered to hundreds of softies, both as the facility supervisor and, when it was her turn, as a Caretaker. Right now, in fact, she was Caretaker to an especially poignant softie called Lesser Hedrick. Seeing softies up close could still break her heart. She wondered if her young self would be appalled at that too. Had Charlene Rutkowski become something of a softie as well?

Determining post-mort decomp levels had been part of her job in San Diego. Zombies provided a tougher challenge, one Luis would have relished. Their deterioration moved more slowly. Some theorized it had to do with their ingestion of nerve tissue from victims' brains. Charlie didn't think this held water; reports of zombies craving brains were as false as those claiming zombies had enough healthy cartilage and tendons to run. The stages of rot, however, were scalable to living levels.

This specimen was a classic example. She looked to have been roughly eighteen years old when she'd died. Stages of rigor mortis, swelling, bursting, liquefaction, and adipocere were in her past. Charlie had memorized the order of organ putridity via a vulgar acrostic she'd created with fellow med-school students: *Little boys should investigate short men like Bob Hope likely kneeling beneath every pretty dame's vagina and uterus* stood for larynx, brain (infantile), stomach, intestines, spleen, mesentery and omentum, liver, brain (adult), heart, lungs, kidney, bladder, esophagus, pancreas, diaphragm, blood vessels, and uterus. Every one of these parts was kaput in this softie. Because she'd been lying fallow for some time, weeds had grown through her back, flowering from her pelvis, ribs, neck, and mouth. It was cold now, and the plant matter was shriveled, but the phenomenon was always breathtaking, as if the zombie's own body couldn't help but reflect the earth's revived verdure.

Retiring as Slowtown zombies were, they began to emerge, *crick-crack*, from dark places to seek the source of the ruckus. Charlie and Nishimura took the next block at a trot while the Face and Hoffmann jogged in front, monitoring the shriveled faces surfacing from storefronts and upper windows. Charlie believed their white eyes, many gone marmalade in the dark, focused on the writhing remains of the softie.

The Chief sat beneath the donut shop's shredded awning. She did not note their arrival, but that was normal. Charlie and Nishimura set the stretcher in the middle of the road and joined the others in surveying the area. Charlie thought, as she often did, of how quickly the recovery party would be encircled if all the zombies decided to descend. Decayed or not, on this street, they had the numbers to win.

'What do we do?' Charlie asked.

'What we don't do,' Nishimura said, 'is take undue risk. Everyone got that? Free will exists in Fort York. If Greer, or anyone else, wants to act stupid and chase after a boyfriend, that's their prerogative.'

He pushed out these words well enough, and it was the proper boilerplate to convey, but Charlie could hear the hard fold down the center of his voice. The fact was, Greer Morgan was not an anonymous citizen. She was the legendary Lion, and having her at the fort was a symbol that even those known for violence were better suited in a place of peace. Losing the Lion so quickly after losing the Dove wouldn't look good. On the eve of the Blockhouse Four vote, it might make Nishimura look all the weaker.

'Greer,' Charlie hissed. 'Goddamn it.'

Goddamn herself too. For three months, she'd kept to herself a fact about Richard's past no one else knew. Nishimura said when you entered Fort York, you had the right to shed your past and make a new beginning. Greer Morgan, for instance, had done just that. By the time this bad business with the Blockhouse Four rose up, it seemed too late for Charlie to reveal what she knew about Richard. But she should have. She was starting to see that.

'Let's do a check, three blocks, no more,' Nishimura said. 'No calling out, all right? No getting closer than sidewalks. Walk soft and listen. You hear something, give a snap. Same configuration: Charlie, Hoffmann, left. Me and the Face, right. Ten minutes, then we book it. Show me nods.'

They nodded. Nishimura stepped right, a navy snap to his heels, the Face following, soft as a cat. Charlie decided: when she got back to the fort, she'd tell people about Richard. For now, though, do the job. She took to the curb and, with Hoffmann right behind, began moving slowly down Queen Street.

A record shop, its floor the onyx scree of shattered vinyl. A tea shop, a spicy redolence mixed with sweet zombie spoil. A lingerie shop, empty but for a few lacy puffs and elastic straps. Charlie stepped, stopped, listened, eyed zombies eyeing her, and moved on, Hoffmann so close her breath furled around Charlie.

Three blocks, and nothing. Nishimura pointed back up the street where they'd left the softie, and they performed the routine in reverse, though not really. Nishimura might be doing things by the book on his side, but on her side, Charlie didn't bother. She'd heard nothing but *crick-cracks* and did not expect that to change.

Etta Hoffmann didn't believe in preambles: 'She's gone.'

Charlie replied at a Slowtown volume, 'Or she doesn't want to be found.'

Compared to the walk west, the walk east was dark. Trees, parking signs, and trolley stop shelters dripped into a gulley of shadow. Elevated frameworks clung to pieces of original signage, and the golden light made molten hues from what used to advertise frozen yogurt, mobile phones, desserts. The going assumption was that, at night, Slowtown was as still as Fort York. But did Charlie know that for sure? The *crick-cracks* might combine to create the crackle of a boisterous bonfire as putrid percussionists tightened in a ritual knot.

She was scaring herself. Time for chitchat. A regular friendship with Hoffmann was impossible, but she'd grown attached to the odd, and oddly brave, woman whose first trip outside the D.C. area had been that long, dangerous safari to Fort York with the Archive in tow. During that trip, Hoffmann had latched on to Charlie with an avidity that was as strange as it was touching. Their comparable ages never prevented Charlie feeling like Hoffmann was a younger sister, even a daughter, the child she and Luis never had the time to raise.

'Etta. When do we start getting more sun?'

'Winter solstice. Six weeks.'

'Six. Christ. And daytime peaks in what? July?'

'June 21.'

'Fabulous. Is Luvvie going to send out a reminder?'

'I don't know what Luvvie is going to do.'

Charlie grinned, since Hoffmann couldn't see her do it. Old Muddy's librarian worked too hard, and frankly too much knowledge of how the New Library functioned resided in her head alone. So Charlie had assigned to her an assistant, Luvvie Lafayette. The girl was everything Hoffmann wasn't. Peppy and persistent, the flirty, fast-talking, twenty-year-old lesbian had the brazen practicality that mystified anyone who came of age before 10/23. Hoffmann reacted to Luvvie like a wasp flying too close to her face, but Charlie suspected she'd come around.

'Well, whether it's Luvvie or you, let us know when we're close, huh?'

'Of course. It's on my calendar.'

'These days, we all need something to live for.'

Before arriving at AMLD, Charlie had never met anyone who'd kept an exact day count during the Second Dark Ages. The best unexpected perk of annexing the Hoffmann Archive of Tales from the New World was reclaiming a calendar. Upon meeting Hoffmann and learning of her Archive, someone at the fort had asked, rather offhandedly, if she knew what day it was. Hoffmann had responded specifically and confidently. The man's eyes welled up. He shouted for others to gather.

People kept asking the same question, needing to have the experience of receiving a true answer after a decade of wild estimation. Some broke into laughter: It was a Monday? How could it possibly be a Monday?! Some broke into sobs: How could they have misplaced an entire two years? There was hugging, dancing, celebration.

It was a holiday no one expected, a birthday – a rebirth day – for everyone at once.

Time that had dissipated like dandelion fluff snapped back into stackable blocks: days, weeks, months, years. Nishimura had been pushing folks to adopt calendars and clocks for eighteen months; Hoffmann convinced them overnight. Was it possible to build a clock, they wondered? Hoffmann dug through the sloppy stacks of the mostly ignored Toronto Public Library branch across the street, found the right text, and reported that, yes, they could. Behold: the elegant sundial. Plans for sundials passed like gossip, and soon crude rods surrounded by hemispherical shells marked with hour lines were cropping up everywhere. Within a week, a Master Sundial, plated with valueless pennies, was erected in the center of Fort York: the place of honor within the place of honor.

A team set to work on building an honest-to-God clock featuring brass gearing and a quartz oscillator. It didn't work yet, but when Charlie heard it go *click-click* – so close, yet so different from *crick-crack* – she accepted it as the world's heart, resuscitated from the brink. Being able to measure the time going forward gave dimension to time passed. Luis's death by her bullet was no longer smeared over her entire past. Rather, his death had occurred a specific, identifiable quantity of time ago. Now she could hold the instant up to the light and see it, and grieve it, and for the first time, *put it behind her,* back in the lineup of hours, days, months, and years where it belonged.

One page of her past, cataloged in the Archive, held the biggest regret of her post-10/23 life, and that was saying a lot. It was, in fact, the first page of her record, the night of October 23 in Autopsy Suite 1. According to Etta Hoffmann, John Doe was among the first, if not the *very* first, zombies to revive in the United States, and wow, did Charlie wish she had never learned that.

What if John Doe had been the ambassador of a new race? What were the chances the first zombie would manifest beneath the gentle hands of two people whose sympathy to the dead should have made them the least likely to panic? All John Doe had done was look at her and reach for her, and what had she done in response? She'd dropped his heart, kicked it with a bootie-covered shoe. She'd set the tone for everything that followed.

What if she'd committed the original sin?

What if all of Earth was paying for it?

A preposterous, self-important worry, one that nonetheless kept her awake for months. When she felt Face-like levels of honesty, she admitted the John Doe regrets were why she'd made herself the leading force of Hospice, the whole reason recovery missions like this existed. No offense to Hoffmann, but right then, she wanted to see Lesser Hedrick more than anyone. The crisis of the Blockhouse Four might be inevitable in the social experiment of Old Muddy, but she'd still feel safer balming her past scars at the softie's side.

'What do you think?' she asked. 'We all going to be okay?'

'I don't know,' Hoffmann said.

'Based on history, I mean. The new history. You know it best.'

'Then no. We aren't.'

Charlie sighed. 'You need to learn the art of the white lie.'

'Yes. We are going to be okay.'

'It's just, I don't know, everything, all at once. Richard, the Blockhouse Four. Muse leaving. Now Greer. People are going to feel vulnerable. It's all going to play right into Richard's hands. It's like we're cursed.'

'There's no such thing.'

'But you don't think we'll be okay. You feel it, same as me. We're on the ledge.'

'If Richard weren't here, it wouldn't be "the Blockhouse Four" at all.'

Coming from Hoffmann, this was sweeping oratory and deserved Charlie's consideration. By the time she arrived back at the softie on the stretcher, she understood. If Richard hadn't come, puffing his flames of justice, the Blockhouse Four would simply be known as Federico, Reed, Stuart, and Mandy. The chasm between these four people everyone knew and liked and Richard's foreboding epithet was deep and throbbing with monsters.

Nishimura and the Face caught up, and the four gathered around the softie. Nishimura checked the yellow razor of sun before sighing.

'Anybody got anything? A button? Piece of foil?'

Pockets were checked, but no one did. Nishimura nodded grimly, took a deep breath, and headed over to the Chief. Charlie believed in Nishimura's policy of addressing the Chief as rarely as possible. The zombie was physically delicate, and her relationship to the living more so. Pushing a minor miracle like that, Charlie thought, was like petting a butterfly. A reasonable instinct, but you'd probably rip off its wings.

From Queen Street's defunct trolley tracks, she watched Nishimura's slow approach and respectful bow, and then, to her surprise, his gentle kneel, his forward knee nearly touching the Chief's ankle shackle so he could look up at her rather than down. Charlie was touched. Not only for the respect it showed the Chief, but for how it revealed how badly he wanted to find Greer. Nishimura's cool rationality made it too easy to forget that unfenced love for his fellow human fueled most of what he did.

'She's not looking at him,' Charlie observed.

'Sometimes she doesn't,' the Face said.

'She's not gesturing at all.'

'It can be subtle. A little roll of the eyes.'

'No,' Charlie determined. 'It's not working.'

'Then she doesn't *want* it to work,' the Face pointed out, and Charlie had to agree.

It was only because Nishimura had kneeled, she thought, that he noticed two little wads of paper beneath the Chief's withered feet. Much later, Charlie would think that this moment, as much as any, had pointed a path forward: it was when you humbled yourself before another that secrets were revealed to you, right there in the dirt. Keeping one eye on the Chief, Nishimura picked up the wads and flattened them over his palms.

For the first time Charlie had heard, Nishimura didn't use a Slow-town voice.

'It's a picture of Muse. And the Chief, she's got a new button. Greer, and maybe Muse, they must be right—'

From the third floor over the donut shop came not a woody, duster, screecher, or any of the sounds that narrated this gradually changing world but the kind of noise one didn't hear much these days: the deliberate, vehement crash only a living person could make, followed by a sharp, piercing shout.

Little American Flags

Personal History Transcript #1
Location: Fort York New Library
Subject: Charlene Rutkowski
Interviewer: Etta Hoffmann
Time: 4,217–10:05

Notes: This is the first Personal History transcript recorded at Fort York in Toronto, Ontario (Canada).

Q.
The exact literal precise minute I was forced to shave my head. That's when I knew: this was not going to be a good time for women. It could have been. Zombies didn't go after women more than men, or Black people more than white, or Republicans more than Democrats. If things had gone a different way, I don't think we'd even be calling it the Second Dark Age. We'd be calling it the Great Equalizer.

Q.
I do think that was a good question. You're doing great. I think this whole thing is going to be really great.

Q.

Early. Way before you were taking calls. No one knew a single
clue about a single thing. Was it airborne? Was it foodborne?
One guy with us had the idea it could be mites, or ticks, or lice,
and that was that. Off came the hair. Not with an electric razor
either. We were on the move. We were in cars and garbage
trucks. For us it was scissors and disposable razors, and dull
ones too, because we only had one pack, and at our peak, there
were forty-eight of us. The men didn't care. It was actually scary
how much they didn't care. You shave the heads of a group of
guys, any group of guys, and you start getting skinhead vibes.
Something about looking the same – they start acting the same
too. The women, it was . . . fraught. I don't want this to sound
like the women were weaker. But I cried when they shaved my
head. What can I say? Hair is all wrapped up in emotional stuff,
you know? You can't control that. Maybe if it had been the Great
Equalizer, it wouldn't have mattered.

Q.

Clothes too. Of course clothes too. They had to eradicate those
nonexistent mites, didn't they? Funny how the men and boys
got their clothes back a lot sooner than the women and girls.
They said it was because they had limited soap, and had to get
clean clothes to the ones working outside the caravan, and those
were all males, no exception. It was California, they said, we'd be
fine. I guess we were. But it didn't feel fine. Bunch of naked
women, crammed in a car? Does that sound fine to you?

Q.

The worst part of it, easily. You were instantly helpless. I'd only
been with Luis a couple weeks, but I'd done everything, *everything*. With the garbage crew, they'd fight with zombies and

people would get killed right in front of me, on the other side of the car window, and I couldn't do anything. To help them, to protect myself. We were a fucking Happy Meal in there, just waiting to be eaten. They had the child locks on, and there was always a man guarding both front doors. You could try squeezing out, but – see this here?

Q.

Shotgun butt to the chin. I tried to get out, got butted, and now there's blood all over the inside of the SUV. What do these other women know? Maybe this Rutkowski bitch is going to bleed to death and in a few minutes they'll be locked inside a car with a zombie. You see what I'm saying? The fear just doubles and triples until you're dependent on the men. You're doting on them so you'll get clothing and food. You're seducing them. You have no choice. It's the old world all over again. It happens so fast.

Q.

Relatively speaking? Yeah, it ended quick. But the psychological effect I think took years to play out. The end of the garbage-truck caravan was nothing special. One of the cars broke down in a big-box shopping area. Best Buy, OfficeMax. Zombies rolled out like a fog. This was only a few months in. People had plenty of spit and vinegar, as old Maury Rutkowski used to say, but no procedures yet. I'm sure that's all over your Archive: procedure saved asses. Zombies had us totally circled by the time the women were able to get out of the SUV's front doors, and I'd say half of us died. Rosa made it into a car with some men and got away. You don't need to know who she was, but I was glad she got out of there. I think. It's a screwed-up world, right, when you don't know if someone's survival is good or bad?

Q.

By another car! There's something very American about it, don't you think? You watched a lot of TV. *Happy Days, Dukes of Hazzard*. What says 'U.S.A.' like a car? Henry Ford lived right here in the good ol' U.S.A., remember. He was also a racist. American to the core, right?

Q.

A van, to be exact. What we used to call a child-molester van. Big white box, no windows. They picked me up on a frontage road off Highway 52. What do they teach girls? Never go to a second location. But I'd been on my own for a week, and was starving, and thirsty, and sleepless, and pretty much definitely going to die, and here was this vehicle that *ran*, you know? Second location, third location, whatever. I was in. I waved my arms, and I guess they didn't think my peach-fuzz head looked too weird, and that's how I got mixed up with the Patriots.

Q.

Different, right from the get-go. The garbage-truck gang, they were anonymous, no one in charge beyond men in general. The Patriots had a leader, this guy Kristoffer Skipp. He wasn't in the van. He was in Salina, Kansas. The guy driving the van worked for him – he'd been doing some job for Skipp in San Diego on 10/23 – and though Kristoffer Skipp got all the credit for the Patriots, I think it was this guy, the driver, Byrd Entwistle, who made the whole thing take off. Something was screwy with Byrd. He'd lost his nut in those first weeks. But he'd lost it in a really persuasive way. This boss of his became like a god in his head, and he went on about him for fifteen hundred miles, the great Kristoffer Skipp, how no one would be able to weather the storm better than the ingenious Kristoffer

Skipp. You say that stuff enough to a van load of people who'd lost all willpower, they start to believe it.

Q.

I was the sixth person in that van: three men, two women, twenty-some cans of fuel. Near San Bernardino, we hooked up with another van of people, and they liked what Byrd was saying, and then the whole group picked up a third van full of folks at the Utah border, and a fourth and fifth in Colorado Springs. All thirty of us made it to Kansas. When we got to Salina, there was this big billboard: *KRISTOFFER SKIPP, GENERATOR KING.* I think I started to get the picture then.

Q.

Would you call it a cult, though? Maybe I'm being defensive. He certainly had the compound for it, his outdoor showcase arena. Totally walled in, because he'd been obsessed with people trying to steal from him. Probably untrue before 10/23, but definitely true after. Think about it this way. Luis and I had one single generator we stole from his neighbor, and for two weeks, we worshipped at it like a metal temple. It let us watch DVDs, listen to music, put up Christmas lights, feel like human beings. Imagine if you had a couple giant outbuildings full of generators and another full of fuel. Not only would you have continual electricity, your bartering power would be through the roof. We had food, we had desserts, we had entertainment.

Q.

Girl, you *know* he had heads on pikes. A hundred? Two hundred? Kristoffer Skipp was a big-dicker. He was one of those guys just waiting for something like 10/23 to happen. He sort of reclined into it, you know? His house was right there on the

premises, a big, electrified palace. I saw things there I thought
I'd never see again. Working toasters. Irons for clothes. Electric
can openers. Those air fresheners you plug into outlets. All of it
flooded in light, day and night. You could see Generator King
from miles away, like the sun. And we were like moths. We
would've sizzled ourselves crispy to keep close to it.

Q.
I'm not defending him. But everyone back then wanted to get
rid of the zombies. They truly believed that was the only viable
option. Kristoffer was different because he actually had the
means to do it. *Jihad* wasn't the best choice of words, that's all.
I don't know. Maybe I *am* defending him.

Q.
Mostly overnight trips at first. Great Bend, Dodge City. Wichita,
after a while. Topeka, Lawrence. Eventually north into Lincoln
and Omaha, south into Tulsa and Amarillo. Jihads could take all
kinds of shapes. IEDs, primarily. Like I said, we had gasoline like
crazy and the know-how to pump gas from beneath gas stations –
tens of thousands of gallons, whole lakes of the stuff untouched.
Trigger mechanisms were easy. Old cell phones were like acorns,
all over the place. Half of what Kristoffer traded for was C-4 and
Semtex from construction sites, so there's our explosives. Naturally only one thing reliably attracted zombies, so we hid our
IEDs inside fresh bodies.

Q.
Dead bodies. Freshly *dead* bodies.

Q.
Not that I know of. Though I guess I can't rule it out.

Q.

We'd fill a car with gas, set it on fire, and let it rip into a crowd of zombies. A few times we tried suicide bombers, attaching the bomb to a zombie and waiting for it to join a larger herd. Blast wave, shrapnel, fire. It really tore them up. Every time, after the zombies were in itty-bitty pieces, we'd take these little American flags – Kristoffer had boxes of them, stupid give-aways for customers – and we'd plant them right in the middle of the carnage. In a few years, there were thousands across the lower Midwest, whole fields of American flags like wildflowers. Anywhere bodies were blown to bits, that was the land of the Patriots.

Q.

Proud, yes. Flippant, no – I don't think I'm being flippant. We were killing beings who'd invaded our country, who were try-ing to replace our culture with their own.

Q.

I do, in fact. I do know how that sounds, Etta. Not to tell you how to do your job, because you're doing a fine job, but maybe the better question to ask is why it took me so long? It's not an answer I'm proud of. With the garbage-truck gang, everything had been so overtly awful. At Generator King, everything seemed so idyllic. But the two places shared one thing: women, how they used us. They always took a couple of us on jihads, but why? To make sure anyone who got zombie guts on him got cleaned off. To make sure everyone got fed. Back at the com-pound, what did we do? All the women and girls? We kept house. We cooked meals. We had sex with the men. And the people who read this transcript one day might judge us, but I ask you, what were we supposed to do? What were any women, across history, supposed to do? The worst part was, while you were prancing around the sparkly kitchen in your heels and your dress with your hair grown back pretty, you could feel your survival skills drain away. I'll tell you something. You can be infected with an idea that same way you can be infected by a zombie.

Q.

I can isolate it to a single moment. The men were sitting around the table, Kristoffer at the head, while a few of us women buzzed around, pouring coffee, picking up dishes. They were discussing what to do with us. Should girls learn first aid at ten years old instead of fifteen? Should the pregnant women be moved to the second floor where the generators weren't so loud? Should we get the older women knitting sweaters and darning socks? I don't know why, but it hit me. They were talking about me, my life, my future, and I wasn't even being consulted.

Q.

Waited, that's what. One thing you can count on from any patriot is they can't resist spreading patriotism. It was Year Fucking Six, maybe Year Seven? Somewhere between zombie rats and zombie dogs. By that time, the Patriots were blowing up whole towns. That's the kind of stock we had. We'd carpet-bomb the place. We'd squeal this police siren, our signal for anyone alive in town to get the hell out, and then we'd descend, wire the streets and buildings with explosives, and *boom-boom-boom-boom*. Bonus was, it took care of rats like pretty much nothing else. Some of us women were sewing great big US flags by then, and there were always a couple rolled up in the back of a van, ready to plant on poles above the ruins. Smoky, black, bloody ruins – it was the country we wanted.

Q.

I walked. What could be simpler? But is there anything that's
ever been stronger? People getting to their feet and walking?
The Patriots' wiring had gotten sophisticated, which meant the
actual detonations were easier, but there wasn't any stopping
them once they started. We were in a town called Guymon in
the Oklahoma panhandle, and as soon as I heard the first bomb
go, I dropped a pitcher of lemonade right in the dirt and walked
straight into town.

Q.

I'm sure they tried. But how could they really follow? Guymon
was ten seconds from being an inferno. A fast-food joint: *blam!*
A police station: *boosh!* Geysers of fire, and even though I knew
where some of the bombs were, I sure didn't know all of them.
Pieces of brick whacked me on the shoulders. I got shrapnel in
the back of my legs. I had to pat out a fire in my hair, all that big
blond hair I'd grown back. This thing, this metal coil, came
flinging out of the fire, red hot, and ripped open my cheek and
neck – that's how I got this. Even then I kept walking. I walked
through hell and somehow, some way, didn't get burned alive.

Q.

Perfect question, Etta. They did, in fact. Some of the men drove
around the other side of town to catch me if I came out. I saw
them right before I passed right by this nice brick building and
noticed all these faces staring out the windows. Zombie faces.
What do I care? These were women's faces, though. Only
women. I got closer and saw the windows were shatterproof
plastic. That's why they'd never gotten out. And even though
the whole world was blowing up, I got closer and really looked
at them. I could tell when they'd died, they'd had black eyes and

fat lips and bruises, because they'd never healed. The place was a women's shelter. A safe house. And this line just came to me. I don't know where from. Did someone famous say it? *Haunt them like you're already dead.*

Q.

Haunt them like you're already dead.

Q.

Haunt them like you're already dead.

Q.

Because I want you to remember it. Because one day, you might need it. When I let those women out, it felt like letting every woman out of every car in the garbage caravan. Don't ask me how I knew it, but once those zombie women came upon those Patriot men hoping to catch me, there would be a fight, a real fight, and finding worthless old me wouldn't be a priority anymore.

Q.

Eventually. Once I made it out of town. Eventually, I did look back, and a fair number of zombies had made it out too, and you can call me crazy if you want, and I know I'd sucked down a lot of smoke and lost some blood and wasn't in a super-reliable state of mind, but I swear all those zombies were women too. Like they'd remembered they could run, and hunt, and I was glad, even if the one they were hunting right that second was me. The one closest was so strange-looking it makes me doubt the whole memory. She had these hatchet wrists and, of all things, a bow – like a bow-hunting bow. She had these metal legs, like racing prosthetics, and they made her move really fast. I thought, damn, this robo-zombie's going to get me. But she didn't. She looked at the sun, like she was relieved it wasn't hidden behind smoke, and headed due west.

Q.

Yeah, the rest of the zombies chased me. Look, this is the first interview. Let's set a precedent for not prattling on forever. Plus, I'm tired. Aren't you tired? Talking is tiring. I'd forgotten that. Who's had time to talk much for fifteen years? Long story short, the Patriots didn't mean to teach me about getting gas from gas stations, and hot-wiring cars, and all that, but they did, and it helped me get going, and fast. All I wanted was to get as far as possible from the land of little American flags. After a while, it only made sense. I was headed to Canada.

Astonish Ourselves

Twenty years ago, Greer had been woken from sleep by a pounding on the trailer door. It was early; only Daddy was up, doubtlessly fumbling with his HortiPlastics uniform and monitoring the coffee maker's black spits, but he'd come alive at that, using his most resonant voice to scare off whatever druggie had chosen to pester them. But talk ensued, and when Greer crept into the main room, she and Conan, peeking from under his sheet on the sofa, watched one of the Sunnybrook owners enter, accompanied by a white guy with a big gut hanging over a holstered sidearm.

The stranger started poking through their shit while Daddy sputtered. This was illegal! You need a warrant! The owner rolled his eyes and said, Mr Morgan, didn't you want to figure out who was selling drugs and making beautiful Sunnybrook a hellhole? The humiliation was hot, and Daddy gulped it in place of his coffee. Big-gut man found no evidence of drugs, but plenty of evidence of a lousy life: a pail catching rainwater; window glass repaired with tape; a system of bent hangers keeping the refrigerator door shut, innovations the Morgans had been proud of until these men sneered at how these animals lived.

Greer was the big-gut man now, sidearm traded for a bow, nosing where she wasn't wanted: behind Slowtown's closed doors. She had good reason, but hadn't the owner of the Last Resort thought the same? Greer opened the ground-floor apartment door. A zombie looked up at her from an easy chair so wasted that exposed springs corkscrewed through his rotted thighs. The tufted, polyester carpet was littered with crap: an oven mitt, half a briefcase, loose synthesizer keys, the bones of a squirrel. Her first thought?

Animals. They live like animals.

Humiliation burned for both the zombies and herself, sharp at either end like all the pikes out there holding severed heads. Thinking of zombies as animals was no better than what Mama Shaw's orderly had said a million years ago: *Maybe They're smarter than They seem.* She strode in, too quickly for the zombie to do anything but stare in blank surprise, and checked to make sure the other rooms were vacant. They were not: two zombies in one, three in another, and in the bathroom a dozen zombie rats drawing their whiskers back from yellow teeth. But no Muse, so she hustled out, shut the door, closed her eyes, and listened. Still there, that low, musical vibration. She leaned to see up the stairwell. Two stories, four more units. She could do this.

Consensus estimates were that Queen Street buildings hid one or two shamblers each, but after Greer finished her second-floor census, she was up to fourteen. In a single building. Either a lot of zombies wanted to live near the Chief, or Slowtown was far more populated than anyone had guessed. Greer's skin burned hotter, baking her bones. Keep up the pace, stay vigilant. Glancing down the stairs, she could see the first-floor zombie had pulled his thighs free from the easy chair, opened his door, and climbed the first flight of stairs. *Crick-cracks* could be heard behind every second-floor door too. She was an outsider being reminded of it – gently so far, though she couldn't rely on that goodwill to last.

RESIST: Had they received the message already?

Steps were missing on the flight to the third floor, giving glimpses of zombies gathering below. Greer reached the landing and felt the flooring sway. Unless it was the effect of the music, so close now she didn't have to investigate both apartments. It was a guitar, no question. She placed her hand on a hard plastic doorknob, feeling for vibrations in her fingertips, knuckles, and sternum, all places that had been touched before by 'Walk Away', as well as by the hands that played it.

She opened the door, crossed the threshold, and thought, *That was too easy.* There had to be a twist; twists were all the past fifteen years had supplied. But what she saw was exactly what she'd hoped to see for three months, not a creased magazine photo of eighteen-year-old Muse King, but the real-life late-thirties version, playing the 1978 maple-necked, mahogany-bodied, custom Alpine White Les Paul Gibson called Hewitt. Though he did not sing, the gray puffs of his breath in the cold air might as well have been whole songbooks. He was alive.

Every possible emotion shot from Greer's body, a maelstrom of relief, gratitude, betrayal, and rage, that last of which, of course, because she was the Lion, dominated. She slammed the apartment door behind her and let out a single ice-pick shriek.

'You're here? All this time? I'll put *your* head on a pike! Asshole!'

The prehensile scrambling of his fingers paused a beat before continuing. Less than one second, and yet it cleared a space inside which she could clear her eyes and try to think. It was Muse, all right, but not the Muse she remembered. He was pungent, too sweet. His meager sweater draped over the knurls of skeletal shoulders. His face was whittled to a thin pyramid and coated with a beard like black mold, and his skin was the color of sandstone. The red bulbs of his eyes shone through the churn of his breath, into which she wanted to dip her face until it turned to tears on her cheeks.

Stairs creaked behind her. Zombies were coming, slow and weak, and in numbers she hadn't expected.

'Get up.' She snapped her fingers. 'We'll talk it out later.'

He smiled, a pale purple slash. 'Remember this tune?'

'Remember *this* tune? Me yelling at your ass to get the fuck in gear?'

'Shh.' He nodded dreamily. 'Listen.'

The Gibson was scored with the surface damage of the Second Dark Age, but a music-store raid in Year Two had supplied Muse with enough strings to last a lifetime, and the guitar sounded good, with the homemade tractor-tire buffer still secured over the sound hole. Greer had no wish to squander seconds, but knew, as anyone did after fifteen years of living with someone, the exchange rate of giving a little to get a little. She made fists and pretended to listen, and then, quite by accident, recognized the *plink-plink-plink*.

'Walk Away' had segued into the song Muse had been playing when they'd first met at a dirt crossroads in a Missouri field. She had too much control to let a gasp escape, but felt it jab like a ripped-out rib. Muse, his voice a ravaged rumble that only made it prettier, grated through the second verse.

> *Take my burned old bones*
> *Cool them in the river, y'all*
> *Take my burned old bones, ooo-ee*
> *Cool them in the river, y'all*
> *So all the pitch-black things I done*
> *Slide right down the waterfall.*

Muse had again heard Greer's approach and played to guide her way. It was the only reason to pine for those fearsome days: wishing to feel how she'd felt the morning they'd met. She remembered how their conversation had played out. It was easier than inventing new dialogue.

'You thirsty?' she asked, an echo wending through the years.

Muse smiled. He hadn't forgotten his line: 'Need to piss.'

Greer's turn: 'You eat like a dog.'

'Woof,' Muse recited.

Greer managed to swing her arms, heavy as dead anacondas, at the collapsing apartment. 'This your place?'

Muse, as tired and ill as he looked, had the reply ready: 'Nah, girl. Just wandering around and got to feeling Faustian. I'm ready to cut me some Robert Johnson-type deal.'

Greer needed a cane, so she lodged her bow against the floor, its hard thump announcing the end of playacting. 'I know who that is now. "Kind Hearted Woman Blues".'

'Then you know what he did out there at the Devil's Crossroads.'

'Sold his soul.' The words frightened her, and she waved a hand to conceal it. 'Come on. Put it away.'

'Can't go with you, baby.'

Her sigh became a thorned hairball. To clear it, she aimed her face at the floor. It looked like a junkie lived here. Canned foods opened with the stomp of a boot heel. Crusted stains where the jellied contents had squirted free. Plastic cigarette lighters. Scorch marks and ashes from half-assed fires. Old socks and rags soiled with what might be blood. A bucket in the corner that could be holding piss and shit. She kicked one of the emptied cans and followed its wobbly roll.

Cat food, its label photo of an orange Persian degraded to a chiaroscuro. The sight stung her eyes; her heart too. This was bad. She wanted to fold herself onto the mucky mattress and hold this once-beautiful boy, but worried after she was buckled in by his bony arms, she wouldn't get back up, not even when the zombies closed in with their vestigial teeth and dry tongues.

'This has to do with all that stuff you were talking about,' she said. 'For months. Years, really.'

He chuckled softly. 'You never listened.'

'I'll listen now, back at the fort. There's a vote tomorrow. You don't know anything. It's Richard, he wants to – it's too much to explain.'

'Richard,' he sighed. 'He's why I left when I did.'

'Now he can be why you come back. You can talk to people, make them understand what they should do. You're good at that.'

'It's too late. I have to be here. For my people.'

'Your people are at the fort.'

His smile looked like it hurt. He rolled his neck, which crackled like rice cereal, an odd backdrop to his string-picking.

'You know Hoffmann, yeah?' he asked. 'The librarian?'

Greer jumped on it; she'd jump on anything. 'She's down there on Queen Street right now. Let's go see her.'

'We all knew it deep down, but it didn't sink in till that lady laid it out. "The zombie virus isn't cannibalistic, it's antihuman."'

Squeals, creaks, moans: doors opened, banisters gripped, stairs climbed.

'No one wanted to hear that shit then,' she said, 'and we don't have time to hear it now.'

'Hoffmann got a lot of things right. But she got one thing wrong.'

'Enough with the drama. Say it, then we go.'

His five right fingers sprang out, deserting the strings, while his left fingers smothered the neck, the silence of snow.

'The zombies aren't the virus. We are.'

A long, cold hand slid down her throat, taking hold of her hope like viscera and yanking them out her mouth. It wasn't the specifics of what Muse said; she didn't give a shit about specifics. It was that tone of stubborn belief. Nothing was going to get him out of here besides a brute force she'd never manage, not with zombies amassing. Tears rimmed her eyes.

'This is what you're doing out here? Deep thinking with the white-eyes?'

'What did I say at the crossroads? Best place to hide is right out in the open.'

'In the freezing cold? Eating cat food?'

'Just listen, Greer. Just listen. I'm going to play some more.'

'*This* is what the fuck you're *doing*?'

'It soothes them when I play. It'll soothe you.'

'*I'm* not dead!'

Or was she? Standing above a demolished donut shop with a cat food-eating blues guitarist? Sounded like afterlife nonsense to her.

'What do viruses do? Hear me out.' He was playing again, heart-beat patterns, lovelorn dips. 'They multiply, adapt, and kill. People did all that first, didn't we? We were on our way to take down the whole operation. *We* were the disease, Greer. What does that make the zombies?'

'You want me to say "the cure". There, I said it.'

'They're the antivirus, that's right. Go easy now. Feel the music. I'm telling you now why I can't go with you.'

'You left me. You *left* me.'

'Just for a bit. We're all coming back together.'

'What does that even mean?'

'I used to sing a lot about soul, but I never gave it a single real thought. I think about it now. I think about it all the time. Because we let our virus run wild, the world had no choice but to put up a defense. It tried to stop us. It ripped our soul right out of our bodies, made it into halves: the living, the dead. We're all at the crossroads now, baby. We got to put body and soul back together if we're going to have a chance. If the world's going to have a chance.'

'We already have the chance. It's Old Muddy, KK.'

'KK? Uh-oh.' He laughed. 'I'm in trouble now.'

She felt a flicker of the old anger and snatched it. 'Let me get this straight. You figured this all out. You. King Kong. Musician. Fifteen years, no one has shit-all of a clue what the hell went wrong, but you eat cat food for a few weeks and suddenly you're Socrates.'

'It's not me. It's the music. I don't think it even had to be music. Could've been poetry. Painting. *Art,* is what I'm saying. Art, all of it, went down the tubes after 10/23, right? Except me. I kept playing. I kept the flame. The only reason I was able to do that was you. You did the fighting. You did the protecting. You made art, *all* art, possible again. You helped keep our souls alive. You should be proud.'

'Proud? I'm not proud of anything. You think those St Croix kids aren't screaming in my skull every fucking day? If I'd bashed that guitar of yours into a hundred pieces, maybe I'd be proud of that. Maybe.'

'I think you have to go through some shit before you can see it. And you've gone through some shit. Will and Darlene, too – I think that's why they sent me their son's guitar. We got to bring people together, animals together, plants, trees, fire, water together, the whole thing, and accept all of it, find beauty in all of it. That's art. That's art.'

'You sound like someone who's about to do something stupid. Muse. Please. Come back to the fort.'

'The fort's a step that doesn't go anywhere. Greer, we got to stop trying to own the world. We tried that already. We fought over it like wolves over a carcass. Forgetting, you know, the world's not ours to fight over. We're here to live *with* it. Musically. Poetically. Artfully.'

'All right. Okay? *All right.* I'm not arguing. You hear those sounds on the stairs? Fuck! I've got a *bow* here, Muse, not a machine gun. You're going to get us both killed; how poetic is that?'

Muse's ring finger dandled the B string, a tremorous lament.

'They won't hurt you. Not while you're with me.'

'A little blues is going to keep them away?'

His lips now, the same tremor, the same lament.

'Because I'm like them now. Or will be, right quick.' He smiled sadly. 'My old spirit's going to slide right down the waterfall.'

As if on a hinge, her head tilted back down toward the floor. It wasn't only burn marks and food cans that made this place look like a junkie's den. There was a used syringe. Several syringes, actually, probably scrounged from the vet clinic a few blocks north. If Muse had been honest about his past, intravenous drugs were out of his comfort zone, which meant this was something so awful she didn't know how she guessed it.

'Did you . . . ? Muse. Did you make yourself . . . ?'

Both sleeves of his sweater were ripped and unraveling, and along his left arm she saw the black entry points of injection. He was nodding, soft and metered, the way he might reassure a child who might be thinking about sobbing. His playing, too, had mellowed into a lilt that sounded rather Irish. Only now did she sense how much of a struggle it was for him to make his fingers move, to keep his body upright, all for her.

'Don't get spooked,' he urged. 'Took me a time to find a vein, that's all.'

Tears ran, hot grease down her cold cheeks.

'Muse, no.'

'I took it from the Chief. From the best of them all. She's the mom I never had. The dad too. Though Will and Darlene, they came awful close.'

Greer let the bow fall, holding her head with both hands, her fingernails ice chips along her scalp. 'I know you didn't want to kill them. Or even hurt them. But *become* them? Muse, you *moron*, you dumb *fuck*, why did you do that? It's way too fucking far!'

'You're upset,' he whispered, 'and, baby, I hear that, I honor that. But you got to ask yourself, what other kinds of people did they say that about? That they'd gone too far? That they had to be put back in their place?'

Snick – fingernails against the door. More likely, finger bones. No depth of melancholy could dull Greer's instincts. She pivoted on a heel, locked eyes on a metal chair, grabbed it, and levered it beneath the doorknob. It might hold back a few zombies. But the chair was welted with rust; the knob hung like an eyeball in a rotted socket; the wood of the door looked ready to split like an old pumpkin. She veered back to the bed.

'You arrogant asshole! No one listened to your rah-rah shit at the fort, so you came here to find people who couldn't tell you to shut up!'

'Be mad. It's okay. But I'll be one of them soon. They can tell. You stay in my arms, none of them will hurt you.'

'No fucking way. In *your* arms? You going to bite me? That your big plan?'

He grinned. His teeth were brown. 'Not unless you want me to.'

'I am not going to die up here with you, dumb fuck!'

'People, zombies – we're all dying,' he said gently. 'Here's what we need to accept. We're smart zombies as much as they're dumb humans. Any second now, those two lines are going to converge, and us and them will be *exactly the same*. Body and soul back together. I can feel it. The Chief can feel it. All of Slowtown can feel it. Why do you think Richard's fighting so hard, like a fish on a line? He feels it too. I knew you were coming to see me, baby girl. I've been waiting. Because you can feel it too, can't you?'

Fuck no, she couldn't. She didn't feel anything but furor, and under that, grief, and under that, the unrest she'd known since she was born. Fighting was what she knew, and he was telling her to lower her fists. That's what she called giving up. But what if it wasn't? Muse asked if she felt it too. Willpower streaming from her eyes, she let herself believe she did. It had come in the stirring of trees that now owned the world, their branches reaching only halfway down so she'd reach up, or a pattern in the sparrows, ovaling near before darting off to show her the sky's immensity and how puny humans were in comparison, or the way Slowtown zombies' eyes followed her like sunflowers followed the sun, their rib cages pre-sunken as if to allow room for her inevitable surrendering embrace.

She slapped herself on the forehead to drive out these thoughts, then thought she heard a second slap, a third. The apartment was too cramped for the bow, but she'd fended off plenty of zombies by boot and fist alone. She coiled defensively, hearing the slaps draw near. Once she'd spotted Muse, she'd forgotten all protocol, which insisted, above all, checking every other fucking room in the place. Such a rookie move – she deserved whatever she got.

What she got was a dog. It rounded the corner with a loping, irregular gait brought on by a missing back left leg. Not missing entirely: half of it dangled, the snapped bones swaying. It was a zombie German shepherd, the distinctive qualities of the breed transformed. Its weighty chest held its barrel shape, though half its organs had fallen out through wide cracks in exposed ribs. Its once-fluffy tail was as bony as a string of beads, with remnants of fur hanging like Spanish moss. Its ears, once pointy radars, had rotted down to nubs. Its low-positioned head, a signal of aggression when it was living, now signaled nothing but a decomposing neck. From this position, the German shepherd's trademark long tongue trailed, even longer, a twelve-inch strip of dry, gray flesh dragging along the floor – the source of the slapping sound.

Greer adjusted her stance. Oversized jaws made zombie dogs, unlike zombie people, dangerous right up until they went softie. The German shepherd plodded forward, its white eyes two penlights in the dark, its canines two more. It entered the main room inches from Muse's mattress, and Greer didn't care if he was doomed to death, she didn't intend to stand here and watch it happen at the teeth of this three-legged monster. She lifted a boot, reared back.

The dog sat. It was the least likely thing imaginable. It propped itself up on its ruined front legs, as properly as possible, wrapping its bone-tail around the mangy puffs of its hindquarters. It looked at Greer, its dead tongue dangling, not in happiness exactly, but a kind of contentment.

Muse stopped his plucking to touch it. Greer inhaled sharply, picturing his talented fingers reduced to spurting stumps, but the dog did nothing. He scratched its head. He'd clearly done that many times before: the fur there had been rubbed off, and Muse's finger-nails rasped over the animal's exposed skull.

'This is Willy,' he said.

That was it. She'd seen too much. Greer dropped to her knees, slicing her calf on a cat-food can, and let her face fall hard against Muse's damp, feverish neck. He slid the guitar aside and she twined her arms around his shivering, skeletal back and found, despite the things that had ravaged them both, they still fit together, living and dead, body and soul.

Greer waited to feel Willy or Muse bite her, or to hear the clack of a syringe full of the Chief's fluids being lifted from the floor. Instead, she was the one who lifted, back onto her feet, and though she made her tired legs do the hard work, because Muse was so weak, she let him do what she'd never done out in the wild: take control of where they were going. He walked their joined bodies to the apartment door, slid aside the chair, and turned the knob. She searched herself for fear and found a curious lack.

'We're going to astonish ourselves,' he whispered. 'All I ask is, don't tell them I'm up here. All right? You – you come back when you're ready. For now, I'm going to give you a little taste of what we can do.'

The door opened. White-eyed skulls bobbed toward her as if loosed from the bottom of a lake. Their slushy shreds of skin smeared mucus over her neck. Their spiny fingertips danced like kitten claws up her arms. Their cold teeth pushed like corn kernels into her cheek. But those fingers did not dig, and those teeth did not sink. Greer tucked herself deeper into Muse. His body was weak but his fingers, ever strong, locked at the small of her back. Taking the cue, a dozen other hands pressed against her, innocent as children, rever-ent as priests. They carried her; Muse carried her; she carried herself. It was a bewildering, intoxicating motion, not life, not death, but a path that cut through both.

Suddenly Sadness

There should have been order. When a developing situation required assertive action, the ten seconds it took to parcel out duties could feel like ten years, but those few moments could save lives, often everyone's. The lesson was fifteen years proven.

Charlie had suspected the last couple of years of relative peace had loosened these codes, and here was the proof. Nishimura plowed into the donut shop without explaining the plan to the Face, Hoffmann, or Charlie. The Face rushed in after him. Hoffmann, consummate follower, went third. That forced Charlie, who'd yet to move since Greer's shout, to take the critical position in the donut-shop doorway. A team never left its rear unguarded.

From two stories above the donut shop came the whale songs of straining wood, the sandpaper hiss of bodies along walls, the rattle of a few ankle-chains, the *crick-crack* popcorn. There were zombies up there in unforeseen numbers, though if anyone had the skills to slink right past the slowpokes, it was Greer Morgan. Charlie's concern was Nishimura. She pictured his brain like a ball of twine, pulled too tight by Richard. Greer had snapped it.

His voice, fractured, from inside: *'Greer!'*

Charlie bit back terror and surveyed Queen Street as her post required. In the center of the street lay the poor softie, still strapped to the stretcher. Other zombies didn't appear to like that; Charlie believed twice as many were visible from windows and doors than she'd ever seen before. She tried to exude calm, the opposite of the donut-shop clamor, before permitting herself to look at the zombie sitting three feet away.

The Chief's skull faced straight, but her eyes, the color and luster of a seashell, had rolled upward to stare at her. Charlie liked the Chief. This was, she now realized, a radical thought. Over the past decade and a half, she'd felt spates of sympathy for individual zombies, even affinity, as in the case of the safe-house zombie women of Guymon, Oklahoma. But she'd never felt inclined to spend time with one, until the Chief. The ancient one seemed wise, and Charlie supposed she craved that wisdom.

Everyone said the Chief's fascination with shiny objects was an amygdalic anomaly. Yet it imbued her with the maturity one saw in veteran zoo animals that had made peace with captivity's rules and allowed you to study them as they studied you. For Charlie, looking at softies – whether as a Caretaker with Lesser Hedrick or out here in the field – was looking over the waterfall of death itself. You learned nothing, yet came away awed and rejuvenated. Even the frailest softie contained this power; at Hospice, where several were always present, their lost moans harmonized into a single, forceful fermata.

From inside the donut shop, more shouting, a door kicked, floor trash booted. From higher up, fracturing wood. Instead of feeling tense, Charlie felt exhausted. For so long, she'd heard this life-or-death bickering, each noise daggering into her shoulders like vulture claws, bowing her spine under the weight of vulture meat, the black density of vulture feathers.

'No shooting!' Nishimura cried. 'Everybody hold! It's her!'

Greer had been found. That was good. Charlie, though, felt no uplift. Suddenly sadness soaked into her. There was something mournful about the Chief, or, more bitingly, about Charlie *herself* when she stood before the Chief. Fort York protocol dictated that, when you died, your brain was incapacitated at the instant of zombie revival and your body burned. That meant, though Charlie was a loyal handmaiden to zombies, she would never exist as one herself. That had to be a positive thing. But what miracles zombies had been! And how little headway the living had made in grasping their meaning, even as they hurtled toward obsolescence.

As if of its own accord, her hand floated toward the Chief, a vast spacecraft sailing amid stars of dust. Charlie wore pink faux-leather winter gloves with faux-fur trim, the fingers scissored off. She'd chosen them from Old Muddy's stockpile because they fit. But in the tepid gray light, they felt like a glimpse of a future when people once again had time for things like style. The bright pink outshone the brown, perishing Chief; what if one day this venerated zombie was thought of less frequently than which shade of pink was more flattering to which shape of lips?

She touched the Chief's braids. They were wire. Nishimura would kill Charlie if he saw her caress a zombie like this. She didn't care. It hit her the Chief looked a bit like her mom, Mae Rutkowski, or what Mae might look like now. Charlie moved her fingers along the Chief's rot-mottled cheek. It sank under her touch like wax. Just like that, she'd changed the Chief. Everything was changing, every day, and only the Chief saw the end as well as the beginning – whatever it had been, what it might be again. Charlie drew her fingers across the purple, festered bottom lip, a gesture of the acceptance she'd failed to give John Doe.

'I'm sorry,' she whispered.

A dross of metal whanged across shattered tile as four people stumbled out of the donut shop. Greer was among them, flailing to remove her wrist from Nishimura's grip. Charlie recognized her lividness for a far rarer emotion: shock. She'd witnessed something notable, and in the chaos only Charlie noticed.

'—had to have heard us down here,' Nishimura hissed, 'calling your name—'

'Let go,' Greer growled.

'She said Muse wasn't up there,' the Face told Charlie.

'But a lot of zombies were,' Nishimura said.

'Will you get your asshole hands—'

'A *lot*, way more than anyone—'

'I will *hit* you, Nishimura.'

'We should move,' the Face said, spying dozens of white eyes in the dark.

'Better to hit me,' Nishimura said, 'than put the whole group at risk like that, ever again, do you hear me?'

'Snoop.'

This last word was a soft gasp, nearly lost in noise too loud for Slowtown, all those scuffling feet and jangling buckles. *Snoop* – a name only ever used by one person, and not in four years, which suggested it was blurted out in shock.

Here was the pattern she'd replay until the end: Charlie looks at Hoffmann; Hoffmann looks at the Chief; Charlie looks at the Chief.

Only after seeing it did Charlie feel it, no more painful than an overfirm handshake. The Chief's jaws were fastened over all four of Charlie Rutkowski's fingers. She absorbed the dreamlike sight of her own guaranteed death for a few seconds. It was a mirror of Luis's bite from Mamá Acocella – a warped mirror, since the Chief's excluded Charlie's thumb. The zombie's milky white eyes contained no malice. She had only done what was in her nature. Charlie found herself nodding, hastening to forgive. The living, after all, had done what was in their nature too.

The Chief blinked. No biologic reason for it. The blink felt like a small gift.

Did that mean the bite was a gift too?

'No!' Nishimura bellowed.

He pulled on Charlie's coat. Her left arm yanked straight, each bone and tendon a link in a tightened chain, but the Chief's teeth did not yield. Nishimura swiveled, agile for an old guy, and kicked the zombie in the chest, hard. Words screeched from Charlie's lungs as if she were the one struck.

'What are you doing?' she demanded.

Nishimura kicked again. The Chief's chest caved like a cardboard box, ribs snapping from the sternum in puffs of powdered bone. Three teeth, black as three drops of oil, flew from flaccid lips and Charlie pinwheeled free, past the curb, expecting a hard Queen Street crack to the skull. Arms caught her. She heard the clatter and ping of a bow dropped to pavement. Greer maneuvered from under Charlie to snag her wrist like the neck of a rattlesnake. Charlie took in the askew angles of her pointer, middle, and ring fingers. Each one had taken a tooth to the second phalange. As the two women stared, the wedge-shaped holes began squirting blood.

'This is impossible!' Nishimura cried.

Hoffmann crashed to her knees before Charlie, lips making fish motions, possibly trying to breathe, possibly muttering, *Snoop, Snoop, Snoop.* The librarian hurled her rucksack to the road, peeled the Velcro, and pulled out the first aid kit. Good, solid, proper procedure, but Charlie was dizzy and couldn't pay attention to the right things. She looked at Karl Nishimura, his hands open and trembling, as if even clutching his head was beyond him.

He sobbed, 'How could things go so *wrong*?'

Charlie felt her coat sleeve being pushed back, heard her shirt being ripped. She felt a tourniquet bite into her forearm. All she could think of were Nishimura's words. He saw more than a bite, more than a dead friend. He saw the loss of one of the fort's most vital citizens – sentenced to death. Charlie knew that Nishimura understood how the loss might reflect upon him, given that he'd gone against all norms to protect zombies at the risk of the living. In his eyes, Charlie saw the potential turn of the vote and the ruin of the fort, all from one instant of inattention.

Charlie wished he wouldn't worry. She'd touched the Chief to make things right, not wrong, but the Lion was roaring—

'Was she bit? Are we sure?'

—and Charlie didn't have the energy to outshout her. She regretted it right away, as she watched Nishimura's wide, rattled eyes land on, and latch upon, a particular object slung to the Face's right hip.

Don't, she wanted to beg, but in place of words from her throat came blood from her fingers. Greer dodged the blood, maybe already poison. First aid kits no longer included butcher knives. Fifteen years had taught them that chopping off bitten parts only prolonged the misery. The tourniquet served a purpose opposite to its original intent, not to slow blood gushing out but rather to slow poison flooding in, to delay it long enough to get the infected to Hospice.

Absolutely no one knew the routine better than Charlie. Next from Hoffmann's rucksack would be cable ties to bind her ankles and wrists in case she turned early. *Her* ankles, *her* wrists – it was really happening.

Nishimura lunged for the Face's holster – a sight more surreal to Charlie than her onrushing death. Karl Nishimura, figurehead of peace, minister of nonviolence, founder of the Armory that kept guns out of everyone's hands, grappled for a firearm. Hands that looked to recall navy training ripped away the safety strap, and Nishimura got a palm on the grip before the Face clamped his hand and whirled to catch his ambusher. There was a tussle: Nishimura going at the gun with both hands, the Face, in shock, blocking him.

The Face's right hand slipped off the holster, surprising both men. Nishimura's left hand, abruptly freed, arced across the air, his pinkie grazing the Face's mangled cheek. Despite having no air, Charlie gasped. She knew the Face thought seeing his face was bad enough. Making someone touch it, even by accident, was unthinkable, and the man recoiled like an unmasked movie phantom. Nishimura's face curdled in self-disgust, but he withdrew the gun anyway, took two big steps to the Chief, and shot the oldest zombie in recorded history, point-blank, between her iridescent eyes.

The detonated skull hit the entry alcove, an aerosol of yellow bone chips, black clods of brain, and a gray miasma of everything else, the stuff of incalculable years lived, and died, and lived, and died. The shackle on the Chief's ankle jerked, rang once, and was still.

'We've been so good to you!' Nishimura howled at the headless body. 'Why did you do it?'

Charlie shivered. Could be the blood loss. Could be death's microscopic claws sinking into individual cells. She let her heavy, grief-pounded head loll back until the Chief, Nishimura, the Face, Greer, and Hoffmann all vanished from sight. Her scalp touched pavement; she was looking across Queen Street upside down.

The incapacitated softie swayed in her stretcher. Multiple white eyes glowed from every dark opening; the density of zombies above the donut shop was no fluke. Rather than groan, they exhaled, dust billowing from dead chests; a mournful lowing like that old soul singer Sam Cooke.

A change gonna come, oh yes it will.

Not only eyes now. She saw lowered heads, slouched shoulders, and curled backs: *crick-crack, crick-crack.* The locals were stirring as they never had before. First, the maltreated softie, and now, far worse, their elder, dispatched in a fashion against all Slowtown accords. Their limbs jerked in ways only a great dancer might manage. Charlie's brain betrayed her: they were Fred Astaire, all of them, holding out long, white hands, asking the unanswerable question: *Who's got the last laugh now?*

Warmer hands brought her back to a sitting position, back to reality. It was Etta Hoffmann. From what details Charlie had been able to pry over the years, Hoffmann had withstood batteries of psychiatrists and therapists to remain her unemotive self, and Charlie had never been more thankful for that than right this second, when she was fucking dying and everyone else was losing their goddamn minds. Hoffmann abhorred touching more than absolutely necessary, and Charlie wanted to make this easy for her. With her good arm, Charlie took hold of Greer instead.

'We need to leave,' Charlie said into her ear.

Greer nodded. Hoffmann removed a garbage bag from her pack. She wrapped it around Charlie's left arm to prevent blood leakage, and secured it with tape. Behind them, Nishimura quit gaping at the mess he'd made of the Chief and gazed at the others with childlike puzzlement.

'Unstrap the softie,' he croaked.

The Face was already doing it, on his knees in the middle of a street being usurped by a couple of dozen zombies *crick-cracking* onto the sidewalks. The Face had neither the time nor leverage to remove the softie from the stretcher without damage. His gloved hands skated through the softie's mucid flesh to the rib cage, which he gripped like handles. Though he slid the softie to the road as gently as possible, she lost her left arm in the transfer, and Charlie's poisoned brain tried to excuse it. Her left arm for the softie's left arm, fair trade. Please let it be a fair trade.

She heard the stretcher clack down beside her. She watched Hoffmann wipe it clean of softie slurry. She heard Nishimura set down the cursed gun before easing her onto the canvas. She felt the Face cable-tie her ankles and wrists. She saw Greer buckle and tighten the stretcher straps. Her body sailed upward, the sagging trolley lines seeming to dive at her like nooses. It was happening too fast. She didn't know who to think of. Luis? Her mother, who looked like the Chief? She laughed, tasted blood. She was going to have a second chance at being a daughter, rebirthed by a Mother Earth gone mad.

They were on the move at last, booking it in Old Muddy's direction. Thinking of that good place, the home she'd come to love, her unglued thoughts strayed to another person: Richard. She had to hold out, had to tell them. When Richard arrived four months ago, when Charlene Rutkowski had heard his voice, his full name, she had known, even all these years later, that she and Luis had spoken to him on that first night, right after John Doe's disposal.

Richard Lindof.

WALK
AWAY

Beowulf

Winter of discontent. What asshole said that. Who cares. The
asshole was right. It was winter, and Richard Lindof had himself a
whole heap of discontent. He'd gotten to Fort York in mid-July, when
it was eighty-plus. Jesus Hayward Christ, wasn't Canada supposed to
be the land of igloos and all that? But it didn't take long before polar
bear weather set in. He'd always hated the cold. Why do you think he
kept places in Miami, Vegas, and Hollywood? Miami, he knew, was
sayonara. He'd been watching when Fox News, as if it'd been Election
Day, called Miami as the first city to go solidly zombie. Owner of a
battery of off-road vehicles, Richard had hightailed it the other direction, to Hollywood, where he witnessed firsthand the holocaust of
fire that burned the city to ash. But Vegas?

Vegas was still standing.

Even without the evening pyrotechnics, even halfway crumbled,
the memories of Sin City's casinos, towers, spires, pyramids, and
pavilions lulled him to sleep each night at Fort York and got him up
each morning. The glories of Vegas – the sex-and-fireworks arousals;
the on-demand delights of lips and tits and pussies; the sperm-like
spilling of two million bucks per day – might yet return, if men like
him had the gonads to wise up the delicate flowers.

He'd get it done. Four months at so-called Old Muddy, and he'd
already engineered a major vote. Small steps first, giant second.

That's what Pop always said. If he could see Richard now, he'd be proud, for once in his life.

At his peak, Pop Lindof's energy conglomerates boasted revenues topping fifty billion. You name the fuel, Pop produced it: petroleum, gasoline, diesel, jet, ethanol, as well as the thousands of miles of pipelines to transport crude oil, refined petroleum, and natural gas. His eldest son, Clark, had scooped up the family football, making millions in fertilizers and pesticides, as well as in the cheap production of resins, chemicals, plastics, and polymers. Clark also picked up Pop's custom of funding lobbying firms that made sure no green groups could impede growth.

To Joe and Jane Average, too busy struggling to pay rent or whatever, the Lindof name meant nothing, but to titans of business and politics – the only sectors to matter – the name was a bellwether of profit. Richard Lindof, the younger son, learned quickly this was as much a curse as a blessing. He was expected to trail-blaze new avenues of earnings. It was tough. Damn tough. Richard might have the headwind of a millionaire's bank account, and the benefit of being able to fail spectacularly without repercussions, but he also had challenges Clark didn't.

To start with, he'd been born ugly. Pop and Clark were no George Clooneys, but Jesus Hugo Christ, Richard had truly gotten the scant end of the stick – 'More like a handful of bark,' his grandmother had said right to his face. His absurdly long nose had been pared down between senior year and college, but there wasn't anything to do about his too-short left leg. A built-up shoe was uncomfortable, awkward, and, in Richard's assessment, unpleasant to look at. So he went without. The result? A permanent limp and a corkscrewed, hunched back.

Worst of all was a withered left arm. The arm was a well of humiliation that never dried. It didn't matter what his last name was or which fancy academy Pop sent him to after he flunked out of the previous one. He hid the arm with scarfs or book bags when he could, but eventually, it showed itself. It was a hand-length shorter than the other, skinny as a broomstick, and had the pink slickness of burn tissue.

The Lindofs, of course, could afford the best medical care, but the arm was beyond what any surgeon could repair or augment. Pop advised him to seek counsel with the Lord in private, but in public, to never let the arm get in his way. Pop was a religious man. Ribbon-cuttings were preceded by Bible verses, stock-price spikes celebrated with prayer, God's grace evoked for executive bonuses as well as mass layoffs. Clark wore duplicates of his father's cross-themed jewelry. Only Linda Lindof, Pop's wife, referred to as *Mother* by everyone, right down to boards of directors, was cool on the God stuff, and Richard had loved her for it. If God was good, he wouldn't have crippled an innocent kid like him! Mother Lindof didn't hedge; she wrapped her arms around his hunched back, snuggled his long-nosed face, and conceded the point.

Richard spent much of his young life crying about the unfairness of the world. The tear ducts at the corners of his eyes swelled so large, they looked, and felt, like bloated ticks sucking on his eyeballs. Boys laughed that his arm looked like a giant second dick – he should be proud of it! If only that were true. The girls he met, affluent and unmagnanimous, didn't hide the repulsed curls of their pretty lips. Tears gushed some more, the ticks returning to his eyeballs. Humili-ation made him angry. Now *that,* he was proud of. A stubby leg, an anorexic arm: those were deficits. Anger, on the other hand, he could use.

Mother died of a heart attack when Richard was nineteen. By then, he'd quit crying. He'd never cry again. He turned her death into a bucket of coal, Pop's favorite fossil fuel, and pitched it into his heart's red-hot furnace.

As an adult, he got into movies. Of course he did. Movies had a grand history of unattractive men splashing their fetishes onto huge screens, making bank, and getting to screw enterprising starlets along the way. There was no lack of would-be auteurs willing to adjust their principles in exchange for funding. Richard dreamed of being a good sport from the front row of the Academy Awards, as the host poked fun at him for hours before handing him an Oscar. The problem was he didn't like any of that Oscar crap. Action movies, TV sitcoms about fat guys and their sexy wives – that's what he liked.

So he threw money at supposedly acclaimed filmmakers anyway – and lost his shirt. Sure, they'd included the T&A he'd required as part of the deal, but Jesus Humphrey Christ, the idiots had drained out all the sexiness! At Christmas dinner, Pop told him to seek Christ for guidance. Clark tsked Little Richie for choosing the riskiest possible market while holding the saltshaker just out of reach of his under-developed arm. Richard's face boiled. Ticks crept back over his eyeballs and fed.

Then, finally, jackpot: Nicolò Bonfiglio, an Italian *artista* who bounded into Richard's office in sunglasses and beret, jabbering how he made films not only for the mind and the heart but for the cock and the cunt! Richard, a dick hair from quitting the biz, was transported, and right there shook on a deal to give Bonfiglio the million he needed to make his hot-blooded adaptation of what he avowed was the most revered Old English epic poem.

'Richard Lindof, you resemble Bela Lugosi,' Bonfiglio proclaimed. 'You will cameo in my little art film, no?'

Having heard the rude comparison before, Richard had avoided all old vampire flicks, but from the Italian's fluttering lips, *Lugosi* had a buccaneer's brio, and Richard grinned, feeling pleased. Sure, why not? He'd embrace it.

Richard didn't know what rated as an 'art film' in Italy, but he was thrilled by Bonfiglio's product: *Beowulf vs. the Spider Women*, a big, sweaty, lusty, bloody flick in which all characters, regardless of gender, went topless. There wasn't much plot, just how Richard liked it. Beowulf, played by the unknown Stefan Ratzenberger – soon to be known as 'the Ratz' – a guy so muscled he looked like a bunch of grapes, used swords, spears, tridents, and hammers to devastate scores of monsters before pounding (in both senses) the spider women themselves. The climactic scene was staged by Bonfiglio to get as much stage blood as possible splashed across the actresses' heaving breasts.

Beowulf vs. the Spider Women didn't win any Oscars – in fact, it won something called a Razzie – but it generated five times its budget worldwide, two-fifths of which Richard funneled into Bonfiglio's sequel, *Beowulf vs. the Wasp Women,* which made seven times its budget, three-sevenths of which went into its sequel, *Beowulf vs. the Cobra Women.* Richard loved snipping and framing profiles of Bonfiglio and himself, though he rarely read past the intros. He never had much patience for words, and the articles' opening paragraphs always had mocking tones he didn't like.

He heard the same tone from Pop and Clark. Even though Richard no longer cried, ticks still clung to his eyeballs. He didn't get it. He was a successful Hollywood producer! His name was ten feet tall on movie screens! Every time he had a private viewing of a new sequel (most recently, the excellent *Beowulf vs. the Women from Uranus*), he looked at the actresses' delectable bodies and the Ratz's muscled arms and felt ownership. They made up for what he lacked. Mother would have appreciated it. Like Beowulf at the end of the fabulous *Beowulf vs. the Colosseum Bitches of Rome,* Richard Lindof had an empire.

How quickly it collapsed. Bonfiglio had thus far cunningly convinced the Ratz to remain a man of mystery, but now the Ratz demanded a publicity tour for their biggest film yet, *Beowulf vs. All Women,* and he got it, despite Bonfiglio's frothy cautions. The problem? The Ratz had always been dubbed by the growly basso profundo of a retired sports announcer from Detroit. The actor's own voice was airy and finicky, and online jerks quickly called him a faggot. Seemingly befuddled, the Ratz came right out with it: he *was* gay and proud of it. Richard didn't give a hoot; the revelation might gin up interest.

But once opened, the Ratz's mouth would not shut. He might be gay and proud, but he was also sexist and proud, racist and proud, and anti-Semitic and proud, and before the tour was finished, the new film was finished. Production on the Lindof/Bonfiglio magnum opus, *Beowulf vs. the Entire Female Population of the Universe,* was shit-canned.

Richard's Google Alerts exploded. The Ratz got the most vitriol, and after him, Bonfiglio, but trailing not far behind was Richard Lindof, the 'talent-free' son of an 'unsparing tycoon', a 'hunchbacked', 'Lugosi-looking', 'Shit Midas' who peddled 'soft-core smut', 'too stupid' to realize 'camp value' was the reason 'low-IQ idiots' watched the Beowulf 'films'. In short, it was everything Pop and Clark had ever said. Jesus Hieronymus Christ, the ticks, how hard they'd sucked at his aching eyes, and to bear the pain Richard thundered around his Hollywood mansion, breaking things, fucking pillows, going a little crazy.

Pop sent him a crisis manager, but Richard turned the man away. He didn't need help! There was no crisis! The movies were good! He'd make fifty more! None of that was true, but if he let the Lindof estate dig him out, Clark would lord it over him for the rest of his life. Little Richie, who had his nose cut off and now couldn't smell garbage when it splattered across his face; Little Richie, whose hobble sent him tripping into every business pothole; Little Richie, whose stubby arm couldn't grab money when it was sitting right there on the table.

No one in the biz would touch him. He was whispered about at restaurants, mocked on the Sunset Strip. He was a sniveling boy again, except without Mother to run to. Richard had no joy. No job. No prospects. No pride, no self-respect. Neva was no help. Did he forget to mention he had a wife? He usually did. Her name was Neva. She lived in his Hollywood place, sometimes. He went the other way: Miami. The Magic City, capital of beach, booze, and boobs. It'd fix him up, inspire him toward his next venture.

It did no such thing. He fell like a bag of dog shit into a dumpster. Coming up fast was the annual Lindof Thanksgiving bash, the point of which was to brag about your successes. Richard would be a punching bag. He started considering the guns he kept – for display only, until now – at the Miami place. Maybe he'd end it all. Why not? He'd never produce another incredible film. Nobody loved him, or even liked him.

Vegas was the place for it: no winters there, no discontent. He chose October 23, a day with no obvious historical import, to minimize the chance his suicide would be overshadowed in the press. He began arranging the final blowout. Pull-out-all-the-stops time. The biggest, highest suite he could find. Exhaust his contacts, see who might show. Stick coke up one foreshortened nostril, Adderall up the other. Dancers, stripteasers, hookers: invite 'em, keep coaxing them with Benjamins. Give a couple of off-strip homeless dudes fifty bucks to fight in the bathroom, let people place bets. Rent a chimp, you know, just to have it around, doing funny chimp shit. It was going to be great, really great.

He didn't know where he'd do the deed (the balcony? the hot tub?) or when (the stroke of midnight? in the midst of a three-way?), so he stowed his smallest handgun in his right jacket pocket, where his normal-sized arm could extract it when the time was right. He felt good. For the first time since the Ratz opened his dumb mouth, Richard Lindof felt like his swaggering old self again. Not *a* Lindof, but *the* Lindof, at least for one more night.

The A-listers didn't show. That was okay – they'd hog the attention anyway. The B-listers didn't show either. Fuck 'em, those suck-ups were worse than the A-listers. To cover his ass, he sent invites to the VIPs of several conventions. The result was a spiky, surreal mix of Pop's defense-department associates, forgotten '80s singers, the mayors of a number of midsized cities, third-rate Vegas magicians, plastic-faced ex-models, dorky app creators, a boxer who'd once fought for the heavyweight crown, and a crop of coroners and medical examiners in town for a training symposium. Lindof loved it: once he'd blown his brains out, he'd have a dozen pros on hand to examine every glob.

Lindof started fondling the gun at eleven. He was high as a comet. A shirtless rapper with gunshot scars had done some freestyle, and it had been awesome. The girl he'd paid to suck his dick had been a sweetheart, and when he gave up trying to come – because he was high as a fucking comet – she petted his arms, even his withered one, and he imagined divorcing Neva and marrying a good-natured, dick-sucking sweetheart like this. Sadly, there was no chimp. He'd spent half the day trying to find a chimp. On the upside, he'd given the winner of the bum fight another fifty to hop around the furniture, hooting like a monkey.

Ten minutes before midnight, as Lindof stood on the balcony, gazing across the pulsing quasar of the Vegas strip, the desert breeze ruffling his hair like Mother used to, he became aware of a hubbub. It had been some time, he realized, since he'd been inside. He reentered the suite to find it mostly emptied, glasses dropped on carpets, drugs abandoned in varicolored anthills. That wasn't good. If he shot himself and nobody saw it, what was the point? By the time he got to the foyer, he found twenty-some people thumbing phones and listening to one of the medical examiners talking about ... well, it didn't make much sense.

Dead bodies reviving in their morgues back home?

Pop's defense-department pals were setting up shop in the parlor, opening laptops while speaking into phones set on speaker. A few blanched coroners and MEs remained, murmuring into phones with voices gone cold sober. Lindof was sobering too. He took stock of the suite, soiled now with everything but his brains. His gun hung heavily in his pocket like a lethal case of blue balls, the climax of his exploding head having been rudely interrupted.

His eyes fell upon a fellow who'd introduced himself earlier as JT, some kind of morgue guy from one of the Sans, Francisco or José or Diego. He'd been partying hard earlier, singing at the top of his lungs, grinding men and women alike, drinking what looked like a giant piña colada out of a steel mixing bowl. He looked like shit now, curled and shivering in the corner of a sofa, his phone cradled to his face like a kitten.

Forget Adderall, forget coke. JT's slide into quivering jelly filled Richard's body with what felt like quick-drying liquid plastic. He felt brand-new. He felt indestructible. When JT tossed himself off the balcony, Lindof's urge to do likewise vanished. Feeling frisky, he plucked up JT's phone and gabbed a bit with a guy named Acocella, who'd just dealt with one of those walking corpses in person. The more agitated Acocella got, the more his wetback accent emerged. That really revved Lindof's engine. This guy was falling apart, same as Clark's employees would stream from their factories when they heard. Pop's stocks would scream into the gutter.

Jesus Hernando Christ, it was perfect.

Power brokers all over the world headed underground. Most people didn't know the rich had priority phone networks, but they did, and Pop reached Lindof after most people's infrastructure had failed. He urged his youngest son to join him in a luxury bunker in Colorado before they sealed it. Pop's iron voice had melted to a whimper. It felt good telling the old man, nope, that's okay, go ahead and brick yourself up, God bless. Up top, that's where real power could be taken, and Lindof intended to have the grabbiest hands.

The key was training your nose to the smell of roadkill – and everything was roadkill now, the rancid new colors of the American flag. Lindof got to where the smell made him hungry, and people were drawn to anyone who still had appetite. They were also desperate to be told what to do, one thing at which Lindof excelled. In fact, every quality Pop and Clark said doomed Little Richie to mediocrity (lazy delegation, lack of curiosity, blind greed) now brought him success. Zombies were the dead-eyed workers at Pop and Clark's factories; they posed no real threat. While everyone else boo-hooed about *why* and *how,* Lindof scooped up everything he wanted.

He was Beowulf, killing who needed killing, fucking who needed fucking, king of wherever he was.

Lindof thrived. For about twelve years, anyway. After animals started going zombie, even his most fervent followers lost their will. He was increasingly alone, which meant he was nobody. He did the only thing that made sense, returning to his beloved Vegas. Trump International Hotel, apparently having been built of the chintziest material, was gone from the skyline. But the lower buildings of the strip were mostly as he'd left them. Vegas, as ever, was filled with *stuff,* providing plenty of gigantic fiberglass props, echelons of dead slot machines, and moldy card tables to shield him from zombies. Even zombie rats, at plague levels in Year Twelve, were sparser in the desert, and their skeletons made nice, crispy sounds when he squashed them.

Hoping for uplift, he skulked into his favorite haunts: MGM Grand, Paris, Caesars Palace. Lindof hated how easy it was. No security guards, no guest lists, no all-access passes. Even the private high-roller rooms had been opened to a dirty, shambling, undeserving public. It might be the worst thing ever to happen in Vegas, which was saying something.

One last time, Vegas delivered. At the Venetian, inside the Grand Canal Shoppes, he came upon the famous Madame Tussauds wax museum. Sunlit via ceiling cave-ins, it was the tidiest post-zombie setting he'd ever seen. It made sense; a wax museum held nothing survivors needed. It wasn't until he stood face-to-face with Khloé Kardashian that Richard Lindof realized he, however, did need something here.

Most of Khloé's face had dripped to her shoulders, slopped about her neck in a shawl of peach wax. Her long hair existed in patchy ponytails, swaths having been gnawed off by starving animals. Stripped of fake flesh, the exposed clay skull still had Khloé's bright blue glass eyes, begging to be put out of their misery. Lindof wouldn't oblige. Though her big breasts and renowned booty had also melted, her lingerie top, jeans, and stilettos kept the pooled wax roughly in place and turning him on. He could do what he wanted and Khloé couldn't complain. She couldn't even say he looked like Bela Lugosi. Though, for once, he felt like Lugosi, drawing sustenance from this bitch, same as if sucking her blood.

He'd seen zombies rip open dozens of people. It was kind of erotic, if he was being honest: people forcibly stripped until there was nothing left to take off. He gazed around the shadowed wax museum. Angelina Jolie, Brad Pitt, Halle Berry, Johnny Depp, Jennifer Lopez, Katy Perry, Rihanna. The prettiest people in America, turned into the ugliest. Richard Lindof, he of long nose and short leg and stubby arm, was lording over superstars he'd once dreamed of meeting at the Oscars – and he was better-looking than any of them.

He'd never paid heed to rumors of Toronto. Hauling his ass through a jungled country just to be someone's second banana held little appeal. But standing before all these fabulous people he'd outplayed, he changed his mind. He loitered only enough to fuck Marilyn Monroe (when was he going to get that chance again?) and got moving. What a wild, colorful world those zombie bastards had ushered in. Pretty, he admitted, though it'd look better with streets and sidewalks. To keep things tidy. To let you know who owned what. They'd get back there, and he'd be the one to make it happen.

Fort York, once he got there, was a letdown, especially its de facto captain, a walking headache named Karl Nishimura. It was also just what the doctor ordered. Nishimura claimed Fort York was representative of a lot of emerging societies. If so, all the better, because it meant those places needed Richard Lindof too. He'd go Lugosi on them, suck out their insides, bring them to their knees like Beowulf did – *Beowulf vs. Everyone.* Jesus Henry Christ, he'd make the bastards feel what he'd felt the first four decades of his life.

Ticks all over their eyeballs.

No Long Goodbyes

First rule, only rule: wash your hands. In a world lacking antibiotics and antivirals, humans were as vulnerable as goldfish in a bag of water. A minor cough, a sniffle, a little scratch. Anything could take you down for good. Karl Nishimura's time aboard aircraft carriers had prepared him for the task of organizing a society, and no area of that education was as valuable as hygiene. Long before zombies had redefined the idea of communicability, sicknesses had swept through *Olympia* like gales. Officers lectured their staffs on the simple thing every sailor could do to squash future contagions. Soap, warm water, scrub, repeat.

Upon arriving at Old Muddy and eyeing the runny noses of those he shook hands with, he made hygiene step one. Soap was quite harvestable. Wrecked buildings often had full, boxed bars, and a hotel score could set a person for life. But a trade-and-barter society could only last so long. Nishimura was all about *production,* teaching a man to fish and all that. Fort York was hardly Colonial Williamsburg, but its museum and collections had examples of older technologies: the tools of a blacksmith, a wheelwright, a brickmaker, a shoemaker, a weaver.

Nishimura canvassed residents to find those best capable of operating the tools. Next, he befriended a man who'd been a middle school chemistry teacher, and together they reproduced one of his classroom experiments: making soap. It was complicated, involving boiling embers and mixing the residue into simmering lard. Soon entrances to all fort structures were stocked with soap, water, a heating element, and a volunteer who ensured your grubby hands did their civic duty.

Naturally, people got lazy, but never enough that reports reached his ears. The first person Karl Nishimura definitively knew to have violated the rule – or was just about to – was Karl Nishimura. Nai Nai, the elderly, farsighted soap sentry on Wellington, sang greetings to the recovery team in the order she recognized them.

'Right before the sun falls, Face, very good. *Nǐ hǎo,* Greer and Etta. Karl, everyone is saying, "Where is Nishimura, we can't find Nishimura." The voting, it is causing much, much—'

The Face motioned Nai Nai aside.

'No soap, not now.'

Nai Nai's skin folded into a frown. 'Karl?'

'No soap,' he snapped.

'Why are you bringing a softie through the fort?'

Greer, far less polite than the Face, sent Nai Nai's water bucket flying with a kick while keeping both hands on the stretcher. Aggression was rare at Old Muddy and likely brought back fifteen years of trauma to Nai Nai. Her quick cry for mercy pierced Nishimura's heart as she collapsed into the soapy spill. Any other time, the Face or Nishimura would have knelt to check on her, but the former was racing for the railroad tracks to head off anyone else who might slow them, and the latter had half the stretcher to worry about.

From the tracks, Nishimura saw it: Fort York. The name was not a misnomer, but neither was it sufficient. Located near the city's Bathurst Quay lakefront, the historical site itself was about five blocks long, a roughly triangular park bordered by highways. The eight original buildings might have squeezed in two hundred people, but residents had outgrown the space well before Nishimura's arrival. What they'd begun to do, a capital idea Nishimura helped them pursue with navy rigor, was rehab bordering properties as living quarters, allowing historic Fort York to serve community, administrative, and ceremonial functions.

The fort's hundred-year-old stone walls were head-high and served no real defensive purposes; the train tracks, Bathurst Street overpass, and elevated Gardiner Expressway offered superior vantage points for spotting zombies, back when they were a threat. Hospice was situated in a former commercial complex off the fort's southeast corner, next to their cobbled-together hospital. Softies, as Nai Nai suggested, were transported around the fort's eastern edge. Who they carried today, however, was no softie, and the fastest route to Hospice was straight through the historic site.

The stone walls were slotted with embrasures through which soldiers had once fired cannons, and Nishimura and his team dashed through one. It was eighty yards to the opposite edge. Jolted by adrenaline, Nishimura and Greer should have covered that in under a minute, even carrying a stretcher. But the historic site was the settlement's hub and heart, and this sundown was thick with people wrapping up their daily activities – reviewing building plans, testing inventions, giving lessons, and playing with children. It was always a bustling, clamorous mess, but a satisfying one, the way Nishimura's home with Larry, Atsuko, Chiyo, Daiki, Neola, and Bea had been, once upon a time.

Today, the fort was twice as busy. Nishimura had the sickening thought that everyone already knew that he, the unerring Saint Karl, had botched a recovery operation so badly that beloved Charlie Rutkowski was dying and the Chief had been blown to bits. In seconds, the dozens of loose groupings would constrict around him, the way zombies once had, their eyes blankly disappointed, their mouths drooling for his blood.

The real reason they'd amassed, of course, was the vote, only hours away now, which would decide the fate of the Blockhouse

Four and decide the future of Old Muddy. The vote was scheduled to begin at sunup, using the same simple process they'd used for smaller matters. You wrote your vote on a slip of paper, dropped it into a box, and got your name checked off a master list. Before the trip to Slow-town, Nishimura believed his proven platform would win the day, and easily.

No longer was he sure. He heard people arguing at frequencies foreign to Fort York. He saw invisible lines drawn through a popu-lace that until now had eschewed any, Karl Nishimura followers to the east, Richard Lindof devotees to the west – and more than Nishimura expected. He was disturbed by all the backs of heads, the unmistakable look of people gathered for a speech. He didn't see a speaker yet, but it had to be Lindof. His followers were gathered before the Brick Magazine, inside which the Blockhouse Four were kept, and which itself was fifty feet from East Blockhouse, the scene of the crime.

Nishimura, Greer, the Face, and Hoffmann got as far as the Offi-cers' Blue Barracks before people blocked the way, bidding for attention.

'Karl, folks are getting riled up here—'

'If he's going to talk, Mr Nishimura, you really ought to consider—'

'If Lindof sees you've brought a softie in here, he's going to—'

'Move back!' Nishimura shouted. 'We have a woman bit here!'

His own words made him shiver, and he watched the shiver trans-fer to people's bodies. If only the children's instructors were here, he thought. Astonishing numbers of kindergarten and preschool teach-ers had survived the Second Dark Age, and no one could calm a crowd like they could.

'That's terrible. But, Karl, the situation here—'

'Put her down. Someone fetch a bolt gun.'

'We'll take care of her. You go talk to the people—'

'This is Charlie Rutkowski!' Nishimura cried. If these people took the stretcher, they'd have to learn urgency, which he'd already accepted as his god. 'We are not bolt-gunning her right here like a cow! Doesn't she deserve to die right? We're taking her to Hospice. Get out of our way, *please.*'

Greer took up the charge, elbowing ferociously while the Face made a wedge of his arms and bolted forward. The crowd, at last, parted. The only ones still in their path were three children playing hand-clapping games like centuries of little ones before them, except instead of Patty Cake or Miss Mary Mack nonsense, their rhymes had been learned in Fort York's small but growing school:

> *Zombie, zombie*
> *Bite me not.*
> *But if you do*
> *I'll take the shot.*
> *I will not cry*
> *I will not moan.*
> *Oh, zombie, zombie*
> *Take me home.*

The 'shot' in question was the aforementioned bolt gun, the kind used for rendering livestock brain-dead before slaughter. Children accepted the practice as readily as their parents had once accepted the equally mystifying ritual of burying corpses in body gardens. Other chants and songs involved what to do if someone got bit or died off-site, and how Slowtown was to be left to the zombies. The surprise to Nishimura was how the rhymes also soothed adults as they bore down through the world's rebirth.

The team veered around the children, trampling the edge of the Garden. Long leaves of dead corn whipped their cheeks. Nishimura ignored it, but saw Charlie press against her straps, as if wanting the tendrils' witch doctor touch, anything to stay alive for a few minutes longer. Like the fort itself, the Garden was triangular and took up one-third of the lawn. Even with the corn, strawberries, marigolds, black-eyed Susans, primroses, lilies, and philodendrons shriveled for the season, the wildness was evident. The lushness that had swallowed North America belonged to the dead, and in humility, Fort York had built the Garden to prove humans, too, could let beauty exist without destroying it.

Space opened up. The Face broke into a run. Greer and Nishimura did likewise, with Hoffmann right behind. They passed the fort's center point, the Master Sundial: four thirty, daylight nearly snuffed. Due west, straight down a concrete path, Nishimura glimpsed the Armory, the settlement's most potent symbol.

Few people made it all the way to Toronto without a gun, if not several, but upon joining Old Muddy, those firearms were placed inside the Armory, which was more than locked up – it was bricked up. The proximity of firearms was like the proximity of Slowtown: the point was to actively choose not to possess them. Humans had built countries of annihilation with their militaries, whole cities of destruction like *Olympia*. Master Chief Boatswain's Mate Karl Nishimura had been complicit in the world's eager pursuit of death and sympathized with death's choice to fight back.

Because a herd of fresh zombies hadn't been spotted in years, a cache of only three emergency firearms was passed person to person on the fort's revolving Custodial Council – *custodian* had been purposefully chosen, to remind councilors they were servants, not leaders. Even that small allowance had dropped poison into their cups. The Chief flashed through Nishimura's mind, not the wizened, wrinkled, ponytailed sage children drew but the scattered shards of her skull after he'd pulled the trigger.

The Face scared off a pair of necking teens. They'd been kissing at the Circular, a semicircle section of wall with two embrasures, both outfitted with rusted, nonworking cannons. Greer hoisted the stretcher above them and passed through an opening, forcing Nishimura to do the same. His fifty-eight-year-old muscles wobbled and the stretcher dipped, but Hoffmann was right there, stilting an arm to support it.

'Whoa,' Charlie huffed, her first word since being strapped in.

It was a sign she would live long enough to die with the same care she'd extended to others. This was all Nishimura's fault. He could have wiggled out of the recovery assignment if he'd wanted. With the vote looming, no one would have blamed him. But pride, like a swallowed seed, had flowered in his chest. He'd wanted to prove he was Saint Karl, the best of them all.

What was that, in a word? It was politics. The antithesis of what he wanted Old Muddy to be. If Richard Lindof had changed him that much so quickly, perhaps the result of tomorrow's vote was inconsequential. There was a larger fight happening here, and he might have already lost it.

It was a relief to leave the crowd behind. They galloped across Fort York Boulevard and waved aside Hospice's soap sentry. The sharp scent of homemade soap battled with the scent of the hospital next door. Depending on the day's disaster, this stretch of sidewalk might smell of urine, feces, blood, or even alcohol if someone had scrounged up an old bottle and drank themselves sick. Today's smell was simply of bleach, and he welcomed it. It spiked up his nostrils like steel prongs, keeping Hospice's own scent, that sickly sweet fetor, at bay for seconds longer.

Hospice stank of rot. Nishimura did what he always did, gulping it fast to acclimatize, the way one cannonballed into a cold lake. No element of Fort York was more crucial than Hospice. It was the children's rhymes writ large: acknowledging, knowing, and accepting death was the thing that might finally perfect life.

He did not remember what the building had been before. A nail salon? A kickboxing studio? It had been remodeled, though not into the antiseptic beige bilge of pre-zombie medical centers. Hospice was not, in fact, medical in nature. All that divided the entry space from the realm of the softies was a single rail of mismatched curtains: one with pink polka dots, another with little football players on it. One had a Christmas-tree pattern. The unifying factor was real people chose them.

Greer and Nishimura set the stretcher on the floor. No one was better at delivering bad news than the Face. Without being asked, he slipped through the curtains to tell Hospice workers one of their own had fallen. Greer backpedaled into a wall, as if only now, their package delivered, could she start to process her culpability. Hoffmann kneeled beside the stretcher, her inexpressive face shiny, as if bloating with tears that might explode her head just like the Chief's.

The farewell had come fast. They always did. Nishimura wiped his mind of all else, lowered himself, and looked at the dying woman, whose eyes had mellowed beneath a yellow film. He'd uttered enough comforts to the dying to have a script, but now he could not summon a word. This was Charlene Rutkowski. Charlie! Who'd played catcher in softball games at Coronation Park, the only player able to throw out a runner stealing second. Who'd once chased off a nagging Nishimura with two biting staple removers. Whom he'd found, one evening, weeping alone in a pretty dress that meant things to her he couldn't guess. Who'd danced so hard to *Born to Run* when they'd gotten a turntable working her face was lost in all the frolicking hair. If Nishimura was the fort's brains, Charlie had been its heart, and now they would have to survive on what she'd pumped out of herself. All told, it was quite a lot.

'I'm . . .' he began.

'No sorries allowed here,' she whispered. 'You know that.'

He nodded. 'But why did it have to be you?'

'No long goodbyes either.'

He nodded again. Charlie Rutkowski's life would be celebrated soon, with so many tears shed into the soil he imagined the Garden bursting into winter bloom. Zombies, dumb as they were, had taught humanity a lesson. Death had multiple stages. Possibly stages the living still had yet to uncover. There was peace in that if you let it wash over you.

'I ran in there without warning anyone,' he atoned. 'I lost control.'

'Lost control?' Charlie smiled. 'Did you? Or did I?'

He put his hand – so old – atop hers – so old.

'You did perfect,' he said.

'I reached out to her. My mother. She was sitting right there.' Charlie smiled. 'She always loved donuts.'

He nodded a third time. Most people dying from a zombie bite stopped making sense, and Charlie was not so skilled at Hospice work she'd be able to slow the fallowing of her own mind. Nishimura cupped a hand to Charlie's face. Her skin was icy. Her blistering sweat made a wispy steam that hovered over her cheeks.

'You were the best of us,' he said.

'Ha.' Her grin cracked the sick glaze hardening her mouth. 'You were, dummy.'

He smiled.

'Will you go back to the Bronx?' It was the Face, having surfaced from the rippling curtains. The gun he'd carried, the one Nishimura had fired, was gone; it was customary to turn it over to Hospice, who would, in turn, turn it over to the Council. The Face's voice was dulcet; his arrival had been silent; he kept his distance even now. 'If you have your choice, I mean.'

'San Diego,' Charlie said. 'Chet Musgrave's generator was the best generator.' Her grin widened. '*He* was the Generator King.'

The Face looked at Greer. Nishimura did the same. Backlit by dusk's scarlet shimmer, Greer's face was cloaked in shadow. Her bow clacked against the wall as she shrugged, the gesture a kid too self-conscious to mutter a socially prescribed politeness. It also served as an admission. Nishimura could tell Greer would wedge her jugular into Charlie's mouth if it would transfer the venom. She'd already lost Muse, so why not? It was enough apology for Nishimura, and he figured it was enough for Charlie too.

Curtains billowed, and a woman appeared at the Face's elbow. Next to Charlie, Marion Castle had the most Hospice experience, and pre-10/23 had worked in a nursing home. She was a five-foot-zero spark plug wearing the usual smock, gloves, and medical mask. Not usual at all was her expression. Charlie was not only her boss but a valued friend, and the free fall of losing her, paired with the sudden responsibility of replacing her, created a vertigo Nishimura recognized from the navy, where one person's dismissal or death meant promotions all up the line.

'Is one of you coming with her?' Her voice shook. 'No one has to.'

'I will,' Hoffmann said.

She looked at Nishimura, not asking, but curious to see if she'd pulled rank. Nishimura nodded gently. Of course Hoffmann should be the one to escort Charlie through her final exit. He made a mental note to speak to Hoffmann's assistant, Luvvie Lafayette, before the night was through, and another to check on Hoffmann herself. He did not know how she would handle the loss of the one person she trusted. His hope was that the irrepressible Luvvie had made enough inroads to hold both library and librarian together.

Marion snorted, storing her sob for later. Crying was encouraged at Old Muddy, but Nishimura admired the effort. There was more work to be done tonight. Marion bent with her knees, lifting the head of the stretcher. Nishimura stood to make room for Hoffmann, who took the foot. Marion nodded the count, and they lifted on three. In an instant, Charlie Rutkowski passed from Nishimura's view, and he knew he'd never again see her big, brash, scarred, amused, blond-framed face, though he did hear one last word from her as the Face held open the curtains and her bearers carried her away.

'Oh, it's *you*,' she said, and Nishimura wondered who her unraveling mind believed it saw. Whoever it was, he was glad. People used to say you were born alone and died alone. Perhaps the zombies' biggest gift was discounting the latter. Ushers waited for you now, just past the curtain, happy to show you to your seat.

Half-Bomber, Half-Bombed

Personal History Transcript #215
Location: Fort York New Library
Subject: Karl Nishimura
Interviewer: Etta Hoffmann
Time: 4,359–8:39

Notes: None.

Q.

First, number one, now that we're on the record, I want to formally apologize. I should have been the first one in to sit with you. I've been so busy. The expansion. You know how it is. But that's no excuse. I hope you know there are few endeavors here at Fort York that I find more worthwhile, and on a personal note, more gratifying, than everything you've got going here at the New Library. Whether we change the world or not, who knows. But to have a record that we tried? Indispensable.

Q.

Mind? I *insist*. This is where you lead and I follow. I have a hunch you don't see yourself as a leader, Hoffmann. But what's

a leader? It's one who takes action so inspiring that others follow her. When I got here in Year Ten, there were, oh, three
hundred people. Do you have any idea how many of those three
hundred had heard of you? One woman here had called you a
few times over the years. Lizzie Bonaparte. I don't know if she's
shown you yet, but she's a tattoo artist, and you know what she
tattooed on her left arm?

Q.
ARE YOU OK? CALL ME. I have some regrets. It felt like we
were common looters. I understand your plan was to leave the
Archive to be found at some future time. But we knew people
needed it now. We knew we could nurture it into a dynamic living thing. Lizzie had your number tattooed too, and we had
that incredible phone still working. Landlines, can you believe
it? Charlie's calls . . . they were dishonest. Traveling to D.C. to
rob you – and that's the right word – was a calculated wrong,
done for what we determined was a greater good. That you
agreed to come with Charlie – I'll just say I was overjoyed.

Q.
It had to be Charlie. Who else would you trust? We figured she
could make it the five hundred miles to D.C. She came to us
from San Diego, which is twenty-five hundred miles. She's even
got me beat. Puerto Vallarta to Toronto is twenty-three hundred. I'm competitive. I did the math.

Q.
I ejected from an F-18. That's a fighter jet. The pilot, a top-notch
sailor named Jennifer Angelys Pagán, had been stabbed before
takeoff, by me, by accident, and we drifted way off course while
I slept. She turned zombie just before we reached land. 'Will one

pinche man on this boat listen to me?' [Laughs.] I did listen. I
ejected just like she explained. Everything, I suppose, went
according to Hoyle. The chute deployed. I even steered it a little.
When I hit the water, I did it like I learned in a class. Side of
the foot, side of the hip, beneath the shoulder. Spread out the
impact. Even so, I don't recommend the experience. Every bone
pounded to dust, I swear. You're underwater, you're choking,
and then there's the chute to deal with, like a sheet of wet
cement. I couldn't do it today. Fifteen years older? No way. But
I got untangled, grabbed my seat kit, and started paddling. It
didn't even occur to me, even though Jenny told me, that both
seats would eject together.

Q.

A parachute line? Some coral? It felt too much like a hand for it
to be a hand, if that makes sense. I was pulled under so fast my
eyes were open, and there she was, Jenny Pagán, weighed down
by her flight suit and helmet, but doing just fine because she
didn't need to breathe. She'd saved my life a few times by then.
It was like she regretted it. She had both hands around my
ankle, and I started kicking, but I was spent. I was done for. She
just reeled me in, right into her cloud of blood.

Q.

Would you believe a shark? Her blood, I think, is what did it. It
snapped in like a big silver rubber band, chomped right into her
waist. Soon as the blood cleared, I saw other sharks. I guess I
had some strength to swim after all. Funny how apex predators
will do that. I made it to the beach and just lay there for hours,
and it was a good thing I got the rest. You know how the tide
brings in seaweed and shells and flotsam. That's what happened,

except zombies. I don't know if a ship went down, if there was a mass suicide, or what, but wave after wave of them rolled in, all green and bloated, so waterlogged they couldn't stand. But they clawed right through the sand toward me. If I was ever going to give up, Hoffmann, on myself or the world, it was right then. Let them take me.

Q.

It's a concern, and I appreciate it. But I'll bet the Archive is going to be North America-centric for another decade. I wish I could tell you more about Mexico. I know I kept to the Gulf of California. Durango, Sinaloa, Sonora. Poor towns with buildings in baby-room colors. I don't know what the Mexican government did or didn't do, but it looked like guerrilla units had been through. Just death, death. Kids, babies, old people, everyone machine-gunned in the head. Sometimes I'd wake up to two different hums. One would be zombies in massive numbers a few miles away; I could see them undulating on the sides of mountains. The other hum was gunfire, like a swarm of bees. All I know is it was warfare, and I didn't want any part of any war ever again.

Q.

Years. A few. A lot? You lose track. Compared to *Olympia*, it was easy. Story for another time, but I'm telling you, *that* was hell. This was like ... paperwork. Like something I had to power through. One more mile. One more town. One more block. It wasn't all on foot. There were caravans, all headed north. Things had to be better in America, right? I got onto some. But you don't speak the language, you might as well be making zombie moans. Anytime someone had to be kicked off, it was me. I didn't fight back. The time for fighting was over. Even then, in my Mexico years, I had that in my head. Zombies, they're so slow, so stupid. If the living had known how *not* to fight, we'd be fine today. Fine? We'd be *enlightened*.

Q.

I did. My husband, Larry, and our kids, Atsuko, Chiyo, Daiki, Neola, and Bea. I got so hot sometimes, so thirsty and tired, I couldn't even hold that many letters in my head. I shortened it to L-A-C-D-N-B. Me and those six letters crossed the border near El Paso. Felt appropriate, to be honest. My family was one of immigrants. Except at this border, the only ones being shot at were zombies. The ones crossing borders – all kinds of borders.

Q.

I heard lots of things, but what do you trust? I heard about rich guys using zombies like armies out east. I heard about the Lion and the Dove carrying on like Robin Hood in the Midwest. I heard about the Patriots, this cult blowing up whole towns in Kansas. The only legend I laid eyes on myself was this one particular zombie who'd been through hell, all torn up, half-burned, close to softie status. She had these metallic legs and just would not go down. I ran into her in Taos. I was navigating this fallen ski lift and there she came, metal legs scissoring through the snow. I got my ax ready. When I told you I wouldn't fight, I didn't mean I wouldn't defend. She came right up to me. The whole left side of her clothing was gone and her skin sparkled. It was frost. She'd partially frozen. It was actually pretty, and Hoffmann, I don't know if you could tell it from D.C., but *pretty* wasn't something anyone had seen in a long time.

Q.

Yes, the whole country would be beautiful soon. You might remember, scientists said climate change had doomed us. Our offenses were irreversible. Our grandchildren would be wearing oxygen masks. But they never counted on early human extinction, did they? You could *hear* it. Nature, inhaling and exhaling. Leaves trembling in pleasure. We died so the planet could live. I believe that. Maybe the zombie in Taos could tell I believed it. She left me alone. I left her alone too.

Q.

I found a motorcycle buried in snow with a sidecar full of fuel, and I took it, and I tell you, I nearly wrecked ten times a day because I couldn't stop gawking. The life. The life that had come back. I knew chances were slim, but I kept hoping that L-A-C-D-N-B were alive to see it. Because you can't see it and not be changed. You can't see it and not realize how badly we'd messed up the whole thing.

Q.

No, I did. I did find them.

Q.

[Long pause.] I was a different person by then. What would have broken me in half back on the boat – I understood we were part of something larger. You ever see how a group of zombies works together without saying a word? They know they're part of something larger. Maybe with the machines dead and the white noise gone, maybe we can start to hear what the zombies, and the dogs, and the rats, and the trees hear. Larry . . . he did what he felt was best. They were all inside our house in Buffalo. What a number they'd done on it. It took me a half day to get through the barricades.

Q.

Six lumps under cobwebs thick as a quilt. I thought they were
dead-dead until one of the lumps shifted, then all six did, like
they'd been woken up. Larry, Atsuko, Chiyo, Daiki, Neola, and
Bea. I used their full names when I took care of them. Today, I'd
do it differently. They were softies before we had a word for it.
Afterward, I wandered around looking at pictures of our
extended families. Of course, I got to thinking about the last
time the world almost killed itself. And I had this thought. And
it's vain. And I don't want it to come out wrong.

Q.

I'm Japanese American. Half-bomber, half-bombed. Me, and
others born like me, we were the solution to that war, the only
possible solution. What if that means I have, mixed up in my
genes, the qualifications to bring together both halves of this
war too? A stupid notion, undoubtedly. But it kept me going to
Toronto. I'd been hearing things about Toronto for a long
time.

Q.

Three hundred people living together and not at each other's
throats? That alone was notable. Yes, they had heads on pikes.
Yes, there was the shackle situation in the Stone Magazine. But
they were doing *something* right. I came in via the Gardiner
Expressway, which was coated with bright-green grass, and
way up there, looking down on Fort York, you see how defensible it is. Did you know the fort used to be on the water's edge?
That's why they used to call it *Muddy York* and why we started
calling it *Old Muddy*. It took a couple centuries of landfill to
push the water back, but by Year Ten, the natural borders were
coming back. Pretty soon, the fort's going to be waterfront

property again, and that's *really* defensible. People would need to arrive in boats to attack that.

Q.

I know, I know. It's a tough mind-set to break. Defense – it's all we thought about in the navy and all I was thinking when I got here, even though, by then, I was seeing softies by the side of the road every day. What stood out to me were the crops. In Garrison Common. In the lots across Bathurst. This had to be a special place. When I went down and said hello, the people were open. The people were kind. You didn't travel much, so I'm trying to convey to you, and to anyone reading this in the future, how incredibly, preciously rare that was. I was wiping away tears. Later, when I thought about Fort York, what it meant symbolically, it all made so much sense.

Q.

Navy officers generally know their military history. The Sacking of York. April 27, 1813. The US invades Canada. This is what's going through my head while I'm taking a tour of the place. *America* invaded *Canada*. If they'd won, there wouldn't even be a Canada. Why did the US need all that extra land? Because the British had it, naturally. The US sails up in its boats, there's only a few hundred British regulars, some militia, a handful of Mississauga and Ojibwe. Not only do we roll over them, we're appalled by them. Any Brit caught fighting alongside one of those Indian savages will be executed, we say. We end up torching York. A year later, the Brits revenge our revenge and burn down the White House. When the Treaty of Ghent is signed, guess what's changed about the US/Canada border? Nothing. Twenty thousand casualties, and the answer is nothing.

Q.
Exactly Earth's estimated population in Year Ten, that's right. Eerie, huh?

Q.
Uselessness. That's what Fort York represents to me. Before the War of 1812, most people in Upper Canada were American. We were fighting ourselves, you know? 10/23 hits and again: we're fighting ourselves. That's human history, and it has to end, Hoffmann. That's what we're trying to do here.

Q.
Which brings us back to the Stone Magazine. Let's not be afraid of it. Let's spell it out for posterity. The Stone Magazine is a bombproof, windowless storage building built in 1815 to keep powder safe. When I arrived, it was filled with zombies. Those crop fields I'd seen? They had zombies working them, pushing plows and harrows. They dangled meat in front of the plows – human meat they tried to keep fresh in buried boxes. Disgusting on numerous levels. The zombies had shackles on their ankles to keep them controllable. People here called them *domesticated*. They were not domesticated. They were enslaved.

Q.
We could. But we could also focus on how receptive these people were to a dissenting alternate viewpoint. I came in with a lot of ideas. They didn't shut me up. They didn't kick me out. They wanted to be better people. They were excited about it. All I said was we shouldn't do a thing until we freed the zombies. We couldn't build a new world on the mistakes of the old one. It was the very first vote we held, Decree One. It wasn't unanimous,

but it was a plurality, and we led those zombies out to Stanley Park and started breaking off their chains, and then they . . .

Q.

I'm sorry. Do you have a . . . thank you.

Q.

If you could have seen it. Larry had family enslaved in Trinidad and Tobago – if only he could have seen it. If only video cameras were still around, and WWN, so the whole world could see. Once a few zombies had been freed, they didn't come after us. They started trying to free the other zombies. Trying to chew through the chains. Breaking fingers off on the shackles. I didn't know what to make of it, exactly. No one did. But one thing was for sure. We knew, without a doubt, we had done the right thing. We got out of there, climbed up the expressway, and watched the zombies walk away. To where? Queen Street. Slowtown. They chose it. Our second vote, Decree Two, was to let them keep it.

Q.

I made it clear from day one I was no leader. A leader, in fact, was the worst thing we could have. What we needed here was the opposite of *Olympia*. We needed to disperse power. End the patriarchy. Share burdens and blames. Be brothers and sisters, not leader and followers. You begin doing it, it starts to feel so obvious. We'd make a haven. Maybe a *heaven*. At least give it a shot. We'd never have so clean a slate ever again. Hence the Custodial Council.

Q.

It's how we end up at the Armory. It's not so radical when you think about it. The fact that it felt so scary was the proof we needed to do it. We needed to break bad cycles. The Armory was our chance to put our money where our mouths were. Well, that's a bad metaphor. Seeing how Decree Three was prohibiting the use of money.

Q.

Everything! Guns were everything. How you caught your dinner. How you protected yourself from zombies. How you asserted yourself against rivals. But guns were also how you stole food from children. How you murdered. How you raped. Having guns was handling fire. Eventually, it engulfed everything. Look at me. It engulfed my whole *life*. So we took what we'd believed were our most valuable possessions and locked them up. Bricked them inside the Stone Magazine, the same place we'd enslaved the zombies. They're right there. You can get to them. But you'll have to spend some time breaking them out, right in front of everyone. It'd feel like defiling a temple, wouldn't it?

Q.

To that I'd say, ask the children. Are you going to interview children? To them, the Armory isn't some reservoir of latent violence. It's a tombstone. If they grow up viewing guns the way older generations viewed medieval torture devices in museums, nothing would make me prouder.

Q.

That's the best question of all. Because if it's just us, what good will it do? I take back calling Old Muddy a *special place*. We can't hope for that. We've got to hope it's not a special place at all, that all budding societies are headed in the same direction. My last stop before Buffalo was Detroit. Jenny Pagán was from there. That's how we named our escape plan: Operation Bills-Lions. I promised I'd get her home, and obviously, I failed. But I went there to see if I could find anyone who looked Puerto Rican, and I actually did – Jenny's parents, Jorge and Lorena. They were living in a high school gym. All my military stuff came back. I stood straight, and saluted, and didn't move until they saluted back. I told them what an exceptional sailor their daughter had been, and how, if there were honors left to give, I'd recommend her for all of them. I said I was sorry. And they said, no, they were the ones who were sorry, and they cried till they slumped to the floor, and I thought to myself, *Whoever these people were, whatever they're sorry for, they've changed. We've all changed. We just might have a shot.*

Libido Dominandi

The Face devoured the New Library's history books, but it was still WWN's offbeat, end-of-broadcast 'kickers' that stimulated his strangest musings. One kicker profiled a Palm Springs high school teacher who'd created a utopia exercise for his brightest seniors: a homespun biodome in which they'd have to live for two weeks. WWN's soft-news correspondent kidded that it could get a little Stanford Prison Experiment in there, prompting the teacher to catalog quirky historical notions of utopia. The one the Face remembered was Cockaigne, a medieval fantasyland with wine rivers, pancake trees, pastry rain, and roast geese flying overhead. To get there, you had to eat through three miles of rice pudding.

Compare that to Fort York's squat, utilitarian, two-hundred-year-old wood, stone, and brick structures, which looked no better with four hundred anxious people turning the grass to mud. This rinky-dink hodgepodge was going to be their paradise? The Face lodged his fists into the aching small of his back and watched Nishimura plod, rather like a zombie, back toward the fort. He had a sudden worry Nishimura would turn around and, knowing full well the Face never lied, ask him if he still believed Old Muddy could pull it off. Right now, the Face would be forced to reply that he wasn't sure.

When he'd arrived in Year Eleven, he'd been a quick convert to the navy man's sweeping vision. It was a tough row to hoe, Nishimura told the Face, while literally hoeing a row of sorghum. He was right.

The urge to own was so overpowering even the Face had to force himself not to hoard what he scrounged. An intact love seat, for example, better used in the fort's commons, or the perfectly preserved carving knife, best employed by those on cooking duty.

The Face's face made him an unlikely spokesman for Nishimura's designs, but the anchor desk had given him persuasive chops, and he'd helped convince Old Muddy residents to gamble a passable present on an idealistic future. The first phase was heavy on classic, commune-style egalitarianism. If you labored, you got everything for free. The Custodial Council served short, monthlong terms, responding to ideas, filling out labor sheets, and overseeing workaday choices. Nishimura said the Council was conceived opposite to military hierarchies.

'Being on the Council should suck,' he said.

Mission accomplished: the Face could report firsthand that council work was like being chased by chickens – the squawking kind, not the zombie kind. Someone turns up a trove of canned soups, delectables like Broccoli Cheese and Chicken Won Ton and French Onion, and guess who got the fun job of choosing who got them? One of the waterwheels powering the fort's machines breaks at three in the morning, and guess who had to rustle up the repairman? In those too-late or too-early hours, shivering and yawning, the Face felt as slow as any zombie.

What Nishimura got right was this: it felt good to finish a custodial spell. *Public service* was a phrase WWN folks loved using to describe their jobs, forgetting their six- or seven-figure salaries. The Face recalled a partisan talking head complaining that President Bush, after 9/11, had missed a once-in-a-generation chance to galvanize Americans toward a volunteerism not seen since World War II. A few decades late, the Face agreed. Selflessness would save the world.

Nishimura slipped through the Circular's embrasure. The Face watched residents swarm him like a zombie horde. Beyond that, he could not see much; the sun had dipped, and he barely noticed Greer slinking south toward the bay, the curve of her bow looking straight next to her bowed back. He didn't know what to do. Follow Greer, make sure she was all right? Stay here and wait for Charlie to finish her journey? Or go after Nishimura and be the loyal deputy he'd always been? There was no real choice. If the results of tomorrow's vote were in danger, his responsibility was telling the truth to those who might ask him for it. He walked down the Hospice stairs, his ankles, he thought, giving out a small *crick-crack*.

The Face greeted the soap sentry, washed his hands, and leaned against the cannon, glad that the dim, flickering light of the fort's tiki torches hid his face. The people inside these stone walls were sick with worry; the odor resembled that of the zombies who'd crawled from General Spalding's battlefield. Maybe Muse King had been wise to vacate after Richard Lindof had landed.

The world is rough, Nishimura once said, *but utopia is delicate.*

The Face let the cannon take more of his weight. He wished it could take the weight off his mind. He thought back to the long night of conversation he'd shared with Nishimura and Charlie after he'd arrived four years ago. It was his best memory since 10/23. It might be his best memory, period. When else in his life of disinterested models and disdainful coworkers had he felt truly accepted?

The three of them had been in Fort York's Mess Establishment, built in 1815, or so said the placard, and the cleanup of a community meal had turned into one of those magical nights you quit having after college, when like-minded souls intoxicated you with directionless joy and daylight had yet to find the cracks in your notions. They'd lollygagged like they'd had a case of PBR to plow through. Nishimura, looser than the Face ever saw him again, put his feet on a table and expounded on ideas he'd developed across Mexico, the United States, and Canada.

'You two religious?' he asked.

'My folks bled rosary beads.' Charlie lay flat on the floor like a girl at a slumber party. 'I wonder if faith gets stronger when you don't think about it. Is that blasphemous? But doesn't it feel true?'

The Face blew out a whole row of candles before taking a closer seat. He was still new and eager to spare these people from a clear sight of him. 'I never thought much about it back in the day.' He shrugged. 'Never thought much about anything.'

'My people were Shinto or Buddhist,' Nishimura said. 'I never practiced any of it, and what I saw on *Olympia* didn't particularly endear me to Christianity. But that's the kind of fervor we're going to need. We need people to make a leap of faith.'

'Not going to happen,' Charlie said. 'Everything they had faith in went kaboom.'

'What did they have faith in most?' Nishimura pressed.

Charlie sighed. 'I knew a guy whose faith was gadgets.'

'I was like that,' the Face said. 'I was logged on 24-7. I don't know why. They told us all the time our devices were being used against us, to steal our information, or sell it. But I kept believing anyway.'

'Little nuclear bombs we carried around like kittens,' Nishimura agreed. 'The problem with so-called smart devices was you could personalize them. You could follow who you wanted to follow. See and hear things you already liked. They were hand mirrors. Of course we were obsessed with them. The trick now is to replace that mirror with a window. No more seeing ourselves; we see each other.'

'It won't work,' Charlie said.

'That's the spirit, Rutkowski,' Nishimura said.

'Everyone's going to feel like we're moving backward. Even I feel it!'

'You're talking about inspiring people with ideas like they used to be inspired by religion,' the Face said. 'The problem is, religion relied on miracles. We used up all we had. People in biblical times would have thought our pre-10/23 life was *full* of miracles. Our blind could see. Our crippled could walk.'

'Our dead,' Charlie added, 'could live.'

'And all we used it for was to hurt each other,' the Face said.

'That's what gives me hope,' Nishimura said. 'One thing I know for sure is, we weren't happy back then. We weren't satisfied. What's different now is we can actually see the world again, beautiful and unspoiled. I really believe we can use it safely if we operate under animal philosophy, taking only what we need.'

'How many people are there here?' the Face asked.

'Hoffmann's running a census,' Charlie said. 'But it's got to be, what? Five or six hundred?'

'With that many, you might be able to pull off what you're talking about,' the Face said. 'You might be able to say, "Don't split the atom again." "Don't make mustard gas." "Whatever you do, don't invent social media." But with a thousand? Two thousand?'

'I read a population needs ten thousand to avoid inbreeding,' Charlie added.

'Libido dominandi,' Nishimura said. 'Lust for domination. Meet enough sea captains, you learn the phrase.'

'Latin,' Charlie groaned. 'Give me a choice, I'll take apocalypse over med school.'

'Somewhere in Connecticut, I was poking around an old shopping center and saw this security camera,' the Face said. 'Few minutes later, I saw another one. When I started looking, I saw them all over the place. There must be thousands of cameras like that, some still running on wind or solar, and all they're staring at is *other cameras*. A feedback loop, no humans in sight. That's our legacy. A world we're not even part of. We can't do that again.' He shrugged. 'I think that means I'm with you.'

'Oh, great, the men have a plan,' Charlie snorted. 'Surely this ends well.'

But before the night was over, all three were high on the hope of the blank canvas. They gasped in enthusiasm, oohed in agreement, laughed at everything. At one point, Charlie covered her face, mortified by their ambition. The Face snagged her elbow to reveal her grinning embarrassment, and she batted at him playfully, and he had to sit back, way back, to calm his heart. No one had touched him with kindness in eleven years. His resolve to help turn Fort York into paradise doubled. Anything was possible.

In that single dizzying eve, seeds were planted for the fort's two guiding protocols: the Armory and Hospice. In the meantime, they had a philosophy to follow and a direction in which to head. With Charlie and the Face's help, Nishimura's big ideas spread faster than a *PERPLEXED* meme. To the Face, it felt natural. Zombies were dying out. The Fort was growing. In the New Library's collection of vintage magazines, the Face found a yellowed 1950s ad for suburban development, which he tore out and tacked to the door of his room.

An Experiment in Better Living!

Was the experiment failing? The Face strolled into the fort. Every tiki torch blazed, painting the crowds on either side in a thin orange wash. These were people who hugged and held hands and gave piggyback rides to any kid who wanted one. Seeing them split in half was shocking.

The people outside the Brick Magazine, the holding cell of the Blockhouse Four, were the loudest. If the Face's forthrightness was needed anywhere, it was there. He walked down the central sidewalk, still in place from the fort's days as a historical attraction. It bisected the Garden, passed both the Armory and Master Sundial, and curled into the waiting crowd. Richard Lindof had not yet appeared, though a large crate had been situated before the Brick Magazine for his eventual boost. The Face nudged his way closer until he could read its faded stamp: DRY AGED BEEF. It felt fitting. Fort York, as well as every other known settlement, might have gone vegetarian, but the ghost ache for flesh lingered, and red meat was what Lindof had been tossing since the day he'd arrived.

The Face rubbed warmth into his arms, thinking through what he'd heard about other communities from Fort York newcomers. Their reports described colonies like Old Muddy but for their lack of Arcadian underpinnings, which made them more volatile. Generally encouraging news, as were the stories of the collapse of less palatable societies.

Fort York's closest neighbor was Fort Drum, a former military training base on the US end of Lake Ontario. Prior to 10/23, eighty thousand troops had trained there annually. Today, from all accounts, it was a quiet, walled village occupied by industrious workers who'd come to kindred conclusions about softies, choosing to leave them be rather than mop them up. Fort Drum had a peculiarity confirmed by two visitors. Like Fort York, Fort Drum dreamed of a world divested of its self-destructive impulses, but they approached the goal through brain science. Among Fort Drum's population were three neurosurgeons studying the ventromedial prefrontal cortex and the insular cortex, areas of the brain controlling egalitarian behavior and kindness. If they could manipulate these areas, they theorized, they could neuter antisocial urges.

While it would be nice to rid the world of future Lindofs, the thought of DIY neurosurgeons made the Face queasy. He was glad Fort Drum was there, glad they were forward-thinking. For now, he was also glad they were at least a day's horse ride away.

The crowd quaked. The Face lifted onto his toes and saw a group of seven or eight people entering the fort from the East Gate. There was no question it was Lindof. There was a chest-puffed pride in the strut of those serving as unnecessary bodyguards, while the man in the middle indulged in a slow strut that didn't quite hide his limp. The fanfare turned the Face's stomach.

No one at Fort York had fewer exchanges with Lindof than the

Face. The reason was simple. Lindof found the Face repulsive. When Lindof caught a glimpse of him, he turned away, his face clenching into a child's dinner-table mask of disgust. At first, the Face hadn't held it against him. The reaction was honest, and there was no quality he prized more. This benefit of the doubt lasted one week. Like other Fort Yorkers, Lindof had complaints. Unlike other Fort Yorkers, he did not submit them to the Custodial Council. He bad-mouthed, got personal. Council idiots. Those morons who did whatever they said.

People strong enough to have lived through the Second Dark Age should have seen right through such middle school whisper campaigns, but a surprising number gravitated toward it. The Face watched people's lips relearn the workings of sneers.

The Face had kept these observations to himself; it didn't feel good to be the subject of such open revulsion. Now he regretted it, violently. He should have walked straight up to Lindof and forced him to look at his mangled face, if only to make him acknowledge what everyone at Old Muddy had been through. What had been the purpose if they were going to revert to petty, despicable behaviors?

Once he'd amassed a disgruntled clump of followers, Lindof began trumping up minor incidents as major scandals. A month after arriving, a yacht beached nearby with a manifest of zombie rats, and two days were spent torching the vessel in the water. If Fort York had a policy of proactively patrolling the Lake Ontario waterfront and firebombing empty boats, a red-faced Lindof cried, threats like this would never happen.

If Lindof had presented valid concerns, Old Muddy would have addressed them with frank debate, same as always. But Lindof's discourse was so absent of intellect, so focused on base urges, it glissaded under higher echelons of reason and caught everyone by surprise. For the first time in five years, confidence in their way of life was eroding.

Maybe the Fort Drum folks have it right, the Face thought, imagining a trio of neurosurgeons piercing lobotomy lances through Lindof's eye sockets. Instantly, he chastised himself. These were the sorts of spiteful thoughts that made people rebel against the Custodial Council – an infection was spreading. Charlie Rutkowski had once confided in the Face she might have known Patient Zero. There was a new Patient Zero now: Richard Lindof.

The Face didn't want to attribute cliché qualities to Muse King strictly because he was an artist, but the Face noticed things. For three years, Muse had been the fort's warmest, gentlest resident. The Face, capable only of blurting unvarnished facts, envied Muse's ability to wrap hard truths in cozy fables. But he'd seen Muse go cold observing the rash-like spread of Lindof apostates. Seven days after Richard arrived, Muse went bye-bye, as if to protect something pure inside him. Now the Face wondered, if the vote went Lindof's way, if those on the west end of the fort would follow Muse's lead.

People cheered as Richard Lindof rounded East Blockhouse, the scene of the crime, and gave it a little pat, perhaps assuring the building that he would protect it from future wrongs. Inside the blockhouse were the most valuable, delicious, spoil-resistant, shelf-stable relics of yesteryear, and by and large, residents did a solid job bringing such finds to be stored. If they quietly took for themselves a finder's fee, who really cared? The Council doled out the rest for birthdays, weddings, deaths, other occasions. Campbell's soup. Boxes of salt, cornstarch, powdered milk, Jell-O. Containers of rice. Bottles of soy sauce, corn syrup, vanilla extract, vinegar, honey. Cans of dried beans. And, of course, alcohol: beer, wine, and spirits, all of which the Face knew made Nishimura nervous, but none of which could be ditched without being tyrannical.

Even rarer than alcohol at Fork York were drugs, but Federico, Reed, Stuart, and Mandy had gotten high on some sort of inhalant before deciding their case of midnight munchies could not be denied. They pushed past a seventeen-year-old named Shyam Iyer, on duty at East Blockhouse, and began loading their arms with food. Shyam tried to stop them. They resisted. Shyam shouted. Fifty-two-year-old Yong-Sun Tang, pacing with insomnia, came to his aid. The delirious foursome beat both Shyam and Yong-Sun. The young man suffered broken ribs and lost teeth and was still urinating blood, while the older man broke his hip and five ribs, which set off a lung infection that just might kill him.

For their trouble, Federico, Reed, Stuart, and Mandy absconded with a carton of assorted ramen noodles, sixteen packs of instant cocoa, four bottles of wine, two bags of sugar, one bottle of maple syrup, and a fistful of bouillon cubes.

Now the Blockhouse Four were locked right here inside the Brick Magazine. Fort York, by design, had no jail. Loss of community status, Nishimura contended, was a more productive punishment. But angrier people made a decision before most were awake, and so in the Brick Magazine the foursome remained, going on six days now. They were brought food and water, and allowed out to relieve themselves, wearing shackles left over from the enslaved zombies. Why didn't that detail have the impact it should have?

If he were in charge, Lindof crowed, those chains would never come off.

Tomorrow's vote was not about the Blockhouse Four. Ostensibly it was a no-confidence vote against the Fort's Custodial Council (An Experiment in Better Living!), which would then permit the permanent exile of Federico, Reed, Stuart, and Mandy. But anyone with a set of eyes could see the real purpose of the vote: the growing shadow in the shape of Richard Lindof.

He climbed atop the crate. He was far from graceful. The man was late sixties and out of shape, and his shorter leg and half-length arm required the assistance of four men. But Lindof knew how to play a crowd. Once standing, he raised a victorious fist over his head, making light of his struggle to get there, though in reality he wanted that hooray that, sure enough, burst from everyone. The Face jerked in fright. He knew every one of these people's names, a trick he'd picked up as a roving reporter. But the way tiki fires danced in their pupils and flames slithered across their exposed teeth? He swore he didn't know them.

They quieted only when Lindof signaled with his good arm he was ready to speak. As the din died, the Face again ached at the loss of Charlie. Once while walking with the Face and noticing Lindof holding court, she'd muttered, 'If they only knew what I knew.' The Face, as always, held nothing back and asked her what she meant. Charlie, however, was true-blue, honor bound to the Old Muddy principle of allowing people to remake themselves. The Face wished he had pressed the issue. He pictured Charlie as she'd been that magical night, lying on the Mess Establishment floor, drunk on hope, brighter than all the candles, her scarred face beautiful with gaiety and her blond hair spread like the sun.

Past Due

My God – if Charlie believed in God, which even now, at the draining, dizzying end, she wasn't sure she did – my God, Hospice was beautiful seen from this floating, gliding stretcher. The physical details might be dismaying, but added together, they created not oppressive despair but soaring inspiration. Both in med school and at the morgue with Luis, she'd spent untold hours with the dead, but never had she expected her concerns for them would evolve from corporeal to, let's face it, spiritual. Life, it really knew how to surprise a gal.

All she could see were the two people carrying her stretcher. Marion Castle looked beaten by grief, though her unflappable professionalism held strong. Charlie detected grapefruit essential oil under Marion's medical mask, often used to combat Hospice odor, though in truth, the odor wasn't as bad as one might expect. Degraded past their most fetid phases, softies exuded nothing more than a rancid cinnamon stink.

Charlie might still be the only one able to interpret Etta Hoffmann's blank looks. Right now, the slight bulges of her locked jaws and her gently pulsing temples were what indicated she was barely keeping it together. Charlie tried to smile at her. Did she do it? Her lips had gone numb.

She visualized their path through the maze of tables with the stretcher's every turn. She saw posters drawn by schoolchildren, supplying encouragement to caretakers. MAKE FRIENDS WITH DEATH, read one, with a painting of two clasped hands, one tan and thick, the other green and bony. WE ARE ALL THE SAME, read another, featuring a dramatis personae of humans, zombies, giraffes, horses, cats, and birds in a smiling line. Only after Lindof's arrival had Charlie felt a twinge of doubt about these charming messages. She recalled the rage she'd felt when antiabortion protestors made children hold hateful placards. This was different, right?

Richard Lindof. What were the chances he'd end up at Fort York? She recalled with chilling precision his smug, callous voice through Luis's speakerphone, editorializing on JT's suicide with *He seemed like a fun little gay guy.* It had been the instant of the Earth's pivot – John Doe's brain incapacitated; other dead bodies animating all over; chaos at Trump International Hotel – and yet nothing had been as sickening as Lindof's bemusement. It was as if he'd been a long-dozing, cold-blooded reptile waiting for the sun to die so he could crawl out and own the night.

You should be pissing your shitty little diapers, he'd said as Charlie had piloted Luis's Prius into the gridlock of apocalypse. *Because you know what I think? I think your world is about to fall into the ocean, Acocella, and my world is about to rise up like a fucking mountain.*

Charlie had fuzzy recollections of a Richard Lindof being the son of some industry giant. Had he maybe produced a few soft-core action films? All of it was slipping from her brain in a long, final exhale. She closed her eyes and tried to bury the pain beneath the falling-soil shushes of Caretakers murmuring to softies. Actual burial might be a thing of the past, but at Hospice, symbolic burial was very much alive. Charlie breathed through her nose and repeated the wisest words she knew. Make Friends with Death. We Are All the Same.

Nishimura had wanted Hospice smack in the middle of the fort, right in Centre Blockhouse. Charlie, as she often did, nudged his ambitions to a realistic level, suggesting a spot just outside the fort's walls. Ideally, an actual former hospice facility or nursing home. Hoffmann took to the idea instantly; nursing homes, she'd said, had been part of the VSDC network, and Charlie had to smile at the woman's steadfast dream of getting the system back online. Unfortunately, they found no such place, but the only tools really needed were tables, chairs, and curtains for the Caretakers, and a smaller space in back to serve as the Dying Room.

That's where Charlie was headed. What could be luckier than kicking the bucket in a room expressly made for bucket-kicking? She tried to smile, but damn those numb lips. Too bad. She'd come to believe that softies responded to smiles. It made sense. Pre-language babies did; the post-language senile did too. Tonight she'd have to hope tone of voice alone carried meaning too.

'Stop.' She rapped her fist against the stretcher bar. 'Table 20.'

Marion would have disregarded anyone else's request. Above her mask, the woman blinked once, telling Hoffmann to pause. Charlie was jostled against her binding buckles – a reminder she'd become as dangerous as softies were harmless. She strained to see over the stretcher's edge. Marion again took pity: she nodded for Hoffmann to lower the stretcher so Charlie could see what she so badly wanted to see.

The softie on Table 20 had been recovered from Slowtown six weeks ago. While securing him to the table, Charlie had discovered in his shredded pants a moldy wallet. Inside, she'd found faded photo evidence the man once had multiple brothers, all much taller, and their shared last name was Hedrick. Hence the softie was dubbed *Lesser Hedrick*. Caretakers were encouraged to name their softies if it helped, and here was proof it could: the name endeared this softie to Charlie so much, she'd fudged the books to be his Caretaker.

Charlie rested her cheek on the side of the stretcher. There he was, her elder, her child, now her brother too. The wallet photos pictured

Lesser as white, male, midtwenties, average in every way but height. He'd hate to learn he'd lost a few more inches: his feet had fallen off in Slowtown. He'd also lost his genitals, and his skin had gone brown-black. In short, he was no longer white, or male, or midtwenties. He'd become what all softies in their last days became: everyone.

His body was shriveled inward, shoulders close to touching, wrists crossed, a posture Charlie found saintlike. Since being emplaced in Hospice, everything south of his ribs (abdominal muscles, stomach, liver, appendix, pancreas, colon, intestines – she felt like a diener again, listing them off) had crumbled to flakes, piled atop loose vertebrae and draped with skin the color and texture of black banana peels. Lesser's sternum had fallen in, creating a cage for the shriveled sacks of heart and lungs.

Lesser's lone eyeball rasped as it rotated toward Charlie. Like most softies, his eyelids had been picked off by scavengers, giving him a statue's severe, impartial stare. Such stares invited truth-telling, the same as the dark windows of Catholic confessionals she'd been shoved into at age eight. Everything came round. One of the unintended surprises of Hospice: things you hadn't been able to say to people before the world fell apart, you could say to softies. They'd lost most of their features, become anyone you needed them to be.

'Lesser.' Her croak frightened her, but she thought she saw in Lesser's eye an interest in hearing her voice. Charlie no longer valued understanding as much as she did the desire to understand – as Greer Morgan had once put it, the *want*. She didn't care what naysayers like Lindof said. They weren't here every day like she was. What softies wanted was tenderness, and Charlie was determined to deliver it.

'You'll have to pass without me,' she said. 'I know you don't have much time. My brave boy. But don't be scared. We'll get you through. My brave, brave boy. Marion will find you a new Caretaker.'

'I'll do it myself,' Marion said.

Charlie's relieved sigh shot acid into every bronchiole of her lungs, and she mashed her lips against what had to be a coming upchuck of blood. Moments from now, she'd be in the Dying Room, where she, per rules both biological and cultural, would die. Out here, Lesser Hedrick and the other softies would continue shuffling off their coils. So much death, so much life, in this sighing little cathedral.

During that all-night bull session in Year Eleven, Nishimura had spoken of Jenny Pagán, whom he'd stabbed, who'd saved him anyway, who'd then gone zombie and tried to kill him, only to be killed a second time by sharks. It was the *cycle* of it, Nishimura said, the cycles *within* cycles, that obsessed him. Everyone's death allowed everyone's life. Why did it have to be a traumatic exchange? If people could lose the fear of death that had hounded them since humankind's first flicker of self-awareness – and without the dangling carrot of religion, so much like the dangling red meat of Fort York's former enslaved – we might also lose the compulsions that drove violence, cruelty, and jealousy.

No one liked the word *hospice*. No shit they didn't. It brought back the wretched, dragged-out deaths of loved ones, the shame of a society that forbade euthanistic dignity. In Year Fourteen, Marion said something Charlie never shook. 'Zombies were old hat to me way before 10/23. I spent my whole career around them – terminal patients hooked up to breathing machines. You want more proof this is all our doing, there you go. We went ahead and invented the undead without bothering to figure out what we'd do when they learned to walk.'

The idea of the Caretaker program was to take your turn sitting with softies until fear turned to acceptance, disgust to empathy. Most people spoke to their softies. Some read from books. Some whispered songs. Some screamed, close to ripping their softie to pieces. In short, people worked out their shit and put it behind them.

After DOD – Death of Death – a softie was wrapped in a sheet and carried to a waterfront wood-burning incinerator at Bathurst and Queens Quay. When the wind was right, the ashes would self-scatter over Lake Ontario, some of it rippling the water enough that fish darted up to kiss them from the surface, swallow them, and get the cycle going again.

A Caretaker could never predict the state of their assigned softie. As with sounds of collapsing buildings, terms of art had developed. *Talcum* described a zombie so fragile it barely survived transport to the fort; they might last days, if the sighs of their Caretakers didn't blow their bones to powder. *Lace* described a zombie months into inertia, whose flesh yielded to the touch; like Lesser Hedrick, they might last for weeks. *Eggshell* described a zombie picked up from Slowtown just after losing mobility; like eggshell china, they were delicate but firm, and might last months in Hospice before passing.

Tonight, that last category included Charlie Rutkowski. She almost smiled. Lace? She'd always been more of a denim girl.

Call it her imagination if you liked. It really didn't matter. In the twitch of Lesser Hedrick's eye, Charlie saw forgiveness for her early departure. More than forgiveness. Lesser and the softies all around him were bequeathing the planet back to their former rivals, trusting them to be Caretakers of it. Charlie held in a ragged sob only because of the physical pain it might cause her. The solace she'd always taken from Hospice had achieved its final form.

She nodded at the Dying Room.

The stretcher lifted. The upward disequilibrium made Charlie feel like she was back at the Acocella house, rushing upstairs to check on Luis. He'd been right about a lot, but he'd been wrong about one thing. The zombie genesis was no Miscarriage. It had been a successful delivery. DOD, after all, was a double negative. Wasn't the Death of Death the same as the Birth of Life?

'Goodbye,' she called to Lesser Hedrick, who stood in for Luis

Acocella, Mae Rutkowski, and so many others she felt fortunate to have met. So many people worth missing. The tear that rolled from her eye burned down her cheek like mercury, flaying open the flesh so she could feel the teeth that had chewed so many delicious foods, the tongue that had wrestled in so many exciting kisses. The world had fucked hard with everyone, her more than most, but goddamn, she'd miss it anyway.

Ecclesiastes Something

Personal History Transcript #1530
Location: Fort York New Library
Subject: Richard Lindof
Interviewer: Etta Hoffmann
Time: 5,745–15:22

Notes: Also present: Luvvie Lafayette.

Q.
I'm a movie guy. Never was much for books. This is what you do all day? Sit in here with these dusty books? I'm also a business guy, and what I know about books is, they don't make business sense. Reading a book is like hiring the slowest, most expensive workers in Vermont. Watching a movie is like applying the screws to your workers in China, who give you a better product in a fraction of the time. Lady, you're telling me you'd rather spend weeks reading *The Da Vinci Code* when there's a perfectly good movie out there telling the same story?

Q.
Nice. Very nice. 'Books still worked when we lost the grid.' I guess you think that's cute. You're one of those people who's

going to stand in the way of progress. I knew it before I sat down. You can always tell. It tends to be, I'm sorry, but it tends to be bitter females of below-average attractiveness who carved themselves a little corner of power and don't want anything to change. Well, baby, it's going to change. Jesus Hubert Christ, it's going to change big-time.

Q.

Because I'm a nice guy? Because they asked me to? Your little board of directors. I caught their drift. I wanted in, I had to do this little sit-down. It's no skin off my ass. My legs are beat anyhow. But don't go thinking I need your little fort. Which, by the way, is the least fortlike fort I've ever seen. I could just keep on walking. Probably should. What am I doing in Canada? America was number one in the past, and it'll be number one again. Forget it. I'm here. Do your questions. I'm hungry and want to check out what kind of food you have in this joint.

Q.

To be honest, I cannot say I'm impressed. So far, I cannot. I'll tell you the first thing I thought after washing my hands like a five-year-old. Where are the heads on sticks? You can make a pretty fair judgment of a place by how many heads they've got on sticks. So that doesn't bode well. Then they start showing me, what? The Armory? Are you kidding me? You got all those beautiful weapons and you've bricked them up? You people are mental. Forget the heads on sticks. I didn't see any handcuffs, leg irons, pillories. You don't even have a jail. Look, lady, take my free advice. See if your little CEOs will take up a motion to remove all heads from all asses.

Q.

That's kumbaya stuff. That's Sunday school. Let's hold hands and think positive thoughts. If that's the best you got, baby, you deserve what you're going to get. Look, you got a nice little spot here. It's cozy. You got some nice overpasses to shoot off of. I'd hate to see it all go up in smoke. Couple hours, the right kind of bad guys? Poof.

Q.

You got book dust in your ears? That's what I'm saying. The bad guys don't have to come galloping over the hill like Lee Marvin. They could come from right here. A cancer from within, as they say. How would anybody stop them? Let's recap. You've got no jail and your guns are all bricked up, and what you've spent all your time on is – what do you call it? Sick bay? Nursing home?

Q.

Jesus Heathcliff Christ. You're certifiable, you people. I've seen things, baby, that would wipe that smug look off your face. This takes the cake. I asked to see it. I thought someone was yanking my johnson. We wash our hands like we're in kindergarten again, fine, and go inside this normal-looking building, and I'll be a monkey's uncle if you don't have – lady, I was rubbing my eyes like a cartoon character. You've got dried-up old zombies in there with people reading them stories and whatnot. Let me tell you what you do when you find yourself a dried-up old zombie. You take your boot and go smash. You be glad there's one less of them the world has to deal with. What you don't do is go goochie-goo like they're cute. Are there some kind of toxic fumes here I'm not aware of? Has something happened to your actual, physical brains?

Q.

You're saying a living corpse is both disgusting and . . . what? Sacred? No, no.

Q.

No, no, no, no, no.

Q.

No, no, no, no, no, no, no. Shut up. Not to be rude. But shut up. That Asian fellow with the flagpole up his ass fed me all of that sap. Sounded pretty proud of it too. Normally, I would've helpfully explained to him that he was a retarded individual. But you understand, my jaw was on the floor.

Q.

I'm not a weirdo freak, am I? So, no, I have not. My pop was a true-blue believer in all that God stuff. Let's bow our heads in prayer, yea Christ has risen, all that, and it made about as much sense as what you all are saying here. He wouldn't listen to sense either. I'd say, 'Pop, what's the meaning of life?' and he'd say, 'Richie, you have to have faith,' and I'd say, 'But didn't we come up with faith in our brains?' and he'd say, 'God made your brain,' and, well, you see how productive that all is. If Pop were here now, he'd say something like 'Zombies don't have souls, which proves we do.' [Exaggerated shrug.] Instead of heading for the hills, he should have come here and become a zombie-lover like your Asian fellow. The way zombies went around and converted people, so to speak? That's A-plus missionary work. That's what he'd say.

Q.

Just so I have this straight, you're saying maybe zombies are holy because they show us *our* sins? I suppose Fort York is

Noah's Ark, then? And this whole thing's supposed to teach us some big lesson? Let me guess – the same one people like you always hope is true. 'The meek shall inherit the Earth.' But did they? Take a peek into your Hospice and tell me if the meek in there inherited anything good. Pop's favorite Bible verse was, 'Men go and come, but Earth abides.' Ecclesiastes something. We read it differently, me and Pop. He read it like Earth shows us who's boss. I read it like, no, you don't get it, Pop. Men will keep coming, and coming, and coming.

Q.
Where did you hear that? One of these books?

Q.
Did I say I'm denying it? I'm not denying anything. I told you I was a movie guy. I admitted it first thing. The limp, the arm, they confirm it, don't they? Oh, you're clever. You think you're clever. Waiting to reveal this now. You know what I think? I think you're a bitch. Your whole no-smiling thing. I see right through it. I see through everybody. It's my little talent. You know what? I did this as a favor. In good faith. Well, you got what you wanted. Now I'm shutting it down. Good riddance.

Q.
I'm walking back over to your table to say this so your recorder gets it nice and clear. With you? No. No second session, not with you. No way. With baby darling over there, though? That I'd consider. Didn't catch your name, darling, but you want a private interview sometime, you just let me know. You're a little darker than I usually like my girls, but this is Canada after all.

Eskimos, Inuits, Aboriginals. You take what you can get, right? Jesus Harrison Christ. I'm leaving. Your Asian fellow wanted to show me a few more things, and I'm going to need all my energy to pretend to care.

Throw the First Punch

Nishimura's specific goals: check off the one pending obligation he had at the fort, break the news to Luvvie, and go to bed early. Hopefully, daylight would dry the spatters of Richard's bile from people's faces – and clear Nishimura's own head about what had happened to Charlie and the Chief. His broader goal of being a good person got in the way, as it often did. When he entered the historic grounds to review, as promised, a team's progress on a telegraph machine, he could not bring himself to rebuff an overture from a group calling themselves the AV Club.

They were devoted to bringing art back to the world via whatever media they could muster. Until he vanished, Muse King, skilled at nothing but making people take a knee when they heard him play, had been the AV Club's patron saint. Without him, the club carried on. Their current efforts included mixing paint so there could be painters, getting analog four-tracks rolling again so there could be recording artists, and producing fresh film so they'd have something to run through rejiggered 8 mm cameras. The club members were young, sixteen to twenty-five years old, and were as flushed and flustered as Nishimura had been in his youth. He adored them, but for now, showed them the glow.

'Karl, you have to do something,' Georgia said. She was their de facto leader, six feet four, shaggy-haired, outfitted with thick-framed black glasses.

'I am.' Nishimura tried to smile. 'I'm going to play with a tele-graph machine.'

'They're like wolves,' said a boy named Jack. 'Since your team left, there's been fights, all afternoon.'

'Not as bloody as the Blockhouse Four fight,' added a girl named Marilyn. 'But worse. That fight was because of drugs. It didn't mean anything. These were *for real*.'

Nishimura's sigh felt like glue, oozing up his throat. He gazed across the fort with hard reluctance. Past the Garden, swaying like the Garden's windblown leaves, was Richard Lindof's flock, and beyond them, the makeshift crate stage awaiting the arrival of their leader. That's what he was, a leader, the very thing Fort York had tried to avoid.

'The will of the people,' he said, 'will be what it will be.'

'Bullshit,' said fraternal twins Rudi and Russell.

Nishimura hated to survey the AV Club's expressions. He knew what he'd see. Bright, attentive agony, the tiki light painting passion-ate patterns across clean, ardent faces and hair grown to snatchable lengths, unthinkable just a couple of years ago. That they'd been barely self-aware on 10/23 meant nothing. As proven in the 1960s, the 2010s, and every era between, young adults did not need to know the feel of a fist to understand it; they'd absorbed truths from their parents' quivering hands. It took the undamaged to fight the hardest fights.

Jack pointed at Richard's crowd. 'If they win that vote, we're out of here. The whole club. Along with everything we've built, all our ideas. We mean it, Karl.'

It was one more spear into his side, each spearhead carved from a dead person's bone – the Chief, Charlie, Jenny, Larry, his children. The combined weight made him heavy and slow.

Didn't they know the clear, common sense Nishimura might espouse to the masses would only wilt in the red blood Lindof would be spewing? He shook his head, hoping the motion would free him of these burdens; hot sweat rolled laterally across his cheeks.

He started to go around Jack, but a kid named Gary blocked his path. Nishimura redirected, only to be hindered by a girl named Vincenza. These weren't aggressive moves; the AV Club was large. Nishimura's chest clenched at the sheer number of young people refusing to back down. Perhaps he, Karl Nishimura, age fifty-eight, should forget everything he thought he knew, and listen to them, and trust them.

Georgia was back in front. Her large hands were pressed together, nearly in prayer.

'We know you don't want to engage him publicly. You think it will legitimize him. We understand that. Everyone does.' Georgia winced. 'But, Karl, man, there's no choice anymore. This is the wire we're down to. I'd walk over there and do it myself if I had the right words. But we all know you're the one. It sucks. I know. Being the one sucks. But sometimes, that's what life makes you.'

Nishimura's face broke open like pond ice after a thaw. It felt as if he'd been bitten back in Slowtown and this was the ripe tearing of decay. It was more shocking than that: it was a grin. This kid. This Georgia of the AV Club. Already people were following her like they'd followed him. One day, whether at Old Muddy or somewhere new, Georgia *would* have the right words, perhaps through her art, and growing numbers of people would listen to them. Whatever happened tonight did not have to be the final word.

Nishimura took hold of the side of Georgia's neck. Beneath his soaped and scrubbed hand, he could feel the young woman's unwashed hair and sweaty skin, and he was glad for it. They'd need plenty of grit for where they were headed. Not just ten years from now but ten minutes from now.

'Hold on tight, Georgia,' Nishimura said, and Georgia did, gripping the wrist that gripped her neck. 'Here we go.'

Releasing her and being released by her, Nishimura turned from the AV Club and ducked like a boxer past other citizens petitioning for his attention. He broke from the pack at the Master Sundial. It was night; there was no telling the time. That was good. Let this event exist outside of time, outside the record of what they tried to do with Fort York. Let this night and morning be one last, loathsome dip into a past of aversion and antipathy. He realized both his hands were in fists. The impulse that had made him shoot the Chief was back. It should have repulsed him. It really should.

Halfway across the fort, Lindof began to speak, in the low, scratchy tones Nishimura had come to loathe.

'Look at this crowd. This beautiful crowd. I recognize so many of you. Hi, William. Hi, Lewis. You're all here. And it's cold! Isn't it cold? But you're all here, bundled up, aren't you? You're here because this is important. Because you care about your community. Because you have common sense. And what's common sense? When a guy comes up to you and socks you in the kisser, you don't stand there and wait for him to sock you in the ball sack too! You sock him back. Better yet, the whole community comes together and socks him back together. That's called *punishment*. That's called *common sense*.'

When the cheer went up, Nishimura was on the path through the Garden. He'd heard plenty of cheering at Old Muddy. When the first waterwheel went operational. When they got a moped engine to run on vegetable oil. When a woman woke successfully from a spleen operation, proving the viability of homemade ammonium-nitrate ether. This cheer, however, was a kaboomie, screecher, duster, and marimba all at once. Vegetation blocked Nishimura's view, but he pictured it just fine. He knew William. He knew Lewis. He liked them. He had no desire to see their kind faces warped by wrath.

Nishimura emerged from the Garden at the back edge of the crowd.

'I don't need to tell you these things,' Lindof boomed. 'You're smart. You're the smartest bunch of people I've come across, and I've traveled many, many miles. Because you're so smart, you're going to appreciate what I'm about to say. Those people on the other side of the fort, they're smart too. You think they can hear me? Hey, people! Come on over! We're just talking! Look, here come some. Right through the Garden, isn't that a pretty sight. The ones who don't, have a chat with them later. Explain our side of things. No need to be violent or anything. Not unless you have to!'

Lindof laughed, and the crowd laughed back. Nishimura was inside the throng now, able to identify individual chortles: the biology teacher who made the soap, the preschool teacher who kept things equitable at mealtimes. He loved these people. He *loved* them. He kept moving.

'Since we're talking about violence. We know why we're here, don't we? We're standing right in front of – what do you call this thing? The Brick Magazine? The Brick Shithouse is more like it, right? Do you Canucks know how to build houses or what? Those four deadbeats in there aren't getting out. Those four hoods. Those four thugs. Can we be honest? Those four are no better than zombies. And what do we do with zombies?'

A man: *Shoot 'em!*

A woman: *Kill 'em!*

From the instant he'd slipped his hand from Georgia's neck, Nishimura had felt as if he were running on rails. Now he skittered offtrack, taking elbows to the ribs and fingers to the eyes, the whaling of frenzied applauders.

'All I'm trying to say to you smart people is, there's this old idea called *scared straight*. Any of you remember it? I'm seeing some nods. Preventive justice, my friends. Who really ought to throw the first punch? The bad guy? Or do you punch the bad guy before he even gets the chance? The sad truth, folks, is that's never going to happen with this sad-sack Council of yours.'

Nishimura pushed through the last line of fanatics and stared right up Lindof's nose, which, in the stark firelight, had the subtle notches of plastic surgery. Things had been removed from Lindof, but not nearly enough.

As Nishimura took a step toward the crate, Lindof glanced down. His foreshortened nose wrinkled back, his thin lips curled in victory, and his glassy blue eyes flashed in hot glee. In that instant, fifty years peeled back: Lindof was a fifth-grade harasser fueled by a rage he'd never get to the bottom of, and Nishimura was a twiggy, obedient Japanese boy who always came when bullies ordered.

A cuff clasped over Nishimura's biceps and slung him back into the crowd. He whirled and saw a monster, worse than any childhood tormenter, worse than Soba Ayumi's Millennialist. He blinked; this was no monster. It was the Face. His mangled features were cryptic, but his bright eyes said everything.

'You sure about this?' the Face hissed under the clamor.

Because the Face allowed no lies to cross his lips, Nishimura replied with a question: 'What do you think?'

The Face nodded, his pale blob of a head tossing tiki smoke. 'Get up there,' he said, without hesitation, and to thank him, Nishimura, also without hesitation, placed his hands atop the waist-high crate and hoisted himself up. Lindof did not make room for him to stand, a power play, and Nishimura was scared he'd totter off. That would be that, five years of work undone by a slip of the foot. But he bore down, stood tall, and gazed from a higher vantage than he'd ever wanted over his fellow Fort Yorkers.

Nishimura looked at Lindof. Lindof looked back. The Face proved it better than anyone: in the new world, it was more foolish than ever to judge people on their looks. But he wanted to. Lindof's underdeveloped arm and hunched back made him stand out. Otherwise, he was wildly unexceptional. He had no big ideas. No guiding ideology. He was not particularly intelligent. He was a slob, a lout, a boor. The bad things he'd done, he'd done them simply because he could.

There used to be millions like him.

Lindof stepped to the crate's front edge. If his left hand wasn't so small, Nishimura thought, he would be rubbing them together.

'Look, folks! We've got Karl up here! You all know Karl. He's the guy who told you the Council was a great idea. He's the one who said, hey, let's not have guards guarding anything at all and see how that goes. We saw how it went, didn't we? Personally, I'm thrilled Karl has decided to join us, because I, for one, would like a few answers. Wouldn't you? If he can't give them, we'll send him a message tomorrow morning, won't we? Unless we go ahead and send it tonight. Unless we go ahead and send it right now.'

All That Mattered

The Dying Room was small and Spartan. Its native furniture had been cleared before Hoffmann arrived at Fort York, but she could imagine it well enough. Cheap desks with chipboard drawers, metal rack shelving, a rickety end table that held a broken printer. She had lived with similar décor during her long years at the American Model of Lineage and Dimensions.

Here, all had been replaced by a single stool, a small table, and a dentist's chair. The last did not exactly put people at ease, though the scariest accoutrements had been removed: the suction tools, the spittoon, the adjustable light, the rotary arm. This left only the adjustable seat itself, which could handle any size of person and, thanks to its nonstick vinyl, was easy to wipe clean. The room's new-world innovation was chair straps, rigged from old seat belts, and an unassuming wooden box that held the bolt gun.

By dumb luck, Charlie Rutkowski's old friends Lenny Hart and Seth Lowenstein had been at Hospice when she was brought in. Lenny Hart cut free Charlie's cable-tied wrists and ankles and strapped them down flat, whispering apologies the whole way. Seth Lowenstein removed the bolt gun and fondled it like a rosary. Hoffmann thought it might as well be. It was the holiest object at Fort York, a tool capable of taking life, death, and undeath all in a single shot.

Either man could prepare the substances used to lessen a dying person's final minutes of agony, but Marion Castle was the expert.

Charlie Rutkowski did not need instructions. She popped open her mouth to accept the willow bark that, when chewed, offered minor relief, and tilted her head to allow the application of menthol and chili pepper capsaicin to her temples and sternum, which generated a cold burn that helped mask pain signals. There was fort-made ether too, but Hoffmann knew Charlie Rutkowski would shake her head at it, which she did.

The room could be better, Hoffmann noted with pinpricks of regret. Plans were in place to create a dimmable light system. Hoffmann's assistant, Luvvie Lafayette, who was loud but not too difficult to work with, wanted to poll every interviewee during Personal Histories to find out what music, if any, they would like playing when and if their turn in the Dying Room came. Charlie Rutkowski had cried when she'd heard that idea, explaining through tears how she had played music from a movie called *The Quiet Man* while Luis had died. The idea inspired Hoffmann toward another one. In the library's special collection room, they could keep file folders of a Last Image for every resident, something for them to focus upon in their final minutes.

Karl Nishimura liked that idea so much, he had given Hoffmann the only family photo he had. The photo was pale and wrinkled, like he had spent fifteen years rubbing his thumb over it. Hoffmann felt strange taking it. The Last Image was still only a concept. But Karl Nishimura insisted she keep it. Should he be mortally wounded, Hoffmann would bring the picture to the Dying Room, wouldn't she? Of course she would. Unlike every supervisor she had worked for at AMLD, Karl Nishimura was someone it gave her satisfaction to assist.

Over four years at Fort York, especially with the help of Luvvie Lafayette, Hoffmann had learned enough about herself to know she had a way of distracting herself from what was happening. In this case, Charlie Rutkowski's death. Hoffmann regretted moving so slowly on things. Charlie Rutkowski would die under blazing oil lamps, not dimmable light; staring at blank walls, not a picture of her beloved Luis Acocella; in crashing silence, not along to a Bruce Springsteen power ballad. In the absence of those comforts, Hoffmann needed to offer her own. That meant doing the thing she had never been any good at: talking.

'Charlie Rutkowski,' she said.

Charlie Rutkowski turned her head in response. Her bright blond hair contrasted with her gray skin. Her eyes, like anyone zombie-bit, had gone a creamy yellow, but for now, they remained her eyes, flickering with stubborn life as her pale purple lips attempted a smile. Hoffmann could not return it. She had never mastered smiling.

'You don't have to say anything,' Charlie Rutkowski rasped.

'I'm going to . . .'

'You're not a blabberer like me. That's okay. That's good.'

'I'm going to miss you.'

Charlie Rutkowski cried, long fingers of salt scrubbing paths down a dirty face. Her torso wrenched and flopped, the seat belt straps squealing in sympathy. She balled her fingers, the nails still bearing red smutches of polish she had turned up weeks ago. She gave a great, trembling heave, as if trying to void herself of tears in a single sob. Lenny Hart looked away. Seth Lowenstein wrapped his face in his elbow and cried too. Marion Castle tented both hands to her mouth as if whispering a blessing, and who knows? Behind that hospital mask, she could be doing anything.

Charlie Rutkowski's wet eyes sprang open. Tears wobbled on her lashes, raindrops on spiderwebs.

'Few things,' she gasped. 'Real quick.'

'We have it under control,' Hoffmann said.

Charlie Rutkowski waved this off as best she could with bound wrists. 'Few things I haven't had time to think through. Horses. We tried giving them squirrel meat and it didn't work. Why horses? You think because horses were in league with humans? Stupid thought. Half-baked theory. Tell it to someone. Or not. There it is.'

'All right.'

'We're never going to make it to the Global Seed Vault in Sweden. We need to stop pretending that's going to happen. The Seed Savers Exchange in Iowa is the next best thing. We need to send a delegation. Tell people that was my vote.'

'I will.'

'Now here's the important one. Richard Lindof. I spoke to him on 10/23. I know it sounds crazy. But I did. Time, man. Blows by so fast. Knocks you clean the fuck over. Lindof doesn't care about us. About any of this. He's out for himself. He needs to be stopped. At all costs. *All costs.* Tell Nishimura to do whatever he has to do.'

'Okay.'

'Last thing. Etta Hoffmann? You safeguard the Archive. Hart, Lowenstein, Castle – you help. Without it, we're fucked. Without it, it's all going to happen again. Maybe it won't be zombies next time. But it'll be something. Some other kind of sarcophage. Luis called his zombie infection the Big G. Guess now we'd call it the Big Z. Luis. Oh, Luis.' Her laugh was a single icy scrape. 'He gave me orders up to the last second too.'

Charlie Rutkowski's fingers shot outward. Her back arched. Marion Castle tried to apply more menthol-chili balm, but Charlie Rutkowski's head was thrashing, and so she nodded at Lenny Hart, and the most unpleasant piece was put into place: a thick leather band strapped around the lower half of the face, with small holes drilled so the wearer could breathe and talk for as long as they were able. It also held the head securely in place, which would make it easier for Seth Lowenstein, when the time came for the bolt gun.

The word *muzzle* was not used, but Hoffmann knew that's what it was, the person on the chair having neared wild-beast status.

Hoffmann felt hot liquid push through her pores and into her eyes. She wiped her face and looked away. Nothing but blank walls. What Last Image would she choose when her time came? Would it be a still from one of her favorite shows, *I Love Lucy* or *This Is Your Life*? Would it be a photo scoured from a real estate brochure of the kind of tiny, comforting D.C. apartment she still missed? Would it be a rendering of the New Library, all that inspiring order? No, none of that. When she thought of it, the correct answer was obvious.

As much as Karl Nishimura warned against the pitfalls of materialism, people at Old Muddy filled their living spaces with trinkets or pictures reflecting the person they wanted to be. Hoffmann's belongings were few enough to fit inside the camo fanny pack she wore everywhere. Included were the color printouts she had taped together on 4,187–05:18, the day she had left AMLD at Charlie Rutkowski's side. On the left, Annie Teller, robust in her soccer jersey, and on the right, Tawna Maydew, in bed with her calico cat – an odd couple every bit as heartening as Greer Morgan and Muse King.

Already the photos were the last thing she looked at before sleeping each night. She had taken more than one thousand Personal Histories; across them had emerged strange parallels, unexpected repeating details. She puzzled over them by candlelight in the New Library, long after Luvvie Lafayette had wiggled her hips out the door. Twelve separate interviews referenced what sounded like the same zombie. A zombie Karl Nishimura had chanced upon in Taos, dazzling beneath a negligee of frost. A zombie Charlie Rutkowski had spotted outside the firestorm of Guymon, Oklahoma, released amid a flood of undead women. A zombie who had stolen, and even fired, one of Greer Morgan's bows during the St Croix catastrophe. A zombie the Face had witnessed clawing from battlefield mud, equipped with steel leg prosthetics and wrist hatchets.

According to the Face's unbelievable testimony, this zombie had worn a name tag reading ANNIE TELLER. Hoffmann was prepared to believe in radical coincidence. But she was not prepared to believe that Annie Teller had died. The battlefield zombie had been clad in clothing that belonged to an 'Annie Teller', that's all. The only detail to make her doubt was the one shared by all twelve accounts, that the metal-legged zombie was heading west, always west.

Can we make that our emergency plan? If the world goes gooey, we'll meet on the banks of beautiful La Brea!

Hoffmann tried to accept she'd never know the end of the story of Annie Teller and Tawna Maydew. This was difficult. The two times she had been unable to finish a TV show's full run still tortured her. To get her mind off it, she focused on a truth almost as inspiring as the photos. Living in close quarters with other people had provided her with drama better than any TV series. If she was lucky, *The Old Muddy Show* would never go off the air, with reruns forever accessible via the Archive.

Even now, two women were working on a printing press. One used a repaired wood chipper to pulp plant matter for paper and mixed ink from iron sulfate and oak tree gall. The other forged metal mods from which she planned to cut upper- and lowercase letters and punctuation. The printing press's first project would be the Hoffmann Archive of Tales from the New World. Once mass-produced, it would be distributed to every community they could find.

This would be good. It would be Hoffmann's legacy. It was all she had left, now, for Charlie Rutkowski was leaving her. Blood vessels extruded like red yarn from the yellowed eyes rolled back into her head. Pale slime oozed from the mouth holes of the leather band. The yank of her body had reversed, like she was trying to crouch beneath the pain. The very end could be the worst part. Hoffmann leaned in. She did not like to touch people. But people, she knew, sometimes liked to be touched. She tried to do it right. Not a poking finger, but a whole, open palm. She settled it on Charlie Rutkowski's shoulder. The heat of the woman's body baked right through her clothes into Hoffmann's hand.

'Remember when we met?' Hoffmann asked.

Charlie Rutkowski's bottomless black pupils rotated down from their sockets. Tears had thickened into a gel that jiggled when she nodded. Her voice crackled through rabid froth.

'Our phone calls.'

Hoffmann shook her head. 'No, when we *met*. When you broke into my home.'

Charlie Rutkowski laughed hard enough for beads of red spittle to escape the leather band. Above her medical mask, Marion Castle flashed Hoffmann a cautionary look. At the foot of the chair, Lenny Hart was pulling on rubber dish-washing gloves. Behind the chair, Seth Lowenstein wiped sweat from palms and regripped the bolt gun. Somewhere outside Hospice, a low-voiced man was hollering, and another man was hollering back, stuff about the Blockhouse Four, though it might as well have been every unwinnable argument ever. All that mattered was right here.

'Your clothes,' Charlie Rutkowski managed. 'Staples and tape. A cup of dead bugs.'

'Yum,' Hoffmann said. It was, she thought, a decent joke, which might mean the advice Charlie Rutkowski offered at Slowtown had sunken in: *You need to learn the art of the white lie.*

Charlie Rutkowski's laugh distended into a pealing wail. Hoffmann did not have to think first. She held her friend's shoulder more tightly.

'You were pretty,' Hoffmann said. 'Even in a hockey helmet.'

The only sign of Charlie Rutkowski's miserable grin was the bunching of her cheeks above the leather muzzle. Her reply was labored, gruff with sick lather, hiccuped with pain.

'I was – scarred up – by then. Hair was – too short. But thank you – thank you. I shouldn't – care. Here I am – about to – about to die – talking about if – if I was pretty. Fuck it. I – was. I'm – glad I was. I was the – sexiest – goddamn bitch – who ever survived – the apocalypse.'

'Damn right,' Lenny Hart whispered.

'Still are, babe,' Seth Lowenstein said through sniffles.

Foul-smelling sweat clung to Charlie Rutkowski's every pore. Her hair had gone amok with grease. Her skin went from gray to seaweed. But she beamed, and because of it, the Dying Room did not need fancy lighting, a fresh paint job, or record albums. She was the light of the world and all its music. Personal History Transcript #1, Charlie Rutkowski, was kept in a binder in the New Library, and it might have its uses, but this, right here, was all anyone needed to know about this woman. Hoffmann once read of the bokor who stole the Haitian nzambi's soul. No one would ever steal Charlie Rutkowski's. Everyone in this room would make sure of that.

'I love – you guys. I – really fucking – love you – guys – love you – Luis – love you—'

'Snoop,' Hoffmann said, and when she took hold of Charlie Rutkowski with not just one hand, but both, it felt like the embrace they'd been owed since their first phone call a million years before.

'Haunt – them, Poet – like – you're – already—'

Eviction

'**Let's tell the truth. Can we agree, Karl, to do that much? The** truth is we shouldn't be up here. We shouldn't. We might have our differences, but when it boils down, we should all be on the same side. What side is that? That's easy. We should all be on the side of *the living*. But that's not what I see. Maybe it took a fresh pair of eyes to see it? What I see is your Council doing an excellent job. A fantastic job. An excellent, fantastic job *protecting zombies*.'

'I didn't come up here to debate you. I came up here to remind all of you, my friends, that we built Old Muddy as we did because we didn't believe in sides. Zombies are not what brought us to this point in history. It was sides, the long history of taking sides.'

'Sides, a bad thing? This is what I can't understand. Sides are what keep psychopaths away from children. Not having sides at all, that sounds like a dictatorship to me.'

'I don't know how you get from a council to a dictatorship. We are empathetic people. That's all we have ever tried to be.'

'We are this, we are that. You're going to speak for all of them.'

'That is exactly what I am not doing.'

'Frankly, I'm surprised more of your "empathetic people" haven't killed themselves. It's an awful thing to say, I know. But you kill yourself around here and you've got it made. Few blocks north, there's a whole neighborhood waiting for you, rent-free. Once that's not good enough, we've got cozy beds for you right across the street. It's a tempting offer. Maybe the reason more people don't take you up on it is all their suicide weapons are all bricked up. It's an awful thing to say. I know.'

'No one here does anything they don't want to do. Except wash their hands.'

'That's what people in cults say. "Everyone's free to do what they want." But they're really not, are they? Because they're being manipulated. All you people, take a look at yourselves. How you dress, the kind of food you eat, where you sleep. Is it how you'd be living if you were making your own choices? Of course not. Because there's a council saying, you have to put whatever you find, no matter how hard it was to find, in the communal pot, so someone who didn't work at all can have it.'

'I don't know why this is so difficult for you to understand. The Council doesn't set rules. They carry through ideas *we* decide upon.'

'There's Karl's "we" again. Hear that, people? "We" is the chain gang of words, my pop used to say. "We" is everyone tied ankle to ankle – of course we're going to move slowly, chained together! We need more "I" around here! Who's with me on that?'

'I am. We all are. That's why the Custodial Council rotates. Every voice has equal weight. You've been here four months, Richard. Your time on the Council will come up soon, and you'll see for yourself it's a job of responsibility, not power.'

'Responsibility, not power.'

'If you're clear on it, we can climb down and go about our evening.'

'I see why they hired you, Karl.'

'No one "hired" me.'

'I see why they hired you because you make my case so elegantly. If you're a person with responsibility, but no power, what are you? I'm asking you, what are you?'

'A valued citizen doing your part.'

'You're an *employee*, baby. You guys remember McDonald's? Wendy's? Burger King? You think those minimum-wagers weren't popping their zits all over your Big Macs? You pay people squat, you get squat. That's what tomorrow's vote is all about. I say we scrub the Council, where good ideas die deaths longer and slower than zombies.'

'And replace it with what? A leader, I suppose? Someone like you?'

'I didn't say that. I'm not advocating for or against that.'

'Let me tell you who never had a leader. The zombies – and they took over the whole world. What other proof do we need that a united purpose is the most powerful force there is?'

'I get a little offended when I get compared to a zombie. Maybe it's just me.'

'Here's the problem with leaders, Richard. When you poke a hole in a community and say, "Here's the leader, this spot right here," all the water drains into that hole. No one does anything for the right reasons ever again, because they need that water to survive. I spent two decades in the US Navy. That was how we operated. Because the world was already ruined, and the best we could do was dress up in matching outfits and point weapons at each other.'

'We would have fared better against zombies without guns? You're actually saying that?'

'I'm saying it wouldn't have mattered. Any way you game it, we end up right here, right back at "in the beginning". But that's an opportunity. That's the rarest chance a species ever gets. We were given a chance to start over here at Fort York. By this beautiful lake. With the means to grow this beautiful garden. You know what? I'm happy I'm up here speaking about this. Because I don't get to say it enough: I'm proud of you. I'm proud of all of us.'

'Karl's getting in the mood! All right, Karl, if you're so happy and proud, let's talk about Fort York. Let's talk about what you built here.'

'Happy to.'

'You've been here five years? And there's still no defenses?'

'All the colonies we've been in touch with are peaceful.'

'For now. For now they're peaceful.'

'They're striving for the same things we are.'

'That's right. They are. They literally are. I call them the *Beachcombers*. They land on our beaches at night, we've all seen them, little boats at night with two or three people. I don't know what so-called peaceful community they're coming from. Fort Drum? I don't care. They come to Toronto to take our stuff.'

'How is everything in Toronto ours?'

'Because we were here first, baby.'

'Were we? Who gets to say who owns what?'

'These fine people standing here in the cold get to say! Because they've put in 100 percent of the work around here, Saint Karl. They call you *Saint Karl*, don't they?'

'Some do. I wonder what they call you.'

'My bet is no one's going to be calling you Saint Karl once people start dying. Once a lot of people start dying. No place I've been, and I've been everyplace, has had the hubris to not have even the flimsiest defensive wall. You don't think some of those Beachcombers aren't going to want what we have here? The guns in the Armory? The food poor Shyman and Sung-Yung were guarding?'

'Shyam and Yong-Sun.'

'Neither of whom will ever be the same again! You need a wall, for starters, which I will help build after we get rid of the Council who says we can't build it! No one gets in without proving their worth first. The days when someone could just waltz in are through.'

'Isn't that how you got here? Just waltzing in?'

'I'm not talking about the past, Karl, I'm talking about the future.'

'Everything you say is about the past.'

'If that were true, you think I'd have a crowd like this? No more freeloaders. No chance of zombies getting in either, unless we're the ones shipping them.'

'Shipping them? What does that mean?'

'We find the right partner out there, who knows? Zombies are a good source of labor if we can find a fresh-enough crop.'

'Richard. You don't trade people.'

'Don't act so shocked. What's shocking is you tucking them into little beds across the street. If you won't give us our guns to shoot them with, and you won't let us build a wall to keep them out, we might as well get something out of them, am I right? Jesus Herschel Christ, we give those deadheads everything, and what do they do for us? They're leeches. They're worse than food-stampers. They're an invasive species, that's what they are. Asian carp. Burmese pythons.'

'They do share one thing with most invasive species: we brought them here. It's our fault.'

'Well, if we brought them here, it's our right to get rid of them! After we win tomorrow, folks, we're going to tear down the Armory. You hear that reaction, Saint Karl? The people speak!'

'They speak because they're not remembering. Friends, come on! We don't eat meat. We don't need guns for hunting. The zombies who are left, you've seen them, you've all done recovery jobs in Slow-town. They're no kind of threat.'

'"All these streets are yours except Slowtown." Nice catchphrase, Saint Karl. But what kind of sense does it make to give zombies a major street running straight through the area we ought to be developing? If we don't claim it, the Beachcombers will. We could gun up right here, right now, head over there – *bang, bang, bang* – circle back through Hospice – *bang, bang* – and have our hands clean of the whole mess by breakfast. By breakfast, baby! Ladies and gentlemen, after fifteen years, the odds are in our favor! And we're just *standing* here. Building *clocks*. Inventing better *soap*.'

'We cannot build a better world on violent acts.'

'When was the last time you people left the city? If it ever warms up, I'll tell you what, I'll head up an excursion. You won't believe your eyes. Millions of acres, untouched, and the only things standing in our way are a few little tribes of zombies.'

'Enough. We're done. I'm not going to try to reason with a man—'

'In the old days, a place like Slowtown, the poor or the sick? Eviction.'

'Excuse me—'

'Zombies, unfortunately, don't mind being poor or sick. They require a firmer hand.'

'—excuse me, this is our way of *life*. To stand up here, after four months – four months of doing nothing remotely productive, I might add – and think you have the first idea what makes this place work? This is our *home*, Richard. It works. We know it works because we know how it makes us feel every day. If you want to go back to the old ways of blowing things up and shooting people, I suggest you look behind you. See that building? Just across the bridge, still standing? That's the New Library. I suggest you go in there, pick up a few books, and reacquaint yourself with the old world you're so attached to. See how close we came to ending it all, before the zombies.'

'I've been to your library. I sat for an interview with your librarian. Jesus Heinrich Christ, she's a piece of work, isn't she? I have a humble suggestion about what to do with her beloved Archive. You want to hear it, folks? It sounds like they want to hear it, Karl.'

'Friends, ask yourselves why this man appeals to you.'

'Burn it, baby. Every single binder. Soak them with gasoline and burn them.'

'We can't listen to this. We have to be good to one another.'

'*We* don't have to do anything. This isn't your ship anymore, Captain.'

'It's . . .'

'Ah, the big talker has run out of – oh. Is there news? It looks like news.'

'People, whatever it is, let's not—'

'Lots of whispering going on. Who wants to let us in on it?'

'We shouldn't rush to—'

'Is this right? Am I hearing this right?'

'It's not what it . . . People, please.'

'Karl? Saint Karl? Is there something you want to tell us?'

'People. Please. Yes, it's true. There was an incident.'

'This is unbelievable. They're telling me—'

'An accident. A terrible accident.'

'Charlie Rutkowski is dead. Folks, she's dead.'

'This isn't – we were going to tell everyone tomorrow.'

'After the vote, you mean. Oh, Karl.'

'Because it's late, that's all.'

'This happened in Slowtown?'

'On a recovery mission. But—'

'On one of those "safe" recovery missions in Slowtown?'

'I know how it sounds. But none of this changes anything we've—'

'I'm hearing she was bit by the Chief? That's the old zombie everyone claims is so peaceful!'

'Accidents like this have always happened. There has always been a risk.'

'How is blowing the Chief's head off an accident?'

'I . . .'

'That's what I'm getting from the front row, Karl. Did you use a gun, an actual gun, to shoot that zombie in the face?'

'I'm not going to let you twist this.'

'The guy who took our guns shot the Chief – with one of our guns?'

'You all know how important Charlie was to me. How important she was to all of us. It was a moment of poor judgment.'

'I think you did the right thing, Karl.'

'No, I didn't. I did not.'

'Of course he shot that nasty old woman in the face! Poor, sweet Charlie—'

'Don't you dare use her name—'

'Karl said when he came up here we had nothing to argue about. I'm man enough to say he was right. He's taken action today in Slow-town that every single one of us should follow. Yes, that's right. Go ahead and cheer. We should all cheer at what Karl did! How about we don't stop yelling hooray until we've finished the job? You want to wait until tomorrow to do it? No? Me neither, baby. Who wants to act right now? Who wants to see justice, Karl's kind of justice, laid out right this second?'

Faster, Brighter, Deeper

Electric tongue tip to tongue tip, a million nerves snapping, la petite mort, the little death, the flash blackout of orgasm, the body seized in pleasure so arresting it might as well be pain, and gratitude too, for at last your body ceases to exist in the troublesome way it always has, and your mind, just as troublesome, also ceases but to acknowledge it's all gone, the fear, anger, sadness, disgust, shame, dejection, indignation, envy, contempt, helplessness, despair, suffering, guilt, pulled from your body the way a titan's fist might extract your spinal cord, leaving you deboned and featherweight, a slip of flesh, a mere notion of a woman, and unclear if *woman* was a good idea at all, if *man* was either, here in the ether, they both seem so clunky, those beefy stacks of flesh with their pulsing organs and leaking orifices and the raw, wet, spilling disgust of their reproduction, more pleasure, more pain, la petite mort all over, except these little deaths make a life, a squealing piggy of hot, angry flesh to suckle and nourish only so it can wreak its own trail of joy and misery, the point of which seems clear now, the point being there was no point, but the universe is a big place, so what does it hurt to gamble on one world and see if its ants build anything but hills, see if its bees serve anything but queens, see if the species on top does anything but subjugate and terrorize every other tier, only for the dice to come up mixed, of course they do, it's always been a cold table, and you're busted, ass on the curb, body broken, heart and lungs kaput, and you are here, wondering why you ever bothered in the first place, for it's so much better here, effervescent in electric eclipse, which you might have guessed would be lonely but is not, where you have taken the hand offered in what you used to believe were nightmares – *Shall we dance?* – and discovered there is no learning curve here, you are not born into it a squealing piggy but instead drafted to the highest level, all knowledge yours, because this is life and death at once, and what a surprise to learn the two states never had to be divided, and you understand what happened down there on the blue rock you used to crawl around was nothing less than this perfect form visiting Earth, the zombies, life and death, each powered by an all-consuming sin-gularity of *la petite mort,* where the You and You and You was just another way of saying Us, and now you, former woman, have been invited into that effort, and you are happy and grateful, until the touching tongue tips slip, and something goes very wrong, or pos-sibly very right, and the formless idea of you curdles back into physical form, just look, your chest, your belly, your arms, your hips, your legs, your feet, we shall *not* dance, not just yet, and you are upset, and a single sob from you could shatter the blue rock into pebbles, but you accept the relapse, as those you briefly became have given you the gift of a lesson, one you first saw on a plaque above the door of your old boss and former lover, HIC LOCUS EST UBI MORS GAUDET SUCCURRERE VITAE or THIS IS THE PLACE WHERE DEATH REJOICES TO HELP THOSE WHO LIVE, and that's here, that's now, they have rejoiced to help, and now you must live, toward the promise that, if we work as one, the secrets of our gorgeous, messy, thrilling world can be ours, and you, woman, will be the one to tell them, if you can only remember it when you wake. We could have it all.

Charlie Rutkowski didn't die.

She tasted something. Like dirt and kerosene, a little floral, slightly sweet. Next, she smelled it, a lardy, oily odor. Finally, she felt it, a kidnapper's hand clasped over her mouth, his fingers digging into her cheeks. She rolled her jaws and felt the grip extended all the way to the back of her skull. She stuck out her tongue and explored small holes drilled into hide. It was leather over her mouth. Through the jailhouse bars of her crusted eyelashes, she saw the buckles pinning her wrists and ankles. Everything was soft and fuzzy until she felt the cold iron poke of a blunt object to her right temple.

The bolt gun. She'd pressed it to dozens of temples herself. She was in the Dying Room. She'd been dying. Now here, so fast, came another death.

'*Stop!*'

A twisting body – Etta Hoffmann – landed hard atop her. Charlie felt all breath shoot out of both their bodies. Never in her life, she felt certain, had the stiff librarian moved with such spontaneity; it was a wonder her tendons didn't audibly snap. Yet there Hoffmann was, flopped over the dentist's chair, heedless of the potential contagion of Charlie's saliva. Her left hand slapped so hard at the bolt gun she boxed Charlie's ear three times, more than enough to yank her from the bog of willow bark, menthol, and chili pepper.

'Ow.' Charlie's first word after rising from the dead.

Hoffmann straddled Charlie on the dentist's chair. Her face was pale and perspiring, and dipped low enough that Charlie could bite it off if she wanted, which she didn't.

'You are okay,' Hoffmann said. 'You are okay.'

'I'm okay.' Charlie's voice was marbles. 'Etta, shh.'

'The fuck,' Hart panted.

'Look at her eyes,' Lowenstein said in an awed hush.

'This isn't—' Marion began. 'This hasn't—'

'They're clear,' Lowenstein said. 'They're totally clear.'

'The *fuck*,' Hart repeated.

Images from the San Diego morgue spouted from her mind as if from a hatchet wound. She saw John Doe's head turn on his neck, the simplest thing, followed by the sour-milk orbs of his eyes looking first at Luis, then her. *Madre de Dios,* Luis had said. *How long after a body dies?* she'd stammered.

This time, she was John Doe.

Hoffmann crawled off Charlie, collapsed to the floor, clambered back up, and raided the table drawer so brusquely the bolt-gun box atop it skidded off the edge. Charlie's mind coruscated, every memory too colorful, swelling, ready be plucked like berries. She saw Lowenstein cradle the bolt gun to his chest, inadvertently aiming it at his chin, and heard, clear as music, her last conversation with Luis: *Right in the middle of the head. Straight at the brain.*

'Lowenstein.' Her tongue was far behind her brain. 'Be careful, would you?'

He glanced at the bolt gun, shuddered, and held it away from his body.

The drawer rattled. Hoffmann swiveled. In her hands were all the tools the librarian ever needed: paper and pencil. For four years, Charlie had watched with pride as Hoffmann weaned herself from obsession. Still a zealot for routine, though. She commandeered the room's stool, perched atop it, and used her own thighs as a writing surface. Personal Histories were her job, and she knew, before Charlie appreciated it herself, that no page in any Archive binder had a record of anything like this.

'What happened?' Good old Hoffmann.

Charlie tried to think. Her memory was cratering. Details were going like the teeth once pulled in this dentist's chair. That included the sensory recollections that would have been most pleasing to translate, if it had been real. She thought it was? Most of what she'd experienced seemed separated from her mind by a thin layer of algae. She only had to dip a finger beneath it, a full hand if she were feeling bold, to have it back in her grasp.

'I'll tell you what didn't happen. She didn't get bit. Who said she got bit?' Lowenstein grimaced. 'I almost bolted Charlie in the fucking head!'

'She *was* bit,' Marion said.

'Not by a zombie, she wasn't!'

'This is what I *do*,' Marion snapped.

'Not anymore, it isn't,' Lowenstein growled.

'It's what we *both* do!' Marion gestured at Charlie. 'Were you bit by a zombie or weren't you?'

Charlie withdrew the finger she'd been trailing through the algae's psychedelic sheen. She blinked at the eight waiting eyes. Had she been bit? She pictured the Chief's apologetic face as she closed her jaws on Charlie's fingers. Or was *apologetic* the wrong word? Maybe it had been sympathetic. Maybe the Chief had known she was passing to Charlie not a death sentence but a birth certificate.

'She's groggy,' Hart said. 'She doesn't know what you're saying.'

'No one in here knows what they're saying!' Lowenstein cried.

'What did you see?' Hoffmann pressed.

'Etta, please!' Marion shouted.

Charlie's face ached; she realized she was wincing. There was so much she'd felt in those minutes of death; there was so much more she'd felt while dipping back into it. Oceanic depths of peace, cheesy as that sounded, and an infinity of unrestricted love, even cheesier. It had softened her, Mae Rutkowski's Bronx bombshell, which is why these people's hard noises, amplified by the Dying Room's bare walls, made her recoil like a child. These were the emotions zombies had tried to end. To have them run this hot, this fast, scared her.

'Please.' Her voice was muffled under leather, and a flash of the room's anger infected her. 'Can someone take this fucking thing off me?'

She heard the clunk of the bolt gun placed on the floor and felt

Lowenstein's hands on her head. Her hair got caught in the band and she cried out, not from pain but more anger, spraying in a gush. Seconds later, the muzzle was gone and other smells and tastes poured in – the ripe sweat of these people, the precise piquancy of their panic. Charlie wiggled feeling back into her numb face, and hoped the prickling sensation was death, calmly inching back through her body.

'I can't explain it,' she gasped. 'I'm sorry, I can't.'

She blinked at Marion in apology, realizing she'd failed to absolve her. Marion's jaw dangled like the medical mask from her ear.

'Hart,' she said. 'Get those straps off.'

For half a minute, the only sounds in the room were the soft chimes and thwaps of Hart unbuckling the chair straps. Charlie only noticed the rasp of Hoffmann's scribbling when it stopped. Unlike the other three, the librarian was undamaged and undaunted.

'What did you learn?'

Relief broke inside Charlie. Hoffmann might yet save them all.

'You've gotten so good at this, Etta,' Charlie said. 'You ask all the right questions.'

Hoffmann, per usual, had no use for praise. Charlie smiled. Hoffmann hadn't changed that much. The librarian raised impatient eyebrows, but how could Charlie speak past a grin that kept growing? These were the four best living beings on Earth, and it was shit luck the task of articulating death's inexpressible glories had fallen to an ineloquent broad like her.

'Charlie?' Hoffmann prodded.

Charlie hugged herself. It felt good. She ran her hands up her neck, the sides of her face, into her hair. She didn't care who saw. Around her breasts, over her stomach, along her hips. She didn't care. Down her thighs, against her crotch. For a handful of seconds, she'd been the whole universe, and it had been wonderful. Just as wonderful was having this body. Its fragility was the point. A single body like this couldn't win shit. But a single body could inspire other bodies toward the same goal. This was what she had to tell them.

'Are you the . . . ?' Lowenstein sounded adrift.

'It can't be true,' Marion whispered.

'The last?' Hart managed. 'Charlie, were you . . . the last?'

'The first.' Hoffmann's look challenged anyone to disagree. 'She was the *first*.'

The Dying Room doorknob rattled; Marion was gripping it to steady herself. She tore her mask the rest of the way off, and it floated to the blood-spattered floor like a document of outdated rules. Marion pressed the heel of her free palm into one eye socket, then the other.

'We can't rush this,' she mumbled. 'It could be a fluke.'

'No fluke,' Charlie said. 'I can feel it.'

'We have to tell people,' Hart insisted.

'I can hear it in my blood,' Charlie said.

'There will be pandemonium,' Marion said. 'We have to confirm it.'

'How?' Hart cried. 'Go kill someone?'

'Can't you see it?' Charlie asked. 'In the air?'

Lowenstein snapped his fingers. 'A rat. We find a rat, kill it. If it doesn't come back . . .'

Marion nodded. 'Okay. All right. Where do we—' She laughed. 'The one time you want a rat.'

'The bay,' Lowenstein said. 'The pier ruins. There's always rats.'

He scrambled. Charlie heard the bolt gun kicked across the floor, no longer needed, maybe not ever again, and when Lowenstein passed the foot of the dentist's chair, he squeezed Charlie's calf, and though it wasn't sensual in the way Charlie had always defined it, a voltaic sensation shot up her leg, erotic in the way everything now felt faster, brighter, deeper. She gasped, and it turned into a laugh.

Marion blocked the door. 'Bring your stompers! Some of those rats will be zombies! Hart, go with him, don't let him do this alone. And be careful!'

Hart nodded, heaved for air, broke into a delighted grin, and dropped Charlie a wink. It was nearly as good as a touch. She hugged herself more tightly, digging her fingernails into her ribs, twisting her legs, curling her toes. Marion stepped away from the door, and Hart and Lowenstein scrambled out like eight-year-olds on summer vacation.

Marion braced her arms on the chair. Charlie reacted without thought, twining her arms up Marion's the way she'd done with lovers. She had no plan to kiss Marion Castle, that cool-headed pro, the idea was preposterous, but look at that: Marion let the weight of Charlie's arms pull her into the chair, and they kissed, lips plumped to lips. Marion broke it off and snuggled into Charlie's shoulder, and Charlie roped her in her arms, and they stroked each other's hair, and learned their tears had the same temperatures and weights. Charlie extended a hand to Hoffmann, knowing the librarian would give it an alien's stare, but look at that: Hoffmann took it, and Charlie held on hard – no take-backs, like the girls used to say in Parkchester – and the three women held together, one silent, two laughing and weeping, because it was over, it was over, it was over.

'No more zombies?' Marion whispered. 'No more softies?'

'No more Eggshell,' Charlie whispered.

'No more Lace.'

'No more Talcum.'

Charlie wiped Marion's tears; Marion wiped hers.

'I'm glad you sent the boys away,' Charlie laughed.

'Critter huntin',' Marion giggled. 'All they're good for.'

They both angled their heads toward Hospice's main room, as if they might hear the two idiots spreading the word before they should. What they heard instead was the burble of Caretaker talk, rarely ever this loud and never this fearful. Hart and Lowenstein must have left Hospice's front door open in their haste. A louder, lower noise snaked all the way to the dentist's chair like a browbeaten dog.

These voices were not the two she'd heard shouting before she'd died. These were voices in the dozens, a freight-train roar. Charlie's cozy, cotton swaddling began to cool, crack, and flake. The people she heard were unified, the thing for which she'd hoped, but for ugly reasons. Marion grabbed her hard, and when Charlie heard the splinter of disemboweled wood, she grabbed back.

We Made This Happen

Bare hands ripped down the door. Previously, the Face had only seen destruction like this carried out by zombies, who didn't care when fingers snapped back or palms got shredded. The first strikes had been with solid objects, including a board stamped DRY AGED BEEF, wrested from the crate on which Lindof and Nishimura had been standing. Mad-dog mania took over fast. The Brick Magazine might be brick, but the door was wood. With so many people heaving at it, it was going down.

The Face was knocked about. He spotted Nishimura through the tumult, on the ground beside the crate's remains, holding his bloodied forehead. Nishimura's mouth was moving, but the Face didn't believe audible words were making it out; the man looked to be in shock.

Forty or fifty people pressed at the Brick Magazine; the first few managed to push past the long shards of the broken door. It was too much for a single man like him to fight. Wasn't it? The Face pictured Nathan Baseman making Chuck Corso his offer: risk it all, take Feed 8, and become what ChuckSux69 only pretended to be, a *TRUTH TELLER*.

The Face dove into the scrum, peeling people away from the door. Some whirled, teeth bared, ready to punch, only for their frenzy to collapse upon seeing the Face. He kept driving until he lodged himself, bloodied by elbows and knees, against the brick surface beside what used to be the door. People poured inside. Screams came from the second floor. No teleprompter here, but the two weeks after 10/23 proved he could monologue when his back, literally now, was against a wall. He grabbed the lapels of the next person trying to get inside.

'Think what you're doing! It isn't just those people inside! It's all of us! Think what you're doing to all of us!'

The man flung his arms away and dove inside. The Face snagged a woman's wrist.

'Karl was right! We have to be better! We have to be better *right now*!'

She contorted her face at his misshapen visage and kicked him in the shin. He cried out, releasing her; she tumbled inside. An old man was next, reaching for the sharp splinters of the door with what looked like starving hands. The Face grabbed the back of his coat collar.

'We have to remember! Witch hunts, and lynch mobs, and frontier justice—'

'Let go of me!' the man growled.

'Do you want us to go down like that, in the new history?'

The man punched the Face in the nose. His head shot against brick. Black starbursts, red agony, first at the rear of his skull, next torrid from the center of his face. Like that, the Face was back in Slowtown, the instant Nishimura had gone for the holstered gun and grazed the Face's cheek with a pinkie. It had been a slap to everyone's face, a sudden, blasting reminder of the truth they'd pretended to forget; he was hideous, and no one but a zombie wanted to be close to that slick, seamed flesh, the sole ear, the half nose, the scar-tissue eye hoods and lipless mouth. The blood gushing from his nostrils looked black in the night, and that felt right; a monster like he was would not have red blood.

'Let go of me, you ugly, ugly fuck,' the old man spat. 'Ugly fucks like you ought to be put out of your misery.'

The man clambered inside like a rat, whiskered face pushing past slivered wood. Others burrowed in behind. The Face's hands crept over the remains of his face as he slid down the wall to the cold ground. He was Chuck Corso again: coiffed, outfitted by Armani, a pole on which models could swing, an idolator of reflective surfaces.

A renewed huzzah went up as what was left of the door was kicked open from inside. A train of savagely grinning Fort Yorkers dragged out the Blockhouse Four. Their features were inflated from beatings: noses flattened or sideways, dislodged teeth stuck to their bloody cheeks and necks. One held his arm oddly, a bone jutting from the skin.

First was Stuart Shardlow, Old Muddy's best hope when it came to ham radio, who'd donated his staggering collection of driver's licenses to the New Library, a handsome, blond-haired, all-American sort able to recite bygone baseball stats like psalms, and whose ubiquitous, bloodred, St Louis Cardinals cap had been replaced by actual blood. Next came Reed Hollis, a guy who exasperated Nishimura, but whom the Face liked, as he could see how badly Reed desired a couch-potato life, not to freeload but rather to spend more time with his de facto wife and their two adopted girls. Mandy Moundson was third, the only woman in the foursome, and the only one, of course, stripped of her shirt, who'd become famous at Old Muddy for styling hair and giving professional shaves, and whose beach-gull laughs could be heard for blocks and bore a similarity to her sobbing. Last came Federico Riera, a quiet, brave man who'd been patiently, gradually cross-referencing New Library texts to log new species of plants and animals, a task he wouldn't soon return to, given that compound fracture.

The Face believed he heard Lindof shouting orders, but the voice was puny beneath the din. A detached section of the Face's brain noted how quickly Lindof had stopped mattering. He'd been a fuse, that's all, and post-explosion, he was little but a sulfurous smell. No one was chanting the names of Shyam and Yong-Sun either; they'd been but excuses. While many had fled, masses crowded close, tiger-striped from torches, emitting screeching, noxious clouds of combustible hate. The mob formed into a procession that curled south, along the stone wall, toward the Circular's embrasures. They licked their lips. They rubbed their crotches. They wanted it so badly and had been chaste for so long.

A hand grabbed the Face and pulled. He pulled back.

'Let go!' he shouted, no different from the old man, no better.

The voice was calm. 'Face.'

'Don't look at me!'

How could any voice be calm? 'Face.'

He let his arm be pulled from his face, the cracking open of a lobster, his flaccid white meat exposed, to be slobbered down a buttered gullet. A woman knelt on the grass before him. He rolled his head to avoid her, but she mirrored it with a roll of her own, and that bit of tenacity was enough to break his spirit. He scrunched up his face, which only made it uglier, and looked back.

Etta Hoffmann still wore her boots, rucksack, and fanny pack from Slowtown. She looked as unbothered by his disfigurement as ever. Perhaps it was because she'd just seen worse: the death of her only friend. She read his mind and shook her head.

'She's not dead.'

'What? Who?'

'Charlie.'

'Etta, I'm sorry. I'm sorry, but she'll die. Sometimes it takes longer.'

'No. She's normal.'

'It's a disaster here, Etta, they broke in, dragged them out, they're crazy—'

'Charlie came back. She came back normal.'

Her everyday tone was what let her words slip into him, like a hand through drilling rain. What she said was simple and impossible. The Face believed no other imaginable statement, at this instant, could have had made him stop and think. The Face might have the rep for truth-telling, but Hoffmann was a step beyond, constitutionally incapable of distortions, aggrandizements, or hyperbole. If she said Charlie Rutkowski had survived a zombie bite, then—

The Face bolted upward, the Brick Magazine furrowing his back.

Then it was true, and it should, it would, it *must* change everything.

'Nishimura.' A miserable sound, not fit for broadcast. The Face cleared his throat of swallowed blood, self-pity, and fear. '*Karl!*'

He grabbed hold of Hoffmann's rucksack and hauled her with him up the small slope to where Nishimura sat, dazed. The Face dropped to the ground, taking splinters in his knees from the busted crate, one more injury to ignore, and shook the man's listless wrists as he might to two ends of a jump rope.

'Karl! Wake up! Look at me!'

Nishimura, his eyes red blotches behind tears, squinted at the Face and Hoffmann.

'I'm sorry,' he whispered.

Hearing these two sad words from the hardiest of Fort York's residents, the Face felt his marrow expand until it cracked his bones, the best thing that could possibly happen. His former trainer, Xander, had always said real strength came from the body repairing itself from wounds. The Face took Nishimura by the shoulders.

'You were wonderful, Karl. You made me proud.' It was true, and he felt himself begin to rebuild.

'They didn't listen . . .' Nishimura said.

'Karl, I need you to hear what Hoffmann has to say.'

'There's no point. They'll never—'

'Master Chief Karl Nishimura!' the Face shouted. 'You listen to Hoffmann right now or I'll court-martial your ass!'

No one submitted to military orders their whole career without the sound of one striking fear. Nishimura's eyes widened and cleared; his gaze sharpened.

'Affirmative,' he said. 'Let's hear it.'

While Hoffmann talked, the Face gazed across Old Muddy. It was all but emptied. Resounding off the highways overhead and the high-rises all around were the earthbound hollers of the vigilante convoy, trackable by the miasma of sparks lifting from toted tiki torches. By the time he looked back at his friends, Hoffmann had done it again.

'Help me up.' Nishimura extended both hands. 'We have to tell them.' He was pulled to his feet. 'We have to *run*.'

This was no tiptoe down Queen Street. The three of them sprinted in the direction of the torchlight. In their urgency, in traces of the mob's destruction, the Face stomped plants in the Garden and Nishimura knocked a piece off the Master Sundial. Hoffmann took the worst of it. She was already lagging when the Face heard the thump. He looked back to see her down in the grass, having struck the unlit Well House outside the Armory. She pushed herself up on two hands but was clearly dazed.

Nishimura shouted from the vicinity of the Dry Moat.

'We need to move!'

Hoffmann's face was lost in moon shadow. His face, then, was lost as well, and as awful as he looked, the Face regretted they couldn't see each other, as this might be their last chance. At the same time, he was heartened. The librarian had pulled him from quicksand. She was not going to be able to keep up with the men, but one of her good qualities was an immunity to feeling slighted. The Face whispered goodbye and ran after Nishimura, who was climbing over the inoperable eighteen-pounder gun positioned at the fort's southwest corner.

These were the streets of the greater Fort York, former lakefront Toronto. The svelte ribbon of Fort York Boulevard; the ovoid towers of the Waterpark City condos; the Fleet Street trolley tracks, kept up to snuff in hopes of eventual revival; the cute, red-topped Queen's Wharf Lighthouse, daytime meeting spot of teams of workers, nighttime meeting spot for new lovers. The Face caught up to Nishimura on the seven lanes of Lake Shore Boulevard. Stomped weeds revealed the path of the caravan.

Coronation Park was barely larger than the three softball fields it once contained, two of them plowed now in favor of crops. A group of sports fans, Stuart Shardlow included, had kept the last outfield mowed, the infield soft and level with raked dirt. Stuart, Reed, Mandy, and Federico had been forced to their knees on the pitcher's mound, a dough of tears, spit, and blood dangling from each of their faces. Shrieking, jeering, hissing people encircled them, all but the children, who skipped the baselines, delighted by tonight's distraction.

One man sat separate in right field, head dipped between his knees. Nishimura ran over, squatted, and the Face pulled up behind. It was Seth Lowenstein, a close friend of Charlie's, and the Face's first thought was he'd come to the lakefront to mourn her death. If that were the case, they had astonishing news for him. It was not the case: Lowenstein's knees were spread to allow him to cough up blood.

'What happened?' Nishimura demanded. 'You okay?'

'We tried to tell them about Charlie,' Lowenstein mumbled.

'Who's we?' the Face asked.

'Me and Hart. They wouldn't listen.'

The Face pivoted and searched, like an outfielder after a mishandled ball, and saw, not fifty feet off, a second body in the grass, motionless.

'We tried to stop them,' Lowenstein moaned.

If Hart was alive, Lowenstein would have to be the one to help him. Nishimura sprang to his feet, a young sailor again instead of a fifty-eight-year-old organizer, and darted for the swarm of bodies, bright orange from torchlight, their heckles louder than any blubbering for mercy. The Face took off after him. From Lowenstein to the Blockhouse Four was one hundred feet; it should have taken only seconds to cover. The Face wondered why it took the duration of four entire lives.

He saw a lot of things in that time. He saw a resurfaced Richard Lindof, beaming at the apex of the tightening circle, his teeth reflecting fire. He saw arms as long as grasshopper legs – because they held baseball bats. It was not irregular for equipment to be left beside the rusted chain-link backstop. Some bats were pulled back in proper Major League stance, others rose like caveman clubs. Yowling faces, misshapen by flames, urged the hitters to hit.

He saw the first swings, the rocket into Federico's ribs, the pile driver onto Reed's shoulder, the torpedo into Mandy's stomach, the level, professional swing into the center of Stuart's face. So much blood jetted so quickly it struck other jets midair, making plasma dance as playfully as hummingbirds. The Face, who had drowsed through thousands of dull sports reports, instantly grasped how these baseball bats were inevitable, an American symbol as potent as any the US carried when last ravaging Fort York.

The Face heard infield dirt under his boots but seemed to be going nowhere. Bats rained blows until a knife made its obligatory appearance and sank into Federico's jugular. Arterial blood shot three feet. Everyone at Old Muddy had a knife; they were handy. Mandy was stabbed in the chest, her tongue flapping amid black spurts of heart blood. People were jumping up and down as if this were a concert, as if they were young and indestructible, and it was murder that had performed that miracle, not Charlie's defeat of undeath. Stuart, blinded, his face staved in, crawled toward first base until he was knifed in the back what seemed like a hundred times, until his wool coat, cotton shirt, skin, and muscle formed a thick purple stew. Reed was stabbed in the face repeatedly, slivers of cheeks, chin, nose, and ear pinwheeling astray, destined to look like the Face if he lived, which he would not.

Exactly when he hit the crowd, the Face didn't know. He only knew he felt bodies, sticky and squirming like newborn mice, knocking him back and forth. Nishimura was nearby; they collided repeatedly until a huge man lifted Nishimura from his feet and carried him off. From the dirt near second base, the Face saw the Blockhouse Four's corpses being hit with boots, dirt, rocks, streams of urine. Knives stayed brandished; the fun part was still coming. No Hospice for these four, no Dying Room, no bolt gun. People paced, waited, flicked blood off their weapons. The Face dug his chin into the dirt, afraid that to get up now would attract the baseball bats still glistening in the flame.

Everyone knew zombie revival was fickle. It could take two minutes or twenty; in frigid climates, it could take two hours. The Face didn't know how much time passed, but it was enough. With four chances at revival, it was more than enough. The Blockhouse Four did not stir. There were murmurs of confusion. Cries of disbelief. Startled recollections of Hart and Lowenstein yelling something about Charlie Rutkowski. Was it true? A few shrieked when the news drove home. A few began to cry. The Face wondered if he should feel relief. But after living through Rochelle Glass and Nathan Baseman, Scotty Rolph and Ramsey Dylan, Generals Spalding and Coppola, and Richard Lindof, he could read bad news like Nishimura could read a ship's log. Safe waters were nowhere near.

'We made this happen!' Lindof cried. 'All of us together!'

Gasps, sobs, expletives, keens, yawps.

'No,' the Face said, cold dirt swirling into his eyes.

'Let's finish it! Let's end it! This is our chance!'

Cheers, hoots, shouts, claps, hails.

Men came forward like men always did, dropping to their knees and plunging knives into dead flesh. They sawed like the carnivores they still were in their hearts. One of the men, on his non-cutting hand, wore a baseball glove, and when it was fully opened, it made the perfect cushion for Stuart's severed head. The other three men gathered the heads of Reed, Mandy, and Federico, and held them high, greeted by the mad wails of the other meat-eaters, newly hungry for fresh blood.

Someone had already embedded the baseball bats into packed dirt.

The bat handles were dull but the severed heads, with their torn trapezius muscles, snapped tracheas, and dislodged vertebrae, put up no resistance when thrust downward. Stuart Shardlow, Reed Hollis, Mandy Moundson, and Federico Riera became mottled, bloody hams steaming with heat, staring with bright red eyes at a world that had no use for them, not in any state of life or death. Heads on pikes at last! The status symbol Lindof treasured! He strode through the prizes, their extruded tongues painting delicate lines of blood across his sleeves.

Half the crowd was already gone, rushing to the next stop. Lindof, though, did not look as if in any particular hurry. He stopped in front of the Face. For the first time, he didn't recoil or gag. He grinned straight down, the licks of flame behind him completing his Bela Lugosi metamorphosis.

'To Slowtown!' he shouted to scattered whoops and ovations. 'Everyone to—'

A globule of blood and rind of flesh popped into the air. A metal arrowhead poked through the center of Lindof's chest. His jaw opened, empty of words at last. His fingers wiggled daintily before his arms, both the normal-sized and shrunken one, dropped to his sides with butcher-board slaps. He fell like an axed tree and was blanketed by a cloud of infield dirt. Richard Lindof died, Jesus Hercules Christ, right when a zombie's revenge became unavailable, and when the Face peered past the stunned crowd and the four leering, severed heads, he saw, still in her bowhunter's stance, Greer Morgan.

Carve the Heart

Greer had never adopted the gung ho attitudes of Old Muddy true
believers and so was surprised at her feelings upon seeing Fort York
burn. Her breath was reeled from her chest like a tapeworm, and she
choked violently, coughing until it felt like her lungs were dangling
down her abdomen.

The Face fared little better at her side. He clung to her to remain
upright, which almost toppled her; she had to cling back, and between
them, they found equilibrium. The first thing she thought of was
white fire melting the gas station awning in Bulk, Missouri, and how
it went ignored in favor of the brawl between Raskey Apartments
refugees and Team HortiPlastics. Same damn thing: the Brick Magazine might be brick, but that didn't mean fire couldn't gut its insides
and roof. The terms for collapsing buildings cycled through her head.
She'd be able to call this one a *duster* soon, if she was still around.

Also on fire were the Officers' Brick Barracks and Officers' Blue
Barracks, which made unfortunate sense. They were the fort's birth-
places of revolutionary ideas, and though Greer used to roll her eyes
at the public brainstorming sessions, as she'd once rolled her eyes at
the Sunnybrook Club, she understood now, at a visceral level, that
she'd believed in all of it. Why else had she given it three and a half
years of her life, all her energy, her courage, her arrows and bows?
Some of it had been for Muse, but not all of it.

Trees were aflame. So were sections of grass. Most upsetting of all, the Garden was an inferno, individual plants hissing and popping as they curled into skeletons of ash. One person was on fire, screaming as people whipped at her flames – unless, of course, they were beating her, wanting whatever pillage she'd nabbed first.

The Face pointed, and Greer looked. Silhouetted before the Brick Magazine flames were the frolicking forms of people dashing in and out of East Blockhouse, arms overloaded with soup, rice, beans, and most of all, alcohol, the flames making caramel swirls through translucent bottles. She could feel the Face's tears, icy against the wild heat of the bare arm she'd flung over his shoulder, and she understood why. These people were committing the same crime as the Blockhouse Four – whom they'd just gleefully executed.

After Marion Castle and Etta Hoffmann had stretchered Charlie Rutkowski toward the Dying Room, Greer had hightailed it out of Hospice. She couldn't take the Face's monkish acceptance or Nishimura's aggravating sympathy. Greer's pursuit of Muse was to blame for Charlie's bite, simple as that. She'd hung a sharp right at Bathurst and gone all the way to Little Norway Park, the new border of Lake Ontario. She sat on a bench near the softie incinerator, cradling her bow in her arms like a loved one's corpse. Daddy? Mom? Conan? Or Charlie?

Deep down, she'd loved Charlie. Who hadn't? Why, then, had she behaved like her love for Muse was more important? Perhaps because he was the Dove? No zombie dog named Willy was going to protect him. He needed a Lion.

The pep talk did no good. After all, the shit Muse had spewed was moronic. Only a man with an unwell mind would inject himself with fluids from the Chief, wanting to be part of some antiviral solution. *We got to put body and soul back together if we're going to have a chance,* he'd said. Sounded like bullshit, though, hell, sitting here looking over the cold gray bay, who really knew? Muse also said, *The fort's a step that doesn't go anywhere,* and from distant howls she heard, he might have been right.

The sound of Lindof's mob grew closer and louder. Greer let it. She pulled her legs onto the bench and breathed in the cinnamon spice of zombie ash, wondering if inhaling enough of it would have a similar effect to Muse's injection. If she were a zombie, she could walk into Slowtown without guilt or fear, find Muse, and go on loving him as she had for fifteen years.

She dipped so deeply into that strange, pleasant thought that she didn't register the sobbing until it became screaming. She snapped her bowstring to sting her forearm. That did it; she leaped to her feet and put her ear to the wind, same as she'd done while traveling the eastern half of America. The upheaval came from Coronation Park, and she could tell by its sharpness it had nothing to do with zombies.

What in old Toronto would have been a brief three-block walk was complicated by the eroded bay. She had to backtrack to Lake Shore and cut down the Martin Goodman Trail. She had to admit, it was invigorating to creep again, to hunt again, to duck beneath overgrowth and navigate rubbly paths. But it was slow work, and when she emerged from foliage, she found only twenty people. Twenty-four, if you counted severed heads.

She'd seen hundreds, if not thousands, of heads on pikes since the Second Dark Age. Never had she seen any this fresh. Their eyeballs still glistened. The bat handles, visible through their open mouths, still ran with blood. The heads were so deformed she might not have identified them if she hadn't already guessed their names: Stuart, Reed, Mandy, and Federico, the first casualties of a different kind of dark age.

Greer killed Lindof. She felt nothing but regret she hadn't done it sooner. She found the Face stumbling sideways, trying to stand. She steadied him. He babbled, told her how Charlie hadn't died, gestured at the fort, and only then did she realize it was hours too early for dawn to be lighting the sky.

Now this: fiery cataclysm, the whole utopia crumbling, and not from a thirst for justice, as Lindof's masses might claim, but a hunger to possess objects that, in the light of day, of *all* days, would do nothing to make them happier. Look how they tore at walls with bare hands. Look how they gathered at the northern embrasures, jabbing torches toward Slowtown. More, more, more, until they had nothing at all.

The Face moaned at the plundering of East Blockhouse. But Greer's eyes rose higher and farther, just across the abutting street. It was the largest fire in sight, as smoke-frothed as a storm-maddened sea, each whip of flame a piece of civilization peeled away to reveal a white nothingness. The billowing sparks, Greer realized, were bundles of paper spat into the sky. Books, magazines, hundreds of binders of paper. The New Library, wholly consumed.

Etta Hoffmann, standing in the middle of Bathurst, gazed up at the blaze, her deadlocked posture a jarring contrast to the ungovernable twists of flame. A blizzard's worth of spewed paper settled atop Hoffmann's head, shoulders, feet, and that stupid fanny pack. Her bearing was calm, as if she'd seen it all before. Or at least read about it.

Fifteen years of tireless work, gone. The Hoffmann Archive of Tales from the New World, vaporized. Its planned reproduction and distribution never to happen. Once Greer had scoffed at the project; now she felt its loss like that of a major organ. *Mi corazón,* she mourned, *mi corazón.* Everything they'd lived through, now fated to slip the collective mind.

No millions had died.

No billions of bones were strewn across the land.

None of this had ever happened.

The Master Sundial proved it. The gnomon was busted, the hour lines scratched to nonsense. There was only right now, and Greer was moving. The Face was tugging her down the path bisecting the blazing Garden. Long flames met over their heads like they'd just been wed and were dancing beneath red-and-orange-flowered arbors.

They emerged into the west half of the fort. What had been known at its 1815 founding as the Stone Magazine was so besieged it looked to have been built from the nightmare lumber of human limbs. These days, it was called the Armory, and a horde wanted inside. Some drove hammers and tire irons against the walls, but most used the tools that ruled this night – their bare, bloody hands – to dislodge shattered rock. A small hole had been bashed all the way through the wall, and a woman was caught inside it, screaming to be pulled out as men pushed her farther in. Maybe it was the nearby fires, but Greer swore she smelled the ammo inside, baking toward explosion.

The Face pulled her off the path, past the Armory. He was leading them toward what had been the Garrison Common battlefield and now was the way out. She was awash in gratitude for his effort, but didn't intend to run. Everyone had business in Slowtown tonight, including her.

Greer pulled her arms free. The Face looked pained.

'You can't reason with them,' he said. 'They won't listen—'

Abruptly, he looked to the right, and Greer looked too. Two children were skipping around the Well House, dizzy with destruction, chanting an educational rhyme gone sour: *Zombie, zombie, bite me not.* As the info plate described, the Well House's gazebo was a modern reconstruction, complete with an old-fashioned bucket on a chain, built to protect the well itself, a seven-meter drop dating back to 1802.

It was also a safety hazard kept boarded shut, until now. The children accented their dance by pitching rubble from the Armory walls down the well. Negligible havoc in the greater scope of things, but the Face was famous for noticing details, and when he left Greer's side to approach the well, she made sure to beat him to it. The children cheered, happy for new playmates. She elbowed one aside, not giving a shit about his age. He'd grow up to be as rotten as any of them; she knew it even before looking into the hole.

Twenty feet below, barely visible, was Karl Nishimura. In her over-long thirty-two years, Greer had seen carnage of the worst sorts, but anyone knew when a body looked wrong. A right arm that had to be dislocated was trapped under Nishimura's back. His left leg was bent the wrong way at the knee. His gore-striped neck was arched too drastically, and his mouth, garish with blood, was open as if dying of thirst. Greer believed him dead even as she called out his name.

'Greer,' he replied instantly.

'Karl! We'll get you out.'

'They're coming to get you.' His relaxed tone chilled her. Conan had told her the same thing fifteen years ago before slaughtering more former classmates: *They're coming to get you.*

'If we send down this bucket, can you grab hold?' the Face shouted.

'They'll throw you down too, and we'll all be a pile of limbs. We'll all be the same thing. We'll be Legion.' He chuckled. 'How about that. Legion is us.'

'Your other arm,' the Face demanded. 'Is it okay?'

In the deep dark, Nishimura's grin held the pale contours of a skull. He raised his left hand into the moonlight. All four fingers lay broken against the back of his hand.

'One of us will have to go down,' Greer said softly to the Face, who pulled experimentally on the bucket's chain to gauge its strength.

'The golems,' Nishimura mused. 'Greer, you remember?'

'You're hurt,' she called down. 'Try not to move.'

'You said, "Isn't that a Tolkien character?" and I said, "No, no. They're monsters. Monsters we call forth to wipe us out."'

'The chain might be strong enough,' the Face whispered. 'But this bucket. We'll bust it to pieces.'

'Jenny said she had to tell me in case she died. Now I'm telling you, Greer.'

'Shut up, we're trying to—'

'I'm telling you because it looks like we'll need them again.'

Nishimura's laugh echoed up the well, the circling of a clumsy ghost. Greer felt the sound as if the tuning fork that made it had been stabbed into her ribs. The Face let the useless bucket swing free, his eyes stricken behind their fleshy folds. Greer's sinuses thickened with tears. She could fill the bucket with them, make this well wet again, let Nishimura float his way out.

'Learn to call them back, Greer. The rules are in the old books. Not all the libraries can be burned.'

The end of zombies, all they ever wanted; the urgent need to bring them back. Greer snatched the chain. She'd wrap it around her foot if she had to, toss Nishimura over her back.

'I'm coming down!' she cried.

'No!' the Face shouted, while Nishimura said, quietly, 'No.'

She had a foot on the well's edge, but the Face pushed it off.

'I'm going down!' she roared.

'You can't,' the Face said.

'I will!'

Nishimura: '*You will not, and that's an order!*'

Greer stumbled off the Well House's floor and fell to the cold dirt. The children danced around her. Ribbons of soot-black slobber swayed from their lips. Their pink mice eyes shone. Their beastly little hands the stone shards they'd use to carve the heart from the world.

The Face swooped down next to her and shoved the children aside. They didn't lose their balance, though, and their sickly sweet song kept circling: *I will not cry, I will not moan, oh, zombie, zombie, take me home.*

A united roar rose up, almost a cheer, except without a trace of joy. Greer thought it was the sound a pack of hominids might make when, through combined effort, they pulled apart the ribs of a mammoth. A whole corner of the Armory had collapsed. At least one person had gotten pulverized, her muffled screams futile icicles against the destroyers' furor. People poured into the Armory like ants. They grabbed the smooth thighs of the guns, caressed the long barrels, and unboxed ammo so they could slot it in, hard.

Once armed, they stood, and saw in the weapons' steel the reflection of torches held by those hollering for Slowtown. Both guns and torches lifted higher, two separated lovers in a train-station crowd. The weapons lusted for the good times they remembered so fondly.

Nishimura's voice rose from the earth.

'Don't worry about me. What's the worst they can do? Put me in a camp? For my sympathies, of course. My sympathies to the enemy. My ancestors lived through this. I'm Japanese American. You know what I'm saying?'

Greer looked at the Face so hard his scars seemed to run with fire.

'All right,' she whispered.

'Japanese,' Nishimura croaked, 'American.'

'All right!' the Face shouted, and Greer was glad, because outrage was what they needed if they were going to move. The Face grabbed Greer's arm to help her up, but she was already up and sprinting toward the embrasure by the North Soldiers' Barracks, which fed out to Strachan Avenue – not the quickest way to Slowtown but their best shot at beating the mob. The Face was behind her, and again, she felt a sobby gratefulness, now that she was leading them into the fray rather than out of it.

She kept hearing Karl Nishimura's voice, drifting on smoke, his final word repeated like a curse.

'American . . . American . . . American . . .'

Let the World Rise Gently

The second sacking of Fort York lit their way. The brighter fires of torches indicated the mob was heading up Niagara Street, which would land them east of Slowtown's center. Greer, better schooled in these streets than anyone, hurtled north on Strachan, which should feed them onto Queen Street two blocks west of the mob's mass. What then? The Face had no idea. If Nishimura couldn't avert Old Muddy's fall with common sense, what could he and Greer do? They had no weapons besides Greer's bow. They were insignificant.

His history reading, done at the dearly departed New Library, gave him one sliver of hope. *Insignificant* described most great people of history.

Greer was half a block ahead. Fort York's blaze turned her quivered arrows into candles, each one seeming to carry a flame. The Face ran faster, his heaving gasps covering the bellowing of those on Niagara Street as well as the distant whinnies of Old Muddy's three hundred horses, penned up in the path of the fire. He didn't even hear Greer's clomping boots until she abruptly stopped. She stood at Queen Street in what looked like delicate surprise, arms outward as if pinching an invisible gown off the ground. Her head rolled left, then right, with an awed slowness that made no sense. Slowtown never changed; that was what made it Slowtown.

The Face heard it before he saw it: a sustained tone as multifaceted as any choir, those Italian distinctions he'd never really grasped, mezzo-soprano to contralto, baritone to bass, lifting and sighing like snow drifting down before sweeping back into the sky. Beneath this shifting drone was soft, irregular percussion, like calloused fingertips brushing over weathered drums. By the time the Face halted – by grabbing hold of Greer – the sounds had grown to be no different from those of his blood, bones, and meat. It was him; he was it; they were us. They had always been us.

Hundreds of zombies filled Slowtown. The Face remembered, after the Chief was shot, the unexpected galaxies of white eyes glowing from every window and doorway. Here they were, emptied from florists, coffee bars, shoe stores, dress boutiques, secondhand shops, bookstores, ice cream parlors, diners, cafés, and the countless apartments above them. Three hundred zombies? Four hundred? Five? The Face couldn't tell.

Too many shuffling feet trailing too many Fort York shackles; too many dangling arms and those arms' dangling flesh; too many torsos so eviscerated the Face could see other zombies through the holes; too many heads hanging from too many exhausted necks, though these heads were lifted – he swore to whatever was left to swear to, *the heads were lifted,* bony chins thrown to the moon, the fire, to whoever or whatever might look them in the milky eyes and know them at last.

When the mob emerged, it looked like fire itself; the torches, of course, but also five years of firearms flashing, being leveled. This was why Greer swung her head: the zombie herd to her left, the mob to her right. The two parties would meet roughly in front of where Greer and the Face stood. Front-row seats for the final clash everyone had feared, or anticipated, or hoped they could eternally avoid.

At the front of the zombies stood Muse King; at his side, a zombie German shepherd dragged its gray tongue across pavement. Muse was gaunt, gray, and filthy, but still magnetic. The shudder of his gait told the Face he was weak, until the fact that zombies weren't biting him suggested another possibility. The Face found he didn't care. He wanted to run up to Muse, shake his hand, tell him how good it was to see him again, how nice it would be to hear him play one more time.

He did not have to ask. Muse's alabaster guitar, still outfitted with its threadbare strap, hung over his shoulder. His gray fingers, slow but steady, plucked out a four-bar tune, simple but compelling, sad but inspiring, wistful but exhilarating, the kind of tune that, once in a generation, became the anthem of protest, its own kind of fire. The Face thought he might be crazy, but the moans of the zombies seemed to be duplicating the tune's base chord, getting as close to a single song as any mass of marchers ever had.

The truth broke over the Face like a dawn.

'This isn't an attack,' he said.

'Walk Away,' Greer gasped.

Her hand was pressed to her face, burying her mouth, flattening her nose, halfway covering her wide eyes. The Face thought of the RESIST button Greer had given the Chief. A coincidence, had to be, but why not believe in the impossible? Why not now, at the end of everything? Maybe that tiny little trinket was the last push they'd needed.

The Face smelled soot in the air. The New Library, the Personal Histories. He'd spent hundreds of hours reading them, and a line from Charlie Rutkowski's transcript came back. *I walked,* she'd said. *What could be simpler? But is there anything that's ever been stronger?*

Acting either on an order or simply on the ingrained instinct to kill, the armed mob spread out in a line across Queen Street. Though their guns were ready, the triggers were not yet pulled. These people, roaring for blood, had bled plenty themselves. They wanted a way to release their pain, even if that meant shooting it from weapons, hoping it might embed in someone else.

That wasn't how viruses worked – a disease passed to one person remained in the other. Everyone ended up infected. With the zombies a single block from collision with the militia, the Face knelt and pulled Greer down with him. To the mob, he thought, it must seem like there had never been anything like this. But there had been. This march felt like all marches put together. Flesh loss made the zombies roughly the same shape. Deterioration had made them roughly the same color. Their oldest, the softies, were disabled, yet had been brought along – softie ribs entangled in zombie legs, softie skulls lodged in zombie ribs. Most improbably, the Chief was there too, her unmistakable, button-covered torso being carried by a zombie walking alongside Muse King.

They came, the dead bodies; they stood in wait, the living souls.

'Body and soul back together,' Greer whispered.

The zombie front line passed so close the Face might have plucked free a scrap of moldered skin. He could feel the heat of the maggots being circulated like sluggish white blood. The torches carried by the militia could never run so hot, for fires, even ones the size of Fort York, eventually died. Maggots, though, you never squashed them all. Some would hatch and become flies, and their descendants would be waiting when you died. Waiting for *you* – you, specifically. It didn't have to be gruesome. It could be miraculous.

He saw torches dip, rifles and revolvers lower.

The music, that heartbreaking four-count, kept going.

Tears found odd routes down the Face's perfect cheeks.

'You did it, baby,' Greer wept. 'You did it.'

He nearly did, but for a single bone. The underlying percussion the Face had first heard had been the dry-bone *crick-crack!* trademark of aged zombies, except layered hundreds of times until the sharp pops achieved a cloudburst's softness. The zombies were fifty feet from the mob when one of the thousands of zombie bones broke in half. *Crick-CRACK!*

It sounded like a gunshot.

That was all it took. That was all it had ever taken. One of the militia fired. A zombie's head exploded. When the skull bones clattered down, they sounded like projectiles. Bullets erupted from the mob, hundreds at once.

Greer screamed. The Face covered her head in his arm.

The zombies were ripped apart. Faces punching inward; the backs of heads exploding; tongues landing, still licking, among clumps of brain. Teeth sprayed in kitelike arcs, catching torchlight, escaping like fireflies. Pulpous limbs split and went tumbling, ankle chains ringing like castanets. Spinal columns blew out intact, bone pythons glissading across concrete. Hanks of gray muscle flew all over, as if great hands were prying zombies open, seeking pearls. Automatic revolvers put so many holes in chests that torsos ripped along the perforations, dumping full trash-bag loads of organs. Shotguns blew massive holes through stomachs, flinging intestines over other zombies like nets and taking them down. Shooters closed and kept firing, turning skulls to dust, bodies to sludge. Those with blunt weapons pummeled brains into puddles of mucus while anyone with boots smashed loose eyeballs and blobs of flesh. Queen Street was a meat grinder; Slowtown was a slaughterhouse. The gutters, so nicely tidied by zombies, pulsed with a thick, fibrous mire, part congealed blood, part liquified tissue.

'Nothing's happening,' the Face said into Greer's ear, his first lie in fifteen years.

Only after a large number of the zombies fell did the Face see the animals. They'd crept from side streets, behind the farthest rows of marchers. Not undead dogs, and not, for that matter, undead rats or zombie chickens, but living animals of every stripe. A bear. A cougar, a bobcat. Wolverines, foxes, coyotes. Smaller beasts too, mammals and reptiles and insects, rushing like brown water around the larger contingent's paws, claws, and hooves. Lording over all was the giraffe the Face's recovery team had seen just that morning, its lippy mouth held in the same grave line.

The Face was sobbing when he had a sonic hallucination. Minutes later, when the shooting ended, he'd blame it on the fired ammo, the expended shells ringing off the street, the crunch of bone and pound of flesh. But in that moment, what he heard was voices. The zombies' voices. Had Greer heard it too? Had everyone in the mob heard it as well, and was that why they kept firing, to cover it up? Or was it only him, because he was a reporter by trade and might yet serve again as witness?

The zombies referred to themselves as *You*. You were a family called the Coopers, dead in a moldy basement, wishing you could have ended your lives in love. You were a man named Roger, wondering if what you died for meant anything at all. You were a group of friends named Sarah and John and Bill, dead on a deserted tropical island, even in victory wondering how you might have saved others. And on, and on, a litany of regrets, so incredibly sad, because it did not have to be like that. We all could have been so happy.

The Face buried his ashy face in Greer's ashy hair, and smelled in her sweat and tears the parts of her that would one day turn her body into spoil, from which would rise new kinds of life. He forced himself to smile; his lipless mouth unwittingly kissed her scalp. The kiss made him feel better, just a little. Inside us, there is no original evil, nothing to fear, no reason for regret. Our bodies contain everything. Let the world rise gently from them.

All Her Favorite Songs

The explosives for which Richard Lindof had advocated had already been built. Greer had learned enough to know things like that weren't whipped up in an hour. The first major kind of explosives relied on gunpowder, which required charcoal, sulfur, and saltpeter, and that last ingredient was a real bitch to manufacture, involving soaking limewater through dung and other unpleasant tasks. In hindsight, the second major kind of explosive had been inevitable at Fort York. It relied on nitroglycerin. And where did one find the chief component of nitroglycerin?

It was an offshoot of the production of soap.

Her bitter laugh had the sound of taking a punch. The people of Old Muddy, their hands had been so clean! Now they were so dirty. Hearing people explain the handmade dynamite to kids, Greer understood the production of it predated Lindof's arrival. Maybe Lindof had never mattered. Maybe Lindof's death from her arrow was inconsequential. Maybe this night was always going to come.

She and the Face hadn't budged from their forlorn embrace on the edge of Queen Street. For a while, he'd had to hold her back. She'd wanted to find Muse, pull him from the line of fire. But once marchers began being torn apart, the Face had covered her eyes, and she'd lost him. He hadn't tried to drag her away, and for that, she was thankful. They had to watch this slaughter play out. For punishment. They were not blameless.

Few noticed them. Those who did didn't care. They might have been Nishimura allegiants, but the time when that mattered was over. The ravagers appeared to believe this was a new beginning. Greer believed the opposite: this was the start of another long, slow, ugly end. She pressed her cheek harder into the Face's. She could feel every hill and valley of his scars and wondered if she pressed hard enough, her face would take on the same contours, allowing her to mask her guilt from everyone, herself included.

Gasoline was a rationed substance at Fort York, but you wouldn't know it from the dousing of Slowtown: zombies, softies, weeds, trees, buildings. A dozen bonfires were already going, flames two stories high. Zombies were being tossed into them, some still twitching, some still moaning. Dry, papery flesh went up quickly. Soggy organs melted into black puddles that sizzled like grease. Scorched bones collected at the foot of each fire, interlocked like fingers.

Those who'd stolen liquor bottles from East Blockhouse did not wait to use them. As strong as the stink of the dead was the stench of alcohol. People's faces and chests glistened with it. There was cheering and singing. A man licked whiskey off a woman's face while cackles rose from her arched throat. Another man knelt beside a boy, letting him sip from a rusty beer can. Two children kicked a zombie's head down the street like a soccer ball, celebrating when it caromed into a fire. A dozen young men and women stripped bare and danced a ring around a bonfire, crooning bygone hits, sweat glistening off their ribs, so heaving, so hungry. She saw sex: women with women, men with men, men with women, men with zombies – or at least with parts of zombies. It was an orgy more untamed for the five years of decency that had preceded it.

'The animals.' The Face's voice was hoarse from smoke.

Greer kept her eyes on the revelry, still hoping she might see, silhouetted against flames, a thin figure with a loping step, a guitar on his back, and a dog at his side. Or hear the faint, hopeful notes of what should have been a prophetic song. A gunshot snapped, close enough to make her jump.

'Actual animals,' he continued. 'I swear I saw them at the back of the crowd. Giraffes, bears, raccoons. Nothing now. I guess I'm crazy.'

Crazy didn't mean untrue. Meeting Muse King on a dirt path was crazy. Traveling with him across America was crazy. Finding him living among zombies was crazy.

'Not crazy,' she replied, somehow wringing sound from her raw, aching throat. 'Astonishing.'

With the magic word spoken, there he was, Muse King, a.k.a. King Kong, a.k.a. KK to his friends. Hewitt, the 1978 maple-necked, mahogany-bodied, custom Alpine White Gibson Les Paul, was gone, but Hewitt's strap still dangled from Muse's neck, clicking across the pavement. Greer would have known him anywhere: the long limbs, slightly sunken chest, scraggly beard, the outline of his lips. He was being carried by two men, one at his skinny shoulders, the other his shoeless feet. Greer's heart exploded, fueled on Missouri nitroglycerin. The men carried Muse like he was a bag of trash.

Greer bolted up, ripping free of the Face's grip. Muse's condition had been unclear earlier, his ragged gait either that of a zombie or of someone starving and sick. He might still be alive, or something on the borderline, close enough, but the men carrying him were too drunk, on booze or power, to see anything other than one more worthless ghoul.

She sprinted into a scene that looked like an old battlefield photo, and why not? This was the Second Civil War. She was outside of her body, operating it like a kite caught in a gale. She'd never make it in time. Her legs were older now, and tired, and wounded. She'd need a miracle, a real one, and selected one from her past: Fadi Lolo and his Schwinn, not all that fast really, but enough to do the job. She felt the blue bike's rumble through her thighs and the silly slap of Fadi's fluttering scarf. It was enough. She doubled her speed, hearing what

Fadi had said before leaving her: *The fight waits for me. I should have stayed with my people.*

Ride fast.

She shouted Muse's name, knowing that if he heard her, as he always had, he'd turn his head and chuckle, same old Greer, same old heroics, the Lion coming after her Dove. The men would see their mistake and set Muse on his feet, and when Greer collided with his chest, his hands would settle upon her as expertly as they always had. Just like Hewitt, Muse knew how to play her, knew all her favorite songs.

Her mistake was forgetting who she was. Just like that, it mattered again. She was Black. She carried a weapon. She should not have been surprised to feel a bullet punch into her side, Slowtown whirling into pinwheels of flame as the impact spun her in a complete circle. She staggered, but kept going. Fadi's Schwinn had wind at its back now. Muse was a few feet away. She could be astonishing too. Look at her go.

When a second bullet lanced her throat, she barely noticed. One of the fires set off planted dynamite, and there was a thunderous, blinding explosion that ripped a hole through reality, and through the world's new wound, she saw Muse's world, the place of astonishment, the place of Urschleim, the life between people, animals, plants, everything. Too bad the Face was behind her, screaming. There was no reason for screaming. He'd learn that soon enough.

The third bullet entered her skull, and the last sight Greer Morgan had in this particular world was of Muse King as she collapsed onto him. Her weight drove him from the men's hands and to the ground. His body was warm, though not as warm as the body from the first song she'd heard him play, *Take my burned old bones, cool them in the river, y'all.* She was cozy there on top of him, a repeat of the hundreds of times she'd pinned him to kiss him, and though her eyes burst with hemorrhaging blood, his were soft, and kind, and waiting, and not white, not white at all.

The Gauze

Charlie found Hoffmann sitting near the Little Norway Park
incinerator. The coals were dead. The only light was that reflecting
off the bay: blue moonlight and the red ripples of the Fort York fire
raging to the north. Charlie had come here often to dispose of softies, but as far as she knew, no one ever sat here by choice. The spot
had a nice view, but cremains got everywhere.

She joined the librarian – former librarian, now – on the bench.
Hoffmann said nothing.

For a while, they listened to the distant crackling of the fire, and
beyond that, the muffled blasts of mysterious detonations. They
watched a thin fog roll over the water. Fog was rare this late in the
year, and Charlie wondered if the heat of all that fire and spilled
blood made Lake Ontario exhale this disappointed breath.

'You need to go back?' she asked. 'Get anything?'

She could see that Hoffmann was wearing her old, ugly fanny
pack and was unsurprised when the woman shook her head. Hoffmann was not one for belongings. There were bits of paper in her
hair, drifting out like dandruff. Charlie watched a burned bit of page
settle on the librarian's fanny pack. Typed on it was a single
unanswered letter: *Q*.

Being careful of her bandaged, self-splinted fingers, Charlie
shook her backpack straps to make the carabiners jingle so Hoffmann knew she was ready to go.

'I took some stuff from Hospice. Willow bark. Some ether. I left most of it. People will need it. They'll need it tonight. They'd better hurry, though. Fort York Boulevard is all weeds. The fire will burn right across. Lesser Hedrick, all the softies, they'll burn too. I don't know. In there, out here – maybe it doesn't matter.'

Hoffmann tilted her head and looked north. It was a night to expect anything: Charlie looked too, and saw no one at first. Moments later, at the limit of her vision, she spotted a group of people gathered in the lot of the old Waterfront Neighborhood Centre. She felt a short, unraveling loss. Nishimura had wanted to rebuild the center as an improved version of its old self, a lively meeting place for when Old Muddy's population outgrew the immediate area. What plans they'd had. How outrageous had been their visions.

'I think that's the AV Club,' Charlie said. 'That tall girl, I think that's Georgia. They've got bags. They must be getting out. I remember Muse King used to say it was art that was going to save us. I hope so. I hope those kids do all right.' She looked at Hoffmann. 'You want to chase them down? See if we can go with them?'

Hoffmann squinted for a while, then shook her head. Charlie wanted to watch the AV Club hike away. They'd do it with energy and purpose, still confident they could achieve anything. But she turned away, knowing it would only hurt. Because *that* was utopia, wasn't it? Nishimura, who'd gotten so much right, had whiffed at the concept's essence. Utopia had nothing to do with settling in. It had everything to do with keeping moving, never stopping. The fear of death was the same damn thing. It had nothing to do with dying, everything to do with failing to have lived.

'Right,' Charlie said. 'They're young. We'd only slow them down.'

Giving it no advance thought, she one-upped the handhold she'd given Hoffmann in the Dying Room. She stretched her right arm along the back of the bench, gripped Hoffmann's far shoulder, and nestled the strange woman into her side. Hoffmann's failure to recoil was its own reply.

Charlie rested her head against Hoffmann's head and watched the weaving threads of gentle currents. She sat as still as possible and listened to her body, every minute part of it, searching for signs of sickness. She'd been doing this since she'd woken up in the Dying Room. There was nothing to be felt, aside from four smarting fingers. It was a good sign. So why did she feel so disheartened? She thought of plastic Jesus, lording over Mae Rutkowski's dining room. Be merciful, he'd preached. He hadn't been wrong. All the people of Fort York had needed to do to thrive was be merciful to themselves.

'I'm sorry,' Charlie said.

'Why?'

'For bringing you here. The Archive would have been safer in D.C. You were right to keep it a secret.'

Hoffmann shook her head.

'No?' Charlie asked.

'People read it. The parts they remember, they'll tell others. It'll be passed along. Stories never really end.'

'That's nice of you to say, Etta, but I don't know—'

'Luis Acocella,' Hoffmann said.

Charlie's mouth shut with a snap. She didn't believe she'd ever heard Hoffmann interrupt anyone before. She was a listener, not a talker. Hearing Luis's full name in Hoffmann's voice, a voice that only ever spoke of business, that mostly asked questions, made Charlie press her lips together. She wouldn't cry. She couldn't. Tears dripping onto Hoffmann's neck? It would be too much. Hoffmann would pull away in disgust.

'Luis Acocella's been gone a long time,' Hoffmann said. 'But his story keeps growing. Doesn't it?'

Charlie nodded. Tears spilled, everywhere, all at once, over her face and arm, down Hoffmann's chest and back. Afraid of who her sobs might attract, Charlie wrapped her free arm around her hitching torso. Her hand grazed her belly. Thin, hard, and leathery from years of scrapping for food, but once it had been soft and fertile, capable of growing a life. Sitting here on the edge of another uncertain world, she had no regrets about never having given birth. Especially now that she'd become a kind of child herself: the first should-be-dead reborn into life. Luis would challenge that. Rebirth or Miscarriage, he'd ask. Given the rumbles coming from Fort York and Slowtown, Charlie admitted the prognosis didn't seem good. She focused on the sounds closer to hand. The huffs of her crying, Hoffmann's exhales, the whispers of hands stroking arms.

'I hope this means we get dogs back,' Charlie said. 'I miss dogs. Would you help me take care of a dog?'

'Yes. But I am uninterested in dogs.'

Charlie laughed. 'Love you, weirdo. You ready to go?'

Hoffmann, true to form, only nodded.

One more sound joined the mix. It was the gentle, plinking noise of water being forcibly pushed. Charlie straightened, wiped enough tears to loosen her finger bandages, and stared straight ahead. Lake Ontario was rippling. The sandy shoreline frothed. Something was in the water. Something coming closer.

The fog was as white as a zombie's eye. The center of it darkened like blood spotting the strip of gauze that held this fragile world together, then released a canoe holding two men. Their dark clothing and black-painted faces had kept them hidden. The man in the rear plied an oar with expertise. The man in front wore a belt with a gun strapped to either side, though it was the old coffee tin of tools on his lap that squeezed Charlie's throat.

She'd learned about these tools in med school. Wire saws. Cranial rongeurs. Scalp clips. Laminectomy punches. Tumor forceps. Drill guides. Micro knives. These were neurosurgical instruments, which meant these men, whom Lindof might have called *Beachcombers*, came from Fort Drum, where leaders promulgated good behavior through corrective brain surgery.

Unimportant details, really. How they got you, exactly, didn't matter. Once again, the time had come to run. Cutting from the fog were two more canoes, four after that, another eight, another sixteen, another thirty-two, the gauze shredding now. Charlie realized that zombie resurrection hadn't ended only in Toronto; it had happened all over, including Fort Drum. That, plus the chaotic signals of smoke and fire from Fort York, told these would-be conquerors now was their best shot. *When my utopia doesn't align with your utopia,* Charlie thought, *this is what happens.*

Never would the living stop trying to turn themselves into the dead. The lead boat struck sand. The name of the boat came into view. It was *Antonia.* The men climbed out. Charlie Rutkowski stood, grabbed Etta Hoffmann by the hand.

Shall we dance? she almost asked.

Are You OK? she almost asked.

'Here They come,' she said instead.

Beautiful

At the first flower of dawn, Annie Teller crossed Wilshire Boulevard and entered Hancock Park. Somewhere in her shadow memories, she knew what it should look like. It did not look like that anymore. The Los Angeles County Museum of Art had fallen, spray-painted and shattered, cousin now to the broken segments of the Berlin Wall on display across the street. The Pavilion for Japanese Art, a curvilinear structure that, even in death, had never left Annie's dreams had collapsed inward like a folding fan. The park itself had none of the scruffy, green-brown Los Angeles charm she'd seen in so many photos. It was all red dirt and scorched earth, the trees and plants replaced by drifts of nondegradable plastic trash.

Half of Annie's legs were metal. She had a sense they were why she kept going when others of her dead generation fell. Blades, dulled by time, had been screwed into her wrist bones. Only patches of her clothing survived. Large swaths of her skin were fire-damaged. Ice-burn scars from winter journeys had turned the rest of her flesh a stippled gray. Chunks of her fell off every day. Just as Hancock Park had become unrecognizable, so had she.

But the La Brea Tar Pits were still here.

Sourceless facts swirled in the twitching glob of her brain. Crude oil had seeped from this ground for tens of thousands of years. Bones recovered here dated back thirty-eight thousand years. No race of animals, no matter how inventive their self-destruction, was going to change that.

Her brain, active for so long, was winding down. She could feel it, the unspooling of the thoughts she'd replayed for unknowable years. She was here, though she did not recall why she'd come. *LA BREA TAR PITS:* the words had hunted her like the rest of her kind had hunted fast-moving ones. The words once had been written on her chest. She needn't have worried when they faded away. She'd lost her way many times, but never her purpose.

Why, then, did she still feel her journey was incomplete?

Annie Teller had fallen down thousands of times, and every time, *LA BREA TAR PITS* ordered her to get back up. Here she believed she'd find something to keep her down for good. The notion came to her simply, gently. Tar was sticky.

A whisper of memory informed her that Lake Pit was to her right. She moved toward it, but progress was slower than usual. She looked down with a right eye that still worked and observed her metal legs being gripped by hot asphalt exuding through the grass. Crossing a stony granulate that had once been a sidewalk, she then found a way through the latticed remains of a chain-link fence. She hobbled to the bank of a black pond bubbling with methane.

Annie had seen many beautiful things on her journey, things that made her pause despite the ferocity of her calling. Endless freeways of gleaming vehicles like giant dead cobras. Collapsed bridges like slain dragons, visible beneath bodies of water gone lucid as diamond. Bison in such incredible numbers their herds looked like the shadows of skyscrapers long since fallen. None of that could match this.

Lake Pit's surface was browns, yellows, and purples, gliding through and past each other in iridescent patterns like smoke, or clouds, or intermixing pools of blood, all slowed to prehistoric speeds. Evidence of the dead was everywhere. Festoons of feathers where birds had been sucked under. Filigrees of bone from small mammals that had edged too close. A conglomeration of skulls, all different, all wide-jawed in a silent, happy chant.

Annie Teller's good eye surveyed the opposite side of the pit.

Tawna Maydew stood in the golden rays.

Memories, though incomplete, filled in fast. Annie recalled, in the first hours and days, everyone wondering *why*. Here was all the *why* she'd ever needed: one person needing another to make the pain of life bearable. She had a vision of shooting an arrow from a window of the Mansfield-on-Sherwood rehab center, choosing and pinpointing the end of her first long walk. Now, at the end of her second, after overcoming the physical and mental struggles of recuperation, the alienation of being something called a senior statistician, the loneliness of a sterile workplace, Tawna was the only point Annie had yet to reach.

Tawna Maydew stood beneath the tusks of the largest of three fiberglass mammoths. The paint had been blistered away by fifteen years of sun, but otherwise the statue looked as it had in so many photos. Tawna, too, did not look so different. She was still tall, still curvy, still tanned, still shaggy-haired. Perhaps she'd been here the whole time, standing, standing, standing, while Annie had been walking, walking, walking.

Annie's heart had perished years earlier, shaved away like rust by her own wind-sharpened ribs. But she might be confusing the heart organ with the heart concept. She felt a stirring, akin to how she'd felt seeing those stranded vehicles, collapsed bridges, drifting continents of bison. It was the feeling of mattering.

She'd only seen Tawna Maydew in the flesh once, at a place of illusions called Disney World. This was no illusion. There she was. Standing. Moving. Tawna was lifting her arms. Tawna was walking forward.

Tawna was entering the pit.

Annie understood basic physics. Lake Pit was eight to ten feet deep in its center. The asphalt would roll over Tawna's head as she progressed. The accumulated weight of it would pull her to the bottom. Annie would never see her at a closer distance, never touch her, despite the thousands of miles, the incalculable years.

So Annie Teller entered the pit too.

The asphalt suctioned to her bladed legs. It was worse than being snagged in the wild vines of the Arkansas Ozarks or the depths of Colorado snowdrifts. To move a leg, she had to shove aside an entire lake of tar. Her efforts created ripples that moved outward, rainbows corkscrewing the pond's lustrous surface. Rival ripples came from Tawna's own trudging thighs. How could she move like that, with legs of mere flesh? Annie wanted to touch those legs as others of her kind wanted meat and blood. She pushed harder. The hot tar reached her knees, her waist.

When Annie Teller and Tawna Maydew reached each other, the asphalt was at their chests; their silent trajectory had avoided Lake Pit's deepest area. Black oil, however, had splashed across Annie's face, partially obscuring her good eye. Tawna, she thought, was reaching out to her. Tawna's mouth, she thought, was making a noise that Annie, missing both ears, could not hear.

A sound surfaced from the dry crevices of her brain – the beep her phone had made when receiving a text. It was in texts she'd first seen pictures of La Brea, usually in the background of Tawna's sultry selfies. That's right. Tawna lived just a street or two away. That might explain why she wasn't in pieces. Maybe she'd kept her end of the emailed bargain, and had been waiting safely, patiently indoors.

If the world goes gooey, we'll meet on the banks of beautiful La Brea!

It was as beautiful as billed. As warm and cushy as the blankets on Tawna's bed always looked, tugging Annie toward well-earned sleep.

Annie forced an arm through the black mire, found Tawna's hand. Tawna Maydew was real.

Annie felt Tawna's fingers close around her wrist, unmindful of the blades. Ripples hit ripples, rainbows ate rainbows. The sun had risen, turning the asphalt gold.

They were chest to chest. Annie's chin struck Tawna's. The sticky tar glued them together. That was fine. Annie did not plan on ever moving away. Tawna's arms wrapped around her back. She returned the embrace, an achingly slow movement. She felt her right hand fall off. It did not matter. Tawna's eyes widened, opalescent goo stretched between her lashes. Her eyes were liquid and blue – they were blue. Annie's brain, sluggish now, took valuable seconds to appreciate this.

Tawna Maydew was a fast-moving one.

Tawna Maydew was alive.

The fact that it did not matter, mattered. Annie folded her arms around Tawna. Her warm, pulsing meat, her hitching puffs of breath. Nothing had felt so good in a long time. Annie thought about biting and changing her, like a woman named Katrina Goteborg had bitten and changed her. She chose not to. Annie and Tawna could get no closer than this. Tar sealed their bodies, two into one.

Annie believed she heard Tawna's thoughts. Euphoria at their reunion. Gratitude their odysseys were complete. Happiness they were home. Or were those thoughts Annie's? No longer could she tell the difference. No longer were there boundaries.

As the sun rises higher, you realize the two of you are not alone. Over there is another you, and over here, another. You look and see yous to the left, and yous to right, and you can hear before, behind, and all around you, yous closing in, their cricking, cracking dead parts going silent in the ancient asphalt. The yous are not only two-legged. Yous come with four legs, and tails, and claws, and fangs, and snouts, and forked tongues, and pointy ears, and antlers, and horns, and fur, and scales. Finally, the yous with feathers drop in and bite off parts of you and you and you, and spirit them into the air to be scattered all around, so you will be planted everywhere. In time, you will grow back.

You begin to sink. You share a thought, your last one. You have always been the living dead. You will always be. It was the coming of death that allowed you to live. The dead yous tried to teach this to the live yous for so long the dead yous had no choice but to begin shouting it. Now it is up to you, and you, and you – it is up to us, at last, *to us* – to remember, to rise up just like we in this pit sink down, to live among our living in peace, to die among our dead in harmony, for both states will persist, clinging to the other like shadows. We are not ghouls. We are not zombies. We are our own mothers, fathers, daughters, sons, sisters, and brothers. We have been waiting for us to accept us, to open arms for embraces. We are gone now, but we will be back. For now, the dead sink. For now, the dead die. For now, the dead win.

Stay Scared: a Coauthor's Note

Lugosi always lived in a castle while the zombies
went out to pick the sugarcane.

George A. Romero, Film Comment 15, no. 3 (1977)

It begins and ends with *The Tales of Hoffmann*. Not just the book
you're holding but possibly George Andrew Romero's whole career
and, by extension, my career too.

George's obsession with the 1951 Michael Powell and Emeric
Pressburger film was so well documented that the Criterion Edition
DVD features an interview with George, wherein he describes his
unlikely and fortuitous viewing of the film at age twelve. If you
haven't seen the movie, I understand. Unlike George's other avowed
influences, like Christian Nyby and Howard Hawks's *The Thing from*

Another World or Richard Matheson's *I Am Legend,* it's not horror, fantasy, or sci-fi. It is, rather, an adaptation of a Jacques Offenbach opera, itself adapted from E. T. A. Hoffmann's short stories.

I suggest you see it for three reasons. One, it's a stunning, phantasmagoric example of how a limited budget can provoke genius. Two, George and I would both argue that it *is* horror, and fantasy, and sci-fi too. Three, it's the piece of art that made George Romero, as he says in the Criterion interview, 'find out how to use the pencil' – and if you're bothering to read this unusually long author's note, that's probably of interest.

Nearly everyone believed George's pencil was used exclusively in the service of film scripts. But he'd been speaking publicly about working on a novel as early as 1981, when *Rod Serling's The Twilight Zone Magazine* asked, 'Is it true that you're writing a novel yourself?'

George's response: 'Yes.'

Over the next thirty-six years, ancillary evidence suggests the idea of writing prose fiction rarely left his head. Until the 2017 short-story collection *Nights of the Living Dead,* edited by George and the indispensable Jonathan Maberry – which includes an earlier version of this novel's opening – George's only traditionally published piece of adult fiction, outside of novelization credits, was in a 1982 paperback anthology titled *Modern Masters of Horror.* The unnerving twenty-one-page story, 'Clay', is a knockout and exercises two of George's recurrent themes: religious faith, primarily its futility; and humans' inability to communicate.

Two other offbeat pieces of fiction are worth mentioning. The first is a catalog, created for an art exhibition by George's friend George Nama. Printed by Jack Rutberg Fine Arts shortly after Romero's death, the catalog includes the fascinating, allegorical short story 'Liberator', which inspired the golem myth woven into *The Living Dead.*

The second is a children's book written and illustrated by George: *The Little World of Humongo Bongo.* Published in Belgium in 1996, it was inaccessible to English readers until a 2018 reprint by Canada's ChiGraphic. This edition concludes with an interview, in which George, who hadn't directed a movie in nine years, says, 'I get sick and tired of trying to promote films. . . . It's just pretty tiring, so I have been wanting to just write.' George's lifelong frustration with Hollywood is evident not only in this quote but in lines from *Humongo Bongo* itself, like this one:

'It was terrible to have your heart hardened.'

Few lines George ever wrote spoke to me more personally; I lent the line to *The Living Dead*'s Karl Nishimura. You don't have to be an artist to understand how gradually a person's fire can be extinguished. Don't get me wrong. Novel-writing is a business too (trust me on this), but your legs are swept from under you less frequently than in the movie biz. Just to ruin your day, here are only some of the film/TV projects George was attached to over the years:

Apartment Living, The Assassination, Beauty Sleeping, Before I Wake, The Bell Witch, Black Gothic, Black Mariah, Carnivore, Cartoon, Chain Letter, City of the Dead, Cryptid, Cut Numbers, Deep Red, Diamond Dead, The Divine Spirit, Dracula, Empire of the Dead, Enemies, Expostulations, Figments, Flying Horses, The Footage, From a Buick 8, Funky Coven, Ghost Town, The Girl Who Loved Tom Gordon, The Golem, Goosebumps, GPS, Gunperson, Hell Bent, Horror Anthology, The Ill, The Innocents, Invasion of the Spaghetti Monsters (a.k.a. *Shoobee Doobee Moon*), *It, Jacaranda Joe, Jack and the Beanstalk, The Long Walk, Mannequin, Masque of the Red Death, Mickey B* (*Macbeth* with robots), *Midnight Show, Mongrel: The Legend of Copperhead, Moonshadows, The Mummy, Native Tongue, Night of the Living Dead: The Series, Orange Project, Pet Sematary, Phibes Resurrected, Phobophilia* (a TV special for Penn & Teller), *The Power, The Princeton Principle, The Raven, Resident Evil, Salem's Lot, Scream of Fear, Seeing Things* (a TV anthology based on the stories of Shirley Jackson), *Sharing Joy & Sorrow, Shop Till You Drop . . . Dead, Solitary*

Isle, Something Outside, The Stand, Stranger in a Strange Land, The Tales of Hoffmann (as a space opera!), *Tarzan of the Apes, Three at a Time, Trick 'r Treat, Turn of the Screw, Tusk, Unholy Fire, Untitled George Romero Wrestling Project, Wake, War of the Worlds: The Night They Came, Whine of the Faun, Whiz Kid, The X-Files, The Zombie Autopsies,* and *Zomboid.*

It is no wonder, then, that a novel appealed to him. No one had to give him a green light. No one could force rewrites via a slashed budget. No one could make him cut his best effects to protect the sensibilities of a delicate populace. However, like thousands before him, he found finishing a novel to be grueling work. In the 1992 book *Dark Visions: Conversations with the Masters of the Horror Film,* George told Stanley Wiater, 'I often thought about writing a novel, but then I realize what a commitment that is. Screenplays are in fact about one-third the size.'

For a while, that seemed to be End of Story.

Eighteen years later, in the Fall 2010 issue of *VideoScope,* at the end of an interview regarding *Survival of the Dead,* his final film, George states, so simply anyone might have missed it, 'I have been working on a novel.'

When I heard about George's death, I was visiting family in Virginia. The news came across my gadget, something George would have hated. I had to sit down. All I said, I think, was, 'Oh no.' When I was asked what was wrong, I said, 'George Romero died.' My sisters and father had sketchy ideas of the significance of this, but my wife, Amanda, understood right away.

To say I grew up with George Romero is fanciful but true. The first film I actually recall watching is *Night of the Living Dead.* I must have been five or six. I saw it with my mom, Susan Laura Kraus, who had a penchant for fright flicks. It may sound like bad parenting, but was, in fact, the best parenting. As *Night* obsessives know, one of the film's magical feats is how well it plays to different audiences. (How many films boast a stately Criterion Edition as well as two different RiffTrax versions?) Probably to ward off heebie-jeebies, my mom liked to laugh along to it, razzing the hapless Barbra and booing the cowardly Harry. Crazy though it seems, given the film's plot, *Night of the Living Dead* became a safe space for me.

It helped that the movie was always on. Skip this paragraph if this stuff is old hat. When the Walter Reade Organization, the film's original distributor, changed the title from *Night of the Flesh Eaters,* it neglected to put the copyright bug on the title screen. That was all it took for *Night* to plop into the public domain. For George, this was both bad and good. The bad: he'd never make the millions he deserved. The good: because it required no rights payments to screen – and because it was really damn good – it was shown everywhere. If someone in a movie is watching a movie, odds are it's *Night,* and my educated guess is that no movie in history has been released on VHS and DVD more often – many hundreds of times.

By every logical measure, the colorized version put out by Hal Roach Studios in 1986 is an atrocity. But let's get illogical. If you can find a VCR, watching the colorized VHS is the closest you can get to feeling how beat-up and put-upon the film had become. The 'colors' are thin and sickly, like tattered flags, yet a nobility lurks in that analog sludge. It's accidentally beautiful in the way of tenth-generation tapes traded by pre-internet movie buffs. Their ugliness proved how beloved they were, how hard people were willing to work to see them anew.

It's another of *Night*'s magical feats. The film was like the zombies it invented: overused and abused, but unwilling to die.

Night barely feels like a movie to me. It's more like an album I love; it's part of my waking thoughts, my blood and oxygen. Hearing of George's death reminded me, yet again, how much his stories felt like family stories, how much he felt like family. I engage in little fandom.

My home is nearly devoid of media mementos. The one exception is George. The *Night* poster behind my writing desk. The weird piece of *Creepshow* fan art I bought the day George died. I keep three framed photos in my office: one of my wife and me, one of my mom, and one of George and me from the only time we ever met: March 6, 2006.

In January 2006, I read an article about George, probably about 2005's *Land of the Dead,* in which George's manager, Chris Roe, was thanked. *This can't be the same Chris Roe from my hometown,* I thought. The idea was preposterous. I grew up in the hamlet of Fairfield, Iowa, not exactly a hotbed of Hollywood talent. But my memory of Chris was that he'd been interested in genre film and television. I scoured the internet for an email, wrote him, and days later, we caught up on the phone.

Chris had indeed become a successful talent manager, and one of his clients was George Romero. I told Chris what a fan I was, and he suggested the three of us get together the next time he was near Chicago, where I lived.

Three months later in Rosemont, Illinois, at Fangoria's Weekend of Horrors, I met Chris in his hotel room, and soon after, George lumbered in from the adjoining room. He looked like George Romero, all right: roughly seventy stories tall, shrunk down to size only by his trademark oversized glasses. He wore his usual green vest, his hair in its usual white ponytail.

He also looked like shit. He was sick. Sick enough, in fact, that he should have canceled the appearance. But he refused to; he took his fans seriously. Eleven years later, his wife, Suzanne Desrocher-Romero, would show me a notebook in which George practiced his signature prior to signing events so it would look all right despite his trembling hands. Regarding the kind of person George Romero was, there is no more poignant piece of evidence.

The three of us had a nice chat, or as nice a chat you can have when the man of the hour can barely stand. George was interested in hearing about my novels, though he was more interested in the small-town history Chris and I shared. Soon, it was time for George's event. Chris and I escorted him down the elevator and through the halls, serving as guards to keep signature hounds at bay. We stopped only once for George to buy cigarettes. It's a painful detail. Eleven years later, he would die of lung cancer.

That was it for eleven years. A month after George died, I received a call from Chris. We'd stayed in loose touch over the preceding decade, during which both our careers developed. By then, I was hard at work on my second collaboration with Guillermo del Toro, *The Shape of Water*. I was delighted to hear from Chris, but fully unprepared for the new kind of collaboration he proposed: completing the epic zombie novel George had left unfinished.

There were more obvious choices. Authors more famous, authors known for zombie fiction. I'd circled the topic before, if obliquely. My *Zebulon Finch* duology features an undead protagonist, though he's agile and debonair, about as far from a Romero shambler as it gets. In the second volume, I pay explicit homage to George, with Zebulon going mad in the Arizona desert and believing George Romero is sending him instructions via *Night of the Living Dead,* à la Charles Manson and *The White Album*. (The book also includes a conspiracy theory based on a detail in *Night* I'm convinced no one but me has noticed. Sorry, you'll have to read the book.)

After I recovered from the shock, I had no choice but to convince myself I might actually be up to the task. My interest had always lay in George Romero, not zombies per se. I knew from interviews George felt similarly. As grateful as he was for the undead that gave his career life, they forced him into the smallest of spaces, the same as they did Barbra and Ben. As the above list of unmade projects illustrates, he struggled to get anything else made, even in the realm of horror.

It must have hurt a little, especially for a guy who virtually never watched horror movies. Classic Hollywood cinema was what he loved, films like Olivier's *Richard III,* Wyler's *Ben-Hur,* and whatever was queued up next on Turner Classic Movies. Though it sounds counterintuitive, horror fans would do well to celebrate the distance George kept from the genre – his films stand out for precisely that reason. Capital-*H* Horror was very rarely his primary concern. What shook him up was rooted in daily life.

Nowhere was that clearer than in *The Living Dead.*

The novel reboots the zombie crisis to Day One. George did that before with *Diary of the Dead,* a through line he continued with his final and most underrated film, *Survival of the Dead.* Though he'd intended to make more movies, you can't complain that *Survival*'s last image is the final picture George ever put on film. It synopsizes his Dead cycle with savage efficiency: two dead, old, white men, standing across from each other at the sunset of humanity, pulling impotent triggers on emptied guns.

Chris and Suzanne gave me plenty of pages of George's novel, but surprises were yet in store. On February 14, 2018, the project was made public in *Entertainment Weekly.* The story was picked up all over, including on the AV Club. I don't recall the last time I'd read internet comment boards. But for whatever reason (George would have scolded me), I scrolled down to read them.

There I found a comment from the user TTTWLAM, who wrote, 'Around the year 2000, Romero had a website where he sold an each-chapter-is-a-few-bucks story *The Death of Death*. It was supposed to be his "definitive" take on how *Night of the Living Dead* played out on a global scale [but] he quit by about Chapter 3.'

I knew a whole lot about George Romero, but this was news to me. I searched the net. I searched it harder. I asked fellow Romero fanatics if they'd ever heard of it. I consulted Homepage of the Dead, a fan resource that's been around since 1997. Nothing. Finally I turned to the internet archive project the Wayback Machine to see if I could find artifacts of George's short-lived website. Lo and behold, there it was, in an imperfect but semi-navigable state.

Eventually, I hit upon a page that made me gasp. A mocked-up book cover proclaimed *The Death of Death,* along with the tagline 'Hell is upon us'. Elsewhere on the site, in a post dated July 21, 2000, George wrote, 'My zombie films focused on small groups of people dealing with their immediate problems. *The Death of Death* will be an original novel with much wider scope. . . . I let it all hang out here, guys, without a thought for budget or propriety. . . . It will be available for downloading, one chapter at a time.'

Exciting stuff, but it had been a subscription-based offer. You sent your money, and pages showed up in your in-box. I wasn't going to find actual pages on the site. What I did find, however, was plenty of evidence that George, avowed technophobe, had been briefly excited by the prospect of the internet. 'There's no "Middle-Man" anymore,' he wrote. 'It's just you and me.' He even spoke of offering his next zombie film exclusively on the web.

Having been through the Hollywood grinder (talk about 'Hell is upon us'), who could blame him for what in hindsight looks like heedless optimism? Around 2000, there was a feeling the independent film world was on the brink of a paradigm shift that would allow directors to bring their work directly to the people. It didn't happen, for lots of reasons. Chris Roe recounted to me how the site's chat rooms got nasty – of course they did – and George pulled the plug. It was one more heartbreak: his hopes lifted by a new democratic ideal only to see it ruined by familiar, ugly behaviors. Exactly the sort of thing he made movies about.

I discussed the mystery of *The Death of Death* with Suz. She believed she might know someone who might have a copy: longtime fan and filmmaker Christian Stavrakis (who sculpted the bust of George installed in Monroeville Mall, *Dawn*'s filming location). A few days later, I received an email from Suz, subject line: 'Death of Death.pdf'. I was gobsmacked by the contents. TTTWLAM was right: George had only written two chapters. But those two chapters equaled over one hundred pages.

Written fifteen years before the bulk of *The Living Dead*, they revealed George making a trial run at a similar concept. (These pages also proved his fixation with names like Charles, Charlie, Charlene, and Chuck.) While the *Death of Death* pages lacked the structure of *The Living Dead* pages, they were brasher and darker. Some of it had no place inside *The Living Dead*, no matter how much I adored them. (Case in point: a bonkers sequence in which a woman is rescued from ritual genital mutilation only for her rescuer to crash their getaway jeep and be thrown into a river, whereupon he turns zombie and starts after her, only to be suddenly ripped apart by hippopotamuses.) Other sections, however, could be meshed into the work, especially if I tweaked this, adjusted that, merged Character B into Character A, and so forth.

As a grace note, the old website featured a short story by George, 'Outpost #5', which had been lost to time. Written from a zombie's POV, it lays out, clearer than anything before, the underlying facts about zombies – how they use their senses, to what extent they have feelings, and so on. This story, combined with careful readings of the Dead films, helped me to create a master profile of a Romero zombie I referenced throughout writing. Suz granted me permission to use both *The Death of Death* and 'Outpost #5', and I was off to the races.

The surprises still weren't over. Months later, Chris called with a discovery: he'd turned up a nine-page letter George had written, describing where he'd intended to take various plot threads. At this point, I was four hundred pages into the novel. This new information was, to say the least, a pain in the ass. Nevertheless, I was thrilled. The bits of synchronicity were startling. Both George and I had independently plotted the news anchor character as ending his career the same way, and we'd both invented a heroic fighter pilot named Jenny. On the other hand, a couple of things he planned I put the kibosh on, including two apparently minor characters he'd envisioned as having 'many frightening adventures'. I'd already killed them off, and they stayed dead. Sorry, George.

Suz was adamant that George anticipated the book having a pessimistic ending. However, he ends the nine-page letter with this: 'It might even be possible that some people could survive the plague.' What, I wondered, did he mean by 'survive'? As in, 'not get eaten by zombies'? Or as in 'survive past the plague's end'? I like to imagine the act of writing a novel was so liberating that George, the pessimist who let Ben get shot in *Night,* might yield to the same pinch of optimism that made him, at the last second, deviate from his own screenplay and let Fran and Peter live at the end of *Dawn.*

The result of this constant trickle of new material was a collaboration process more typical than I could have anticipated. It was like George was still hard at work in Toronto, typing in his usual spot on the sofa, CNN playing in front of him, Suz buzzing about, their birds squawking, and every now and then he'd send me some new pages. Like any effective collaboration, it was part jubilation and part fist-fight, and we came out the other side like John Wayne and Victor McLaglen in *The Quiet Man,* bruised and drunk, but with arms slung over each other's shoulders.

One thing was certain: he intended the novel to be epic, a real doorstop, a conversation starter as well as stopper. I had a big job in front of me, and as much groundwork as he'd laid, there was plenty I'd have to do on my own. To begin with, I needed to come to grips with where George was heading with the zombies; he left a half-finished picture. That meant establishing a firm timeline of the Dead films, which isn't as simple as it sounds.

First, obviously, I rewatched all the films. If you ignore the decade shifts (as George did) and focus on how long after the zombie uprising each film takes place, here is the chronological order that emerges.

1. *Night of the Living Dead (1968).*
2. *Diary of the Dead* (2007). This occurs more or less simultaneously with *Night,* though I'd give *Night* the edge based on various pieces of contextual evidence.
3. *Survival of the Dead* (2009). In this sequel to *Diary,* a title informs us we are six days after the dead walk.
4. *Dawn of the Dead* (1979). The best clue offered by the film is the one-legged priest who remarks, 'Many have died last week on these streets.' More telling is the 1978 novelization of *Dawn,* credited to George A. Romero and Susanna Sparrow, which firmly places the events at three weeks after *Night.*
5. *Land of the Dead* (2005). According to George's commentary on the *Survival* Blu-ray, *Land* takes place 'three years or so' after the plague begins.
6. *Day of the Dead* (1985). The original script begins with a title reading, 'Five years . . . since the dead first walked.'

So that's 1968, 2007, 2009, 1979, 2005, 1985. Clear as mud? For the purposes of *The Living Dead,* George's movies had established what to expect in the first five years after the plague begins. The novel's brief second act hurtles through this time frame, since the movies cover it well enough. He had some thoughts on the years after that, but a significant chunk of the conception of Years Six through Fifteen was up to me. My two best sources of study were *Day* (the final film in the timeline, and the film originally intended to conclude the series) and *Survival* (George's last film).

The two films might be the series' most tonally divergent. *Day* is nearly as cynical as *Night,* except for an epilogue so sunny it makes you wonder if it's supposed to be a dream. (George is cagey: 'It doesn't really matter,' he said in a 2000 interview with *Quarterly Review of Film and Video.*) Meanwhile, *Survival* is a hopeful film, showing zombies adhering to harmless behaviors and being compelled to quit attacking us.

With this framework in mind, I had a long meeting in Toronto with Suz to discuss subjects that might help me carry on in George's spirit. We spoke about George's overall impressions of the novel, his thoughts on zombies in general, his opinions on religion and technology (startlingly similar), his dream projects, and his greatest fears. Most affectingly – and with apologies to Suz for making her cry – we spoke of his death, which came a quick three months after his diagnosis.

'I intend to keep [the chapters] coming until I'm diagnosed as terminal, at which point I'll, real quick, whip up an ending,' George wrote on his old site. You can hear his fiendish cackle, even as you wince at the bitter taste. The day *did* come when he was diagnosed as terminal. At that moment, according to Suz, all business ceased. He wanted to be present with his loved ones, hard stop. Although Suz isn't absolutely sure, it's likely he passed while listening to the soundtrack of *The Quiet Man* – probably his favorite film after *The Tales of Hoffmann.*

Suz told me 'Luis' was her name for George when he was being difficult. After learning that, I realized the relationship of Luis and

Charlene in *The Living Dead* somewhat mirrored that of George and Suz. I have tried to honor that as best I could.

I watched the movies yet again, with their commentary tracks. I read the original screenplays, as well as earlier drafts where they were available. I read, listened to, or viewed every interview with George I could find. I read critical and scholarly analyses of his work. Most of all, I did some long, hard thinking on such wide-open questions as, 'What does it all mean?' I have talked of little else for the past couple of years. For those who know me, I apologize.

My choices were guided by my own interpretation of George's inclinations. For starters, it's common knowledge George regretted *Night*'s implication that the radiation-charged Venus probe produced the zombies. He worked to scrub our memory of it over the next five Dead films, and that effort guided me here. Naturally, characters in *The Living Dead* would speculate on the cause of the zombie plague, but any conclusions would extend only to the philosophical. No Venus probe, no government bioweapon gone wild, none of that. As George asserted in his original novel manuscript, 'No one ever would, ever could, figure out why.'

Romero purists might scoff at the idea of zombie animals, but this, too, began with George. On his commentary track for *Land of the Dead,* he speaks of a zombie rat scene cut for budgetary purposes and adds, 'It's a topic I might have to visit.' In a May 28, 2010, interview in *Vulture,* George mentions the zombie rats again, saying, 'I'm thinking about it.' *Land*'s shooting script bears this out, portraying the characters of Riley, Slack, and Charlie (what did I say about George and the name Charlie?) being attacked at the J&L Drawbridge: 'SKREEEEEEEE! ZOMBIE RATS crawl up onto the roadbed. DOZENS.'

He wasn't only thinking of rats. Just prior to *Land*'s release, DC

Comics put out the six-issue comic book *Toe Tags* (subtitle: *The Death of Death,* if you can believe it), a wonderfully illustrated but not-great tale written by George and featuring zombie chimps.

What did George's zombie rats and zombie chimps have in common? What I realized, and let Etta Hoffmann realize in the novel, was neither were attacking other rats and chimps. I think George knew what he was up to. Here's a bit of dialogue from *Dawn of the Dead:* 'Cannibalism in the true sense of the word implies an intraspecies activity. . . . These creatures . . . prey on humans . . . they do not prey on each other.'

Once you accept the gradual zombification of animals, it's only logical that Earth would redevelop Edenic qualities. *Day*'s final scene points the way by showing its protagonists happy, on a tropical isle unspoiled by humans. *Humongo Bongo* is George's bluntest take on the Eden concept, depicting a lush world cyclically ruined by exploiters. All this is reflected in *The Living Dead*'s penultimate scene.

Regarding the novel's final scene, I have only one comment, regarding the last sentence. A somewhat obscure fact is that *Night, Dawn,* and *Day* were all loosely based on what George describes as 'a little short story' he wrote, 'an allegorical thing' entitled 'Anubis'. (An earlier title of *Night of the Living Dead* was *Night of Anubis.*) Written by George when he was roughly in his midtwenties, the story has been lost. But in a November 8, 2013, interview with BFI, George revealed the story's final three words, as he remembered them. In a nod to this genre-spawning short story, these are the words I used to conclude *The Living Dead.*

Slowtown is my own idea (though Nishimura's 'All these streets are yours. Except Slowtown' is a nod to *2010: The Year We Make Contact,* another Eden story). Slowtown has a history. Around 1996, while still in college, I wrote a screenplay that was an homage to *Night.* Youngsters, lend an ear: in ye olde 1990s, zombies were persona non grata. It had been a decade since *Day* (generally considered a failure at the time). Danny Boyle's *28 Days Later* wouldn't come along for six more years, and it would be another eight until the premiere of AMC's *The Walking Dead.* As is surely becoming obvious, my obsession followed no trends. I toyed with the script for a decade, and though I never produced it, I'd always believed its final act cut to the heart of something. After reading what George had written of *The Living Dead,* I saw how my idea could be reworked to bring closure to George's premise. The concept had to do with old age.

What I didn't know back then was George had directed an entire movie about old age. It was called *The Amusement Park.* Written by Wally Cook and produced in 1973 for $34,320 by Communications Pittsburgh at the behest of the Lutheran Society, the fifty-minute dramatic film was intended to highlight the deleterious effects of ageism. With George as the director for hire, boy, did it ever. The finished film was successfully screened at community centers, but because it was an industrial project, it faded into obscurity. Lucky for me, I hadn't forgotten the film's mention in *The Cinema of George A. Romero: Knight of the Living Dead,* Tony Williams's compulsory 2003 scholarly text. I asked Suz about the film, and she revealed, to my shock, that it had been found. Even more shocking, she let me see it.

If you're a Romero fan, you might recall what happened next. *The Amusement Park* had been produced as an industrial, but I found it exciting and unnerving. It had all the stamps of a George Romero film. I started a Twitter thread about it, the story blew up, and suddenly, I was fielding press and distributor queries. I forwarded them all to Suz, who, just three days before I finished writing this page, premiered the restored film at the Romero Lives! tribute in Pittsburgh. What mattered in terms of *The Living Dead* was that I had fifty minutes' worth of visceral, unexpected insight into George's thoughts on old age, hospice, end-of-life care, and more.

I set the old-age section of the novel in Toronto. The Romero faithful may wonder why I callously renounced George's longtime Pittsburgh home. The reasons are simple. George used a Pittsburgh backdrop for *Night, Dawn, Land,* and *Diary,* but not *Day* or *Survival* – which, as you recall, are the two 'final' chapters in the series. Pittsburgh had its due, especially with *Land,* which gave it a proper send-off. It's also worthy to note that the *Dawn of the Dead* novelization reveals our survivors' ultimate goal: reaching Canada.

Additionally, as much as we fans love Pittsburgh, we also have to accept George's new home of Toronto. Evidence suggests he loved it with all his heart. He loved being with Suz, he loved the local film crews, and it was there he wanted to be buried. Although Toronto works as a setting in other ways too (it certainly brings clarity to certain political notions), these were the main reasons I set the novel's would-be utopia in what, for George, was nearly that.

Finally, whenever in doubt, I defaulted to the inspirational text upon which we began. Over the two years of writing the book, I kept a piece of paper taped to my computer so I would never forget what *The Tales of Hoffmann* had to tell me. It's no coincidence both *Hoffmann* and *The Living Dead* have three acts. It's no coincidence the *crick-crack* sound I attribute to old zombies is found in the chorus of one of *Hoffmann*'s songs. I could go on and on with what you might call Easter eggs but I hope are more like nudges to dig deeper. Only if you're so inclined, of course. Offenbach completed *Hoffmann* in 1880; it'll still be there when you're ready.

The novel is filled with scads of references to George's universe, but the only one I feel obligated to explain here, for newcomers who might be confused, is the word *ghouls,* which is what the undead were called in *Night.* The word *zombie* didn't show up until in *Dawn,* when at 1:44:53 (of the US Theatrical cut), Peter says, 'There's going to be a thousand zombies in here.' It's a funny line, in hindsight. George had no idea how true the statement would become in the 2000s. A thousand? Try a million.

Suz didn't show me any notebook pages on which George practiced writing 'Stay scared!' but it wouldn't surprise me if they existed. The line was his trademark. Merely a cheeky expression, I'm sure he would have told you. But I like to think George, that long-haired '60s radical whose ideals were too inflexible to squeeze comfortably inside Hollywood's boxes, was using the slogan as a subtle warning to avoid complacence. To stay vigilant. In other words, 'Stay scared.' My longest work is not, in fact, this one, but the two-volume, 1,457-page *The Death and Life of Zebulon Finch,* which I organized entirely around the phrase, 'You gotta have fear in your heart.' It took the completion of *The Living Dead* for me to realize George and I had been saying the same thing for a long time.

Don't let your heart get hardened.

You gotta have fear in your heart.

Stay scared.

In the writing of this book, during the times I break through the fog and feel anew the awe, responsibility, and gratitude, I feel like it's March 2006 all over again, and George, tired but resolute, is lumbering down the hall, not unlike one of his creations, heading toward his final event of the day, and I'm still there escorting him, I'm still there guarding him. I'm still determined to help him get there. Only this time, we're not stopping for smokes.

Daniel Kraus
October 15, 2019

Acknowledgments

Chris Roe and Suzanne Desrocher-Romero brought me into the book; Richard Abate sold it; Brendan Deneen bought it; Melissa Ann Singer edited it; and I will never be able to thank these five people enough. Michael Murtagh's personal tour of the USS *Intrepid* was invaluable, as were Adrian Durand's insights into navy life. When it comes to understanding dead bodies, you can't ask for a better corpse club than Mary Roach, Judy Melinek, and T. J. Mitchell. Phil Morehart provided a trove of published Romero research material. Adam Hart's early ideas regarding a post-zombie society were a guiding light. Steven Schlozman made an offhand remark at the University of Pittsburgh's 'Reflections on Romero' event on October 19, 2018, that crystallized a major theme of the book for me. John Stone's beautiful 'Autopsy in the Form of an Elegy', my favorite poem, appears with the kind permission of Mae Nelson Stone, James Stone, and John H. Stone. Finally, Amanda Kraus did the most important work of all: reminding me the world of the living required attention too.

The following people and institutions helped in ways too granular to get into here: Terry Alexander, Ashley Allen, Tara Altebrando,

Bryan Bliss, Jill Bruellman, Christa Desir, Corey Ann Haydu, Jennifer Kearney, Affinity Konar, Adam Lowenstein, Carrie Mesrobian, Anne Elizabeth Moore, Bill Morrison, Vincenzo Natali, Tina Romero, Grant Rosenberg, Benjamin T. Rubin, Michael Ryzy, Marcus Sedgwick, Francesco Sinatora, Julia Smith, Christian Stavrakis, Andrea Subissati, Christian Trimmer, Katharine Uhrich, Jeff Whitehead, Tony Williams, Sara Zarr, the George A. Romero Foundation, and the University Library System at the University of Pittsburgh.

Additionally, I'd like to thank the following people: freelancers Laura Dragonette and Sara and Chris Ensey and at Tor, Greg Collins, Theresa Delucci, Tom Doherty, Oliver Dougherty, Fritz Foy, Rafal Gibek, Jordan Hanley, Eileen Lawrence, Devi Pillai, Sarah Reidy, Lucille Rettino, Alexis Saarela, and Jamie Stafford-Hill.

While I used far too many research materials to list them all, here are a few that greatly impacted the writing. *Working Stiff: Two Years, 262 Bodies, and the Making of a Medical Examiner,* by Judy Melinek and T. J. Mitchell; *The Chick and the Dead,* by Carla Valentine; both *The Cinema of George A. Romero: Knight of the Living Dead* and *George A. Romero: Interviews,* edited by Tony Williams; *Night of the Living Dead,* by Ben Hervey; *Murder in the News: An Inside Look at How Television Covers Crime,* by Robert H. Jordan; *Carrier: A Guided Tour of an Aircraft Carrier,* by Tom Clancy and John Gresham; *Another Great Day at Sea: Life Aboard the USS George H. W. Bush,* by Geoff Dyer; the PBS series *Carrier; When There's No More Room in Hell: The Sociology of the Living Dead,* by Andrea Subissati (which helped me connect Haitian zombies to Romero zombies); *The Knowledge: How to Rebuild Civilization in the Aftermath of a Cataclysm,* by Lewis Dartnell; *Utopia for Realists: How We Can Build the Ideal World,* by Rutger Bregman; *Martin Heidegger's Grouch,* by Yan Marchand; *Gospel of the Living Dead: George Romero's Visions of Hell on Earth,* by Kim Paffenroth; Powell and Pressburger's *The Tales of Hoffmann,* and, of course, the films of George A. Romero.

About the Authors

Legendary filmmaker, writer and editor **George A. Romero** is celebrated for his series of gruesome satirical horror films about an imagined zombie apocalypse, including the classic *Night of the Living Dead* and *Dawn of the Dead*. He died in 2017.

Daniel Kraus is a bestselling novelist whose work includes co-authoring, with Guillermo del Toro, both *The Shape of Water* (the film version of which won the Best Picture Oscar) and *Trollhunters* (adapted into the Emmy-winning Netflix series). His work has been translated into over twenty-five languages. He lives in Chicago.